WATERMELON
NIGHTS

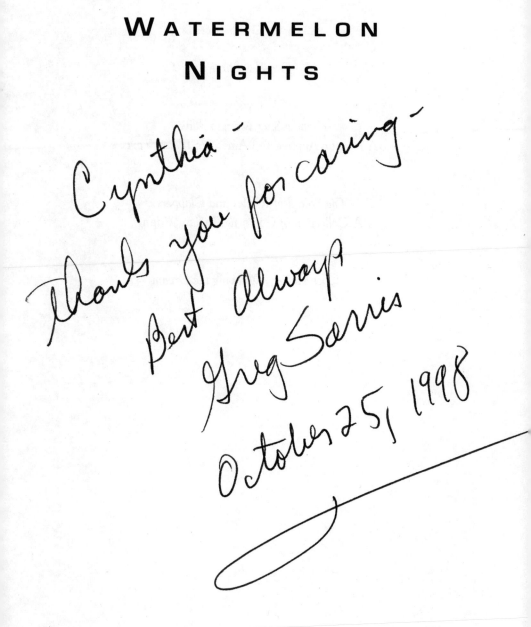

Cynthia —
Thanks you for caring —
Best always
Greg Sarris
October 25, 1998

Also by Greg Sarris

Grand Avenue

Keeping Slug Woman Alive:
A Holistic Approach to American Indian Texts

The Sound of Rattles and Clappers:
A Collection of California Indian Writing

Mabel McKay: Weaving the Dream

WATERMELON NIGHTS

a novel

GREG SARRIS

HYPERION

NEW YORK

ISBN 0-7868-6110-X

Text designed by Nicholas A. Bernini

First Edition

10 9 8 7 6 5 4 3 2 1

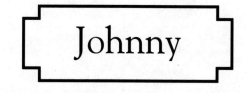

Johnny

O N E

No doubt I come home with a hole in my face and words of leaving and Mom and Grandma gone right to work on the situation. For once, their heads was in the same place on the subject of me: Neither one wanted me to go. Mom knows whatever Grandma might've told her about what happened. Grandma, she sees more than even I can tell you of my own story; her sense of things is clear. Me, I'm talking just to try and make sense of it.

Smiling and white teeth. Felix. If, like they say, a picture's worth a thousand words, then this story's got to start there—with Felix smiling at every turn, for if everything else in my brain has dribbled out that hole, this picture has not. His smile, which I might've understood for all it had to tell if he hadn't looked up so fast and said, "You and me, homeboy. We're gonna change the world, eh?"

This pronouncement after reading a flyer about a rinky-dink tribal meeting, like it was God's last word. I never seen the guy before. He stood just inside my cousin's house, and it was Auntie Mollie or my cousin Alice I expected to see when the door opened. I'd been walking the neighborhood, passing out flyers for the tribe.

He looked back down at the flyer. It was red, with black lettering that told the time and place of the meeting. At the top was the tribe's name, Waterplace Pomo, and below that a drawing of a pond with rocks and grasses around it. I knowed because I made the flyer and had fifty more in my old knapsack. Then he looked up. "We'll have ourselves the biggest bingo hall this side of Vegas," he said.

He'd answered the question that hadn't had a chance to form in my brain. He'd said "we." Which meant he was part of the tribe. Which meant he was Indian. Which meant he was a cousin.

"Yeah," I said, but what was I talking about? The flyer didn't say anything about a bingo hall.

"What's up?" he asked. He stuck out his hand and told me his name: "Felix."

I locked fingers, bumped knuckles. "Johnny," I said.

He didn't have a shirt on. His hair was messed up.

"See you at the meeting, bro," he said.

He looked me in the face, still grinning, all the while slowly rolling up the red flyer in his hands. Then, when it was too late, I seen he had just said Good-bye, this meeting on Auntie's porch is over. I'd been doing nothing, just standing there. I felt like a fool. I'd been half a minute behind him all along.

Then I thought quick, reached into my knapsack, and pulled out a blank genealogy chart, which I just happened to have a few of. "Here," I said, handing the paper to him, "you got to fill it out before the meeting."

He took it but did nothing more than keep up that grinning—This meeting on Auntie's porch is over.

"Cool," I said, and then I turned and split.

When I was down the steps, halfway to the street, I heard him call after me. "Hey," he said.

I turned.

"Come back tonight and help me fill this thing out, will you?" He was waving the genealogy chart. In the other hand, he held the red flyer still rolled tight.

"Yeah," I said, "OK." Then I made off again. I never looked back; but I felt he was still standing there, smiling.

* * *

Then I could've kicked myself. What did I mean, Yeah, OK? Back in my truck, rounding the corner away from Auntie's house, I thought of how the guy stood in the doorway, telling me he had enough of me, making me feel like a fool, then asked me to come back and help him fill out his chart and I say, Yeah, OK. Who was this guy who come out of nowheres and planted himself like he'd been in that doorway forever?

I didn't think whether or not I'd go back to Auntie's later. I tried to push the guy out of my mind. I had work to do, a few more places to hit. The Bills and then the folks living on the other side of the fairgrounds, the Joneses and the Ramirezes. The Bills, they're two sisters, one bigger and meaner than the next. I wasn't up to that situation so I drove back to headquarters.

We called it headquarters but it was really nothing more than a few filing cabinets and a table and chair in Steven Pen's garage. His son Raymond sat there acting all-important, like he was tribal chairman, not his father. He had big ears, the kind that made you think of a dog seeing something, and he looked about twelve, when he was twenty, my age. Two years of college and he couldn't get a summer job, which is why he sat at the desk every day. I understood the reason he talked down to me, like he was in a higher position and knowed more—he had to make himself feel good somehow.

"Good job," he said when I set my leftover flyers on the table. Then he looked at the flyers like he was seeing one in particular and asked, "Did you go to the Bills?"

"No," I told him.

"You should've," he said. "This part of town would be finished."

Yeah, right, I thought. I'd like to see you at the Bills. My mind spit up a picture: six hundred pounds of flesh and purple sateen and pink polyester swallowing him whole.

"I'll get them tomorrow," I told him, "first thing."

He pulled out his genealogy chart and placed it on the table so I could see the work he'd done. Which was another thing to lord over me. Each one of us was supposed to complete our charts. It was one of a list of things we had to do to prove to the government that we was real Indians. Our tribe was trying to get what is called "federally acknowledged" so we could have a reservation and gossip and fight with each other there instead of in town on Grand Avenue, where most of us live. That's what the upcoming meeting was about, these charts each of us was supposed to fill out and turn in, which, if you ask me, look no different from dog pedigrees. But Raymond had his all filled out, or at least he thought he had. I spied the half that wasn't complete, the part for "mother."

His mother ran off after he was born, rumor has it, with some junkie from San Francisco. His father left him with a relative here and then finished college. When he come home, he had a new wife.

Raymond caught my line of vision. "My mother's from another tribe," he said. He looked at the wall, like he was gathering strength from something he seen there and then shot back with all his might, "But I'm full Indian."

He fixed his eyes on me, daring me to match him. Like he knowed he'd turned over the card that ended the game. I'm light-skinned, hardly a quarter Indian. These days the more Indian you are the better, the more white the worse. Truth is, we're all mixed up. Which I could've pointed out if I'd had half a second with his chart. We all come down from one woman. Her name was Rosa and she was half Mexican. Her mother was named Rosa, too, and she was the wife of a Mexican general. Truth is, she was his wife in name only: She wasn't treated any better than a whore, a slave. Pride is a game none of us should play. But, like I said, Raymond Pen was desperate.

"I got to work on mine," I told him, looking back at his chart. Then went one step further in letting him feel good. I told him what time I'd come by tomorrow and that I'd hit the Bills first thing. He nodded and sat back, confident. If it was possible, his ears would've rested down.

* * *

Indians is a mean, unhappy bunch. Grandma says all peoples is that way, then she comes back around to my point of view. She says Indians can't help it on account of Rosa and that Mexican general. Meanness. It's a song, she says, that keeps getting told over and over, passed from one generation to the next. The words might change, the melody don't. She sits in the aluminum folding chair in her garden, plunk in the middle of her hollyhocks out back, and tells me, "Yeah, Johnny, heartache is an Indian's middle name." Then, looking at the sky-reaching rods of pink and white flowers, she says, "But there's more," and with that she points out things, the flowers, for instance, and says to look at them for you'll see Old Uncle smiling . . . listen to the birds, the frogs at night, and you'll hear him singing. And then all the stories about the old man she knowed as a kid, the medicine man who could fly to the moon and back. Them stories over and over, sometimes changed and reconnected to one another in different ways, but the same nevertheless, ever since I was a kid. And to this day, I like it there, sitting beside her. If she's in the garden, where she likes it best, I'll sit on the ground. Sometimes, if the world's eaten too much of me, I rest my head in her lap, like I done when I was a kid.

But as much as Raymond laid one into me, I didn't go out back where I seen Grandma was sitting. I come into the house and went straight to my bedroom. Raymond wasn't bothering me at all. It was the face I seen: Felix in Auntie's doorway. And more, the man standing before my eyes, all six feet of him. Yes, he was tall, and as dark as anybody who claimed full blood. But that wavy hair and the smile, the smile that told you at least two things: that everywhere else you looked, his shoulders and chest, his skin, a thousand others had looked, too, and every one of them found what they seen perfect. His carved chest, the ripples in his stomach. The last couple hours twisted in my head. I should've been angry at Raymond, I often was after dealing with him; but all the anger in me just then was focused on

Felix. Who was this stranger in my neighborhood telling me this meeting on the porch was over?

I jumped up and ran out to Grandma. She had built a little fire on the ground, which she does sometimes, and was watching the smoke wind its way through her hollyhocks. I sat and leaned against her.

"Long day, eh?" she said, poking at the gray hairs under her red scarf. "Mean Indians."

Any mention of mean Indians signaled the likelihood of a story-telling session. I had to head her off.

"Auntie Mollie, she got any cousins?" I asked.

Grandma laughed. Her shoulders lifted and shook quietly. Her face moved in and out of the sunlight. I knowed what a dumb question I asked, and neither one of us said a thing for the longest time. Then, when I figured she'd forgotten everything, she leaned over so she was close to my ear and started laughing again. "Lots," she whispered, and gave me a gentle push.

* * *

That was in the afternoon, about three. At eight that night, after dinner, I found myself at my desk in my room, filling out my chart. The meeting was hardly a month away, when all of us was supposed to have our charts done, and here I was Mr. Pass-Out-the-Flyers-for-the-Meeting, and I hadn't done my chart. But guilt about not doing my chart wasn't what moved me. If I was going over to Auntie's, I had to have a reason besides the fact that I simply agreed to go. I'd have my chart done so I could show him how he was supposed to fill it out. That and a quick visit to Auntie Mollie and Alice and the boys, make sure their charts was completed also.

While Grandma banged pots and pans in the kitchen, I filled in the empty spaces on my chart, tracing from me and Mom and Grandma back to the first Rosa, which is what everybody was supposed to do to prove we was a tribe. A tribe, hell, it's a family. One big family. If Felix was a cousin, part of the tribe, I could help him fill in anything after his mother and grandmother if he got stuck, since that is where everybody's lines start crossing together, after the grandmothers and great-grandmothers. I finished my chart, using what I knowed from Grandma, then sat for the longest time, deciding whether or not I should go to Auntie's. I went to the front room, sat in front of the TV without turning it on. The kitchen was quiet, empty. From the couch I could see through the kitchen to the open back door, and beyond that, the top of Grandma's head, the red scarf in the kitchen light, like a flag signaling where she sat outside in the warm June night. I folded my chart, which was in my lap, and left.

* * *

When I got over to Auntie's, I seen things different in the house. Something bright, something about the lights, like none of the lamps had shades; and the two little boys, their faces was full and happy while they played Nintendo on the front room floor. But mostly it was Mollie. After Justine, her oldest girl, just sixteen years old, stepped between one of the Estrada brothers and Kolvey Green when they was unloading automatic rifles on each other and got herself killed, Mollie walked like she'd been packing a hundred-pound sack of cement for the last five hundred years. Slow, bent over, and heavy. Mollie was never Miss Sunshine Ballerina. She's a big woman, heavy, not on the order of the Bills, which is weight off the scale, but heavy nonetheless, and she always moped around, like she was half awake and mad she wasn't full asleep. But tonight she was awake again. Her black eyes was full of the light there. For the first time I actually seen her pretty; how smooth and young her skin was; her lips, thin but shaped clear, the way flower petals is; and her hair, which she'd cut in a straight line just above her shoulders, it was shiny, like wet black olives.

She was sitting at the kitchen table with Felix, who had a small treasure chest of beads and half-finished necklaces spread out in front of him. He wore a sleeveless white T-shirt, and I seen how the naked lightbulb overhead reflected up and down the length of his arms; and he caught me looking, if even for that brief moment. He nodded for me to sit down, as if Mollie hadn't greeted me and said to do so already. Alice was there, too, the second daughter, a year younger than Justine. Only she didn't hold the light that was everywhere else. She wasn't grumpy, or even uptight, worried about things the way she is a lot, but when I sat down, saying hi and catching her eyes, it was like there was nothing in them, the way water don't reflect trees on a gray day. She looked over her shoulder once at the boys in the front room, then glanced back and forth from the Indian basket she was working on in her hands to the beads on the table.

With his pointing finger, Felix pushed his beads one at a time to the center of the table. He told where each come from and what its history was. Black glass beads from China. A turquoise chunk from Arizona. Coral disks from Egypt. He said the Egyptian disks come out of an ancient tomb, King something or other. I thought, Why in the hell are we fooling around with stuff that come out of a grave? Old-timers say never to touch that stuff. Might haunt you. But I said nothing. I didn't want to draw attention to myself. Besides, there was no time. He was pushing up one bead after another and talking nonstop. He covered a dozen countries and at least four times as many different kinds of stones. Sounded like he'd been all over the world and hand-picked each bead. All the beads was precious. Each could affect you special: The Chinese beads was for thinking, mind work, he said; turquoise had to do with the earth; and the Egyptian beads, I forget. Then there was the necklaces, most of them just started or half complete, with their combinations of beads that could affect you special too: the glass beads strung with turquoise and silver for love; cobalt blue with the coral disks for good luck. His eyes followed his fingers and below his sleeveless white T-shirt, he lifted and straightened his arms with each bead he pushed forward, causing a panther tattooed on the ball of his shoulder to stretch and step.

When he was finished, he sat back and locked his hands over his chest, satisfied with the show he'd given. He looked over what he'd set out, all his beads and necklaces, mostly just giving us time to take them all in. Then he looked up. His eyebrows was raised, like he was asking, Well, what do you think? But his eyes told you he knowed you couldn't think nothing but it was all just great. Alice, she wasn't paying attention; she was weaving, stitching her trimmed sedge root around a willow rod in the way I seen old Pomo ladies do. Mollie was caught though, her light-full eyes moving back and forth, landing on this stone or that necklace, the way bees do with flowers, stopping a moment, drinking in what they need, and then moving on. The beads was pretty, some of them beautiful actually.

"Where do you get them?" I asked.

"Junk shops, flea markets, yard sales," he answered without unlocking his hands over his chest.

"They're beautiful," Mollie said.

Which was what he was waiting to hear. He stretched his arms over his head, his hands still locked, and grinned ear to ear, that solid row of perfect white teeth. Like he'd just got a king off your chessboard. Then he come forward in one fell swoop and took something from the small treasure chest opened in front of him, and when he opened his hand, a necklace, sky blue and aquamarine set off with one black and bright red stone, spilled from his palm and caught perfect on his middle and index fingers so it hung before your eyes in all its splendor. The showstopper.

"Wow!" Mollie said, her eyes opening like a kid's at a Fourth of July fireworks show.

"It'd be perfect for you," he told her.

And then I knowed for sure he was a con. Despite the way he'd caught me off guard before, I still had the ability to see clearly, and I seen this strand of blue beads wasn't right for Mollie; didn't suit her at all, no more than a sixties ass-high miniskirt would. For one thing, my business is clothes, used clothes, matching them to people, so I have a sense of these sorts of things; for another, I seen he was doing nothing more than charming her, stringing along her attention. Even Alice was looking over, marveling at the necklace he kept stroking with his long brown fingers. He talked on and on just like before, nearly ten minutes, since this necklace had I don't know how many beads from I don't know how many different places and he wanted you to know as much. What it all added up to—happiness, good luck, peace—I didn't know then. I wasn't listening. Felix was a good talker with a smile to match.

After a while Mollie got up and dished us out some ice cream. With the beads and necklaces still on the table like charms, we talked about different things: Mollie's job at the cannery, certain folks in the neighborhood, the hot weather. I told them about my having to visit the Bill sisters the next day. Talking kept me from being rude, from completely tuning out or just leaving altogether. It wasn't that I was disappointed with Felix, like I was expecting more from him, but that I seen what he was about so fast and clear.

"God-awful," Mollie said about the Bills. "Hateful bitches."

"Gives Indians a bad name," Alice said, picking up her basket again.

"Act so dumb, don't they?" Mollie said. "Life's too short."

She smarted, stung herself with her own words, and everybody got quiet with a picture of Justine somewheres in their minds. A short life.

"Maybe the meeting'll change things," I said finally, changing the subject.

"Hope so," Mollie said, pushing back from the table and getting up.

"Did you start your chart?" I asked her.

"Yeah, I did," she said and then started moving around the table picking up the empty ice cream bowls. When she turned for the kitchen sink, Felix got up. Even while I was sitting, I seen he wasn't no taller than me, about the same height actually, average, which surprised me since I'd been picturing him a lot taller, six feet or more. But he was put together good: broad in the shoulders, narrow and lean below, and his clothes—the sleeveless white T-shirt and the 501 Levi's cinched with a silver-studded black belt that matched his leather boots—was nothing special, but he wore them the way a healthy animal wears its skin.

"Help me with mine," he said, and nodded for me to follow him out the back door.

"Smoking'll stunt your growth," Mollie called after him, teasing, light and happy again.

I looked at her and then at Felix already in the doorway, then got up and followed after him.

We plopped ourselves on the porch steps and Felix pulled a flattened

Marlboro from the soft pack he kept in his front pocket. Then he held the pack out to me.

"Want one?" he said.

There was one cigarette left in the pack. "Don't smoke," I said.

"Worried it'll stunt your growth?" he said, laughing as he lit his cigarette.

"Yeah," I said and watched the smoking match he flicked away fall in one long arch to the bottom of the steps.

It wasn't any cooler outside, but the air was fresh, not kitchen smells. Only Felix's smoke, sharp and floating in waves in front of us. He smoked holding his cigarette between his thumb and pointing finger and leaning forward, like he was meeting the cigarette partway each time he puffed.

"Here," I said after a couple of minutes, taking the chart that was folded in my shirt pocket and showing it to him.

"Oh, yeah," he said as if just remembering what we was doing. He pulled the blank folded chart I give him from his back pocket, where he'd no doubt put it after I give it to him.

"Here," I said, pointing to my grandmother, Elba Gonzales, and then back to her mother, my great-grandmother Carmelita Gonzales. "Somewheres in here our lines'll cross. Always does."

He studied my chart, following from Carmelita Gonzales to Juana Maria and Josephina, the ones with no last names, all the way back to the first Rosa. Then his eyes jumped and I seen where they landed.

" 'Father,' " he said. "You ain't filled out nothing for 'father.' "

Either he was dumb or just plain rude. Maybe he didn't care. Point is, a blank space there, or anywheres on the chart, meant one of two things: Either you didn't know who the person was or, if you did know, you was ashamed. Both of which causes embarrassment. Particularly if you're Indian, since lots of us have blank spaces; and now with everybody wanting to be full blood and all, nobody wants to claim relations that ain't Indian.

"John Severe," I told Felix. "That's my father's name. Like mine."

Then I went one step further. I pointed to the empty line for my mother's father, just below the line with Grandma's name on it. "My mother, she don't even know who her father was."

I expected him to ask questions, you know, like if Grandma was a whore, what the situation was that she didn't know the father of her baby. But he come back to my father.

"Did you know him?" he asked. "Your father."

"Uh-uh," I said. "He was Italian. Last name was Severino. Mom got me stuck with just Severe. John Severe."

"My father was Mexican," he said and then took a drag off his cigarette and exhaled a long cloud of smoke before he added, "Didn't know him either."

The crickets was loud just then, like that part of the night had all at once turned itself on.

"Why didn't you put your dad's name there?" he asked. He was looking again at the empty line on my chart for "father."

"Just did the Indians so far," I said. "I was in a hurry." Which was the truth, of course.

"Why didn't you know your father?" he asked.

Something had a hold on his brain, locked in place so his thoughts stayed focused on this empty line—my father. In case he hadn't noticed, I had no pretensions about this stuff, my family history, so I told him: "Mom and him had a thing, you know. Never stuck around. He was already married, I think."

Just because I'll talk about stuff in my life don't mean I expect others to do the same. And even if I did want to know something personal about somebody, I don't have the nerve to ask. So I never asked Felix about his father and why he didn't know him neither. Time passed with us quiet. No sound but the crickets and him taking another drag off his cigarette. Then I seen him looking back at the empty chart on his lap, and I pointed to the line for "mother," my finger touching the piece of paper, and said, "Start there. 'Mother.' "

"Rose," he said. Then I seen his face settle, that thing in his brain let loose. "She got killed," he said.

"How long ago?" I asked, not knowing what else to say just then.

"Fifteen years ago; I was seven," he answered. He flicked his cigarette butt the same way he flicked the match, with his thumb and middle finger, and the cigarette, its end all aglow, sailed in an arch to the ground below.

Without intending to, I'd pushed him into a land mine. All those questions about my father, my empty line, was a way for him not to think about that empty line on his own chart, where he knowed he'd have to start. Maybe I'd have some heavy story like his own. Maybe my father got killed. But I had no such story, and before I could say something else, I had pointed him to "mother."

It's natural a person would want to know what happened to his mother. He must've figured as much, even though I was no ways going to ask. But he didn't answer. He talked in another direction.

"My auntie Daisy raised me," he said. "You ever heard of her, Daisy Green?" He chuckled hearing himself say the name, and then he said it again in case I didn't get the humor in it the first time he said it. "Daisy Green, can you believe that?"

"Wild," I said for lack of anything else to say.

"She is . . . You heard of her?"

"Uh-uh."

"Crazy. She *is* wild. Taught me to steal, all kinds of shit."

"My grandmother mostly raised me," I said.

"She's a nice lady."

"You know her?"

"No."

"You ever seen her?"

"No."

"Well, how do you know . . ." But I couldn't finish my question because just then I seen how he took me in. Both of us busted up.

"Make a new friend, hell, gotta say something good about his grandmother, right?"

I nodded and we laughed again. Then, all at once, he got up and went inside, leaving me with the night and his footsteps behind me sounding across Auntie Mollie's kitchen floor. Then he was back, plopping himself down again.

"Here," he said, and when I looked I seen the sky blue and aquamarine necklace, his showstopper, coiled neatly in his open palm. "It's yours."

He pushed his open hand towards me, urging me to take the necklace. I took it finally.

"I thought you was going to give it to Mollie," I said, running the necklace bead by bead through my fingers, stopping where the blue and sea green was set off by black and bright red.

"Nah," he said, "it's yours."

He watched me examining the necklace. "Wisdom," he said. "Things come together in that necklace so it's wisdom."

I couldn't see no meaning in the necklace, not wisdom or nothing else. But I got the idea while we was at the kitchen table that he was giving it to her and I think she did too. Then something rolled out of me.

"Ain't right for Mollie anyways," I said, seeing the necklace rested in my palm now. "It ain't. Finish the one with the glass beads and turquoise and give that to her."

"The one for love?"

"Whatever," I said. "Yeah."

"But she don't have a boyfriend."

I shrugged. "Don't know," I said. "Just an idea I got."

"Hmm," he said, resting back with his elbows on the top step. He stared out to the crickets, like he was seeing something in the night.

When I looked over at him, I seen on the top step, behind him, his empty chart. Where it fell when he got up to go inside, or where he set it even before he got up. Either way, it was out of his way now. He didn't have to look at it. He'd gotten me completely off track, away from the chart business, away from Rose. I seen his routine clear. But I felt no need to let him know, or to match him. Earlier I'd wondered who his mother was and thought to ask how she was related to us, to Auntie Mollie or to me, but now I knowed better than to bring up the subject. That was for him to do.

A sadness come over me. I watched him sit up and light his last cigarette. The panther stretched and stepped, but it was alone.

Neither of us said nothing for the longest time. Then he asked me if I liked my necklace.

"Yes," I told him, though I hadn't really thought about it.

"Put it on," he said.

And I did, just to go along with him.

"Looks great," he told me. "Wisdom."

I wondered how he'd come up with that—wisdom—and how he knowed so much about each of his beads. But again I said nothing. I let the quiet between us be our words. Later, we talked some about our jobs—his work a few months back on a pear ranch, my work on the dairy and the used clothes I sold on the side. I told him I went to junk shops too— Salvation Army, Goodwill—for the clothes I patched up and sold. When I got up to leave, explaining about morning milking and feeding schedules on the dairy, he nodded, letting me know he understood.

"Better say good night to Auntie and Alice," I said, facing the kitchen.

"Nah," he said. "Auntie's getting ready for bed."

"Tell them then," I said and turned, making my way to the side of the house.

"I will. See ya."

"See ya."

I looked back once before turning the corner. He was watching me, I could tell. But I seen only his white T-shirt and the orange glow of his cigarette.

TWO

It occurred to me that it was all a story, this thing about Rose, his mother. I realized, while driving home, that I knowed no more about Felix than I did when I first seen him that afternoon. It wasn't just that I hadn't found out who his mother was and how, or even if, she was related to us, but I hadn't found out a thing about him, who he was, where he was from. But who would make up a story about their mother like that?

At home things was quiet, dark. Grandma sat at the kitchen table, with only her sewing lamp for light, working on an Indian baby cradle. She makes things like that, baby cradles and gathering baskets, stuff with willow rods, that she gives to people. Bent over, concentrated on her work, she never looked up. It was a quarter past eleven.

I should've gone to bed. Instead, I sat at my desk and pulled out my genealogy chart, which I left folded in front of me. I dropped the necklace down too. I was thinking of Rose. What happened to her? How was she killed? Then I thought of my own mother. We weren't close, me and her. Like a horse and a cow in the same pasture. The horse eats the grass so short the cow can't eat and then the cow tears up the ground so the grass can't grow. Both starve. Can't live together, which is the story of me and my mother. She sees black, I see white, ever since I can remember. By the time I was fourteen, just before I come to live with Grandma permanent, things was out of hand. She seen college and good grades for me; I seen school as a place with a bunch of wasteful words for what you already knowed, if you had any sense. Skills, she kept saying. You need skills. Something to do. She seen me in clothes from JC Penney, where

she works as a manager of women's accessories, bracelets and purses half
this town can't say no to. Or even Macy's, she'd say. I'll give you my
credit card. But I seen used clothes, a fifties button-down shirt, white with
a black collar, or an old uniform jacket from Union Oil, orange and black,
cool with a gold stud and black chinos. I seen what I wanted; she didn't
want what I seen. So I run away a couple times, me her only kid, left her
house on Parsons Way in the neighborhood where it's new Honda Civics
and pets from the animal shelter. I always come back to Grandma, and,
like I said, landed here permanent.

Though she don't want to say it, I know what Mom thinks when
she comes to see me at Grandma's: See, I told you so, nowheres in your
life, twenty, nearly twenty-one, and no skills. She's confused now, anger
and love for me banging in her stomach like two round rocks shook up in
an empty paint can. I make the visits nice, ask her about her work, her
miniature collie, Chef. I offer to paint the back door where the dog's been
scratching. I tell her she looks nice. Maybe one day our wants will land in
the same place, like two pebbles tossed into the same pool of water. If I
ever lost her, I hope we'd been in that place first.

I glanced down at my chart, unfolded it. I pushed the spools of
colored thread and unmended used clothes aside, grabbed a pen and wrote
"John Severe" on the line for father. Of course I couldn't fill in anything
for "father's father" or "father's mother." I didn't know anything. Neither
did Mom. John Severino, father. Mom changed the name to Severe in the
hospital.

She was still married, had been for sixteen years, to Harold Pettyjohn, her boss at JC Penney, when she met my father. The circumstances of my coming into this world she explained early on in a way I
would be able to put together and understand when I got older. Like giving me a poem whose words took on a deeper meaning with time. Stuff
like: A baby is the most beautiful thing in the world. A gift from God.
When it happens, how it happens, doesn't matter. You accept it no matter
what. Even if people don't understand. A man and a woman, sometimes
they don't stay together, they don't marry. You're special that way. A gift
from God.

Still, for all her clever talk, it was a sensitive subject, the subject
of my father. Not for me—I never knowed the man. But for her. And I
used the very mention of him against her. I could win arguments, throw
her off course if nothing else, just by bringing up his name. A kid's way to
war. Cruel. A jab to the heart. "If I really do have a father, tell me what
he looks like," I said once, standing with her next to the ticket booth for
the kiddie train at the park. I'd been on the train half a dozen times al-

ready, and she'd told me no more train. I was five. "Tell me what he looks like," I blurted out again, making a scene for all the mothers and kids to see.

She took my arm and dragged me to a park bench away from the crowds. I'd crossed the limit, she said. She was fuming; and embarrassed, I'm sure. She said something about behaving in public, a lecture. A few minutes later, when the air had cleared and she mentioned my father, I'd forgotten I'd brought him up at all.

"He was tall, very handsome," she said and paused.

It took me a second to figure out what she was talking about, that she was actually answering my question. Which just shows you how much I really cared then. But I seen how she was looking, staring like she was seeing him five feet in front of her. Not the line of people in front of the ticket booth or the kids loading onto the train, not the things I seen, but him, my father, the person I never seen. Kind of spooked me, like if I looked I'd see him standing there too. Her lips moved, quivered, and then she talked, like the words that fit what she was seeing had finally come to her.

"He had curly hair, bright eyes like you, Johnny."

It was a one-night affair. She gave up everything, even before the first sign of my coming showed itself. Husband. Home. Not because she was in love with John Severino, but because her time with him one afternoon at the racetrack was enough to let her see her life for what it was. Nothing. Alone. A prune crate empty and left on the side of the road. And even if she wanted my father, if for a split second she thought of following him, she seen it was useless. Not on account of whether or not he was married. But the way he left, she told me many years later; how he walked to his horses without looking back at her. So she had no fantasies of him and her and life happily ever after. But that day in the park, when she was seeing him close enough to touch, she no doubt seen again what she seen her first and only time with him—her own loneliness.

* * *

I should've gone to bed then. Instead, I did something foolish. I wasn't thinking. I jumped up and ran to the kitchen and phoned her. It was dark. Grandma had gone to bed. I heard surprise in Mom's sleepy voice through the phone. She kept asking if I was all right.

"I been thinking about things," I told her.

"Are you all right?" she asked again. "Not in trouble, are you?"

I pictured her scratching her hair, wrinkled brow, trying to wake up. She didn't like people seeing her unless she looked perfect.

"Johnny . . ."

"I'm fine . . ."

"It's midnight, what is it?"

Suddenly I was stuck. What was I calling her at midnight for? "I was thinking about things," I said again, then added, "what you and I talk about."

"We'll talk tomorrow," she said.

And that was it. We said good-bye. She was perturbed; she would have a hard time getting back to sleep and then call Grandma in the morning while I was at work, asking what was up with me calling so late at night.

I flicked on the light. Standing at the kitchen counter, I seen the table set for breakfast.

* * *

The next morning, six o'clock, I was at Del's, where I always was six o'clock in the morning, racing up and down the calf barn dropping half-gallon plastic bottles of milk into feeders for ten hungry calves. The minute I unlatched the door and turned on the barn light they was up and bawling, all ten of them, like they was screaming, Don't forget me, don't forget me. Far as they knowed, I was the cow. I gave the nipple. A couple of older calves always finished first and pushed the youngest ones from the bottles. I had a backup though: number Seventy-two, a solid black Holstein that was a quart low, and I don't mean with milk. She was the last in the milking barn morning and night, and if there wasn't a cow in front of her, she'd stand and bawl, totally lost. I'd go up to her before she got milked—she was real friendly, slow creatures usually is—and get me a couple of quarts, which I took back to the younger calves and fed special.

I didn't let Del see me, though I don't think he would've cared; and God knows, if Seventy-two couldn't do nothing else, she did give lots of milk. For Del each calf was a miracle. Especially if it was pure dairy, Jersey or Holstein, and all the calves in the barn was. Del made each miracle happen. He bred the cows dairy, when orders from the boss was to breed them beef. At eighty-two Del wasn't going to stop milking cows.

He come here sixty years ago, when dairies was everywhere. Him and his brothers, fresh off the boat. They come down from Seattle, looking for work. Filipinos. They picked hops, cut grapes. Filipinos, in kitchens scrubbing dirty dishes. On weekends it was cockfights in Sebastopol, come Monday clean hands peeling apples, folding starched white sheets in laundry rooms behind big houses on MacDonald Avenue. Del was a butler at first. Temporary work—he replaced another butler away on vacation or something. When the regular butler come back, the boss told Del he'd help him find a job in another house, a permanent job. But the boss never made that happen, didn't get Del another butlering job. Then Del found the cows: a herd of them packed under the big oak by the road, and in the 100-degree July heat they had the right idea; and Del, he wanted to be there with them, resting peaceful in the shade. So he crawled through the barbed-wire fence and sat down, and when they started moving up to the barn at five o'clock, as they done out of habit every day, he followed them. He was delirious, hot and thirsty. Hadn't eaten for two days, he said. When Old Man Wilson come out and seen him at the gate, Del thought he'd seen his last day. He give his full name—Delfino de la Vega—and stood waiting for Wilson to shoot him or at least call the sheriff. Next thing he knowed he was cleaning out the milking barn, a rubber water hose in his hand. Water, cool water everywhere, and he knowed right then he was saved. He looked at the cows standing in the wooden stanchions chewing their cuds peaceful, and said, "Thank you, for taking me in."

The dairy was small then. About sixty cows. Jerseys and Holsteins, all grades, none of them registered pure. Del seen the milk barn go from wood to metal and concrete, from hand-milking to machine, from sixty cows to nearly three hundred and back down to eighty. When it would be only sixty cows again, he said his life would be over because that's where it was when his life had started. Cyrus Wilson, the son who never cared for the cows like his father, told Del to dry up the dairy. Breed them beef and sell the calves to the market. But when the artificial inseminator come—there was no bull left on the place—he couldn't get things straight always. Jersey or Holstein, it was a dairy after all, and Del wasn't around at these times to remind the man of Wilson's orders.

I been coming to the dairy since I can remember. Grandma brought me. Del, he's shrunk some, and his dark skin is even darker, about the color of blackberries. His hair, once black, is now a silver cap. But it's not much different the way he hoists sacks of feed nearly as heavy as himself or slips through fences I can't get my leg through. Little and wiry, he ain't changed. When I come in the barn after feeding the calves, he nodded to the light Jersey with the black-rimmed ears, letting me know where to help finish the milking. There was only about six cows left to milk, and we finished as always with Seventy-two. I swear she turned her head in the stanchion and winked at me, like she knowed our secret. But then Seventy-two couldn't remember minute to minute, much less a half hour before.

We washed down the barn, then locked the milk tank. Outside, Del took my arm. "Payday," he said.

It took me a minute to catch on. It wasn't Friday. What he meant was a new calf. We walked across the road and found Fourteen, an old Jersey with a white splotch on her face, busy licking a heifer, fawn brown like herself with a smaller white splotch. The calf wobbled on all fours, then steadied herself with each brush of Fourteen's long gray tongue. I couldn't believe I'd missed it. I checked for new calves each morning when I put out hay. If it was a heifer and pure dairy, Del flipped me a silver dollar—he always kept a couple in his pocket—and said, "Payday."

"Lot of milk," I said, looking at the cow. Her udder was like an overpacked suitcase caught between her hind legs.

"Colostrum," Del said and pitched me the silver dollar he was holding in his hand. "For the baby. Colostrum."

He looked back at the calf and rested his hand on the low fence post. I knowed he'd stand awhile. I left him in his reverie. Like I said, cows was his life, and this Jersey calf, it was another good day.

Walking back to my truck, I flipped the silver dollar in my hand. Thirty to forty heifers a year meant thirty to forty extra bucks a year. Add that to a silver dollar each Friday and my yearly gross sat at a little under a hundred bucks. For two hours' work in the morning and about two and a half at night. Sometimes mending fences or cleaning calf stalls on the weekends. I find peace with the cows, something like Del. And Grandma says it's a good thing, what I do. She knowed Del when she was young. Lovers, she says, and she says it's a complicated story. "He was always there for me, even after, especially after." Indian girls chased around with the Filipino guys. Moonshine whiskey and cockfights, the dance halls in Fulton and Windsor, work camps in Santa Rosa and Sebastopol. Helping Del is natural to me; I been doing it all my life. But now, at twenty, nearly twenty-one, in fact, a hundred bucks a year wasn't going to get me the new truck I needed, and I sure as hell wasn't making much from the used clothes stored in my grandmother's house. Driving down Petaluma Hill Road that day, back towards town, I felt like I been nowheres all my life. Like there was a shell around me that hadn't bust yet, and when it did I'd be somewheres else, somewheres new. The only thing I knowed might bust just then was the 1970 Ford pickup I was driving, and when she stopped, when her banged-up red sides dismantled themselves and fell out all around me, I'd be sitting in the middle of the road in a car seat someplace between Del's and home.

Grandma was watching the morning news with her toast and instant coffee. My eggs and bacon was at the table, hot as always. Grandma and her perfect timing. For once I wished for an empty plate, nothing.

* * *

I ate my breakfast, then went to my room, closed the door. I was tired; I tried to sleep but couldn't. Seemed the events of the day before was forever with me. They was on my mind, turning in my head, even when it didn't seem I was thinking about them. I thought of this: what I'd put on Felix, what clothes. Maybe a colored T-shirt, black on red; maybe a button-down long sleeve. Not because I wanted to cover him up, but because it was my job: I took Goodwill clothes and dressed folks so they looked good, so they was the ground zero of fashion. Most of my bedroom and all of Grandma's back porch was hangers of clothes: rows of shirts and blouses, pants of all kinds, suits and boxes and boxes of shoes stacked against the walls. Everything but underwear because you sure in hell can't sell that used. I made use of my special abilities; I looked at a person and seen what fits her inside, what made her heart comfortable and secure, and I put whatever that was on her body. Might be something totally out of style, like a forties jacket or fifties tapered pants, but you got a whole neighborhood of poor people feeling like movie stars every time they walked into the Safeway supermarket. It was them whose divorces and affairs you was reading about.

I could do more than just see how clothes fit a person. I seen a lot of things in this world special. When I was five I seen a frog had a missing toe. It was a little green-sided thing, on a flat rock under Grandma's irises. Nothing special. But when I looked close, I seen it had one of its front legs stuck out, like it was wanting me to see something, and where the middle toe should've been was nothing but a little nub. When I told Grandma, she said it was a good thing. I never thought much about it. Then I seen it again the next summer, and again the next summer, and the next summer after that. "Four times now," Grandma said. "Means you got that spirit—you're gonna see things." Not long after that I seen in Old Man Toms's black eyes the crystal vase he wanted to steal out of Grandma's cupboard. With Grandma out of the room and me not budging from the chair by her cupboard, the geezer never got his buzzard claws anywhere near that vase. Then, a couple of years ago, I seen how Dollface was about to bust an artery in his heart. Dollface, the three-hundred-pound white guy who lived around the corner with his four dozen cats; and it was the cats that told me, something in the way they was sitting still and close to him while he sat on the porch and smoked his pipe like he had a million tomorrows. I told Grandma and she had an ambulance there before Dollface felt the first pull in his chest. Two weeks later he was home with a set of stitches and a lot of happy cats. Grandma said one day I could heal people. But I'm no doctor. I never gone that far.

And just then, as I was laying on my bed thinking of what I'd put on Felix, my special abilities shut off. My eyes ranged over the racks of men's shirts against the wall, back and forth. I knowed my merchandise without looking at it. Still, nothing popped out, not one shirt, long-sleeved or short, not even a color. I thought again of his smile. I couldn't tell with him what I seen and what I didn't.

* * *

About ten o'clock Alice showed up, and before I let her in and found the sleeveless flannel shirt she was wanting and didn't know it yet, I told myself that I would get her to fill me in on Felix.

Alice rummaged through the racks of shirts on the back porch. It's something I let customers do, take time to look over things, even though I already seen what it was they wanted. You had to let folks feel they was discovering for themselves. Alice, she was unsure of herself, like only yesterday she found a mirror and discovered she had a body. And if she could say as much, she'd tell you she wished she had never found the mirror. Too much to think about and where to begin? She had a boy-friend, Anthony, but he was the same, figured a body was something like Mars, a planet a million miles from earth. So Alice wanted something that would show a little of herself, but not enough so people would look and remind her she was a blossoming fifteen-year-old. And then it had to be kind of hip, cool, like what other kids wore. "A shirt," she said, and I seen the sleeveless flannel.

It was a little loose on her, which of course was perfect, since it hid her body and was neighborhood hip at the same time. It showed her arms, which was just enough, and reached below her waist. After the red fake silk she tried on, the blouse that collected itself around her cupcake breasts, the flannel was just the thing. She flipped her long straight hair and flattened her bangs in the mirror. Which was another sign she really wasn't used to seeing herself. She kept looking at her face, like she was seeing it for the first time, instead of looking right away at how the shirt fit her.

Most of the time I ask customers to make me an offer, then I hag-gle. But if they're old, I say nothing, offer things cheap. Or if they're poor; and Alice, she was as poor as a field mouse in winter. Not to mention the hard luck of losing her sister. "Two bucks," I said and even then I felt low-down, seen how she dug and pulled up the change from her purse.

But, like I said, my mind was fixed elsewheres, and I needed Alice the way a man in the middle of nowheres needs a map. It was perfect that she had showed up now, almost like I willed her to the house, even if, truth be known, she had told me a week ago that she was going to come over for a shirt.

I offered her a Coke, which was nothing unusual, and we sat on the back porch watching her two little brothers feed bread crumbs to Pete, Grandma's white Muscovy duck. Her brothers, Sheldon and Jeffrey, had as much fascination with that duck as Grandma, and always brought him something to eat when they come with Alice. Grandma says Pete's as smart as a talking mynah bird. I kept thinking how to start the conversation I wanted without making it look like that was what I wanted. Then Alice talked up.

"Things is better around the house," she said. "A little, anyways. Mom's happier."

"I seen it last night," I said.

I thought about Auntie Mollie being happy; and, all at once, the odd idea come to mind that Felix was her boyfriend. Overweight Mollie, sad Mollie with the curlers in her hair?

"Who's Felix?" I blurted out.

I wanted to take my words back, take a deep breath and swallow them. Of course Alice never witnessed my foolishness around this guy, the way I'd been slow. So it was only me seen myself dumb again, but that was enough.

"You met him last night," she said, surprised I asked the question.

She looked out at the boys, the late morning sun catching her cheekbones, the outline of her face. She's Indian-looking, straight hair, dark, her eyes slanting a little. And she's quiet, a lot like the old-timers. But where so many of them got hate, Alice got only worry. Worry about her brothers. Worry about her poor mother, and probably her sister asleep in the cold, cold ground. And right then I seen a trace of worry in her eyes, like a school of minnows that surfaces in the water then disappears below as fast as they come up.

"Did he do his chart?" she asked.

"I don't know. I showed him what to do," I answered.

"Still got to finish mine," she said. "Meeting's in a month, right?"

"Yeah," I told her.

She wasn't really interested in charts or the meeting just then, I

could tell. Her mind was moving like the arm on one of them old juke-
boxes, feeling over each of the selections. I knowed she'd hit the number
I pushed sooner or later. And I was right.

"Felix," she said, like she was just remembering. "He's staying
with us."

That much I'd figured. Still, the way she said it was like a door
opening. You knowed you would get a peek inside before long.

"He's a cousin, from Lake County."

I looked at her. She was still watching the boys with Pete. "What
cousins we got in Lake County?" I asked, which was about as smart as asking how many blackbirds in a field is a blackbird.

"No," she said, "he's Mom's sister's kid. Rose."

Close, first cousins was what she was saying, as opposed to the
countless second, third, fourth, and fifth cousins each of us got here and
there a hundred miles around. Mollie and her family only come to the
neighborhood a couple of years ago. I didn't know that much about her
close relations. She wasn't a first cousin to me, or my mother. Second or
third, maybe. I'm not sure. I was thinking of none of this, though. My
mind was locked on the fact Felix come from Lake County. Seemed
strange; I pictured him from a faraway place, Los Angeles, or even if it
was just San Francisco, which is pretty close. Lake County, an hour north
of here, ain't nothing, and if an Indian's from there, you can bet both
shoes he's from a reservation.

"Lake County," I said again; I named a couple of the reservations,
Elem, Robinson.

"Robinson," she answered.

"He told me his mother died . . . was killed."

"Yeah," she said, watching the boys empty the last of their crumbs
out of the plastic Wonder bread bag for Pete. "Yeah," she said again.

But this time it wasn't as if she was opening a door with her talk;
she was closing it. I knowed not to inquire further. She might've been
close to Rose, her aunt; and maybe Rose died some way horrible, a car accident, drowned.

She looked down at the flannel shirt in her lap, folded and tied
with a thick string. "Thanks," she said. She was ready to leave.

"How long's he staying with you?" I asked.

"What?" She looked at me, dumbfounded.

"Felix," I said.

"Don't know," she said, registering finally what I was asking.
"Mom says he moves around a lot. He did up there."

"In Lake County."

"Yeah," she answered. Then she looked back at the boys and said, "He's nice."

It was only after her and the boys was gone that I seen how her face was just then: plain, without the little smile she had before; not worried or upset, just plain, the way a field is solid yellow in July.

* * *

I didn't linger on thoughts of Alice though. And I should've been upset with myself for asking so many questions about Felix. But sitting on the back steps after Alice left, I felt only excited, stirred up. Like I had something under my belt. Like I knowed something, which I did. He was my size again, not somebody over six feet tall; that nowheres place where he drawed himself up big in Auntie's door had trails, a path I'd set my foot on and could follow. He was from Lake County, Robinson Rancheria. Jewelry, Lake County, and a mother named Rose, Auntie's sister. And so how did Rose die? If Felix had nothing special beyond that smile, if he was just a fast-talking con, he did have a way to make you wonder, and if nothing else pushed me just then, that did.

I gone straight to Grandma.

She had her three-ring circus going, which meant she was sitting in the front room with *General Hospital* on the box, her game of solitaire spread out on the coffee table in front of her, and on the couch next to her, the morning paper opened and folded back on an article about South American killer bees. She sits like that, roving from one activity to the next, watching TV for a while, then turning up a few cards, reading the paper, then back to the TV or the cards. "Keep busy this way," she says, and she doesn't like interruptions; she won't answer the phone, nothing. Still, when I approached, she patted the only empty spot next to her on the couch.

I sat down, careful not to mess up her newspaper, or bump the table so her cards would jumble.

"Mollie," I said. "Did Mollie have a sister named Rose who got killed?"

She picked up a three of hearts and held it, looking back and forth from it to the cards turned upright on the table.

"Grandma . . ."

"Hmm," she said, still studying her cards. "Yes, I heard that. Don't remember their names though. Moved to Lake County long time ago. Yes, one got killed."

Then, like she finally figured out what to do with the card, she held it up in front of me and said, "Three of them. There was three sisters."

She plunked the card down, setting it separate from the others so she wouldn't forget it. Before I could say another word, she turned to the newspaper and placed her pointing finger on the article. "Killer bees," she said, "they're coming north," and with that I heard a car on the gravel driveway.

I looked out and seen the red BMW convertible. Julie Brigioni.

"Customer," Grandma said.

"Yeah," I said and sighed, getting up and making my way to the back door, where my customers know to knock.

Julie Brigioni, impatient as usual, flipping her perfect-cut blonde hair in the sun and watching for Pete to waddle out from behind the hollyhocks and chew her tanned ankles to the bone. Of course Pete never bit nobody; he'd come out, if he heard someone on the steps, only thinking he was going to get fed. Where she comes from, Montecito Heights, folks don't have ducks in their backyards. No poor folks. And Julie, she tells you through her candy-apple smile, no matter what she's actually saying, that she wouldn't trade places with you for all the world. You live in a dump and she don't.

I put up with her—sold her clothes that her friends called "used junk with a twist"—because she's Cyrus Wilson's niece, the guy that owns Del's dairy. She drives over once a month in her fancy car to check out my new merchandise. Early on she said something about her uncle Cyrus, and I put two and two together without ever letting her know I worked on the dairy. I figured I could spy, find out if Cyrus Wilson had a buyer yet for the property. Yes, if it wasn't for that, I'd have found a way to put up a closed sign every time she pulled into the driveway. She is beautiful, she's college educated and classy, all of which I can handle. It's her attitude that bugs me, and there's enough of it to sink a ship.

Like always, I let her squirm awhile, with Pete coming within inches of the bottom step for a handout. It's the only way I can handle her attitude once she gets inside the door. She talks all cool and nice while letting you know she's above God's green planet. I just listen and remember them panic-twisted lips I seen a minute before outside the window.

"That is the ugliest duck in the world," she said when I finally let her in. She rushed past me, inside, where she figured she was safe, and then straightened herself, like she'd just strolled into a boutique in the mall. She glanced at the racks of clothes and then looked back at the door, which I always left open after she come inside. "You know, that duck looks like a buzzard."

Even though I'd explained a hundred times over the type of duck Pete was, that Muscovies have fleshy red faces, she always said that about him.

"It's hot today," she said as she started sorting through the clothes. I watched her and knowed nothing would appeal to her. Nothing jumped out at me, nothing I seen. But she made sure, going back through the racks a second time, her long fingers stopping half a second on each hanger before the flat of her palm pushed the entire piece of clothing aside. She worked fast.

"Well, not today," she said with a bored sigh.

"Yeah," I said, watching how she was stalled at the door, looking outside. Last revenge, I thought: Pete was still at the bottom of the steps. But before I could enjoy her fear, I sensed a shadow, something from outside, and all at once; and I should've seen where she was gazing, not down the steps, but straight ahead, eye level, for it wasn't Pete she was looking at but Felix. He must've been standing on the second or third step, because I heard him before I saw him. I heard him ask for me. "Johnny?" he said.

Julie turned towards me, her shoulders in my direction, her eyes still fixed on Felix. She collected herself fast, though, and said to him, "He's here." Then she walked out and I come forward and seen how she brushed past him and made her way out of the yard. His head was turned, following her, and he was leaning against the porch railing, bracing himself with one arm. He was on the second step. He was wearing the same clothes from the night before: sleeveless white T-shirt and 501 Levi's cinched with a silver-studded black belt that matched his leather boots. When he turned around, he was smiling.

"What'd you do to her?" he asked.

"She's like that," I said.

"All the time?" His grin reached ear to ear, showing that row of picture-perfect whites. And it wasn't like the smile before, when he seen me slow or idiotic, but more like I was something cool, like I had in me something he understood and we was equals because of it. Of course he thought it was Julie, that maybe he'd dropped in on the tail end of a fight, seeing her take off the way she did—ha! upset over a duck.

"She's just a customer," I told him.

"Yeah, you sell clothes," he said.

"Yeah," I answered.

"We're cousins, third, I think." He paused. "I seen it on my chart." He was all of a sudden serious, his smile vanished, like I'd known him all my life and had forgotten something important he'd told me and it bothered him.

"It's kind of cool, ain't it?" I answered after a moment, for lack of anything else to say.

"Blood is blood," he said, as if I still hadn't understood what he'd said before and he was now giving me a clue. He searched my face, looked me in the eyes, for any sign I might've caught on.

Slow or idiotic, no. This time just plain rude. It hit me, and I did what I should've done before: stepped back from the door and asked him in. Slowly he mounted that last couple of steps. Once inside the porch, he stopped, glancing back and forth on either side of him, like he'd just walked into a dark woods, and then his eyes caught and settled on the racks of clothes stretching from the sink and Grandma's washer to the two wide porch windows.

"That's just part of them," I said. "I got all kinds of clothes."

Little by little and like his eyes was leading him, he made his way across the porch to the clothes. He didn't touch nothing; he just stopped and looked, his back to me.

"Alice said you got some good stuff," he said, "and she was right— you got some *damn* good stuff."

He parted the hangers directly in front of him, looking at something. "You sure you're not going with that white chick?" he asked, his back to me still.

"Uh-uh," I said. "She's a snob."

"White chicks is that way, trust me," he said. "Ain't worth their nice cars." He talked as if his mind was elsewheres, like on the piece of clothing he was examining.

"You seen her car?" I asked.

"The red beamer that was out front, yeah," he answered in that same faraway voice.

And then he turned full around, facing me again, and he was holding up a black vest, velvet-soft material, silver buttons. I knowed even before he tried it on that nothing I had could've been more right for him. Black and silver. His black hair and shining eyes. I'd forgotten all about that vest.

"How much?" he asked, slipping into it.

He caught me off guard, but then my brain righted and shot back with something just in time to save the day.

"Nothing," I said. "Trade."

"Serious?" he asked. He looked surprised, though he remembered, no doubt, the necklace he'd given me.

"Serious," I answered.

He looked at me a minute. His eyes narrowed; they told me I understood finally what he'd been trying to say: We're cousins, we make and sell things, we ought to trade, exchange merchandise. Then, in case there was any doubt, he said as much: "You and me, we're into stuff, hitting the junk shops for what we do. You can show me where the places is at in this town."

"OK," I said.

He took off the vest, letting it slink down one bare arm, and then he folded it over the other arm. He started out, but before he got to the door he stopped, just a foot from my face, gave me his hand and said, "Cousins."

I felt then as if I hadn't said enough; after he'd said we could work together, I'd only said OK when I should've said more. I knowed I should've said more. But nothing come, nothing that made sense. As he ambled down the steps, I called after him:

"So you done your chart?"

"Started," he turned and said.

"The meeting's in a month," I said, trying to hold him, as if while he waited I might find the right thing to say.

"Yeah," he said, shaking his head, "I seen a lot of Indian politics—too much, in fact."

"Yeah," I said, just to agree with him, and then he was gone and I was looking down at Pete, still at the bottom of the steps waiting for a handout.

Cousins. Ha! A con, I thought. Slick. Here and gone. He didn't like Indian politics, seen too much, he said. But what did he say at our first meeting on Auntie's porch—"You and me, homeboy. We're gonna change the world, eh? . . . We'll have ourselves the biggest bingo hall this side of Vegas." I looked at the hole in my rack of shirts, seen the empty hanger. Then I went back to Grandma.

Coming through the kitchen, it occurred to me that she had deliberately attempted to distract me from the subject of Rose by pointing to her article about killer bees. She's like that sometimes, she'll try to distract you from a story, or even just tell you part of it so that you have to find out or figure out the rest for yourself, like it was a puzzle. She knows all the answers, but she won't tell you. Of course, she denies this when you confront her; but then, when you come back a week or a year later with the answer to something you asked her about before, she'll say, "Oh, yeah, I heard that." So why didn't she tell you what she'd heard before? She'll squirm her way out of that too.

So I had full intentions of playing hardball with her now. She was still on the couch, now gazing at the TV. I sat down in the cleared space where I sat before. Picked up where we left off.

"How did it happen?" I asked.

"What?" she asked, not turning her head from the box.

"Rose, Auntie Mollie's sister, how did she get killed?"

Grandma craned her head, looked me in the eyes. "Someone said something about a man; I don't know."

"A man?" I was surprised: At least she'd heard me and responded.

"There was three of them, three sisters. One got killed." Back to her unclear answers.

"How?" I pushed. "I mean, how did it happen, Grandma?"

"Sadness. How does any of them things happen? Them Bill sisters . . . Rosa."

I'd mentioned the day before that I was supposed to drop flyers off at the Bills's and dreaded it. I was worried she might get me off track with a lecture about how so many of us is sad cases; specifically, I was worried she'd go into her storytelling mode, tell the story of Rosa for the umpteenth time. Which she did.

"The Mexicans, Johnny, they come in and killed and kidnapped everybody. Raped the women. Sold the men and boys—girls too—as far away as Mexico. Sold them as slaves. There was one young woman left—the Mexican general kept her here as his wife. They baptized her and named her Rosa. I don't know, but they say them Mexican folks named this town after her: Santa Rosa. The Mexican general, he didn't treat Rosa so good, not good at all. But they had a daughter, the second Rosa, and when she was old enough, she run away; and when she come back years later, she had her kids with her, and, that way, with her and them kids, this tribe started up again. The kids was Indian, from a man over by Sebastopol Lagoon. So we're all mixed up with the other tribes too. But, no matter, what we got in common is that one ancestor, the first Rosa. She never did see a way past the adobe's four walls where the general kept her; never seen the whole tribe back to life, when it had been killed off to just one person."

"Who killed Rose, Auntie's sister?" I asked, as if she hadn't gotten off track with the story. "I mean, who was the man?"

"Not sure what happened," she said. "It was sad." She looked back at the TV for a moment, as if she was thinking, perhaps trying to remember who it was that killed Rose. Then, with one quick turn of her head, she was looking at me again.

"That's why you help the tribe," she said. "Sadness. Like the Bills. Give them those flyers."

There it was: not a story this time, not even a puzzle, but a trap.

"Grandma—" I began to protest, but she quickly interrupted me.

"Pete," she said, "he wanted a snack and you didn't give him nothing."

"That was Rose's son who was just here," I protested.

"Pete," she said, looking past me to the back door.

"See," I said, "you know stuff and won't tell . . . You knowed he was outside—at the bottom of the steps, begging. You see things . . ."

She shook her head no, then nodded to the back porch.

When I looked, I seen Pete on the top step, in the doorway, waiting, like a dog that was obedient and knowed not to come inside.

Grandma, it was no use fighting her. The world and her was in cahoots with one another. She tugged at her apron, then picked up her folded newspaper and started fanning herself. She was looking back at the TV. I got up and found an old tortilla in the kitchen for Pete.

* * *

Indians is like weeds. You know the difference between them and other plants, and wish you didn't, because every time you look into your garden you see where they're growing. You got to deal with them. Unless you're Raymond Pen, who gets others to deal with them. Fools like me. And I seen what weeds was in my garden that afternoon, besides him. The Bills; and if Indians is weeds, then them two is thistles. Still, I kept my promise and took them a flyer.

Both of them appeared pleasant enough, which must've been on account of the full bowl of popcorn between them on the couch. Food was the one thing that might slow their meanness; all that popcorn was a good sign. Always best to catch them on a full bowl. They eat like that all day and quit only for regular meals—breakfast, lunch, and dinner. Ain't a *Oprah* or *True Stories of the Highway Patrol* they can't tell you about. Mona, the older one, the one with the brows, looked at the flyer, then handed it over the popcorn to Lena, the younger one, the one without brows. I sat in a chair they wore out and probably didn't use no more; they couldn't, the stuffing was worn down to the metal springs. Lena kept studying the flyer, turning it this way and that, like it was a painting and she couldn't tell if it was up or down. Part of my job was to answer questions if folks was confused about something. After what seemed a half hour of Lena looking at that flyer, I figured I better talk. With the Bills it's a crapshoot, anything you say; popcorn or not, you don't know how they're going to react.

"It's about putting our charts together," I said.

"Yeah," Mona said.

Lena didn't look up. She kept gazing at the piece of paper, and now she was feeding her face, her big skin-hanging arm working back and forth from the bowl to her mouth, automatic. Mona looked slightly interested, her pencil brows coming together in a straight line over her nose. Like she was thinking of something. I thought I was in the clear. Then I rolled the dice and lost.

"We're all related," I said.

"Ain't that a pisser," Lena snapped, letting go of the flyer.

"Yeah," Mona said, like she all of a sudden understood what Lena was thinking.

I seen the flyer catch on Lena's round polyester pink knee, then, when she moved, sink to the floor.

She looked at me straight on and pointed to her chest. "Me, I don't claim none of these people as relatives."

She dropped her hand and sat back, letting me digest her first dose of poison. Then she mashed her teeth, like she was preparing the next batch, and leaned forward again, her forever stomach in a purple sateen blouse resting on the tops of her legs.

"Why should I?" she asked.

"Yeah," Mona growled.

Lena's eyes pushed out with the meanness that was swelling her brain just then. She reached for a handful of popcorn, then stopped herself. Mona leaned forward then. Her stomach, reaching her knees, was even bigger than Lena's and her face was filling with red. I was a goner.

"Federal acknowledgment for what?" Lena asked. "A bunch of thieves, cheaters? Uh-uh, not me."

"Me neither," Mona said.

"We had a reservation already, two of them," Lena went on. "You know why we lost them?"

She turned her head sideways and jutted out her chin, like she was waiting for an answer. Made me think of hide-and-seek the way the chin appeared all at once from her massive jowl. Of course she wanted nothing from me. She was setting things up to spit out the answer herself. But then she couldn't get started. She'd gotten so riled up her throat squeezed. She coughed and tapped her chest, like that would open her pipes.

"Because . . . Because," she stammered. She was like an engine trying to turn over. Then she took a deep breath and caught herself. Pointing her stubby finger up Grand, she said, "That woman up there. That same woman! The one calls herself a fucking medicine woman. Nellie. Nellie Copaz, it was her mother made a deal with the white man and got Mama and Papa and the rest of them throwed off. Poor Mama and Papa . . . you know why?"

Her head was sideways again. But this time, before she could answer, Mona jumped in. "Because she was fucking that white man," she said and then her little snake mouth snapped shut.

"Fucking him," Lena said in case I hadn't heard the first time. "And you know what?" she asked, pointing once more. "That same woman, the one calls herself a medicine woman? She fucked the white man's son."

"Sure did," Mona agreed.

Then Lena sat back and folded her arms, confident. "Now wouldn't you say that's a case of like daughter like mother?"

She gave me a minute to fully comprehend the connection. Proud of herself, she patted the top of her frizzed perm.

"Now, the second time," she said, "right up the street." Her arm shot up as straight as a gun, and now she was pointing in the opposite direction, down Grand. "You know who I'm talking about. Zelda Toms! At least she don't claim no pretensions like the other one. How could she when every dipstick this side of Mexico been in her oil? You know what she done?"

She dropped her arm, again let me consider a minute, which was her way of setting things up for what she was going to say next.

"You know the last place we had was over in Sebastopol, right?"

"Yeah," I said.

Lena hunkered herself to the edge of the couch and rested her hands on her knees. Her fingers was spread and turned in so her hands made me think of alligator claws.

"Zelda Toms had the deed," she said, "don't ask me how, and she lost it in a card game."

"A fucking card game," Mona added for effect.

"And you're wanting me to be in a tribe with them, a bunch of whores and thieves?" Lena asked. "People don't change. And that fucking Steven Pen calling himself chief! He ain't no chief. He's a sellout, a god-damned apple—red on the outside, white on the inside—just like his father was . . . And you! You're so desperate for friends you believe anything anybody tells you. They're using you. Don't you see? Every one of them sold us out. My mother and father died in the park on lower Fourth because every one of them sold us out!"

I wanted to say her mother and father died in the park on lower Fourth because they was drunk in below-freezing weather. But what come out surprised me. I said, "My grandmother, she didn't sell anybody out. She left because of all the hatred."

Complete silence.

"Hatred," Lena finally said, all choked up. "That's it. That's what I'm talking about. This whole damn tribe. Hatred."

She turned back to Mona, the red out of her face, the hot wind emptied from her body.

"That's right," Mona said quietly, looking back at Lena.

And with them calm and looking at each other, I figured I better make my move before the tide turned again. "Well, gotta go," I said and slipped out the door.

* * *

It was warm outside, hot, the afternoon sun in tar bubbles on the street. But I could breathe. I was out of there. I walked half a block, then seen the corner grocery, which was across from Mollie's. When I seen the two big cypress trees on either side of Mollie's porch and the chocolate brown front door between them, I realized a truth: The only thing more troublesome than seeing the Bills was seeing Felix. But what was all the fuss about besides my pride? And Felix, who was he? A fast talker maybe, but just another Indian, a rez Indian at that. I looked at my watch: four o'clock. I had to be at Del's in an hour. Better do something useful with my time, I thought. Finish passing out flyers and make everyone happy. Hear Raymond say in that I'm-important voice, "Good job, Johnny."

South Park, where a lot of us live, is on the west side of the fairgrounds, just behind the racetrack. Some folks live in Roseland, further west, and others, the Ramirezes and the Joneses and a couple of other families, live east, on the other side of the fairgrounds. Which is where I had to finish my flyer run. I knocked on doors, answered questions if folks was home, stuffed a couple flyers in the mailbox if they wasn't, split. It was four-thirty when I pulled up to the Ramirezes, my last stop. A little extra time to hang with my friend Tony and get something to eat before heading to Del's. But just as I come up to the screen door, I heard all hell breaking out. Pauline, Tony's mother, on a rampage.

"How could you just let your sister walk out that door?" she was yelling. "Didn't you watch her? Can't you keep an eye on her, like I asked you? Can't you do anything right? Lazy, lazy, lazy . . ."

Her voice was high-pitched, stopping and starting in fits. And the baby, the four-year-old, she was crying in the background to match her mother. Poor Tony. If I took two steps and peeked through the hole in the rusted screen that was the size of a person's head I knowed what I'd see: Tony sitting on the edge of the couch looking straight ahead, and Pauline pacing back and forth in front of him with that long hair of hers hanging in her sunken face and catching on her foaming lips so she'd have to keep spitting and swiping at it.

You'd think she was yelling about the baby, but I knowed it was about the older one, Tony's sixteen-year-old sister. He was supposed to watch both of them, the La's, La Tonya and La Angelique. But watching the older one, La Tonya, that was no easy chore. Keeping her in the house was about as easy as holding an entire rainstorm in a thimble. The streets was her life; already she'd been busted twice for shooting and stuff, gang-banging with the Estradas. Still, Tony tried his best with her.

He took care of both them girls, that's on top of stocking shelves at Payless every night. Plus he checked in on his grandmother, Zelda Toms, too. He done things right. He wasn't lazy. What he was was Steven Pen's son. That's right, Raymond's half brother. But Tony looks like Steven, and ever since he found out a few years back that Steven was his father Tony got more like him. Not the square build, the straight nose, not that stuff, but the eyes, something that says they seen sadness and ac-cepted it. The way a mother sees her crippled child. And it's that same-ness in them drives Pauline crazy, especially when she wants to blame someone for her life. She'd like to blame Steven, but she's too proud for that, all smiles and ain't-I-a-survivor when she sees him. So it's Tony who gets it. And Tony, who knows Steven and knows Steven is his father, takes the blame. He thinks that somehow he had something to do with his father's decision to follow what was between his legs instead of what was in his brain. Like Tony had something to do with the mistake. That he wasn't just the mistake itself, but that he'd had the hammer and nails that put it together. And that's how he meshed with Steven, even if he didn't see him that much. A sadness in the eyes, an I'm-sorry look that Steven, regardless of his button-down oxford cloth shirts and paisley ties, has too. Father and son.

Lately, things was particularly tough. Pauline was three months off crystal and starting to face things. She was at full blast now. I left a flyer by the door and left, headed for Del's. I couldn't stand thinking of Tony taking all that crap, staring straight ahead like he does—them eyes. Like a mule that keeps staring no matter how much you load on its back.

He was the first guy I met when I moved in with Grandma per-

manent, when I was fourteen. A lot of the other guys picked on me because I come from my mother's place in a better part of town. Once,
coming home from school, Ernesto, Tony's older cousin, and a couple
other thugs got a hold of me—they was going to rob me of the whopping
fifty cents I had. Tony was with them. I figured enough of their hassling
me. I pulled out my two quarters, offered them. I took my chances. "You
want this, take it," I said. "But it ain't nothing. You want small change?
I'll show you how to get lots of it." And with that I led them over to the
corner grocery where I unloaded the gumball machines with a trick
Grandma taught me using a dime and twisting the knobs a certain way.
She said she learned the trick when Mama and her was poor and she had
no other way to get Mama a candy. "Don't do them things unless you're
desperate," she warned me, and I guess I figured I was desperate enough.

    And what happened? They thought I was a major criminal. I told
them I knowed a lot more, too, like how to rob a store; and with that Ernesto spread the word that I was pretty cool and nobody picked on me
again. The point of all this is that the next day Tony come over to
Grandma's house by himself. "Sorry," he said. "For what?" I asked, after
which he explained how it was his idea to have Ernesto and them rob me
on account of how he thought I was rich. "I wanted to be cool," he said.
I forgave him and we become best friends. But, to this day, I can't forget
how he kept saying he was sorry, even after I forgave him. "Promise," he
said, "promise me we'll never hurt each other. Make no pain. Promise." If
only the world could promise Tony as well.

    Things just wouldn't be pain-free for him, if they are for anybody.
His girlfriend, Vivi, for instance. She was going to have a baby. Of course,
Tony had full intentions of marrying her. The problem was how to tell
Pauline. Who'd take care of the little La and the big La if not Tony? "We
kind've put the cart before the horse," Tony told me. But there was no
"we" in the matter, at least in terms of the decision to have the baby.
Vivi seen two things clear: one, Tony had no immediate plans for moving
out of his mother's; and two, he was the kind of guy who made a promise
to the world not to hurt nobody. So Vivi pulled the snap tight; she got off
the pill and told Tony nothing about it. And now Tony's heavier in his
shit than ever, which is another reason I couldn't stand there listening to
him take abuse from Pauline. Think what it's going to be like when Tony
drops the bomb about him and Vivi. Vivi, she'll get just what she wants:
a hard-working, only-wanting-to-please husband, and, in time, she'll have
a house with a dog, daffodils, all the rest. And Tony, when he finally
breaks from Pauline, he'll sit the same way, taking crap, only now from
Vivi. I can see it, him grown old that way.

Love is like a tightrope walk. It's a balancing act, and even if you think you've made it across the water, when you got one foot on solid ground, a wind can come up and blow you away. Sex, that's something else again; it's like jumping into the water without even trying to get to the other side. And, of course, the two get mixed up so most folks hang from the rope by their fingers, going this way and that, and most of the time nowheres at all. I come up with a solution: instant replay. Think how you feel just after you come, and ask yourself, Would I go through this whole thing just to get to that place? Of course, lots of times you're so set on the major motion, you don't want to think that you got a machine with a replay button. But it's like they say in AA, it works if you work it.

It's what helped me see after a while what I had with Trina, and how I could've found myself in the same place as Tony. Not that Trina, who's Vivi's cousin, is anything like Vivi; she wouldn't have fooled me and come up pregnant. But she might've let things go on forever, and things was nowheres. She come to the neighborhood, her and her mother, to live with Vivi, and the first time I seen her all I could think of was dinner. This beautiful black girl walking up Grand all legs and breasts, not tits but breasts, all woman and pushed up and out under a low, square-cut blouse that made you think of a fancy tablecloth where you wanted to sit down and eat and eat. Which I did, and it got so bad, with me running over to her place every night, I lost weight and got sick. Some meal. Grandma; who knows life inside and out, said if I'm going to do them things, I ought to at least take vitamins or something. "That's what they give them bulls, ain't it?" But then after a while, things slowed down, big spaces opened up, and what filled them spaces wasn't stars and flowers like before, but just meat and potatoes. And then my instant replay kicked in, and it worked. Showed me things for what they was: boring, nowheres. So I told her. I told her the way I asked myself how I felt about her after sex, thinking that might be a way for me to start off honest with her, but she got so insulted, she took off and never let me finish what I wanted to say. No chance of us being friends after that.

* * *

So it's no wonder, pulling into Del's after I left Tony's, that I felt depressed, thinking of him and all that stuff with Pauline. I got out of my truck and stretched, as if that might pop the sadness out of me. I seen number Fourteen and her heifer wasn't in the calving pen, which meant the calf was in the barn and I'd have another mouth to feed. The old grease-sputtering generator was grinding outside the milk barn, and from

THREE

That night I had a dream. I was naked in the dairy barn playing with the water when Mom come around the corner and said: "Johnny, what are you doing?" I panicked, holding my hands over my crotch, anything to cover myself. My drawers was around my ankles; I tried to pull them up but they kept falling down. Nothing worked. She was as mad as hell. Funny thing though, it had nothing to do with me being naked, if she even noticed. She was going on and on about why wasn't I in college and how I needed job skills unless I wanted to be a bum the rest of my life. Then the next thing I knowed I was outside and Grandma was sitting on the cement water trough in the middle of the cow pen. Cows everywhere and Grandma just sitting there. She adjusted the red gingham bandanna on her head and said: "Gee, it's hot." I panicked again, remembering that I was naked and thinking I must've been barefoot in six inches of cow shit, but when I looked I seen I was dressed: T-shirt, jeans, and on my feet my every-day rubber work boots.

I never quite figured out that dream. Of course, I didn't try to. Grandma says not to analyze them. She says a dream ain't nothing but what it is. The way a cow's a cow, a tree's a tree. It don't mean something else, the way lots of folks think. Point is, it's real. Yet it's real the way the world is real to her: a frog with a missing toe is Old Uncle, the medicine man showing himself. You can see him in anything, not just in the frog but in the trees, in a pair of old people's shoes; and not just see him, she says, but hear him, hear him singing his song, which she calls an angel song. So if things in a dream is real the way life is real to her, then the stuff of dreams might not be just what it is—a cow, a tree—after all. Which is the way it is with Grandma: Certain things she says, when you do analyze them, prove contradictory.

Whatever the case, the story shifted gears after that dream. Went from first to second, and then right into third. The pieces of the picture begun to take their places. Without me seeing any of it. Me and Felix was friends. We hung out. Beads, clothes; the things between us. Junk shops, flea markets, yard sales, Goodwill. I learned all about finding beads; Felix, he seen how I picked out clothes. We done everything together. In my rattling old pickup—since Felix didn't have no car—we scoured the town for what we needed. Left nothing unturned. My clothes racks growed heavy, bowed in the middle. Felix, his treasure chest spilled over. And then we put our heads together. Got a gig selling stuff at the farmers' market Thursday nights uptown. Beads, a few choice clothing items. But it was more than just business with me and Felix. We talked, talked about a million things. Anything you could think of.

The end of the world, for instance.

"It's here now," Felix said. "Everywhere you look."

We was parked by the alley, a block from the Goodwill, waiting for the big Wednesday morning drop-off, which we would raid. Felix was looking at a black woman on the street, about fifty, as plain as can be in a print shift, gazing into a shop window.

"What's she see?" he asked.

"A bunch of lamps," I said on account of how it was a lamp and fixture place.

"Uh-uh," he said. "Dead wrong. She sees nothing."

"She sees a lamp she wants," I argued.

"Yeah. Nothing."

"What do you mean?"

"Wanting something ain't anything," he said. "Where does that lamp come from?" He looked at me like I didn't know which way was up. "And where does the light in that lamp come from?"

Crossed my mind he was into some kind of nature shit. Which he was on occasion. You know, the wisdom of the elders. Prophecy. That stuff.

"Wood," I said finally. "The lamp's made of wood . . . The light, I don't know. It come from some generator someplace."

"But that lady there," he said, nodding with his chin towards the woman, "she ain't thinking that. She ain't gone that far. And you, you ain't half sure of nothing yourself."

"And you are?" I said.

"No. And that's my point, man."

"What?"

"That nobody knows nothing," he answered. "Nothing. Don't you get it?"

"No," I said. "I don't." And now I didn't care how he looked at me. He made no sense. He must've seen me thinking as much, on account of how he started a lecture.

"Humans, man, we fucked up," he said. "Pulled out the stitch in things so nothing's connected. That lady, she don't know nothing. Indians is just as bad as anybody else now. You and me, we don't know shit. Not where the light in a lamp comes from, nothing."

He lifted his hands like he was holding the world, one of them plastic globes you see in classrooms, and motioned with his eyes for me to see it. "When we look at things in this world, it looks like they're holding together. Truth is . . ." He stopped, letting his hands collapse on his lap, fall at his sides. "Truth is, they're not. They're apart because nothing's attached. The end is here."

I thought, What the hell, you're the one dropped your hands. What kind of argument is that?

Four Mexican kids, gang types in baggy getups, crossed the street going in the opposite direction.

"See," he said, like to drive home his point. "See them kids? What are they, fourteen maybe? Old clothes. Raiding and shit. They know even if they don't see it. They know it's the end of the world. Nothing means nothing to them. Just sorting through the pieces, the leftovers."

His eyebrows come together; his face, it growed dark with what entered his mind just then. He looked at me and you'd have thought he was about to spill the life secrets of Jesus Christ.

"Look at us," he said. "You and me. We're doing the same thing. Dealing junk at the end of the world. Dealing the leftovers. We're there. Only difference is, we see it . . . I see it."

He waited for me to agree. But my mind jumped elsewheres, to the only thing I seen just then: that big old truck with Goodwill painted on the sides in big yellow letters turning into the alley and full of leftovers from the end of the world.

"It's everywhere you look," Felix said, paying no attention to the truck.

"Everywhere you look," he said again, as if closing his argument, like his words was the wax over a jar of fresh-cooked fruit.

Wished I half-believed him. If only he'd made a nickel's worth of sense on the subject. It'd be a good rap to use on Mom. Why I didn't need no college skills—the end of the world was here.

* * *

Which brings up another subject we talked about: Del and the dairy. "Hopeless," Felix said.

Putting hay out for the milkers. That's what we was doing. Cutting alfalfa bales open with Del's tiny wire cutters and spreading the loose flakes in the wooden troughs. Hot as hell, and alfalfa flying up in tiny pieces like dust that caught at the back of your throat and covered everywhere on your face and arms with itchy specs of green and gray. Felix wasn't happy.

Of course he wasn't one for the dairy in the first place. "Stinks like shit," he'd say when he come to help me. Which was four, maybe five times total. He said he had enough of ranch work. Up in Lake County where he growed up. Picking pears, apples. Pruning trees each fall so his hands callused permanent. He worked with animals too. Not dairy. Beef cattle and sheep; and he told me his first piece of ass was a sheep. "We was shearing them," he said. "Me and some older Mexican guys. They put this sheep on the edge of a truck bed and pushed her like they was going to push her off. Ha! The poor son of a bitch sheep she bucked back."

Felix sighed with disgust, brushing the tiny pieces of hay off the front of his T-shirt. "The old man's senile," he blurted out. Luckily, that old generator outside the milking barn was sputtering loud; and with the cows stacked up in the holding pen and Del inside, I don't think Del heard a thing.

Felix climbed out of the trough and leaned against a fence post. Like he was quitting. Like he'd had enough.

I looked at him, questioning him with my eyes, saying nothing.

"Doing this shit," he said, throwing his hand towards the troughs and barn. "Day after day, for how many years?"

"Sixty," I said.

I jumped out of the trough then, too, just in case our words might carry into the barn. The slightest breeze could push the generator grinding in the other direction, downwind, and float our words as smooth as a meadowlark's song into Del's ears. I didn't want him to hear a thing.

"He likes it," I said. "I told you he likes it."

I'd told Felix the whole story: Del coming in thirst and hunger, and how Del seen life in each cow. Everything.

"He don't even know if he likes it. You know why?" He paused, like he was waiting for me to answer, all the time both of us knowing he'd give it himself. "Because he don't know no difference," he said finally. "He ain't done nothing else—for sixty years, you said. He don't know the difference."

"Don't mean he don't like it," I said.

He kicked a pile of cow crap, then looked at me point-blank. "Do *you* like it? Honestly? Do *you* like this?" He was throwing his hand toward the troughs and barn again.

"A fish lives in water. A dog lives on land. Different strokes for different folks."

"Whatever," he said, like I was a fool he couldn't waste no more time with.

He started to come back to the trough, then he stopped.

"Look," he said, pointing to the row of new houses bordering the pasture below the barn. "What do you see?"

"Houses," I said.

"Yeah, houses," he said like I'd been a smart-ass. "And that old man in there, he's slaving away like them houses ain't going to bust through that fence and gobble this whole place up."

"Maybe he does know."

"Then he is senile, right? Crazy. Because it's hopeless. He ain't going to last much longer and neither is this place. Either way, hopeless."

I seen all along what Felix was up to with his business about the new houses. He knowed I seen too. I just should've figured what come next. The wrapping for his gift box of words.

He looked again at the houses, then at me. "Remember the end of the world," he said. "That old man in there, he's like everybody else. The signs is right in front of him and he keeps working like he's got eternity."

"He knows what he's got," I said.

"Hopeless," Felix said, meaning both of us, me and Del.

"Gobble, gobble," I said.

He blinked, looked at me like he was asking if I was getting smart with him. I shrugged my shoulders.

"This whole place might get eaten up," I said. I didn't care what he thought just then.

A couple big Holsteins come up from the barn towards the troughs, finished milking. More would be coming. I turned and started spreading the alfalfa even. Del's got a thing about it. Wants each of the cows to have an equal share. Eat peaceful. Sometimes the bigger cows—the older Holsteins—get pushy with the smaller ones. Felix come and started spreading hay too.

"Hope he pays you good," he said through the green dust flying up. His words was soft feeling on purpose, like to meet me in the middle with a truce after all he'd said about Del.

"He does," I said. How could I explain the truth?

With lots of the things Felix said you'd think he was nothing but out and out cruel, negative. He was cruel. He was negative. But most of all he was moody. His moods was like the weather in spring and fall, going back and forth from sun to rain, changing sometimes without the slightest warning. When alfalfa flew in his face, when he was hungry or bothered about something, he could be a son of a bitch, cruel and pigheaded. He knowed what was what and anybody who didn't know what he knowed was an idiot. Then, when the sun was out, he'd have you wait in the middle of the road while a hundred little old ladies crossed one by one in front of you. For instance, on the way home from Del's that day, after we got ourselves half a gallon of cold Gatorade, things changed.

We was just getting back onto Petaluma Hill Road from the supermarket when he said: "Del must really love them cows. Jesus."

"Yeah," I said.

I learned to ride his moods the way you learn to ride a raft downriver, looking ahead, keeping your eyes peeled for the rough spots, where the water's churning, and never getting too comfortable where it's smooth, for you never know what's around the bend. I seen a lot with Felix. I seen what other people didn't. I knowed the habits of the cat. I watched.

We'd sit behind our table Thursday nights at the farmers' market and talk about the white folks strolling by. Hundreds and hundreds of them. They come looking for vegetables and stuff people was selling in booths up and down the street that was closed down for the market. A couple of cucumbers here, tomatoes, a dozen brown eggs down the way. They filled the cloth shopping bags they brought with them each Thursday night, showing each other how they was environmental and wasn't wasting paper.

"Makes them feel like they're real," I told Felix.

"Yeah, like they're keeping the world from ending," he answered.

We got to where we could read people, tell you exactly what they was going to buy, and how many. For example, nothing deformed or dirty. No tomatoes with blight. No apples with fly spots. If them brown eggs had chicken shit on them, forget it. Miss Back-to-Nature, she'd search and pick through things so what she pulled up and dropped in her cloth bag was near as pretty as what she found in her local supermarket. And never too many of one thing in case she got home and found out what she paid for was no good, rotten on the inside or all seeds and skin. Felix could really make fun of them. He'd get up, tighten his ass the way they do, walk two steps ahead of them, and then stoop over a basket of eggs or a box of apples and pick out the ones he knowed they had their eyes on. Then he'd turn and see their faces for what they really was—bitch tight and gruesome. Then, after a minute or two, he'd put the things back down. And do you think any of them ladies caught on, or cared if they did? No pride. They'd grab up what Felix put back faster than you could blink an eye.

"White people," he'd say when we was done laughing. "So fucking greedy, ain't they?"

It was true. They was a ball of contradictions. Peace and love and they didn't know how close to the surface their own greed and hate lived. Had to agree with Felix on that one. They couldn't see how nothing was connected to nothing else, much less the parts that made each of them a person.

But they wasn't the only contradiction. It was Felix himself. Much as he made fun of the white people, he played up to them like they was, in fact, God's special creation. First off, he sat behind our table with his shirt off, at nine o'clock at night, even with the fog in, letting them take in what I seen the first time he opened Auntie Mollie's front door. Breathtaking, what takes the breath and catches it so time stops and nothing's moving but the rise and fall of his breathing in all that beautiful face and chest. Like a thousand before, each person thought it was the first and only time in their life they seen perfection. Hair, smile, chest. Perfection. Men, women, and children. How they later thought what they seen depended on who they was. Maybe envy. Sex. Whatever. But at that moment it was perfection. And it was a trap, a metal cage Felix could look in and inspect his prey for as long as they was caught in it. A second, maybe two. A minute. I seen a woman Mom's age step back and stare a full five minutes. And at that time, during the time they was caught, Felix sized them up, figured how he could play them, if he could play them at all, how to sell them a necklace, how to bullshit.

Most often it was the girls, of course, white girls. And here he'd rag on them to me. He had a theory about them. They liked dark guys, he said—Indians and blacks—the way they liked horses: They wanted adventure, something to ride, but they always held the reins and when they got tired of the horse, or if it growed old, they got rid of it for a new one. Didn't stop him, all his theorizing; if you ask me, he done a pretty good job of lassoing any white chick he wanted, and if anybody was holding the reins it was him. His gig: See them looking at you, smile, invite them over to look at a necklace, ask what they liked, and go from there. He led them like they was puppies on a leash. Stroking them this way and that, how beautiful their hair was, how a color of a bead matched their eyes, how it was them and only them. He led them in circles. He led them out of our booth, down the walk. He come back with sandwiches, drinks, once even his own cloth shopping bag full of vegetables he would take home to Mollie. Another time, after leading a redhead away, he come back and asked: "What do you do if a chick's on the rag?" "Talk to her," I said. "See what kind of a mood she's in." He laughed, clipped me on the shoulder, and said: "You idiot, go for a blow job." Then, not a minute later, the same girl, the redhead, walked by, smiling embarrassed-like at Felix and keeping on her way. Something had happened. Whether or not it was what Felix said it was, I don't know. Twenty minutes is awfully fast.

But I do know this. He got Julie Brigioni's phone number. Julie, the grand duchess of bitch who sorts through what her friends call my "used junk" every month and never lets you forget how rich she is. Felix got her number. One night we seen her passing on the promenade—she didn't notice our table—and after I convinced Felix she wasn't ever my girlfriend and what a stuck-up piece of work she was, he made me a bet he could get her phone number. And damn if he didn't go after her and come back ten minutes later with the number. The right number; he gave me the torn piece of paper she wrote on, claiming he didn't want it, and I checked the number against the one I had for her in my customer roster at home. Same number.

So Felix said one thing and did another. A ball of contradictions. Which he didn't argue with when I called him on it. Might be a contradiction, but there's sense in it, he claimed. "Got to make a living," he said and shrugged. "You don't think white folks ain't screwed us all along?" In other words, he was using people. Just because he chatted them up didn't mean he liked them. Surprise, surprise. How was he any different from what I seen so fast and clear at Auntie Mollie's that night: a fast talker, a con. A con's sense. And he'd go on and on about it, share with me all his thinking on people and situations, what he was going to say and do and why. He showed me everything. Except how he might be using me. But I watched and seen nothing he could pull, and figured he knowed better with me. And in his own way, a way he could never say except in the ways he avoided it, he needed me. He was lonely too.

If anything, I was jealous at times of his manipulating ways. It kept him ahead. His thinking was like a fox, mine a dumb hen caught in the coops. I couldn't keep up with him. I couldn't think that way. Like a kid who ain't got it in him to swing the bat so he hits the ball. I couldn't do it. Thursday nights he sold necklaces. I didn't fare as good.

Now with Indians, Felix was different, but not much. Got to handle them with fine kid gloves, he'd say. Go the extra mile. They're tricky. They don't show what they're thinking. They hold back, watch for the other person to show himself or herself so they can figure out how to handle the situation and protect themselves. It's ancient. It's in the blood. In the old days, they studied strangers close, watching for ways the strangers might poison them. Then it was with the white man; they had to watch his every move, hide themselves in any way they could. Keep themselves behind flat eyes that revealed nothing. Players at a poker table. Fear.

"Can you blame them?" Felix said. "Look at all the shit that's happened."

We was on our way home from the Thursday night farmers' market, and the discussion come up how Indians was different from whites—after he was laughing and talking about how easy the white folks is to play. I asked how white folks was different from Indians, just to see what he'd say. Just to see if he'd come out with the full range of his ways, admit the fact he had no limits on who or what he'd do. But after his small talk about handling Indians different, he got quiet, sad-like.

"My mother was sad," he said. "And look, now she's dead. Hell, and Daisy, she's in jail again."

I never asked questions. About how Rose died, or what his Auntie Daisy done to get locked up. Like I said, I'll talk about myself, but I don't push it with other folks. Pretty dumb Indian, I guess. Must be all the white blood. Which is what Grandma teases me with when I can't see things her way. And she always says, Watch yourself around Indians, especially if you don't know them.

Felix did watch himself, he was cool, slick. Charming. But it looked like that sadness from his home calmed his conniving. A good muffler over a loud exhaust pipe. Oh, he'd talk a lot of shit like how he had come back to the tribe to be chairman and lead us into the biggest gaming enterprise this side of Vegas. Full of himself. Like he was Moses. And Raymond Pen thought Felix was the best thing since electricity. Steven Pen seen in Felix everything his own son wasn't: strong, a natural athlete, outgoing and likable, a leader. Which should've bothered wimp Raymond but didn't because Felix, ever so smart and hip to what was going on, seen where Raymond had points of strength—college and book learning—and he took them points like they was precious gems and polished them so they glowed beautiful. "If it wasn't for you checking in all these genealogy charts and keeping the books in order, we'd never get nowheres," he told Raymond. "And, see, I can't even speak correct English, saying stuff like 'nowheres.' Should be 'anywhere,' I know. Maybe one day you'll have time to help me." From the look of things, you'd think Steven would nominate Felix the next chairman, with Raymond ready to sit in the street and keep records for Felix if he had to. Felix was working it.

But like I was saying, there was something else about the way he worked with Indians. And you seen it most clear in how he done things for people sometimes for no other reason than the sadness he seen in them. And he seen it fast. Water, and him the divining rod. With Tony, for instance. Like everybody else in the neighborhood, Tony worshiped him. Wide eyes, taking in everything Felix said, how Felix done things, buckled his black leather belt, tucked in, or didn't tuck in, his T-shirt, how scuffed his boots was. He never knowed he was studying so hard because the studying come out of his amazement and amazement never lets you see nothing but what you're wondering at in the first place. Breathtaking. "It's cool you know him," Tony said. Meaning it was cool that Felix hung with me special. Others seen it, too, how me and Felix hung close. Felix basked in the sunlight of folks' worship, though he never said anything about it. I just seen it on his face: the cat that's ate the mouse. But after we first met Tony, Felix was quiet, different.

It was inside the corner market. Tony and Vivi was in front of the magazine rack arguing about whether or not Tony could buy the *Sports Illustrated* he was reading. Never mind she had *Essence* in the shopping cart. "We gotta think of this," she said, patting her stomach that wasn't sticking out yet. Tony dropped the magazine into the cart, and just when they started off up the aisle toward the checkout counter, I called after them. Tony turned and you'd have thought it was Felix that called him. Tony's eyes filled with Felix. Completely, like the entire store—me, Vivi, the aisles of groceries—all at once collected in that one person. I introduced them.

"Heard about you," Tony said, wonder full on his face.

"Cousins," Felix said, extending his hand and working his charm.

Tony took his hand, locked. "Yeah, I know. I heard," he said.

Seeing Tony distracted, Vivi grabbed the *Sports Illustrated* out of the shopping cart and tossed it back on the magazine rack.

"That's a cool magazine," Felix said, drawing everybody's attention to what Vivi had just done.

Vivi whipped her head around and picked at that processed short hair of hers that no doubt come out of the last *Essence* she bought. She was giving Felix the fighting eye. Like asking, What did you say?

Felix had challenged her, and she wasn't taken in by wonderment of him. And now he was answering her silent question, as good as calling her down, and looking nowheres but in her eyes. She held a moment, then backed off. She looked at me like she was blaming me for bringing Felix into her world, for starting the trouble. Then she sighed, like it was all nothing but a nuisance too small for her to bother with. "Come on, Tony," she said, patting her not-sticking-out stomach again. "Better get home with these groceries before Grandma Pauline gets upset." She took hold of the grocery cart, then lifted her chin and rolled her head away from us and started for the checkout counter. Slowly, her attitude a mile high. She'd brought up two things—Tony's baby growing inside her and Pauline—magic things that pressed his buttons. She'd reminded him. He shrugged and followed her away.

"Pitiful," Felix said, low, so Tony couldn't hear.

And right then Felix seen the whole story. Without me telling him a word; he didn't know nothing but me and Tony was friends. Not the details, not how Tony made a vow to the world never to cause trouble, not about meeting his father, Steven Pen, none of that. But the hurt, the sadness.

"He thinks he deserves that shit," Felix said on our way out of the store that day. "He thinks fighting is a sin. That's a slave."

"That's exactly right," I said.

Then he stopped. He was looking at me hard. "Then why the fuck ain't you helped him?" he asked. "Said something. He's your friend, ain't he?"

"Yeah," I answered. "I have helped him, tried to."

Which was the truth. I'd told him he didn't need to feel so bad about things. Just recently I told him he didn't have to live with his mom, that her problems—getting off drugs and taking care of his two sisters—was her own, not his. I asked him to come live with me and Grandma. And I told him that just because Vivi was pregnant and wanted to have the baby didn't mean he'd have to marry her and be stuck to her the rest of his life. I reasoned with him this way and that, inside and out. But nothing touched him. Which is what I explained to Felix just then.

"Well, if you can't do nothing for him, I can," Felix said.

And then he turned and walked up the street towards Mollie's by himself.

That night after dinner he come to Grandma's with determination in his face as forceful as a bulldozer pedal to the floor. "Take me to where Tony's at," he demanded.

So we went over to Pauline's. Vivi wasn't there. But in front of Pauline, who was taking in all of her new long-lost cousin, Felix handed Tony a bracelet. It was beaded, red and white, diamond patterned Indian style, beautiful. Lord, you couldn't miss it.

"For all them that ever wants to hurt you," Felix said for the room to hear. "For strength."

Tony held the bracelet up, studying the design.

"Means strength," Felix said again.

Then vision kicked in. I seen things. Fury and fight, all them things in that bracelet. Strength, what Tony needed. It was there, perfect for him. But it was made from the battle Felix was fighting; his own battle, his own mad stitching and beading against sadness, which Tony would never raise a finger against, bracelet or not.

And then something strange with the Bills. Between Felix and the Bills, of all people. I seen something there too. He turned them soft. Served sadness to them like it was their own hearts on a kitchen plate. I couldn't believe it.

Sure I'd prepped him, told him in detail of their mean and crazy ways. But he wasn't afraid none; and nothing, no matter what I said, could've helped with what he done. It was none other than his own instinct for this kind of thing, like I said. Nothing he planned ahead.

He found a picture of their parents. On the wall just above the TV. An old black-and-white from the thirties: Mrs. Bill in a scalloped dress, stylish for the times, her hair cut flapper style with two perfect spit curls like tiny corkscrews over her broad forehead; and Mr. Bill, already a heavy man and no more than twenty-five, in a dark suit with a white handkerchief folded in a perfect triangle in his coat pocket, his face gloomy, the wide mouth turned down under a low brow of coarse straight Indian hair packed down and combed back slick. All the time I'd sat in that room before and I'd never seen it.

"Your Mama and Papa," Felix said before anyone could say anything else. Before I could introduce him. Before they could ask us to sit down. It was like radar. We'd only been in the house half a second and he'd made a beeline for the picture. It was our last stop on the rounds that day to remind folks about the tribal meeting the next night.

Felix worked fast. He didn't give the Bills a chance to say anything about the photograph, whether or not it was even of their parents, though you could see it was—Mona and Lena looked identical to the father, Mr. Bill—or where it was taken, though the ramshackle cabin they stood in front of in their Sunday best was no doubt on the old reservation.

"My mama, I got a picture of her young too," he said.

You'd think it was a gimmick, a put-on. But when he turned from the picture, giving the Bills their first chance to see who was actually standing in their front room, his face was flat, empty. Then his eyes focused and what they seen was not us or something beyond us, not even that picture of his mother young, wherever it was, but that part of his mother, no doubt her death, that was the hole in his own heart. Trouble was all of a sudden all over his face.

Shocked the Bills so they hadn't time to take in his beauty. Mona pushed the worn, stuffing-empty chair for Felix to sit down on, a kindness from that woman the world had never seen. Her penciled brows was collected over her forehead in deep consternation. She covered her tiny, spitting mouth with her fat hand, and when Felix sat down, she nudged Lena with her other elbow.

"Water," she said without looking away from Felix. "Get him some water."

Which Lena done. I might as well been invisible. Mona and Lena sat on the couch opposite Felix, and, like I said, was so taken up with his sadness they never seen his looks, or for that matter, the king-size open box of Cocoa Puffs between them. I leaned against the wall. But I seen plenty, and learned something too: Felix's mother—Rose—was murdered.

"It was the closest to her killed her," he said.

"Your mother was Rose!" Mona gasped, both fat paws over her mouth now.

"Oh, Christ . . . Oh, Christ," Lena said.

Then there was the tears in her eyes, and in Mona's too. Not Felix, who kept focused, only looking away a couple of times, maybe so he wouldn't get choked up too. But them two, teary and looking at him. It was their own story: how they seen it was Indians, them closest to their mother and father, who killed them, traded off the reservation and put them out to die in the park on lower Fourth Street. They knowed what I didn't—the story of Rose, how she was murdered, who murdered her, why—and because they knowed they didn't have to go back over the details with Felix. And wouldn't. Which left me with more questions than I had before.

I stood a while, until Felix got up and hugged them good-bye. Then, on the way out, I had the presence of mind to mention the meeting, why we'd stopped over in the first place.

"Yeah, you ought to come," Felix said after me.

They nodded, like he'd said the sun was out, and Mona held the rusted screen door open for us, sniffling and patting her brow with a paper towel.

On the street Felix was quiet, and then, like the time he was mad at me over Tony, he walked back to Auntie Mollie's by himself. Sure sign things struck deep.

Then something else. That night after dinner, pretty late—I was getting ready for bed—he come over and give me his chart.

"Something's come up," he said. "Don't think I can make it to the meeting."

We both knowed he was lying.

"What do you mean?" I asked.

"I'm not sure," he answered. "But I filled out my chart there. Auntie helped me."

I looked at his chart that I was holding and sat down on the bed. He'd done it, he'd filled it out complete, all the way back to the first Rosa.

"Just turn it in for me, would you?" He was jittery. I could see he wanted to leave, not talk about why he was backing out of the meeting.

"Sit, why don't you," I said, motioning with my chin to the desk next to my workbench.

"Should split," he said.

Then I pushed. "Why ain't you coming to the meeting?"

"Orders and stuff, man."

"For beads?"

"Yeah."

Once again, we both knowed he was lying. And we knowed, too, if I pushed he'd lie again. Whatever. I let him go.

I sat a minute after he left, staring blank at his chart. Didn't see none of the names, only the questions in my mind. Then I went to Grandma, surprised I hadn't sooner.

"Rose was murdered," I told her.

She sat at the kitchen table, with only the light from her sewing lamp, making something with willow rods, like I seen her do a thousand times. A baby cradle or a gathering basket; she had just started it, twined half a dozen small rods around and through a spray of slightly bigger sticks.

"Oh, I think I heard that someplace," she said about Rose without looking up from her work.

Times like this I could grab that whatever-she's-making right out of her hands and pull the willows apart stitch by stitch. The problem is, you can never know if she forgot or just never thought to tell you, if she set the puzzle out on purpose.

"Why didn't you tell me?" I asked.

"What?" she said, looking up from her work like she just realized I was talking to her.

"That Rose was murdered . . . Why didn't you tell me before when I asked about her?"

Grandma thought a moment, checking the index of all our conversations. A long moment. And then she landed on it.

"One got killed. One of them three sisters. Didn't remember which one, though. I told you that, ain't I?"

She didn't miss a beat, Grandma. Throw a question back to me that I can only answer yes to: Yes, Grandma you're right. That's what you told me, one got killed.

"Didn't remember their names," she added, further reminding me of what she'd said before. "Never seen them for so long until that one, what's-her-name, moved up the street."

"Mollie," I said.

"Yeah, Mollie."

"What happened to Rose?" I pushed. "Do you know how she got murdered, what happened? Did you hear anything about it?"

A whole slew of questions, which I didn't expect her to answer. The puzzle again, something vague, certainly not the full story, if anything at all. Then she surprised me.

"Husband. Zelda told me. We was talking about it."

"Felix's father?"

"The one that got killed, it was the husband done it. That's all we heard. Don't know if it was the boy's father."

Grandma's point: Rose could've had—and probably did have—more than one husband, more than one man other than Felix's father. But I was on a roll. I had Grandma talking straight and didn't want to lose her.

"Yeah, Rose. She's the one got murdered," I said, as if repeating what we both knowed might knock something else loose from her memory bank so it fell out as plain and straight as the last piece of information done. Maybe something else her and Zelda talked about. But no such luck.

"Sad," Grandma said and picked up her willow work again. Then she stopped a second, and staring into the air beyond me said what I'd heard her say before: "Moved to Lake County long time ago. There was three of them, three sisters."

I thought right off of Felix at the Bills', the scene there, how dark he got. Would the Bills have carried on so if it wasn't Felix's father who done the deed? Wouldn't they have said the name of the guy who done it, if it wasn't Felix's father, cursed him out loud just to share with Felix their rage? I told Grandma about what happened at the Bills' and what I was thinking just then. She kept working, bending and twining her willow sticks under the sewing lamp.

"So it probably was Felix's father," I said.

"Might be," she said without looking up. Then she said what she did know, what she was certain of, what she said after the first time she met Felix and at least a dozen times since: "Funny, that boy."

"That boy." Her words for Tony and Raymond, guys my age, my friends. The word "funny" was new, different. I knowed what it meant though, at least the range of what it could've meant. There was parts of him she didn't understand. Pieces that didn't match up. The too fast smile with his gifts of French bread and doughnuts. The necklace he gave her and his polite talk. His love of elders. His tight clothes. Bottom line: She didn't know how to trust him, she couldn't see how the words fit together to make a whole story. She never said, Don't trust him. She never warned me, nothing. Only the word "funny." And she done a couple of strange things: She

fed the French bread and doughnuts to Pete and she hung the necklace—
wisdom, like mine—over a fence post in the backyard where she could see
it from her chair in the hollyhocks. I seen her glance at it a couple of times
when I was sitting out there with her. I guess, like me, she was watching to
see how the words come together. Waiting.

That night I knowed nothing else would come out of her. Did Felix's
father kill his mother? And if he did, would that explain Felix, string the
words like a finished necklace? Whatever the case, Grandma didn't have
the answers, and even if she did, I wasn't going to hear them just then.
Nothing moved. Nothing talked but her fingers, and it was a language of
them willows.

I went back to my room and picked up Felix's chart from the bed.
I looked at the names, Rose on back to Rosa. Of course it told me nothing
I didn't know before.

FOUR

The meeting started off with two surprises: Felix and the Bills. They was both there. Felix I was certain would back out; and the Bills anybody would've bet the shirt on their back them two wouldn't show up—they never did before. The place was packed. The corner Baptist church on the south end of Grand. Folks squeezed into the pews, sat in the aisles, lined the walls. The whole tribe. Wasn't nothing like it in years, Grandma said. If Felix had something to do with the turnout, if he persuaded people to come with his smile or just plain made them curious, I don't know. But the Bills, no question, it was Felix who got them there. Too bad he couldn't get them to leave.

Things started off regular enough. The usuals showed up early to help. Alice with Nellie Copaz and Nellie's grandson, Edward, the gay guy who went to Stanford and wears a sport coat to the corner grocery. Me and Tony. Grandma with Zelda Toms. And of course the Pens: Steven and his pretty Apache wife, their daughter, and Raymond. We put a long card table up front next to the pulpit for the tribal council and another one against the side wall for refreshments, food. You'd think Raymond was Inspector General the way he went around checking things. Steven and his wife and daughter greeted folks, the welcoming committee, and me and Tony served as slaves, carrying and setting up the tables, getting the trash cans, sweeping. Grandma, her and Zelda they come early for one reason and one reason only: to find where they wanted to sit and sit there. Oh, they fiddled with the tortilla chips Steven brought, opened the bags and poured them into bowls. But don't let them kid anybody, they come early to pick out their seats. With Indians it's important. Especially the old ones. They got to be where they can watch everybody else with nobody else able to see them watching. I seen it a million times. Once I called Grandma on it and she looked at me like What-in-the-world-are-you-thinking. Then she turned to Zelda and talked Indian, shut me out. I know a few words, but never learned the language complete, not enough to keep up with Grandma and Zelda.

Zelda, she's Tony's grandmother, Pauline's mother; a funny old gal with her worn slip always hanging a couple inches or more below her housedress, but she can whisper and gossip to beat the band when she gets around Grandma, and Grandma keeps right in step. Nothing can get between them. The church posed problems: Everybody would be facing the front of the room. Grandma and Zelda would have to be content with the backs of people's heads. They sat together in the last pew, in the corner where it was darkest.

Folks filled in all around them, right up to the front pew. Fast it seemed, all at once. Which was strange. Most times they wander in a few at a time, most of them late. Only at funerals do you see Indians on time. That's because if they're late, they'll miss the body being dropped in the ground and not get to see who cried and passed out. Food was everywhere: The card table against the wall was heaped with pies, pots of spaghetti and chili, salads, even plates of homemade tortillas. Which was something else made me think of a funeral—all that food. Eerie. Thank God, there was plenty of talking, folks visiting with each other. Mollie and her two boys found a seat near the back, and Felix was with them. The Bills sat up front, a couple of rows from Alice and Nellie and Edward. I stood in the line against the wall.

When the church could hold no more, Steven called the meeting to order. All of them was up there with him, the council members—Frances Toms, Anna Silva, Annabelle Burke, Trick Burke, and Raymond. People hushed some, but not completely until Steven asked Nellie to come up and open the meeting with a prayer.

"That's a holy person?" snapped Lena Bill, the younger one, the one without eyebrows, the one who talks the most. She said it so simple you'd think she was still in her front room with a bowl of popcorn and the TV going.

But her words had power. Like a sponge on a small puddle of water. Sucked everything up, every sound, every last voice, faster than you could take a breath. Nellie, who was already standing up, hesitated. Then Steven urged her forward with a nod of his head and Edward got up and let her out of the pew.

At the other meetings we've had she prayed in English. Grandma

says Nellie don't speak the Waterplace Pomo language as good as her and
Zelda on account of how she left the old reservation when she was young—
after her mother hung herself in the white man's barn—and went and lived
with her father's people, the Pomo by the Sebastopol Lagoon that speak
another language. But her songs—what she uses to heal people—sound
clear, Grandma says, and they're ancient, which is how Grandma knows
Nellie's the real thing—she couldn't have learned them songs no other way
but through the spirits. And when she prays in English, Grandma says that's
true too. Good stuff: peace, what the Creator wants from us. Same as if she
said it in Indian. But today, she made a turn. She prayed in Indian. She
waited a moment at the pulpit, like she expected someone—one of the
Bills—to tell her to get down, and then she started, soft at first, then
stronger, louder. *Wadu*: come. *Qa cha*: Waterplace. Them words I understood.

    She stepped down, went back to her seat with Edward and Alice,
and folks started up again with the busy chatter. Then just as fast as they
started up they closed down when Steven stood up to speak. On and off like
it was a switch someone was pulling. Steven said we done good, 137 completed genealogy charts turned in with more still coming. "One hundred
and forty," Raymond announced, holding up three new completed charts
for everybody to see like they was winning lottery tickets. Just then it occurred to me that I'd left Felix's chart at home. I forgot it, plain and simple.
I looked and seen him quiet next to Mollie. Not the same Felix, the one
that shines, looks bigger and stronger than the rest, but something else,
someone quiet, shrinking, like he'd pulled inside himself all that glowed, all
his size, to the point where he was no different from anybody else. Like he
was hiding behind the looks of someone average.

    From where I stood against the wall I had a good view of things. I
seen where everybody was sitting, squeezed in here and there. Tony's mom,
Pauline, with his two sisters, the La's, and with Billyrene, her sister, Tony's
aunt, who the Bills referred to as "the biggest whore of all." Looking at
Billyrene you'd wonder, not about the big part—with that flour-sack belly
she can't keep tucked in between her white blouse and black stretch pants
she gives the Bills a run for their money in the size department. It's the
whore part that's curious. Like, who'd want to, free or not? But nothing, and
I mean nothing, looked stranger—or bigger—than the Bills. Muumuus and
flowers in their hair. They dressed up. I'm not kidding. Bright flowery muumuus, two or three red roses in their hair, and their faces covered with thick
pancake and rouge so they looked like giant plastic dolls propped up side by
side in the pew. So unreal they was, you sighed with relief when one flicked
her wrist or smirked her snake mouth. They whispered back and forth with-

out turning their heads from the front of the room the whole time Steven was talking. Everybody else was quiet.

Steven said with so many completed charts we'd more than finished the first part of our job to get the U.S. government to acknowledge us as a tribe—so we could get land and build another reservation, a place for all of us to live and go back to if we wanted. A place with houses and a cultural center; and, depending on who you talked to, a bingo hall. It's a crazy thing, having to prove to the United States that we're Indians when they seen us as Indians once before, and then, when we left that last reservation west of Sebastopol, decided that we wasn't. White people! Grandma says. I say, what's to keep them from changing their minds again, even if we do prove ourselves Indians to their satisfaction? And since we all get along so good, what's to keep us from killing each other and losing our reservation again—for the third time! Steven says it's just a matter of completing the steps and things'll turn our way. Stuff like: We can control our fates, be as one as a people again, have a home that is ours and truly ours. Sounds good, I think. What does it mean? Anyway, we done good with the first step. It was the second step, what Steven was explaining—writing a report showing how we always continued as a tribe—where things come unglued. He said him and Frances Toms, Tony's aunt who sat on the council, was going to write it, with Raymond and Edward checking it over for punctuation and spelling.

"Who's going to write it?" Lena shouted out. "Did I hear you say Frances Toms, daughter of . . . Zelda Toms?"

"You have a problem with that?" Frances challenged. You could hear a pin drop. The room held its breath. Frances is plain, neither flashy cheap like Pauline, Tony's mom, or fat gross like Billyrene. But she'll fight like either of them. Now she acted professional, at least on the surface, like she was a nurse asking them what flavor cough drops they wanted.

Lena patted her puffed hair like it was a contraption that would tell her what to do next. And just then I seen it: a flaw in the makeup; she'd left a pink roller in her hair, at the bottom of her neck where she couldn't reach or hold a mirror to see. Again, I thought to myself, Why do I see shit like that? A hair roller at times like this when everybody else is holding their breath and seeing nothing but the way out of the door should one of the two big dolls explode. And that's what I seen just then too: how folks was afraid. Auntie Mollie and Felix quiet. Zelda with her head down. Even Pauline, three months off dope and not a budge. All that talk, the talk that turned on and off so fast, it was nervous talk. Nice stuff about nothing. They sat, each of them like a bull rider on a bull the moment before the bull's let loose.

But not Lena. Her puffed-hair machine kicked in and she spat back at Frances.

"Yes, I have a big problem with that!" She hesitated so as to make what she was going to say next dramatic. "Tell us how we lost the land in Sebastopol. Since you know history so good, tell us."

"The land was actually closer to Graton," Frances answered, still the professional. "The apple grower tricked Mom—"

"What, in the card game she lost?" Lena snapped, as mean as sin.

"No—"

"Wait! Wait!" Steven said, holding up his hands. He looked over at Frances, who was coming undone quick, then out to the giant doll with her reptile lips so tight you couldn't see she had a mouth. "Listen, no use hashing over the past," Steven said, now the teacher with a bunch of mis-behaving kids. "We got to be positive. We got to look at the ways we've hung together, not split apart."

Everybody knowed he was pointing at Lena. He waited a minute, catching our attention so we'd all listen, and then said: "We're a tribe. One people. One blood. Each of us is related—"

"Well, you done plenty to help that!" Lena blurted out.

"That's for sure," Mona added, adjusting her weight from one hip to the other.

Steven was stopped dead in his tracks, interrupted and confused. What in the hell was they talking about? But I knowed. I seen what poison dagger they was firing and right where it was aimed.

"You know what we're talking about," Lena said. "Don't act so dumb. You like for people to think you're so high and mighty. Teacher, ha! Let's start naming your kids."

Steven's eyes widened, registering at last where the Bills was going with all this.

"First, there's the one got killed," Lena said. "Justine, Mollie's girl. She was yours, wasn't she? And that boy there," she said, pointing her spiteful finger at Tony, who was standing just behind me, against the wall. "You fucked Pauline, good ol' Zelda's daughter, to get that one, didn't you?"

"He sure did," said Mona.

"Two kids and done nothing to claim them. Fucked two of your cousins, so-called tribal members, ain't they? Then run off to college and come back an apple. Now tell me, how's that positive?"

I didn't dare look over at Auntie Mollie or back at Tony. Didn't have the nerve to see how they was taking this. I stared straight ahead and amused myself with Raymond, who was upset only because Lena identified Tony and not him as one of Steven's bastards. Steven stood awhile like he still couldn't believe what he'd heard. Looked like he didn't know what to say. But folks was waiting. The chairman of the tribe had to say something. He straightened his shirt collar and stood tall. He forced himself calm.

"Lena," he said. "I don't believe you or your sister have turned in your genealogy charts, have you?"

"Why should I?" she asked.

"Well, at this point you're not on our tribal rolls. Which means at this point you're not a member of this tribe."

She freaked. She sputtered, tried to talk, but her throat squeezed, like I seen at her house, so nothing come out.

"Members, ha!" she shouted all at once. "Me and my sister here is the only ones got Waterplace Pomo full on both sides. You," she said, pointing her finger again. "Your father's from Kashaya Reservation and your mother might as well been pure Mexican."

Steven smarted, but she moved on, away from him to Raymond, who finally got recognized but hardly like he wanted.

"Him, that boy of yours there. His mother ain't from this tribe. Was a drug addict, wasn't she? Explains why he's got AIDS. He ain't that sick and skinny for nothing."

Poor Raymond, his worst nightmare: someone saying out loud that he's a wimp. But I didn't hang on the problem of his embarrassment. The way Lena was firing I might've been next.

"Speaking of AIDS," she said, and pointed to Edward. "Look at that." Then she turned back and pointed at Frances.

"Shut your mouth. Don't be saying I'm gay, you fat bitch!" Frances said with nothing less than a barroom challenge now.

But Lena ranted on, right over her head.

"It's because of what their mothers and grandmothers done. Whores—"

Steven banged his fists on the table. "Lena!" he shouted.

But she kept on.

"Yep, whores that stole our land, both of them," she said, meaning Nellie and Zelda, but when she turned looking at the empty seat where Zelda had been sitting and seeing no one there but Grandma, she quieted.

And just then, as if to stop her from talking again, three of Zelda's daughters—Pauline, Billyrene, Frances—was on their feet, each moving from different parts of the room toward the two big sisters. People cleared away, some slipping out the side doors. I had a quick vision: flesh fat and flushed red raging wild, torn muumuus and polyester, hair-pulling, food everywhere, chili on the floor, broken pies splattered on the walls, the whole thing. But it didn't turn out that way. Tony took hold of his mom. Three of Billyrene's daughters held her, and Steven jumped down from the table and grabbed Frances. But it was more. The Bills. With Zelda's daughters tied up on either end of their pew, them two sat calm and collected, like they knowed nothing was ever going to happen, not a hand would touch them. Even with folks cleared out so the pew was empty, leaving clear access for anyone to attack the two of them sitting there, they didn't budge, not a twitch.

Lena looked one way at Pauline, then the other way at Billyrene. And then she looked straight ahead and said as calm as spring rain: "Touch me or my sister and you'll go right back to jail."

It was the winning card, all right, but not enough to keep Pauline and Billyrene from turning things upside down if they'd wanted to. Point is, they didn't want to. In that quiet moment before Lena talked, while old Zelda's girls was caught at either end of that pew, a question come up that the folks that had left and was leaving had already answered. Why sit here and put up with this shit? Embarrassment. Shame. It was enough having to turn in a chart with empty spaces. It was too much to have somebody else fill in the spaces for the whole world to see. After Pauline and her two sisters sat down, the Bills got up and left, quiet. But nothing was the same. It was like they took the life of the meeting with them.

Steven finished business as best he could, then set the date for the next meeting, in two months. I thought of Grandma and seen her sitting in the corner alone. Zelda would be home by now. Of course, Mollie and Felix was gone, too, like half the room, probably home also.

Grandma said it was a nice night outside and she could walk home by herself. Tony disappeared with an upset Pauline, and so it was me and Raymond that was left to clean up. And Steven, he stayed too. I actually felt bad for Raymond, seeing his little arms with the broom. Sweeping, it didn't fit him, but he tried. None of us said a word. What was there to say? We finished the floors, then emptied the tortilla chips back into the bags. Everything else folks took back with them. I did find something interesting though: Lena Bill's pink roller; it must've come off when she was pointing, jerking her head here and there. I found it under the pew where she was sitting. The damnedest thing. Again, leave it to me. I should've smashed it under my boot heel. Instead, I took it home and put it in my cigar box of collectibles: ticket stubs from concerts, spools of old thread, the piece of paper Julie Brigioni wrote her number on for Felix. I found Felix's chart on my desk, where I'd left it, and put it in the cigar box too.

* * *

Next morning, after the chores and milking, I helped Del run a springer—a cow that's just calved—up to the dairy barn from the calving pen. It was her first time, her first calf. First-timers don't know the routine; they fight like hell when you separate them from their calves. But old cows, I seen old cows walk away from the calf the minute you open the gate. But this one was worse than any I seen, first time or not. A Holstein. White with black-ringed eyes and a few dollar-sized spots sprinkled over her back and sides, she was the color of a dalmatian dog. Spooky-looking with those eyes. Long and rangy. She'd take two steps forward, then turn, cut back quick toward the calving pen. She got away from us once and tore clear to Petaluma Hill Road. She bawled out loud; and after we finally got her into the dairy pen, I swore she'd come back over the fence, jump it or run straight through.

"Good luck getting a chain around her neck," I said.

"One-forty," Del said, watching the young cow pace back and forth in the pen.

Of course there wasn't one hundred and forty milkers, or a hundred and thirty-nine before this one. About eighty is all. But Del keeps the chains with their metal plate numbers from every cow that's ever left the place. He fastens them over a stainless steel rod back of the dairy barn by the milk tank, and each chain waits its turn to be born again around a first-timer's neck. Each chain—and there's about two hundred of them now—moves up a notch with every new cow that comes into the milk herd. Del wanting life to go on forever. One-forty is up. A white Holstein. In a past life maybe a Jersey or another Holstein. Del could tell you.

One-forty had a bull calf, an Angus, as black as the bull she met up in the hills. Only the first-timers Del bred beef. Smaller calves, easier on the cow. So no surprise, no silver dollar. In time, a few days, maybe a week, I would take it to the auction. I spread fresh straw, fixed it a bed in the calf barn, then helped it get started on the rubber nipple. And right then, holding the plastic bottle of yellow colostrum milk, something come over me, like a weight, black clouds letting loose rain as thick and heavy as lead. Everything that happened the night before, I thought at first. But thinking back on it, the more comical it struck me. No, it was Felix. What happened to Felix? Must've left the meeting with Mollie. He was quiet, not like himself, and he hadn't wanted to come to the meeting in the first place. Was there something he didn't want let out in the open? Did the Bills know something besides what happened to his mother? The black calf took the last of the milk, then butted the nipple for more.

Caught on quick. I could hear One-forty bawling up at the dairy barn. The calf watched my every move, already traded its mother in for me. The end of the world, Felix would say about the meeting. Folks fighting. Ha! He'd say it, too, about this foolish calf: disconnected and not knowing it. But my knowing that—what Felix would say about the meeting—wasn't enough. I had to find him.

He was on Mollie's front porch, stretched in the sun on a kitchen chair. Smoking, beads on his bare chest. Felix. What was the hurry to find him? Smiling. Showing off for all of morning. Nothing different. The night before and whatever fears and secrets he'd had was a hundred feet beneath him. But he wanted to talk about the meeting.

"Survive the riot?" he asked.

I sat on the porch steps. Inside the house Mollie was yelling at one of the kids. Something about leaving his toys on the floor.

"Wasn't no riot," I told Felix.

"I know, no hair-pulling shit. Alice told me."

"So why'd you ask?"

He looked at me smart-ass-like and shrugged. "Was a riot all the same."

"Why'd you take off?"

"Auntie wanted to," he answered, nodding towards the screen door.

"Yeah, like you would've stayed anyways," I said.

I was pushing and he knowed it. But why not? I'd rushed to find him; I wanted some payback, not his smart-ass shoulder-shrugging attitude. Then Mollie's voice cracked like thunder just inside the door.

"God damn it, Sheldon, I could've broke my leg!"

Felix stood up, stretched. "She's on the rag," he said. "Let's get out of here."

Saved by the bell, I thought.

We drove to Windsor, north. Monday mornings the Salvation Army on Sulphur Springs Road. Big store, good place if you can have at the drop-off bins. Usually too well guarded. The store is run by the alcoholics who live there, each of the men—it's men only—doing six months' recovery time. Monday mornings, though, the store is closed, all the men at a prayer meeting with no one to monitor what gets left in the bins back of the building. Mack Green, a black guy from the neighborhood who's done a couple stints in the place, tipped me off. Pray to Jesus, save our pickled souls, here comes the devil to rob your blessed clothes.

It was easy; we drove right up. Cardboard boxes was piled alongside the big green metal bins and me and Felix wasted no time sorting through the clothes. What we didn't want we tossed into the bins, which saved the men some work since they'd have to open the boxes and toss the clothes in there if we hadn't done so in the first place. I say, help folks when you can. Vision kicked in and two items jumped out at me and dressed themselves on people: a print dress for Grandma, lightweight, cool for these hot days, with endless tiny white stars in the dark navy material; and a flower-print kimono-type blouse for Mollie, full sized and orange, with plenty of black to pick up her eyes and hair. Felix held up a pair of khaki trousers for himself. Perfect. Patch the knee and perfect. I would never have guessed—they wasn't tight-fitting. But with Felix I'd given up. I couldn't match clothes to him. Like with myself. I seen nothing. But after he held up the khakis I seen how they would work—what he probably seen the minute he spotted the pants. With his black boots and leather belt and a sleeveless white T-shirt. That olive-dark skin of his, rich like the earth under trees, and his black hair. The cat would melt the moon.

"You'll sew them for me, won't you?" he asked, holding the pants close to his face now, inspecting the torn knee.

"Maybe," I said. "C'mon, let's split. It's almost noon."

We packed the stuff we wanted back into the cardboard boxes, loaded the boxes onto the truck bed, and took off. We wasn't a mile on the 101 when Felix said he didn't want to go home. "I'm sick of shit around there," he said. "You know what I mean?"

"You mean with the tribe?"

"All of it."

"What, you only been here a little more than a month."

"That's enough."

I seen the sign—River Road—and I turned off the freeway. Without thinking.

"Yeah, the river," Felix said, excited, sitting up in the seat. "Let's go swimming. The Russian River, I ain't done nothing but cross it a couple times up near Healdsburg. Let's go."

"I got shit to do," I said.

Which was true. Lots of people, my mother for one, think I'm irresponsible, fly-by-night. But there is a method in what I do. The clothes business, I keep logs of everything that comes in, everything I sell, and at what price. I know what I make each month. OK, so I don't earn enough to pay rent and feed myself someplace other than Grandma's, but I'm running a business, and what the hell, when I get a business that makes a lot of money, I'll know how to run it. Practice makes perfect. Point is, I have a goal. I'm working towards something. Which is why I had no business turning off the freeway. I was behind with my book work, not to mention

Annabelle Burke and her daughter who made an appointment to look at clothes at one o'clock. But when we got to the stop sign in Fulton, what did I do? Instead of turning back, I went straight on.

I drove steady, the old truck banging on the open road, and the vineyards and open fields and trees washing the town away behind us. Horses. Cows. Thousands of blackbirds all at once lifting and dropping and lifting again over the cornfields.

"It's beautiful," Felix said. "It's beautiful to get away."

A few minutes before he'd been a begging kid. Something else had crept in now, colored him. Heavier. All the stuff that was at home. And the question just fell out of me.

"Why was you so scared about the meeting?"

Plain and simple. But he looked at me like I'd asked him what kind of plants growed on Mars.

"The tribal meeting," I continued.

No way was I going to let him off the hook now. He didn't say anything, so I went on: "Look, all that crap the night before about you having something else to do ... And then at the meeting, you should've seen yourself—like a fucking deer caught in the headlights. Why?"

"Hey, don't swear at me, man," he said.

"What was it?" I asked, not letting him sidetrack me. "What was you afraid of?"

"How do you know I was afraid?"

"Something was bothering you."

I gave him a full minute. Still, he said nothing. "What was it?" I asked again.

"What if I told you it was none of your business? I don't like nosy people. Catch on, friend."

Completely dark. Lights out and a gun to my head. Shut up or else. Goosebumps come over my skin. I went too far. Kindness and care was the wind in my horn, no matter how hard and loud I blowed at him. But he heard none of it, cared less for kindness. No. No. No. No. Shut the fuck up. What business of mine was it anyways? I caught my breath, then turned onto Waller Road. I knowed a swimming hole not far from the bridge.

A weekday. The dirt parking lot on the side of the road was empty.

"It's here," was all I said, getting out of the truck.

I thought of the boxes, my merchandise. I stacked a couple in the cabin, then closed the lid tight on the others. Who'd steal a bunch of old clothes out here in the middle of nowheres anyways? I knowed Felix was

watching me—he didn't help with the boxes none—so when I finished I
cut down the path below the bridge. He stopped me.

"Hey!" he yelled from the road. "Wait up!"

I waited, staring into the thick gray willows, until he reached me.
When I started walking, he stopped me again.

"I got something to ask you," he said.

I seen the game, how he was playing tit for tat, as if he hadn't
ended it in the first place with his threat. Catch on, friend, I thought.

"OK, what?" I asked.

"How come you never wear the beads I give you?"

"I do," I said. "When customers come."

Which was half true. I wore the beads sometimes, around the
house. But never outside. Why? Mollie. I didn't want her to see me with
them. I still felt he'd promised them to her first. Which I didn't tell Felix
just then. Why was I telling him anything? Because in his own way he
was trying to tell me he was sorry. He'd splattered me all over the windshield and now he was picking off the pieces and trying to put me together again. And, who knows, maybe it did hurt him I never wore his
beads for him to see. We each had questions.

"You know," he said, "you could've said that your not wearing the
beads was none of my fucking business."

"I know what you're doing, Felix," I said and started walking.
"Playing with me."

Then I felt his hand on my shoulder and I stopped and turned
around.

"Hey, man!" he said. Even before he said anything I seen his face
change, how he turned once again further than he'd ever gone before.
"I'm sorry," he said.

I looked at him and held the words like they would be his last.
Never mind I knowed he was sorry before he said it. Never mind. He said
it, put himself out on a limb, and there was nothing for me to do but be
the net below the tree. Jump, Felix.

"I was kind've an asshole," he said.

"Who ain't?" I asked him.

"You," he said. "You're perfect."

He needed to catch his breath now, feel himself on firm ground.
"I don't like people playing with me," I said, imitating his threatening
voice. "Catch on, friend."

There. Tit for tat. His game.

He busted open a wide smile. "Fuck you," he said. "Where's the
fucking swimming hole anyways?"

We walked on, below the bridge and upriver through green and gray willows, until the brush cleared and emptied us out onto a place where the river stretched wide, the water glass smooth and a good patch of sandy beach. I knowed the place, been up and down the river a lot. First with Grandma when I was a kid and she used to cut willows and pick herbs. I can see her tying a bundle of willow branches with thick cord, her orange rubber gloves, sand on the knees and back of her housedress. Smell the sharp scent of the sticky mountain balm leaves. And after tying up the cut willows and filling our brown paper bags full with tea leaves, how she'd pull out a couple tortillas from her purse and toss them on the ground. Wonder bread if she had nothing else. "For the spirits here," she'd say. Later, I come with my friends to fish, hike the trails. And after that, I come with Trina, my ex-girlfriend. Not much different except about five years ago folks found this place and started sunbathing naked. That's when Grandma quit, went up to Healdsburg to get willows and herbs. "The nude people?" I asked. "No," she said, "not that. I just don't want them seeing me." Go figure. But nice summer days two things never change: families in them rental canoes and a big silver osprey in the sky above.

Which is what me and Felix seen when we first sat down—that wonderful bird. Gliding, following the path of the river, as smooth and quiet as a feather floating. Felix never seen one before, didn't know what one was.

"Like an eagle, only silver," he said.

"Yeah," I said, and pointed to a stand of redwoods about a half mile downriver on the other side of the water. "That's where it lives."

"How do you know?" he asked, looking at the trees.

"Grandma told me," I said. "Seen it every year I come."

Felix leaned back on his elbows, then sat up again and wrapped his arms around his knees. Swallows played over the water. Acrobatics in the air. They danced, flipped this way and that so back and forth you seen their white undersides then their metallic blue-green backs. Hide-and-seek. Now you see, now you don't. Dark and light. Color, then none.

"It's beautiful here," Felix said.

But he wasn't relaxed. He couldn't get comfortable. He shifted himself in the sand, unwrapped, then wrapped his arms around his knees again.

"The meeting," he said finally.

I thought maybe he brought it up on account of me. Like, to finally answer my question so in his mind things would get settled and we would be full friends again. But he didn't have to answer my question now, not ever if he didn't want to. That much I told him after he put himself out on a limb and said I'm sorry. So I joked about the Bills in their doll getup. Then I pictured for him an all-out fight between the Bills and Billyrene Toms, yards of dimpled belly flesh on the floor, fistfuls of hair and torn-up flowered muumuus.

"No, I'm serious, man," he said.

"You just got to laugh about it," I said. I was caught on a fence. I still wanted him to know we didn't have to talk about the meeting. At the same time, I didn't want to push him away if he really wanted to talk.

"You laugh too much," he said.

He turned again with his talk, went around a corner and left me scrambling to catch up. I sat, quiet. We said nothing. A blond family in a canoe passed, big puffy-yellow lifesaver jackets on them. We watched the canoe until it disappeared beyond the redwoods.

"You're good at describing things," Felix said, picking up where he left off. "You got a way with words, making things funny . . . but they ain't, not always anyways."

"I know," I said. "But sometimes they are, things is just plain funny."

"Yeah, well, sometimes things is just plain sad and laughing ain't right. You know what sad is?"

"I seen it plenty."

"Seeing it ain't knowing it." He paused, collecting in his head what he was going to say next.

Now that he was on the topic of the meeting, was he going to punish me with it? Is that what he was doing: punishing me finally for pressing him so hard in the first place? Talking down to me the way he does sometimes, making me the dumb ass?

"Them Bills, for instance," he said, starting up again. "You laugh. Poor bitches. Poor, miserable Indian bitches. You know why they're like that?"

"No," I said.

"Because they ain't done nothing. Sit and rot and every time any-body else starts to move, they got to stop them, knock them down. We're at the bottom of the barrel, man, and nobody wants nobody to get out. It'll make everybody confused because if we're all not at the bottom of the barrel then who are we? Them two, they ain't no different from other In-dians, only thing is, they're out with it. Ain't you heard Indians talk about each other behind folks' backs? It's the same, man."

"Not everyone's like that," I said.

"All Indians is like that," Felix said right away. "Last hundred years—this entire century—what've we done? This tribe? Lost. Lost. Lost. Lost. A hundred years of doom. And now things is winding down complete."

"There was a lot of folks at the meeting," I said.

"Yeah, you and me, we did a good P.R. job. But it ain't even that. You know what it is? It's greed. It's because they think getting acknowledged by the government and getting land will get them a bingo hall . . . And then what? We get money for the first time in our lives and then we'll really be killing each other. Look at that place up in Lake County. They get a gaming operation going and now they're shooting up each other so bad the National Guard's got to come in and stop them."

Then he give an answer to my question about why he left the meeting, what was bothering him about it all along. "I left last night because I couldn't stand to see it go on and on—the sadness."

It was an answer I'd half-expected. Nothing new.

He took a breath, tossed a small stone into the water. The swallows kept on. He wasn't finished.

"You see, we're cut off, disconnected. We become like the white man . . ." He was looking at a canoe—a man and a lady—paddling down the river. "It's been downhill. We fell right into the hole *they* dug. But you know what we are now?"

I shook my head.

"We're the canary in the cave, man. Why are we the canary? Because we're the keepers of this place, and when the keepers ain't keeping it, it's over. You know about the frogs, man, what's happening to the frogs?"

I shook my head.

"They're dying. Me and Alice, we seen this program on TV last week and it showed how frogs all over the world is dying. Entire species of them. Frogs and toads, man. They was here before dinosaurs and they're dying! And the scientists, they don't know what's doing it. But it's something in the environment, the ozone maybe. But, you see, Indians, if they was living right, they would've seen that. They would've seen what was happening to them frogs. No, man, it's the same everywhere and nobody's seeing it."

He stopped, like he wanted me to say something, agree with him, give a nod.

"Johnny!" he said, excited, so I'd look at him.

I looked.

"Mollie, you know Auntie Mollie?"

I nodded yes.

"You know why she was so damn quiet at that meeting? Because she seen them Bills for the first time in over twenty years."

"But she lives right down the street from them."

"She's only lived there, what, a year or two? And you know them two Bills hardly come out except late at night—to hit the twenty-four-hour Safeway."

"Mollie's heard me talk about them a hundred times."

"That's my point, man. She didn't know what their names was. She didn't connect. She told me after the meeting, when we left, that twenty years ago her and my Mom and Auntie Daisy beat the shit out of those bitches in a bar up in Healdsburg. Daisy stabbed one with a knife and then her and Mom and Auntie Mollie took off back to Lake County. Man!" he said, gesturing wild with his hands to make me see his point. "Don't you see? They're fucking cousins and they was killing each other and not even knowing it! What's that? I ask you, what's that?"

"It's crazy," I said. I wasn't thinking really; I was still caught up on Mollie and the Bills not knowing each other, if that was really possible.

Felix looked at me, letting me know I hadn't given him the answer he wanted.

"Disconnected," I said.

"It's sad," he said, not giving me another chance. "That's what sad is. And that's why it ain't funny. I seen too much of it. I seen it all my life, and it ain't funny."

OK, he'd made his point. I was off the mark, but not that far. I thought he was empty then, cleared out, point made. But this time I was way wrong. All he'd done was make way for what come next.

"I seen my father kill my mother," he said.

He pulled his knees to his chest, wrapped his arms around them, and then talked down to the dirt below the bow in his legs.

"I did," he said. "I was small, seven years old. I seen the knife, her screaming, everything. Everything but the blood. I can show you the exact prune tree where it happened. But I didn't understand he was killing her. She was always screaming and fighting, screaming and fighting, that's what I remember. After my father left that night, I was just happy she was quiet. Like maybe she'd gone to sleep. Or passed out, which I didn't understand then. She had this big army coat on; the blood must've been underneath it. When Auntie Daisy come in the morning I was sleeping right there alongside her, snuggled up to that coat . . . But that's what I remember—how things was peaceful. Then I learned what it meaned."

He uncoiled himself, picked up another stone and tossed it into the water.

"Felix," I said, "the Bills knowed your story that day we went to their house, I mean about your mom, Rose, didn't they? Wasn't that why they was carrying on so?"

"Yeah," he answered, looking at me like he couldn't believe I was questioning.

Pretty low, I know. The guy just told me how he seen his father kill his mother and I'm cross-examining him. But I kept on: "Well, you said the Bills and your mom and them didn't know each other when they was fighting in the bar."

"They didn't," Felix said.

"Well, how did they know your mom's name and her whole story? Seemed like they knowed her when we was at their place."

Felix shrugged. "Easy, man. You know how Indians talk. The Bills must've heard it somewheres—about my mom—maybe read it in the paper and figured by the name it was a relative that got killed. Probably they remembered Mom and her sisters as little kids before they left this area. The Bills is older than Mom and Auntie Mollie. Mom and Auntie Mollie and Auntie Daisy, they left here when they was little."

"I know," I said.

"How'd you know?"

"Grandma told me."

"See, Indians talking. Would she recognize them later when they was all growed up? No. She might know the names, but that's all. If she was drunk in a bar someplace and my mom or one of my aunts pushed her, would she say, 'Oh, you're my cousin. I recognize you. Hi.' See my point? . . . Everybody knows the stories, they just don't know each other."

"Sorry," I said.

"For what?"

"I don't know how I got into that."

"What?"

"Asking questions."

"Who cares?"

Two more canoes passed, families paddling down the river. We watched them. I felt bad; I guess I'd been asking him questions to get the facts straight, as if to make sure his story was all true.

"Dumb-looking fucks, ain't they?" Felix said like his old cocky self. Then he looked at me serious.

"You ever have anything like that happen to you? I mean, like with my mother."

"Uh-uh," I answered without thinking. Then a funny thing: I looked at him and knowed what he meant all along. He wasn't mad or punishing me for pushing him into this place about the meeting and his mother; he wasn't trying to score points or make me understand some philosophy of his. Not now anyways. He was looking to see if he could meet me in that same place, under that prune tree where he hung on to peaceful that wasn't peaceful. He was looking to see if he was alone there. I could only be honest, tell him what I couldn't say after he told me of that place: "I don't know what sad is."

My insides pulled. I'd let him down, I felt. More than anything else I wanted to be there for him just then. But I was far away, and, as it turned out, he's the one come back for me, gathered me up.

"You do," he said. "Everybody knows what sadness is one way or another."

He looked back to the river, his eyes catching the canoes making their way to the bend below the redwoods. "Dumb-looking fucks, ain't they?" he said, going back to where we was before.

More canoes come up, a whole gaggle of them just like the two that had passed: families, some kind of church outing for the entire congregation. Felix turned to me just then and I seen excitement in his eyes. "Come on," he said, clipping me on the shoulder and jumping to his feet.

I followed him up the bank and into the willows. He tromped this way and that, zigzagging, branches hitting me in the face behind him, until he come to a clearing that overlooked the river. He glanced at the canoes on the water, then picked up a clog of dirt that crumbled to sand in his hand. "Shit," he said. Then he spied a buckeye tree, the ammunition he wanted: walnut-size green balls hanging from the drooping branches.

"There's apples across the river," I said. "A whole orchard."

"Naw," he said, "we can't go across the water. Besides, nowheres to hide in the orchard."

He filled his pockets, then pulled off his T-shirt and used it as a bucket to carry off more buckeyes. "C'mon," he said.

I did the same, loaded up.

"Grandma said the old-timers used to poison fish with these things," I told him. "Used to grind up the nut inside and put it in the water. Fish would float up, like they was drunk. It's how folks fished."

"C'mon," he repeated.

We hiked upriver, pockets bulging full front and back, T-shirt bundles tied in a knot and tight in our arms. I followed him into a redwood grove, and not more than a couple of hundred feet into the shady trees he found his spot: a fallen redwood trunk, enormous across the forest floor and reaching to the riverbank. He set his shirt of buckeyes on the ground and, jumping up onto the tree trunk, slipped backwards, the hard soles of his boots tearing away the trunk's old bark. "Son of a bitch," he said, catching himself from toppling over on the ground. He jumped down and took off the rest of his clothes, boots, then pants, everything. He looked at me. "Wild Indian," he laughed, and then he turned and climbed onto the log.

Crouched a little at the waist and taking careful steps, he creeped along the tree trunk towards the water. The muscles in his back shifted and bulged like tiny islands with each step, and when he got as far as the riverbank with its view of the water, he crouched lower and I seen where the straight groove in his back arched and ended above his ass, and below, where he was dark, and further, where from behind you seen he was a man. Then he stood up, straightened, and turned around.

"C'mon," he said. "Hand me some of them buckeyes. What the fuck you waiting for?"

Waiting? No. Stopped in time. Caught in understanding at that moment. Understanding why I could never match clothes to him. What could match what was standing in front of me? And I knowed just then how white folks come up with the story of Adam being alone and perfect in a garden: One of them seen something like Felix. Everything fitting. Nothing God made better.

"C'mon," he yelled, all excited, "there's a bunch of them coming downriver."

"OK, OK," I said, finally catching myself.

I rushed over to him with my shirt full of buckeyes and started handing him one after another, as fast as he could toss them; and he was throwing fast, rapid-fire. The canoes, a hundred yards away in a line and calm and full of nature lovers, was sitting ducks. And Felix was a good aim. *Ping! Ping! Ping!* Hit. *Zap! Bang!* On and on. First a chubby woman full of red cheeks hit *pow!* just above the big baby feeders. "Oh my God!" she screamed, grabbing her chest. Then a fat, bearded guy on the shoulder. A couple of times the sides of the canoes. And then a young husband type, maybe twenty-five, hit square in the midsection so hard he folded over.

"We're being attacked," yelled Big Baby Feeders.

"What do we do?" called another woman.

"Somebody's throwing things," one of the kids said, as calm as Christmas.

"Up there!" another kid said, spying Felix and pointing.

"Up here," Felix echoed, jumping up and down on the log for all to see . . . "Up here, you dumb fucks."

Heads spun, focused. A dozen "Oh my Gods" and then even more "Honey, turn your heads." Heads went every which way and then speechlessness until Fat Beard, who was hit on the shoulder, said, "I'll take care of this," and started paddling his canoe with his sunglasses wife towards the shore. "No, honey, don't," she kept telling him, but his angry red neck was swelled with determination, a bull charging, and nothing would stop his mad paddling. He was going to save the tribe.

"Felix," I said, "c'mon, let's get out of here."

He turned and looked down at me. He was smiling, as cool as a cucumber. "What, you're afraid of this fat white fuck?"

He glanced back at Fat Beard, who had reached shore and was climbing out of his canoe, the wife still begging him to stop. He secured the canoe, pulling his end onto the short beach there and then starting up the bank. But the bank was steep, straight up-and-down black muddy clay, and Fat Beard slipped, rolling and sliding like a pig tossed down a chute. Unholy words, and then he tried again and slipped worse. The third try it was clear he was going to make it. He hung on, pulled himself up by a huge tree root sticking out of the bank.

"C'mon," I said to Felix again, letting what buckeyes I had left fall on the ground.

He looked at me and smiled like I was stupid. Then he jumped off the log and, as naked as Creation made him, walked over to meet Fat Beard where he'd be coming up the bank. Fat Beard was there before Felix took even five steps. Huffing, out of breath, his legs and Hawaiian shirt and corduroy shorts smeared with black mud, he was raving mad. Made me think of the Bills the way his beady eyes bulged in his flushed fat cheeks. And his neck, it was swelled wider now than the head on top of it. Then he seen Felix and stopped cold. Ten feet in front of him and Felix wasn't moving one iota.

"You, you son of a bitch," Fat Beard wheezed. His voice sounded small, far away, like his throat was full of straw that muffled his words. And with his eyes fixed on Felix, who wasn't moving none, the color in his face all of a sudden growed pale. "What's the matter with you, boy?" Not threatening Felix, but scared now, like he was saying, You might be crazy enough to kill me, boy.

I sidled up to one of them big redwoods, and when Fat Beard seen me he growed even paler and shrunk. "Oh my God," he said, and I knowed what he meant: How many of you is in these woods? I'm surrounded! He looked back to Felix and Felix never moved.

"Fuck you, white man," Felix said.

Fat Beard, a mountain of mud, turned around and was gone, down the bank, as quiet and soft as a deer in the brush.

Felix won. He pushed the man back. Sheer intimidation. I was relieved nothing happened, and I felt strong, so strong with what Felix done I joined in the victory and yelled after Fat Beard: "This is Indian land, you fuck! Get out!" Then I run to Felix, who was still standing there and said: "I can't believe how you done that."

He spun around, like I broke his spell there, and made a beeline for his clothes. "What'd you say that for?" he asked, grabbing his pants.

"What?"

"About this being Indian land."

I shrugged, not knowing what the problem was.

"Look," he explained. "That dude goes to the cops and tells them what you said, then they know it's Indians done it, right?"

"What else?"

"Mexicans. If you hadn't said that Indian stuff, they'd think we was Mexicans."

"But if we get caught . . . the guy seen us."

"Quit arguing with me. And we ain't getting caught. C'mon." He picked up the rest of his clothes, boots and everything, then dropped them on the ground. He leaned against the tree trunk and put on only his socks and boots. "C'mon," he repeated, picking up his clothes again.

I picked up my shirt and followed him upriver. He tromped in his black boots along a narrow path for about a half mile, out of the redwoods and through some willows and alders until we come to a small creek that met the river. Horsetails was tall there and the water was shallow and smooth; when Felix throwed down his clothes and sat naked in the sun, I seen how the horsetails made a wall hiding the little creek's beach from the river, which was just a stone's throw away. He took off his boots and socks and, using the boots as a pillow, he laid back. I sat down next to him.

"You think they'll call the cops?" I asked.

"Naw," he said. He stretched, put his hands behind his head. "You know what?" he said then. "You talk too much."

"Among everything else that's wrong with me," I said.

Felix chuckled to himself. "Oh my God . . . Oh my God . . . Oh my God," he said, imitating Big Baby Feeders. Both of us busted up, and over and over we described for each other how she looked when she got hit, and then busted up some more.

Birds sounded, sparrows, squawking blue jays, a lone heron far up-

river. The sun beat down. Hot. A line of swallows come in from the river
and went up the creek dipping and twirling in the air. I never been this
far upriver, I thought. I watched the swallows.

"You know, I never told you something," Felix said after a while.

"What?"

"Remember that first day you come to Auntie Mollie's? Did I look
messed up, kinda like I was sleeping?"

"I think, but I don't remember."

"I was in a hurry though."

"Yeah."

He laughed. "You know why?"

"Uh-uh."

"I was beating off. You fucking come over and interrupted me."

"Sorry," I said. I kept watching the birds.

"You ever beat off?"

"Of course."

He was looking at me. "When?"

"All the time, man," I answered.

Then the birds give out, none come. There was alders, some of
the tiny square leaves yellow on the edges and shimmering in a breeze I
couldn't feel. But shimmering all the same, everywhere just then, and I
meant to meet Felix in the face, where he was looking at me, but my eyes
fell from the leaves elsewheres: He was full, all of himself, and when he
sat up and said, "C'mon, let's go swimming," I followed.

I peeled off my clothes and before I took one step in the sunlight
towards the river where he was going, I seen what I felt before, why I
hadn't taken off my clothes until now, how I was just like Felix, heaven-
wards.

We went in until our feet wasn't touching. We was about halfway
across, paddling to keep afloat. The water was calm. Felix looked up and
down the river for canoes. There was none, and I just watched him. I
didn't know what to do. He played first, dived down and pulled me under
by the ankles. A couple times he done this, and I struggled each time getting away from him. We wrestled and then he was on my back and I
knowed to quit fighting. I knowed to go with him. He wrapped his arms
around me, up under my chest, and I felt him behind, pushing, pushing,
pushing, pushing, where he couldn't go, not in the cold water and without
more time, and then I felt him between my legs and I squeezed, feeling
him just below where I was touching myself; like that, both of us kicking
wildly to stay afloat, until I heard him whisper in my ear, "Now."

We got back to our place behind the wall of horsetails and

stretched in the sun. Said nothing, until about four o'clock, a couple of
hours after we'd come out of the water, when he joked: "Coast is clear. I
think the cops give up trying to find two Indians."

"Yeah," I said, "I got to get to work."

Vineyards, trees, and open fields, and then the tract houses pushing back the old prune and pear orchards. Things in the reverse of our
coming. I turned off River Road onto the freeway.

"You ever fuck a white girl?" Felix asked.

"Yeah, my first," I said after a minute. I told him about Jennifer,
the girl who lived around the corner from my mother. Both of us fifteen,
in the old cemetery on Franklin Avenue, our first time, both of us, and
blood all over.

"I know," Felix said. "I fucked a couple of virgins before."

"Who was yours?" I asked. "Your first."

"Some chick on the reservation."

Four forty-five and the freeway traffic was thick. Somehow I had
to drop Felix and our merchandise off on Grand and get to Del's in fifteen
minutes. I took the College Avenue exit and drove the side streets towards South Park.

"You sure you ain't fucked Julie, that white chick?" Felix asked.

I was amazed. "Julie Brigioni? The girl we seen at the market?"

"Yeah. The one who buys clothes from you."

"No," I said.

"You sure?"

"Yeah, I'm sure. Besides, she ain't going to like some dark guy
from South Park."

"She likes dark guys, trust me," he said, sure of himself, then
added real quick, "I got her phone number, didn't I?"

I remembered how Felix first seen Julie: upset and leaving
Grandma's back porch. I'd told him before that she wasn't my girlfriend; I
hadn't told him the reason she was upset that day: not at me but at the
prospect of getting bit by Pete. I thought I'd tell him about Julie and Pete.
That way maybe he could get it out of his head that me and Julie knocked
boots. But, as it turned out, I didn't have a chance.

"What would you think if I fucked her?" he asked all of a sudden.

I looked at him. His eyes was wide. He was grinning, playful, in
one of his joking moods, looking at me.

"I got an idea," he said. "You're so hell-bent on helping that old
man save his cows . . . I think I can help out."

I looked back at the road but he must've seen the question in my
face: What in the hell are you talking about?

"With Julie, man. I'll make Julie tell her uncle, the one who owns the dairy, I'll make her force him not to sell it. How?" He looked at me waiting for an answer, then clipped me on the shoulder and laughed out loud. "I'll make her beg for my dick, man. Can't you see it? I'll hold her down. 'No, honey. No pee pee until Unkie promises to keep the cowies. No, no, no, honey.' "

He laughed at himself, carried on. He described things, her panties caught on one ankle, her saying please please please while he teased her, pushed himself so all he did was touch her and then more and louder please please please. I laughed, I guess because he was so lively and funny the way he told things. Truth is, I didn't want to see any of it.

"Naw, you know my theory, man," he said when he was done laughing at himself. "White chicks, they like dark guys the way they like horses."

"Yeah," I said, turning onto Grand finally.

* * *

First off, another dream. That night after my chores at Del's and Grandma's French bread and fried chicken dinner, I dreamed of Jennifer, my first girl, the one I told Felix about. Actually, not about Jennifer and our first fling in the old cemetery on Franklin Avenue, but about what happened after. When I got back to Grandma's, not in the dream but after me and Jennifer left the cemetery, I seen the damage, what was wet and cold on me there. I'd gone to take a pee and found blood, blood everywhere, on me, on my white Jockey shorts. I figured out what'd happened. Then what to do with the bloody shorts; no way was I going to put them in the wash for grandma to see. Not that she would've punished me; she's comfortable about stuff like sex, she talks about it. It's just that it was something personal, like them parts of your body you don't hang out for the world and your grandma to see. So I grabbed Grandma's black Bic lighter, tore off to the ditch behind the fairgrounds, and set my bloody shorts on fire. Burned them.

But in my dream things was different. I peeled off the shorts, put my jeans back on, but I didn't have the lighter. Nowheres. I dropped the shorts on the ground, searched my pockets, looked all around, turning over leaves and twigs, and come up with nothing. I'd lost the lighter. Matches. I would go to the store and get matches. Then I seen the shorts, smeared blood and white against the gray-clay earth like a flag. I kicked leaves and dirt on them, stomped them with my boots, until the red and white was camouflaged, and then I wandered up the ditch to the road just behind the fairgrounds. Cars raced back and forth; odd since the road normally wasn't that busy, and when cars passed there, they was slow, maybe twenty-five or thirty miles an hour. I felt I was standing on the edge of a freeway. Then all at once a car pulled up, a green Chevy, old, maybe a '68, and when the passenger door flew open I seen it was Del, and he was furious, mad like I'd never seen him mad. "The heifers on the hill, they've busted loose," he tells me. His face was the color of a beet, his eyes glassy wild; he talked like he was asking me where in the hell I'd been. He wasn't happy. "I'm coming, I'm coming," I said and hopped in the back-seat of that old car. Who was driving I never seen.

Like I said before, I don't try to figure out dreams. Don't mean the dream don't think of you though. What I mean is, pieces of it float up, pictures you seen, when you ain't thinking of it at all. Maybe in the mid-dle of the day, you're eating a tuna fish sandwich and right before your eyes is a picture, not the whole dream, but a picture, and there you go re-membering and talking back to the dream, thinking about it when you never wanted to before. Dream tricks you.

Which is what happened with this dream. It kept floating up. Tapped me on the shoulder while I was pitching hay or sorting clothes, and when I turned and looked, there they was—the bloody shorts. Or Del's pissed face. Or me picking through leaves and twigs looking for Grandma's Bic lighter. And then I was caught. Call it guilty that I was fooling around with a girl and guilty I wasn't at work. Or Felix. But I never felt guilty about what me and Felix done. Not when I thought about it anyways. That wasn't what was bothering me. What bothered me was that I was thinking about him in the first place.

I worked hard them days afterwards. Labeled all my merchandise, even put price tags on everything, something I never done before. I weeded Grandma's roses in front and trimmed the privet hedge along the driveway. At the dairy, I changed the straw in all of the calf stalls, twelve in all now, and I mended the old wooden hay feeders and checked the barbed wire fences in the hills where the heifers and dry stock run. Busy, and still I'd blink and see them shorts or that green car pull up and its passenger door fly open. And then, same as always, it was Felix I seen. Fe-lix smack in my mind's eye.

* * *

Felix was restless. Jumpy. Like he was itching and couldn't scratch. Clothes day at Goodwill and all he could say was, "Let's hurry." At a garage sale on Montecito Avenue he jumped out of the truck, and then without looking at the stuff for sale on a table just ten feet from where we was parked, he climbed back in and said: "Ain't nothing worth-

while here, let's go." I hadn't even gotten out of the truck. But I didn't argue. Which brings up something else—his moods. Dark. Dark. Dark.
Dark. You had the sense if you sneezed he'd fly off the handle. Nothing
was right: the quarter pounder from McDonald's, it was dry, not enough
ketchup and wasn't there supposed to be pickles?; Mrs. Johnson, who lived
next door to Auntie Mollie, she played her funky music too loud; the
color of my truck and the fact it needed a paint job.

My first thoughts about what happened—how Felix changed—
was that it was on account of me. Or us, what we done at the river. Like,
maybe he seen things got out of hand that day and was mad, mad at himself and mad at me. Maybe he was ashamed. Maybe ashamed to be with
me, like, if folks seen us together they could tell what we done. But then
he still expected me to pick him up each morning, and we talked with
folks we knowed just the same. And then the more I thought about it the
more I seen it wasn't what me and him done that was bothering him, or
if it was, it wasn't the only thing.

Mollie. I remembered how on that morning—the morning before
we gone to the river—Felix was outside, waiting on the front porch and
he never went back inside the house, just grabbed his T-shirt from the
back of his chair and we left. Mollie yelling at the kids something about
leaving their toys on the floor, and Felix said, "She's on the rag." These
days Felix wasn't even waiting on the porch, but on the curb, sitting
there; and if I was half a minute late, I'd find him walking up the street
towards Grandma's. And, according to Felix, Mollie was a nag and she
stunk. "Sounds like you guys ain't getting along," I said one day.
"Women," he said, "all of them—bitches."

And something else. Felix quit showing up for things. Like the
farmer's market Thursday nights uptown. First week, he handed me his
treasure chest with jewelry to sell; after that he didn't even bother. "Naw,
waste of time," he said. Fact is, I was the one wasting time. Wasn't selling
shit. Felix, he made a killing, sold necklaces and bracelets to the charmed
ladies until there was none to sell.

And the Monday night tribal council meetings. Seven o'clock,
the corner Baptist church on Grand, the same place we held the general
meetings. Anyone can go, listen to the council members discuss stuff, join
in if you have something to say. I never went regular until Felix come
along. Once he started, walked over with me and introduced himself, he
was gung ho, never missed a one. Until now. Of course after the flare-up
at the last big meeting no one asked why certain Monday night regulars—
Billyrene Toms, Edward Copaz, and a couple of others—didn't show. You
knowed. Enough was enough. But Raymond come up to me after the

meeting and looked like he'd wet his pants if he couldn't find out what
had happened to Felix. Steven looked over when desperate Raymond
asked about Felix and so did Frances Toms, both of them waiting to hear
my answer too. "Couldn't make it," I said like I knowed.

I didn't know. I made a point of not asking, lest Felix think I was
nosy, or worse, that I cared. And these days, with Felix as touchy as a
scorpion caught in a jar, I wasn't about to test that truth. We'd do our
clothes and jewelry rounds, hitting the regular spots—Goodwill, the Salvation Army, garage sales—and then before I went to Del's for the evening chores, I'd drop him off at Auntie Mollie's. "See you tomorrow," he
always said. Which meant, Don't ask me what I'm doing tonight, if I'm
doing anything it ain't with you, I'm none of your business.

Then he surprised me. A couple of weeks after our trip to the
river, I'd barely gotten home from Del's one morning and Felix was at the
front door. I offered him coffee but he didn't want any. Grandma, who
was doing dishes at the kitchen sink, slipped out the back door. I pulled
up the heavy glass ashtray Grandma keeps below the sink for folks that
smoke and set it on the kitchen table. But Felix didn't want to sit down.

"My pants," he said.

Then I remembered his khakis, the ones he'd gotten at the Salvation Army the day we went to the river. He'd given them to me a couple of days before to sew.

"You got them yet?" he asked.

"Yeah," I said, and he followed me into the bedroom.

The pants was over the wooden chair next to my desk. Luckily,
I'd sewn them just the night before, stitched the torn knee, and done a
pretty good job too. You couldn't tell nothing from where they was torn.
I lifted them off the chair and handed them to him. He inspected my
work close, holding the sewn knee close to his face, and then, satisfied, he
clutched the pants to his side and with his free hand reached into his
pocket and pulled up a folded five-dollar bill.

"Here," he said, offering me the money.

"Felix," I protested, "we're partners." Then, as soon as I said that,
I didn't like the sound of it. Not sure Felix did either; his eyes looked
steady, but I got the feeling he was smarting all the same, asking what in
the hell did I mean.

"You know, like friends," I said to make what we both just heard
sound different. But it seemed saying more only got me in deeper. Ain't
correcting a wrong only a way of admitting the wrong was there in the
first place? I turned around like I had other things on my mind. I focused
on the flannel shirt with the torn pocket, folded on my desk.

"Yeah, well," he said. "Thanks."

I heard him slip the money back into his pants pocket. But the whole time I knowed he was looking at me. I felt them same steady eyes. Then he said: "Do you want to go to Vivi's party tonight?"

"The one she's having for her and Tony?" I asked, turning around.

"Yeah," he answered.

It was some kind of engagement party where Vivi was going to announce to half the neighborhood that her and Tony was finally going to get married and show how she got things straightened out to her advantage with Tony's mom, Pauline. I was surprised that of all things to do Felix wanted to do this.

"OK," I said. "I think it starts about eight."

"Pick me up," he said, and then he was gone.

I looked back at my desk, still wondering why in the world Felix wanted to go to this party. He didn't like Vivi, didn't like how she owned Tony, and now he wanted to go to something celebrating as much. Then I thought of what I'd said, the word "partners," and how the room had gotten quiet; and I felt like a fool. I hurried back to the kitchen table, where my half-finished scrambled eggs and bacon was waiting, but before I sat down I caught sight of Grandma through the open back door. She was sitting in her aluminum folding chair, with the wide-opened newspaper pulled up to within inches of her face. I walked over and stood in the doorway. She didn't budge. Felix's necklace, the one he give her, still hung on the fence post where she left it, its bright colors, sky blue and red, glinting in the morning light. Then I seen it was yesterday's paper that Grandma was reading. I thought of saying, It's OK, he's gone, you can come out now, but I didn't. I turned around, went back to my breakfast.

* * *

I picked Felix up at eight, figured we'd get to the party fifteen or twenty minutes late. I wasn't crazy about the whole idea, to see Vivi celebrating what folks said could never be done: whipping Pauline into shape and hooking Tony. As usual these days, he was waiting on the curb outside Auntie Mollie's place, first a silhouette against the bloodshot orange night sky, and then as I got closer, his own colors, the white sleeveless T-shirt, his hair and skin, the khakis I sewed. He was nervous, edgier than usual. "Let's get the fuck out of here," he said. "What took you so long?"

No surprises at the party: packed and getting worse by the minute, loud music, enough cologne and perfume in the air to give you an asthma attack. I couldn't breathe; I was pushed up in a corner so any way I turned

I was either stepping on somebody or facing the walls. Felix slithered away right off, made his way to the punch bowl and then I lost him. I figured he was still in the house somewheres. He didn't drink or dope, something me and him had between us, and the folks doing that stuff was outside, on the front lawn or in the cars parked up and down the street.

Of course, what always happens at parties? Well, let's put it this way: Besides getting slammed into a corner, what always happens to *me* at parties? The first person I talk to is the last person I want to see. She finds me and then I'm in the corner trapped worse than before. Trina. My ex-girlfriend. Should've figured she'd be there. Vivi's her cousin after all. She comes up with a sweet, "Oh, hi, Johnny," like she's surprised to see me and maybe even happy about it, and then with one roll of her head, she's back where we left off and not an ounce happy about it.

"So say something," she said. "Don't just stand there."

"Like what?"

"Like what?" she snapped and put her hand on her hip, like she was talking to Creation's biggest idiot.

She did look incredible, what with the skimpy pea green dress she was wearing that Rachel Rickford give to her—Rachel Rickford, this half-black, half-Mexican girl who wears clothes like no other girl dares; Rachel, beautiful Rachel with her long thick hair, she'll do any guy in town as long as he's got expensive wheels. I wasn't in the running. But seeing Trina in that dress and fancy getup—thick black bracelet, gold necklace and big hoop earrings—I could say I had, or rather had had, someone close enough to her.

"Like what?" she said again. "Like, for instance, this shit about why you didn't want to have sex with me."

"It's not that exactly. It's—"

"It's what?" she demanded.

How to come out and tell her I just wasn't interested in her no more? That there was nothing between us but sex. Both my attempts to explain the situation only messed up the truth, got her on the wrong track and me starting over again worse off than before.

"It's what?" she asked, shifting her weight to the other hip and setting her other hand on it. She cocked her head to the other side then too. Well? she was asking.

Saved by the bell. The music stopped and the next thing I heard was Vivi hollering over the crowd, "Listen up, everybody! Everybody listen up!"

Folks turned around, paid attention, and I slipped through them, made my way around the wall-to-wall folks until I found a spot on the other side of the room where I could see Vivi. I wasn't close and there was a horde of girls with piled-high hair in front of me, but I could see good enough. I could see Tony, Pauline, and La Tonya, Tony's sixteen-year-old gang-banging sister, sitting on the couch, like they was waiting for emcee Vivi to introduce them. They was quiet, serious, like they was thinking of the speech they'd give when Vivi called out their names. The Silvas, Frankie and them; even Jeannie Silva, who Nellie Copaz cured of cancer with a song, she was there and looked great. All the Toms clan, the off-spring of the endless Toms sisters. The Joneses. Billy Peters, who just got out of the service. And Crystal Peters, his sister who had twins last Christmas. Where was Felix?

Vivi was fiddling with the switch on the standing lamp, trying to turn up the light so more folks could see her. She wore a white dress, tight around the middle and showing every inch of what soft rise she had there.

"All right, everybody," Vivi said, turning away from the lamp she couldn't get to go brighter. "Listen up now. Listen up."

She picked at her short, processed hair, which was flat and combed forward so it looked like a black swimming cap on her head, and then patted her stomach. Folks quieted; the talking, which had shrinked to whispers when Vivi first called out, stopped altogether.

"Now this party we're having," Vivi started, satisfied she had everybody's attention, "it ain't no regular party. It's something special—"

And just then Billy Peters started clapping, interrupting her, and he didn't stop until it occurred to him half a minute later that nobody else was clapping.

"Like I was saying," Vivi said, picking up where she left off, "this ain't no regular thing, this here party. It's something special. As most of you know, me and Tony, we're having a baby—"

And again Billy started clapping, cheering her on, and like before, quit only when he realized nobody else was clapping. I looked and seen what them close to him seen: He was dead drunk. His head hung to one side, and his big glassy eyes stared up out of his pockmarked face, making him look like a poor hound dog waiting to be fed.

Vivi gave him a look that said, If I could make you disappear, I would. She took a long breath, letting you know she didn't find Billy Pe-ters amusing in the least, and then she started again. "What I been trying to say is that this is something special. This is a celebration. What you-all don't know is that . . . well, me and Tony's getting married."

Clap. Clap. Clap. Only this time Billy started going wild, cheering and jumping up and down like he had a horse just come in first at the races. And this was when folks was supposed to clap—Vivi had paused for that effect—but they was so distracted by Billy's outburst they just stood there looking back and forth from Billy to Vivi.

A couple of the guys with Billy, two Mexicans I didn't know, tried to calm him, grabbing at his clapping hands that was going like propellers on an airplane. Vivi throwed a hip to one side in a sign of frustration, and rested her hand there, the long black fingers and pink painted nails tapping against her white dress, while she waited for the two guys to quiet Billy's hands.

"I am telling you," she said rolling her eyes, "I am telling you." Her words was full of her disgust, letting Billy's friends know she was reaching the boiling point and they better hurry the hell up controlling him. After all, she'd been working to put on this show since the day she met Tony, and this drunk fool was messing up two years' worth of hard work and manipulation.

Each of the guys took one of Billy's arms, quieting him some, and then looked back to Vivi.

"May I please continue?" Vivi asked, real pissed off.

"Yeah, yeah, yeah . . ." Billy mumbled.

"Go ahead, girl. Ignore him," Trina called out from her corner.

"Thank you," Vivi said. "Thank you very much."

"Go on," Trina assured her.

Vivi glanced around the room and then, before she continued, found Tony and Pauline on the couch. "It's not just that we're getting married," she said. "It's more. It's about two families coming together to help each other. I'm moving in so I can help my mother-in-law here with stuff around the house. La Tonya here, she can help baby-sit the new baby, and while she's at school, I'll be able to look after the little sister, La Angelique."

I looked around the couch, where Tony and his mom and sister was sitting, for the little sister, La Angelique, the four-year-old. Who was baby-sitting her now? She was nowheres that I could see. Pauline looked relaxed, like she was tired but happy all the same. No frown lines, no down-turned mouth, but happy, like what Vivi was saying was music to her ears. What was it changed her mind about Vivi? How'd she know she'd still have Tony as her slave? And La Tonya, who used every swear word in Creation when you mentioned Vivi, she sat there the same way, as peaceful as an old lady in church on Sunday while Vivi told half the neighborhood how things was going to be in that household.

"But it's more," Vivi said after she let folks digest the fact that she was calling the shots and had figured a way to solve the family's problems. "It's about something important. This marriage coming up, it marks the best of our neighborhood. An African American and a Native American coming together—"

"What, you think you're the first black fucked an Indian or something?" Billy growled. He was focused now, seen her attitude and not just heard her words. His two Mexican friends shook his arms, like, to quiet him. "Well, it's true, ain't it?" he asked them. "Who she think she is anyways?" Then Billy seen the two guys was holding his arms for the purposes of restraining him. "Hey, let me go," he said.

Vivi was like a balloon that popped, all that she was holding inside come out with a bang. "Motherfucker," she snapped, "get that goddamned drunk out of here . . . Now!"

"Vivi," Tony called from the couch to calm her.

"Don't 'Vivi' me," she told him.

She looked at the two guys trying to turn Billy towards the door. Folks was opening a path for them to get by. "Hurry up!" she yelled after them.

"Vivi," Tony said again. "Vivi."

She turned to him and barked, "What? What the fuck do you want?"

Tony motioned with his eyes and a nod of his head to the crowded room. Vivi followed his eyes, and when she seen the stunned room looking back at her, it was like she waked from a bad dream. She excused herself and disappeared.

Slowly folks picked up where they had left off. Chattering, gathering around the punch bowl, but nothing was as loud as before, not the talking, not the music. The party had peaked, come to the top of the hill and now was toppling down the other side. People would begin to leave. They'd find who they wanted to talk to but hadn't yet. They'd say hello and then say good-bye. Some would be relieved their boyfriends or girlfriends hadn't flirted with anybody else. Some would be disappointed. Some wouldn't know. That tall black guy eyeing Linda Toms would have to make his move soon, if he was ever going to do it at all. Trina was talking to them girls with the big hair. I couldn't see Felix anywheres.

I waited a couple of minutes, and when a space opened, I made my way to Tony, who was standing with a half-filled plastic cup of punch by the tall upright CD player. I waited again, this time while he finished saying good-bye to Frankie Silva, funny Frankie who forever wears them loose-fitting dark brown cords that make him look from behind like a fifty-year-old schoolteacher. When Frankie split, I stepped forwards and told Tony a host of lies. Congratulations. His getting married was the best thing. I was having a good time at the party. "Yeah," he said, happy that whatever I said had nothing to do with Vivi's show or with anything that might cause him more grief.

"How long you been here?" he asked.

" 'Bout an hour," I said. "I come with Felix. You seen him?"

The question just slipped out; for the moment I'd actually stopped thinking where Felix was.

"Felix?" Tony asked, raising his eyebrows.

"Yeah, Felix."

"He . . . You didn't see?" Tony asked with disbelief, his eyebrows raised even higher. "Rachel Rickford, man." He paused like he had given me another piece of a puzzle and was waiting for me to see how it fit in. "You didn't see it?" he asked after I said nothing. "They was all over each other, in front of everybody, right here." He pointed to two empty kitchen chairs next to the CD player.

When Crystal Peters come up to Tony and started apologizing for her brother, I cut out.

I drove directly home. It was a warm night, star-filled. No moon. I parked the truck in the driveway, then I couldn't get out, couldn't move. I sat for the longest time just staring at the house. A couple of mocking-birds chattered crazy, back and forth the way they do sometimes on sum-mer nights. I thought nothing, just listened to the birds' senseless ranting. Funny how they sing, imitating all the birds of daylight, first a blue jay, then a wren, a quail, even a crow; one of them calling out in one song and then the other following suit, a couple of ghosts laughing into the night at everybody.

Twice Grandma looked out the lighted window. Looking at me in the truck like what was wrong with me, why didn't I come in. Used to be when something like this happened I was stoned or drunk. No, Grandma, not this time, not anymore. It bothered me when she checked a second time, and something about the house too. I didn't want to answer to no-body just then. I didn't want to go in and see Grandma with a glass of milk for me, which she always has when I come in late at night. She'll set it on the kitchen table with a paper towel folded in half just so, her way of letting me know she knows I'm home safe. I didn't want to see that. I didn't want to see anything in the house, the ugly plaid couch with Grandma's star quilt over the back in the front room; or my bedroom with clothes folks throwed out piled on the desk, or the sagging single bed with its corny wooden headboard carved full of floating leaves and flowers.

I started the truck and backed out of the driveway. Grandma be damned. I was twenty, nearly twenty-one years old, after all. Things was cramped, my life was too small. I drove to Del's, why I don't know. I guess

because I figured it would be dark there, quiet; I could pull up to the milk
barn and just sit or walk around with nothing to bug me but a herd of
cows. Which is what happened. All of them damn cows getting up from
their peaceful sleep and bawling like it was time to come into the barn
again for milking; they heard my truck and went on automatic pilot, and
by the time I backed up and turned around, I seen a light come on in
Del's little cottage across the road. Narrow escape. I tore out of that pot-
holed driveway with nothing but a cloud of dust behind me. What Del
seen I don't know. He never said nothing. Neither did I.

Where was I going to go? There was no escape. There was no
place to go. Not here. Not where I knowed everyone. Nowheres where
family and friends surround you like a fifty-foot steel wall. Nothing. Nowhere.

So I headed back to Grandma's. At least I might try and sleep.
But I took the long way, turned on Pressley so I come up Grand past
Auntie Mollie's, and when I seen the lights on and the open front door, I
stopped. Why not? If all the lights was on and the TV going, why not
drop in? Pull yourself together. You're doing nothing but saying hello because you seen the lights on and, Hey, Felix, I never seen you at the
party, what happened? Yeah, I was just on my way home. When did you
get home?

No, he didn't get home. Still talking to myself when Alice seen
me from the kitchen, and before she come walking ever so quietly past
the two little guys sprawled in front of the TV and took my arm, even before that when I first felt the quiet of that house, the way the front room
shrunk the voices on the TV to secret whispers, I knowed Felix wasn't
there, and more, that things wasn't good.

"C'mon," Alice said.

She led me around the side of the house to the back steps. Walking just like she done coming to the door, softly, one foot in front of the
other like she was passing along on the narrowest of paths and didn't want
nobody to take notice of her.

"What's going on?" I asked.

"Shh, Mom's in the front bedroom."

"Close the door," I said, nodding to the open kitchen door above
the steps.

"Nah, she'll see it, and if she opens it and finds us here, she'll
think I been telling you things."

"What?" I asked, and then followed her lead and sat on the bottom step.

Alice looked over her shoulder, then said: "She's pissed at Felix. She's really mad. They was fighting terrible."

"About what?" I whispered.

Alice looked at me with them eyes that's as flat and even as hay fields in July. You see nothing. An even color forever. She looked out to the dark yard, and when she turned back to me, she was different. Something come in her eyes. "You know," she said, picking her words slow and careful, "Felix, he ain't all you think."

What she was referring to exactly, or where she wanted to go with what she said, I wasn't sure. But I understood two things: She knowed a lot about Felix and a lot of it just wasn't good.

"I know," I said.

And then she let out with: "Mom and him was fighting wild . . . Called her names."

"Felix?"

"Yeah." She looked over her shoulder again and then whispered, "Said he was going to kill her. Then he run out."

"When?"

" 'Bout a half hour ago. The boys, they're scared, and Mom, she ain't come out of the bedroom."

"Well, he must've come right back from the party," I whispered, thinking out loud. What happened with Rachel Rickford? Must've been one of Felix's quick finishes, if it was anything at all, since he couldn't have had that much time between the time he left the party with Rachel and come back here. All this I was calculating in my head while Alice said, "Yeah, he come back from the party," as if she cared a thing about him going to some party. Then she looked out into the night again and said: "That wasn't the problem."

Of course when somebody says something like that you ask, What was the problem, which I did.

"He started to go back out," she said.

I looked at her, and she knowed I was needing to know more, the rest of the story, if I was ever going to understand what she said just then. She coughed a little, the way folks do when what they're about to say ain't easy.

"He . . . all he does is come here and eat," she said and stopped again. Even with her staring into the night, I could see her thinking, creases in her forehead, her mouth closed and tight, how steady her eyes was but still moving ever so slightly, as if she could see a foot in front of her all the different ways she might tell her story and was looking for the

right way to tell me. She flipped her long hair back, swallowed, took a
deep breath.

"He eats breakfast, goes out with you, comes back and sleeps, has
dinner, and then he's out again."

"Where?"

She blinked, then said, "Him and Mom got this agreement. Made
it when he come here. She's supposed to help him and he's supposed to
help her."

"Where does he go?" I asked again.

She looked at me, then away. "He was supposed to fix things
around here, like painting the house . . . And with the boys, he was supposed to help with the boys. And I'd have more time with Auntie Nellie
for learning to make baskets, that's what Mom said."

She got on to her baskets, how Auntie Nellie said she had a gift
for weaving, even about how Auntie Nellie said she would *see* things one
day, have special powers. I had to get her back on track.

"Where does Felix go at night?" I asked.

I seen her smart, caught. "I don't know. Just out."

"All night?"

She nodded, "Yeah. That's what him and Mom was fighting
about. He come back here after the party and then he was going out
again."

"He stays out all night?"

"Yeah."

"Where? . . ."

"I don't know, I told you."

If Alice knowed where Felix gone at night, and I don't think she
did, she wasn't going to tell me. It made no difference to me just then
anyways. Something like a magnet formed in my brain; things come together and stuck in one place plain and simple for me to see. He had a
gig, something going on. All this time I thought it had to do with me, or
us, about what happened at the river. Knocked the wind out of me. Stars.
Just seeing stars. My whole insides stopped, and it was all I could do to sit
up straight and not upset Alice more with me keeling over.

Really, if I hadn't looked and caught Alice seeing me, I might've
passed out. I thought she seen the inside of me just then. Her eyes peeled
wide, like what they was seeing was no less than pure scary and awful.
Then she said:

"Didn't you hear me? Felix said he was going to kill Mom."

I was taken aback. "No," I said.

"Yes," she argued, her voice above a whisper now. "They was

screaming and he pushed her against the wall and said he was going to kill her."

"People talk like that when they're mad," I said.

"He had his hands around her throat like this," she said, putting her hands together with the fingers spread and curved, like they was around a person's neck. "She couldn't breathe."

"He left and she's OK, right?"

She looked at me the way a kid might if you was about to leave her on the side of the road someplace. Hurt and scared, disappointed and disbelieving all rolled up into one.

"She's OK, ain't she?" I asked again.

"No."

My head shot up.

"No, I mean, yeah, she's OK, but . . ."

"But what?"

She looked me straight in the face. "I'm scared he'll do it. Maybe not now, but sometime. You know, his father—"

"Yeah, he told me," I said, interrupting her. "But that don't mean Felix is going to kill someone. That don't make sense. Like he's going to get mad and kill his aunt because his father killed someone!"

"That's not all," she said, and then paused like she was trying to pick out her words again.

"What?" I asked.

"He's the type that would do it," she said, sure of herself. "Like I said before, you don't know him."

"Nobody knows him," I said, and then seen a pathway back to what was on my mind. "Like, where do you think he goes at night?"

"Who cares?" she said.

I said nothing.

And a voice answered: "Johnny does."

A man's voice. A guy. Behind me, Felix, before I could turn around to see him.

Alice and me jumped, bumped into one another, and when we looked up behind us, there he was in the doorway. A giant. A ghost, the white T-shirt. Both of us caught. How long had he been standing there? And before he left, stepping silently across the kitchen floor the way he come, he spoke to us in a voice no louder than a whisper, and what he said fell on me and Alice as soft as a nylon net over a couple of sleeping birds.

"Tell him, Alice. Tell him since you know so much. He wants to know."

Alice gathered herself together, then stood up. "Leave," she said, "before Mom comes out."

I did. I left. Got in my truck and went straight home. Two in the morning. Three in the morning. And only this: Felix seen. He knowed how much I cared. And I knowed I couldn't stop. What had happened to me? So many blows to the gut, and all in one night, and still I was standing, eye to eye with him.

FIVE

Morning comes so fast when sleep's so short. I'd closed my eyes and I was up again, hurrying myself to Del's. Then Felix. A half hour before I was supposed to pick him up, he was at my door. A hundred thoughts run through my mind and added up to one thing: fear. Fear of what he'd do or say to me. But just then he said nothing. Business as usual: He come in and sat himself at the table; and as usual, Grandma slipped out the back door. I finished my breakfast, scrambled eggs and toast, just to keep my mouth full, to keep from talking. I think he did too; I pushed the plate of stacked toast in the center of the table towards him, and when I looked up again the plate was empty. Then it was time to leave.

Somewheres between Goodwill and a garage sale on Morgan Street he started talking about the party, how fun it was, who was there.

"You got lucky," I said. I was walking on eggshells. Anything to be normal. Anything to pretend all that happened last night never happened. Anything to lie. Felix went along with it.

"You mean with Rachel?" he asked.

"Yeah," I said.

"Ah, man, we been going out for a while."

"She's hot," I said, each of my words like a hundred-pound dumbbell I was trying to push over my head.

"Yeah," he said.

Then at McDonald's, while we was in the drive-through lane waiting to pick up our lunches, he told me what he meant to tell me all along.

"I'm moving," he said.

He waited, like, for me to ask where or when.

"Point is," he said after a minute, "I'll be going out of business for a while. This here business," he added, pointing with his thumb to the back of the truck.

Translation: Don't pick me up or expect me coming around in the mornings anymore.

"So I won't be hanging with you anymore."

"Right," I said and pulled the truck forward.

"But I'll be around," he said.

Translation: I'll be in the neighborhood. If we see each other, it will be only when I want to.

I pulled up to the window and a round-faced white girl with a voice like Daffy Duck said: "Nine eighty-seven, please, sir."

Felix shot a ten-dollar bill in front of my face. "Don't say I never give you nothing," he joked.

I took the bill and handed it to the girl.

"Right," I said.

* * *

Does anybody know what love is? Can a person know before he's smashed like an almond in the jaws of a nutcracker? I needed to know. I asked for nothing more. Not Felix. Not nothing. Just to know what was happening. What slow death Creation picked for me. Was it love? Felix kept his word. I never seen him after I left him off at Auntie Mollie's that last day, after McDonald's, and I didn't go looking for him neither. I quit eating. I couldn't sleep. I couldn't match clothes to people. "Pick for yourself," I said.

I went to Del. I asked Del. I knowed the story, how his heart was broken, how his heart was healed. I always suspected it was Grandma he loved, that him and Grandma was both telling me the story of their love without identifying the other person; and because they didn't name the other, I didn't feel it was right to ask. Now I'd listen again. Maybe I'd understand something.

"Tell me again," I asked one morning after we finished the chores.

It was a warm morning, as clear as a bell, and me and him was leaning on the fence behind the hay barn where the cows was moving single file out of the corral, making their slow dusty way to the open pasture up the hill. Used to be all green up there when Del had enough help to set irrigation pipes, grass all summer. Now it was dry, bone dry like everything else this time of year; but the cows liked it anyways, liked to browse as if they was still looking for grass there, and by twelve noon, when the silver mercury thermometer outside the milk barn read ninety degrees, they'd be under the old oak trees on the far side of the pasture, the coolest spot on the farm.

"I loved a woman," Del said, the way he always started the story. "She put her arms around me." He run his hand over his blackberry face, then held the back of his neck for half a second, like that would click on his memory and take him back in time. "Only one woman before that. Not long in this country, and the boys, it was my cousins and my brother, they took me to that first woman. Over in Fulton, she had a place there. Oh, we was all just young punks then. Anyway, this girl, you give her the money, then she takes you inside—inside her house. And she's in there like this." Del stepped wide and lifted his arms, demonstrating how the woman lay spread-eagle on the bed. "So I was there like that, with her. Then what happened, I looked once, maybe over at her arm, how it was across the bed, and seen the bull. The bull, he's the one watches nobody hurts that lady. He stands in the corner of the room. Only I didn't see him before. Then it was all over for me. Nothing doing."

He paused, thinking, then said, "I don't think she liked Filipinos, that lady. White lady, you know. My cousins and my brother, they go back sometimes. But not me."

A fly buzzed in front of Del's face. He swatted at it, then rested his hand on the back of his neck again, this time for a while before he continued with his story. I looked over at the cows, all of them out of the corral now, the last of the long dusty line plodding up the hillside, big udders swaying back and forth with each slow step. Number Seventy-two, the empty-headed black Holstein, pulled up the rear, and behind her, the very last cow in line, was number One-forty, the dalmatian-spotted first freshener, the skittish cow me and Del couldn't get up to the milk barn from the calving pen.

"We work in the fields," Del said finally. "Pick prunes, apples, whatever. Laundry in a big house on, uh . . ."

"MacDonald Avenue," I filled in for him.

"Yeah . . . All of us Filipinos, that's what we done. Weekends we go out to Windsor, a ranch there; or maybe to where brother's living west of Santa Rosa, Sebastopol."

"Cockfights," I said.

"Yeah . . . Just young punks then, all of us. Drink. Dances too. Women come. Indians. Some of the Mexican girls too. And that's how I meet her . . ."

"This Indian girl, the one you loved."

"Yeah." Del looked over at the cows, then back at me. "And you know how she done? Done like this." He made a circle with his arms, like he was holding somebody. "And I see her again and again, and every time like this." Then he dropped his arms. "But she said 'no more.' Just left."

"Maybe she liked somebody else," I said, giving him the same answer I always did when he got to this point in the story. "Maybe it was an excuse."

"No," he said. "I don't think so."

"Was that love?" I asked.

He peered up at me with his face one big question mark.

"Was that love?" I asked again, slowly.

"What?" he asked.

"When she left, did you feel love? Was that love then, the feeling you had?"

He shook his head. "No. When she left, you're talking about . . . Wouldn't you call that after love, something like that?"

"What was love, then?"

Again he looked at me as if I'd asked him to explain gravity.

"When did you know you loved her?"

"When she done like this," he answered, lifting his arms to a circle again.

"That's all? Only then?"

"No . . . Talking to her. Sitting by the water with her."

"What did it feel like?"

"Good."

"After she left, what did it feel like?"

"Not so good."

He looked up at me, waiting for the next question. I led him back to the rest of his story, what I'd heard countless times before. "So then you come here," I said, and he told the rest. Hot and thirsty, with nowhere to go. The cows and Old Man Wilson. The cows. Home.

"That's how it happened," he said, "me coming home."

No matter what you asked him, what part of the story you was curious about, he always wound up in the same place—how he got to be where he is today. He turned, and resting both hands on the wooden fence, looked up the hill. All of the cows, except Seventy-two and One-forty, had vanished over the crest.

"See that. That's good," he said, watching the two cows. He turned to me then, his little eyes clear like nothing else just then. "The old one there, she's helping the young one, showing her the ropes."

Love: One mindless old cow leading the other.

I don't know if I ever expected to learn from Del what love is. After all, what could he do besides tell his same story over and over again? What can anybody do but tell their story over and over again? Grandma. Del. Me. Maybe use different words, describe it different. But it's all the same. Good or not so good, like Del said. Point is, I couldn't fool myself no more. I was living my story, I was in over my head. Yes, love and not so good. But it was something I'd never considered, this love. So I'd have to ask questions, and I had no one to ask but Edward.

Like I said, I wasn't eating. I wasn't sleeping. I needed to know something. I'm not sure what. I needed a piece of wood, a raft to hold on to, to keep from drowning in the whirling river that had become my life. Somehow I managed a few sensible thoughts on the way to Edward's. Don't tell him it's you you're talking about. Make up a story. Watch that you don't slip.

Edward lives with his grandmother, Nellie Copaz, the lady who sings and makes baskets. I been in her house before, neat and clean, African violets in the windows, doilies, as white and light-looking as cut-up binder paper, over the chairs and sofa; and in the kitchen her table stacked with willows and sedge roots for her baskets. And then Edward's room, which I'd never been in before. Through his door and you was no longer in Auntie Nellie's place; for that matter, you wasn't even on Grand Avenue. It was England or something. Pictures of horses jumping, fox hunts and English saddles, all of them pictures in glass frames with no edges. Guys rowing boats in matching tank tops along a narrow bay of water someplace, the sun coming up in the distance. Everything was neat, his two dressers each with a square mirror on the top, the way his hairbrush and a nail file was laid out on one of them dressers just so; and next to his bed that was made as tight as something you'd find in a hotel room was a fancy-carved nightstand with a book on it as thick as a Bible and called *The Golden Bowl*. The lampshade there was shiny, a golden color, and maybe that was supposed to go with the book. The lamp was on, and a good thing it was, otherwise it would've been pitch black in there. The blinds over the one window in the room was pulled tight.

I sat on his hard bed and he sat in a chair next to his glass-top desk, and already I didn't like the situation. Like I was the patient and he was the doctor. He wore a pink oxford cloth shirt with a monogram of some sort above the left pocket, and loafers with no socks, and jeans. The jeans was new, creased down the front of the pants legs, and he wore them as if they was two-hundred-dollar slacks. He was strange to look at: small eyes, a color I could never tell, in a large face, a face made even larger and more square-looking by the short hair parted and pasted down on the top of his flat head. His skin was white, ghostly; his hands looked like two little round sugar cookies below the pink cuffs of his shirt. We talked about tribal stuff, the last meeting, the next meeting. I'm sure that's what he thought I'd come for. And I didn't let him think otherwise. I made up agenda items that I wanted to run by him—that I was going to run by all the tribal members. Fund-raisers. We needed to have bake sales, garage sales. Ways to make money and get more people involved. What about bingo at our Monday night council meetings? Bingo and we could invite the whole neighborhood. Why not, the Catholics do it.

"We need a counseling program," he said.

"You mean alcohol, drugs?" I thought immediately of Pauline, Tony's mom.

"Well, that wouldn't hurt. But I was thinking of the insecurities people have . . . you know, what most of you call hatefulness."

"Hatefulness?" I asked.

"Yeah, you know, the way people talk to one another. The way they act."

"It's bad," I agreed. "Maybe we could make some money and then get a program, a counselor."

His little hands opened and closed, opened and closed on the tops of his legs. Red color filled his cheeks and ears. "No," he said, leaning forward. "We can't do anything, not a single thing together, nothing will work until we deal with the hatefulness . . . the insecurities." He stopped and looked at me. "Johnny," he said. "the way we talk to one another. The way they talked to me!"

And the picture come to my mind that he wanted there: the Bills at the last meeting calling him an AIDS-ridden faggot. My first thought was to argue, to point out that while, yes, folks is hateful, the Bills is an exception, plumb off the scale. Then reason kicked in, my mind worked faster than I might've expected at that moment, and I remembered my purpose for being there.

"How'd you get like that?" I asked. I seen him smart, so I rephrased the question. "I mean, how'd you know you was gay?" Then to soften things more, I said, quick, "I mean, it's cool with me. I don't care what a person is."

He looked at me like he didn't know what I was talking about at first. Maybe that picture of him and the Bills at the last meeting wasn't the picture he wanted in my brain. Then his small eyes got even smaller. He studied me, as if what he might find would give him an answer.

"Yes, I've known for a long time that I was gay." He sounded like someone on *Oprah* after she's asked them the big question folks can't wait to hear the answer to.

"How'd you know?" I'd play Oprah. Keep it that way.

He shrugged. "I liked men."

"But there must've been some signs or something."

He looked at me with them small no-color eyes again, but not as long this time. "Yes," he said. "There's some things."

"Like what?"

"Well, first of all you're attracted to men. Like, maybe a friend, or somebody you saw taking a shower, maybe at a gym or someplace."

My heart knocked at the mention of a "friend," but I kept my composure, didn't blink. I was on a roll, with Edward exactly where I wanted him.

"But then there's a lot of specific things," Edward said.

"Like what?" I asked.

"Questions," he said, sitting back in his chair.

"Like?"

"Oh, I can't think of all of them. You know, like, do you like Madonna? Or, put it this way, do you like female singers better than male singers? Would you rather listen to Alanis Morrisette or to Tom Petty? Bonnie Raitt or Bruce Springsteen?"

I hadn't thought about it.

"What do you think of when you masturbate? Men or women?"

Haven't done it for a while. But when I did my instant replay with Felix, just thinking would I do again what I done at the river, I would have to answer yes.

"Do you think of ways to see men naked? Do you take long showers in gyms or at the swim center?"

Don't even go to a gym or the swim center.

"Do you think of ways you might get to have sex with a man you've been watching for a while?"

Don't think so. Wasn't passing this test, it seemed.

"Do you get jealous and upset when a guy you like is with a girl?"

That one caught me, but again I didn't blink.

"You think about this guy all the time?"

Then Edward leaned forward and cast his net. "You and Felix, you guys did something, you're doing something . . . You want to do something with Felix."

"What?" I snapped. "This is about you, not me."

"You two guys are always together."

"So?"

Edward sat back and folded his arms across his chest, confident, like he knowed enough not to believe me, like it was him who'd led me exactly where he wanted me and not the other way around. If I could see his puny eyes they'd tell me as much. If he could see inside of me he'd know he was right. Still, I managed a cool front, or I thought so anyways, as much as I could. And then, when he gave me the opportunity, I hit hard.

He uncrossed his arms and leaned forward again. "Is Felix gay? Tell me." He was begging to know, all of a sudden a desperate schoolgirl.

"Not unless you want to get your ass kicked," I told him.

That stopped it. He pulled back, straightened, and looked at me like he was seeing a rattlesnake coiled and ready to strike again. I seen his eyes; they was wide-open and the gray-brown color of oak bark.

"So anyways, what do you think of the idea of a fund-raiser?" I said.

"It's a good idea," he said.

We talked a little more, mostly about starting bingo Monday nights at the council meeting, long enough for both of us to part company comfortable.

I'd gone to his house about noon, not long after I'd gotten back from Del's that morning. Cleaned up and walked over there. Coming back up Grand on my way home, I passed Mollie's house. Was Felix in the house? Had he moved yet? I'll be around, he'd said. Don't ask questions. Don't ask questions. If not still at Auntie's, then someplace close by. Rachel Rickford's, no doubt. She had her own pad, a green apartment two blocks away, on Deturk Street. Him and Rachel. We been going out for a while, he'd said. Do you get jealous and upset when a guy you like is with a girl? You think about this guy all the time?

I turned up Pressley. My mind was a junkyard. It was filled with things that would never fit or match with anything again, half an axle, a refrigerator door, rusted box springs as bent and flat as cardboard in places; and these things was piled thick and stacked nearly as high as the solid walls that held them in and the rest of the world out. A bullet to my brain wouldn't loosen the mess that was in there. The world was still and heavy. It was hot. Up ahead the street looked like a painting, oil colors, thick greens and grays, a smeared white-picket fence. The sun was tilted a little in the sky behind me, but it wasn't going nowheres. It was the middle of summer, the middle of the day, and all of Creation was caught there.

Then I seen two little kids, the Lopez girls, cross the street going towards Dollface's place. Remember Dollface, the three-hundred-pound fool with four dozen cats whose life I saved when I seen he was going to bust an artery in his heart? The girls disappeared behind a truck parked there. It was a Humane Society truck; and when I come up to it, I seen two people in leaf green uniforms, a tall guy with wire-rimmed glasses and a thickset blonde woman with a single short braid at the back of her head, holding wire cages in their leather-gloved hands and chasing Dollface's scurrying cats around below the porch.

"What the hell you doing?" I yelled.

The two little girls come over and stood behind me, like it was them I was sticking up for. The blonde woman looked at me and dropped her empty cage. She started for the truck, then stopped, seeing I was standing right next to it. I laughed. She was trapped in this godforsaken neighborhood and couldn't get to her truck and radio for help. Like me and a couple of skinny Mexican kids was going to riot and jump her. The tall man, with his cage hanging from one hand, took her arm and said, "It's all right." Then he looked at me. "We have an order," he said.

"What happened to Mr. . . ." It occurred to me that after all these years I didn't know Dollface's actual name.

"Dollface," one of the Lopez girls filled in.

"He got sick," the other one said.

I stood a moment, face to face with the tall cat catcher. Then I seen behind him Dollface's empty easy chair on the porch and I knowed right then that Dollface was dead. Wasn't no vision, nothing that come to me unusual. A fool could figure out as much. If Dollface was alive, no matter where he was, hospital or whatever, nobody would be catching his cats and carting them off to the pound. I turned around and ushered the girls back across the street. "Go home," I told them.

I thought about Dollface, how I'd seen him just a couple of days ago sitting as always on his front porch with them cats of every color everywhere you looked, lining the porch railing, on the steps, here and there around his feet, each of them like a piece of clothing, a balled-up shirt or sweater he placed just so to admire in the morning sun. And a week before that, maybe less, I walked past his place on the way to the corner market. He was watering his camellias and the cats had followed him to the front of the yard and spread themselves in all their oranges and grays and stripes across Dollface's small patch of lawn. "Hello there, boy," he said, lifting the hose like he would wave with it. "Boy" is a word you wouldn't want to use in this neighborhood, especially if you was white and talking to a black guy or an Indian. But Dollface, who was white, didn't know it was a bad thing and folks knowed he didn't know. He said "Hello, boy" to those of us he liked.

I had no more special abilities. Vision wasn't kicking in no more and it wasn't going to. I knowed I was distracted, knowed I was low and

couldn't work to match clothes to folks, but I didn't know how much I'd
lost until now. In them days before Felix come into my life I was on a
steady rise. A person could walk in the door and I'd see the blouse she
wanted even before she mentioned she was shopping for a blouse. I seen
the pains in Billyrene Toms's big stomach was stones—gallstones. And
when Frances Toms had a headache and was dizzy at a council meeting, I
seen the Reese's peanut butter cup she was eating turn into an ants' nest,
a clump of brown dirt filled with ants' eggs; and with each bite, she was
taking in them near invisible white eggs that would hatch into more of
the insects that was already inside of her and feeding off her blood. Dia-
betes, that's what the clinic doctors told her a week later. The candy I
seen, that was the poison killing her—sugar. Same thing with Trick
Burke. Only with him I seen the poison in the can of Coca-Cola he was
drinking. And on Constance Trujillo, the Mexican lady at the end of
Grand who gives out big red apples on Halloween, I seen little purple
roots growing underneath a pimple between her eyebrows. Cancer, which
her doctor caught just in time. Things like that, diseases and pains, I seen
more regular, maybe a couple of times a week, before Felix. Now that I
was thinking about it, I seen that my special abilities had faded away gradual, without me taking much notice. The last time I could remember vision kicking in was at the Salvation Army. When I seen the print dress
perfect for Grandma and the kimono-type blouse for Auntie Mollie. That
was just before me and Felix gone to the river. No, Creation wasn't punishing me for what I done with Felix. That felt good to me. The way vision did. Parts of you is alive that's bigger than the life you normally
know. It's after, after it's gone that feels bad. Felix was gone and vision
tiptoed out behind him. Them poor cats, I thought, picturing the gray and
orange creatures balled up and trapped inside those cages. But then, how
was I any different?

I walked away from Dollface's slowly, heading towards Grandma's.
I felt the heat. The world was still and heavy again.

* * *

Where I'd left my French toast and eggs, I found a tuna fish sandwich and potato chips. Different food but the same green ceramic plate—
Grandma's got a set, each plate a different color. Same folded paper napkin. Same fork and knife. I sat down at the table, but still I wasn't hungry.

"Why didn't you tell me about Dollface?" I asked Grandma.

She was in the kitchen pouring boiled tomatoes from a pot into
half a dozen canning jars lined up on the counter, a dish towel wrapped
around and hanging from the pot handle. Her first tomato harvest of the

year. By the end of the summer there'd be cucumbers for pickles, beets, green beans, and eggplant, more tomatoes. All the stuff she gets out of the little garden she plants in the corner of the backyard each spring. She weeds and waters; Pete eats the snails and slugs. How she keeps him from eating the vegetables is beyond me.

She emptied the pan into the last glass jar—just enough tomatoes to fill her six jars—and then set the hot pan into the sink. "Oh, yeah, I heard he died," she said, turning to me and wiping her hands on her stained apron.

Oh, I thought to myself, we was going to play games. Her puzzle game. You put the pieces of what she knows together like she don't have it together already herself. You don't know what she knows or how much or for how long she knowed. Cat and mouse. Then when you get something right, she'll say, Oh, yeah, I think so, that's right, when it's something she could've come out and told you when she first heard it or when you first asked her straight. The problem is, you never know for sure if she forgot the answers or just never thought to tell you, or if she's setting the puzzle out for you to play on purpose.

"Yeah," I said finally, "they're taking his cats."

"Oh?"

"Yeah," I said, "to the Humane Society."

"Maybe find a good home," she said.

"Forty cats? Uh-uh, they'll gas them."

She shrugged and turned back to her pot. She turned on the water and started scrubbing.

"Gee, Grandma, you don't have much heart," I said, taking a jab at her. She had her puzzle game. I had my straight shot.

She stopped, her shoulders not moving, only for a split second, long enough to let me know she heard me, then she started scrubbing again. She turned the water on more, louder.

"How'd he die?" I asked over the noise.

"Sick," she said without looking up. I didn't think she'd heard me.

"Heart probably," I muttered to myself.

Grandma turned off the water and set her pot upside down to dry in the dishrack. "Yeah," she said.

Yeah. And she'd waited a minute at that to respond. Yeah. She come in my direction and looked at the full jars on the counter.

"How'd you know I'd be home for lunch?" I asked.

"What?" she said, looking up.

"How'd you know to put this food out, this sandwich? . . . I hardly ever eat lunch at home."

"You don't go to the rummage sales no more."

She was right, but it had only been a few days that I hadn't stalked the Salvation Army and Goodwill.

"You're on a different schedule," she said. "A schedule where you don't eat." She wiped her hands on her apron again, then slowly made her way to the table and sat down.

What she had said and the way she sat down—folding her hands on the table—was a sign she wanted to talk. My turn to talk straight when she hadn't? No way. More than ever I was tired of her help. It was a lie: this sandwich on a clean plate, the potato chips; this house; her knowing about my life. She couldn't help me. Not anymore. Not now. And I was pissed that she was even trying.

"Different schedule don't mean I come home for lunch," I told her.

"You're here, ain't you?"

I'm not eating, I wanted to say. But then I'd only put myself in deeper. Because you're trying not to eat so you'll win the argument, she would answer.

"So, how'd you know about Dollface?" I asked. "Who told you?"

"What?"

"Dollface! Who told you about Dollface? How did you know?"

"Who told me?"

"Yeah. Who told you?"

She unfolded her hands and scratched her brow, like she was calling up her memory. "Let's see," she said. "Mrs. Lopez across the street, she's the one told me. And Constance, she told me. And Nellie. And Zelda—"

"Why didn't you tell me?" I said, interrupting.

"You didn't know?"

"Grandma!" I said, my face full of heat. "Why do you do this? Why do you play games with me? Why don't you just tell me things?"

"Tell you things?" she said. She looked down, hurt, as if I had insulted her in the worst way possible. Then she looked up at me, her eyes heavy and full of disbelief. "Tell you things? What you want to know, Johnny?"

And then it fell out, like she'd pulled the cork in my heart. "What's love, Grandma?"

She folded her hands and looked down at my sandwich and potato chips, thinking. Then she looked up at me again, her eyes narrowed and focused now. "The way Rosa was."

"Trapped and miserable," I said.

"Yeah, like that, ain't it?" She was looking right at me.

"Can't it be like anything else?" I asked. "Can't it be like the second Rosa, the one who got away?

"The second Rosa?" she said, cocking her head to the side, amused. "Hmm. She had problems too."

"Can't it be like good things? . . . Like what you say about Old Uncle. Like flowers and stuff."

"Yeah, Old Uncle's things. But it's more too. And it's got to have a story with it." She stopped a minute, then repeated, "It's more."

"Happy, beautiful, spiritual," I said.

"Them's just words," she said and started laughing. I had to laugh too.

She unfolded her hands and pushed herself back from the table. Her face slackened and that heaviness come back to her eyes. "A story," she muttered.

"Story, that's just a word too," I said, still upbeat.

"Yeah," she said and then quickly turned her face so I couldn't see her. And just as fast, she got up and started back to the counter with her six jars in a tidy row. "Better eat your sandwich," she said over her shoulder. She didn't turn her head or look back when she spoke. But I already seen what her face looked like. Seen it before she turned her head away from me at the table. The heaviness in her eyes had flooded her whole face, poured out. Not hurt or disbelief, but worry. She'd gotten me right where she wanted, eating out of the palm of her hand—got me talking, and for a moment I was detached from my misery. Then she couldn't keep up the talk. She couldn't keep me floating and she knowed it. Worry hit too hard. So hard she didn't want me to see.

I didn't run to her and say, Things'll be all right. I said nothing, even though seeing her like that made me uneasy, scared-like. At the same time I was pissed; she had opened my life like a school paper she could read. She read the paper, only she couldn't correct the mistakes. I was mad that she seen my life and at the same time mad that I was worrying about her worrying about it. I ate my sandwich, most of it anyway, then went to my bedroom. Fell asleep.

I woke, hearing Grandma in the backyard talking to Pete. Picturing her out there, I seen something else: the necklace Felix made for her hanging on the fence post. Bright, all of its colors against the weather-battered wood. She never let that necklace in her house. I got an idea. I jumped up and grabbed my old cigar box from under my desk. I flipped open the worn lid, and reaching below Felix's genealogy chart folded neatly on top of my memorabilia, ticket stubs, and Lena Bill's pink hair

curler, I found the necklace he give me. Wisdom, he'd said. I'd leave it
outside too.

I went to the river. Parked my truck and followed the same path;
walked under the bridge and upriver through the willows, stopping once
at that place where me and Felix first sat down, where the brush cleared
and the river growed wide, and then again where Felix climbed naked on
that enormous tree trunk and chucked buckeyes at the folks canoeing on
the river below. Then I kept on until I come to that spot where the small
creek meets the river. There I sat down. Behind the tall wall of horsetails,
where me and him sunned ourselves and nobody could see us. I looked for
signs, footprints in the sand where we'd walked, buckeyes that might've
fallen out of our pockets and balled-up shirts. But there was none, no
trace that we had ever been there. The sand was smooth, the horsetails
and low-growing weeds undisturbed; and the river, it was like it was the
first time a human seen it, the water a clear slate with not a sign of time
or history on it. Could I be like that? Could I walk away as clean and
empty as the water? Leave my necklace and continue my life without a
trace of what was before? That's what I had been thinking.

I hung the necklace on an alder branch. It shone bright in the
sun, its colors of sky blue and aquamarine with black and bright red. Then
I grabbed it and tossed it hard into the river. A tiny splash. A ripple.
Smooth water and nothing else.

I stood awhile looking at the water. Swallows come and dipped. A
mallard hen, brown and as plain as sand, flied past. She was low, so close
to the river that the tips of her noisy flapping wings beat the water as she
went. Then it was quiet again. Just the birds and the trees. Nothing
knowed what was beneath the water. Nothing. Not the mallard hen, or
the birds or the trees. Only me.

A canoe appeared, coming around the river bend. A young couple, white folks, the kind me and Felix seen, vacationers. I hid behind the
alders and watched them. "Dumb fucks," Felix had said. And just then I
hated them too. For no other reason but the way they could paddle over
the water knowing nothing. I had to leave this place. I thought of an offering. I left my shirt, hung it over the horsetails. Then a prayer. Stay
beads. Stay. Stay. Stay under the water.

* * *

They must've washed up. Surfaced in all their beautiful colors and
climbed aboard the wind. Something happened, something come back
and took hold. Four days later Felix was standing outside my front door.

"Where the fuck you been, homeboy?" he said, all smiles when I opened the door.

Eleven o'clock and me still in my work clothes smelling of cow shit. He was bright, as handsome as the morning itself. He was wearing khakis, the ones I patched, his trademark sleeveless white T-shirt, a black belt and boots.

"Come in," I said.

"I can't," he said. "In a hurry." And he talked about us folks getting together, us young people, that night for a meeting about what we could do to help the tribe and would I come. Informal, he said.

"Where?"

He thought a minute. Where, something he hadn't thought about. "Well, can't use the church Thursday nights. Let's say Tony's. Tony's, eight o'clock."

And then he was gone. I found myself looking down Grandma's porch steps, down her empty walkway to the sidewalk where a lone hollyhock stood waving back and forth ever so lightly in the morning breeze. A rooster crowed in the distance. Gone, as quick as he come.

I'd been OK. Busy at Del's, and even a round to the Goodwill. I worked on my books, thought about my life, how much money I had and how much it would take to move. It was time for me to start over, broaden my horizons. Maybe San Francisco. Somewhere. And I figured the kind of job I'd get: clothes; merchandising they call it, sales. Maybe one day run a big store, Macy's. Ha! End up doing the same thing as Mom. So what did I need a college education for? I felt good. I felt normal. I was more than moving on with my life, I was going, going somewhere else. And when them weak moments crept up on me, and they done it, in the evenings or during the day driving around by myself, I thought about the necklace, how I tossed it. I had something on him, on the memory, that was my secret, that I done, and it made me feel OK.

Then he shows up. But still I was all right. I grabbed on to my secret and my plans for a different life and stayed afloat. And that's how I pictured sitting through the meeting. Afloat, interested only in the things going on, the topics up for discussion. Felix had plans. He had reasons for charming folks. I'll be around, he'd said. Yeah, he'd stay in the neighborhood. No doubt get himself elected chairman. Sit tall. His scheme. Be on top when we get land and a bingo hall. So much for his talk about nowheres Indians and the end of the world. Even if he did see things the way he talked, he'd be watching for how he could turn it all to his advantage, sell the sinking world a necklace and keep smiling. I seen it. I seen

what he was up to. How we can help the tribe, he'd said. I'd have a suggestion of my own: bingo Monday nights at the council meetings. Beat
that. And then I'd go, just as I'd come.

All this I thought out standing in the doorway. Nothing to think
about after that except what I was going to wear. And that come quick
too: loose Levi's and a new print shirt, one I picked up at a garage sale. It
was a little extravagant, wild for my tastes, with its mod, thick collar and
bright red colors, but I'd wear it as a sign that I wasn't all me no more,
that I was going somewheres else.

* * *

I seen the cars parked at Tony's—Raymond's Honda Civic, Edward's VW convertible, the Silvas' gray van—and figured I was late.
Everybody was there. Must've been a dozen cars. It was only seven fifty-
five. Maybe the meeting had started earlier. Did Felix give me the wrong
time? Eight o'clock, he'd said. I went up the porch steps. Pauline was
standing inside the screen door, like she'd been waiting there for me or
she'd seen me coming. She didn't move. Drugged? Drunk? Frances Toms
appeared behind her. Their faces was unclear, shadows behind the rusted
screen.

"In the back," Pauline said, low.

Never stand and try to figure Pauline out. Drugs or not drugs. Up
or down. Take the hint, move, leave.

I walked around the side of the house to the backyard. It was
dark, the big black walnut tree on the side of the yard hiding what light
was left in the evening sky, and just below the tree I found a circle of
folks on folding chairs and upturned prune crates around a fire. The fire
burned high and bright, at least three feet of yellow flames shooting out
the top and rust-corroded sides of an old garbage can. It blinded me. I
couldn't make out anything but light-colored clothes and teeth, no faces,
no one I could recognize in that first instant. Then Felix, his grinning face
just two feet in front of me, was up from nowheres and offering me his
seat. "Sit down, homeboy," he said, and I followed the long reach of his
extended arm and pointing finger to an empty chair.

Sitting down, I watched him, and kept watching him until my
eyes adjusted to the blinding light from the fire. He stood at the center of
the circle, so close to the fire you'd think he'd burn himself. His sleeveless
white T-shirt reflected nothing. Only his arms and dark face caught the
fire's shadows. Behind him, directly across the circle from me, I seen Tony
and Vivi. They was hand in hand. And next to them sat Trina. What was
she doing here? Or Vivi, for that matter? Vivi never followed Tony to In-

dian meetings. The Silvas sat to my right, Frankie and Jeannie and some of the younger brothers. And on my left the Tomses, Linda and the rest of Billyrene's kids. And then I seen Rachel Rickford; the night air blowed the flames so I seen her all at once in a chair behind the fire. She was sitting up straight, all of her thick black hair blending into the dark behind her, her hands crossed on her lap, and she was looking at me. She kept staring, as if she didn't know the flames had shifted so I could see her watching. She was dead serious, focused, like she was trying to hear something too.

I felt funny, eerie, seeing her seeing me like that; and then I noticed that everybody was watching me, all of them faces in the circle, and each of them was the same way, serious. Like maybe I'd interrupted something and they was waiting for me to apologize or make some excuse for myself. I looked on both sides of me and found Raymond Pen on one side and Edward on the other. Raymond's weak heart must've kicked just then and put fear into his open face. He blinked, like he couldn't believe what he was seeing, then looked away. Edward, pale as usual, was the only one not watching me. He followed Felix's every move.

"Now," Felix said, taking a step towards me, "we can get to the second order of business here."

What was the first order of business? I thought. So I was late. What time did the meeting start?

"We have to deal with lying, people putting down tribal members," Felix said, and he kept walking towards me until I was looking right at his teeth. And then before I felt a thing, I saw it, saw the black panther move on the ball of his shoulder; and not his arm in my face, for I was watching his arm, but his boot so hard to my jaw that I was knocked out of my chair, landing on all fours at his feet. And still I felt nothing. I watched, listened, as if nothing had happened and I was still in my seat.

"Lying," he said to me.

I looked up at him and followed his black eyes to Edward.

"Didn't he lie, Edward? Didn't he tell you me and him was faggots?"

Edward cut his eyes to me. They growed wide with fear. His skin, it was so pale and thin-looking now you'd think if you went close enough you could see through it to the insides of his square head and out the other side.

"Didn't Johnny say that?" Felix asked again, this time lifting his fist like he would strike Edward. "Isn't that what you told me?"

I looked around the circle. Nothing had changed; each face was heavy and staring at me. Then I looked at Edward and seen his wide

scared eyes moving as fast as hummingbirds back and forth from me to Felix. He was trapped. And just then, I seen the cage he put himself in. The
whole picture of what happened come together quick. Edward told Felix a
lie, in hopes of getting Felix for himself. He believed me and Felix had a
thing and told Felix I'd said so myself. And thinking of what happened
and realizing all of a sudden where I was—knocked down in front of
everybody—only one thing come into my mind. Save myself. And as fast
as I thought that, I knowed somehow that there was no saving myself.
The damage was done. Who was on the ground, after all? Then what
come was what was left and growing—anger. And I was so black with it,
I seen only one thing; one thing, like I was looking at it through a tele-
scope, and that was Edward's neck.

He had no time to answer Felix. From where I was on my hands
and knees, I lunged at him, lifted clear off the ground and grabbed his
neck. He flew backwards in his chair, both of us, me still on top of him
after we fell, and then I knowed nothing but my hands closing tighter and
tighter on the soft skin, the tiny Adam's apple that slipped and stopped
beneath my strength. And then the blood splattering over his face, his
twisted mouth, movement behind me and someone yelling, "He's killing
him! He's killing him!" Then nothing at all.

When I come to half a moment later I was against the back of the
house and sinking to my knees. Somebody—maybe Felix—had pulled me
off Edward and thrown me across the yard. I hit the old batten-board siding hard. Enough to wake me. I caught myself from falling forward flat on
my face. Memory stirred and anger boiled again in the blood. I looked for
Edward. But I couldn't see him. People stood in a dark and solid line in
front of the fire. They was looking at me; I could tell even though I
couldn't see their faces. Somewheres behind them was Edward. I got to
my feet, and holding on to the side of the house, I seen Pauline and
Frances in the porch window, their round dull faces like wax above the
window's reflection of fire and the line of people. Ghosts. I looked back at
the people. I could make out only light-colored clothes. Ghosts. I would
never get past that wall. I turned and left.

I drove back to Grandma's. I wasn't thinking. When a rabbit gets
shot, it'll run and hide in a place it knows, behind a rock or knoll, even
if it's as good as dead already. A sixth sense kicks in. That's how I was.
That's how I got back to Grandma's. I sat in my truck for what seemed
like the longest time. Then I felt the wet and seen the stains in my red
shirt. Blood. Edward's? When you can think that rational, when you start
to ask what and whose, your body comes alive and hooks up with your
brain again. The first step outside of shock. Which is what happened to

me. I felt pain; pain on the right side of my face. My jaw ached, throbbed, and my cheek burned, like someone was pushing a lit cigarette into my skin. When I felt my face, I found a hole. It was so wide and open my pointing finger fell clear through to the inside of my mouth. I was touching my teeth. Then more pain, like salt on the torn-open skin. I tried to swallow, catching nothing but caked blood in my throat. My jaw pounded worse. I looked in the rearview mirror. My face, it was Edward's, what I seen in his face, a bloody mess, only I had a tear the size of a nickel, a black hole in my cheek I could've breathed through.

Where I had been empty of reason, now I was full of it. My mind worked fast. Never once did I think of going into Grandma's. I only thought not to go in there. When I seen the curtain pull back in the front window, I started the truck and backed out of the driveway. I knowed what I had to do. I knowed how bad off I was. I drove to Community Hospital and checked into emergency.

Lucky I had my wallet with me, a card showing I was on my mother's insurance policy from JC Penney. This tired Asian woman in white and thin as a rail took the card at the check-in counter and started punching in numbers on her computer. She looked up at me while she was waiting for the computer to talk back and asked, "How bad are you hurt?"

"Enough to be here, don't you think?" I said, turning my cheek so she could see the hole.

She glanced at my wound like she'd seen 290 such things already that night, asked me to have a seat, and then looked back at her computer, which was spitting out a piece of paper, no doubt with my entire life history in numbers on it. I asked if I could have my insurance card back. "Oh, yeah," she said, picking up the card and handing it to me. "Take a seat."

"Yeah, you said that already."

She cut her eyes at me. She wanted things a straight line, no curves in her world.

I took a seat. Others was waiting in that room with light so bright it hurt your eyes, as if enough of you wasn't hurting already.

Hardly two minutes after I sat down, a rosy nurse with a clipboard come into the room and sauntered over to me. "How bad you hurt?" she asked. You'd think she was asking what flavor ice cream I wanted, chocolate or vanilla.

"Enough to be here, don't you think?" I said.

She bent down and looked at my cheek. "I see," she said, and then went to a black man sitting a few chairs from me. He wasn't that old, maybe fifty or so, but his bony body was hunched forwards like he was a hundred; and he was fighting for air, his humped back rising under his overalls with each toilsome breath. After a minute, she took him by the arm, helped him up, and led him out through the doors.

I wondered how long I would have to wait. Pain was shooting through my jaw into my neck and head; my cheek was on fire, the gaping tear with countless tiny nerves pinching and pricking in the open air. Signing in with Happy Face and then watching the nurse go around the room had helped keep my mind off things. Now, for the first time since the accident—if that's what you would call it—I had my pain and all my senses and time to think. I knowed where I was, I knowed why. Holding my cheek in one hand and the insurance card in the other, I seen the line of people at Tony's, the faceless black wall. Then I seen Felix; I was looking right up at his teeth again.

"Lying," he'd said to me. And then all of a sudden my mind shifted gears. What was in my brain was what was right in my hand—the JC Penney card. I got out of my seat and went to the check-in counter.

"It'll be a minute," Happy Face said.

"I got to change something," I said. I held my jaw.

She looked at me, asking with her hard eyes and closed, down-turned mouth, What?

"Don't want this on my insurance card here," I said.

"Huh?"

"I don't want to put the bill on my insurance. I can use the clinic card." I reached in my back pocket for my wallet and pulled out my card from Indian Health. "I'm an Indian," I said, handing her the card. But no sooner had I said that than I saw big-mouth Annabelle Burke sitting at her desk in the clinic with a bill from Community Hospital in her pudgy little hands.

"Come to think of it," I told Happy Face, who was anything but at this point, "I'll pay with a check."

I felt someone tapping on my arm and turned to find the rosy nurse.

"Mr. Severe," she said, "we can take you now."

I looked back at the receptionist. "Please," I said. "I got ID. And if my check bounces or something like that, you got information already from my other card for backup."

"Go ahead," she said with a wave of her hand. She was glad just to get rid of me.

I followed the nurse towards the double doors and heard Happy Face call after me, "You'll pay on your way out then."

The nurse left me in a cubicle made of curtains. Then a guy come, an orderly, and wheeled me on a stretcher to a big, machine-filled room for X rays.

I thought of Mom and Grandma and in my mind seen them standing side by side next to the stretcher looking down at me. I wanted to reach out, take their hands. But I didn't. I looked at the orderly so I wouldn't have to see their faces. He must've seen me looking from the corner of his eye and figured I wanted to talk.

"Is this gang-related?" he asked. He was folding back the plastic hood of a machine.

He caught me off guard. Straight off I didn't know what he was talking about. Then slowly I seen the picture he seen. Me brown-skinned with a hole in my head, the shit kicked out of me. Maybe he seen my address too. It pissed me off. I wanted to ask him where he got off asking folks questions like that. But no words come. I looked up to the ceiling, the bright lights, and closed my eyes. I knowed the picture that was in my mind even before I seen it there again. It was what looking at Mom and Grandma would've made me see, why I turned away from them and looked at the orderly. Like Mom and Grandma and Annabelle Burke and every other Indian from here to Lake County wouldn't find out anyways. Like they wouldn't hear what happened and see the same thing, the solid wall of people and me against the back of the house, clinging to the batten-board siding long enough only to catch my breath to leave. Everything was different now. I'd see it in people, what I seen in folks the minute I walked into Tony's backyard. No matter how kind or gentle, no matter what folks wanted to think, whether or not they'd be friendly with me, I'd see it. It would be in their eyes. Something that called me a stranger.

"Yes," I finally answered the orderly, "was a gang."

"Have the police been notified?"

"No need," I said. "Everything's been settled."

I felt my insides roll and squeeze again. I kept my eyes closed. The orderly moved the stretcher around a bit, I suppose to line me up with the machine and get a good picture of my head. Not long after somebody else come in, the technician who worked the machine. "After we get some pictures, we'll give you something for the pain," the technician said. "Nothing to be afraid of."

He talked quiet and close to my head, almost into my ear. He was trying to assure me things would be all right. I appreciated it. But after he talked I felt the warm tears just come harder.

I don't know how many X rays. Lots, it seemed. Turn your head this way and that way and the clicking sound of the big contraption over and over. Didn't open my eyes until after I was back down the corridor and behind them green curtains again. Then a shot for tetanus in my arm and two more in my cheek to numb me so this hairy doctor smelling of garlic could wash my wound and sew it up without me feeling anything. About the time he was done with me, the rosy nurse come in and handed him a package of X rays, saying, "Looks OK." The doctor set down the silver instrument in his hand and held the pictures of my head up to the light. "Good news," he said. "Nothing broken." A hole's enough, I thought. The nurse took the pictures and left. Then the doctor taped white gauze over the side of my face. "OK," he said without looking at me and left. He didn't care for lowlife. Bad enough paying taxes for welfare and jails, let alone having to work in a county hospital sewing up us scum after we poke holes in one another.

I wasn't out of there yet. The nurse slipped back in and gave me a small bottle of pills—codeine for the pain. She told me not to open my mouth a lot and to take the pills only when I hurt. She said I could get a refill by calling the doctor. "You're OK to go now," she said. But she was wrong. She hadn't seen who popped in behind her. Happy Face, complete with her clipboard of papers and my bill. Happy Face, there for the curtain call. She pushed towards me and the nurse disappeared behind her.

"You said you were going to pay with a check?" she asked, looking down at her papers.

"Yeah," I said. I could hardly talk. My face was numb from the pain shots. I slowly got off the table and reached into my back pocket for my checkbook. "How much?" I muttered.

She tore a copy of the bill from her clipboard and handed it to me. Five hundred and ninety-nine dollars.

"Can you cover it?" Happy Face asked. She must've seen shock on the good side of my face.

"Yeah," I said.

She offered me her pen and I took it. Then she gave me her clipboard to write on.

What she didn't know was what a close call it was. I had six hundred and three dollars in my checking account. My life's savings. My ticket out of town. Hardly a few days ago I'd moved my savings—six hundred and fifty dollars—to a checking account. Part of gearing up for my big move. The day after I had paid forty-seven dollars for antibiotics at the feed store. One of Del's calves was sick with snot nose and scours. That check was the first I wrote in my life, but at the time I figured it was no big deal; forty-seven dollars wouldn't put me under. But five hundred and ninety-nine dollars! I'd be left with less than four bucks.

I handed the receptionist back her pen and clipboard with the check. "Can I go now?" I asked.

"No," she said, taking the clipboard and looking down at the check. "Meet me at my desk."

She flew through the curtains. I went back into the lobby and up to her window. She was punching numbers from my check into her computer. And, just then, panic come over me. Not because of the check. I knowed it would clear. But the thought of going back to Grandma's. The neighborhood. Grand Avenue. How was I going to get out now? I had no means. Out already with no way out.

Happy Face tore my receipt from the computer printer and handed it to me. "Now you're finished," she said.

I took the receipt. "You got that right," I told her.

* * *

I drove with the right side of my face as numb as an ice cube. There was a low ache in my jaw; my head felt heavy, like a balloon filled with water. But nothing hurt the way it did before. The pain shots worked. If I was anything, it was tired. When I pulled into the driveway, I quickly killed the lights and shut off the engine. Not that Grandma wouldn't hear me. She sleeps with one eye open. I just thought the quieter I moved the quicker I could get into my room. I slid around to the back of the house, crept through the kitchen; and if you ask me if I remember coming into my room and collapsing on my bed, I'd have to say no. I was asleep before my head hit the pillow.

What I knowed next was more like a dream: Grandma standing over the bed and looking down at me, saying, "Johnny! Johnny!" Like a dream because she never comes into my room. I must've left the door open—which normally I don't do—and she seen me fully dressed, lying on the bed. Maybe thought I was passed out drunk. I squinted my eyes and seen the full sun coming through the window on both sides of the blind. I panicked. Jumped up and pushed past Grandma. Didn't have to look at the clock. I knowed it was at least eight o'clock. I was two hours late for work.

My head pounded and felt like a brick, still too full and heavy. I had the sense to gulp down a codeine pill—without water—before I left the house. I didn't think of much else then except getting to Del's. No second thoughts. No first thoughts, for that matter; nothing about how I was sick and Del could manage just this one day by himself. Nothing like that even as I was tearing down Petaluma Hill Road towards his place.

When I pulled into the dairy, I found Del washing down the holding pen just outside the milk barn with the rubber hose, the last chore of the morning. I jumped out of my truck and hurried over to the metal pipe fence.

"I'm here," I said over the fence.

Without looking up at me, he quietly turned the knob on the nozzle, bringing the gushing water to a gentle spray, a leak at the end of the hose.

"Calves fed?" I asked.

He looked at me then. "You been in a fight," he said matter-of-fact. I glanced at my red shirt and Levi's. Stains, blood everywhere.

"Yeah," I said.

He said nothing, only kept looking at me. Not a sound but the soft hissing from the leak in the hose, which Del held off to the side.

"The calves?" I asked again.

"Look at you," he said. "It's no good fighting, hitting people." He turned the knob on his nozzle, letting the water blast full, and continued with his work.

Still, I wasn't thinking. I turned and went into the barn to get the answer to my question myself. Yes, the calves had been fed, not only fed but the plastic buckets and bottles had been washed, left to dry upside down in the racks next to the deep metal sink in there. So he's done everything, covered me, I thought. Then I remembered something: number Five's calf, a new Holstein bull calf down in the barn. And wasn't today Friday, auction day in Petaluma? I knowed Del hadn't taken that calf over to the auction yet. Besides, who done most of the deliveries to the auctions anyways?

I went through the barn and found Del. I stood on the clean concrete where there wasn't no fence between us. He had to look at me. "I'm taking that bull calf to the auction," I yelled over the shooting water.

He didn't look up.

"I'm taking that bull calf to the auction," I yelled again, louder than before. Felt like my stitches about come apart when I opened my mouth that wide.

Del turned off the water again, slowly, and without looking up, adjusting the knob on the nozzle until there was nothing but the leaking spray again. He turned to me, holding the hose at his side. "Huh?" he said. He seen me but his black eyes, little and plain, showed no particular interest in what I had to say, nothing special. I might as well told him the water leaking out of his hose was wet. Still, I repeated so he could hear—I wanted him to hear—"I'm taking the bull calf to the auction."

"Oh. Oh, yeah," he said, as if just remembering the calf. He opened the nozzle then and turned back to his work.

Might as well have said water's wet. But at least he heard me.

So I went down to the calf barn. With a rap-rap against the corrugated aluminum siding of the stall, I woke the black-and-white spotted calf, then pulled him out through the narrow makeshift gate. He balked and bawled a bit; and when I bent over to scoop him up in my arms, the blood in my head surged and I near blacked out with the pressure and pain. Still, I managed to get him to the truck and secure him with ropes on the bed. Then I drove—no radio, nothing—straight to the Petaluma auction. I left the calf with the fat walrus-mustached manager. He handed me the receipt, saying the same thing he always does, as if he never seen me before and this was my first time leaving a calf: "Mail the checks out Monday for the full price received minus the handling fee."

"Calf's off colostrum. It can take regular milk now," I told him.

"Yeah, yeah," he said, looking behind me to the next truck coming in.

I looked back at the pen where he'd put the bull calf with a dozen other calves. Most of them was bawling. Hungry? I couldn't see my calf. Lots was Holsteins.

I seen things like Felix just then. Not just on account of the creeping housing tracts and the fact that Mr. Wilson would sooner or later sell off the place. Not even about how Del went about his hard work because for sixty years he done it and knowed nothing else. None of the things Felix said. But more. About the dairy itself. The so-called love of cows. Calves yanked from their mothers; the bulls sent to auction, heifers kept only to grow up and have their own calves yanked from them. Years walking up that hot dusty hill and back. Love. Is that what Del seen in number Seventy-two showing One-forty the ropes, the old cow letting the young one follow her back and forth to the milk barn, helping her adjust to the routine? Several weeks ago, One-forty fought like all hell when we took her calf, run away down the road when we tried to put her in with the milk herd. This was good that she followed a senile old cow and now found her way with the rest of the herd? This was love? No, it was a circle of stupidity. A circle that taught the cows to forget the cruelty. A circle Del lived in. It went nowheres. It would die just as each old cow had died and then it would be nothing. The end. The end was happening all the time and would happen sooner or later once and for all.

I had to tell Del. I had to come clean about my leaving. Which I hadn't. No need to explain how I seen things. I couldn't stay. I had to go, take care only of myself until the end. That's all Del needed to know. What else would he understand?

I wasn't mad anymore. On the way back to Grandma's that morning I felt nothing but the need to get things done. Sew up the past and get on with things, the next chapter. I thought of Grandma. How much did she know by now? Had Pauline or Frances told Zelda so that Zelda called Grandma and blabbed? Or was it the other way around? Grandma seen what a bloody mess I was on the bed, and then after I left so fast panicked and called Zelda to see if she'd heard anything from her kids or grandkids. Probably that since Grandma, like most Indians, don't want to come out and say to everyone who knows her, Hey, and I got yet another thing happen in my family. And that was it: I was now a thing. Not a bad thing the way a murderer or a thief is, not that bad. But something to talk about . . . that wasn't like talking about just buying a new car. The blank spots on folks' genealogy charts. The story nobody wanted told about themselves, the one they tried to forget or change into something other than what it was. I'd be wearing a story now like a shirt I couldn't get off. Before I was nothing, slipped up and down Grand as good as invisible. No story. Elba Gonzales's grandkid. Light-skinned. Sells used clothes. Pretty nice. Maybe talks too much. Now it was different. In Grandma's eyes, too, I'd see it. But she'd have to be the one to get me out, lend me the money to leave. I knowed—I'd have to talk to her for that.

She did just what you'd expect. Played cool. Eggs and bacon was on the table. She was drying dishes at the sink and she didn't turn or even look my way when I come in and sat down. Times like this she waits with her silence for you to pull out all the questions in her brain. I didn't know how much she knowed. I didn't care. I was going to play it straight with her.

"Grandma," I said. "Sit down."

I was starving. I sloshed up my eggs even though it hurt to eat. My appetite suddenly come back; my body waked up to the fact it hadn't been nourished right for some time.

"Yes?" Grandma said, looking up from her dishes. Still, she didn't look over at me. She stared out the window above the sink.

"Sit down," I said again. "Over here."

She looked in my direction, set her dish towel down, and slowly come to the table. She stood a moment, like she was still thinking how she was going to handle what I would tell her. Then she sat down. She placed both her hands on top of the table, waiting.

I swallowed a mouthful of the scrambled eggs and set my fork down. "Grandma," I said. "I got beat up last night." I paused, letting her get full on track. "My own people. Members of this tribe, the tribe you always want me to help. The ones I make flyers for, sweep up shit after meetings for. Them. You say they're mean, hateful. Well, you're right. Only I can't see the good side no more, no reason for helping them, if I ever did. I did it for you anyways . . . It's too small here, Grandma. The neighborhood's too small, the Indians too close. I got to go."

There, it was out. She didn't flinch, bat an eye. Her way of saying, After all I done for you, fixed them bacon and eggs on your plate there day after day, and this is what you do, run out on me.

"Grandma," I said, attempting to reason with her, "this neighborhood, everybody's trapped. The same old crap over and over—sadness."

She didn't want to talk.

"Grandma," I said. "Felix beat me up. Tony and everybody watched. See, they're all part of the wall. They said I said . . ." Then I stopped myself. Why try and tell her the whole story? That wasn't the point now. "I'm leaving," I said again. "Moving."

Still, the staring eyes, the stiff upper lip.

"And Del," I said, agitated now, "working for a silver dollar a week. Do you realize, Grandma, that's what he's been paying me all these years—one damn silver dollar a week?"

"How much you need?" she asked all at once.

"Well, more than a dollar a week!"

"No, to move," she said.

Her staring eyes didn't shift, yet they filled with her knowing she'd put down the winning card and beat me to the punch.

I decided to keep things up front, straight. "Five hundred dollars," I said, "maybe six hundred." But talking to her wasn't that easy. More was on her mind, I could tell.

"Grandma," I pleaded, sincere, "don't you understand?"

She pulled at her red bandanna, adjusting it over her parted hair. Then she got up, and turning back to her work at the sink said, "We'll go to the bank."

I didn't move. I didn't say anything else. She wasn't happy in the least and I seen no way just then to do anything to help her. Besides, I had only one thing to do now and that was to take care of myself.

I finished what was on my plate and went to my room. I took another codeine pill, as my face was starting to hurt again. I plunked myself at my desk and put things together. Six hundred dollars from Grandma— which I would pay back—would cover one month's rent. A small apartment. Didn't matter really, just a place until I got settled and could find something else. And before I even started looking for an apartment in San Francisco—since that was where I'd go on account of how it was far away, a whole other world—I'd make a couple trips down there and line up a job. Sales. In a department store. Macy's. My plans locked in place and presented themselves clear. And how did that happen? By the mere fact that getting kicked in the face forced me to do more than just think about moving.

And another thing: I had at least four hundred dollars' worth of merchandise in this damn house. Even if I sold the stuff for half price, which was about as good as giving it away, I'd have two hundred dollars more. Food while I was getting settled and waiting for that first paycheck.

There was no end to my mind opening to possibilities. Once you see the wall for what it is, you can see beyond it and then the world is endless. Better yet, so are you.

I peeled off my bloody clothes and showered. Then I napped, a peaceful, empty sleep. Grandma's rapping at the door woke me. I jumped up, thinking I had overslept and was late for work again, but the clock above my desk said three o'clock. I had two hours before work.

"Yeah," I said through the door.

"Somebody's here," she said back.

I figured a customer. Which was good since there was no time like now to get the word out about my closing one-half-off sale. I pulled on a pair of Levi's cutoffs, a fresh T-shirt, and rubber thongs and hurried for the back door. Near the kitchen table, Grandma stopped me and pointed in the other direction to the open front door. It was Tony.

"Your face!" he said when I come up to the door.

"Yeah, what did you think?" I said to him. "I got kicked in the head. Don't you remember?"

He smarted. If he had an I'm-sorry speech prepared, he'd just forgot it. Still, his eyes was desperate for forgiveness, the eyes I knowed so well. I'd forgive him, but I wanted to get a couple of things straight first.

"Come in," I said, stepping aside so he could get by.

The way he walked through the front door you'd think he was expecting a gang to jump out and pounce on him. He was hunched some and wide-eyed, looking back and forth, left to right. I didn't make things easier for him neither.

"Sit down," I said, nodding to the couch in front of the TV.

Again, he smarted, then looked at me and sat down. He didn't know what to think. Was I going to tell him off? What would I say? Whatever it was, it was serious. We always visited in my room or on the back porch. Never in the front room. But I had one other reason for keeping him there other than letting him squirm in his seat for a while: I wanted Big Ears in the kitchen to get the details she wanted without me having to bother to tell her.

I sat in the chair opposite Tony, where he could see me straight on. I turned on the table lamp so he could see my stitches like they was half an inch from his staring eyes.

"I'm sorry about what happened," he said.

"What happened?" I asked, smart-ass-like.

"You getting hit . . . kicked in the face." He had a hard time getting his words out.

"Didn't you know about it? Wasn't you and everybody else in on it?"

"No. Well, yeah but . . ." He stammered, then stopped. I had my hand on the carton of eggs that was his guilt.

"I seen it in everybody's eyes the second I walked into your backyard," I filled in. "I seen it in everybody, even your mother and aunt. They knowed too."

"Johnny," he said, pleading for me to understand. "I didn't know he was going to hit . . . kick you."

"But *what* did you know?"

"All I knowed was he wanted to talk to you about it. He wondered if you was saying that to folks about . . . I never knowed he would hit you."

"But you knowed he was talking about this thing I supposedly said and you didn't come and tell me about it."

"Johnny, he just come around that morning. Hell—"

"You had all day to find me."

"Johnny," he begged.

"So let me get this straight," I said. "Felix went around calling a meeting—supposedly about what us young people can do to help the tribe. That was one agenda item. The other just happened to be this thing I was saying about Felix. Right? And everybody knowed what was up—"

"Johnny—"

"—everybody but Edward, because if Edward knowed he would never have gone and got himself in that situation. Edward, who said all that to Felix in the first place. Felix set up a trap for the both of us to fall into right in front of everybody."

"I know it's not true."

"What?"

"What . . . you know. What Edward said. Shit, I know you're not gay because if you was and tried something on Felix, Felix would've kicked your ass a long time ago."

That stopped me. Not just how simpleminded he seen things, but how he seen Felix—just how Felix wanted Tony to see him. Tony must've understood my quietness just then as a sign he was making inroads to my forgiveness. He pushed further.

"Edward's the gay guy, not you. He's the liar. And he got off without a scrape. You should've busted him up more."

Then I was more than stopped. I was sorry for Tony. He was trapped. A mouse on a treadmill. He would forever ask forgiveness for breaking his promise only to break his promise again. Promise, no pain. He couldn't promise. Pain, and then more pain. Me, then Edward. On and on and his eyes would always be begging.

"I'm moving anyway," I said, finally talking again. "Been planning it for a while."

"Where?" he asked, caught off guard.

"Frisco . . . maybe L.A. eventually."

"Why didn't you tell me?" His voice was full of hope that I'd pardoned his sin and that we was now on to other topics of discussion.

I was going to make a joke and say, I was afraid you wouldn't tell folks. But if I said that he might take it as a sign that everything was OK. Which it wasn't.

I never answered his question. Instead, I asked for his help. I asked him to tell folks about my closing-out sale, one half off everything. Then we talked about a couple of meaningless things—I forget what. When he got up to leave, he was pretty certain all was forgiven, I could tell. Not 100 percent sure, but about 80 or 85. We was talking civil, not like when he first come in and sat down. His face was relieved, his eyes calmer. He was in a hurry, he said. An errand to do for Vivi.

"Tell me something," I called after him as he was making his way down the porch steps.

He got to the bottom and looked back at me.

"What ideas did you come up with at the meeting—for helping the tribe?"

"Bingo at the Monday night council meetings," he said, his face beaming now.

"Felix's idea?" I asked.

"Yeah," he said, like, How did you know?

"Thought so," I told him.

He looked at me, then shrugged his shoulders.

"See ya," I said, and he left.

I walked back through the front room. First thing I noticed, Grandma wasn't anywhere in the kitchen. She was in the backyard, under her hollyhocks reading the newspaper. Had she just snuck out? Had she heard anything? The wide-open newspaper was pulled close to her face, a sign she knowed I was there—me or somebody, it didn't matter—and she didn't want to talk. Just a couple feet away from her Pete stood on his short yellow legs preening his white feathers in the afternoon light, paying me no attention neither.

I went to my room and laid on the bed again. A quarter to four. I set the alarm. I had an hour to sleep. But my mind wandered, wouldn't close back down. Pictures come and went. People and places in the neighborhood: the Bills sitting in front of their TV with a bowl of popcorn between them, the picture of their parents dressed in their Sunday best just above the TV; Pauline, Tony's mother, on the couch in the middle of that party-crowded room with a hollow smile on her face while Vivi tells half the world how things will be in Pauline's house from then on; Tony with his please-forgive-me eyes; sad Auntie Mollie at her kitchen table, looking down with eyes full of light at the show of beads. Then Felix. But now not his face; not even that forever smile, but his words. His words that day on the river: We're at the bottom of the barrel, and nobody wants nobody to get out. It'll make everybody confused because if we're not at the bottom of the barrel, then who are we?

Hadn't I just said the same thing to Grandma—Indians here build up them adobe walls against each other. To keep each other in, in the same situation. The same crap over and over again. I seen in detail how what he had said works, how it happens. How it works with them thing stories folks pin on one another and then talk about endlessly. Thing stories like drunk parents dying in the cold on lower Fourth, fathers that don't up front claim you, white blood, being a queer. Thing stories that make folks bow their heads in shame only to look up a day, a week, a year later with suspicion and hate at all the world and everybody they know. And then, so they won't be alone, singled out in their shame, they take to the business of collecting and spreading thing stories about everybody else. A poisonous basket weaved together with their fear and hatred. My Indian community. And Felix knowed it well, well enough to see the weave and know how to carry his life in it. Grab a hold of people's fear—Tony's eyes, Raymond Pen's insecure heart—and turn the screws.

I wasn't ashamed of what I done with him. Never was, deep down. Never regretted it. Because at the time there was nothing else to do; and because in a time like that I knowed I would do it again. Only hoped it would be someone different, not a person who seen only what he wanted in the moment he wanted it; someone who would talk to my own loneliness, visit it kind-like instead of using it with no more care that he used his own hand on himself. But still I didn't regret him. He gave to me a way of seeing the world. Clear. Cold. Sad. And in that way, I knowed he would be with me forever.

That afternoon I told Del I was leaving. He was in the barn, halfway through the milking, squatted next to a big Holstein whose tits he was washing with a wet rag. The milking machines sounded *swish-swash, swish-swash.*

"You're in trouble," he said, getting up and sticking the rag into his back pocket.

"No, I'm not. I'm not running from the law. It ain't nothing like that," I said.

He looked at the cut on my face, then reached for the milking machine hanging overhead from the stainless-steel pipe and squatted next to the cow again.

"I'll keep helping you for a couple of weeks," I hollered loud, over the machines. "Can't go nowheres until my face heals up anyways. A couple more weeks," I repeated.

He put the milking machine on the thick-spotted tits, suck-suck, suck-suck, and then straightened and walked past me without a word, to the next cow.

He acted the same way he did earlier—like I done something wrong. Like I hit someone out of sheer meanness and now I was leaving him the same way. And again he didn't ask no questions, didn't bother to find out who, what, or why—my story. Before I was mad; now I was just relieved. I told him finally that I was going. He could give me all the silent treatment he wanted. Grandma too.

Word spread about my clothes sale. Tony must've talked and others too. That next week and a half folks lined up each morning below the back porch steps. I found them there as soon as I got back from Del's. No frills, no help, no matching clothes to their bodies, which I couldn't do anymore anyways on account of how I lost my vision. Just find what you want and it helps if you have correct change. All kinds of people. Folks I didn't know and then the ones I did, my regulars, Indians—the Tomses, the Silvas, the Pens, the Burkes. They're the ones—the ones I knowed—that didn't look at me; or if they did look at me, looked as if they wasn't looking, trying to hide that story about me and whatever they thought about it behind their eyes. I seen all what wouldn't sink deep enough for them to hide. It didn't take vision.

Grandma didn't much like the onslaught of folks. She's private, you know, old-time Indian. When folks come one or two at a time, she could busy herself in the front room, or if she was outside, slip behind the hollyhocks, but with half a dozen or more in the house at all times, she couldn't do nothing but keep in her bedroom permanent, grab her newspaper and willow rods and lock herself in until I left for Del's in the afternoon. When it was over, when what I had left of my store was racks of empty hangers, she would have been happy, thankful, if it wasn't for the fact that it meant I was leaving.

The morning I come back from getting my stitches out, we gone to the bank. Sort of embarrassing standing at the teller's window while your grandmother is drawing money out of her savings account for you. The teller, this prissy snob with blonde curls piled on her head like coiled intestines, did nothing to make me feel better neither. I seen what she was thinking behind her thick glasses. She seen me looking and dropped her eyes quick to the money order she was pushing over the counter in my direction. "Severe," she read off the money order. "What kind of a name is that?"

"It's the name of someone who's broke and needs his grandmother to bail him out," I told her.

Even Grandma, who'd been quiet and shut off for the last couple of weeks, had to laugh at that one.

When we got home, things wasn't quite so funny, however; and I knowed they wouldn't be the second I seen the new Mercedes C230. The cheap version with that not-quite-leather interior they call leatherette. Still, a Mercedes-Benz, black and shiny, a sign of I've-made-it-in-this-world. Mom.

I hadn't seen her since the start of summer, over two months ago. Which wasn't unusual. A month or two would go by and we wouldn't see each other. But we hadn't talked since that night I called her up at midnight. Which was unusual. Normally we talked at least once a week. That last visit, which was at Grandma's, got difficult, hit the places our lives aren't happy together, where them certain parts of one person come out and sting and hurt the other. Things started off fine and then, in no time, we started fighting and Mom got up in a huff and marched out the door, mad at Grandma, too, since Grandma had stuck up for me.

But her and Grandma talked since then. And I don't mean just the time Mom come and left me that college catalog. I knowed the minute I walked into Grandma's, before I even sat down across from where Mom was sitting alone on the couch waiting for me, that her and Grandma talked, if not just that morning already, then every day, once or twice, since I got kicked in the head. Mom knowed everything, and who would've told her but Grandma. Mom don't mix much with other Indians.

"Johnny," she said without a hi or hello first, a sign she was serious and whatever she was going to say you couldn't argue with. Something I experienced lots growing up with her; that and the way she sits straight and stiff during times like this too. "Johnny," she said again. "It's OK to love . . . whoever."

First: embarrassment. Mom seeing something, true or not, about my sex life. Then: speechlessness. What to do? Say? Say I never done what you think? Talk? Change the picture? Jump around the truth? Try to explain it? Maybe just tell her why I'm leaving, that the neighborhood's too small. Yes, move on from that picture she has in her head. I hadn't told her myself that I was leaving, and now wouldn't this be a good time? And I'm going to do what you want, Mom—get a real job. Yes, and I was about to speak when my eyes adjusted to the dark room—only the small table lamp next to the TV was on—and I seen her face clear. She was undone. Stiff and straight, yes, but undone. Cracks in the surface. Her hair, for instance. Set and cut across the ears like always, parted just so on the side, but gray; for the first time I seen gray, gray strands that seemed to stand out, as if each one had lifted itself from under the dark tight curls and placed itself so you could see it and she could do nothing to hide it. And that nothing-to-do-to-hide-it was in her eyes, the most telling thing about her just then. They was naked. Not just on account of how she wore no eyeliner or mascara, something unusual for her, but the way her eyes was small and so big and full at the same time, small that was a sadness over all the big things inside of her. The things she'd never have enough words for.

"Johnny," she said. "I loved your father and that was wrong—people would say that was wrong. But look . . ." She lifted both hands for a second, pointing to me. "Look," she said again.

God, I thought, she did know everything, probably thought more about it than it actually was. Did she think me and Felix was full-on lovers and that he turned on me when I told somebody about it? What kind of drama did her and Grandma have in their heads? I looked to Grandma, who'd found something to busy herself with in the kitchen. She had never come into the front room, where Mom was sitting—proof she'd been talking to Mom. She knowed Mom wanted to talk to me. Proof, too, Grandma'd been talking to neighbors, that she knowed more than what she might've caught that day from my conversation with Tony. It oc-

curred to me just then that maybe the two of them was in this thing together: a plot to have Mom here when me and Grandma come back from
the bank so Mom could talk to me and change my mind about leaving
home. But that's not what she done.

"Go," she said. "Go wherever you can be happy." And what was
full in her eyes was coming down her face now.

Both of us stood up at the same time. And then there was no
space between us. She squeezed me with all her might. Sobbing, she said,
"I'm so proud of you, Johnny." And I held tight, crying just as loud.

Then she was gone, out the front door, and Grandma was gone,
too, probably out the back. If I wasn't so busy wiping the snot from my
nose with the bottom of my T-shirt I might've started laughing, or maybe
started bawling again, with what I was thinking: Me and Mom finally
come together, met in the same place, all over the notion I sucked a guy's
dick. Go figure.

* * *

Alice come over with the excuse she wanted to see what was left
in my store. Of course her two little brothers had plastic bags of stale
bread to feed Pete. I started to open one of the cardboard boxes I had
taped up—I'd finished packing the last of my leftover merchandise a couple of days before—when Alice tugged on the tails of the sleeveless flannel she'd bought earlier in the summer and said, "Really, this shirt I'm
wearing is fine."

I straightened and looked at her. "You didn't come for no
clothes," I said.

"Uh-uh," she said, smiling with the slightest embarrassment.
"No."

"Didn't think so," I said. We laughed at each other. My heart felt
good just then. We went out and sat on the back porch steps. The late
morning light was on our faces and warm. The boys was feeding Pete,
having fun. Me and Alice was quiet for the longest time, but it was no secret to either of us what we had on our minds, or rather who. And then
we come out with it, as easy and gentle as letting go of a balloon on a
blue sky day.

"Remember when I bought this?" she asked, tugging on the long
tails of her shirt again.

"When you and me first sat here and talked about Felix," I told
her.

"Right," she said. "You asked me about him."

"Right," I said, using her word to let her know we each had the same situation pictured clear. "How long had he been living with you at that point?"

"Just a few days, maybe a week," she answered. "That was the beginning of summer, huh?"

"Yeah."

She looked at me and then looked out to the yard, over the heads of the two boys tossing bread to Pete, as if she was focusing on the leaning back fence. "I knowed everything," she said.

"What?" I asked.

"I knowed everything about Felix then."

"What do you mean?"

She let go of her shirttails and grabbed the tops of her knees, her fingers spread and clutching like she was holding a grapefruit upside down in each hand. She was still staring straight ahead when she started talking. "First, the parole officer was in our house. He was talking to Felix. They didn't think I was in the bedroom listening. I was, though, through the door. And then later I heard Felix and Mom talking about it. I listened the same way, sneaking." She took a long, deep breath, kept staring. "He was in jail before he come here . . . He beat up some girl. On the reservation. His girlfriend, I guess; and then he drove her someplace and left her to die, tossed her out of a car. That's what he was accused of. He was telling Mom that it didn't happen that way exactly. But I believe it did."

I believed it did too. No doubt, it was the real reason Felix hadn't wanted to go to the tribal meeting. It wasn't just about him not wanting to see the sadness, being reminded of what his father done to his mother, but about how he continued the sadness himself. If some folks knowed at the meeting about what he done with this girl—and certainly some of them must've known—then their faces would've been reflecting this truth back to his face. And I was thinking that was where Alice was going with this story—pointing up how Felix just about done to this girl what his father done to his mother, a sad and ugly circle. But I was wrong. Alice had lots more territory to cover, different places to go.

"That's why I was so scared that night I seen him choke Mom," she said a little faster, easier now. "Remember that night you come over and he caught us talking?"

"Yeah," I said.

Then she hesitated again, considered how to say what she needed to say next. She was looking down at the porch step just below the one her blue tennis shoes was perched on. Her hands still gripped her kneecaps.

"But I knowed before that," she started. "I knowed. I knowed how he was. I seen what he was doing to Mom. Even all that talk of his about how sorry he was for her over what happened to Justine. I seen what he was doing. And I seen Mom fall for it . . . They didn't think I knowed what was goin' on, but I did. They tried to hide it, like when me and the boys wasn't around. But I seen it. Him teasing her, cute-like. Her smiling, happy again. It killed me to see her smiling on account of him, happy because of him. That's why I couldn't do nothing or say nothing . . . I wasn't supposed to know. And think what Mom would've done if I said something. And Felix, he would've killed me."

"You mean . . ." I couldn't finish my sentence.

Alice shook her head yes.

"But he's her nephew, her sister's kid!"

Alice kept shaking her head.

She looked back out to the fence. "I seen everything. I seen the whole story before it even happened."

She seen it before, I thought to myself, and, in my case, I seen it after, after I lived it. And then, as if Alice was reading my thoughts, she turned to me and looked me in the eyes. "That's what I come over here for," she said. "If you could've known before, maybe all what happened to you wouldn't have happened." She looked at the scar forming on my face, then back at my eyes. "I come over to say I'm sorry I didn't tell you before."

I seen her eyes just then; they was full and deep with the way they matched what she was saying. I thought of how I seen them before whenever we talked about Felix: covered, plain and empty.

"I don't know if you guys was . . . did . . . It doesn't matter," she said, fumbling a bit again for the right words. "But . . . But see, he works in places where people won't talk. Like with him and Mom and whatever else."

She stopped then. So much come into my head and so fast I couldn't say all what it was. Stuff about how Alice seen just what I seen: how Felix works. How Alice had vision, how she had pain. How she was as big and as wide as the sky. And more. But most of all, how with her sitting there I wasn't alone.

"I know," I said. "I know how he works." I took her hand then, wrenching it free from her knee, then the other hand. She was still looking at me, and more was in her eyes than what I seen before; she was waiting for my answer.

"It's OK," I told her. "Don't worry about it no more. I'm OK."

She sighed with relief. Her eyes teared up, but before either one of us got to bawling, she jerked her hands free, swiped at her nose, then slapped the tops of her knees and said full of poking fun at herself: "Gee, you ever hear me blab so much?"

"Quite honest, no," I told her.

"Well, I ain't finished," she said, and sure enough she talked straight for the next ten minutes. First, how I wasn't the only one that was OK. Her mother too. How Auntie Mollie didn't start drinking again. She was going to AA meetings and, of all things, thinking of joining Alice over at Auntie Nellie's for basket-weaving lessons. Can you believe that? Aunt Mollie, of all people, settling down to weave baskets. So many rules, sacred songs, and her doing all that? And did I know Alice's boyfriend, Anthony, took her to see the original version of *101 Dalmatians* and afterwards they got an ice cream cone—her, mint chocolate chip; and him, cherry vanilla.

"Oh, and a funny thing," she said after taking a breath. "We seen Felix when we was walking home."

"Felix?" I said.

"Yeah. He was driving a fancy car," she said.

And before I said another word, before I could relate what was in my mind's eye, I sat a moment seeing the car and hearing Felix ask: What would you think if I fucked Julie Brigioni?

"It was a red BMW convertible," Alice finally said for me. "And, Johnny, I know he seen me and he just drove by like he didn't. Just like him. Perfect, ain't it?"

"It's perfect OK," I said, seeing no need to say any more about the story that was in my head. Then I was curious. "Wasn't he living with Rachel Rickford?" I asked.

Alice shrugged. "I heard that. I don't know. When he left our house, he never said where he was going. He'd been sneaking around at night for a while, which is why him and Mom started fighting."

"Yeah," I said.

"He's still around," she said and sighed. Then she looked at me again and said, "You're a nice person. That's why I felt bad about seeing you with him and not saying anything, what I knowed."

"I found out," I told her.

"I hope you won't forget us after you move."

"How can I?" I said.

We talked a little more, mostly about her boyfriend, Anthony, and then she gathered up her two little brothers and left. Pete followed them to the end of the yard and then stopped, looking after them as they made their way along the side of the house to the front yard. Funny how Pete does that, stands on his squat little legs watching after folks when they leave, like he was saying good-bye and wishing them well. Funny, too, that there is no gate or fence there and yet he always stops at the same place, never venturing further. Any time you're sitting on these steps, Pete's in view.

With Felix, things was always a question. You could think and ponder forever; just when you got it clear, just when you think you got him nailed down, he'll surprise you and set you back to thinking and pondering again. But that day, sitting on the porch steps after Alice left, my mind took another turn after a while. No questions anymore. Only a picture: A boy, a small Indian boy holding to his mother, holding to her oversize army coat that hid her blood, that hid the fact that she was as cold as the night itself; yes, under that prune tree in the middle of a starless night where he hung on to peaceful that wasn't peaceful. And then something else: When he woke; days or years later when he found out that what he was hanging on to wasn't what he was hanging on to and then, out of fear and anger and all them other things that come from what he found out, he started swinging, hitting back at the world, at the mean trick of his life, hitting back whether or not the world hit him again, and then he never stopped. It gone past sad. It gone to frightful.

SIX

The next day I made final preparations for my leaving. After morning chores at Del's, I drove uptown to Sawyer's Newsstand and got a *San Francisco Chronicle*. I read the classifieds top to bottom and called and set up appointments to look at three apartments on Thursday. I got directions and made a reservation for one night, Wednesday night, in a Motel 6 just south of the city. I figured I'd get down there and get a good night's sleep and that way have all day Thursday to find a place to live and maybe even have enough time to check out the big department stores for a job. Everything I owned, which was already packed into one big suitcase and two medium-size cardboard boxes, I'd have with me. If things worked out perfect—a place to live and a job—I'd be ready to stay put and start work right away. I wouldn't have to come back.

Which is how I set things up on this end. I told Del that for certain Wednesday morning's chores would be my last. Today was Monday, so tomorrow and Wednesday morning and that was it.

The next day, Tuesday, I took the boxes of merchandise I didn't sell to the Goodwill. It was funny leaving things there when all I done before was took. "Thank you," some lady there said to me. "And thank you," I said in return, and she smiled at my appreciation of her time spent helping the poor. I had to laugh. The world sometimes is just one big place of all the things a person don't know.

Later that afternoon, I cleaned my room. Dusted, wiped down the insides of the dresser drawers, washed the one window inside and out, and scrubbed the cracked wooden floor. I didn't have to do any of it. The room was clean enough. I was avoiding the last two pieces of business I had to take care of before leaving: apologizing to Edward and saying good-bye to Grandma. Finally, when there wasn't a surface left to sponge or another wall to wipe, I left for Edward's.

It was my last talk with Alice that made me think clear about what I had to do with Edward. Nothing she said about him, for the subject of Edward never come up in our conversation. But something she said to me, something she needed to do to clear her own mind and because it was right, which was to say, I'm sorry. Yes, I knowed my blacking out and attacking him was wrong and dangerous. At the same time, Edward lied, as far as I could tell, and caused a mess. But that kind of back and forth thinking and making excuses was all just part of the same thing. It was hitting back. Better to say I'm sorry and go out that way.

I walked up Grand. It was hot. Late August and summer had turned its switch to high one more time. Tar bubbles come up in the street. A crow perched on a low picket fence in the shade didn't flinch as I passed by; its heavy wings was drooped, its black beak open, panting breaths of merciless air. I turned into Nellie's place and passed along her narrow marigold-lined walkway to the front door. I knocked for what seemed the longest time. Finally, Nellie answered. She opened the door just a sliver, showing only half of her tidy gray face.

"Hi, Auntie," I said. "Is Edward here?"

"Just a minute," she said and closed the door tight.

Half a second later, she was back, peeking out the door again. I seen strain in however much of her face I could see just then. "He . . . he don't want to see you," she said.

No words come to me. No response. Why I'd assumed he would want to see me I don't know. Fact was, he didn't.

"Got to close the door now," Auntie said with some embarrassment in her voice. "You know, to keep the cool air in."

"Yeah," I said, and she closed the door.

The thought come to me to knock again and ask her to tell Edward for me that I was sorry. Just so he knowed. But if he didn't want to see me, why would he want to hear what I had to say? I made the effort; he knowed at least that I knocked on his door. And I knowed. Auntie Nellie was caught in the middle. It wasn't like her not to ask you in. She's an Indian doctor. Peace is important to her. Maybe her vision was on and she seen why I was there. I hope so. She'd know, too, that things don't always heal perfect.

Grandma was next. As it turned out, life didn't go the way I planned there either. I had a talk ready, all the stuff I wanted to say to her: Thank you for all you done for me and no matter what, no matter where I go, no matter who I meet, you will always be the most important part of my life. I start to talk, saying, "Grandma," and what does she do? She looks away from *Oprah* and tells me, "It's hot." She might as well have said bullshit. She'd been avoiding my eyes the last few days even more than she had during the last few weeks, since I first told her I was leaving. When I come back from Edward's, I found her plopped on the couch with the TV on, a game of solitaire spread out on the coffee table and yesterday's paper next to her and folded back to the weather page. No beating around the bush, I had thought to myself. No trying to catch her eye. No warm-up discussions about how I knowed my leaving was hard for her. Just out with it.

"Grandma," I said, demanding she pay attention to me.

"Huh?" she said, only half looking away from the TV again.

"Do you hear me?"

"Yes," she answered. You'd think I had asked if she thought the sun was out.

The last twenty-four hours I had a lot of peace in me about the world. Edward's rejecting me, I accepted it for what it was. I couldn't fix things between him and me just because I wanted to. I was OK with that. But Grandma sitting there pulling one of her mind trips undone me. I tried to keep myself calm. Again, I thought of the things I wanted to say to her: Grandma, it's OK to tell me you don't want me to go; it's OK to tell me what you want, please just say it. But she was up before my mouth opened and heading for the kitchen. "It's hot," she said, walking slow and tugging at the collar of her dress. "Going to have to water the plants again tonight."

I gave up, went to Del's. Later, during dinner, I thought of trying again.

"It's our last supper," I said.

"Enough green beans there?" she said. "Just picked them."

"Yeah, they're good," I told her.

Then we went back to eating the way we begun. In silence.

It was hot. The day pushed through the walls of Grandma's house so that at eight o'clock at night the place was like an oven. I thought of taking a drive, but where? What's new to see in an old place? I thought. Instead, I laid on my bed with my window wide open listening to Grandma watering her vegetable garden out back. Pete would be next to her, swiping with his bill at the water falling from the hose. They'd be out there until midnight, having fun, cooler than me. What did Grandma want anyway? How could I say good-bye to her so she'd hear me?

Eventually I fell asleep. Then it was time for my last round at Del's. I said good-bye to all the cows, with a special pat for each of the calves.

Then I gone to Del and told him I was leaving now, good-bye. He nodded and other than that I might as well have told him there was a fly in the barn. He kept busy, never looking away from his work, which was sweeping up the grain the cows spilled under the metal milking stanchions to take home to his chickens. I asked if he was sure he could handle all the work by himself, at least until he found someone else who could help him, and again he just nodded. I told him, just as I had tried to explain before, why I was leaving—that I had to get on with my life. I told him I'd come back and visit him. Still, nothing. The slow steady strokes of his broom over the concrete floor. But as luck would have it, I stood in the door half a minute, why I don't know, and then looked back. He must've thought I was gone. With his one free hand, he held his flimsy old white T-shirt up to his face, his black-brown belly showing, and wiped his nose, once and then again.

Then he was looking at me.

I gone and hugged him, all the while him thanking me and wishing me well in his Filipino English. Then he let go, and from his pocket he pulled out a silver dollar, which he pressed into my palm. "A good day," he said. He had found a place inside himself to be strong. I didn't fare so well. I hugged him and then it was me wiping snot from my nose with the end of my T-shirt.

Grandma didn't let down her guard. Not like Del. She kept tough. Breakfast as always, a shower, my one suitcase and two cardboard boxes in the truck bed, and she's doing the dishes.

She hugged me; she had to on account of how I went up to her, turned her around, and held her tight. She even followed me halfway to the front door, as far as the kitchen table, but that was it. I was on my own.

It was about one-thirty. It was also 104 degrees. If yesterday summer had turned its switch to high, then today it just let the world simmer in that heat. Unbelievable. The air outside pushed, squeezed you into yourself, the way the sun dries a raisin. I checked my radiator to make sure it had enough water—my truck was old, after all—and then I left. I turned off Grand onto Pressley, heading for the freeway. I drove slow.

Things looked the way they looked on Sundays when I was a kid. You could see how the neighborhood fixed itself each day while you was in school, what you missed sitting in a classroom: shadows from Grandma's hollyhocks at nine in the morning, noon shining on car tops, the Pens' sheepdog spread out on the front lawn in the early afternoon, Auntie Nellie taking her daily walk. And more. It was as if on Sundays, not Saturdays, but Sundays when everybody was around, that the world slowed down with the weight of all that was in it and let you see every sleeping dog and cat, every kid playing in the street and old person on a porch, every flower, every rose, as if it was passing you in a parade. Driving down the street, I seen the neighborhood like that because leaving itself made everything stand out clear and present itself slow; and like on Sundays when I was a kid, I knowed I wouldn't see things like this for a while.

Then I seen the truck. Because it was no regular part of this neighborhood. Because it was so big parked near the end of Pressley up ahead. And when I focused, I seen the watermelons heaped above the wooden truck walls that held them, heaped in a mountain that peaked near the center of the truck bed. I drove forward, slow still, until I seen the outline and shape of each green beauty. Water on a hot day. Sweet watermelon. I thought of Grandma.

I parked and grabbed a watermelon off the truck. Why I didn't think about getting caught I don't know. The large black truck was parked in front of Magdalena's place, Magdalena who grows giant white calla lilies in her front yard and sings Mexican love songs from her porch with no shame. At fifty, she still had many men friends. Probably the truck driver was one of them. But I didn't think about it then. Neither did I think about the two teenagers, Vince Green and Jaime Martinez, who watched me from across the street. I held the watermelon next to me on the truck seat and went back to Grandma's.

I wouldn't have stayed, I would have turned around and left after I set the watermelon on the kitchen table if it wasn't for the fact that she was finally looking at me. It wasn't her dead-serious expression. That could've been a scheme on her part to keep me there an hour longer, maybe a day longer. But her eyes, which I'd wanted since the first time I told her I was leaving. I had them now.

"Grandma," I said and then blurted out all the things I'd planned to say earlier—You're the most important part of my life, I love you, I know you'll miss me.

She didn't blink. "What does this mean?" she asked after a minute.

"What?" I asked.

Standing by the table, she began rolling her fingers over the watermelon's humped green back. Slowly, gently, the little finger, the ring finger, the middle finger, the pointing finger, the thumb.

"You mean the watermelon, Grandma?"

"Yeah. What does it mean?"

"What do you mean?"

She looked at me straight on, hard. She said nothing.

I sat down opposite her. "You mean, like a flower or something . . . Something like Old Uncle," I said, letting out whatever came to mind.

"Yeah," she said.

"How's that?" I asked.

"You tell me."

Then nothing again. Slowly, gently, her fingers tap tap tap tap tap over the watermelon's humped green back. On and on. Almost an hour and she was still standing, all the while looking at me. I started talking then just to break the silence. I figured she had a puzzle, a story she wanted me to piece together. "A watermelon is like a flower because it's sweet . . . It's like Old Uncle because you can't really tell what's on the inside, what else it is. It's like . . ."

"It's not *like* anything," she said, firm.

She looked at me, stopped her tapping for a moment, then started up again. If for no other reason than that I'd given a wrong answer, I felt certain now that she wanted an answer from me, that somehow I'd fallen into a trap she'd set. She was waiting. It occurred to me that she would stand there until midnight or until she fell straight over the top of the table, whichever come first. "Grandma," I said. "Don't you think you should sit down?"

"Oh, yeah," she answered and sat down, like she'd all of a sudden realized she'd been standing for nearly an hour now.

And then what do you think? She sat and sat, looking at me and tapping the watermelon. If she could stand until midnight, she could sit until noon tomorrow. And she would. She wouldn't budge. When I looked at the clock again, it was five o'clock. It had been two hours! Things was serious. Of course the notion it was all a scheme on her part kept crossing my mind. But it didn't matter. I knowed me and her was at the place of saying good-bye. We just hadn't said it yet.

I waited another hour. Nothing come to me to say. Then I got up— she didn't move—and called and canceled my motel reservation. Turns out the motel done that for me when I didn't show up by six. I didn't go back to the kitchen table and Grandma after that. I went into my empty room and laid on the bed. I fell asleep.

When I woke it was two in the morning. It took me half a minute to get my bearings. I didn't know where I was. In the kitchen I found nothing but that big green watermelon on the table and Grandma's empty chair pulled back. She'd gone to her room and closed the door. But that didn't mean she was getting tired. It didn't mean she had given up. She was looking at me still.

Again the hot day had pushed itself through the walls. The house was an oven. I went out on the back steps and sat down. It wasn't much cooler. The air was thick, sticky. You didn't breathe it, you swallowed it. I tried to think of an answer for Grandma; I could go in and tell her what I'd come up with, make my peace and leave. I could get to San Francisco in plenty of time to look at the first apartment I had called about. But nothing come. I was stuck. Like the hot, sticky air had sealed shut all the passageways inside my brain.

Then the voices. Next door, the neighbors carrying on in Spanish. They was someplace near the front of their house, maybe on the porch, talking away, laughing. It wasn't like they had just started talking. They'd been there for some time. It's after two in the morning, I thought. What are they doing up so late? It's a work night. And then I heard other voices, fainter, yes, but even the sound of a radio, as if the neighbors' chattering Spanish was a thread, a piece of stitch work, connecting me to all of the other voices in the neighborhood. I got up and walked along the side of the house to the front yard. The honeysuckle on the fence smelled thick and sweet, like perfume on a perspiring woman. At the end of the path I looked over the fence and seen them. The Ochoas: folks young and old, parents and kids, relatives, crowded on the porch, packed together on the steps. I glanced up and down the street and seen people everywhere there, too, and lights and open doors. I focused and couldn't believe my eyes. Like the Ochoas, they was all eating watermelon.

I stepped out onto the street and started walking. Folks was out everywhere talking to one another. They leaned against cars, talked over fences, gathered in circles in kitchen chairs on their front lawns. It was like after a power failure or earthquake. Only there was no disaster. They was happy, peaceful, spitting seeds and talking between bites of the watermelon that dripped from their hands and down their faces. Gnawed-clean rinds was in the gutters and in piles below porch steps; and still people was eating. Them that seen me waved and hollered hello. I seen them, who they was, but at the same time didn't. Nothing registered. I walked and walked, gone around the block and up and down all the streets of the neighborhood. Everywhere it was the same. The world felt inside out. The place of my dreams, which I'd just woke from, made more sense still than the here and now before me. I would've floated, kept on in this way, if Auntie Mollie hadn't reined me in. "Johnny," she called. "Johnny," she said again and again, until I stopped, realizing I was in the middle of the street smack in front of her house.

"God damn it, can't you see who I am, fool?" she hollered. But she wasn't mad: She was playful, asking me to wake up and recognize her and sit the hell down on her steps for a visit. I felt dumb, which meant I was back in touch with things.

"Jesus," she said as I made my way to her, "if I didn't know better, I'd say you was drunk."

"I ain't," I said.

". . . Or had too much watermelon," she said, holding up her half-eaten sliver of melon for me to see.

She was on the top step and I sat just below her.

"Look, look around," she said, gesturing with her sliver of melon again, pointing up and down the street. "Son-of-a-bitch place has gone crazy."

Behind her, through the open front door, I seen Alice and the two boys sitting on the couch eating big squares of melon with silver forks. They was watching some late-night horror show on TV and laughing at it. I never seen Alice laugh so easy. And then I thought of something: what I seen in Alice the day before and couldn't put my finger on; or, rather, what I didn't see in her, what had always been there before and now was missing. Worry. Worry about the sadness that followed and lived with her family. Her sister six feet under. Her tired and worn-down mother. Felix. Alice had let it go for the time being. She'd pushed it aside, put other things in its place. A boy named Anthony. Watermelon at three or four in the morning and a stupid TV movie.

I looked at Mollie. She was sober and clear, like Alice said. Her small black eyes was sad—they always would be—but they was wide open with the streetlights and all the world in front of her fixed within them. She bit into the watermelon and smiled, like she'd just kissed a lover, then spit a mouthful of seeds to her side and laughed.

"Them boys done a good thing," she said.

"Who?" I asked.

"Vince Green and Jaime Martinez," she answered. "They started this whole thing." She was holding up her three-quarters-eaten watermelon again. "They got the idea and then everybody started in. Didn't you know?"

"Yeah," I said, seeing a story of what had happened. I laughed to myself.

Then Mollie brought the watermelon she was gesturing with close to her face, just inches from her lips and nose. Balancing it upright in the palms of both hands, she studied it for a moment, taking it in with all of her senses. "You know what this is?" she said, turning her head just a notch to see me. "It's kindness. It's a kindness them kids done." And then she bit full into the melon again.

Funny how a mind works. I seen this: Mollie weaving baskets with Auntie Nellie. My mind flipped what made no sense before and then let me see as plain as the shirt on my back what I could say to Grandma. Lightning struck, and only after I was hit and come to did I know what happened. BINGO. Each letter was covered with a chip.

I couldn't tell myself then how I knowed so thorough that what Auntie Mollie said was true. It didn't present itself in pictures or maps with connecting lines. It settled in my body like peace.

Auntie finished her sliver of melon and set the rind next to three others in a line next to her on the top step. "I'm going to get me another piece," she said, getting up and wiping her hands on a paper towel that was in her lap. "Want one?"

"I had some before," I said and got up, and without thinking headed for the street.

"Don't say good-bye then," Auntie called from the porch.

I was halfway to the sidewalk. I stopped and turned around. "Good-bye," I said, "and thank you."

"For what?"

"Everything," I said and turned back towards the street.

"You are drunk," she yelled. I heard her laughing.

"Uh-uh," I said over my shoulder.

I walked and walked like before. But now people's faces was clear, matched with the names and stories I knowed. I seen how each of them smiled, the upward curl of their mouths, their teeth and wide cheeks. Even a dimple on this one, a mole on the chin of that one. And when they seen me I greeted them. Hello, Mrs. Burke, Mr. Burke. Hello, Mr. Green. Hello, Mrs. Lopez. And Steven and Mrs. Pen and Raymond, hello. Hello, Zelda Toms and Frances Toms. Billyrene, how are you? And each of them called back to me in the same way, as if it was the middle of the day and not the middle of the night and none of us had anything to do but be polite and keep eating watermelon.

Then I begun to notice who was missing, who I wanted to see but didn't, and what houses was dark, where there was no lights or melon rinds piled below front steps. Edward, I didn't see him. Auntie Nellie stood by her front gate visiting with neighbors and her house was lit up and wide open, but no Edward. What could I do? Knock on the door and holler for him to join in? No. Just hope for his sake he was inside eating melon to his heart's content. And Trina, I didn't see her neither. And Tony and Vivi and Pauline lived on the other side of the fairgrounds. But Tony and Pauline had all of their relatives in this neighborhood and maybe one of them brought over a watermelon. I hoped so.

A lot of houses was dark, some folks I knowed and some I didn't. One was the Bills'. And this is what I done: gone back to that truck, which was more than half empty, and found me the biggest melon I could. I stood there and studied them green melons. A streetlight was on overhead and two plank sections of the wooden guard rails was off and lying on the ground, so I could see good. I found the watermelon I wanted, rolled it to the edge of the truck bed, and carried it off.

I set the big melon careful on the worn rubber foot mat just outside the Bills' front door. I thought of ringing their doorbell. Then I decided against it. Just let them come out and find it, I thought.

When I stepped back to the street I seen the first light of day, a soft pink over the fairgrounds. I seen, too, that the neighborhood was quiet, folks shrunk back into their houses, lights off. They'd left the rinds and half-eaten melon on porches, in the curbs and on the sidewalks, the way people leave beer bottles and empty cartons of food in a house after a party. Some folks had gathered the leftovers into piles. Others hadn't, just left pieces of melon wherever they'd been eating and talking. I turned and headed back to Grandma's.

I cut up Deturk, making my way towards Grand. Roosters crowed. An old dog crawled out from under a junked van and stretched. A line of small birds landed on a sagging picket fence. And then I seen the car, bright and shiny against everything else in the growing light. Half a block away and parked in front of Rachel Rickford's apartment house, Julie Brigioni's red BMW convertible. I hadn't thought of Felix. When I passed the car, I noticed it was warm. Ticking sounds come from under the hood, meaning the engine had just been turned off. I looked at the faded green building, not knowing which of the apartments was Rachel's. Somewhere in there, I said to myself.

At Grandma's, things was just as I left them: watermelon on the table and her empty chair. Maybe she'd fallen asleep after all. She knowed I wouldn't leave without talking to her about the watermelon. It was a little past five-thirty. I thought of knocking on her door, but then I didn't. I thought, too, about my nine o'clock appointment in San Francisco, how I should call the apartment manager and tell him that I might be late or that we should reschedule the meeting. But I didn't do that neither. Something else come to mind. My old cigar box of memorabilia. I gone out and dug through my suitcase and boxes, which was still on the back of my truck, until I found it.

Then I didn't go back into the house. I carried the box to the back steps and sat down. I opened it and sorted through spools of thread and old concert stubs under Felix's folded genealogy chart. Then I took the chart and opened it on my lap. The empty line for "father." Was his father Felix too? Then I seen the name I knowed, where our histories come together in a woman called Juana Maria and run back to the first Rosa. Lots of sad stories, the same stories sung over and over through the generations like a song. Rosa and the Mexican general, for instance. But there was other songs too. Not-hitting-back songs. Old Uncle songs. And if you couldn't hear them, if you didn't know the melody or the exact words, you could see them nonetheless—the angels that was singing for you. Simple: a frog with a missing toe, a tree, old ladies' shoes, a watermelon. Kindness, which is nothing more than the sweetness of watermelon and the thought that somebody might like a taste. It was always there, even in the hardest places, the sad deaths and the loud, hate-spewing meetings, only we needed to see it, like on a watermelon night. It had become more and more of a secret, something we hid with the tough times, but nothing else ever held us together.

As I sat waiting for Grandma to stir in the house, I thought of my vision, what I had lost. I could still see certain things, like the way a person's hand could be a pair of buzzard claws, or the way a person's eyes is a pool of clear water. And I could still see when a person is saying one thing and meaning something else. Which I seen plenty of lately. But it was the bigger way that I lost: stuff like Dollface's sickness, when things in this world jump out at you, turn themselves on before your eyes like a TV. Stuff that leads to being a medicine person, the kind that sees the whole story in anything she looks at.

Pete come out from under the porch finally and flapped his white wings, wild in the morning light. Got so you'd think he was going to fly. I'd have to give him a piece of tortilla or something.

Just then he got impatient waiting for me to feed him and made his way into the yard. He stopped for a moment near the fence, just below where the necklace Felix made Grandma hung on a post, and then continued on his way behind the jasmine. I wondered if she'd like the story I had about the watermelon, if it was right. It was just one story, but it was my story, how things meant for me. I knowed at least it would start us talking. Then I seen the sun over the back fence and thought of Del. What the hell, I thought. Surprise him. One more good day.

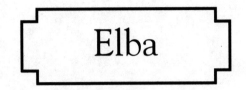

Elba

ONE

We had games. Us poor Indian kids on the Rancheria. Me, Zelda, and Nellie. And competitions. Baseball with the boys and climbing trees and racing back and forth on the dirt road above the creek. We dressed up dolls, castoffs found in the white peoples' garbage or handed to us along with oranges outside the Elks club on Christmas. We jumped rope and played hide-and-seek. In Benedict's barn we played something different, though. It was our favorite, me, Zelda, and Nellie.

First, the arguing over which one got to play Chum, who, in real life, was Nellie's mother:

"I want to be Chum."

"No, I want to be Chum."

"You played her last time."

"But you was her three times last week."

"Play Westin today and be Chum tomorrow."

"And what about me, I gotta be the Indian maid?"

Then, the game:

"Roses. Red roses; I bought them for you."

"Beautiful. Thank you, Westin."

"Let's go for a walk."

"Where?"

"The creek."

"What about the flowers?"

"Give them to the maid."

"Yes, I'll put them in water for you."

Then, one morning, the wagon come, when it was still dark, and it wasn't no pickup wagon to take the men to work. It was the flatbed, pulled by just two horses, and stretched out on the back of it was Chum, the hanging rope still around her neck.

* * *

It was wintertime. Which meant cold and not much food. I lived with Clementine, my mother's cousin, who took me in after Mama died.

All of us lived on what folks called Benedict's Rancheria, the Indian houses, set at the east corner of the big ranch, just beyond the black walnut trees and above the creek. Private land, Benedict owned it. We didn't have a government reservation, which no one seemed to mind, since the tribes that had a government reservation in them days didn't seem to have anything over us. Besides, we was still on our ancestral lands, which, one way or another, we never left. We planted our feet and stayed. The houses, in fact, wasn't but a stone's throw from the time immemorial village. Waterplace it was called, which was why, before some scientist come in and named us Pomo, the other tribes in these parts called us Waterplace—people by the water. That's how it was in the old times: You was where you lived. Now, I guess, our name is Waterplace Pomo. Anyway, at the Rancheria, there wasn't but a dozen houses, and, trust me, not a one worth crowing about. Some was bigger than others, and some had wood floors and some didn't, but every one of them was a shack made from boards and posts that was like everything else from the white people: scraps. I seen families come and go. Shacks burned to the ground and got rebuilt and burned again. But the Rancheria stayed, and I figured, no matter what, it was where I'd live forever. I was ten.

I was a quiet kid. Nothing special. Folks used to say Indians is a quiet, watchful people. If so, then I was a good Indian, typical. Especially with anyone bigger than me, or if they was white. I made myself into a fly on the wall. When grown-ups talked and visited in the house, I kept myself busy, folding clothes or splitting roots for Clementine's basket making. Outside, I kept working, too, picking prunes or pears, whatever; and if I was in a situation where I had to sit still, maybe on the wagon while Clementine chatted with somebody, I set my eyes on a tree, or a clump of blackberry vine, or one of Benedict's cows, if it was nearby. Chum once asked if I was scared. "You lost your mama," she said. "Maybe you're afraid you'll lose me and Clementine." I couldn't say whether she was right or wrong, since, at that age, I couldn't tell you how I was or wasn't in the general way of things. I didn't think about it.

* * *

Chum was the first to find me after Mama died. Well, not the first, actually. It was a man who found me and Mama, a cousin or uncle. It was dark still and he said he wouldn't have seen a thing if it wasn't for my eyes, white and wide, two blinking saucers, that caught his attention and half-scared the wits out of him. "Like a huge owl propped there on the porch," he later said. I was numb, my hands and feet frostbit. Then Chum was there, rubbing me, and I left the porch with her.

What little kid—I was hardly seven at the time—knows how her fate is decided. And if she did know, what difference would it make, for how much choice would she have in the matter anyhow? I don't know who talked, how it was settled which relative would take me. I had no older sisters, so it should've been one of my aunts, my mother's sisters, either Chum or Auntie Maria. When Clementine stood outside Chum's door the morning after Mama's funeral, I figured, if I figured anything, that she was there to borrow something, sugar, a cup of flour. Never did I think she was there to take me home with her, not the old lady who lived in the last shack, the place nearest the hills. Then Chum touched my shoulder, got me to my feet. "*Huu*," she said. "Yes. It's good, it's OK," and I understood. I went to Clementine, took her hand. We started off and I looked back once. Again Chum said, "*Huu*. Yes. It's good, it's OK," and I believed her.

* * *

Chum was right. It was OK. Life with Clementine wasn't bad. Not in terms of having enough to eat or a roof over my head. Though her house sat at the end of the row, separate from the others, it was big. I had my own room. My bed was nothing fancy, an old mattress thrown atop a wood pallet, but in the corner was a chest of drawers with a stand-up mirror, something none of the other kids had. Clementine was one to cut her coat according to her cloth. She portioned carefully her rations of beans and flour. Still, I had three meals a day, more often than not with a piece of dried venison or fish thrown in, fresh meat if she had it. Sometimes, in the mornings, before I got up, she'd come into my room with a plate of fresh-boiled beans and fry bread and set it on the floor. But there was no joy in it, no feeling of warmth or kindness. She never handed me the plate.

She wasn't that old, really; fifty maybe. She just looked old. She was gray and she'd shrunk, the way old people do; her clothes hung on her as if she was about to shed them, as if, when getting up all of a sudden from a chair or turning quick from the stove, she'd finally wrench the heavy sweaters and long dark dresses from her body and step away, free of their weight forever. She'd had thirteen children. All but three died as infants; of the three survivors, one, a daughter, fell to her ugly death under a train, when, drunk, she lost her step dancing with a hobo and tumbled out the back of an open boxcar; and another, her son, drowned in the Russian River with his father when a bridge collapsed under them as they crossed one morning to pick hops. Which meant there was one child left: Ofelia, who married a man in Sacramento and hadn't come back. So Clementine was sad. But it wasn't a sadness she could revel in, enjoy others' sympathy, the way some people do. Indians don't believe things just happen to you; no such thing as an accident, only a reason. With hard luck you either done something wrong to cause it or somebody done something wrong to you. Either way, you're cursed, what we call poisoned. No doubt Ofelia, Clementine's one remaining child, figured if she stuck around death would soon enough find her just as it had the others. I believe now, in thinking back, that Clementine kept me, probably even begged Chum and Auntie Maria to have me, just to prove she could raise a kid and not have it die on her.

* * *

Chum was beautiful, and I don't say that just as a matter of speaking. The word fit her like a glove. Dark, her skin was the color of wet oak bark, her eyes black like a quail's, and when she smiled, she pulled all of the world to her face, for there wasn't nothing brighter or warmer anywhere. Like Mama, and unlike Auntie Maria, Chum was slender. You could see her waist. She wore clean skirts of bright colors—orange, yellow, rose red—tucked just so below her full-cut blouses, most of the time opened at the neck, where a single strand of polished-white clamshell beads gleamed against her dark skin. The girls in town had their movie stars, maybe their mothers or older sisters; we had Chum.

But more than that, she was fun. It wasn't just her smiling face, but everything she done, the funny, funny things that kept you laughing inside long after you seen them. Down at the creek while folks was washing clothes, for instance. When the hens would be gossiping, and by hens I mean Big Sarah and fat Auntie Maria, about who was drinking or chasing around with some man, Chum would catch wind of their words and in no time start hiccuping, swaying back and forth, like she was drunk; or turn to the person closest to her, which was usually me or Nellie, and start raising her one eyebrow in a flirtatious manner, all the while slowly pulling the hem of her dress up over her leg. Of course, her actions was quite exaggerated, which was what was so funny, that and the fact the hens had no idea how she was going on, giving life and gesture to their words; and when they did find out, when they caught sight of Chum's antics, they sure did shut up, pull in their chins and zipper their squawking mouths.

* * *

"Roses. Red roses. They go with your dress."
"Beautiful. Thank you, Westin."
"Let's go for walk."
"Where?"
"The creek."
"What about the flowers?"
"Give them to the maid."
"Yes, I'll put them in water for you."

The game. We didn't play it long. Maybe three months and then Chum died.

Lots was going on around the Rancheria. Not that you could see, but in the roundhouse. With Big Sarah, who was the ceremonial leader, and everybody that was participating in her ceremonies, the singers and dancers. It started after Mama died, Big Sarah preaching about the evils of the white people. Well, I guess it started earlier; after all, Big Sarah had been preaching as long as I could remember. But I noticed it more after Mama died. No doubt because Big Sarah turned up the volume considerable; and, standing in front of the center pole, before lifting her cane signaling the ceremony to begin, she blabbed out the names of the recent dead, Mama's name among them, adding how each of the persons died. Carmelita, drunk, froze. I heard it every night I gone in there.

She talked endless about our ancestors, the first Rosa and the second Rosa. She used the first, the sole survivor of our tribe, the one we all come down from, as a bad example. "She gave up. She died a slave and a whore inside the adobe walls," she'd say, looking in the direction the old adobe once stood. The second Rosa, the daughter, ran away, escaped her Spanish father, reunited with Indian people, and settled this land again. She was a hero. "She fought the white man," Big Sarah said. *Masan* was the word she used, which means white, or white person. But it's a put-down, like the person is no more than the color of their skin.

She'd pound her medicine cane on the hard dirt floor, saying, "We're forgetting the fight." The cane was more of a staff, larger, taller than a regular walking cane. It was beaded white with dark blue stars and crescent moons—that had to do with her dreams and visions. A cluster of cocoon rattles sat atop the crook and, below, up and down the staff's length, hung countless abalone pendants. When she pounded the cane, with all its rattling and clacking, people looked. Thunder wasn't louder.

We started playing our game in the fall, which was the fall before Chum died. I was ten. I remember because we had just started school, fourth grade. The grammar school in town had been forced by the government to open its doors to us Rancheria kids for the first time. No more sitting on the benches outside behind the houses with a volunteer teacher, usually some spinster friend of Mrs. Benedict's. While we had to sit in the back of the classroom—the last row was reserved for Indians—we had a roof over our heads and school every day. In fact, you was expected to show up. But Big Sarah put the kibosh on that. "This is your school," she said one night in the roundhouse after she picked each of us out of the crowd and lined us up in the center of the dance floor, in front of the fire, where our parents and aunts and uncles could watch. She held out her cane, shaking its rattles and pendants. "This is your lesson," she said. Then, with the cane, gesturing to the walls and ceiling, she said, "This is your schoolhouse." Finally letting the cane rest at her side, she looked at each of us, first glancing at our feet, as if she could see something there, a dirty ankle, a torn dress, then raising her glance to our faces, our eyes, making us feel as if we should already be saying, Yes, my ankle is dirty, my dress is torn. She said, "That school in town, all it can teach you is how to be *masan*, traitor. Which of you will become *masan*?"

So we was torn as to what to do. Zelda's sisters, Ida and Sipie, and lots of the other older kids quit school, never went back. Zelda stayed awhile, but, before long, she was out too. Me and Nellie walked back and forth to town every day on tiptoes.

But nights we was at the roundhouse learning how the world was going haywire. Big Sarah talked about the end of the world coming. She pointed to the signs: the floods during the last three winters and the Great Depression, which, at the time, 1932, we was smack in the middle of. There would be a flood, she said, cleaning the earth of white people. The faithful Indians would be planted back here with all the animals and plants the way it was before the white devil come; the unfaithful would drown, their souls left wandering, like the souls of white people, caught between this world and the next.

That time, too, lots of other folks showed up, Indians from the coast and up in Clear Lake. They jammed the roundhouse at night. Sometimes they brung their own preachers and dancers. The preachers, a man or a woman like Big Sarah, had the same idea: White man was the devil. They'd stand in front of the center pole, just the way Big Sarah done, and talk about history things, tell stories. The men preachers was plain, dressed in work clothes, maybe just a string of beads, but the women was colorful, fancy long dresses and scarves, sometimes a headband with pendants of beads and shells hanging from it, covering the women's faces like masks.

There was a woman who wore a black dress that, like the other women's dresses, hung to the ground, but over the top was a half skirt made of straw-colored tule grass, the kind of skirt women wore in the old days; and from a headband tight around her forehead hung a veil of obsidian pendants, covering not just her face, but below, past her neck. She told about the afterlife, describing a land of flowers that was more colorful than anything seen on earth. But if you mingled unnecessary with a white person—in particular, if you married a white person—you wouldn't get to see this place; neither would your children if they was mixed blood. "I know some of you is mixed with the white blood," she said, no doubt referring to those of us in the congregation from Benedict's ranch, where, in fact, all of us was mixed to some degree or other with Spanish and Mexican blood, "but now is the time to stop—or pay the price." Then she said, "Look at the signs: The white world is coming to an end."

True, I guess, the world appeared to be in an uproar. Farmers, folks we'd worked for, some who'd treated us like dogs, had lost their land, and was themselves living like dogs, begging now for work on street corners. Vineyards and orchards was left unkempt or, in some cases, ripped out and plowed under. Old Man Benedict kept solid, didn't forfeit no land or stock, but land was about all he give us. Some work in the fall picking pears and pruning, maybe some fence mending. Mostly, we depended on other farmers, going from place to place following the crops. Now what we picked was the windfall, old fruit on the ground under haggard vines and drooped trees: grapes, apples, and pears that we tried to sell on Fourth Street but mostly packed home and cooked up for jam. The big barns, where we once lined up to get a day's pay, no matter how small the amount, stood empty, hollow shells.

But it wasn't just the white world that was in trouble. Even before the hard, hard times hit, Indian folks was faster than ever giving up the old ways, the fight, as Big Sarah would say. People enjoyed the convenience of the white world; no doubt, white folks, with such things as indoor plumbing and electricity, had figured out how to do things comfortable. Roundhouses was closing down; Indians flocked to the Catholic and Pentecostal churches, where, in exchange for listening to a sermon, they got day-old bread and small jobs cleaning and carpentering. Which Big Sarah, for certain, worried might happen with us. "*Masan*," she called them tribes that give up.

She pulled the reins tight. She wanted all of us in the roundhouse each and every night. Before long, you couldn't speak English in the roundhouse; if there was no one to translate a visiting preacher's Indian language, the preacher had to whisper the words to Big Sarah in English and she'd give them back to us in our Indian language. And after the visitor finished talking, Big Sarah would lift her cane, point to a star or crescent moon with her other hand and say, "Yes, that speech matches my vision right here— it's prophecy laid out to us."

I liked to watch the dances. That is, if I could last through the long speeches without falling asleep. We didn't go into the roundhouse until nine or ten o'clock at night, when it was full darkness outside, and by the time Big Sarah, or whoever, got done preaching, it might be midnight. I'd fall asleep, pass out right where I was sitting. Remember, I was sneaking off to school in the morning. But lots of kids fell asleep, even older people—we never got out of there until two or three, in the middle of the night. The dances was beautiful, though—the men in their flicker feather headbands and eagle feather skirts, the women in brightly colored long dresses and waving fancy scarves as they danced, forming a loose circle around the men. It was a show of colors, a swirl of fluttering feathers, dancing and dancing, singing and dancing.

Late that fall, after the acorns dropped and the cottonwoods lost their yellow leaves, Big Sarah told us about *Moki*. He was going to come one night, unannounced, sometime soon, and bring back the old-time harvest ceremony, where each plant and animal, the water and air, would be named and offered a special prayer. The ceremony would turn our luck around. Each of us was responsible; anyone who drank whiskey or gambled or fooled unnecessary with a white person could ruin things. We had to be prayerful, pure of heart and mind. "We forgot Creation, which is why Creation forgot us," Big Sarah said. "It's why we're hungry. We must bring it back, so I called on this man."

She said he come from far off, over in Sacramento Valley someplace. She said he'd be covered in a cloak of feathers and that you wouldn't be able to tell who he was, man or woman. But nothing she described prepared you for the actual sight of him. That night, when I looked to where the others was looking, when Big Sarah's cane moved as if it was a curtain rod with which she was pulling back a curtain in the dark behind her, what I seen was something darker than the dark, raven black, an enormous cloak of feathers shaped like a Christmas tree, pointed at the top and fuller below, not the size of a man, but bigger, at least eight feet tall. And then it moved, and Big Sarah lowered her cane, but I was hardly looking at her, for the *Moki* was coming in my direction.

It floated, a tree of raven feathers, and stopped so close I could see the frayed ends of some of the feathers. I could smell it, musty and old, dank, like the inside of a deserted house in winter. And while I couldn't tell where its head and eyes sat, I felt it looking at me. I was afraid, and yet I had no reason to fear, at least that's what I kept telling myself. I done nothing wrong: My dress was clean and reached below my ankles; the sleeves of my blouse, also clean, hung far past my wrists, in fact, almost over my hands, and the collar was buttoned tight at the neck the way Big Sarah showed us girls; I was barefoot, which was the rule too; and I hadn't uttered a word of English—I hadn't said anything! And I'd been on time, finding a place between Zelda and Nellie, the three of us seated in a row before Chum.

Then it turned, all of its height and feathers shifting, as if by a machine, and it left the way it come, floating. It made its way clear around the room, stopping every so often, checking out this group or that group of folks standing close together and silent against the walls. One woman, Bertha Bill, started crying and, after a couple minutes, when the Moki still hadn't moved beyond her, she reached into her dress pocket and offered him a dollar bill, which he took. I seen the white-gloved hand shoot through the feathers. A man offered a necklace, without the Moki even stopping, and the Moki took it.

Afterwards, after its full round, the Moki settled next to Big Sarah. Then my worst fears was confirmed.

"He's testing," Big Sarah pronounced, pounding her cane of rattles and shells on the floor. "He's looking into each of you. He's looking everywhere. If something's not right, he can't perform this ceremony. The bad must be cast out."

It wasn't as if I, or anybody else, for that matter, hadn't thought that that was what the Moki was doing—looking for something wrong. It was just now that Big Sarah had said it, and what she said in particular—"He's looking into each of you"—that I thought of more than my dress and blouse, or whether I had said anything in English. What I seen in front of me, all at once, was a girl holding a stack of schoolbooks in her arms and looking back at me. It was as if a full-length mirror had dropped from the rafters and landed upright three feet before my eyes. What I seen was what the Moki would see; nothing I could do would smash that reflection.

And the Moki come right back to me, stood for the longest time. Nothing, no sound; nothing but the dank smell of them feathers and them eyes, wherever they was below the feathers, looking into me. It had a long ember in its hand now, no doubt that it had picked up from the pit fire on the floor; a crooked piece of manzanita, its tip a burning arrowhead, and just as he lifted his hand to pierce me with it, just as I flinched, I caught sight of it sailing over my head, and as I turned, I seen the crooked stick still in the *Moki*'s white-gloved hand, then the glowing tip rammed into Chum's bare throat, all but nailing her to the wall.

* * *

I don't know if Chum cried out. I don't know if she just plain stood there and sobbed, even as folks panicked and made a stampede for the tunnel. Which is what happened. After the *Moki* pulled back from Chum, he gone to the fire and started throwing hot coals around the room, everywhere, so as to burn the place down, all the while screaming, not just one bird-like whistle as before, but a hundred different birds, all of them as if they was in a narrow canyon with their mad screeching and squawking bouncing off the steep walls. Smoke filled the room. Sparks flyed everywhere through the haze. "Keep singing, keep singing," Big Sarah commanded the singers. But she never called the people back, never said, Stay here, don't leave. Probably wouldn't have done no good anyways. Folks figured they was going to burn. I followed, was near the back of the crowd, and still pretty near got trampled.

"We ain't ready, we're not deserving," Big Sarah told us the next night. "Too much sickness here," she said.

But to hear her tell it, all wasn't lost. We still had a chance, she said, if we mended our evil ways. The *Moki* would come back, she didn't know when, maybe not until the spring, and he would test us again. Not until everybody in the roundhouse was clean would he perform his ceremony. Which meant that not until everybody was clean would Creation pay attention to us. Which meant that not until everybody was clean would we have enough food and luck.

The roundhouse wasn't full that next night. Not everybody from our Rancheria come, and no visitors rolled up in their old cars. No horses—no wagons—was hitched outside. "We got to go back," Clementine told me at dinner, which was the second and last thing she said about that *Moki* night; the first thing being, "Take off them smoky clothes and go to bed," when we got home. But I had no problem going back to the roundhouse, even if by chance the *Moki* returned. I felt confident. I didn't go to school that morning. As it turned out, I never gone again.

Chum come back to the roundhouse too. Acted as if nothing happened. Listened to Big Sarah's speech, and when that was done, when it was time to dance, she joined the circle of ladies in their ribbon dresses and danced, waving her scarf and turning this way and that like every one of them. Only, the top of her full blouse was buttoned; you couldn't see her neck.

Nobody said a word. Folks didn't talk about what happened to Chum. But with Indians, in a situation like that, not talking is a sign of lots of talking—the whispering kind of talking between two old hens picking blackberries or washing clothes by themselves. Indians is supposed to be quiet, after all. Then again, how could folks talk in the open, even if they wanted to, what with Chum walking about, doing her business—washing, chopping wood, picking up commodities—right along with the rest of them? Maybe because she didn't hide, or set around crying, folks begun to forget. Maybe they thought she was sorry, even forgiven for her sins. I don't know. Seemed life gone on as usual.

* * *

Then, one day, while visiting Zelda, I heard her mother, fat Auntie Maria, say to Bertha Bill, "Can't believe she shows that scar." She seen me looking and knowed I heard. I was sitting on the floor, by the stove, sewing doll clothes from dress scraps with Zelda, and Auntie Maria she glared down at me like I was the devil itself. Foolish, no-good, nosy girl, her slit eyes said. Of course, according to fat Auntie Maria, I could've sneezed and it'd be wrong. She didn't care for me. Which is why I seldom played at Zelda's house, and why, if I couldn't stay with Chum, thank God I gone with Clementine and not Auntie Maria after Mama died. Why didn't she care for me? Because her no-good, never-around husband, Sam Toms, was my father. Mama used to drink in town with him. Yes, Zelda was my cousin, for all intents and purposes, my mother's sister's kid, but she was also my sister. It was something we didn't talk about. Nellie didn't have a father neither; well, not one that folks talked about or one that was on the Rancheria. But Chum talked about him, a man from the Sebastopol Lagoon people. Apparently, Nellie met him a couple times.

And another thing: Chum had an older daughter, a girl she'd had when she was young, who was living somewheres up north with her father's people—which was something else folks didn't talk about, but Chum mentioned it.

"No shame," Bertha answered, setting her cup of coffee down.

"Right, no shame," Auntie Maria said, but I couldn't tell if she was talking about Chum or about me.

* * *

True, a few weeks after she got burned, after the wound healed, Chum unbuttoned her blouse. She let the whole world see her scar, if they cared to look. And you couldn't help but look. It wasn't what you'd expect, a jagged tear in the skin, an ugly scab; it was round and its dark color was shiny, making it look, at the bottom of her neck, like a fine shell hanging from her white necklace. She said nothing, made no announcements, not even to us kids. She just come out with the top button of her blouse undone one day and gone about her business.

One time, though, she said, out of the blue, "I hope he does come back. I'll pluck him like a chicken."

We was grazing the stock just east of the Rancheria, at the edge of Benedict's property, close enough so we could still see the shacks. We all knowed what Chum was talking about, me, Zelda, and Nellie. The *Moki* was something in the front of our minds.

Zelda stuck her fingers into her mouth and looked back at the buildings, the roundhouse, in particular, which was in plain view.

"Oh, Mama, don't think about it," Nellie said.

But Chum didn't seem to hear her. She followed Zelda's gaze to the roundhouse, and just as her eyes landed there, she said, "Yeah, I'm going to pluck him and kick the son of a bitch where the sun don't shine. Come on, bird man," she said staring at the building.

* * *

"I want to be Chum."

"No, I want to be Chum."

We all wanted to play Chum. We fought like hell. Would've screamed ourselves blue in the face if our screaming wouldn't have brought Old Man Benedict, or one of his sons, Charles or Westin, into the barn. Well, put it this way, me and Zelda fought; Nellie was the adult amongst us, the peacemaker. She was tall, slender, dark and pretty like her mother. But her looks ain't what you noticed; it was her calm, sacrificing ways, which is how she got to play Chum as much as any of us without a word of argument. "I'll be the maid," she'd say, and me and Zelda would stop our bickering, realizing full well Nellie hadn't played her mother for a week. Then we'd feel so bad, we'd volunteer to play the maid, and not argue over the second-best part, which was Westin.

If Nellie was the wise parent, then Zelda was the family brat. She was a nut; some folks said a quart low, what with the way she'd blurt things out without thinking and do everything ass backwards. You'd play hide-and-seek and she'd jump out from wherever she was hiding and say, "Here I am." And the way she dressed: She'd put on clothes that was so dirty you could stand them up; oak moths spun a home for their caterpillars in her sweater each spring. But, worst of all, she was a brat, like I said, the worst. Even at ten, when she didn't get her way, or when she thought you got more beans, a bigger piece of bread, a piece of candy, she'd stomp her feet and fret and then threaten to tell her mother everything she knowed you done wrong since before you was born, like Auntie Maria was God or something. Me and her gone round and round, but Nellie could handle her.

Chum got flowers. The maid rubbed Chum's shoulders. Westin kissed her. They walked to the creek, which wasn't really to the creek, but a special place in the barn, behind the hay bales, where the maid couldn't see.

The barn was enormous, two or three stories high, with thick beams overhead. Mostly, it was used to store hay, which was why, even with the barn full, we had so many makeshift corners, nooks and crannies, to play in. On one side of the barn was a couple horse stalls, which wasn't used, and the wired-in chicken pen filled with red laying hens. That was the only thing we had to worry about: the maid, or sometimes Mrs. Benedict herself, coming in to gather eggs and feed the hens. Other than that time, which was usually a little after lunch, we was free to play. So we'd sneak in after three—I had a pocket watch Clementine gave me—and then, when we got daring, again at night, after we ate and before we had to go to bed or to the roundhouse.

Whoever was Westin had to find long pieces of straw and arrange them just so. The maid had to get out the brush and comb and ribbon bows—we kept these things in a big cigar box hidden under the straw. Chum sat on a bail of hay and waited.

"I'm here now," said the maid.

"OK, hurry, because Westin will be coming."

The maid fixed Chum's hair and put ribbons in. "Do you need me to rub your shoulders?"

"No, no, thank you . . . Oh, Westin!"

"Roses. Red roses; I bought them for you."

"Beautiful. Thank you, Westin."

"Let's go for a walk."

"Where?"

"The creek."

"What about the flowers?"

"Give them to the maid."

"Yes, I'll put them in water for you."

"Here, let's go out this way." And he led her, not outside, of course, but to a place behind the high-stacked hay, in the far corner of the barn, where they sat and talked about the water. "Look at the sky sitting on the creek, how pretty," she'd say—and then he kissed her, on the lips, and kissed her again and they touched each other and kissed again.

"That's bad," Zelda said once when she couldn't play Chum.

"When people love each other, that's what they do," Nellie said, echoing the stuff Chum talked about now and then on our walks into the hills.

"No they don't," said Zelda.

"You don't know," I told her.

"You don't either, dummy," she snapped at me.

"I'm going to get the ribbons. Sit down, Zelda," Nellie said.

* * *

We never stopped playing. Even after Chum got burned. Actually, we played more, on account of how none of us was in school anymore. After me and Nellie quit, an official come out to the Rancheria and asked what the matter was. Big Sarah and fat Auntie Maria anticipated as much, no doubt. The bespectacled white man in a suit and tie pulled into the Rancheria only to find TB-ridden Old Jose, Auntie Maria's uncle, propped in front of her house gasping for air, his bare shoulders poked out of his overalls like busted-off branches. The man got back into his car and tore off so fast it'd make your head spin; probably told the townfolk, who was scared of TB and knowed Indians to be carriers, that he saved their kids by keeping us out of school.

In any event, we was never bothered about school again. No one from town asked for us, and no teacher come back to give us lessons. Nellie and me had a couple books, math and, I think, history, that we kept, since our schooling stopped so abrupt, with us. But, in time, them schoolbooks disappeared. So we had time. Lots of time because all the crops had been picked and there was no work anywheres, except for a few of the men who was pruning trees still. Lots of time and we was at that age between useless and useful, too young or too old, and the best thing to do was to stay out of the adults' hair, not to remind them that you was a mouth to feed and maybe old enough to do more than you done to earn your keep, your share of the pot of beans that come off the stove each day. So we took off when we could, wandered away more and more from the Rancheria.

* * *

What is a kid but nosy? We always wandered and watched: watched from behind bushes and buildings and watched what the big world of people hides from itself. Which is how we first learned about Chum. Creeping here and there, walking past the neighbors ranch, halfway to Santa Rosa, darting into the brush when a pair of headlights come up the road, we seen a lot of stuff. The neighbor man, Mr. Archer, for instance, how he kicked his wife and tied her, standing up, to a fence and then poured buckets of cold water on her. We heard the screaming and crossed the road there to see what it was. Walking along the road, tiptoeing quiet, that's how we first heard the hobo men camped on the creek just below Benedict's barn. That's what Zelda said they was, hobos; but to me they was just white men who worked with us in the fields and orchards. Anyhow, we seen their fire through the trees and sneaked close. Dumb Zelda couldn't hold her plugged-up nose and sneezed, causing the men's loud, laughing voices to stop so you could've heard a pin drop. They seen us. Nellie started to run, but me and Zelda was froze, and then Nellie come back, so the three of us found ourselves eye to eye with this pack of glassy-eyed men.

"Who are you?" one of the men, swinging a bottle of moonshine, asked.

"Indians," Zelda said.

"We live on the Rancheria," Nellie said, "on Benedict's Rancheria."

Another man, next to the man holding the bottle, rattled a can of crackers at us, as if we was dogs. Of course, Zelda gone forward. But, before long, me and Nellie stepped out of the brush and into the firelight too. But there was another reason, besides following Zelda with the thought of getting something to eat, that we'd done so—Westin Benedict was there. We knowed him. You could smell the whiskey on the men's breath, even standing ten feet away, and Westin was drinking right along with them, the men who worked for his father. His shirt might've been white, his pants pressed, but he'd been sitting on rocks, on dirty bedrolls, with the rest of them. The man holding the bottle, the one who first called out to us, passed the bottle to Westin, who took a quick swig, then said, "You kids go home."

"No, no," said the man with the cracker tin. He smiled, his grizzled beard looking shiny in the firelight, and he shook the can, beckoning us further forward. "Watch this," he said to the dozen or so men spread out on either side of him. "Watch this . . . I seen it up north."

He crouched a bit, bending his knees, as if to meet us at eye level, and said, "Do you want a cracker?"

Saltines, I loved them. But I was scared. So was Nellie. Zelda gone up to him, put her hand out.

The man pulled a cracker out of the tin and held it in front of her. When she reached for it, he pulled it back, and, with that, tossed it into the fire and said, "Good toasted. Now go get it."

"Don't do that," Westin told the man.

But it was too late: Zelda was on her knees, scrambling after the cracker. And not just one cracker, but again and again, and not until I was doing the same thing, reaching into the fire, did I realize, yes, you got yourself burnt. "C'mon, you others," he said, and me and Nellie was on the ground in no time. We seen Zelda getting herself cracker after cracker with what looked like no pain. It wasn't the fire that burned you; you could run your hand through it fast. The trick was not to bump your fingers or knuckles on hot coals while you was grabbing and that was hard not to do. Then, worse, you got so excited, you didn't even think about it no more. You just got burned.

"Quit it," Westin said, but he held no sway over them.

And I suppose their laughing wasn't loud enough and our hands wasn't burned enough, for I can't tell you how many times we gone back; gone back and burned our hands, then made it back in time to sit with our bellies full and listen to Big Sarah.

Lots of times Westin was there. Lots of times he wasn't. But the night we seen Chum coming across the back field, out of the orchard, towards the barn, he was there. We'd left, hardly been at the camp an hour, and was coming out of the brush onto the road. This was the early part of the fall, even before school started; way before we stopped going and it was light still, enough light so that the shingled barn roof and the dry hills in the distance was bathed in a blood-orange color, and we seen her, a dark figure, alone, come out of the empty pear trees and walk in a straight line through the white-face cows and their calves in our direction. You knowed by the long dress, the shawl and scarf over her head, that she was an Indian, even though she was thin and so upright, bold, as she walked, without looking this way or that, towards the hovering sun-topped building. And that's what struck me so odd: an Indian alone and on this side of the ranch, so close to the boss man's house.

Who else, walking so tall, effortless, past the cows and their calves? Who else, so slim and not looking back, behind her? Nellie knowed, and she knowed what come next, even before we seen it—seen Westin come up from the camp and push through the brush hardly five feet from our crouched bodies and cross the road, walking not straight up like Chum, but hunched, looking back and forth, up and down the road, before sliding his nearly too big body between the fence slats and disappearing through the chicken coop door. And then we couldn't see Chum neither.

"Talking," Nellie said, as if answering the question me or Zelda might've asked in the next second.

"About what?" Zelda had to pry.

Nellie gave Zelda one of them looks an adult gives a kid after she's stuck her dirty fingers in the food. Even then, before we started playing the game in the barn, in fact, for as long as us kids was walking and talking, Nellie was the parent. Something in the way she done things—like just now, looking at Zelda—told you she was twenty years older than you and fifty times as wise.

"Well," Zelda whined, as if complaining for being punished.

Nellie backed out from under the branches and started up the road. "Tomorrow, I'll tell you," she called over her shoulder to me and dumb Zelda still huddled there.

* * *

The next day we started the game. About four o'clock. An hour or two before dinner. We'd worked all day in the pears, me alongside Clementine, Zelda with her older sisters, Sipie and Ida, and Auntie Maria, and Nellie with Chum. The orchard on the far west end of the ranch. We was finished. Our folks sent us on ahead while they counted up filled crates with Old Man Benedict. Walking past the barn, the subject of what we seen the night before returned to our brains, if it hadn't been there all day long already. We just never said anything, even at break time when we ate together, me, Zelda, and Nellie. And Nellie, knowing one of us would sure as can be say something now, didn't wait for us to start. She herded us into the barn, through the chicken coop door, holding her arms spread as if it was the chickens she was shooing along ahead of her and not two people as big, or bigger, than her.

"Hurry now," she said and latched the door behind us.

After pushing us past bales of hay stacked to the rafters, she sat me and Zelda on a lone bale and said, "Sit there." And she planned it all out, give us the lines, everything.

She gone over the lines again and again, starting with the roses, red roses; after about the umpteenth time, Zelda caught on. By that time, I knowed whatever questions I had about the night before would be answered if I just kept my eyes open.

When we got up to leave, after we had the play down good, Nellie done one more thing: She give Queen Zelda a chunk of horehound candy, our favorite. She wasn't no fool. She knowed Zelda was a squeaker, that if she didn't get her way and wasn't always happy, she'd go home and tell Auntie Maria, which wouldn't only get us in trouble, but Chum, too, what with the way Auntie Maria and the hens talked. Zelda would come back and play this game till the cows come home—and she did, even without the candy.

After Zelda left, skipping up to her place, me and Nellie kept on, past the shacks where the folks was back washing up in big tin tubs and stoking their woodstoves to cook dinner. Nellie reached into her sweater pocket and pulled out another candy.

"Here," she said, dropping it into my hand.

I wanted to know where she got the chunk of horehound, and if she had a chunk for herself. But like before, as if she guessed what I was thinking, she said, "Tomorrow, bring a comb—or brush. I'll bring ribbons and a cigar box to put everything in," and with that, she turned to go into her place and left me walking to Clementine's wondering how I was going to get a comb—or a brush.

* * *

We always played our game in the barn. Nellie made up all the lines. She was the one to set things, to add lines or take them away, not us. And each of us had to have all the parts memorized, especially the part of Chum, exactly the way it was set, the exact same lines with whatever Nellie added or took out, from the last time we played it. That was part of the fun. It kept you on your toes. Poor Zelda flubbed up near about every day. It kept her quiet—she took it as a form of punishment—when it wasn't her turn to be Chum.

We kept prowling, too, watching from behind bushes and the backsides of buildings the goings-on in our part of the valley. More so as the fall settled in and trudged the world toward winter. Nights was longer, dark now after dinner and before the roundhouse activities, our time to creep about. Mr. Archer kept beating his wife, the same way, pulling her into the yard and tying her to a fence, her arms spread like Jesus' on the cross.

Another thing like that: Bertha Bill and Sam Toms, my father, and Zelda's father. The droopy-assed fool, with a gut like a half-filled sack of hops caught between them red suspenders and pouring over the top of his grease-stained pants, come back to Auntie Maria. No doubt because he was hungry and had nowhere else to go. Mornings he was hauling and piling wood for Auntie Maria; nighttime, after dinner, he was down in the creek, near the wash rocks, full at it with Bertha (Auntie Maria's best friend) pushed up against a tree. We seen it, caught sight of Bertha slipping down to the water, and, five minutes later, Sam Toms, and we followed them. Nobody said nothing. But two days later, Zelda shows up with one side of her face black and blue, saying her father hit her for having a big mouth, and then we never seen Sam Toms anymore and Bertha Bill wasn't going to Auntie Maria's in the mornings for coffee.

After that—seeing Sam Toms with Bertha—I thought of my mother. I didn't think, Well, that's what it looked like when him and Mama created me. No, at ten, you don't quite think that way or that far. I wasn't even thinking of him *with* Mama, what they talked about, where they hid from Auntie Maria. He knowed Mama, that's all, so that after I seen him with Bertha and after we got done listening to Big Sarah that night, when I was home under the covers in the dark, Mama come to mind, and, I guess, because I was tired, I seen her dress, the back of it, how her feet kicked up the hem as she walked endless on the road back and forth to town, and how it lifted when she squatted in the bushes or behind the saloon and I seen her bare feet, same as when there was a pair of boots between them and she said, "Turn your head." I was following her again.

Of course, nothing kept us from going back for more crackers. We burned our hands and filled our bellies, night after night. But now there was something else: the chance to study Westin Benedict. Sometimes he was there, sometimes he wasn't, like I said. Though none of us said as much, I know that, as we made our way through the brush toward the hobo camp each night, we hoped to see him. Helped with our game; you know, picturing things: the blond hair that flopped over his forehead, red mustache and sideburns, the way he jutted out his full bottom lip—that was always shiny wet—before he spoke, how he narrowed his blue eyes, even the way he held the whiskey bottle, his fingers spread wide, not grabbing or clutching. As tall as he was—all of the Benedicts was tall people—and considering the fact his father was the boss, it seemed strange to me that he was so quiet. He never pushed his way on the other men, and the one time he tried, when he told them not to throw crackers into the fire for us, it got him nowheres, for they didn't listen. His voice—smooth, steady enough—trailed other voices, never busted the silence itself.

One night, without warning, his father showed up. Come right through the brush, and when us girls turned from the fire, where we was huddled on hands and knees, Old Man Benedict was already loud as a bull.

"What the hell you doing?" he said, but you couldn't tell who it was in particular that he was addressing, for his bugged eyes in that flushed-angry face was still taking in what was in front of him, what he could see in the camp firelight.

"What the hell you doing?" he roared again.

His eyes slowed, settling on Westin, then on a short man holding the bottle of moonshine, then on the grizzle-faced man with the open cracker tin and us. You could see the picture settle straight and clear in his mind, as all of us was froze, giving him all the time in the world. He had blue eyes, like Westin; in fact, he looked like Westin, only gray, heavier around the middle, but the same long sideburns and mustache. As his eyes tracked the crowd one last time and then settled on Westin, they appeared more calm and matched his voice. "What can I do with you, Westin?" Rage had turned to disappointment.

"I'm just down here," Westin said, stating the obvious.

Benedict took hold of his chin, as if thinking, and said, "I can see that," then, dropping his hand, said, "Don't you think you'd be better off in your room on your hands and knees praying to God?"

"Probably so," Westin answered. He sounded just this side of cocky, but, after a minute, he turned and disappeared.

Then Old Man Benedict looked at the man with the cracker tin and the others. "Reckon no more crops to pick, nothing more to do here," he said, "so you boys best be on your way, off my property."

He never did say nothing to us. Just turned and left. We sat back on our haunches for the longest time, watching, like the men, the empty brush. Then a quiet fear rose up like smoke from the fire and seemed to spread itself everywhere. We was scared with Old Man Benedict there, but more so now that he was gone. The dead silence gave no answers. The man with the open tin throwed no more crackers. We left.

Gone out the same way, up along the road, and while I don't think anyone had a notion to make our customary stop and watch for Chum and Westin on their way to the barn, we stopped anyway, crouched just for a second, because we seen Old Man Benedict standing by the chicken coop door, smoking a cigarette and holding a shotgun over his shoulder. I'm sure each of us thought he was watching for Westin, since that was the way Westin snuck into the barn at night. It's what I thought, anyways. But, no doubt, it was Chum he expected there.

*　*　*

"You'll love me no matter what?"

"I will, Chum."

"No matter what?"

"No matter what."

"Promise?"

"Promise. Roses. Red roses for you every day . . . Here, I brought them for you."

"Beautiful. Thank you, Westin."

Nellie never changed the lines after that. We done the play over and over the same way. She kept us to it strict. Got so even Zelda remembered everything and made no mistakes. But then Zelda got bored—a couple times she didn't show up—and Nellie ended up having to bribe her with horehound candy again. Got so Zelda demanded the candy even before we started for the barn.

*　*　*

Chum showed nothing. No sign that she met Old Man Benedict with a gun instead of Westin that night. No sign that her affair was over. Maybe she seen him late, late in the night after the roundhouse, after Nellie and her had come home and Nellie was asleep. She might've snuck out in the cold and dark once or twice that way. I don't know. But, for certain, she never gone back to the barn at her regular time.

The *Moki* had come and gone; winter pushed fall back complete and come in cruel, with fog and constant drizzle, blinding cold and wet, so us kids had to abandon our play in the barn half the time and our night prowling altogether. After dinner we stayed in, found things to do before the roundhouse business started. I always went to Chum's after dinner.

I had fun. Usually, when I got there, they was working, Nellie on her coiled baskets and Chum on her baby cradles. What we're known for, us people, is our baskets. I never weaved one worth half a cent. But Chum showed me how to make a cradle, bending and tying willow rods, and how to use bullrush and redbud for color if I wanted a design, and I got good at it. She tucked bullrush around the rods and made a star, for design, which was always plumb center, where the baby's head would rest. I made a moon, a round circle, no points. It was easier.

Another thing I learned good then: cards. You name it: twenty-one, blackjack, gin rummy, I could play it. Chum knowed every game. "Watch! Think!" she'd say, and she'd slap them cards down quicker then you could bat an eye. School couldn't put my mind to that kind of a test. By the time we got up to hear Big Sarah, my head was worn out, an empty tin can. But I got good.

"OK, now a game of poker," Chum would say and off us three girls would be to test our luck and what we learned. And to up the ante, Chum offered the winner a chunk of horehound candy, which she pulled out of her dress pocket and shook in her hands like a dice while she sat watching us go at it. I won three times out of four, no kidding, with Nellie winning the other time. Zelda, who couldn't tie a knot to start a basket or hold more than two willow rods in her hands for a cradle, wasn't any good at cards neither. She couldn't concentrate, focus. We didn't let her, or help her, win, at least I didn't.

"You're good, Elba," Chum said one night after I cleaned up at a five-card-stud game in no time flat. "You got a good eye."

The way she said that made me happy, and I handed my piece of candy over to Zelda, not because I wanted to, but because I wanted Chum to see what a good person I was.

So Chum never showed nothing. Maybe we was so busy, all by her doing, that we just never seen. But talk was everywhere on the Rancheria. Talk and hushed glances, so you'd have to have been deaf and blind not to have caught at least some of it, for, like water in a tea kettle that simmered quiet at first, it whistled loud and clear in no time at all. The women got quiet when Chum joined the line waiting on the edge of the road for the government commodities truck. Old men turned their backs. Young ones snickered.

It was Clementine who let me know for certain. I knowed she didn't care for me hanging around Chum. I was surprised Auntie Maria didn't out and out stop Zelda from hanging around her, given how Auntie Maria was so direct and outspoken. Clementine was different: quiet, never one to block the door or even pronounce the word "no." She avoided confrontation, never raised her voice. Perhaps she thought she'd wake her bad luck, as if it was a dog sleeping under her porch step that would get up and beg outside her door again. She'd say things roundabout, indirect, which is how she told me about Chum. She said, as I was getting up from dinner one night, "You know, having white babies, that's no good. It's a sin."

I looked at her while setting my plate on the counter. Then, as if to explain why she said what she said seemingly out of the blue, when neither of us, as usual, had spoken a word to each other throughout the meal, she added, "In Lake County, they killed the white babies. I used to hear about that when I was a girl. Yes, they used to do that. They did that," she repeated.

Of course she meant for me not to take off for Nellie and Chum's. I didn't obey her. I acted like I didn't understand what she meant.

But what she said set me straight. Not about what folks was saying about Chum, for I never heard clear, even while I knowed they was talking, but about what I seen: Chum sick. She tossed her guts. Got up more than once from the table and hardly made it to the slop bucket in time. And when I'd go for Nellie, in the mornings now, I'd find Chum pallid at the table or still in bed with the covers pulled up clear to her eyes. Chum had morning sickness. Chum was going to have a baby.

Still, she stood straight in the roundhouse. Stood there, and even danced. With the bad rains, few visitors showed up nights for the ceremonies, and lots of our people didn't come neither, just stayed home huddled next to their stoves. If Chum got sick in the roundhouse, she never showed it, kept her stomach calm in there. Stood and listened to Big Sarah, and danced. No doubt, she thought about the *Moki*, how he would punish her if he showed up now. In the fall, when the *Moki* was here, Chum had been only fooling with the white man.

Christmas was empty, and with the weather spiteful awful, we was shut in, staring at the flimsy four walls, at home with the cold and emptiness of our lives. Empty cupboards. Empty wood bins. Hunger. Cold. A serving of beans and fish broth, maybe a fried potato and watery acorn mush, one meal, not much to begin with, divided into three, a hardly there breakfast, lunch, and dinner. "Put on another sweater," Clementine said when she seen me pushed up, close as I could get to the stove in the still dark morning hours. Already I was so layered with underwear and sweaters you'd think, by looking at me, that I was the daughter of fat Auntie Maria. The tips of Clementine's fingers was blue-purple under the dull lamplight on the table as she held strands of sedge, twining a basket. Pitiful she was, stiff and arthritic, her fingers moving like the legs of a spider caught in mud, but continuing all the same, which, as I understand it, was her way of saying, Don't complain.

We didn't go to the Elks' club neither. Didn't go into town at all. Which I missed. Not only the oranges and other things the Elks give us when we lined up outside their hall Christmas morning, but also the lights and decorations on Fourth Street. That was one day, no matter how cold or wet, I didn't mind following Mama into town; and after she passed on, it was Chum who took me. Big Sarah always said it was no good for us to go there and stand around like beggars. Gives the white people the wrong idea, she said. "Ha!" Mama said. "What does she think we are?" And Chum said the same thing.

So I was surprised that year when Chum didn't take us into town for handouts on Christmas Day. If I figured a reason for this, that is, if I thought beyond my own disappointment, it would be that Chum wasn't up for the trip to town and back, that she was sick. But that morning, Christmas, she seemed to be feeling fine when she got out the cards. "Twenty-one," she commanded, and as soon as we played out one hand, she shuffled the deck again and switched gears on us and announced another game. "Blackjack," she said. "Rummy." "Gin rummy." "Poker." It was like what they call in school a final exam. She was testing all she had taught during the last two months, a major competition, even though, a few days before, she'd run out of horehound chunks, and was now giving the winner only a walnut. Finally, around noon, when I'd collected a dozen walnuts at least, Zelda pushed herself back from the table and said, "We got plenty of walnuts at home."

"Then go home," I blurted out, run out of patience.

"Elba!" Chum scolded, making me feel all of a sudden sorry for what I said. But then she turned to Zelda and said, "It's not for the candy or nuts. It's for fun. Something to do."

Zelda would have no part of what Chum said. She got up and left. Never did come back.

Funny though, a few days later, when the sun managed to peek through the clouds for a few hours, Zelda did sneak over to the barn with me and Nellie. And something else: I brought along the baby cradle I finished making. I guess I was proud and wanted to show it off, maybe use it in our game.

Zelda, who played Chum that day, said, "What'd you bring that for?"

I didn't know what to say. Then, looking from the cradle, on top of the hay, and back to me, she said, "I'm not gonna hold that. It's bad."

"Shh," Nellie cautioned. As always, she was the one to make peace. But, as it turned out, she had more on her mind than our spat. She'd heard the Benedicts' maid coming into the barn late, well past her normal time, to collect the eggs. We seen the top of her powder-blue bonnet above the wire-mesh door and heard her humming. I grabbed my baby cradle and tore with the others to the other side of the barn, to the wide door by the horse stalls that faced the back field and pear orchards.

"Hide it," Nellie told me, and when I followed her gaze beyond the barn, I seen Big Sarah and Auntie Maria and some others heading back to the Rancheria, their backs weighted down by the sacks of trimmings they'd picked up under the pear trees.

We couldn't wait. We had to get out of the barn. I thought of hiding on top of the stacked bales, looked up to the thick beams below the roof. But how would we get up there? And how to get down? In a hurry, I hid the baby cradle in a corner, under loose straw. "C'mon," Nellie said, and we crept out, along the side of the barn, and passed the corrals to the field and orchard, where, like ghosts, we followed the women home.

* * *

At the roundhouse that night, Big Sarah planted guilt the way you plant spring bulbs—deep. To this day, I'm certain neither Big Sarah nor any of them others seen us three girls trailing them back to the Rancheria. But Big Sarah talked—and made you believe—like she knowed our every step. "Kids today is doing bad things, going here and there, where they're not supposed to," she said. "Just today, this afternoon, some girls did like that, done wrong. I seen it in my vision." And it wasn't just us she appeared to have the goods on but lots of other folks as well. "I *see* these things," she said. "In my vision, I *see* them, and so does the *Moki*, even as far away as he is. There is too much sickness here, wrongdoing, for him to come back now. So we have bad luck, hunger. Look at the weather! And things will get worse. There will be death, sacrifice amongst us. But we brought it on ourselves. We did it to ourselves. Our world here is like a baby cradle turned upside down."

My thoughts raced back to the cradle I'd left in Benedict's barn. In my haste, had I not made sure to place it under the straw right side up? Something I knowed, every Indian knowed: Always keep a baby cradle face up, or else you will bring bad luck to the child who sleeps in it, sickness. Poisoners, evildoers, kill children that way—getting a hold of their cradles and turning them upside down. Had I forgotten? Wasn't I paying attention?

I started another cradle. We played cards. Chum showed nothing. If Big Sarah's mention of a baby cradle spooked her, she never let us see. But when I think of all of this, when I think of the time and Chum's reasons, one memory comes to mind, presents itself like a painting, as clear as can be, filling all the space before my eyes so I see nothing else, even if I try. This is it: me and Nellie sitting at the table and Chum on the other side of the woodstove, reaching into a gunnysack on the floor for more walnuts. She left the cupboard open, I'm sure by accident, and I see for the first time where she's kept the horehound candy. I see the empty glass jar, a big jar, the kind you used to see next to the cash register in the general store with a price per chunk—one cent—embossed in the glass. And next to this jar, between it and a stack of plates, I see a bouquet of roses, the dried crimson blooms and pale stems still tied by a bright red ribbon.

I don't know exactly when, anymore, Clementine said to me, "Don't be like your mother," the harshest thing she ever said but, as usual, out of nowhere, so I found myself in bed dreaming about Mama again. It was late, cold, and I was trying to get Mama up, off the porch, tugging, pulling, both of my hands joined under her arm socket; we'd gotten this far, after how many times falling on the road from town, and I was still tugging and pulling when I woke because of the commotion outside. I got up and joined Clementine, the lantern in her hand, below the porch. I was only half awake, so when I looked where all the other lanterns had gathered, my first thought was that stretched out on the back of the flatbed was Mama.

"Hanged herself," I heard a man say.

"Froze," I hollered.

* * *

The maid, coming to work early, glanced over at the barn. The huge front doors, big enough for hay trucks, was open, unusual at that time of morning, which caused her to look. The Indian was there in plain view, even in the dark, hanging from a beam in the center of the barn, for all of morning to find. That's about all we know; that and the fact it was Old Man

Benedict's Mexican foreman who cut her down, and who, with Old Man Benedict, drove her on the flatbed back to the Rancheria.

"Leave it," Old Man Benedict said, meaning the wagon, as he got down and signaled, with a cupped hand, for the foreman to do the same.

He walked home in the dark, left everything, flatbed wagon, horses, Chum.

"Wants us to carry her proper to the cemetery," Clementine suggested. "On a wagon, like they do with white people."

But who really knowed what Old Man Benedict was thinking?

I thought of other things, details. For instance, Chum fixing the rope, and then, with the rope in her hand, climbing the steep-stacked hay bales for the roof beam. But those thoughts was later, much later, for as it turned out, things happened so fast, nobody had time to think of anything. No sooner had they buried Chum just as she was, no coffin, under a mound of sloppy mud and a marker that read JUANA ISIDRA, a name she never used, than Old Man Benedict was back that very afternoon, this time in the family's black Packard, and not with the Mexican foreman but with the sheriff.

"See," Clementine said, "he's come for the wagon, now that we're done with it."

Even I knowed she was plumb wrong.

Old Man Benedict and the sheriff didn't knock on anybody's door. Was there a chief? Maybe Big Sarah. But they didn't go to her place neither.

When enough folks gathered in front of the car, Old Man Benedict said, "You all got to go, leave."

His voice was shaking. He tried to say something else but couldn't. Again, who knowed what he was thinking? Mad about what happened between Chum and his son? Sorry now, grief-stricken, guilty? Whatever, he didn't want to see us and have to think about it, I guess.

"You're doing the right thing. You made the right decision," the sheriff said so as to fortify him, then turned to us and, in a different voice, said, "Him and the Mrs. want you off the ranch in twenty-four hours."

"Sorry," Old Man Benedict said. Then the sheriff led him, as if he was feeble, back to the car, and as they pulled away, he rolled down his window and yelled, "Keep the wagon."

* * *

It come in handy. Not just for the stacks and stacks of boxes and the endless sacks of this and that folks piled on it, but for the center pole that was buried underneath everything and hanging out the back end, like nothing more than a big log. Big Sarah gone crazy that night, saying the greatest punishment in Creation was upon us: We lost our home. She ordered the men to dismantle the roundhouse. "Save the center pole," she said. "It must go with us. Burn everything else."

Which they did. Or tried to. It rained so hard nothing, no matter how big, would burn for long. By morning, slats and roof shingles, heaped in piles over the drenched earth, looked like large pieces of burnt toast.

The rain had stopped, but in its place come the fog, so thick that as we made our way along the dirt road above the creek for the last time, we couldn't see two feet in front of us. It was a pitiful procession, led by the one car that had been on the Rancheria, Bertha Bill's brother's Ford, which he drove loaded down with old people and infants. The rest of us, about sixty altogether, packing in our arms and on our backs whatever we could, trailed the two wagons on foot, Old Man Benedict's wagon pulled now by our two horses, and a smaller wagon pulled by Uncle McKinley's one-eyed mule. On the smaller wagon a spotted pig stood on the edge of the bed, watching the ground roll away underneath her.

Passing the barn, which in the fog looked like a dark hillside from the road, I thought of Nellie. Shortly after Chum was buried, hardly half an hour after our eviction notice, Nellie, bags packed, left in a car with her father's relatives, people from the Sebastopol Lagoon tribe. How was she? Would I see her again? But I didn't think for long. And I didn't think of my baby cradle left under the straw, or of our game, or even of Chum. I was scared, like everybody else, and wondering where I was going.

On the main road, closer to town, the fog hunkered down worse. Uncle McKinley's mule got skittish, slipped a couple times. Uncle McKinley was a short man, his arms reaching straight up to steady the animal. "Shit," he said, "even if the poor bastard had two good eyes, he couldn't see a thing." Then he hollered up to Bertha's brother in the car, "Turn on your headlights. It'll help." But, of course, it didn't.

TWO

We didn't go far. Come up Fourth Street, the center of town, and just stopped, the whole mess of us pitiful Indians. Fourth and Mendocino, the old courthouse on one side of us, the grocery with its fat, hanging salamis in the window on the other. We bunched up, drew together in a ball, not so much to get out of the way of cars and folks on the street but out of sheer panic, dread at the sight of the roads that led in every direction out of town.

But we was in the way. Couldn't plunk ourselves and expect to stay there forever. A couple hours after we arrived, somewheres around noon, folks must've figured we wasn't just another caravan of Indians passing through town on our way to another work camp and stopped for groceries. Too many of us, for one thing, and not a single Indian woman marching through the store's swinging doors for a sack of flour, a tin of lard, not one scruffy, tooth-missing Indian kid flopping a coin on the counter for horehound or licorice. The sheriff, the same guy with the silver star on his chest who stood with Old Man Benedict and throwed us off the Rancheria, come up and asked what the problem was. He talked to Bertha's brother, maybe because Bertha's brother—Elmer, his name was—was the one who negotiated with the ranchers wherever we worked, or maybe because he was the only one of us who had a car. In any event, this is what Elmer worked out for us: a spot to camp at the fairgrounds, south of town, just for the night.

* * *

Why didn't we go to another Rancheria? Indians. They're funny about strangers. Even the ones who danced with us, listened to Big Sarah and shared the spotlight with her in the roundhouse, they'd act funny with a bunch of us dropping in on them. Not just because we might impose on their meager rations, pile up in their already overcrowded two-cent shacks, but because of all the old-time stuff, Indian stuff—fear of poisoners in our tribe, folks who could hoodoo them with special songs and potions. And the same with us, we feared the other tribes too. Old-timers warned: Watch yourself outside your home. Which, I guess, in the old days, before people got so scared and hungry, made you respect one another, made you remember each tribe had something powerful. And that makes me think of something else the old ones said, which explained the predicament we was in: Love your home, know every person, every plant and animal, for without your home, you're like a person without a family, less than a dead fly on the road. At least with that—a dead fly—you could poison somebody.

Some folks did take off. Those that had relatives, a father, a sister, or a brother, on other Rancherias gone begging, took their chances. Even before what was left of us proceeded down Mendocino Avenue under the watchful glare of the sheriff and a couple of his badge-studded cronies, people took off, peeled away from the ball of us like the skin off an orange, piece by piece, a woman with her children, a pack of young men, a girl not much older than me, going on alone.

The place at the fairgrounds wasn't what you might think, a campground with hitches, water, and fire pits. It was the flat, barren piece of ground where they pitched the carnival each summer. That night, huddled in front of the two wagons, fanning worthless fires made from rotted oak wood, we knowed as much about what was going to happen to us as we knowed what was in front of us on that fogged-in road to town that morning—about two feet's worth.

We was packed up, ready to leave at dawn. In the foggy pink light folks gathered around Elmer's car and continued talking in hushed voices about where we might go. "The lagoon," Auntie Maria suggested, "past the Indians there, north." She was talking about a stretch of land where we pitched tents while picking hops on a nearby ranch. Uncle McKinley pointed out that with all the rain, the place was no doubt underwater now. "The lagoon rises up there," he said.

"East, then, Glen Ellen, up in the hills," Bertha said. "Ain't nothing up there."

"What," Uncle McKinley snapped, "and live on grass and tree bark? Ain't nothing up there is right!"

"McKinley," Elmer said, defending his sister, "she was just trying to help; Jesus."

"People got to make sense," Uncle McKinley shot back.

"McKinley," his wife, even shorter than him, said and tugged on his coat sleeve.

"*Mensi!* Keep still!" said Big Sarah all of a sudden.

We looked, followed her eyes. The sheriff was coming up the street, pulling into the empty lot, the squish and splat of mud puddles under tires, as his black-and-white car drew closer and closer. Old Man Benedict followed close behind in his Packard.

"Better have some answer now," Auntie Maria said.

I pulled closer to Clementine and peeked from behind the sliver of space between Auntie Maria and Big Sarah.

"You told him you didn't know where to go," Old Man Benedict said, planting himself in front of the sheriff and a host of the sheriff's badged cronies. He was talking to Elmer, who stood up front, and he was waiting for an answer.

Elmer looked at the sheriff and then answered, "Yes." Elmer was polite.

Old Man Benedict pulled his heavy navy overcoat tighter to his body, hunching his shoulders and tugging from inside his deep pockets. He wore a felt derby. It rested low on his head, but not low enough to hide what was written all over his face, what each of us seen as he looked back at us—shame. It was clear now. Whatever he felt the afternoon he asked us to leave his ranch, we couldn't tell. Now he was an open book. Bagging, red-rimmed eyes, he was a man who hadn't slept. If he'd felt different things before, say anger and disgrace, then they'd come together in him, mixed, like the ingredients of a bitter medicine, to produce this one effect. We seen it in him, and kept watching, no matter how gruff he made his voice sound.

"What do you mean, 'Yes'?" he asked Elmer, after Elmer didn't say any more.

"I told the sheriff, 'Yes,' we didn't have nowheres to go," answered Elmer polite, waiting for the next question.

"Why not go over to Anderson's place, he's got Indians there. Or up to Wicker's or Burke's . . ."

Old Man Benedict rattled off a few more names, and when he run out, Elmer said, "Only the Indians that live there can stay there. It's the agreement with the boss. A whole other tribe can't move on the place."

Benedict nodded. He understood as much from the way things had been on his own Rancheria.

"They got reservations around here," the sheriff said to Old Man Benedict from behind. "That's government land set aside for Indians," he added.

"What about the reservations?" Old Man Benedict repeated for us.

Elmer was calm, no doubt playing his one card—our one card—and having faith in its power just now. He looked into Old Man Benedict's tired, tell-all eyes. "That's set aside for one particular tribe," he said.

"What's the difference?" Old Man Benedict asked.

"We're separate tribes," Elmer explained. "Some tribes got deals with the Bureau of Indian Affairs in Sacramento. Some don't."

Elmer let Benedict chew on that awhile. If the truth of the matter that morning was somewheres between us getting cheated and being happy where we was, you know what Elmer led Old Man Benedict to believe. And he laid it on thick, saying after a minute, "You was good to us."

No wonder Elmer was the one who negotiated with the ranchers where we picked crops.

"Can't you ask for a reservation now?" Old Man Benedict asked.

"Done doling them out the way they used to," Elmer answered.

Clearly, Old Man Benedict was backpedaling. But regardless of how we seen Elmer getting the best of him, we seen, too, for the first time, what them Indians with a reservation had that was more than we did: a ninety-nine-year lease, trust it or not, on a piece of land to live on. It might've been ten, twenty, maybe even a hundred acres in some god-forsaken place in the middle of nowheres, at the edge of some infertile field or atop a mountain with no water, but no one white man could get upset over something and throw you off with a snap of his fingers. That was part of the agreement with the government. Elmer's words with Old Man Benedict fanned the coals of a fire we thought had burned out: hope. Would Benedict change his mind? He had to.

But no such luck.

"I got to think this over," he said, as much to himself as to us.

"This" meaning what he was going to do with us, which, as we seen then, didn't include the possibility of us going back with him. He talked with the sheriff a minute or two and then turned and said, "I'll make a trip to Sacramento."

Which is what, three days later, he done. In the meantime, the sheriff give us a reprieve, let us stay camped there until Benedict and the bureau decided what to do. The town's womenfolk come with everything but their kitchen sinks: casseroles, salads, Jell-O, chicken soup. Pots and pans of this and that, lined up steaming hot on the small wagon bed twice a day, once at noon, then again after it got dark. They even supplied the plates and silverware, and took everything dirty and washed it themselves. The world might have been in the midst of the Great Depression but we was high on the hog in the land of plenty. Even blankets, so we'd be warm at night, and clothes for us children, jackets and sweaters right off the backs of their own kids, clothes with no holes or patches, like nothing anybody ever give us before.

Of course Big Sarah didn't look kindly on any of it. Done her best to sprinkle a few drops of guilt onto every spoonful of tasteful food you lifted to your mouth. "Don't trust the *masans*," she'd say at night after the white women packed up everything and left. "They're making fools of us." More than once she mentioned the big posters we'd seen on lampposts and in storefront windows during our few jaunts uptown from the camp. She couldn't read, but someone told her what the posters said: "Please Help the Homeless Indians."

What Benedict explained to the townfolk about why he forced us off his property I don't know. What gossip, or how much gossip, if any, spread about Westin and Chum I don't know neither. Certainly, Benedict played a big part in stirring up the white ladies' charity, though his wife wasn't ever amongst the women carrying hot dishes from their cars or handing clothes out of wooden crates propped atop the wagon beds.

We wondered what he would come up with in Sacramento. It was the topic of conversation every night, the same conversation. "I'm still thinking it'll be that chunk of land north of Benedict's place, just below Wicker's ranch," Auntie Maria said. "That's government land, ain't it?" Uncle McKinley pointed out that the government was putting a road through there, a highway. "No place for a Rancheria," he told her.

So on that foggy pink morning some days later when the sheriff rolled in with Old Man Benedict behind him we was anxious, hoping for a miracle, if not a good, old-fashioned change of heart on the part of Old Man Benedict himself. And we looked to Elmer to do the bidding for us, guarantee our good fortune. But Elmer wouldn't get a chance to say two cents' worth.

"Sebastopol," Old Man Benedict said, walking up to us from his car, "out Bodega Highway, there's a place." You'd think he had struck oil. He was waving his hands, excited, like a kid, expecting us all at once to join in his enthusiasm. He pointed west. "That way," he said.

A look of surprise come over him, no doubt on account of the fifty or so somber faces that caught none of his enthusiasm. He dug into his coat pockets, his coat flying open now, exposing his sport coat and tie, and he pulled out some folded papers that he held up, above his head, for us to see.

"They're signed," he said, "approved by the Bureau of Indian Affairs. You've got a right to go there."

Still no jumping up and down. Old Man Benedict looked at Elmer, who certainly must've been looking for words. But what could he say, thanks but no thanks? We didn't have no choice. Elmer didn't have a chip to wager with.

"It's a reservation, Indian land, only a few Indians living there," Old Man Benedict offered. "We'll get you materials to build yourselves some places—houses."

He looked at the sheriff. Then the sheriff looked at us. "You can go there today," he said. What he was saying was, Get out of town today. Then, as if to make himself look decent in front of Old Man Benedict, he said, "The ladies are sure going to miss you. You been well-behaved and perfectly mannered out here."

The ladies did come to say good-bye. With lunch and a last crate of used clothes. We was packed, the horses and mule hitched up, ready to go. The sheriff and Old Man Benedict, still scratching his head over our sorry faces, was long gone.

They was nice, the ladies, more smiles and goodness over how good they was to us than ever before. After lunch, when they started handing out the clothes, Clementine signaled with a nod of her chin for me to get in line and get myself something. I was at the back of the line, so by the time I got up to the wagon, the wooden crate was as good as empty. Which is why I seen what I did. The crate, usually atop the wagon bed, was on the ground, and while a round-faced white woman with a broad hat on her head held up a beige sweater, saying, "Here, sweetie," I found myself staring into the bottom of the crate where they'd piled the signs, pulled from lampposts and storefront windows, that read: "Please Help the Homeless Indians."

"No," I said, and turned away.

"Didn't fit, full of holes in the back," I told Clementine, who, even if she thought I was lying, wouldn't argue with me.

Of course them ladies probably thought they discovered us. But I wasn't thinking anything like that just then. It was something simpler—the word "Help." All our belongings packed up, going God-knows-where, and them ladies feeding us for the last time, I knowed the word was a lie. Pulling onto the street, with all of the ladies smiling as they was waving good-bye, I heard Big Sarah's words ring in my ears: "Don't trust the *mas-ans*. They're making fools of us."

* * *

We traveled west, along a narrow road, what is today Highway 12. Orchards: black, twisted branches, naked, a thousand snakes writhing towards the great sky, away from the wet upturned black earth below. Wet everywhere and the cold drizzle. Just this side of Sebastopol was the lagoon. The water had rose up, covering the bridge so that you couldn't see nothing but the line of wooden bridge posts on either side of the road over the lagoon. We stopped.

South and west, across the water, streams of smoke swirled upwards against the gray sky, smoke from some settlement, no doubt. Was it the Indians, the lagoon people, where Nellie had gone with her father's relatives? Was she there somewhere, eating dried fish or meat with a bowl of acorn mush in a uncle or auntie's shack? Was she weaving at the table? Could she look across the water and see us? See me?

No doubt, Big Sarah seen the smoke and thought of Indians too. "Koko," she said. "Paci. Poison. We ain't in our territory."

A car come up behind us and honked.

"Jesus Christ," Auntie Maria said.

"I'm scared of the water," Zelda said.

"Shut up!" her big sister Ida said.

"Shh," her other sister, Sipie, said.

"What're we gonna do?" Uncle McKinley asked.

It wasn't easy. The wagons switched places, Uncle McKinley's wagon up front, between the car and the flatbed now. "So the mule will have support," Uncle McKinley said. "Something in front of him and behind." Then, slowly, they gone across the bridge. We collected together and watched. The car that had come up behind us followed close and kept honking, which didn't help to calm anyone's nerves.

"Damn masan," Auntie Maria hissed.

Once the caravan was across, Elmer come back with his car and started packing us ten at a time across the bridge.

Sebastopol was nothing but one street then, and we crossed it and kept west into the hills. I looked back, seen the streams of smoke behind me now, rising from behind a line of knolls close to the lagoon. Koko, taboo, Big Sarah had said. Paci. Poison. As we climbed higher, the cold mud underfoot, I looked back, expecting to see the place where the smoke rose up, maybe a row of Rancheria houses, but then we turned a corner and the entire valley with its sheet of water disappeared.

* * *

We'd been to the place before. Where we camped once when we picked apples there. An open spot, a few acres, in the middle of an apple orchard. A couple of small houses. A well. Out Bodega Highway, Old Man Benedict had said. The older folks knowed sure enough where we was going. I just never put two and two together, had no idea of where I was until we turned up the path from the road.

Two houses, but they wasn't empty. Only a few Indians living there was the other thing Old Man Benedict had said. In one house was an old man from the coast someplace, Bodega, I think. He had two un-married daughters, ages about twenty, plain, their faces turned down like top-heavy sunflowers, no doubt on account of how the man, dark-skinned and greasy, was no nicer to them than to us. If it wasn't for the fact that the Bureau of Indian Affairs man had paid him a visit ahead of us, he for certain would have unloaded in our direction the shotgun that was forever across his lap or over his shoulder. He spoke a language completely differ-ent from ours and hardly ever said a word in English. In the other house, whose roof was patched together with tin scraps and redwood bark, was a man even more foreign than the other, from a tribe way up north, close to the Oregon border, where the women wear baskets on their heads, Yurok or Wiyot, one of them tribes. How we knowed as much, I'm not sure, since the man, silver haired and wiry, disappeared even before we had our first box off the wagons, left his door wide open with his fire burning and the lantern aglow on the table, which we could see from the path. Nick-named him "the rat" because of the way he scurried off. Still, we talked about him as if he had never left, as if he'd just gone to town for the day, or was sitting alongside Reginald, the greasy-faced man forever looking out his window at us.

He watched everything, could tell you the exact number of boxes each family had. He seen the half dozen or so trucks loaded with lumber spin their fat bald tires in the mud as they made their way up the dirt path to where we had unloaded the wagons. He must've wondered where the lumber come from; probably figured it was the government give it to us since they was the only ones who had anything to spare during them times. But of course it was Old Man Benedict who sent the lumber, paid for it and told the truck drivers the exact spot to drop it off. The drivers told us as much; Old Man Benedict wanted us to know. No doubt that way he could picture our faces turned up in smiles and sleep at night.

The menfolk haggled amongst themselves over who got what pieces of lumber. Women took sides with their husbands, pushing kids and relatives forward who would be living under their roofs. Clementine stood off to the side and said nothing. No matter, though, for Big Sarah, husbandless, stepped forward in a show of strength and pronounced, "The best pieces and all them shingles is for the roundhouse. Ain't nothing going to happen here before that." She nodded towards the center pole, the only thing left now on old man Benedict's wagon. Big as it was, sixteen feet long, a couple feet wide, it looked frail.

Nobody bucked her. Folks left their belongings, yes, even the women and kids, and started hauling lumber, over their shoulders, under their arms, to the spot Big Sarah had picked out. It was at the far end of the clearing, furthest from the main road, and a safe enough distance from the two houses. Also, it was the flattest place, the best spot to build something. But the earth wouldn't hold firm. It sucked, caved in upon itself, so that the men, working fast and furious with picks and shovels, found themselves bailing mud and water out of a shallow hole that wouldn't grow any deeper. Under Big Sarah's watchful eye, they persevered, however; and when at last they erected the pole with ropes and pushed it to the hole, it sunk in a splash of mud that covered the faces and clothes of everyone nearby.

"Keep on!" Big Sarah ordered.

Which they did, wet and cold, into the night. The women built fires, small and not warm, and hung lanterns alongside wherever their man was working. The drizzle let up some by morning, but not significant. The men kept working. Us kids and the women watched. Amazing, the roundhouse was done by noon. The center pole inside and holding up the new roof, new walls. A new tunnel and front door too. The sun peeked out, a good sign, Big Sarah said, but the new lumber paled against the wet earth that surrounded the place in a ring of glistening puddles and footsteps that had filled in with water. It made you think the roundhouse was floating and not planted.

Big Sarah gone in first, alone. She prayed. Then all of us. A small fire burned in the pit. She spoke about the greasy-faced man, said to watch him in case he was *Paci*, and she spoke loud, as if he was listening and she was challenging him to understand what she was saying. She said we'd be safe in the roundhouse. Then she said we was good, we'd done the right thing building it. She appointed Elmer chief.

"We must start right from here," she said, plopping her cane in mud. "Got to be better than ever if we is to survive this exile. Got to survive so that we can go back one day like the second Rosa. This is prophecy, this is history," she said.

When she was done talking, which wasn't too long, thank God, we left. Folks needed to change their muddy clothes. All of us was tired and hungry, not having ate or slept since we arrived the day before.

Auntie Maria and Bertha and Uncle McKinley's wife built a larger fire in
the center of the clearing, a ways from the roundhouse. Folks got out their
pots and pans, throwed in whatever they could spare, a piece of dried fish,
beans. Some ladies done nothing but drop in a couple fistfuls of flour so as
to give the boiling water a milky color, like it was a soup. We huddled
next to the wagons and ate that.

The next day the men settled their differences over who got what
pieces of lumber. Just like before: a row of shacks, only this time the wood
was new—and Clementine's place was small. It was at the end of the row,
closest to "the rat's" ramshackle dump now, but it was only one room. No
doubt, she had a husband who built her a place before; now she had to
stand and wait until someone saw her standing and waiting, until one of
the other women, her needs covered, her house half done with plenty of
lumber to finish, turned and seen Clementine standing there. So we got
the leftovers pasted together into a wobbly one room. At least, when the
men come back from a trip to Benedict's where they retrieved the woodstoves from the empty shacks, they remembered to bring Clementine hers,
which was as big and as good as any.

* * *

Myself, I didn't see the valley again for a couple months. Darkness
and wet, that's what I knowed. And hunger. Wasn't nothing beyond them
barren apple trees that surrounded the place, no other houses to spy on,
no barns to play in. Once me and Zelda walked as far as we could and
found ourselves against a stand of redwood trees that was so tall and dark
I half-believed her when she said, "Bears in there," and I turned around
and come back, never gone there again. Spent most of the time inside
that one-room shack, staring at the four walls with Clementine. "Going to
find firewood," I told her one morning when the sun had made a rare appearance. My idea was to follow the road to Sebastopol. I thought I could
hide there, situate myself behind a building, or maybe the blackberry
hedge I remembered just west of the one street, and wait for Nellie's people to pass through. I'd see her atop a wagon, or maybe getting out of the
car, a Ford like Elmer's, that she'd left the Rancheria in. When her folks
gone into the general store—was there a general store in Sebastopol?—I'd
rush out and embrace her. We'd be so excited that by the time her folks
come out loaded down with groceries, they'd find us still together. And
when they asked who I was, Nellie would tell them "my favorite cousin,"
and they'd take me with them even though I was a stranger and no blood
kin to them, and I'd learn to speak their language and Clementine and
Auntie Maria wouldn't come for me for fear I would poison them.

But I got as far as the third bend in the winding road, before I could even see the valley, when a car come barreling around the corner, bathing me in a shower of mud. Which wasn't what stopped me on my trek. It was what happened after the driver stopped, no doubt thinking he hit me, and backed up to see if I was all right. A white man, black mustache with the tips waxed and turned up, said, "Oh, an Indian, eh?" which scared me enough with the way he said it. But then he begun smiling, turned himself so he was sitting with both feet on the ground, like he was going to get out of the car. Then he gestured with one hand for me to come forward, and with that, I just turned and bolted up the bank and run through the orchards for home. I don't know. Maybe he meant no harm. In the valley, at Benedict's, we knowed everybody who'd come and go on the road.

So I stayed put. At night we gone into the roundhouse. No excitement, no show of visitors from other places anymore, just us, a handful of folks now in a big place that made us seem even fewer than we was. After that first day, right after the place was built and we gone in for the first time, we didn't go back for a couple weeks. Big Sarah burned fires in there day and night to dry up things. The earth firmed up OK and the benches along the walls where we sat in scattered clumps and watched the dancers was dry, but there remained a dampness that never left.

Big Sarah kept on as you might expect: The white man was the devil, with the added stuff about our exile from the valley and how, like the second Rosa, we would return one day. "It is our duty, each one of us, to work towards that goal," she said. "Help the old ones to see Waterplace once again before they pass on. Help the children go back so that they can grow and have their children there."

I wasn't scared anymore about going in there. What did I have to be afraid of? What did I have to hide? No games, no sneaking here and there, no school. I done like everybody else: nothing. And like everybody else, if I felt anything while sitting in the roundhouse listening to Big Sarah go on about our duties to the tribe, it was hunger.

Old Man Benedict struck some deal: The bureau give him a place for us to stay as long as they didn't have to feed us. Which was legal because it plain wasn't our reservation. It was Reginald's tribe's. And where was the rest of them? Didn't come on account of how he was so mean, with that shotgun of his and all. Which folks learned the next summer while working with other Indians, including some of Reginald's people, in the crops. Said he was so mean his own mother gone to another reservation to live. Why he let "the rat," who was from a different tribe altogether, live on the place nobody knowed.

So the situation was this: The government car dropped in with one sack of flour, powdered eggs, and two sacks of pinto beans—for Reginald and his two daughters. Elmer pleaded with the government agent, pointed out that the government gave us commodities while we lived on Benedict's ranch, that we was the same Indians then as we was now. To which the agent, closing his trunk, said, "Yeah, I know. Problem was, there's too many Indians in the valley. Our drivers didn't know which was government Indians and which wasn't. But we're sorting that out now, checking our lists to see what's a reservation and what isn't."

"You had enough for all of us before."

"Maybe so. But things are tight nowadays," and with that he was in his car and rolling back down the hill. And Reginald was hauling his supplies into his house with a wheelbarrow, his two girls following with their heads down.

Got so we ate grass. At first, Elmer and Uncle McKinley gone into Santa Rosa, picking up an odd job here and there but mostly raiding the garbage bins behind the restaurants. The hobos usually beat them to it. Then they gone to the sheriff for help. He said they wasn't part of the town anymore. "And don't go bothering Benedict," he told them. "He done enough for you already." So it was grass. Miner's lettuce, which come up with the rains, that was our salad. And oat grass shoots, which folks throwed in to flavor broth made from a handful of flour. Birds was a luxury, no matter how big or small—robins, finches, quail. A rabbit was a feast. But who was going to hand one over to me and Clementine?

Even the horses and Uncle McKinley's mule looked pathetic, like us, bones and staring eyes. Fat Auntie Maria shrunk, her shoulders and chest, so that what was left of her was collected in a big belly, like a potato sack hanging in front of her. We ate the cows, ate the chickens, everything but the spotted pig. "It's pregnant," Clementine, who never said anything else, protested. "We'll have more pigs," she explained. "They can eat roots, don't need to feed them."

Which got the pig a reprieve, but only temporary. Sometime later, a couple weeks or so, when she was swelled, her belly two rows of milk-full tits, Uncle McKinley said, "Hell with it, we're starving."

Clementine said nothing.

Uncle McKinley had the sow straddled between his legs—she was tame, a pet—and he was bending over with a long butcher knife, ready to pierce the underside of her neck, when the government agent, unexpected, come rolling up the hill.

He got out and opened his trunk.

"It ain't legal, but I got some leftovers," he said, nodding for the men to come get the full sacks of flour and beans.

Reginald come up and said to the agent, "It ain't a month yet, you ain't due for near a week."

"I'll be back," the agent said. "You got enough to tide you over?"

Proud, Reginald answered, "Sure I do."

That night the pig had her babies. Eight, and all of them alive, Zelda reported, standing outside my door.

* * *

Clementine didn't talk much, ever. She was quiet, never one to argue, which I pointed out before. Why she spoke up for that pig I have no idea. Maybe she couldn't think of the pig losing all its babies—even if it was dead itself—on account of how she lost so many of her children, twelve of the thirteen she'd had. Maybe she just seen the plain sense of waiting, so that instead of eating one pig now, we'd have half a dozen, maybe more, to eat in the future. I don't know. I never asked her. In fact, the brief conversation we had that night, after the agent come and the pig had her babies, was about as much as me and Clementine ever talked to one another after we moved to that new place. From then on she talked even less, nothing but a nod, a yes or a no. She was dying and it was up to me to keep her secret.

After the agent returned a second and third time with sacks in his trunk, "leftovers," he called them, and Elmer and Uncle McKinley got a job skinning horses at the slaughterhouse in Santa Rosa, for which they got paid with the animals' livers and kidneys, when color returned to our faces and fat Auntie Maria swelled in her shoulders and limbs again, Clementine remained shrunken and gray. As long as I had known her, her clothes had never fit, was always two sizes too big, as if once before in her life she had shrunk, been sick or upset somehow, and never returned to her normal weight. But now she was hidden in her clothes, twig fingers, bone face, a skeleton withered beneath her blue scarf and dark sweaters and dresses. No sign of life, save that coughing and the blood sputum she spit and I cleaned off her neck and sweater with a washrag.

The bad luck she feared had gobbled up her children had now come back for her, the way a weasel returns for the hen after it has found and eaten her eggs. No doubt, that was how she seen things. And I knowed how she was about it, quiet and ashamed, as if it was her fault, as if something she had done lured the weasel to her nest. So I done as I thought she would want—I kept quiet, acted as if nothing was wrong. Being it was dark and cold with not much to do, and being she was never one to visit much with other people, it was easy for her to hide. And it helped that our house, like before, was at the end of the row—folks couldn't hear her coughing since they never passed by there. Oh, she'd brace herself, stand in the doorway and wave occasionally, just to let people think things was normal, in case one of them might've noticed she hadn't been at the well lately fetching water, or that I was the only one gathering firewood and hauling rations from the agent's car. What they didn't know was that I was building the fires and cooking all the food. And washing clothes: I'd scrub in a metal bucket on the floor and string the wet clothes across the room on a piece of old baling wire. She'd half sit up in bed, the pillows behind her, and I'd support her head with one hand if she was too tired or weak, and with the other hand I'd spoon beans and flour broth past her withered lips. I don't know if she appreciated it. She never said nothing. It didn't matter. I'd done these things with no warmth or kindness in my heart. As long as I kept her alive, and as long as the situation was a secret, I didn't have to face the prospect of what would become of me.

Come late February the first buds showed on the apple trees. Further down the road, a ways from the reservation, the plum trees bloomed, full of pink blossoms. I turned eleven. Said nothing to nobody. Not even to my only friend, Zelda, for fear her or her mom might come to the house to give me something, which, of course, was unlikely. Clementine forgot or was just too sick to do anything about it. In the past, she'd make something, fry bread heaped with jam, and put a small strand of ribbon on the plate. I'd find it on the table with dinner. The last birthday I had with Mama she took me to On Chong, the Chinese restaurant on Second Street in Santa Rosa, the only place in town Indians could sit down. Noodles was ten cents a bowl. Mama ordered a bowl for each of us, and slurping the hot broth, we watched people on the street through the window. We named them and laughed. Turtle. Rooster. Raccoon Eyes. It was like being with Chum.

* * *

I don't know what I had been thinking. Over a month and Clementine not a step outside her front door? Even if people was far away when she was waving, when they looked, wouldn't they have seen the stand of bones? And where was she night after night when everybody else collected in the roundhouse, listening to Big Sarah? Never mind my scurrying around, hauling water, collecting wood, dragging half-filled sacks of flour and beans back to the house. Who was I kidding?

They knowed what was wrong with Clementine. They knowed

disease better than health, after all, for they seen more of it. What Indian reached twenty in them days and didn't know the signs and stories of every disease better than she knowed the palm of her own hand?

"Consumption," Big Sarah said.

Actually, she said, *"Da chuken,"* no breath, the Indian word. Consumption. Tuberculosis. TB. I understood her. I knowed what she would say the minute I opened the door and found her there.

Big Sarah said nothing else. She didn't have to. She cracked my cover with one blow. Auntie Maria was behind her with Zelda and Zelda's little brother, Dewey, in tow. Bertha was there, too, and Elmer and his wife.

"You don't play with these kids no more," Auntie Maria said. "Don't you breathe on them on account you probably got the sickness too, *da chuken.*"

"Mensi," be quiet, Big Sarah told her. Then she looked back at me. "You have her dressed tonight. We'll take her to the roundhouse."

I nodded and watched them leave.

I sighed with relief. At first, I had felt as if I'd done something wrong and just been caught. I took Auntie Maria's harsh words banning me from her children as the first of a pelting that would come from all of them. But now I relaxed, believing that the main reason they'd come was to ask me to have Clementine dressed for the roundhouse, not to punish me. I didn't think what it meant that everybody knowed that she was sick.

And I didn't think what it meant to her.

When I closed the door and turned around, she was crying. Minutes before she had been propped up, half-sitting against the pillows, but now she was slumped down, trying to cover her face with the blankets, crying helplessly, choking. I propped her up again, patted her face with the washrag.

"Don't cry, don't cry," I told her. "It makes you cough."

I felt sorry for her. Rather, I knowed how she felt: caught; and more, what she seen: them dragging her out for everybody to see.

Which is what happened.

Uncle McKinley, Elmer, and a couple other men come with a makeshift litter, lifted her onto it, and carried her out and through the rainy night to the roundhouse. I'd dressed her in clean clothes: bathed her shrunken body with the washrag, slipped fresh underclothes onto her, pulled a dress up her twisted-bone legs, and buttoned two sweaters over her sunked and heaving chest. No matter where anyone might look, they'd find her clean. And warm! I wrapped her in the heaviest blankets we had, covered her head with scarves tied snugly under her chin. But a lot of good that done, what with the rain pouring down on her helpless face and soaking the blankets.

Everybody was there, no doubt to get a good look at the woman they'd been discussing amongst themselves for the last month. The men set the litter on the ground next to the fire; and there Clementine stayed, wrapped in the wet blankets and staring up at the ceiling. She looked like a doll, or a shrunken mummy. She was that still, which surprised me since I hadn't known her not to cough or at least wheeze loudly during the last two weeks. It occurred to me she might be holding her breath, barely breathing.

Big Sarah stood in front of the center pole looking down on her. She pounded her cane on the ground and told us, "I'm going to pray for her health. I have songs for that. Many of you have seen me doctor. You know how it works. If it is right—if she is right—she will live. That is what my vision says. Ooooh!" she said.

"Ooooh!" the crowd answered.

Auntie Maria nudged me with her elbow and I let out a slight squeak after all the others. "Ooooh."

Then Big Sarah called Elmer, and that way, with Elmer keeping the beat for her with a clapper stick, she begun her songs. More and more, at the nightly dances, Elmer stood by her side. I guess in addition to her appointing him chief, she also made him her right-hand man. They sung a few songs, three or four maybe, and then she held up her cane, signaling Elmer to stop.

"This is a hard case," she said, her words filling the room and settling in the waiting ears. "She's far along in her sickness." Then she prayed silently, just her thin lips moving, small worms caught and wreathing on hard ground. The fire crackled. Rain on the roof. She lifted her cane, and her and Elmer started up with more songs.

This happened three more nights. Four singing ceremonies altogether. After that first night, I kept hearing Big Sarah's words—"She's far along in her sickness"—and wondered why folks waited so long to come for Clementine. Certainly, they'd known she was sick. But then, who of us hadn't been exposed to *da chuken*? Maybe it was the prospect of more bad luck they couldn't bear to face, until guilt over her condition forced them to turn to Big Sarah. In any event, Big Sarah didn't have the guns.

"This is a hard case," she repeated at the end of the fourth night. "Something is wrong. She has done something wrong in her life."

I immediately thought of myself, what I might have done wrong either in causing Clementine to become sick or in preventing her cure. I'd behaved, washed before eating and helped with the cooking when she was well. Same thing after she got sick. And tonight, as with the last three nights, wasn't I dressed proper—long dress to my ankles, arms and neck covered?

"But it is not all over yet," Big Sarah added, tossing out a morsel of hope. "We must still put up a dinner tomorrow—after this four-night ceremony."

After any healing ceremony, whether one night or four, you had to put up a dinner, a table, we call it. The responsibility falls on the sick person's immediate family or whoever it was that called the doctor in. Well, Clementine had no immediate family, no husband or kids. Ofelia, but nobody had seen her in years. So the whole dinner could have fallen on me since I was considered the closest to Clementine. But everybody pitched in; in fact, at the dinner a couple people told me how good I was to take care of her. Maybe guilt had set in.

It had dried out a bit, and the men set up wooden tables on the backside of the roundhouse. How many ways can you cook beans? Beans, rice, and fry bread. Thank God, they held off on the horse liver stew, which I don't think anyone learned to stomach—not unless they was starving. I made beans and boiled a small pot of rice, which I mixed in with the beans. Made kind of a pretty stew, the grains of white rice like stars in the bowl. I carried the bowl against my chest and set it on the table. The men set Clementine, still on the litter they'd carried from the house, on top of another table. Silent, she gazed with sunken eyes to the clear sky.

"This is good," Big Sarah announced, standing between the table holding Clementine and the one holding the food. "Good to put this food out." She paused, then said, "But the patient is too far gone."

* * *

So Clementine was done for. Nobody talked about it, at least not to me. But, unlike before, they pitched in, helped. They knocked on the door, left pots of food, asked if I needed wood. Bertha left me a jar of dried mountain balm leaves. Uncle McKinley's wife asked if she could patch my sweater. They peered through the door, but none of them come in. We waited.

I got used to folks knocking. I'd answer the door and find this one or that one waiting to hand me something, maybe bent over leaving a steaming pot on the steps. So the afternoon I opened the door, after hearing a knock, and found a total stranger sitting on the steps, I was taken aback, even before he turned around and looked up to me.

"How do you do?" he said in English, tipping his felt derby.

If you was only to hear him, to hear only the voice just then, you'd swear it was a white man speaking, for not even a white man could speak that eloquent. And the derby, something a true dandy would wear, gray, with a maroon band. Wool suit and silk tie, polished black leather shoes that shone like obsidian. My mind scrambled to make sense of what my eyes took in, for I'd never known an Indian to look like him.

He stood up and turned to face me.

"I've come to see my niece," he said, only now he spoke in Indian.

It wasn't that he was handsome; he was at least seventy years old, though sturdy, and he was rather short and square, dark, a full-blood type, but he grinned wide, showing a row of white teeth that made him, even at his age, striking to look at. His eyes twinkled. If I was older, if I knowed more of the ways of men, I'd say he was the kind with life to spare, a genuine handful of a fellow. Behind him, hardly twenty feet from the shack, rested a new dark-green Packard.

No doubt, he wanted to come in, so I stepped aside.

"*Yah we*," thank you, he said, passing into the shack.

I looked once before I turned to follow him, and saw Auntie Maria and Uncle McKinley making their way from their places right next to each other, in this direction. Like me, they probably had just spotted the flashy new car and not heard it as it rolled through the reservation.

He sat at the table. I sat down behind him. He was looking down at the pile of blankets on the pallet bed in the corner of the room. I couldn't see his face. He sat a long time. He adjusted his hat a couple times. Then he got up and closed the door, which I absentmindedly had left open. The room was dark then, so I lit the lantern, and just as the light filled the room, Clementine gasped, "Old Uncle." He was standing over her.

He said something in Indian, which I couldn't hear except for the sharp s's and t's that sounded from where I was sitting like leaves scraping over dry ground in a wind. "Oooh," he said, finishing what he was saying, and I realized then that he had been praying. Then he knelt down, and leaning over her, kissed her forehead and both sides of her sunken face. "I've come to sing for you," he said, and he took off his hat and set it on the floor next to him. And that way, kneeling, he sung a song, a quiet song, soft like warm cotton, the same song over and over, and he swayed, gentle, back and forth, his hands held out above her, as if he was holding something, a swaddled infant, that he was both rocking and offering up to the sky.

When he finished, after he stood up, I got up and peeked at Clementine. She was deep asleep, as she had been most of the last two weeks, but I could see, even in the dim light, that her forehead and mouth, tight in a show of discomfort for ages, had now relaxed; her brow was smooth, the mouth now gaping, taking in and letting out air with no effort.

He opened the door; light poured into the room. I spun around and found half the reservation gathered below the steps, their necks craning, eyes wide, as if trying to see into the room, past the door, no doubt to see if they could spy Clementine. But, in that same instant, just as I was looking, I seen them pull in their stretched necks and settle on the figure in the doorway.

"Old Uncle!" someone said.

"Old Uncle!" another greeted.

And he put on his derby, which had been in his hand, and stepped down to meet them.

* * *

Old Uncle. That's what folks called him. Not Bill or Charles or Henry. I never heard a white name, much less an Indian one. He said he was Clementine's uncle, that she was his niece. But I heard Bertha say he was an older half brother; and Auntie Maria said something else, that he was Clementine's stepfather. The same thing with other folks: One person would say how she was related to him, and then a half dozen others would refute what she said, coming up with their own stories and genealogies. "My mother told me this," one person would say. "Well, my aunt, she told me something different," another argued.

When he come back into the house that afternoon and closed the door, he took off his hat, like a gentleman, and offered his hand. "Old Uncle," he introduced himself, but he was laughing, as if it was obvious that I already knowed who he was and the joke of his formal introduction was something just between the two of us. I didn't know what to do. My head was confused. But in no time my body took over and I was laughing out loud, laughing as if I'd never laughed before, for it had been such a long time, and again I was confused, but not enough to stop my convulsions.

"Shh," he said, leaning close to me with a finger on his lips. "You'll wake the sleeping angel."

Giggling still, but trying to control myself, I looked to Clementine; but I couldn't see her face, if she was awake, for all the blankets piled around her.

"I seen you when you was tiny," he said then in English, the English an Indian would use. "You wouldn't remember. I gone off, ain't been back for a while. Gone south."

Which was one of the stories I'd later hear along with all the bickering about how he was related to this one and that one. That he'd left Benedict's Rancheria long ago and then taken up with a coast Indian, a Miwok, down in Tomales Bay. Yet no one could say who the woman was, even the folks who had close ties, relations, in-laws maybe, with the Tomales people. Auntie Maria agreed with Big Sarah, who said that if he'd taken up with anybody down there, it sure wasn't an Indian, not the way he was dressed. "Only a *masan* can put clothes like that on a man," she said. "Maybe he's got a good job," Bertha said, "which would explain the new car too." Auntie Maria and Big Sarah shook their heads.

I knowed he wasn't a direct uncle to me; Mama never had brothers that I'd heard of. I figured he was a great-uncle, something like that. He never said more to me about himself than his name and that he had gone south. And that he would stay here for four days and four nights.

"And then we'll put up a table," I volunteered.

He hesitated, then said, "Well, yes."

But it wasn't what I expected—ceremonies in the roundhouse. No, he just sat and sung his song; knelt, actually, like he done the first time, and sung that same song plus some others, all behind our closed front door. Nobody seen or heard but me. They might've heard it if they crept up and pressed their ears against the sides of the shack, but I doubt they did. He didn't sing just at night, but at different times during the day, no regular schedule, whenever he wanted, it seemed. And he asked me to cook, keep food prepared and warm. From the trunk of his new car, he brought in fine chunks of dried salmon, which was wrapped in clean sheets, high-quality linen; and acorn powder, half a dozen lug jars filled to the brim with the ground powder, ready for leaching. He dug a shallow hole next to the shack and showed me how to line it with a towel so I could leach the powder the way women used to do it in the sand along the creek.

"Works the same way," he said, emptying half a jar over the towel. "Surprised nobody showed you yet," he said.

"Ain't got acorns left; ate them all," I told him, reminding him of our conditions.

"Do now," he said and winked, sprinkling water from a metal bucket over the powder.

He'd even carry the bucket from the well for me. On my knees and bent over the leaching hole, I'd hand him the empty bucket over my shoulder, and before I could straighten to turn around, there he'd be with a bucket of water already—the well was a couple of minutes away, and he'd stand there with not a drop of water on him, the sides of his polished shoes without a trace of mud. That was the first sign he wasn't a normal person, fancy clothes and new car aside; at least, that was when I started thinking about it. Got so I turned and watched him walk to the well. And, yes, he gone there and come back, step by step, carrying the bucket like anybody else. But then, as if he knowed I was watching him, he worked harder—faster—to fool me.

Then we'd boil the mush on the stove. Acorn mush and dried salmon, the old-timers' favorite. They'd dip the fish into the mush and eat it that way. Clementine couldn't chew, but Old Uncle held pieces of fish dipped in mush for her to suck, and he'd spoon the mush into her with a stick of dried fish. Sometimes he'd mash up the fish with a fork or spoon until it was as fine and runny as the mush. Couple times I seen him do the shortcut, mash it in his teeth, what mothers used to do for their babies. I cooked beans and rice, and we'd mash them up too. And mountain balm tea, I made a lot of it, kept the water warm. He said I done good giving that to her before on account of how it helped clear her lungs.

"Herbs is good," he said, "but this one is king," and he pulled out big pieces of angelica root and set them on the table, dried pieces twisted like an old man's fingers.

With a pocketknife he shaved one of the fingers into tiny shards, then pulled out a small brown pipe, nothing fancy like his clothes, and stuffed the bowl with the shards. He lit the pipe and smoked. He told me I didn't have to smoke a pipe. "May be too unladylike," he laughed, "but you should burn it to keep you strong, keep away evil." He said he'd leave some for me when he left. "Up here," he said, nodding and blowing smoke in the direction of Clementine's cupboard. The house always smelled like angelica.

* * *

A person with consumption in the early and middle stages has a kind of glow, no doubt from the low fevers. I never seen such a flush on Clementine. But by the second day, her face, which had relaxed when Old Uncle first sung, showed some kind of life: rosy cheeks, smooth skin that looked moist, as if she might be feverish, but when I touched her cheeks she wasn't hot, just comfortable warm.

I hadn't had it so good since I could remember. Food like never before. Salmon. Acorn mush. Beans. Rice. Fry dough. All I had to do was keep the pots full, not worry about how they was going to get that way. Even the wood bin behind the house seemed forever full. What's more, I had time, idle hours with nothing to do. In fact, I often got the feeling I wasn't wanted in the house. Like Old Uncle and Clementine wanted time alone. Nothing Old Uncle ever said, but just the way they'd sit, her propped up against the pillows and him in a chair next to the pallet bed, as if they was just waiting for me to leave so that they could start talking. Of course Clementine wasn't talking still, though I did see her whisper a couple times to Old Uncle while he was kneeling over her praying.

So I cut out. Took up with Zelda. Boy oh boy, what I had missed locked away taking care of Clementine. Might've been dark and rain and not much food that first winter on the no-name reservation, but there was more, and Zelda had her fingers in it—another hobo camp, just this side of Sebastopol, at the bottom of the hills. It wasn't like what I seen at Benedict's, a group of men and sleeping bags gathered around a fire, what you'd call a makeshift work camp. It was more like a small town, or a Rancheria, complete with a road to it and a dozen or so shacks just like you'd see on any Rancheria or reservation—small, put together with scraps; but there was only white people, and the most astonishing thing, at least for me, they was all men. Thirty or forty of them, and before I got there, before I come past the tall cypress trees following Zelda following her sister Ida, I smelled them, the rancid butter smell of white men who didn't bathe. That and whiskey.

"Just wait," Zelda said when I asked her where we was going. "Shh," she told me as we crept down the road, trailing about a quarter of a mile behind Ida.

We hid behind trees, waited for her to round the next corner in the road. But I never thought for a second Ida didn't know we was following her, what with me and Zelda waiting around for her to take off that morning. Another thing, we hadn't waited in front of Auntie Maria's place where Zelda's other sister, Sipie, and her brother, Dewey, and lots of other kids hung around. We waited outside "the rat's" place, which, apparently, was where Ida was living now. She walked out the front door of the rat's place and I couldn't believe my eyes: fat Ida, a fifteen-year-old replica of her mother, only darker, in a shiny dress with a pleat in the back; and, in the front, above the wide-open collar, cleavage like two smooth brown melons pushed up by a corset that cinched her middle tight enough so she'd have a waist. Her hair was set, two spit curls reaching down her forehead, flapper style; her eyebrows was arching lines drawn with a pencil. So when I followed Zelda following her to the road, I wanted to know where we was going.

I smelled before I seen, and I seen before I knowed. Come past the tall cypress trees and hid behind a rusted car, and through its broken-out windows seen Ida disappear beyond the men, a dark figure, the pleated skirt hitting the backs of her thick calves, and then no more.

Men everywhere. Clothes flapped on lines in the cool clear breeze, like giant handheld fans blowing the disgusting air in our direction. Men, mostly in their late teens and twenties, sat two and three to a step; they leaned against old cars and squatted around campfires.

"We could get crackers," I said.

"It's different here," Zelda answered, her eyes peeled on all the movement in front her.

She must've sensed my staring at her, my head filled with questions, for she broke her intent gaze finally, and said, "This is a *real* hobo camp." Then, as if she understood I needed to know more, she said, "At night they have card games, and the Filipinos come with roosters for cockfights—Ida seen it."

"She come at night?" I asked.

"Yeah."

"She tell you?"

"No," she said, "I heard her telling Sipie." She looked back to the camp then and said, "It's like nothing you ever seen before."

"You come at night?" I asked, trying to imagine her creeping down the road in the dark and spying here alone.

"Uh-uh," she said. "But I will if you come with me. Now that Clementine's better, you can get away, or if she dies."

I wondered how she knowed Clementine was better; nobody'd seen her. Maybe Old Uncle told folks. But it was the last thing she said—"if she dies"—that my mind hooked on. I hadn't considered that prospect for a while, specifically, what would happen to me if she did die. When it come to the forefront of my thoughts early on, and in them days when she first got sick it come up a lot, I'd wipe it away, push my worries away with the business at hand—keeping her alive. After Old Uncle come, I plumb quit thinking about it altogether.

"Look," Zelda said, nodding adult-like with her chin. "Ain't he good-looking? What do you think?"

"Who?" I said. Where she had nodded, half a dozen men had gathered in front of one of the shacks, talking and laughing out loud.

"Who?" she said, annoyed. "Who else, dummy, the one in the blue shirt, with his sleeves rolled up."

How she expected me to pick any one man out of that group I'll never know. They all looked the same to me, at least at first glance— scruffy white men, red hair, blond hair, brown hair, all the same. The one she was fixed on was brown-haired, balding in the front, curly and unkempt in the back. Red cheeks as if he was cold, and his blue shirt, wrinkled, was open in the front, totally unbuttoned, so you seen his stained undershirt and the curve of a good-size belly. Must've been mid or latter twenties.

"Bill," she said.

"How do you know?" I asked.

"Shhh!" she said, annoyed again. "I'm counting."

"Counting what?"

"Sixty. I count to sixty ten times. That equals ten minutes."

Well, she learned something in school! What the purpose of her counting was I didn't ask, didn't have to, for after another couple minutes, I watched her duck low and creep to a stand of redwoods, small for redwoods, but close enough together to form a wall so that the men down below in the camp couldn't see her, couldn't see when Bill met her there and gave her a few good swigs from a small glass flask and then dropped his drawers so she could play with him. I hadn't seen that kind of playing—not with Mama and her men friends behind the saloon or when we spied Sam Toms with Bertha—playing that was with the mouth. They had a routine. She had to know I could see everything.

She come back to me when they was finished—and it wasn't very long—and then we left, gone back to the main road.

"Where's Ida?" I asked.

"She stays all day. Sometimes all night. Sometimes she don't come home at all."

If I was thinking, maybe if I was a little bit older, I wouldn't have had to ask about Ida, I would've knowed that she stayed. Now I did know, and I understood in this same split second why Ida was no longer living with her family, why she had come out of "the rat's" house, and, come to think of it, why I hadn't seen her at night in the roundhouse lately. My thoughts just then returned to Zelda, however.

"You been drinking," I said. I meant to say she was drunk, or that she had sounded drunk, slurring her words, when she'd answered my question.

"What do you think, stupid," she snapped. Then huffing and puffing alongside me as we walked up the road, she informed me, "Gee, he gave me more than last time. You might have to carry me."

What a thought! "You're fine," I said. She was walking fine, the only sign of her condition being her slurred speech, which, if she tried, she could keep straight. Her eyes was a little glassy maybe. But she did smell to high heaven of whiskey. "Wash your mouth out with soap before you go in the house," I told her.

"It burns going down," she said, "but then it feels real good."

An ugly thought entered my mind. She was talking about the whiskey, of course, but wouldn't she have said the same thing about the man?

When we was high enough on the road, I looked back towards the valley and seen the lagoon, still wide, spread over the land; the bridge into Sebastopol was dry, though; and beyond the water, the orchards bloomed in white and pink blocks of apple and plum trees as far as the eye could see, clear back to Santa Rosa. I also seen smoke in streams rising from behind a line of knolls just this side of the water, and I thought of Nellie. But it occurred to me that the smoke was coming from the hobo camp.

* * *

We got home OK. The only problem was that Auntie Maria was at the well and seen us come up the road.

"Tell her we just gone looking for wood," Zelda whispered and tore off for the outhouse.

I had no trouble meandering up to the well on account of how Old Uncle was there, too, and Zelda's sister Sipie and her little brother, Dewey. Auntie Maria was fast in conversation with Old Uncle, so I made small talk with Sipie, slipping in that me and Zelda had been out looking for wood. Sipie said, "Oh," and looked as if she could care less, which was likely the situation. She was quiet and kindly, plain; nothing like the gossipy, conniving Zelda or the cold, detached Ida, both of whom got equal shares of their mother. She was fourteen, just a year behind Ida, but, like me, in hand-me-downs, oversized dresses and sweaters, she had no sense of her body. She stood, a full bucket of water on the ground on each side of her, waiting for her mother.

"Well, your medicine is good," Auntie Maria told Old Uncle, wrapping up their conversation. "If anybody can help Clementine, it'd be you."

I didn't hear what Old Uncle said after that; his back was to me. They said good-bye, Old Uncle tipping his derby and Auntie Maria picking up her buckets of water and nodding for Sipie to follow suit. Dewey, who was playing by the well close to Old Uncle, picked up his one bucket, and peering up at Old Uncle with admiration, said, "See, I can carry it."

In the short time that Old Uncle had been on the reservation, the smaller kids had taken a real fancy to him. He'd sit at the well and show them card tricks, do magic, making scarves come out of eggs and shiny new baseballs appear in the palm of his hand from out of nowhere. But then I seen what Auntie Maria thought of him, and how she didn't believe what she had just told him, when she turned with unchecked force and commanded Dewey, "Come along!"

"Old Uncle, Old Uncle," little Dewey shouted out when he was halfway along the path, and again Auntie Maria turned angrily.

Funny thing, as it turned out, that boy would forever be calling out "Old Uncle," and it got to be a nickname for him when he was much older. Fat Auntie Maria would be turning in her grave, no doubt.

* * *

The next day Old Uncle took me into Santa Rosa for lunch. For being such a good sport all this time with Clementine, he said. As much as I might've been excited about seeing Santa Rosa again, I have to admit my mind was set on going back to the hobo camp with Zelda. But how could I tell Old Uncle no, what excuse could I give? What else had I to do around the reservation if it didn't have to do with taking care of Clementine? I was stuck. I thought maybe it would be fun if Zelda come along, so I asked him if that was OK and he said yes.

But what was I thinking, what with the way I seen Auntie Maria call Dewey away from Old Uncle just the day before? She wasn't going to let Zelda get into that car with him. Still, I gone over to the shack and knocked on the door. I hadn't seen Zelda since we parted ways; I hadn't gone to the roundhouse the night before—in fact, I hadn't gone since Old Uncle come—staying in and cooking while he sung and prayed over Clementine, and Zelda was nowheres to be seen earlier in the day when I was fetching water and hauling wood. Like I said, I knowed Auntie Maria would put up the negative, I just didn't figure how strong.

"She ain't going nowheres with you," she barked down the steps.

I about shrunk to the size of a pea. All I said was, "Can Zelda come with me and Old Uncle to Santa Rosa?" Knowing how I was extra polite around Auntie Maria on account of how she didn't much like me in the first place, I might've even said "please." I thought just then that she was saying to me what she would really like to have said to Old Uncle, and in the same tone of voice, but didn't have the nerve to. Maybe she was just hoping he heard, or at least seen, since he was sitting in his car waiting for me only a couple hundred yards away, engine humming. She slammed the door fierce. Was it me? Was I something contaminated now because Old Uncle had been staying in my house? Or was that just an excuse she had now to show her true feelings for me? I knowed she was mad when Big Sarah ordered her to be quiet after she told me not to play with the other kids no more on account of how I might be carrying Clementine's consumption. In fact, lots of folks got mad at her later, reminding her how she kept Old Jose when he was sick, and how I'd done such a good deed caring for Clementine all that time.

"What's the matter with her," Old Uncle said when I got back into the car, "roll out of the wrong side of the bed this morning?"

The way he said that, I pictured fat Auntie Maria rolling out of bed, her body coming off her pallet with a plunk and continuing to roll until it was stuck at the front door. I laughed. Old Uncle must've pictured the same thing. He laughed too.

I rode in a car before, Elmer's. Old Uncle's was something else: plush, a boat, a magic carpet that sailed through the countryside. You was as shiny as the lagoon water under the bridge, as soft as the fruit blossoms on either side of the road. You was the first warm air of the year. He sat back, whistled half a tune every now and then as he watched the road ahead. I forgot about the hobo camp after we passed its turnoff, forgot about Nellie too. Might've forgot Santa Rosa if we wasn't going to it.

The town in early spring: new leaves on the trees, flowers in the yards. Kids in short-sleeved shirts. The sun on car fenders. Chum and us kids used to walk the nice streets this time of year, never stopping for long, of course, lest the white people shoo us away, and she'd teach us the names of all the flowers inside the picket fences: foxglove, primrose, dahlia, wild rose, nasturtium, narcissus, trumpet vine, hollyhock. "Flowers is Creation smiling," she'd say.

"Gee, warm, eh?" Old Uncle said, rolling his window down all the way.

I rolled mine down complete, too, took in the smell of bakeries, food, and the sounds of birds and kids playing.

Second Street, where On Chong was—where else could we go to eat?—was run-down, what you call a backstreet. The Chinese restaurant, Chinese laundry, small Chinese store: Chinatown. There was a thrift shop too; and, around the corner, the saloon where Mama used to go, made to look lately—in the days of Prohibition—like a card hall. Old Uncle parked the car and we gone in the restaurant.

He slapped down a crisp dollar bill, enough for ten bowls of noodles, which, even for me, a glutton for noodles, was an impossibility. But we had other things with the noodles, a beef dish, and sweet and sour pork, which was like eating wholesome candy. We sat in the window, and while I tried to mind my manners, all the while still slurping my food, I told him how on my birthday me and Mama come here and watched and named all the people outside: Rooster. Raccoon Eyes.

"Yeah," he said and laughed, turning his gaze out the window.

He fixed his eyes on a well-dressed white man, suit and tie, proper-looking, with spectacles, who hurried past the window and disappeared into the Chinese store. He looked back at me and asked, "What do you think that white man is buying in there?"

"Opium," I answered, sure as a cat's got eyes.

He looked surprised, eyebrows raised.

"Mama told me," I added right away. "She said the white men go in there and the Chinaman sells it in the back."

"Do you know what opium is?" he asked.

"Like whiskey," I answered, telling him what Mama told me when I asked her the same question.

He settled back in his seat, wiped his mouth with his napkin—he was a true gentleman. Then he asked, "Why does the Chinaman use opium?"

"To feel good," I answered, again repeating what I knowed from Mama.

"And what about the white man?"

"Same thing," I answered.

Old Uncle nodded, rubbed his chin. He looked at me, narrowed his eyes. "I seen you when you was tiny. I seen you with your mama."

All of a sudden we was back on the subject of Mama.

"Where?" I asked.

"I gone off. Ain't been back for a while. Gone south," he answered as if I had asked where he had gone and not where he had seen me with Mama. Maybe I hadn't been clear. But then something else popped up in my brain: We was repeating the same conversation we had after he introduced himself formal to me that first day. I thought of asking him where south he'd gone—Tomales Bay?—and did he have a wife—Indian or white?—the other questions folks been asking. But then I thought better of it, not only because I wouldn't ask anyways, but because just then I got the idea that he had understood what I had asked him and throwed me off deliberate in case the question might get us into the particulars of his life, which he had no intention of revealing.

So I said something that meant nothing: "That was a long time ago."

"Not so long," he said.

He ordered me vanilla ice cream for dessert, said he didn't have any because he had to watch his diet, then we left.

* * *

To my surprise we didn't go home. Headed east toward Benedict's. Just before the ranch, however, he turned and we climbed the hills on a dirt road overlooking the valley. That car of his, it just sailed, floated over the bumps and pits; and, before long, we was following nothing but a horse trail and the car handled the same, floated like a boat. We stopped alongside a couple of large rocks that looked like thick chairs positioned so that you could sit in them and take in the wide view of the valley below. And it was some view! As high up as I'd been with Chum, but a ways south so you not only seen Benedict's ranch and Archer's, but the entire town of Santa Rosa, its center, Fourth and Mendocino, and how it spread from there, streets and square blocks.

We got out and stretched, sucked in the air. It felt good, woke me up; I'd been sleepy in the car, full from lunch.

"It's quite something, ain't it?" Old Uncle said.

"Yeah," I answered, thinking that, like me, he was looking at the town. But when I glanced over at him he was peering, eyes squinted, at the road above the creek. I followed the road then, traced it from the place his eyes was set, just north of Archer's ranch, all the way past Benedict's house and barn to the Rancheria, where the shacks, still standing, looked quiet and empty, even from this distance. The large walnut trees looked bare, but I knowed that by this time of year, if I was standing underneath them, I'd see their pointed green tips. Beyond the trees was the graveyard, the white crosses like bones above the green carpet of grass.

Old Uncle scratched his chin, looked around.

"We should sit down," I said, eyeing the two rocks.

He knowed what I was referring to. "Uh-uh, no," he said. "Them rocks is sacred. Spirits is sitting there overlooking things."

He chuckled and I thought he was kidding, but we didn't sit down. Then he turned to a stand of four old valley oaks just beyond the rocks, large trees with twisted branches that narrowed at the end and hung like large roots reaching for the ground. "Them trees is sacred too. Thank them because they watch over you too. If you come here, maybe just to say 'hello,' they'll like it. In the fall, pick the acorns they give, show them you ain't forgot, you remember. If you do that, if you come here, no harm will come to you."

I heard his words all of a sudden like a stream, drops of water that had started with his talk about the rocks and had gathered force, collecting in one place and running in one direction. He coughed then, clearing his throat. Always a gentleman, he covered his mouth.

"And there's a snake," he continued, "a rattlesnake, huge one, old guy. You can see it in summer and fall under them trees. But don't fear it. It ain't what you think. It's the old earth spirit."

Then he turned clear around, east, and following him, I seen a full moon in the late afternoon sky, an enormous white clamshell disk hung on an invisible string. "The old-time medicine people gone there, seen things—the weather, what's going to happen in the future. See the dark spot above the left eye?" he asked, nodding his chin as if the moon was a mere five feet away.

"Yeah," I answered, seeing the shaded ridge.

"They'd go there and sit—"

It occurred to me just then that he was telling a story. "How'd they get there?" I asked, interrupting him.

"Fly up. Turn into a botfly and fly up."

I expected, after his answer, that he would pick up the story again. But he didn't. In the silence, waiting to hear what he would say next, I realized why it had taken me so long to figure he was telling a story. He'd been turning this way and that, in every direction, talking about whatever his eyes found—rocks, trees, snake, moon. When I'd heard stories before, when Mama or Chum told stories, say about the coyote and what he done to get a white tip on his tail, there was a beginning and a end. Here, with Old Uncle, it seemed there was lots of stories, or pieces of one story I couldn't fit together.

For the longest time he said nothing. Then he turned clear around and knelt down on one knee, facing the valley. His eyes narrowed on the road again. Then he repeated what he'd said his first day at Clementine's, and what he'd said hardly an hour before in the restaurant: "I seen you when you was tiny. I seen you with your mama." He paused, then added, "I seen you on that road."

I wanted to ask one more question: When? How old was I? But he started singing. It was the same song he first sung for Clementine, the one he always opened his singing ceremonies with, a quiet song, soft like cotton.

> Yo ho ahay yo
> Yo ahay yo
> Yo ho ahay yo
> Yo ahay yo.

Something like that. And not very long, not over and over like he done for Clementine, but just long enough, it seemed, for me to hear it. Then he turned in my direction and, lifting his hat, took a bow. On one knee still, he looked like a court jester kneeling before me. He winked and I started laughing.

On the way home, starting back down the hill, I thought to look at him, as if to see who this man really was, what he looked like, as if I might find a mole on his face or neck, a telling feature of his hairline maybe, a widower's peak, that would forever distinguish him in my mind. I knowed that what he said and done on the hill was strange yet somehow important, but I had no way to make sense of it except to try and stare at the man. But floating along in that flower-petal-soft car, and still full from lunch, I fell asleep.

* * *

Clementine had somehow propped herself up. When we come in the door, she reached out with both hands to Old Uncle. She was focused, something on her mind. I thought she was hungry. Old Uncle brought her water.

I got busy with the fire; it hadn't burned out, the place was still warm, but only embers was left in the furnace. I chopped kindling, hauled in some big logs for a good fire. I boiled rice and dropped in a stick of dried salmon for flavor, then mashed the grains and fish sticks into a mush Clementine could swallow. Something pushed me, not so much the thought that we had neglected Clementine; we'd been gone only a couple hours, after all, and she'd been resting just fine. But the sudden realization come over me that this time tomorrow night Old Uncle might be gone, that tonight would be the fourth night, his last here. Four days and four nights he had said. Back in the house now, the excursion to Santa Rosa, the lunch and the ride into the hills, seemed a grim reminder, not so much a thank-you but a farewell.

Old Uncle didn't seem to notice my fury. He sat in a chair next to the bed, his back to me. He didn't see that I was running a race to keep Clementine alive, to raise her from her sickbed, and that I'd keep pace with him, run faster if I had to, if that's what it would take.

About seven o'clock I gone for water. It was warm. The full moon was straight overhead. As I come up to the well carrying my buckets, I seen a group of men stopped there, talking and smoking.

"Ain't no woman taking care of him, Indian or white," one of them was saying. "It's a man . . . He's that kind of guy, you know. The kind that likes men."

It was Uncle McKinley and Elmer and some others, greasy-faced Reginald, too, which surprised me. They quieted as I approached. But even

before they noticed me, I seen their faces in the moonlight, how their eyes
was like Auntie Maria's when she was talking to Old Uncle, no matter how
nice she pretended to be.

Outside the front door, I rested a minute, set my full buckets on the
ground. I hadn't felt a warm night in ages. I looked at the moon. A dark
ridge was over its left eye.

Inside, I set my buckets down and turned to Old Uncle, still seated
in the chair next to the bed. I guess I was looking to him as if asking, Now
what? Now what can I do? But he was unmoving, and when I stepped a little
to this side of him just to catch his face, it was Clementine's I caught instead,
caught her staring eyes, staring past me, staring past the door, just before
Old Uncle reached over and closed them with the tips of his fingers.

I caught my breath. Still propped up against the pillows, she looked
as if she was sleeping. But of course she wasn't.

He lifted his hat, held it over her.

"What are you doing?" I hollered, all of a sudden short of breath
again.

He turned some, looked at me, placed the hat square on his head
again. "Saying good-bye."

He stood up then, started for the door.

"What kind of songs did you sing, anyway?" I accused, standing in
his way.

"Good songs," he said. "Angel songs."

"You come to save her," I pleaded.

"No," he said, "I come to help her die."

Then he was gone. I couldn't hold him. The room was empty.

I sat down in the one other chair. With my elbows on the table,
head in my hands, I stared at the wall. I thought and thought. Then it come
to me. I locked the door, which he'd left ajar, then set to making Clementine
beautiful. I cleaned her, combed and braided her hair, the braids tied fancy
on the top of her head. I put her in the finest clothes she had, which wasn't
much—a black dress, which I not only stuffed with undergarments to make
her look fuller once I had it on her, but stripped the lackluster buttons off
the front and sewed on shiny buttons from another dress. When they come
for her, she'd be ready to walk out, or stay put. Another thing, I opened her
eyes; sitting up in bed, she was staring at the front door. Satisfied, I had me
a long, comfortable cup of tea, the store-bought kind Old Uncle had with
breakfast. Then I gone for them.

*   *   *

They took her like that.

By morning we knowed where we was going to put her—at Benedict's. Big Sarah sent Elmer to ask at daybreak. It was OK, Old Man Benedict said. So Elmer was no more out of the car when Uncle McKinley, sitting atop the big wagon, looked back at the coffin him and Elmer built and said, "Guess we should start, then."

No one walked. They got an extra car, somebody's in-law's Ford, and the rest of us, the kids and older teenagers, rode on the back of the wagon with the coffin. The two horses, still thin and not used to pulling for a while, snorted. Sweat showed in wet lines around their ears and down their backs. Down the hill, then. Sitting on the back of the wagon, watching the road shrink behind me, I felt I could turn around at any moment and see Clementine through the different-colored boards of her slipshod coffin. She'd be resting, just as she was when they carried her out and, at the bottom of the steps, put her in the box. Even in the roundhouse, as Big Sarah prayed and then talked with the closed-up box in front of her, I seen her. "He helped her to die," Big Sarah said, answering folks' questions once and for all about what Old Uncle was doing here. "Only helping her to die," she said. Then she proclaimed, "We can't bury her here. Her spirit will linger." And all the while Clementine fingered the new buttons on her dress.

So it took a while, what with a horse and wagon after all, two cars leading, but we got there. Another warm day and this time I was seeing firsthand, up close, what I seen from the hills the afternoon before—the empty shacks, the graveyard with its white crosses, even the unpainted wooden markers, like the one over Chum. The ground was wet still, soggy a couple feet down. They put Clementine in it, left her with her husband and twelve children.

As people started milling around the food that had been put out smorgasbord style on the wagon, I hung along with Zelda and her sister Sipie. Both of them was quiet.

"I come here yesterday with Old Uncle," I said to break the silence as we took our places at the back of a line that was forming.

Sipie fanned herself with her hand. Zelda shrugged her shoulders, unimpressed.

"We gone to On Chong and had noodles," I added, but still nothing from either of them.

I shrugged then and thought, Oh, well. Did they miss Clementine that much?

But I didn't have time to consider the question for long. Right about then Auntie Maria burst through the line on the other side of the wagon, took me by the arm back through the line and out the gate to the road. Bertha and Uncle McKinley's short wife, Marcellena, was there. But it wasn't them I was looking at. In plain view, just across the road, was an old Ford coupe, and standing next to it was an Indian man, about fifty years old, dark and gray. In the car's rumble seat sat a woman, thickset, with scarves tied around her head, about the same age as the man, from what I could tell, and, like him, she was looking at me.

"I don't know, Maria," Bertha said.

"For marriage? Ain't she too young?" Marcellena questioned.

"Hah!" Auntie Maria snapped, jerking my arm as if I had asked the question. "One way to keep her from drinking and pulling all the others along with her." She jerked my arm again, looked down at me. "Don't think I didn't see you come back up the road the other day with Zelda," she said. Then she looked across the road and nodded, saying, "Maybe this'll help so you don't turn out like your mother."

The man walked across the road. I heard him coming, the grinding sound of pebbles under his shoes, and I saw that his shirtsleeve was missing a button when he handed Auntie Maria the twenty-dollar bill.

He took me by my other arm, led me to the car, where the scarf-headed woman was sitting, and said, "Get up."

THREE

Five years. Four babies, two miscarriages. The babies like the miscarriages. Gone. Stillborn. Stillborn. Pneumonia. Pneumonia. Sweet, then gone. Oh, my life! A dog lived better. You feed them and chain them. Not all the rest.

He started me this way: his little fingers first. "So you'll be ready when your time comes," he said, my time meaning my period. Which he was waiting for, he said. At night after dinner, and even sometimes in the afternoon when he come in from work for a nap, he'd nod for me to follow him to his room. Three fingers by the time my period come. I pushed out the first baby when I was twelve.

* * *

I didn't know what marriage was. I could cook, clean, chop wood, and I'd gotten handy with a needle and thread. But the rest, what I was headed for as I rode in the rumble seat of that sputtering old Ford, I had no idea. Oh, I knowed about sex; I'd seen it. But I didn't know about the fences, the walls. The word would settle in, spell itself clear in my brain in the days and months ahead. "Marriage"; it was the word Marcellena had used. I was sold into it.

The place was just this side of Ukiah, about an hour's drive north on the old two-lane highway from Santa Rosa. With the warm wind blowing around and the open countryside passing on both sides of the highway, the ride might've been fun. Every now and then, I was taken with the sheer thrill, and once or twice the fear, of going so fast with neither doors nor a roof overhead. Then, as quickly as I'd forgotten what was happening to me, the predicament I found myself in, I'd remember. And what was happening to me, what predicament had I found myself in? That was just it. I had no idea. But I was going towards it.

We turned off the highway, gone down a small road a ways, then down another road. I knowed the area, the ranches and farms outside of Ukiah, from when we picked pears and hops. I knowed the reservations up there, too, for sometimes we camped nearby and visited when we worked the crops. So that's where I thought we was headed, maybe the Yokayo Reservation or the Rancheria at Pinoleville. Where else would an Indian in these parts live? But I was plumb wrong. Not a reservation at all but a farmhouse, the kind that white people lived in with a brick walkway, a picket fence, and shutters on the windows. It wasn't as big as the main house, which was just across the dirt road through the property, but it was bigger— and nicer—than anything I'd ever seen an Indian live in.

Who was this man?

"Harold Tatum," he said, offering his hand after I stepped down from the car with the scarfed woman. You'd think he'd just seen me for the first time, hadn't any idea who climbed into his car back in Santa Rosa. Tatum; I'd heard the name, knowed it to be a large family from this area, Yokayo Reservation, I thought. But, of course, this was later, when I had half a second to think. And, as it turned out, Harold claimed he had no relations.

"You go with Annie; she knows what to do," he told me, as if all of a sudden I was as familiar as the shoes on his feet.

"C'mon," she said, nudging my arm.

Harold gone into the yard, past the picket gate where he parked the car, and Annie—she never introduced herself—led me back up the road we come into the ranch on. As we walked, she stared straight ahead, the scarves, a red one and a blue one, one over the other, hiding everything but her thick large nose. When we stopped, she pointed to the cattle guard at the start of the road, just a couple feet from us, and said, "You don't go past this. You don't go out on the county road there." Then she traced the boundaries of the ranch, following the rows of budding pear trees on one side of the cattle guard and the open field on the other. On the way back to the house, she had more to show me, what not to touch, where not to go. "You don't pick the flowers in the boss's yard. You don't put your hands on his clean white gateposts, don't even touch his fence. You don't go into the barns." Her voice was flat, not threatening or commanding as you might think; it was as if she was giving me a tour, naming and describing things rather than telling me what I could and couldn't do.

Then the house. The same thing. What I could and couldn't do. What rooms I could never go into—his bedroom and the large broom closet off the kitchen, where, when she opened the door, I seen sacks of food—flour and beans—enough to feed all the folks at home for a month. And I could open the drawers and cupboards for pots and pans and what she called the regular tableware, but not the drawers above the stand-up cold box where the "good silver and plates" was, not until she showed me how to handle them things proper. Which was the main message I kept hearing: I had so much to learn.

The house seemed enormous and complicated, with all I had to know about it; though, in time, with my learning and day-to-day life, it would grow smaller and smaller. Five rooms: kitchen, bedroom, front room, bathroom, and large sleeping porch off the kitchen. Not a big house by today's standards, but, again, bigger than any house I'd known an Indian to live in. What impressed me most was the bathroom: big porcelain bathtub, sink with running water, and, most interesting, a flush toilet. She gestured to the room from the doorway, as if I was familiar with these things, as if I'd used a flush toilet every day instead of an outhouse a good walk from my back porch. "And the medicine cupboard above the sink," she said, nodding her chin, "don't open that either unless you ask. That's Mr. Tatum's too."

When she finished the tour, with her first set of instructions, she turned away from me, slipped on a white apron that was hanging over the door to the sleeping porch, and reached above the cold box for "the good plates," painted stoneware, which she set on the long honeycomb-tile sink counter. "Shoot, I forgot," she said to herself and moved to the other side of the sink, where fat brown potatoes sat in a line. She picked one up, and catching me out of the corner of her eye as she turned towards the faucet, said, "Go on, get ready for dinner. Get cleaned up."

I guess I felt awkward, as if I'd done something wrong by just standing where she left me. I wasn't thinking. I said, "*Hibu,*" which in my language means potato.

She looked perplexed, taken aback. "*Hibu,*" I repeated and nodded toward the potato in her hand.

"Is that Indian?" she asked.

Clearly, she didn't understand my language. But before I could answer her, she said, "We don't speak Indian in this house . . . And another thing, point with your finger if you have to point, not with your chin."

I thought of her nodding with her chin to the medicine cupboard in the bathroom just minutes before. As if she'd read my thoughts, she added, "Not in front of Mr. Tatum. He don't like it." Then she said, "I forgot, you ain't got no clothes."

Which was something I hadn't considered neither, maybe because I still hadn't understood that the situation I found myself in was permanent.

Auntie Maria no doubt had considered the situation with Harold—Mr. Tatum—on the spot, at Clementine's funeral, and made arrangements then and
there with little thought of my belongings, my clothes and few dolls, at home.

"Gee," Annie said, thinking. "Well, go wash up and tomorrow we'll
have to get you some clothes."

I headed for the sink and amused myself turning the water on and
off. Then I sat on the toilet and flushed, jumping up from the swoosh that
I thought might suck me down with it. I flushed again, tickled by the way
the contraption was just as I'd heard it described—simple, easy, down the
hatch just like that.

Afterwards, I waited in the sleeping porch, sitting on one of the two
cot beds against the wall. It had grown dark, so I couldn't see much, and the
bright light from the kitchen, where I seen Annie bustling about, made my
surroundings even darker. When she come to the door to call me for dinner,
she said, "What are you sitting in the dark for? Turn on a light," and with
that she flicked on a switch lighting the entire room from a bulb overhead.

Though Mr. Tatum had turned towards the house when he left
me and Annie by the car, he hadn't been in the house when Annie showed
me around. And I hadn't heard him come in. I should've expected he'd be
at the table, it was his house, after all; still, I was surprised to round the corner
and find him there. And not just him, but a large boy. The boy was about
fifteen or sixteen years old with a thatch of curly hair and a wide moon face.
As big as he was, at least twice the size of Mr. Tatum, he nonetheless had
small sloping shoulders. With not a hair on his face, he looked like an overgrown ten-year-old. And, to my mind, he didn't look like an Indian; more
Mexican, not only on account of his curly hair, but his other features as well,
his round flat eyes and small curved nose. Certainly he didn't look like Mr.
Tatum and Annie, his parents, I assumed. Square and dark, they was typical
Indians. For as much as I'd been with Annie, I still didn't have a good fix on
her appearance, since she forever kept her eyes from me, but from what I
could tell there was nothing distinguishing about her: on the short side maybe,
and from underneath her scarves, which she wore even to the dinner table,
you could see from her low hairline that her hair was coarse and straight, like
any other Indian's. And Mr. Tatum, who I could see in the overhead light as
I sat down, was the same: straight hair, low forehead, dark.

He sat at one end of the table, the head. I sat across from the boy,
who he introduced as Victor; and Annie, after she lit the two candles and
flicked off the overhead light, sat next to me, on my side of the table closest
to Mr. Tatum. What a spread it was: them painted plates; fancy silverware,
including two forks on the left; cloth napkins folded in a V; big glass pitcher
of cold water, another with milk; candles. Food not that you took from a

pot at the center of the table, but that was already on your plate in neat portions: a scoop of fried potatoes, red Jell-O, a slice of ham.

Nobody said anything to me. After Mr. Tatum introduced me to Victor, saying, "This is Elba"—I never told him my name, maybe Auntie Maria did—he talked as if I was a regular fixture there, Annie or the water pitcher. He talked about plowing that had to be done, how he didn't want to hire Mexicans because they was lazy, and how Indians was worse, plus the fact they was all a bunch of drunks. He himself sipped a glass of wine—a half-filled bottle, the cork on the tablecloth next to it, was in front of his plate. I don't know who in particular he was talking to, if anyone; Annie and Victor kept eating, heads down, neither one of them looking up from their plates. Annie, at one point, poured Victor more milk, and as she done so, as she lifted the pitcher, I seen a small bouquet of roses that had been behind it, hidden from my view. Small roses, faded red, dull yellow, the tips of the loose petals brown with frostbite. They was the same that I seen on the bushes in the boss man's yard, the roses by the big white gateposts that, like the other flowers, I wasn't supposed to pick or touch.

"I don't know, it's so hard finding anybody that can work," Mr. Tatum complained to the candlelit room.

He took a sip of wine, then turned to Victor, asking him how school was going and if he had a girlfriend yet. "Fine," and "No," Victor said in that order.

"What's that, I can't hear you," Mr. Tatum said. As the night had gone on, he'd gotten louder, more direct. He seemed to rise and swell in his chair, like a slow-growing balloon, and he expected us, or at least Victor, to have grown with him.

"Elba ain't got no clothes," Annie cut in.

Mr. Tatum stopped, as if the words had hit him and was taking a moment to register full. His body still turned towards Victor, he rotated his head in our direction.

"You . . . we done took her and she had nothing with her, no clothes," she explained.

He looked at me, the dress and sweater I was wearing. Nothing moved, not even his glassy slit eyes, but you could tell the wheels was turning in his head, the tiny sprockets grinding away. Then he said, "Yeah, what she's wearing ain't right, it's kids' clothes." He cut his eyes a tad to Annie. "Take her to town tomorrow. Get her fixed up," he said.

He adjusted himself in his chair after a minute. Looking down the center of the table, he said, "Yeah, so tell me, how's a man supposed to get his field plowed?"

"Want more Jell-O?" Annie asked, quiet-like. "A lot left."

It was good, the food, what you call a balanced meal. Sliced oranges for dessert served on a separate plate. But the Jell-O, that was something special; and, as I was helping Annie with the dishes in the kitchen, I kept swiping at the extra helping she'd heaped on my plate. I kept my plate hidden behind a stack of pots as we sunk plates and glasses into the soapy water; hid, I say, but Annie had to see me swiping away at the plate with my fork. By the time the pots found their way into the sink, I was done eating.

"You're good at dishes," Annie said.

I felt proud of myself, all of a sudden a bit of relaxation come over me.

"I done lots of dishes," I said.

I thought she wanted to talk, but I guess she didn't. She handed me a towel to start drying. I'd dried maybe two plates, careful so as not to drop them since they was the "good plates," when Mr. Tatum appeared in the door.

"You let her finish," he said.

I thought he was talking to Annie, that he wanted Annie for something, but when I looked to her, I seen she was turning to see him. He was looking at me. He'd been talking to nobody but me. Then he nodded.

That's how it started.

I followed. Gone into his room, which Annie said not to, that it was off limits; but it must've been OK just then on account of how he nodded for me to follow him. Then he said, "Get up on the bed."

Which I thought he meant for me to sit on it, and I did. It was a high bed, two mattresses on a wood frame with a headboard, fancy like the big wood dinner table, and it was soft, springy when I sat down, my legs dangling over the sides. "Lie down," he said. I guess I didn't understand him and looked confused, for the next thing I knowed he was pushing me down, flat on my back, and arranging me like I was separate pieces of wood that he was going to build something with, assemble somehow. Put my hands out, away from my sides, spread my legs. Then he put a pillow under my head, the way I done for Clementine, and pulled off my underwear. Kneeling on the floor before me, looking where he was going with his finger, he started, gentle at first, just touching, then the fire, like his finger was molten iron. No doubt, I winced; I felt tears rolling down my face but I was quiet. He said not to worry, that he was going slow, and I, not knowing a thing, blurted out, "No, please go fast."

He kept about his business. His head was so close I could see the flecks of gray in his hair and the large pores in his flat wide nose. His eyes narrowed in concentration and the ball of his shoulder moved, rolled ever so slight under his white shirt, as he moved his hand on me. Once I turned my head to the door, for it was open, and in plain view was the front room and, beyond that, the kitchen table where the overgrown boy was still sitting. He'd been looking, watching, but he gazed down at the empty table when I seen him. I thought of things, counted Mr. Tatum's gray hair, counted the pores on his nose, anything to distract myself from the hurt, pass the time. I thought of the Jell-O, the sweet taste still in my mouth. That must've helped some; by that time the pain was less, or I was used to it. Truth is, he was finished, resting back on his haunches and looking back and forth from me to his hand, which I couldn't see.

"Annie," he called out. He stood up, holding his hand behind him, and looking down at me, still flat out on the bed, said, "You go with Annie; she knows what to do."

Annie come in and looked at me. "There's a mess," he said. "Hope it didn't soak through. Check." Then he gone out.

When Annie lifted me up, taking me by the wrists, I looked down and seen my blood smeared on my legs and in bright red spots on the bedspread.

Annie took me to the bathroom and filled the bathtub with warm water. She told me to get in and wait until she come back. "Wash yourself," she said. She closed the door behind her. I got in the tub. Felt good, except for the stinging. Afterwards, Annie come back with some nightclothes, far too big, must've been hers; and then I followed her to the sleeping porch, where, in the bright light, I seen Victor under the blankets on one of the cots, reading a book. He paid no attention to us. The cot on the other side of the room was made up with blankets and a pillow now too. And there was a makeshift bed—a sleeping bag and blankets—on the floor next to it, I thought for me. But Annie said for me to take the cot. "I like sleeping on the floor," she said, "reminds me of the old days."

Old days, I thought. Already they was here.

* * *

The next day we gone to town. Town meaning Ukiah, which was much smaller than Santa Rosa but bigger than Sebastopol. Annie drove. She drove good. We gone into a hardware store and bought a cot, which the man behind the counter said he would deliver. He wasn't particularly friendly, but he seemed to know Annie when she come in; and after she give him the cash, a dollar bill, he said, "You're from out Ledson's place, right?"

That was the first time I heard the boss man's name. I was yet to see him. Until then I'd forgot there was such a person.

Just like the man in the hardware store, the lady in the clothes shop at the other end of town knowed Annie. Funny, in Santa Rosa I never seen white people know which Indian you was. Like I said, none of these white folks was particularly friendly, but they knowed Annie, or seemed to. I guess they knowed her on account of how she'd been working for the Ledsons a long time. Again, Annie paid cash, a few bills this time, and I come out of there with half a dozen boxes. But it wasn't no kids' stuff. What a lady would wear, that's what Annie told the shop woman, and that's what I got: skirts, a nice dress with ruffles, a blouse, a coat, two pairs of shoes. And here I ain't ever had a new item of clothing in my life.

"For her?" the lady said, disbelieving, and Annie nodded yes. I'm surprised they found things to fit me.

Afterwards, we done something else. We gone to the grocery, where the two men behind the counter was familiar with Annie, too, and got ourselves each a sandwich made of sliced ham and Swiss cheese. Annie asked if I wanted a pickle. I said OK.

With our sandwiches we walked to the train depot, which was just kitty-corner from the grocery, and sat down on a bench where folks waited for the train. The bench was hard: It hurt sitting, like when the car bumped on the road. There wasn't no people around the depot. There was no train there neither. Annie stared out towards the tracks as if there was.

"I come on that train," she said, holding her half-eaten sandwich in a napkin on her lap.

"Yes?" I said.

"Up Covelo. That's where I'm from," she added.

I thought of asking her more questions, like who her people was, how she met Mr. Tatum, that stuff. But then I thought better of it. She was quiet, her face tilted up, taking in the early spring sun. Why bother her?

*　*　*

That afternoon, after we unpacked the boxes on the sleeping porch, where the new cot was already in place against the far wall, I met the boss man's wife, Mrs. Ledson. She was a blonde lady with a brood of unruly kids. She was cutting roses inside the picket fence. Them kids, about a half dozen of them, all seeming close in age, more or less waist high to her, was belly-aching and bickering amongst themselves all around her. Like the kids' faded overalls, the woman's housedress looked old and was food stained and smudged with dirt from the garden. Her hair, which she'd attempted at some point to pull back in a bun, fell here and there in a hundred loose pieces.

"Stop it. Stop it," she yelled as regular as a clock but to no avail. She was dropping the cut roses in a wicker basket, its lid flopping open, and when she seen us approach, she dropped her scissors into the basket and made her way past the griping kids and thorny bushes to the fences.

"This is Harold's niece," Annie said.

"So you're the poor young lady who needed clothes," the woman said. She looked me up and down, then added, "Well, you done picked out some real nice ones there."

I looked down at my new blue dress, felt the sleeves of my new sweater on my wrist. "Thank you," I said.

"You got a name, honey?" she asked.

"Elba," I told her.

"Well, that's pretty," she said. "What kind of name is that?"

I was about to answer, saying, I don't know, Mama give it to me, when she turned fast to Annie and said, "Sure you had enough money?"

Annie nodded.

"Tell me if it ain't, Annie. 'Cause even if things is tight, rock bottom, I'll come up with the money. I'll find it, if that's what Harold wants. It's the least I can do, honest." She glanced once at the kids behind her, then leaned over the fence, her basket wedged between her and the fence, and whispered, "So bad he ain't even got out of bed this morning. Whole place smells like a saloon."

She straightened, looked at me and talked as if I hadn't been standing right there a second before, as if I hadn't heard every word she whispered to Annie. "Honey, you do look nice," she said. She might as well have said the sun comes up in the east. Then she looked at Annie, and slowly turning back to her work and kids, she said, "Honest, tell me if you got enough . . . After all Harold has done here."

Annie nodded.

We started off, back across the dirt road. We was through our gate when she yelled after us. "Annie," she said, "you only took the frostbit blooms, right . . . There just ain't much out here," she complained.

"Yes," Annie answered in a voice that would hardly carry across the road.

"Oh, young lady, I'm Mrs. Ledson, by the way," she announced in a more cheerful voice.

Again, I thought of saying something—Nice to meet you—but before the words could roll off my tongue, she was bent over, busy cutting roses. "Stop it. Stop it," she was saying.

Funny, after that things didn't look the same to me, or maybe for the first time I seen them as they really was. The picture of Mrs. Ledson was one thing; or, rather, the two pictures of her, helped me put the whole picture together. From far away, she was a white lady, tall and straight; even up close she was that way, a boss lady, but up even closer you seen the clothes and hair, where the dirt and stains was. She'd tell Annie to pick only the frostbit roses, never anything fresh, and then whisper to Annie as if Annie was a sister. In the days ahead, I put things and people together on that place. There was a chain of command on the Ledson place and in her way she was at the top. She was concerned for my well-being—for all of us Indians, in fact—like we was a cow, or even one of their children, that her drinking husband was likely to neglect. She looked for things—me not having clothes, no fresh meat or eggs in the cold box—as proof she would have for him that he was a lazy, good-for-nothing so and so.

Ledson, who I didn't meet until later, looked just like her, except for the fact that he was bald and taller, his eyes usually red from drinking. He was henpecked endless. He took out his frustration on Mr. Tatum. One day, while fetching wood from the pile alongside the barn, I overheard Ledson inside complimenting Mr. Tatum on the good job he done cleaning the chicken coop, then complain that Mr. Tatum hadn't cleaned under the nests and in the corners. Which, then, is what I'd hear Mr. Tatum say to Annie about her housecleaning: "You missed places, dust here and there." It made me think of Mr. Tatum setting at the dinner table talking as if the fields that needed plowing was his own. But Mr. Tatum had a angle on things: He knowed the Ledsons' relationship and knowed how to present whatever it was he wanted or needed to Mrs. Ledson as if it was something Ledson again overlooked and that way, not only cause a fight between them, but in the long run get what he wanted.

I seen in Mr. Tatum's house where the dirt and stains was. The dust that, no matter how many times you wiped the cloth over the windowsills and in the corners, stayed or come back as quick as you turned around; the grime, a light film, like a fine layer of oil, that covered the windows, no matter how often you run the soapy water and towel over them; the toilet bowl and bathtub with their unscrubbable rings; even the furniture, the table and chairs, the way they always looked cockeyed, never square and in line with the room. And we was forever scrubbing and straightening things, as if, somehow, at the end of the day, things would be clean and in order. I say we, for my job was to do just what Annie done, what she showed me.

It wasn't just the inside of the house but the outside too. Paint chipped on the wallboards and shutters. Leaves littered the brick walkway; unruly plants, jasmine vines, and broken daffodil stalks, fell over it. The picket fence wobbled, sagged, leaned this way and that. "Stake it up over here, Annie," Mr. Tatum said the same way he told her about the dust she missed above the cold box or in one of the cupboards.

And, lest you think it was just Tatum's place, it was Ledson's too, the entire ranch, in fact. Yes, the Ledsons lived in a big house, but it was a shambles, the outside just a bigger version of Tatum's, a two-story version.

And the barn, which was at the end of the road, beyond the two houses, looked like an enormous accordion folded in on itself. White chickens, always loose from the wire pens, hopped and fluttered in and out of the holes and wide cracks. It was Depression times, sure; and no doubt, the Ledsons wasn't well off. Lots of places in the countryside was in bad shape, but that was usually on account of how they was abandoned, vacant. This place was lived in.

That night, before dinner, Annie cut my hair. I had scraggly bangs that was last cut before we left the Rancheria, when Clementine was still well. The back of my hair was halfway to my waist. She chopped it plumb off; trimmed the bangs and cut the rest just above the bottoms of my ears, flapper style. After dinner was cooked and everything set out on the table, she put me in my new dress, the dark green one with ruffles, and led me out in it. Mr. Tatum said nothing, and later I gone into the room with him.

* * *

He said he was waiting for my time. But once, on a warm night in June, when Annie drove Victor to town to watch a baseball game, Mr. Tatum jumped on me. Things was different from the start. First, no one was watching, the door open but no Victor at the table. Second, while Mr. Tatum was touching me, stabbing with three fingers now, he had his pants down and was pulling on himself with his other hand. He was kneeling on the floor, as usual; so where I was, spread out on the bed, head back on the pillow, I couldn't see the details but I knowed what he was doing. He worked furious, seeming as if he was torturing himself far worse than he done me. He was panting like a dog that run up a mountain and back. Sweat poured from his brow. Then, all at once, he jumped on me; in a heave of sweat and force he was on top of me, between my legs, but it was nothing but bone against bone, hips against hips. He pounded me and pounded me and still it was nothing but his limp groin, a beating with a soggy noodle.

"God damn it!" he shouted and slid to the floor again. "God damn it!" he yelled even louder and punched the side of the mattress. The bed shook and I felt the force of his fist, which was considerable. But there was no question he wasn't mad at me. He was mad at himself; at his man thing that didn't work, no matter how he held and tried to push the soft thing into me—which I knowed then was his problem.

* * *

My time come that November, Thanksgiving Day. Annie showed me how to take care of myself. She showed me where she kept clean cloths and such, which I pretty much knowed on account of how I hadn't done much else for the last six months, the entire summer, but hang around the house, inside and out, working and learning every nook and cranny. It was a nice time, my period, never mind the discomfort and blood. Mr. Tatum left me alone, didn't nod for me to follow him after dinner. Annie and me talked more than before, which, of course, hadn't been much; and she'd pick up the bulk of the work, telling me to take it easy: "You don't need to fold the clothes so fast now." "Don't lift that crate of milk bottles now." It was, in its small way, a special time. But I learned not to trust it. After all, Mr. Tatum would be waiting for me when it was over, as he'd told me since day one; something I hadn't experienced yet and no doubt wouldn't enjoy, something worse than what I knowed already. Wasn't it like that warm first ride in the rumble seat on my way here?

The day after Thanksgiving, as we was slicing the trimmings off the turkey for soup, Annie said to me, "In the old days folks didn't allow moonsick girls to work, touch the food."

"I know," I said, and I was about to tell her how things was still that way on the reservation, that Big Sarah and the others followed them rules now. But what was now? All of a sudden, standing at the sink counter, I had the same feeling I had when I looked at the far hills, when I passed the fields and ranch houses in the car on the way to town with Annie. I thought of home, of the reservation. I tried to imagine what folks was doing just then: Uncle McKinley and Elmer at the well, stopped and talking with their full metal buckets of water; Auntie Maria and Sipie hanging wash in the warm afternoon sun alongside Auntie Maria's house. Only it wasn't afternoon; it wasn't the same time of day it was now, outside the car window or on the far hills. It was night, as if the reservation was on the other side of the world, that far away, another time zone, like what the classroom teacher in Santa Rosa had taught us about time when she was teaching us about different countries. So now wasn't now there, and I found myself thinking somehow of that, telling myself that I made no sense. But, of course, by that time, whatever pictures I'd had in my mind was long gone. Old days. Older yet.

"Course, Mr. Tatum wouldn't stand for one of us taking time off like that," she said.

She carved. I piled the slivers of meat and skin on the plate. "Two wives and it seems just as much work," she added.

That struck me—the word "wives." Wife, that's what I was. That's what I been doing here, I thought. That's what I been learning. Marriage. I'd heard that in the old, old days, before the white man come in, men sometimes would have more than one wife. And they bought them from the families. Chum said that, when she was young, she knowed of a girl her age that got sold. She laughed, then said in the old, old days a woman might have lots of husbands too. I don't know. That's Chum. But, far as I know, I was the last girl, at least in these parts anyways, that somebody sold.

That day I said nothing back to Annie about what she said. When we finished with the meat, we started chopping vegetables, celery and onions, for the broth.

* * *

This is what happened. About a week after my period, Mr. Tatum nodded and I followed him into his bedroom. I'd had some time off; still it was just as if I'd done it the night before, same routine, which is why, as he was pulling down my underwear and spreading my legs, I didn't think anything was going to be different, even though in the back of my mind I knowed he always said it would be. Door open. Victor, head down, at the empty table. Him with his fingers in me. But then, all at once, he looked out the door, his head turned, and, calling Victor, said, "OK, now. Let's go."

Next thing I knowed Victor was standing alongside the bed.

"Take down your drawers," Mr. Tatum told him, and that's what the kid done. Then Mr. Tatum, still kneeling on the floor, took him by the hand and led him to me. He tripped on the jeans wrapped around his ankles, nearly toppled over on top of me, until he caught himself on the bed.

"Now let's see if you remember all I told you," Mr. Tatum said to him.

The flabby-bellied boy stood awhile looking down between my legs, where Mr. Tatum's hand was again. "Indian way . . . father teaches son," Mr. Tatum said, taking his hand away and moving aside.

Supporting himself with outstretched hands on either side of me, Victor lowered down. Gasping for air under the boy's fat chest, I was more worried about being smothered than anything else. Inside of me there wasn't much more than a little tickling.

But it worked. If not that night, then some night not too long after that. I was pregnant. A stick of a child with a seed pushed up her and growing; before long, I was swelled, a thin vine holding a plump grape. "Got to make her eat more, too damn skinny to carry that baby right," Mr. Tatum complained to Annie.

But complaining that I wasn't eating enough was the harshest thing he done them days, which wasn't really harsh at all, for Mr. Tatum turned nice like never before. After I first missed my time, which Annie told him about right away, causing him to raise his wineglass to me at the dinner table, he left me alone. No more nodding for me to follow him and then calling for Victor. Sometimes after that first night Victor got on top of me, if Victor was gone somewheres or too busy studying, Mr. Tatum done just like he done before my time—poking me with his fingers. But now, nothing. No doubt, he figured poking me there with his fingers might upset what was inside of me, which, all of a sudden, was the main concern in that house—the baby.

"Make sure she eats vegetables," he told Annie. "I done got red meat, now make sure she eats it."

One night when we was low on milk, when there was but one full glass left, which sat in front of Victor, Mr. Tatum commanded, "Give that milk to her," and Victor, never lifting his eyes, pushed the glass across the table.

Before, when I was on my time, Annie more or less snuck, covered for me, so I didn't have to work as fast or as hard. Now it was an order from Mr. Tatum himself: "Annie, make sure she don't lift something heavy. Don't let her stand too long."

Another thing, we started taking drives, visiting folks. The three of us: Mr. Tatum, dressed in his suit and tie, a Panama hat; Annie, behind in the rumble seat, two or three scarves secure around her head.

"You ride up front," Mr. Tatum told me the morning just before our first outing. "Can't have you bouncing around back there as pregnant as that."

True, I was a sight. It was July and I was well eight months along. And clothes—full dress, no matter what—done nothing to hide it. But that wasn't the only reason Mr. Tatum wanted me to ride up front with him, if it was any reason at all, as I would find out.

"My wife," he introduced me.

And always the same thing: "Jeez, you got two wives, Harold," whoever it was I was introduced to would say while looking back at Annie still sitting in the rumble seat.

"Old Indian way," Mr. Tatum said, beaming proudly. "If one wife ain't good, got to get yourself another."

And that's when I seen, after a few of these visits, what he was up to: He had people believing the baby on its way was his and not Victor's; simply put, that his thing wasn't broken. It made me wonder when Mr. Tatum started having his problem, how soon after Annie gave birth to Victor.

We gone to his relations' reservation, which, as it turned out, wasn't Yokayo, but a place just south of there, above the Russian River, with a view of the water. Picket's Hill, they called it, or just plain Picket Reservation. Despite his saying he had no relations, he had brothers, lots of family, and all of them said how they ain't seen him for so long.

"Was just in the area looking for workers when my pears is ready," he told them.

He always had a line for why we was stopping in. We also gone to a couple other places, Rancherias and work camps. Sometimes he said nothing more than, "I was just driving by." Them that knowed him good, like his brother, asked about his son, Victor.

"Busy studying," he told them. "Going to graduate from high school next year. Jesus," he'd mock-complain, "one grows up and here another's on the way."

He always told me to be polite. "Say hello and nod friendly," he told me, "and nothing else." Which I would do and stand there quiet while he chatted about crops and weather. Big as I was, my feet hurt, particularly if he rambled on for some time with folks. If anybody offered us water or invited us to come in out of the hot sun and sit down, he'd say no, that we had to get to wherever it was we was going—town, the next work camp, home.

When my feet hurt, and even when they didn't, when we was merely coming and going, driving through the dry summer countryside, I filled my mind with the sights. I'd been cooped up for so long, the rides was a treat, the standing there being polite and saying hello a small price to pay. Except for an occasional trip with Annie to the general store in Ukiah, I hadn't been off Ledson's ranch, never once past the cattle guard, or beyond the row of pear trees along the property line. At the Rancherias and reservations I looked for people I knowed. I'd see people who'd come to Big Sarah's preaching ceremonies when we was still on Benedict's Rancheria, but I didn't see any of my own people. For one thing, Mr. Tatum never traveled south; instead, he gone north and east, which no doubt had something to do with me not running into any relations. Except for picking hops and pears, which come in August and September, Waterplace folks seldom gone north. But at one of the work camps this side of Ukiah, I seen Uncle McKinley's nephew and a couple other young people from home. My heart jumped; but, as I was standing there with Mr. Tatum, who was talking to somebody, they passed right by me. Whether or not they recognized me I don't know.

* * *

The baby should've cried. Should've at least kicked. After what I gone through, it owed me that much.

I knowed that there was going to be trouble. Not that it was dead already, but that I wasn't doing so good. Two days' labor and I was twelve years old. If it was today, the doctors would've cut it out of me; if I was a horse, the farmer would've shot me. Of course by the time there was any talk of a doctor, the still thing was out of me, on a cookie tray below my cot, and already cold. Ledson was on the sleeping porch with Mr. Tatum, looking down at me.

Then Mrs. Ledson come in, and Annie pick up the cookie tray and left.

"Harold's niece done had a stillborn," Ledson said as if Mrs. Ledson hadn't seen what Annie carried out, and in no time the two of them was at it full blast.

"Walter Joseph Ledson, you drunk piece of shit," she hollered, "you work with this man and you didn't know the girl was in labor?"

"Harold never told me," Ledson answered, "he just come for me." But no matter what he said, he couldn't calm her. She was spitting nails.

I couldn't talk; I didn't have the strength to form words, let alone say them. But what would I have said anyways? I watched Mr. Tatum dodge the fight, yet saying just enough, or nothing at all, so that he would benefit from it without Ledson or his wife catching on. Which is what happened. "Harold, next time come directly to me," Mrs. Ledson said before leaving, "and come by in the morning so I can give you money for funeral costs. I'll scrape the pot again. Use my savings."

Mr. Tatum never said a thing to me. I healed. A month later, they was back at it, Mr. Tatum and Victor. I wondered about the baby. Girl or boy? What happened to it? Funeral? The river, no doubt. At least that's what I liked to think—twiddling its tiny thumbs and smiling up at the summer sun, floating forever south.

* * *

Right away, I was pregnant again, and by the time I was showing good, the early part of that next March, a month after my thirteenth birthday, we was sloshing through potholes, over mud and water-slicked roads to visit folks again. This time he said he was checking if folks survived the rains OK, if this bridge or that fence line got washed out in the last flood.

"Jesus, Harold, awfully quick, ain't it?" folks said, seeing me, the men giving Harold a wink. "I know you was sad losing the last, but Jesus . . ."

And that time it happened the same way: stillborn. The next time, which was after a miscarriage, Mr. Tatum gone for a doctor right away, with the first pains, no doubt to see if the doctor could save the baby, but also to keep Mrs. Ledson happy, who blamed him straight out for what happened to the first two. So the doctor come and the baby spit and screamed fury. And it stayed that way, hollering to high heaven, fussing and fighting, as if it was mad the doctor saved its life, slapped its ass and made it to breathe, as if that was some mean trick and no part of its own desire. It was a girl, and what the doctor didn't see until he come back a week later, when she was screaming to shake the house, her body burning with the fever that took her twenty minutes after he come into the sleeping porch, was that she was born with pneumonia. Annie was her name, after the one that pulled her and the others out.

Next, another miscarriage. Then the fourth one. Another girl. Annie, again. Every precaution: the doctor, clean towels and bedding, fresh
goat milk in addition to my own. Declared healthy, no sickness, no cold.
Then, at one month, as quiet and calm as she had been, she died. Pneumonia, the doctor proclaimed. But what signs?

Mr. Tatum wasn't so easygoing about things this time. When he
picked up the dead baby, like he done the others, to take them to
wherever—the river—he had a scowl on his face.

"Almost made it this time. Next time you will," he said, as if to
make me feel all right. But I knowed he was none too happy.

The house growed quiet in the days ahead. The silence made each
and every one of us more aware that the baby was gone than its crying had
let us know that it was there.

"Elba," Annie said, one day while we was folding clothes on the
kitchen sink, "maybe the next one you shouldn't name after me." She looked
out the window to the pear trees. "Maybe that's it. The babies take on my
bad luck."

"Ok," I told her, "but you ain't bad luck."

"Oh, yes I am," she said and turned her head a notch, enough to
let me know she didn't want to talk about it anymore.

Funny, shortly after I arrived at Ledson's, I'd sometimes think of
Clementine and Old Uncle and get mad; at Clementine for dying, and at
Old Uncle for taking off. Mostly at Clementine, since I hardly knowed Old
Uncle, and if Clementine hadn't died, I wouldn't be here. But now when I
thought of them, specifically when I thought of Clementine, I only worried
that I'd inherited her bad luck.

* * *

For the month that last baby was alive, Mr. Tatum didn't touch me.
Neither him nor Victor. Nothing. Not for a month after either, maybe
longer. But I knowed the peace wouldn't last. The baby's silence was shrinking into corners, pushed there by Mr. Tatum's voice returning to its normal
pitch. Again, sounds returned to the kitchen, the hissing of meat frying, the
clanking of dishes in the sink. At the dinner table, the butter dish sounded
as it slid across the wood, milk and water splashed into glasses from the
pitchers. Mr. Tatum talked endless about this and that on the ranch, the
orchards, the condition of the fences, to Victor, who was twenty-one and
still as soft-faced as a ten-year-old. No doubt, Mr. Tatum's room would fill
with its familiar sounds too. Besides, it was December, in no time it would
be summer again, a mere six or seven months, and wouldn't Mr. Tatum want
me big again, when the roads was dry and it was easy to visit folks?

One day about this time I gone to the barn to fetch wood. I didn't carry it, but loaded it into a wheelbarrow, which I pushed back to the house. I was filling the wheelbarrow, lifting one log at a time, taking it easy still the way Annie told me, when the sky let loose so fast you'd think the clouds had a zipper the Creator just yanked open.

I was soaking wet by the time I got back to the house. Which caused me to go tearing into the bathroom for a towel. Why I didn't dry myself at the kitchen sink I have no idea. Maybe I was thinking of changing my clothes on account of how I was so wet. And why I didn't knock on the door, since it was closed, I can't tell you neither. When I pushed open the door, I found Annie in front of me without a stitch on, just out of the bathtub and drying herself. Which wasn't so strange or unusual. Nonetheless, I was shocked, not because I hadn't seen her naked before, but because I hadn't seen her hair. It was beautiful, even as it was wet, a glistening mane to her waist; and when she turned, wide-eyed in surprise, and faced me, I seen she was no more than twenty-five years old. Square body, broad nose, yes; but she was a girl not a whole lot older than me.

"Get out!" she hissed, covering the front of her with the towel.

It wasn't the response I expected. Again, I was shocked. Forgetting the fact that I had barged in on her, I felt she had just shared something special with me—something we now shared with each other. I felt tender, as if I might hug her, and now she was pushing me away.

"Get out!" she snapped again.

I swallowed hard. "There's dust on the bookshelf," I snarled, and then left, slamming the door behind me.

* * *

Safe that night. The next morning Annie made some excuse for me and her going to town. I say made some excuse, for she told Mr. Tatum we was low on flour when the bin was half full.

"You're going to go just like that, just a sweater?" she said, seeing me in the kitchen doorway ready to go. "It's pouring rain, fool; go put on your coat."

She'd never talked to me like that, harsh and calling me a name. I figured she was still upset about my abrupt intrusion the day before. Mr. Tatum, who was at the table, looked up from his coffee and newspaper. "Yeah," he agreed, "what's wrong with you?"

So I wrapped up in my heavy overcoat and met Annie outside, waiting in the car. Indeed, it was raining, an unzipped downpour still. It was tough going, the windshield wipers hardly keeping up against the storm, the road flooded here and there. Annie didn't blink; clutching the wheel with both hands, she drove on.

And not to the general store.

She parked a block from the train depot, the car facing the train, the boxcars and caboose. She glanced up the street to the depot, where the conductor and a few others huddled out of the rain under the small covered platform. Then she looked back to the boxcars in front of us. The doors on a couple of the boxcars was open. The train was pointed south. I knowed she was getting rid of me; until she spoke, I thought it was on account of how I'd been mean to her.

She said, "You been through enough already; I can't stand to see it no more."

My heart turned over and flooded. I said what made no sense. "You're so pretty without the scarves."

She looked at me, then back at the train. "Nobody can see me, but I can watch them," she told me. Then she give out a small sad chuckle and said, "Old Indian trick. It's all I got."

"Come with me," I blurted out.

She said nothing.

Then I said, "Take care of your son." Again, I wasn't thinking, not putting two and two together with what I knowed.

"Ain't my son," she corrected me. She looked back down to the depot. Seeing the conductor still busy talking, she said, "Victor come with his last wife, or so he says. Claims she died. Who knows? . . . Mr. Tatum used to have some Indian from San Francisco come up here to . . . before that kid, Victor, was ready. But it didn't work. I can't have kids, I guess. Tatum was stuck with me."

"Come with me," I blurted out again.

"Button up your coat," she told me. "The second stop is Santa Rosa."

After the conductor mounted the train, when he disappeared inside the engine room and the whistle blowed and the brakes hissed loose, Annie said, "Now, Elba," and I bolted free, through the pouring rain, and climbed aboard.

FOUR

The second stop. Santa Rosa. I hopped down. The train station at the bottom of Fourth Street. East up the street, Benedict's. Over to Third Street and from there west to Sebastopol Road, the reservation. Home? I had to think a minute, get my bearings, let my head sit on my heart. The rain let up, a harmless drizzle, and I walked.

The reservation hadn't changed a bit. A couple more cars, old heaps, that's all. Wasn't much different from when I arrived, or when I left. Winter: cold ground and naked trees. Just before I left, when Clementine was sick, the apple trees was blooming in the surrounding orchards; but I never seen a full spring, a summer or fall.

Reginald, still spying out his window, no doubt was the first to see me come up the road, for all intents and purposes a stranger. I'd left a long-haired little girl, come back a woman. Except for Reginald's curtain that quickly closed and the smoke rising from stovepipes, there wasn't a sign of life. Nobody outside, the well vacant. Clementine's shack was gone; in its place, a good growth of weeds and a couple free-growing redwood saplings. I looked around. Cold and gray. Some of the places had been painted a dull white, which was already cracked and peeling. Auntie Maria's place was painted and next to it a good stack of cut firewood. The sheets over her two windows was pulled tight. I turned, headed for "the rat's," where, I remembered, Ida lived.

To my surprise it was Zelda who opened the door. To her surprise, too, for she jumped back, sure she had seen a ghost.

"Elba," she said, collecting herself, running her hand over her dress.

"Who is it?" someone called from behind her.

She looked over her shoulder and answered slow so the person would make no mistake about what she said. "It's Elba. Yes, Cousin Elba," she finished, then slowly wound her head back to me. Her face had gone pale.

"Jesus," I said. "I ain't going to bite you."

Realizing I'd been standing there for some time, she remembered her manners and stepped aside, inviting me inside.

Once inside the place, it didn't take long to see why she might've been hesitating. It was tiny, one room, the walls patched haphazardly with tar paper and cardboard; and the ceiling, made from tin scraps and redwood bark, was so low that even us short Indian girls had to duck our heads. But hanging from the walls and the roof beams was fancy clothes like I never seen: blouses of all colors with big buttons, skirts pleated and slit up the side; and not just that, but undergarments, some white and some black, with lacy trim and fancy hooks and snaps. Pairs of high-heeled shoes sat neat in a row on the floor against the back wall, besides a sleeping bag and blankets spread out there.

"You can see why they called him the rat," a voice said.

When I looked up I seen it was Ida come out from behind one of the hanging dresses. She looked tired, haggard, her short hair messed up; hugging an old bathrobe to her fat body, she didn't look anything like a person who would wear the clothes around her.

"Made of scraps the way a rat builds a nest," she added.

Of course she was talking about the walls and the roof; maybe she even thought that's what I was looking at, but I don't know how. What with them clothes and the stench of perfume and whiskey, the place was a brothel. I didn't know to call it that then, what exact word to use, but I knowed nonetheless what was going on. If it wasn't the actual brothel, it was at least the dressing room for such. Point is, I knowed what lived there; and I wouldn't have had to know what I did about Ida before I left the reservation to figure it out.

"I thought they called him 'the rat' on account of the way he disappeared, scurried off after we come here." I was trying to be polite, keep my eyes in my head.

"Well, maybe so," Ida said. Then she looked over to Zelda, now biting one of her fingernails, just the way she done when she was a kid. Zelda give her a quick glance, finger still in her mouth, then looked back down to the floor.

"Gee, Elba, sit down," Ida said, looking back at me. "Us girls, we ain't got much here in terms of furnishings."

She gestured to the floor, where there was more unrolled sleeping bags and blankets strewn about. She sat down, center of the room, balling up a blanket to make herself comfortable, and I followed her lead. Zelda sat next to her.

But it wasn't just Ida and Zelda. There was another girl there, sitting in the shadows against the back wall. How did I miss her before? Too busy looking at the high-heeled shoes, I guess; the girl was sitting on the other side of the sleeping bag there.

"Hi," she said, seeing me see her.

"That's Joy," Ida said.

"Hi," I said.

"That's Elba," Ida said, "our cousin."

"Hi," the girl said again.

She was light-skinned and tall, which I could tell even as she was sitting; pretty, thin lips, a straight nose, long fingers curled around her bent knees.

"Not from around here," Ida said, as if answering the questions running through my mind concerning the girl. "Paiute, from over Nevada."

I nodded, though I'd never heard of Paiute.

Ida looked to Zelda, who looked at Joy, then back to Ida. Nobody knowed what to say next. I figured they was nervous, wondering what was on my mind, and whether or not I was judging them lowly and sinners on account of what was before my eyes. None of them was good at idle conversation. Minutes gone by and not a word. It was up to me to break the ice.

"Done had four babies. All died," I told them.

I waited a couple seconds, testing the water with what I said, then talked nonstop damn near half an hour, telling them the whole story of what become of me since I left. I minced no words. I told them the details of my life on the bed with Mr. Tatum and Victor.

I talked not to shock them, or to fill the silent room with words. I just wanted to let them know that nothing they done would shock me, that I was no one to judge. If anything, I was one of them, lost, a sinner. Which, without thinking about it, I must've believed.

"Gee," I said, "when my time come, I followed no rules. Cooked and cleaned like any other time of the month," I said. "Who's going to worry about that when you knowed soon as it was over some old man's going to be sticking his fingers up you and some fat kid jumping on you."

They was quiet, shock on their faces as I gone on with my story. When Zelda was a kid and the wits was scared out of her, her whole hand would be jammed into her mouth, not just a finger or two, but the entire fist, so you'd think she was reaching for something at the back of her throat, which is how she was just now. I pulled back a bit then, gone from talking about sex and dead babies to chores and rides in the car. I seen Joy and Ida drop their shoulders, like they done finally let out a breath. Zelda, she let her hand slip forward, her fingertips locked now between her teeth.

"Jesus," I said, "Chum used to talk about sex being fun. Hell, I ain't seen no fun in it—or money," I added, remembering my purpose of putting them at ease about themselves.

When I finished talking, they was looking at me, all three of them, as if they was not only still processing all that they heard but waiting to see if I was going to say any more. Then, when I seen Ida pull the small glass flask from her robe pocket, I realized I hadn't been talking for them as much as I had been talking for myself. I was cold. I was hungry. I needed a place to stay.

"Nip?" Ida said, offering me the flask, and I took it, thankful.

* * *

Whiskey. Zelda was right. Burns going down, feels good later. I had me a few nips that afternoon; and, with no food in my stomach, I learned of its charm—hollow sleep. Sleep as black and hollow as the inside of a closed empty drawer. Of course, the next morning, when I finally woke, I was retching on an empty stomach, and, God knows, nothing's worse.

"Here, here," Ida was saying, pulling me from under the armpits out of a sleeping bag. Guess she didn't want me messing up things, but, like I said, my stomach was empty, dry heaves.

"Gee," I said, "how long did I sleep?"

"You was tired," Ida said.

I remembered feeling sleepy—it had been a long day and a long walk, after all—and I remembered getting in the sleeping bag Ida fixed for me, and that felt so good . . .

"You need to eat," Ida said.

On the one-burner woodstove she fried eggs and boiled water for coffee. Coffee, something I wasn't used to having. Mr. Tatum was the only one who drunk it at Ledson's. But I got used to it. Eggs and coffee, part of the routine, and from that point on I was part of it.

The clothes. Getting me into them fancy things was something else. Remember, I had nothing but what was on my back: plain shoes and socks, housedress, sweater, and overcoat. But it was more than need that got me to put them things on. When the girls offered their clothes, when Zelda showed me one of her dresses and Joy handed me a silk-soft blouse, saying she could take up the sleeves, I wasn't just saying yes and thank you to the clothes but to them.

It was about noon, after a couple cups of coffee, that they started in on me. Took off my clothes down to my underwear.

"Eeee! That's old-lady stuff," Zelda shrieked.

And with that they stripped me naked.

I was a model, like the dummies in store windows, and they kept matching clothes to me, skirts and sweaters, blouses; and then once they decided on which items, I held still, sometimes tried the clothes on, while they pinned them here and there to fit me. I never before paid so close attention to my body, what I was made of. I hadn't been conscious of myself. When Mr. Tatum and Victor seen me I was but a kid, and by the time I was growed, them looking at me was as regular as me tying my shoes. Now I was in the light of two lamps for all the world to see. And it didn't help the way they pointed to certain features, like I was a horse they was inspecting.

"Gee," Ida said, looking at my stomach, "you sure done had some kids." The stretch marks there was like wide veins of marble or quartz across the top of a big rock.

Ida must've seen me gasp, for she changed the subject, as if to take my mind off my stomach. "Gee," she said, "I got pregnant a couple times myself. Used jimson weed to get rid of them, though."

"That can kill you," Zelda warned, taking a skirt from Ida, who, finished hemming, got up off her knees.

"Yeah, better to watch your calendar. We'll teach you about that too," she said to me. Then she looked over to Joy and ordered, "Hey, bring me that blouse in the corner."

No doubt about it, Ida was the boss. The others took their lead from her.

When she turned back to me, her eyes fell on my breasts. "You're so loose, fallen for a young girl," she said. Which I didn't think was anything to be ashamed of, until she added, "But a good bra will push them up."

She said it to make me feel better, seeing again how she slipped. And again, she must've known I still didn't feel so good about what she said, for she offered, "Your hair's cut fine."

"Yeah," Joy said, as if knowing to support Ida.

Joy held the blouse to my back, Ida now marking and pinning the shoulders.

"No time at all you'll be a real swinger," Ida said, pins in her teeth.

"Shoot," Zelda said from the corner of the room where she had squatted with needle and thread for my new skirt. "Mary Hatcher will probably come and find her before she comes and finds any of us."

"Who's Mary Hatcher?" I asked, folding my arms over my chest.

"Hold still," Ida complained.

"You ain't heard of Mary Hatcher?" Joy asked, surprised. "You can't be in this business long and not know about Mary Hatcher."

"Not in these parts, anyways," Ida said, pins in her teeth still.

"Not in any parts," Joy argued. "Hell, she's famous throughout the west. They tell stories about her everywhere—far away as Nevada, where I'm from."

"You know who she is?" Zelda asked, asking the question that was forefront on my mind. "She's our cousin. She's Nellie's sister."

My mind flipped, switched books so to speak. I seen Nellie, eleven years old, leaving Chum's funeral on that horrible rainy day in her father's relatives' car. Then I remembered that Chum had had an older daughter, a girl who, last I'd heard, lived up north someplace with her father.

"Chum's older girl?" I asked to make sure I had things right.

"Yeah," said Zelda before pausing, taking a breath. Then she let out with the story about how Chum had had a baby when she was young, about fourteen, from a man up north or from Lake County, Zelda didn't know which, who Chum had met while folks was cutting grapes someplace one fall. It was a girl, and she give it up. That much I knowed, but then she went on to say that folks here said the girl was poison on account of how her father's people was that way. But not when the girl was a baby; Chum give her up when she was seven or eight years old. It must've been tough on Chum and the little girl.

I couldn't imagine Chum giving up her kid, not without a fight, no matter what the situation was.

"Anyway, she's famous now," Zelda said, picking up the story where she had first started it. She told how this Mary Hatcher drove in a fancy car, a big new Packard, black opal; she didn't drive—a chauffeur drove her while she sat back in the finest clothes and jewelry you could imagine, silks and diamonds a white woman couldn't afford. Both whites and Indians was afraid of her. She was beautiful. "And she's our cousin!" Zelda said as if to finish the story.

"Which is why we got a chance," Ida said.

"A chance at what?" I asked.

"She comes into the work camps and other places where the men is," Zelda explained. "If she sees girls there, she takes them to live high and mighty with her . . . I heard she don't take Indians, only whites; but that can't be right on account of how she's Indian herself."

"That's right," Joy said, her and Ida fussing now with the blouse they had draped across my back. "Why do you think I come all the way from Nevada? . . . I hope to get discovered. She's in these parts."

"Yeah," Zelda said, "somewhere outside of Healdsburg, but only a few actually knows where her place is."

"You ever seen her?" I asked all of them.

"Seen her car once," Ida answered.

"She's a madam," Zelda said, and then proceeded to tell me how the madam is the boss of a whole house.

"What about Nellie?" I asked. "Ain't she with the people right down the road here, outside of Sebastopol, them Lagoon people?"

"Yeah. Seen her a few times in the crops."

"Really," I said, excited. "How is she?"

"Quiet, plain. She, you know, sings songs and stuff." Zelda's voice was flat, disinterested.

"You're going to look real pretty," Joy said from behind me.

All of a sudden, I remembered that I was naked. I uncrossed my arms, looked down at my breasts and stomach, then crossed my arms again. How could I ever live high and mighty, I thought.

Joy come around in front of me with the blouse. She held it up in front of me for my approval and said, "Looks good on you, honey."

I hadn't seen her in the direct light before. Her eyes was as blue as the sky.

Got to admit, I looked pretty good in them clothes, a complete makeover from the girl that walked up the road in the cold and gray, anyways. Throwed on a little powder and a dash of lipstick and I looked like somebody new. No movie star, mind you; but Ida and Zelda had nothing on me. The only one with a figure to write home about was Joy: tall; full breasts; then again, with her long arms and legs and light skin, she didn't look like an Indian. But, if you looked close, beyond the first impression of her loveliness, you seen scars, from boiling water she said, on her forearms and the backs of her calves. "Mary Hatcher won't care none," she said one day after she caught me looking at her scars. "After all, a man don't look in those places."

When I first walked out in them clothes, which was a couple days after I got there, the sun was out. Bright as a July day is long, and do you think anybody recognized me? Folks was all about, taking advantage of the clear weather to get things done: chop wood, patch their leaky roofs. Maybe I should've worn my plain clothes to reacquaint myself. Folks walked right past me—Bertha, Uncle McKinley and Marcellena, kids I knowed. My plain clothes was dirty on account of that filthy boxcar and the long walk home. Maybe I just should've worn my heavy coat over my new getup. What did people think, I was just another stray, like Joy, that Ida and Zelda dragged home from wherever, that work camp just down the road? Of course, if they took the time to look, they'd no doubt do just what they done when they did find out who I was in the hours and days ahead—keep walking.

At the well, when I said hi to Sipie, who looked no different from when I left, only a little older, Auntie Maria, fetching water next to her, had no trouble seeing who I was. She looked me straight in the face, then sighed with disgust, picked up her water buckets, and starting off, with Sipie trailing behind, said, "He sure knowed what he was getting, didn't he?"

Like I said, what difference would it have made with whatever I was wearing? I picked up my water bucket and headed back to the rat's. Somehow, Auntie Maria didn't bother me. What was different about her for me? Now her—and anybody else—had themselves a clear-cut reason for not liking me, a reason I could see as easy as them and not have to think about. Whether it was real or not, now or later, just having it made things easier than before.

Just as folks heard the news of my return, learned who I was with, whatever stories Auntie Maria or anybody else passed around, so I caught up on what I had missed. Nothing much had happened with Sipie, which you could tell by looking at her. Twenty years old and following her fat-as-ever mother back and forth to the well and to listen to Big Sarah still preaching in the roundhouse every night about the evils of white people and Indians like me. One of Reginald's two daughters, the youngest one, had run away with a Filipino, folks said, to Los Angeles. How she ever got more than five feet away from her gun-toting father to meet a man is beyond me. What happened, he whistled from the bushes, and she run? Like Sipie, the older sister hadn't changed at all; still hauling water and chopping wood with her head down, never looking up at anyone, just what her father wanted. The big news was Elmer Bill, Bertha's brother. He was still chief, appointed by Big Sarah and still doing all her bidding for her, but he had married, taken a wife who was none other than Ofelia, Clementine's daughter.

She'd left whatever husband she had in Sacramento and come back to Benedict's Rancheria, looking for her people, only to find everybody gone and have Old Man Benedict give her directions to the reservation west of Sebastopol. Maybe she had no intention of staying, but when she found her mother had died, she figured the bad luck that had run through her entire family had also died, and that the reservation was now as good or bad as any other place to live. Maybe Elmer, taking an interest in her, convinced her of these things. Maybe she was desperate and didn't care; finding Elmer single and as well situated as any man on the reservation, with a car and a house, she planted herself on his doorstep. I don't know. She never talked to me then.

I would bet on the hard-luck story, desperation. Not because Elmer was a good fifteen years older than her, nearly fifty, or because of her clothes, which, except for the obviously new dresses and sweaters, was old and patched, but because of the way she carried herself, slumped and heavy. She was in her early or mid-thirties, not a gray hair on her head, heavyset, yes, but she moved as if she was eighty. Small careful steps and looking up every now and then as she was coming from her house to the well, empty buckets in hands, as if she was negotiating a hundred-mile trail she figured she'd never see the end of.

And here she was pregnant with the first of the two girls she'd have, Mona and Lena.

I watched her go about the routine of things: standing in line with Elmer when the bureau agent come—yes, he was still handing out so-called leftovers from his trunk; hauling water, chatting with Bertha and Uncle McKinley's wife, Marcellena, at the well; getting in and out of the car with Elmer. One day, after I'd watched her for a while, I found myself alone with her at the well. I introduced myself, just telling her my name, figuring she'd know who I was, that I lived with her mother and had taken care of her before she died. She looked me up and down. "Oh," she said, acting surprised. "Hi." Then she turned and left with empty buckets.

* * *

The routine of things. The tribe had theirs, us girls had ours. Some of the men had found off-and-on jobs on some of the nearby farms and orchards. Elmer and Uncle McKinley wasn't skinning horses in Santa Rosa no more. Elmer was milking cows on a dairy just across the Sebastopol bridge, above the lagoon, where a pear orchard was ripped out for pasture. Uncle McKinley was cleaning dirty coops and polishing eggs white on a chicken farm. Marcellena, she cleaned house and washed and folded clothes for the chicken farmer's wife once a week. So there was a little more money than before, enough food. Though the congregation seemed to have shrunk some, a few people staying in their houses at night, folks still made their way up the path at night to the roundhouse. Women gossiped by the well. Life gone on.

The routine of things: us girls. Life was harder in the rat's place: no bathtub, no running water or electricity, no stove with four burners and two ovens—none of the conveniences I'd gotten acquainted with and used to at Mr. Tatum's. All four of us cramped in that one room full of hanging clothes. Eating off plates kept with the few pieces of silverware in an apple crate stashed behind the tiny stove. But we made ourselves elegant, big city-like, clearing a space in the center of the room, moving whatever dress or blouse was hanging overhead, pushing aside the sleeping bags and blankets on the floor, and setting up our flimsy card table with plates and silverware so we could sit at noon in our robes eating eggs and toast and drinking coffee. And, in the evenings, about five or six, when we was finally washed and dressed, clothes and faces shining, we sat again, crossed our legs, and ate beans or rice like it was filet mignon, sipping at the whiskey or wine we poured into small glasses before we'd started cooking. If it wasn't for having to take my turn fetching water, I might not have seen the light of day at all.

We gone out at night. Yes, to the very same work camp Zelda took me to before I left. She progressed in her habits there, chose her habits over whatever warnings her mother give her, and found herself living with Ida. I never asked the details. The camp had changed a lot; not the buildings, but the people. Not so many white men; in fact, just a few and they was the poorer of the lot. Mostly Mexicans and Filipinos. A lot of Filipinos, Pinoys we called them; and, like Zelda told me, they was the nicest for the most part, treated us women the best, kindest. They was something like Indians, but oftentimes smaller in frame, slighter bodies, straight, straight hair, and eyes more like a Chinaman's. But what dandies they was: pinstriped suits and Panama hats, silver watch chains and corncob pipes. They'd dress so you'd think they was millionaires, a different suit on every time you seen them, when, truth be told, what they was doing was swapping clothes, helping each other impress the ladies. Could be in the middle of a dusty—and bloody—cockfight and they'd keep themselves clean.

Which was what was going on the first night I gone back to that camp with the girls. Yes, walked in our fancy clothes down that main road near as far as Sebastopol. At least them girls figured to walk in flat shoes and carry their high heels in their purses until they got to the edge of the camp. That was, I soon learned, the routine: Walk to the camp and have one of the men, usually a Pinoy, give us a ride home, which was good because by that time, two or three in the morning, we was tired and drunk. Sometimes we didn't get a ride, slept there, passed out in one of the shacks.

That first night back I seen a cloud of dust lit dirty orange by a huge bonfire, and a mob of men was whooping and hollering there. About thirty or forty of them, silhouettes, arms waving. As we got closer, I seen they was in a loose circle, but I couldn't see what was in the circle, what it was that excited them so.

"Cockfight," Zelda said.

"Honey, ain't you seen a cockfight before?" Joy asked, seeing my questioning face. "Where you been?"

We stopped alongside a shack, not far from the mob, with a good

WATERMELON NIGHTS

view. I seen the pitiful birds flopping around, a tangle of wings, killing each other. Two or three fights, one after the other, ongoing entertainment for the men, who quieted long enough to settle bets from the last fight and make them for the next. Men come with the unsuspecting birds clasped in their hands and tossed them into the ring; they took them out, winner and loser both limp, weak; tossed the loser, and sometimes the winner also, to the dogs waiting at the edge of the fire.

"It's awful," I said.

"Exciting," Joy said.

"Should give us them roosters for soup," Zelda said.

"Yeah, and you're gonna carry them bloody things home and pluck them," Ida snapped. "We ain't that hungry."

Ida quickly turned her gaze back to the men, her eyes scrutinizing each of them, fixing on one man at a time. Later, I'd understand this as part of her job—surveying the scene, so to speak. She was our boss lady, the madam and pimp.

Closer to the fire now, I could see the men in the light; no longer silhouettes, but distinct sizes and shapes, colors—whites, Mexicans, Filipinos. I could see the silver watch chains on the Filipinos' suits glint in the firelight, the colors of the scarves folded neatly in their coat pockets. The Mexicans wore hats, not Panama hats like the Pinoys, but straw hats, western style, and sombreros; many of them had thick mustaches twisted up to a point on the ends. The few white men was like the ones I seen before: ragamuffins.

A Pinoy, as dandy as can be, come up to Ida and handed her a three-quarters-full quart bottle of whiskey. She took a swig, gulped heavy, and handed the bottle to Joy, who was standing next to her.

"This is Sal," she said, introducing the man to me.

"Hi, honey," Joy said after taking a swig and handing the bottle to me. Obviously, she knowed him.

I nipped and give the bottle to Zelda. The whole place smelled like whiskey, damp with it. I pulled my coat tighter and looked around. Men was paying up each other after the last fight. Two women—white women—dressed like us stood in front of a shack at the other end of the camp. They had their hands in their coat pockets, too, hugging the coats close to their bodies. A couple men was talking to them and I could see they was all passing a bottle amongst themselves. In fact, as I looked around, I seen bottles everywhere; never seen so much liquor out in the open in my entire life. I said something to this effect to Zelda and she started laughing.

"What, didn't you know Prohibition's been over nearly six years now—nineteen thirty-three?"

"No," I said, which I shouldn't have said, for everybody turned to me, amazed by my ignorance. "I been away," I reminded them.

"Where, the North Pole?" Zelda cracked.

Then Joy said, "That's what it is, honey; you ain't been around things." You'd think she was a doctor and had just discovered the nature of my illness.

Ida kept talking to the Pinoy man, whose face and oiled-back hair shined in the firelight. The bottle kept going around, hand to hand. I'd had a drink at home, before we started on the road, and felt a little high, but, before long, I was feeling warm and downright tipsy. I didn't care that I'd been on the North Pole. I laughed out loud.

"Now what?" Zelda asked as if I was complaining or saying something dumb again instead of laughing.

"She's drunk," Ida said, then turned back to the Pinoy, Sal.

Not long after, a few of Sal's friends, finished with their cockfighting business, come over and started talking with Sal and Ida. A minute later, Ida was pairing us up.

"You go here, with this guy," Ida said, taking me by the arm and pushing me in the direction of one of the men, and as I swung past her, she said, "And, remember, get the dollar first."

* * *

It was easy. Easier than with Mr. Tatum and Victor. Little, if any, poking with their fingers, fast, and then it was over. Easier yet on account of the whiskey: hollow sleep with my eyes open. That first man, I think he was a Pinoy, but I couldn't tell you for sure. I think we gone into one of the shacks, which was the normal course of things; usually a shack, sometimes a car, the bushes if the man didn't have anyplace else. Can't remember most of them, certainly not their names.

We give our money to Ida, who'd chew us out if she seen us go with a man and not come back with a dollar. Which is why she let us get drunk just enough but not too much. "Meantime, get that dollar first." The men was usually good about paying, on account of how Sal and a couple of the others would beat them up if they didn't or if there was any kind of problem. Ida give Sal a good hunk of money and a shopping list of our needs—food, coffee, booze, sewing thread—and he'd drop the bags of stuff off with us at the bottom of the reservation, Monday nights after work, late. Things gone smooth as far as I could tell.

* * *

Until Del.

He come out of the crowd of men. He come out of nowheres and stayed. Sat on the cot in that smelly shack and held out a dollar.

"Again?" I asked, getting to my feet and straightening my dress. "A second time?" I repeated.

But he said nothing. Sat with that dollar held out, the lamplight flickering on his hand and face.

I hadn't had a whole lot to drink yet that night. It was early on. I had my full wits about me. I could see him clearly. He was small, dark, a Pinoy. He'd fastened his pants, and from where I was standing next to the cot, he looked like a doll, or a ceramic sculpture: a perfect picture, suit and tie, neatly cut and oiled hair, his black eyebrows and lashes, even his lips, looking as if they'd been painted on his smooth face. It all struck me funny.

"What?" I asked with a hard-hearted voice.

He looked a moment longer, then gently set the dollar bill on the cot. Then he got up and disappeared, left. I'd heard of tips, what rich men give their girls if they're especially satisfied. Looking at the crisp bill, I tried to remember what we'd done, anything particular. I couldn't think of anything.

The next night he come up to us first thing. He come up with Sal, who, as it turned out, usually arranged things with Ida, like who got matched up with who. Ida nodded for me to go with him; being it was early in the night again, I was thinking fast and imagining us doing something special, I didn't think what, for another tip, an extra dollar. When he set three dollar bills on the cot, I actually worried, wondering if I was up to whatever it was he wanted. I'd heard from the girls of men wanting some pretty crazy things. I sat down on the cot, lay back, and hiked up my dress, which is how we done it then: hiked up, unbuttoned, or unzipped our clothes, let the men take down our underwear and go to work. But nothing happened. I was spread out, dress hiked up, and he was sitting there. I thought maybe he was waiting for excitement to come upon him, which I knowed sometimes was a problem for some men, especially if they had too much to drink. But he wasn't moving, just sitting there, like I said, with his back to me. When that problem happened, most men fiddled with themselves, like Mr. Tatum done, or expected you to fiddle for them. Pretty soon, I was thinking, What on earth does he want? I couldn't see his face, much less any part of him save his back.

Finally, I sat up. "What do you want me to do?" I asked him, straightening my dress over my knees. "What do you want?"

He was staring straight ahead, same ceramic face from the night before. His hands was folded in his lap, as if he was praying. I fidgeted, uneasy on the cot. He looked over at me, glanced down at the three dollar bills between us, then stared straight ahead again. I got the message: I'm paying for this, I'm paying good money, so calm down, sit there. Which I done. But which turned me into a bundle of nerves. Not that I was afraid; I could scream if things got out of hand. I just didn't like sitting there not knowing what was going on. Time stood still. Yet three dollars was three dollars. About as much as I could expect to make in one night—three to five dollars.

"Just want to talk," he said.

I'd heard of them types too. Freebies, Joy called them. "Easy money," Ida said. "They'll tell you how they're just lonely." Although, up to this point, I'd never had one. What was I supposed to talk about? They didn't tell me that part. I'd been at this business for nearly two months, and, until now, thought I knowed it all. Later, they'd tell me the man does the talking, tells about his problems, and you just listen and say a couple of comforting things. Even if I did know that, this guy would've had me worried. He wasn't talking. Finally, he started in.

"I'm Visayan," he told me, whatever that was. "The rest, they're mostly Illocano."

He looked over at me then. Guess I wasn't starting off so good at understanding, not to mention comforting, for he seen I didn't know what he was talking about and sought to explain.

"Different tribes." he said. "Illocanos from the north, us Visayans from the south, island called Panay."

He explained how they spoke different languages. When he got off the boat, which was up in Seattle, he found himself among Illocanos who spoke Tagalog, which he didn't understand and was just now getting the hang of. I remember this because he repeated the story several times. "Still here, mostly Illocanos," he said.

"Like us Indians," I said, attempting my comforting part without even knowing I was supposed to. "We got all kinds of different languages too—even just around here."

"You can tell just by how we speak English—the accent—where we're from," he said. Which was true for some of us Indians, too, them people speaking languages not similar enough to the language of your own tribe. But concerning the Filipinos, they all sounded the same to me, the same thick English accent. They spoke English deep in their throats.

"Anyhow," he said, "I was born in a tiny village—in the trees," and with that he described what sounded like a Rancheria only poorer. Houses on stilts on account of how the water come up. No place to earn money from white people. No big ranches and farms. No orchards or dairies. "But everybody knowed everybody," he said. But that didn't help them get enough to eat. So he gone to Manila, the big city, to find work, and finding work swept him finally to America.

"Yeah," I said, "everybody knowing everybody don't mean you got enough to eat."

We was quiet awhile. Then he talked again about his village, describing his brothers and sisters, his relatives, things they done. He talked for some time before taking his pocket watch from his coat pocket and saying, "Time's up, I guess."

"Guess so," I said, figuring freebie time, or easy money time, gone for the same price as the other. Hadn't been no three hours, one maybe, but if he thought it was over, then it was over. "Man's the boss after he puts down the money," Ida said.

He looked at me funny and got up. Standing there, he kept looking at me the same way, like he'd all of a sudden found an apple on top of my head and was curious about it. I was about to ask "What?" again when he interrupted me. "Don't you get lonely?" he asked.

"No," I answered. Then he left.

Why I answered that way I have no idea. I didn't understand lonely; couldn't match the word to the feeling to know what it was. Maybe I didn't want him to think I was a sad case. Which, when I told the girls at home that night what happened, they said it was the right thing to say. "Never let a talker think you're sad," Joy said. "He comes to you because *he's* sad." Then they proceeded to educate me complete about the talkers.

* * *

So when he come the next night again I thought I was prepared. But he surprised me again. Didn't go to the same shack, which, as it turned out, wasn't his. Gone through the bushes instead. Crept through a tangle of vine and willow until we come out on the main road.

"What's this?" I said. "What's going on?"

I was getting frightened by this time, figuring maybe he was going to do something to me, hurt me, and I was too far from the camp for folks to hear me scream.

"Just a few more steps," he said, "and I got a surprise—around the corner."

We was going west, toward Sebastopol. Judgment said, You're a fool, girl, turn and run. Something else said, What difference does it make, you're already out on this road far from camp. Them two kept arguing in me with the latter winning, I guess, for I kept walking. And then, coming around the corner, I seen the surprise: a spanking-new car parked on the side of the road. In the black night, under the stars, it shined, looked like some great creature, a mountain lion, just waiting to spring to life.

"Why'd you park it out here?" I asked.

"Safer than in that camp," he said. "The guys in there, some of them might fool with it, and it's not mine."

"Ain't yours?" I questioned.

"No," he said, "belongs to my boss—where I live in Santa Rosa."

"Santa Rosa?"

"Yeah. On MacDonald Avenue. My boss, Mr. Spencer, he's a nice American."

Struck me funny the way he called his boss American. White man. *Masan.* "What do you do there?"

"Butler," he answered quickly. Obviously, he was getting bored with my questions. He looked up to the sky, then said, "C'mon now, let's go."

"Where?"

"For a ride. I'll take you to the ocean. C'mon, got a surprise for you there too."

"What?" I asked. Again, judgment and that something else was arguing inside of me, with judgment getting the upper hand this time. He must've seen me hesitating, for, in that instant, he pulled out from his coat pocket three crisp dollar bills and held them up, splayed in his fingers so I could see—and count.

Funny, that money made me comfortable, like it was some kind of agreement I trusted and understood, something that told me, OK, things wasn't going to be any different from before, from last night, and that I would be safe. I got in.

We drove without saying much until we come to the water. I'd been to the coast before, when, as a kid, I traveled with Chum and some others on a wagon over a steep and winding road to pick seaweed and dig clams. Seemed that trip took forever. Here, we was parked off the road and looking over the water in no time. Was it the same road?

"Pretty, no?"

"Yeah," I said. The night was dark, cold, but there was stars and you could see the whitecaps breaking on the shore.

It was late January. In a couple weeks it would be my birthday, eighteenth, which I thought of just then.

As if Del had been thinking along the same lines, he proclaimed, "I'm twenty-five, been in America four years now." He paused a minute, then turned from the water and offered his hand. "Delfino De La Vega," he introduced himself.

I don't know if I even knowed to call him Del at that point. I told him my name. "Elba," I said, taking his hand and letting it go.

"Sounds like a Mexican name," he said.

He gone into a long oration then on the history of the Philippines, how the Spanish gone and took over everything like they done here.

"Similar to us," I said when he finally finished.

But in no time he was talking endless again, this time back on the subject of his work, the details of his serving food and washing clothes. He said his job was going to be up in July or August, when it was hot, on account of how Mr. Spencer's regular butler, an American, was returning from wherever. Mr. Spencer said he'd help him find another job, but Del had little faith in that since, Mr. Spencer aside, most Americans didn't trust or like Filipinos.

"Similar to us," I said.

"Yes," he said, excited.

I guessed that I'd said the wrong thing, for he was talking a mile a minute now, again about his work and how it didn't matter if he couldn't get another house job because he liked the outdoors and working with animals anyways. Wrong thing, I say, because whereas his talk about the Philippines was kind of interesting, his talk about work was plain boring. What, I was going to be interested in whether folding sheets was more fun than milking a cow? On and on he talked. I wanted to inform him, in case he didn't know, that farmers wasn't no less prejudiced than city folks. But I said nothing. That wouldn't be comforting. So I let him talk.

But he must've sensed my boredom, my agitation, for even as he kept talking, he pulled out from his pocket them three dollar bills and set them on the seat between us. So on and on he gone.

Then, all of a sudden, mid-sentence, he stopped. He was looking out at the water. I thought I done been caught non-comforting again and he might be mad. He got out of the car, gone behind it.

"Quick," he called after me, "get out."

A wave of panic crept over me for the first time since I'd got in the car. I got out, walked slow to where he was standing.

"Surprise," he said, pointing and gazing up to the mountain ridge.

A huge moon sat there.

"See," he said, excited, like a kid.

"Yeah," I said.

Then he took me by the arm and turned me around. Clear across the water was the reflection of the moon. Had I not noticed the reflection before as he talked? Had it appeared and spread out so gradual?

"See, see," he said, and again I said, "Yes."

But it was something more he wanted me to get. He gave me a minute, then said, "All the way to the Philippines and back . . . Across the water to here. A connection." He looked from me to the water, back and forth. "Similar," he said, using my word, as if to help explain what he wanted me to understand.

"Yes," I said.

He was quiet then. We stood awhile. When he turned back to the car, looking at me one last time, I seen the moon in his eyes.

Never gone back to the camp that night. Come up to the reservation, which was before the camp, and he asked me if I wanted to get out there. It was early, not even midnight, but I said OK. What the hell, I had my three bucks. Home alone, I was itchy for a drink. Poured myself one but fell asleep before I could finish it.

* * *

The next night, the same thing. The car. Only we gone the other direction, east into Santa Rosa. He took me to On Chong. It wasn't that he knowed I had fond memories of the place with Mama and Old Uncle or that I was a nut for noodles. It was the only place Pinoys could go too. I figured as much, but I thought on account of them having somewhat similar looks as the Chinese, them all would get along special. Which turned out not to be true. Del said not all Chinese like the Pinoys. "We're too dark," he said. "Only like our money."

I looked at him just then. Seemed the first time I seen him. It was under the bright restaurant lights, after all. But he looked different, not the same man I seen the first night; now, sipping his soup broth off a spoon, his face stretching, moving, he had life, the dark eyebrows and lashes, the carved lips belonging to an actual person, this man I called Del. And while he'd told me more than I'd ever wanted to know about himself, I found myself all of a sudden wondering who he was. I looked at his hands, his face; yes, darker than the Chinese, but that told me nothing. I wasn't afraid, just surprised.

Then it was me talking. About Benedict's Rancheria, my life as a kid there, the things us kids done, how I come to this place with Mama, how we watched the people outside. He put his spoon down, listened. Then, when I was done, he asked, "Are you OK?" which confused me. I nodded yes.

We had ice cream for dessert, then gone for a drive. Gone up Mac-Donald Avenue, past them big houses with their big windows lit up in the dark. He pointed to the place he worked, which, far as I was concerned, seemed no different from the others on that street. Then again, it was dark. Next we was parked up in the hills, in the area where I was with Old Uncle, only not as far, not off the road. The valley was below us, and the town.

"Down there," he said, nodding to where it was darker, only a few lights.

I found the floodlight outside Benedict's barn. "Yes," I said.

Something come over me, maybe the full package of memory, but when, after a little while, he reached for me, I reached back. He didn't do anything, just held me. Then he pushed back and looked at me. I was un-comfortable with people, men in particular, just staring at me, but I didn't think nothing, not what he wanted, nothing. It was as if what I'd glimpsed in the restaurant, that life in his face, had spread over his entire being. So I was not surprised, though I'd never knowed this to be the case before, that when he kissed me, his lips was warm; and when he touched me, his fingers was warm; and when, after my clothes was gone, when I was naked, my arms around his back with all my might, he was warm inside of me.

* * *

Same thing the next night. Dinner at On Chong. Dessert. Only we looked at each other a long time in the car before we done anything. The moon come up. A light rain sprinkled on the windshield. But afterwards he talked a lot, about me.

He said, "You're not like them other girls."

"How do you know?" I asked.

"From the first night, I knowed."

"How?"

"No pleasure or meanness in what you done."

"How do you know?"

He touched my nose, playful, looked at the water on the windshield, a thousand drops holding the moon, then back at me. "Your arms limp at your sides, eyes looking up at the roof . . . You looked like you was praying, praying to be home, anywheres but there."

"Wasn't praying," I told him, feeling a bit edgy.

"You looked like an angel," he told me, ignoring what I'd just said.

"Wasn't praying," I repeated.

"Well," he said, "I was right anyhow . . . You wasn't like the rest. Your arms come up around me."

And just then I realized what was bothering me. He'd been holding a mirror up, showing me, letting me see how far out in that swirling river of his he'd gotten me to go. I didn't say nothing, shrugged my shoulders as if it was nothing, and took the three dollars off the dashboard, the same place he left them the night before.

But he shouldn't have brought them things up about me. Or maybe I should've talked more to him about it, argued that I wasn't praying, that I was just like the other girls, and then dropped it altogether. Maybe it would've made no difference. But, as it stood, he gone too far, for what come next? Roses. Red roses. I seen them the next night after I got in the car. If I'd seen them before, I wouldn't have gotten in. I told him to leave me off at the reservation. I told him this deal with us was no good.

* * *

Why I told him the reservation, I don't know. I'd just gotten to the camp. Hadn't made a cent and sure as hell couldn't charge him for the roses and a lift up the hill. Couldn't take three dollars off the dashboard even if he'd already put it there for me to take. When I got home and found myself alone in that little shack, I was fuming mad. You'd think he had pickpocketed me and got my last cent. But it wasn't the money, even though I kept thinking how the night was wasted—I wasn't going to walk back down that hill in the dark by myself. He'd gotten me out in that water when I never asked to swim and then, of all things, expected me to be happy about it and take them roses. I knowed better. Next thing, he'd have asked to marry me. Marriage. Wasn't roses just the bait for the trap? Roses was for hard-luck women and dumb kids to play with.

I stoked up the stove and changed my clothes and got into the big robe Ida give me. Then I found the flask of whiskey and blowed out the lantern. I got into my sleeping bag on the floor. In the dark, beyond the popping of the fire in the stove furnace, I heard clappers and singing coming from the roundhouse. I took a good nip, felt the sting of the first swallow, and thought, Fire, you could start a fire with alcohol. Was there enough alcohol in whiskey? If not, I could siphon gas from Elmer's car. I would burn every last one of them: pour gasoline outside around the entire place, heavy in front of the entranceway door, strike a match. Then I thought of something else: the razor-sharp bread knife. I could wait in the brush; maybe Auntie Maria would come out of the roundhouse to go to the outhouse, maybe she'd have to rush to her place for something. I'd call her, let her see for half a second that it was me, before I raised the knife and sliced her throat in one fell swoop.

* * *

That night I missed the raid. Not long after I'd walked with Del to his car that last night, while the men was still cheering a cockfight, probably about the time I was just home and lighting the lantern, the sheriffs raided the work camp. Took all the roosters and hauled in a couple of the Pinoy men, including Sal. Folks run and hid, but the women, in their dresses and heels, couldn't get far. Sheriff caught them and took down their names, not just the Indians but the white ladies, too, and said if he come back and found them there again, he'd haul them in too.

"Nothing to worry about," Ida said, sitting in a chair and pulling a high heel off her fat foot.

"Yeah, they raid just to scare folks," Joy added. "They raid to keep the townfolk happy; but, hell, some of them that's doing the raiding are the best customers—always been like that."

Both of them was talking no doubt to reassure me lest the news of the raid worry me.

They'd set up the card table in the middle of the room and was setting around it, shoes kicked off. I was sitting up in my sleeping bag, back against the wall, groggy. I'd hardly been asleep, it seemed, when all three come huffing and puffing through the door. They had to walk home and Ida was complaining terrible on account of how in all the excitement at the camp she'd lost her purse which, according to her, had nothing in it but the most important thing: her walking shoes.

"Jesus Christ, my feet," she said, rubbing her bare foot now.

"That *is* a walk up, ain't it?" Joy said.

Ida got up and, bent over, started digging in the boxes behind the stove. "Where's the hooch?" she asked.

Just then, I remembered the flask was in bed with me. "I got it," I said. Feeling around in the sleeping bag, I found the flask and handed to her.

She took it from me, had a good swig, head back, then sat down. "What're you home so early for?" she asked, setting the flask on table.

"Got sick," I said, "my stomach . . . lower stomach."

"Can't work if you got that problem," Joy said, picking up the whiskey.

She'd just solved what could've been a problem for me: I lied to Ida in order to explain why I was there; I hadn't been thinking ahead as to how I would explain why I had no money to give her.

"That was Del you was with again?" Joy asked.

"Yes," I said.

"That boy is sweet on you. Don't you get sweet on him," Ida warned.

"Don't worry," I said.

"What's gonna happen without Sal?" Zelda asked.

Joy and Ida looked at her as if she was a cat that all of a sudden had just dropped through the roof and propped itself there.

"We told you not to worry," Ida said. No doubt, Zelda'd heard the same stuff I'd heard about not being concerned with the raid when she walked up the hill with Ida and Joy.

"Sal's probably out of jail already—that is, if they ever put him in," Joy said. "Probably just took his name, no more than they done with us. They have to take somebody to the station to make things look good, that's all—like they done their job."

Then Ida said, "We'll just lay low for a while, a week or two."

"But how we gonna eat?" Zelda asked, clearly not content with a word of what she'd heard.

"We got enough for a while," Ida told her, losing patience.

"Sal'll slip us a little something," Joy said.

Then Ida quipped, "And, hell, we'll stand in line when that bureau guy comes. What, them bastards out there gonna stop us? I'd like to see them try."

Still, Zelda wasn't assured. Hands folded tight on the table, she looked like a schoolkid who needed to go to the bathroom but was afraid to ask. "I don't like the sheriff having my name," she said.

The night, before I'd fallen asleep, come back to me. Del, the roses, my anger. I thought: One good thing, the sheriff didn't have my name.

* * *

Wasn't no two weeks the way Joy predicted. Three or four weeks was more like it. Turned out the sheriff kept coming back, checking, I guess, to make sure the camp was cleared of cockfights and whores. Got all the news from Sal, who Joy was right about on both counts: The sheriff done nothing more at the station than take his name and he come by the same time—late Monday nights—with groceries. Joy crept down to meet him a day or so beforehand with our list.

"How much longer?" Ida asked every time Joy come up the hill from seeing Sal.

"Says should be a few more days," was always Joy's answer.

"You always say that," Zelda complained.

Zelda had worries. I know, because I had the same worries. Which I found out only after I come forth with my news first.

"I'm pregnant," I said.

Three or four weeks. Long enough to know for sure. I'd been past my time nearly two weeks at this point. I don't know what happened; I'd watched my calendar the way I'd been taught, been careful with the men, with Del, I thought.

We was all four of us sitting at the card table. It was in the evening, after dinner. Ida was shuffling cards. Which is what we done in the evenings now that we wasn't going to the camp, played cards. All kinds: poker, gin rummy, hearts, blackjack. My training with Chum come in handy, for I was winning left and right, though the prize was nothing more than a swig from the flask. I had the sense to take small nips. I liked playing—and winning. But that night we was a couple hours into playing and I hadn't won a single round. "Gee, what's wrong with you tonight?" Joy had asked. I had no concentration. Zelda often begged out of playing because, just as when she was a kid, she had little concentration to start with and didn't like losing. She was leaning back in her chair, arms folded across her chest, watching the three of us play. When I spoke, told them my news, Ida set the cards down and looked at me. Joy looked at Ida, then back to me.

"I got to know what to do," I said. When I got pregnant at Mr. Tatum's, him and Victor laid off of me. "Don't know if I can go back to work this way," I told them.

That's when Zelda bolted out of her chair and, in a rush of tears, lifted up her sweater and said, "Me too."

In front of my eyes, clear and shiny in the lamplight, was the hard melon of her stomach. Dropping her sweater, she dabbed at her watering eyes, sobbing out loud. "I'm sorry, I'm sorry," she cried.

"Sit down," Ida said quietly, and, like a three-year-old about to take a scolding, Zelda sat down, obedient.

My predicament somehow seemed mild in comparison, which made no sense—both situations was the same no matter how you looked at it. Pregnant is pregnant.

Ida pulled herself closer to the table, the front of her stout stomach bumping it and edging it a couple of inches in my direction. "All right, let's think this through," she said, a judge bringing the court to order.

She said she couldn't afford to have two girls not working; she certainly couldn't afford to have two girls having and raising babies.

Joy said she'd been pregnant twice. The first one she lost natural, miscarried early on. The second one she done everything to get rid of it—drunk a whole bottle of castor oil, ate poison oak, cinched herself in a tight corset for a week—until she had to throw herself down a flight of stairs, which done the trick, except she nearly bled to death. "Blood dripping down the bed," she said, "a puddle on the floor." Which caused Zelda to fling a hand deep into her mouth.

"That wasn't smart," Ida said. "Not worth killing yourself."

"Never got pregnant after that," Joy said and sighed heavy. "Guess I couldn't . . . But, hell, good thing since I got the disease."

"What disease?" Zelda blurted out, her hand flying from her mouth.

Joy looked at Zelda half a moment, then said, "Syphilis . . . Comes with the business."

Zelda asked about the symptoms and Joy gone into a long lecture about how you get it and what to look for on yourself. "You'll know," she said.

"How do you get rid of it?" Zelda asked.

"You don't," Joy answered.

"What happens?" Zelda asked.

"You die . . . after a while."

Ida knocked four times on the table. "I'm OK. How about you girls?" She was looking back and forth from Zelda to me.

So far I hadn't seen any such sores of the sort Ida described on my body, and, at this point, it had been more than three or four weeks, the time it takes for them to come out, since I'd been with a man, with Del.

"I'm OK," I said.

"You ain't been at it that long," Joy said.

"Zelda," Ida snapped, "get that goddamned hand out of your mouth."

Zelda dropped her hand, sat up straight.

"Well?" Ida asked.

"What?" Zelda said.

"Are you OK, have you had any of them sores?" She repeated the same question in Indian, as if Zelda didn't understand English. When we was kids, before I left, we almost always spoke Indian amongst ourselves. Since I'd been back, I hadn't heard nothing but English, I guess on account of how Joy was living with us and didn't understand our language.

Zelda focused finally, then asked Joy, "Can them sores come out after four weeks?"

"Sometimes, usually not," answered Joy.

"So you're OK?" Ida asked again.

Zelda nodded yes, then said, "Unless it still comes out."

"Now what are we gonna do about these babies?" Ida asked.

"I ain't gonna throw myself down the stairs, nothing like that," Zelda said right away.

Ida took a good nip of the hooch, then passed the flask to Joy. "Never said you was, Zelda."

Joy swallowed and pushed the flask across the table to me. "What about that plant you talk about, Ida?" she asked.

"Jimsonweed?" she said.

"Look what happened to Moses's mother," Zelda cut in.

Our cousin Moses's mother was Hattie Bill, Bertha and Elmer's sister. The way folks told it, Hattie was pregnant by some Mexican man. I guess Hattie had no husband or regular man she could pin the deed on at that time; maybe she just didn't want another child. She ground up the seeds from a jimsonweed plant and made a tea. Next thing you know some white man found her in a field a half mile from the county hospital. She'd gotten rid of the baby all right; the five-month-old fetus was in her arms, stiff as she was, both of them covered in a layer of frost that looked as soft as wool, their eyes peering up at the empty morning blue sky.

Nothing more was said that night. We gone back to playing cards. If anybody come up with some idea as to what to do about the babies, if Joy or Ida had some notion as to how to get rid of them, they didn't say; for whatever suggestion one person might make, somebody else no doubt would have a story to go along with it.

FIVE

I wanted an answer. But, as it turned out, I never got one, not that night, not ever. Sure we talked again, the four of us, but always come to the same point, a reason for not doing what somebody suggested, a story. And Ida would rant: "This can't be. You girls was careless, foolish." And Zelda would cry: "I'm sorry. I'm sorry."

Zelda was pretty far along, five, maybe six months. No doubt she was pregnant before I come back to the reservation. And before long, if she hadn't done nothing or said nothing about her situation, she would've had to quit work at the camp anyhow, unless she found a host of regular customers that didn't mind working themselves around a woman's swollen belly.

Sal didn't give us the green light for another three weeks, nearly two months altogether. Luckily, he kept taking our shopping list and coming back with what we needed. Joy had a way with him; by this time, with the two of them going off for drives in his car, it was no secret that they was sweet on each other.

For obvious reasons, Zelda never gone back to the camp. Neither did I. For not so obvious reasons. During them three more weeks out of work, that is, of not going to the camp, I found myself thinking. To put it simple, fear, and nothing else, got me thinking of what I could do besides the camp work to pay my way. I couldn't just sit and live off what Ida and Joy earned. God knows, Ida would've hit the roof.

One late afternoon at the well, I run into Marcellena. All along, she'd say hello to me, which was more than any of the others had done. She was the kind of woman that was comfortable with herself; unlike the other women, she didn't have much to hide, no secret affair or a cheating husband. Uncle McKinley was a grump, and that was no secret at all. Her and Uncle McKinley never had any children, but they raised lots of other folks' children; after Hattie died, for instance, they took in Moses. Which may have been one reason she never found it in herself to be mean or ignore me: She seen how I been motherless for a long time.

"You wash and clean for the chicken farmer's wife, don't you, where Uncle McKinley works?"

She was drawing up water and when she got her bucket to the top of the well, she turned around and said, "Oh, Elba, hi . . . Yes, yes I do."

She looked at me as if she wanted me to explain why I was interested. I felt funny, like maybe she thought I was going to ask for money. While we had said hello to each other in the past, we'd never talked. So I blurted out, "Maybe I could help wash or clean house. I'm good at it."

And just then, as she run her eyes over me, I knowed what she was thinking: Poor girl don't want to be a whore no more.

Seemed like forever, then she said, "OK. I go Mondays and Wednesdays now, sometimes Fridays."

"Thank you," I said with great relief.

"Well, I'm gonna have to talk to the Mrs. first . . . And Elba, you can't wear them clothes!"

"Oh, I know, I know," I assured her. "Got my clothes from when I worked in a house before. I worked five years."

"I know," she said, looking away and picking up her bucket.

"Thank you," I said again. "*Ya weh.*"

"*Mensi,*" keep still. "Today's Sunday. Be here Wednesday morning, seven o'clock sharp. I'll know if it's OK then."

* * *

I was at the well at seven o'clock. And she said yes, it was all right. So we piled in the car with Elmer, who dropped the three of us off at the chicken farm—me, Uncle McKinley, Marcellena—before he continued on to the dairy, which was close by. Uncle McKinley gone into the rows and rows of chicken coops, which, even at that time of morning, was alive with enough cackling and clucking to drown the roaring of a train. Me and his wife gone into the house.

Straight off, I proved myself an expert housekeeper. Shocked Marcellena, who said, "Elba, you been trained good." "The girl's a worker," the boss lady said. Did I know how to dust? Did I know how to sweep and mop floors? Not only could I find dust and dirt in the furthest and deepest of corners but I could reach it. Marcellena, if she seen it, had a hard time getting to it, short as she was. She was forever climbing up on chairs. "I'll get it," I said.

I didn't know it, but Marcellena was testing me out for something else, another job. I knowed there wasn't enough for the two of us to do in that house; I knowed that the first day and could've worked faster than I did if I wasn't worried about putting us out of work before the day was over.

After about a week, she said to me, "Elba, I think you can take a house by yourself."

"Yes?" I asked her.

She told me the house at the dairy where Elmer worked was available. I thought that Ofelia had that job, though for the few days I'd rode in the car with Elmer to work she'd never been along. Marcellena said yes, Ofelia had had the job but had to stop on account of how she was getting on in her pregnancy and wasn't feeling so well. "Hemorrhaging, I think," she said.

"I didn't think she was that far along," I said.

"With a big woman like that, who can tell?" she said, chuckling, elbowing me in the ribs. Marcellena was short but she took pride in the fact that she was slender, tight-bodied.

So I gone to the dairy. What I didn't know was that the dairyman, Elmer's boss, was a woman. A woman who put on rubber boots under her old housedress and sloshed right through the mud with her cows during the day; and, at night after dinner, read the books of great philosophers. Her name was Elizabeth—that's what she wanted me to call her. She didn't care so much about me keeping a clean house. It was the other job that concerned her, something else Marcellena hadn't mentioned. Which was taking care of her father, a feeble old man, withered up the way Clementine had gotten. Only there was nothing wrong with him to speak of, except for the fact that he'd lost his mind. If I wasn't with him, whenever I was busy with something else, he had to be tied to the bed rails; yes, with rope, the same way you'd tie an animal. "Call him John," Elizabeth told me.

Turned out to be six days a week, Sundays off. Me and Elmer, the two folks on the reservation with the most work; him outside with the cows, me inside with John. Which, of course, kept Ida happy, or, if not happy, then at least off my back. Zelda was swelled up, useless in Ida's eyes. I didn't make as much money as I did at the camp, but I wasn't eating as much food either, since, except for Sundays, I was taking most of my meals at Elizabeth's. In fact, I hardly seen the other girls, particularly Ida and Joy. Zelda, I seen in the evenings when I come in; in the mornings when I left for work, all three of them was sound asleep. Zelda was depressed, sitting around and crying all the time. At night, as I got ready for bed, I'd see her sitting at the cardboard table staring into space, the open whiskey flask in front of her.

"You shouldn't drink with a baby in you," I told her, repeating what Annie had told me about taking care of myself while pregnant. Of course, I hadn't even considered drinking when I was at Mr. Tatum's.

She shrugged her shoulders, kept staring.

"It can hurt the baby."

"Ain't done it yet," she said and shrugged again.

* * *

At first I was frightened of the old man, John. No reason, for, as it turned out, he was harmless, and didn't know me from Elizabeth. I guess it just took me a while to get used to being in a big house, alone with a man in his bedroom, without him doing something to me. When I got him out of bed, hugging his six-foot frame to my body, his hands was limp at his sides; and, when I walked him back and forth in the front room for his daily exercise, the only thing he said, repeating it over and over like a talking bird, was, "Careful, Careful. Thank you, thank you," which, by the way, was the only words that ever come out of his mouth. I fed him, I bathed him, changed his soiled pajamas six or seven times a day, whenever necessary.

"Hasn't been anyone like you," Elizabeth said. "Where'd you learn to take care of old people so well?"

Before long, I was cooking too; fixing eggs and bacon for breakfast, sandwiches for lunch, salads and meat for dinner. I made soup from chicken bones, I made chili with pieces of steak and carrot chunks.

"Never had an Indian who could cook like this," she said. "Where'd you learn to cook so well?"

She was an interesting character. Not only did she want me to call her by her first name, but she insisted I take a break from her father and take meals with her at the table. For dinner, she'd change from her rubber boots and old dress to a long black gown that had a tunic neck and tiny buttons shaped like pearls down the front. She'd comb back her short chestnut hair, oiled like a man's, and color her thin lips with a trace of dark lipstick. "Shall we begin?" she'd say, picking up her fork from the place setting I so carefully laid out.

She'd talk on and on and ask me what I thought of this or that. Usually, I didn't have much to say on account of how I didn't know much, if anything, about the things she talked about, books and politics. Luckily, I didn't have to stay long; as soon as Elmer finished washing down the milk barn, I'd have to catch my ride home with him, which was oftentimes before me and Elizabeth finished eating.

As far as I seen, she had one friend: Gwendolyn, an older woman with gray hair pulled back in a twist and held tight by a silver barrette above each ear. She wore tunic-cut gowns, much like the one Elizabeth wore to dinner; and, when she walked, or should I say strutted, into the house after driving herself from town, she'd set her black leather purse on the sink, always in the same spot, and say to me, "How are you, dearie?" before finding Elizabeth. She never knocked, just opened the door and there she was. Nor did she give me a chance to tell her how I was, even if I would've said more than "Fine," which of course I wouldn't have. I liked her if for no other reason than that she relieved me, when Elmer didn't finish his chores fast enough, from listening to Elizabeth discuss things on and on that I didn't understand.

She come almost every night, and if I was at the table, I could get up and start the dishes. Elizabeth got out her books—Gwendolyn brung hers too—and they'd read poems and the like out loud to one another. Elizabeth told me that when her father died, she was going to sell the dairy and move to some place, a farm I think she called it, where people done nothing but read poems and discuss things. She had other friends that had already moved there; and Gwendolyn, whose husband had died, and who didn't get along with her kids or grandkids, was ready to sell her house in town and move there. "I promised my father he would die here," Elizabeth said, "but to tell you the truth, I'm sure he has no idea where he is. Still, I got to keep my promise."

One night, when Gwendolyn didn't come and Elmer was kept late with a cow in heat that he had to put with the bull, Elizabeth asked me if I believed in God. Before I could answer, she said that it was so wonderful that Indians believed in nature, that nature was Indians' God. It struck me funny; I'd never heard it put that way: nature as God. I couldn't understand the notion. But, then again, I'd never pondered what God was.

"It's all right to say no," Elizabeth said, seeing me hesitating. "I myself, well, I don't believe in convention . . . I'm more of an atheist. I believe only in the here and now."

"Yes," I said.

* * *

One thing she said was that I needed a new uniform. Elizabeth put a wad of bills in my hand and instructed Elmer to take off that same afternoon and drive me to town. Which he done. It wasn't that I smelled, that my clothes was dirty, for I washed them every night and hung them to dry, but after a while, the same clothes washed and worn six days a week started to fall apart, give in the seams, unravel. I bought plain housedresses and sweaters, similar to what I was wearing; altogether, three new outfits, a new pair of flat shoes, and some socks. I handed her the receipt with the change the next morning. "Take it out of my pay," I told her. "Don't worry about it," she said, and I thought to myself, What will she say in a few months when I can't fit into the clothes anymore?

It was spring, full spring, past the first blossoms and buds; when the leaves is growed, the oat stalks and yellow mustard tall and weaving in the fields. Zelda never seen it, never walked out and took in the new warm air, let the green and flower colors into her eyes. Maybe she knowed, or maybe she wished—her baby was born dead. Not a stir. No easy delivery either, what with her begging for her mother and asking forgiveness for everything she thought she done wrong in her entire life, and Ida telling her to shut up and Joy telling her to push. For me, even as young and confused as I was, the struggle and then the no crying of a baby was hurtful. Not so for Zelda. After the baby was out, you couldn't tell if she sighed with relief because she knowed her labor was done or because Joy told her it was dead.

Joy and Ida was in a hurry to get dressed for work, as it was going on nine o'clock. Ida told me to take the baby, which was blue and in a metal water bucket, and toss it down the hillside. I told her no, a dog might drag it back.

"Please, please," Zelda begged Ida, "you take it. Take it far away." Which Ida done, leaving the reservation that night with the cold lump in a gunnysack.

"What do you think gone wrong?" Zelda asked.

I was on my knees, arranging blankets and pillows, helping to make her comfortable. A wave of anger shot through me. I knowed she didn't care what gone wrong; no doubt she was thankful, as if now the decision she couldn't make earlier because she was afraid had been made for her. Words come to my tongue: she-bitch, worse than a dog that eats her pups. But I said nothing; for it wasn't that I was mad, but jealous—jealous that the decision had been made for her, as if she'd been chosen to have the keys to walk free and not me.

"Maybe you was right," she said, looking me in the eyes for the first time in ages, "you know, about the whiskey."

"Yeah," I said, and I ladled her some cold water from the bucket.

* * *

She never gone back to the camp. Rested a few days, then stole two of my new outfits and gone back to her mother. Disappeared. I come back from work one night and she was gone. A month later we seen her following Auntie Maria into the roundhouse. A month, which is how long a woman's got to wait after having a baby before she can go in again.

"Strange," Joy said.

"No, she was always a nut case," Ida said with a wave of her hand. "She's probably telling Mama all about our wicked ways." Then she started mocking her. "Mama, Mama, I'm sorry," she said, sounding like Zelda in labor.

With Zelda gone, it was quiet in the evenings. I was alone. As the weather got warmer, when summer come and the nights was filled with the singing of crickets, I found myself sitting just inside the house with the door flung wide open. I could see the treetops and the stars. It was relaxing after a long day at Elizabeth's. One night after everybody that was up and about had gone into the roundhouse, I wandered out onto the road through the reservation. The small shacks, the few old cars, the laundry still on the lines seemed frozen on that warm night, stopped in time under the weight of the singing crickets, so thick you could cut the sound with a butter knife. A lonely but at the same time exhilarating feeling come over me; it was as if I had died and come back, as if I was seeing each shack and each person who lived in that shack, the cars and the laundry, up close, from where I was walking or standing, and at the same time from far away, seeing these things without any feelings, without anger or sorrow, seeing them just as they was. I thought to myself, Have you had a drink?, for oftentimes after a first or second drink I felt something like this. But I hadn't had a drink. I hadn't been drinking while I was pregnant; I followed Annie's advice, hadn't had the nerve to jump over the fence into dangerous territory the way Zelda had.

I drifted from one end of the reservation to the other, looking back and forth at the shacks on either side of the road. At one point, I come within spitting distance of the roundhouse. Come so close because it was quiet then, no loud singing to push me back. But I heard Big Sarah talking: "How many springs now, how many falls, and the *Moki* has not returned. Pain and our own people out there living like the worst of white people. Rosa. Which Rosa? That is the question. Sin is all around us . . . ."

For a moment, I felt frightened, thinking she was able to see through the walls. Then I heard Elizabeth asking if I believed in God.

"No," I said.

More and more I wandered out of the house at night, walked up and down the road past the shacks, but always I'd get to the roundhouse, one way or another, stop and then go back inside the house. I learned to avoid the roundhouse, not walk so far in that direction. But pretty soon I didn't go out at all anymore. And, after that, I didn't even open the door to look out.

* * *

How did I explain my missing clothes to Elizabeth? I didn't. She didn't notice I wore only one of the new outfits. How did I explain my swelling belly?

"Elba, you're pregnant," she proclaimed one evening.

I had just set a platter of fried chicken on the table; no doubt she seen the round outline of my belly as I leaned over, my sweater and dress caught against the tabletop, revealing as plain as day my condition.

"Yes," I said, caught off guard, though I knowed sooner or later— these days sooner—the subject would have to come up.

"Well?" she asked. "Sit down, Elba."

"There's still the potatoes to bring out," I said, flustered.

"Elba, you know how I feel about these things. I'm not judging you," she said, mistaking my confusion just then for shame.

I sat down.

She picked at one of the pearl buttons on her black tunic gown. "Do you know the father?"

"Yes," I answered.

She waited for me to say more. While I begun to get my wits about me, I still couldn't think of what more to say. How would I tell her about Del?

"That's all right," she said finally. "What kind of question is that anyways? It's none of my business."

"Oh, it's a man I knowed, but he's from another country," I volunteered, feeling at this point that I was verging on being rude.

"Not an Indian," she asked, surprised.

"No," I answered.

"Well, is he here? Where is he?"

"Oh, he gone away, back . . ." I said, wondering whether or not I should mention the Philippine Islands in the story I was beginning to concoct.

"So . . ." she said, and then hesitated. "He's not going to take care of you?"

"It's all right. I—"

"No, it's not all right!" she exclaimed, pounding her fist on the table, causing the plates and silverware to jump half an inch. "It's not! It's not! It's not! Look, here you are, a young girl, what, eighteen, isn't that what you told me, and he gets you this way and leaves you this way. You're alone, frightened, you haven't had a baby before, what are you going to do? Have you thought of that?"

"I could keep working," I offered so as not to sound as if I was begging.

She reached over, put her hand over mine. "Poor thing," she said and pulled back her hand, dropping it into her lap with the other one. "I'm all talk, Elba. In my head, I understand the here and now. But that's it. That's all, just in my head. I don't live it. I can't live it. And it shocks me to see what it truly is and makes me wonder if it really is good after all."

"Yes," I said.

She looked at me as if I'd said the fried chicken growed feathers and she didn't know whether or not to look.

"Should I get the potatoes now?" I asked.

"Yes," she said, and her eyes was full of tears.

*   *   *

I'd seen just about a full round of seasons. Finally, I seen the fluffy green and flower colors of spring, watched the grasses dry yellow and the apples on the trees grow big and drop with flecks of gold and red in their skins. Then the leaves, with the return of the cold nights in the fall, turned yellow and dropped and scattered over the shacks and across the road, filled the unkempt and spare gardens of broken cornstalks and withered tomato vines. Maybe because he'd been on my mind and I didn't want to admit it, and maybe because, as he walked up the road towards the shack, the red early evening sun filled the sky behind him, I said nothing. I'm surprised I didn't close the door on him and what was left of that late fall day. I was sitting in a chair, just inside the open door; maybe I didn't want to stand up, let him see the full term of my pregnancy, plain and telling before his eyes. I don't know. But there he was, taking off his Panama hat and holding it polite with both hands in front of him, and I didn't move.

"They told me," he said.

I'd forgotten the tilt of his accent, his throaty voice. His silver watch chain hung in a perfect U from his coat pocket. I said nothing.

"I knowed for some time," he said, unmoving.

I wondered if he'd borrowed his boss's car, if he'd parked it on the road just below the reservation. Wasn't he going to stop working for that boss, something about wanting a job on a farm? I said nothing.

"They said it was mine . . . The girls here, you told them, they said."

My careful calculations told me that the baby was his; I did pay attention to my calendar and knowed when I could have slipped: one of them two nights parked on the hill. And I told the girls as much. I said nothing.

He said nothing.

His long brown fingers, nails trimmed and clean, clasped the hat. I tried to imagine the girls—Ida and Joy—telling him of my condition. I pictured a dusty firelit night at the camp. But when? He said he knowed for some time. Had he been going to the camp regular? Other girls? Ida maybe? Joy? And where was the two of them now? How convenient that on this Sunday afternoon they'd gone for a drive with Sal. Was the three of them parked below the reservation, waiting for Del?

"I'll take care of you," he said.

What did that mean? I'd been so preoccupied trying not to look at him, or think of him, that it hadn't occurred to me to wonder what he wanted. Ida and Joy, no doubt they set him up to this. Even if he wanted to come back, he wouldn't have, not without their encouragement, not with the way I sent him off. "Don't come for me no more," I'd told him. So, what? Did they want to get rid of me? Wasn't I giving them enough money? God knows, I wasn't eating but on Sundays. I cleaned, washed clothes for them. So, what? Was this a marriage proposal? Was I being asked this time? Was he asking—asking first—for me to go off with him?

"I'll take care of you," he said again.

I said nothing.

"If you—and the baby—need anything, I'll help. The girls know where to find me."

Just then his hand moved and, without thinking, I followed it to his face as he put his hat on. The sun had sunk further below the barren apple trees in the distance, filling the sky with more red behind him. I couldn't see his face; it was black, a silhouette against the sky.

"I know you don't want me," he said plain.

I might've burst with anger. I might've screamed. But then he was gone; and as he shrunk back down the road the way he'd come, so did my rage, until the tight-stretched skin containing it was no more than the limp rubber of an empty balloon. Not sorrow, not love, not regret, but some combination of them things, so entangled and buried so deep, I couldn't see it to name it even if there was a name; still, I knowed it was there.

* * *

Still, when Ida and Joy come back before dinner, I blowed up. But, at that point, I couldn't tell you if I was mad at them or myself.

"What," I said, accusing, "I don't give you enough money?"

I was looking Ida in the eyes, which tells you how riled up I was. Ida, of course, was the one to talk to since she run the house, but she was no one to accuse, talk rough with. Wouldn't take much and she would raise her fist and let it fly; folks was afraid of Ida, which must've had something to do with Big Sarah's followers never bothering us or attempting to throw us off the reservation. Even Auntie Maria was frightened of her, wouldn't cross her.

But for some reason, she remained calm. "He just wanted to see you," she explained. "He's working at a dairy now—"

"But you set it up," I interrupted, taking advantage of her calm front. "You and Joy—"

"Yeah," she interrupted in turn, finishing my thought for me, "we gone out so he could have a minute with you—that's all he wanted. Jesus, Elba, what's the problem?" Her voice was starting to show agitation.

"Nothing," I said, holding my ground.

"Labor coming on, honey?" Joy asked.

"No, stupid," I snapped.

Ida cut me tough eyes. Her mouth opened, but what filled it, or rather, blocked it from letting loose with fighting words, was a rapping at the door.

She rapped soft because no doubt she was afraid; and when Ida stepped aside, I seen she had my two skirts and sweaters clean and folded neatly across her arms, holding them out to me as an offering of peace, as if she knowed then when Ida moved she would see me.

She come in and looked around, the clothes still held out in her arms. Looking back at Ida, she said, "Mama kicked me out," which was music to Ida's ears.

"What for?" Ida asked, taking the clothes and handing them over to me.

"Wanted a boyfriend; she wouldn't let me have one," she answered.

"Well, what'd you expect?"

Zelda shrugged.

"Gee, haven't seen you nowheres," Joy said to make friendly conversation.

Zelda looked at her, then at me holding my clothes. "Sorry," she said. "I just didn't have nothing I could wear back to Mama's."

She hadn't changed at all, sloppy clothes, nervous eyes. Her hair was longer, pulled back in a loose ponytail. "Why'd you go?" I asked, no concern in my voice. While Ida seemed to have forgotten the anger that had come up in her just before we heard the knocking, I hadn't forgotten any of the anger that was in me. And now, remembering how Zelda had taken off with my clothes, I had no intention of becoming nice, chatty.

She shrugged.

"You got scared of catching syphilis," I said.

Ida stepped forward, I thought to protect her. "We can't feed you," she said.

Zelda, who'd put her head down, looked up. "I know," she said, and with that she pulled out a wad of bills from her sweater pocket and put them in Ida's waiting hands. "Saved it from work in the crops this fall," she said.

Ida looked at the money, taking careful note of the amount. "Well, all right," she said.

* * *

Wasn't all right with me, but who cared what I thought?

I did what I could. Didn't talk to her for a week, ignored her friendly gestures, her attempts to talk to me in the evenings while the others was out. But I give in. I was being as foolish as her, which was pretty foolish. I seen in her attempts to talk how lonely she was. Lonely and desperate. What was she except like any one of us, the only difference being she showed it so plain. So one night after I got home from Elizabeth's and the other two girls was already on their way to the camp, I talked. When she asked if I would like a piece of fry bread she'd made earlier, I said, "That would be nice," and with that we sat at the card table, me with my fry bread and her with a cup of coffee, and we talked like we was old friends who'd just run into each other after a long time.

As I might have expected, she talked straight away about her family, filling me in with news, most of which I already knowed: Her mother was as hateful as ever; Sipie wasn't married; Dewey, with his gentle ways, would no doubt become a homosexual, which concerned Auntie Maria no end, since, according to Big Sarah, it was a white-man sin like drinking whiskey.

What I didn't know was that Big Sarah had appointed Auntie Maria second in command behind Elmer, I guess as vice chief, or second chief. Also, Ofelia, who Zelda oftentimes baby-sat for, was a secret drunk, not so secret if you was in and around her house a lot the way Zelda was. Zelda said she sat on the couch nursing her whiskey bottle all day. "And what's worse," Zelda exclaimed, "she's pregnant again." As Zelda talked on, mostly about what was going on in the roundhouse, which certainly was no new news, I thought of Elmer. Driving back and forth to work each day, alone in the car after we'd dropped off Uncle McKinley and Marcellena at the chicken farm, Elmer and me had become close. We talked. He didn't seem to judge me as most of the others had, if he did at all, and he talked out in the open about how he loved his little girl, Mona; you'd think by the way he talked about things that his life was a bowl of cherries. All of a sudden, I seen his face different; I seen the downward slope of his brows, his heavy eyes, and then his smile, like his talk, empty.

"I don't like babysitting at Elmer's with Ofelia coming in drunk all the time," Zelda said. Then she was on to her favorite topic: men. One man, in particular, a Henry something who she met picking pears earlier this fall at, of all places, Benedict's ranch. As it turned out, this Henry, who Zelda professed to be in love with, was the reason she was at odds with her mother. It wasn't that she merely wanted a boyfriend, as she had first told us, but that she had one, and, what's more, he was white. She snuck around with him at Benedict's—where all the Indian workers, not just those originally from the place, camped at the Rancheria, some folks actually setting up temporary homes in the shacks that was still livable. But, of course, word got out; and, before the pears was finished, she didn't care who seen her. She defied her mother, walked down the road to meet him for all to see. Now she was fixing to see him again, and when she told Auntie Maria as much, Auntie Maria told her if that was what she wanted then she could go and live with the whores. "Which is what I done," Zelda said, all of a sudden proud of herself. "She don't know how I love him and he loves me."

"How do you know he loves you?" I asked.

"He told me," she said.

I took a bite of my fry bread, swallowed.

"I know, you think he's just a hobo from the camp by the creek there, don't you?" she said. Which wasn't at all what I was thinking. "Well, he ain't, Elba." Now she sounded defensive, as if she was talking to her mother instead of me. "He's a nice white boy . . . His father is a doctor and he was earning money for college expenses. Soon as college gets out, he's coming here to find me."

"You pregnant?" I asked.

"No," she said, "hell no." She took a quick drink of her coffee, then said, "Christmas is what, little more than a month away; that's when he's coming for me. I want to look good."

My mind drifted back to where it had been moments before when Zelda first mentioned Benedict's ranch. I knowed folks from here had gone to the ranch to pick pears, but now I was trying to picture them there—trying to picture myself there—with other Indians going freely about the Rancheria, in and out of the houses, living as comfortable, or more comfortable, than us. Was we from that place? Hadn't we lived there?

"Nellie," I asked, "did you see Nellie while you was working in the crops this year?"

"Seen her at Benedict's."

"How was she?" I asked, excited.

"Fine, like I seen her before. She's plain. Folks was saying she's got songs. I heard that before . . . I told you that before."

Clearly, Zelda was not interested, but I pressed on. "You talked to her, no?"

"Some."

"I mean, you was both at Benedict's and . . ."

She looked at me like she was run out of patience and said, "Elba, I was in love." She took another drink of her coffee, and, as she swallowed, setting the cup down, her eyes moved back and forth over the table, anxious with what she was going to say next. "Elba," she gasped. "Do you know how I know he loves me? Know how I know he's coming back for me?"

I shook my head.

"Because," she said, pushing herself back from the table in her chair. "Because," she repeated for dramatic effect, and she pulled her loose dress up over her knee, revealing, just above her knee, the name "Henry" and the year "1940". "He's always right here. He ain't never gone nowheres and won't."

"It's a tattoo," she said, seeing me looking.

"Yes," I said and sat back in my chair.

"That's the trouble—Mama didn't believe me . . ."

I shook my head, agreeing with her; though, in fact, for the first time in my life, and probably the only time, I agreed with Auntie Maria.

* * *

Next day I gone to work, but it wasn't even dinnertime yet when I tied John to the bed and gone to the milk barn to find Elmer. "It's my time," I told him.

"I'll take you to the hospital," Elizabeth said, looking up from where she was milking a cow next to Elmer's cow. "We'll put the cows out and Elmer can watch John."

She had it all figured out. Elmer knowed enough that we didn't have money for a hospital; what's more, he knowed I wanted to go home right then.

"No," he said, emptying his milk bucket into the large can, "I better take her. You let out the cows. I'll be back."   .

Elizabeth was still squatted beside her cow, trying to take in all Elmer said, when Elmer grabbed me by the arm, leading me out. When we got home, he sat watching from his car until I was safe inside my door.

The girls was eating and slowly getting themselves ready for the evening. Zelda was serving them beans and rice—all three was drinking. I said nothing, lay down on top of my sleeping bag and blankets.

"Don't feel well?" Ida asked.

"She's having a baby," Joy observed.

"She is!" Zelda shot out and set her pot of beans back on the stove.

"Hot water," Joy ordered Zelda, and with that Joy took over as midwife, but, as it turned out, she didn't know that much. But then, who in that group knowed more about having babies than me?

Funny, it was easier than any of the others. I kept looking at Zelda, who had pulled a chair up and was watching. I was looking at her and remembering the Rancheria, the way I remembered it as a kid, all the things we done there, the shacks, the creek, the barn, Mama and Chum and Nellie and her, Zelda. Back and forth my mind gone with no rhyme or reason, stopping on this memory, going to the next, coming back again. Which is why, perhaps, it was easier this time; my mind was elsewheres, and the baby slipped out to catch up with it. Amen.

It was a boy, Pinoy to the core: a tuft of straight hair, Asian eyes, the long fingers I remembered holding the Panama hat. Everybody wanted to name him. Each girl had a suggestion and a reason for her suggestion. "Should be a Pinoy name," Joy said, which meant a Spanish name. She wanted me to call him Salvador after Sal on account of how Sal had been so good to us and because Sal and Del was best friends. Ida wanted me to call him Roosevelt after the president, believing that might inspire him to be a leader. Zelda wanted to call him Sam after her and Ida's father, my father, too, which, as far as I was concerned, was completely out of the question. I asked Ida and Zelda if they knowed for certain what Old Uncle's name was. Ida thought his name was Frank and Zelda thought it was Charlie, Charles, but neither one of them knowed for certain. I picked Charlie, if for no other reason than that Ida made more sense and was more likely to know the truth of things, Old Uncle or not, than Zelda. Old Uncle, someone joyful.

Elizabeth was shocked to see me in her kitchen Monday morning. I'd left work and had the baby on a Saturday. I had Sundays off, which meant I'd missed no work, save the last few hours late Saturday afternoon.

"Oh, no," she said, tears filling her eyes, "please, honey, you need time to mourn."

"Mourn?" I said.

Poor thing, she thought I was back at work so fast because I'd lost the baby. She had my thinking process all figured out, believing I'd come back to work so as not to think about the loss. True, Indians and other poor folks lost babies regular in them days; she must've knowed as much. Her mind was fixed.

"I told Elmer that he should've taken you to the hospital," she complained, wiping at her eyes with a tissue. "I would've paid," she added.

"No need for that; I done fine," I said. "The baby's good."

But it took me forever to convince her that little Charlie was alive and well. Then we had to sit down at the table so I could explain in detail why the baby wasn't with me, what arrangements I'd made at home. It was simple: Zelda, my cousin, needed a job and was a practiced baby-sitter; Ida, Zelda's sister, and her friend Joy had a friend with a car who could drive for milk and groceries, which he done the day before, so I could be at work today. Which was all the truth. What I didn't tell her was what the perfect arrangement took from me—how I missed Charlie. How do you explain that you done had five babies, and for the first time you felt as if you actually had a baby, felt he was yours, all his fussing, his soft-hair smell, his little grin, all of it yours, and what it means not to be there to get every second of it?

She sat, chin cupped in her hands, thinking. "Well," she said, "you can take fresh milk from here after work each night."

"Thank you," I said. "Easier for me on account of how the cold box don't keep things long."

"Oh," she said and sighed, as if a pain shot through her kidneys, "I forgot, you don't have electricity." Then she said that because I was such a good worker and all, she would pay me a little extra to cover baby-sitting costs, which I did not see how that had anything to do with me not having electricity, but I didn't complain.

Ida was happy. Already, I argued how I'd been bringing in money and not eating a thing but on Sundays; I'd been paying for nothing but a place to lay my head. But on top of that I made Zelda promise to limit her intake of food; I told her if this arrangement didn't work out, I'd have to take the baby to work with me and she'd have to go back to work at the camp, since the money she'd given Ida would soon run out, and then what would her nice white boyfriend think of her? And I told her no drinking on the job, to wait if she wanted to drink until I got home from work. She promised.

* * *

Why did I make such an effort? Like I said, even if you're twelve and know nothing of the creating and giving of life, there's something in you that wants to hear that baby cry, that makes you want to pick it up, wriggling and hollering, to your body. I found, for me anyways, the same holds for when you done had it for no other reason than the fear of getting rid of it beforehand. It cried, it wriggled and hollered; and, what's more, it didn't die.

Growed happy and strong. A busy little guy, always on the move. Never changed: the tuft of straight hair, which I cut in bangs over his eyes; yes, the Asian eyes, so with his hair cut even and straight he looked like a China baby. But always on the move, into everything, the box of plates and silverware, the box of food staples, the box of undergarments, the garter belts and the fancy bras and panties. The slightest crack in the front door drawed him to it. By the time he was crawling good, Zelda was earning whatever extra food Ida allowed her. Zelda was plumb exhausted by the end of the day. I'd save slices of ham, maybe half a sandwich, from my meals at Elizabeth's and bring them home wrapped in a dish towel for her.

No surprise, Zelda's man never come for her. But it didn't seem to matter. Even though she complained about being tired, the baby kept her happily busy. In the evenings, able to rest and with me to talk to, she didn't appear to pine away. The baby, little Charlie, settled the household in numerous ways. Ida got gentler, softer even; Joy relaxed; and Zelda got respect, even envy, for the amount of time she got to spend with him. All of a sudden, the girls' attention was focused on the baby instead of on themselves. No more complaints from Ida regarding who was or was not bringing in enough money; no arguments over whose turn it was to wash clothes or fetch water; while Ida and Joy dressed in the evenings for work, they didn't quarrel over the mirror, and when one of them was in front of it, they spent more time looking over their shoulders at the baby than at themselves. He was a kind of miracle, it seemed; the girls kept looking at him, stroking his hair, picking him up and holding him, as if to make sure he hadn't all of a sudden disappeared.

All of us talked more. Seemed Charlie called us to that card table and said: Talk, open your lives. It become a ritual: In the evenings Ida and Joy didn't start for the camp until well after eight o'clock, extending the time the four of us girls could sit together by a couple hours. Memories, that's what our lives was. Ida talked about the sweet blackberries that growed along the creek, and how, when they was girls, her and Sipie would eat themselves a mess of them and then, on the warm summer days, lie in the sand and watch the water skeeters dart and slip over the smooth surface of the creek. "Used to hold hands and pretend we was two big skeeters ourselves," she said. Zelda talked about funerals, about how all the relatives would come together, lots of folks who had moved away and others we'd never met before. She talked about how we played, raced up and down the road, hiked in the hills. She talked about salmon and steelhead from the creek, her mother's fry bread and *tup-tup*, or baked bread. Food: She remembered whose mother made the best pies, the best acorn mush, the greasiest fried potatoes; she remembered Chum's horehound candy and talked as if she had lived off a generous portion of it each and every day.

Them stories always got Joy to talking. That's usually the order it gone: Ida, Zelda, Joy, then me. "Makes me think of songs my mama sung to me," she'd say. Her eyes welled up, her face flushed. I'd always thought she would sing, but instead she'd fall into stories. Small stories: her mother fixed sunny-side up eggs for breakfast; her mother powdered her face and wore sweet perfume; she had one brother who was much older, who had left home, so she growed up like an only child. Then, one night, it happened, she sung:

> *Danny boy, oh Danny boy*
> *the hills are green . . .*

Something like that. Just burst out with it in the middle of her small stories. I was shocked. I was expecting an Indian song, really, for no reason save the fact we was Indians. Zelda was surprised too; her eyes opened like saucers. Ida, leaning back in her chair with her thick arms crossed over her chest, had a self-satisfied smirk on her face.

When Joy stopped singing—and she sung for a good while—she fell into her stories again, only this time she provided a detail none of us had before: Her mother was white. Which didn't particularly shock me, not the way her singing that song had. Her eyes was light-colored, after all.

"So your mother married an Indian?" Zelda asked innocent enough when Joy quit talking.

A look of dismay come over Joy's face. "No," she said, measuring her words careful. "No," she repeated. "Daddy was white too."

Zelda's eyes was dinner plates by this time. Ida didn't budge an inch, sat arms crossed over her chest, a self-satisfied smirk on her face.

Joy faced Ida finally and said, "Sorry, I lied."

"I knowed you wasn't Indian," Ida said, her words matching her smirk. "I knowed all along—every time I asked you."

But then I seen Ida start to well up. Joy got up from the table then, and gone out for water. We was quiet for a few minutes.

"She's white, a *masan*," Zelda suddenly said, as if convicting Joy of murder.

"You didn't know that before," Ida said.

"So?" said Zelda.

"So, now you know this about her and want to treat her different?"

Zelda thought awhile, then said flat out, "It's a sin," to which Ida, raising her voice, exclaimed, "You been listening to those no-good bastards in the roundhouse too long."

"Why'd she say she was an Indian?" I asked. I was curious, but, to tell the truth, I was more interested in squelching the fire I felt rising between Ida and Zelda.

"Easier to be a whore if you're an Indian, I suppose," Ida answered. "People don't question it."

At that point, we could hear Joy coming up the path, her water buckets sloshing.

* * *

The following evening, when we all sat down together, Joy said she was leaving. Her and Sal was going to get married. They was going to Tijuana, on account of how a Filipino couldn't get a marriage license in this country; they wanted to be married truly, he wanted her to be a Mrs. Forever, they was going to settle in Los Angeles, where Sal had some relatives that could get him a job in a restaurant.

We had a little party, set the lamp in the middle of the cardboard table, toasted whatever we was drinking, me water, them whiskey, and cried. I give her a pair of Charlie's booties, which I knitted while sitting with John. "So you travel well," I told her. Zelda give her a fountain pen and Ida give her a necklace of false pearls, real pretty, and earrings to match. But what could any of us, me or Zelda, give Ida when she come home that night, after walking back up the path from the road without Joy?

* * *

"What's going to happen to me?" Ida would ask time and time again after Joy left. She didn't like going to the camp alone, although she not only found someone, another Pinoy, to drive her back after work, but to pick her up also, so she didn't have to walk in the dark either way. It wasn't that she was lonely or afraid, or that she missed Joy, which, as it turned out, she truly did, but that, as she put it, being alone there, standing waiting for a man or even while she was with one, got her thinking about her future, what was going to happen to her. "I want to change," she said. "Not going to be like one of them bastards in the roundhouse, no. I'm looking for something else. But what can I do?"

She thought of becoming a maid, like me and Marcellena. Zelda had been talking about signing up with the recruiter who'd been around from Sherman Indian School, the boarding school in southern California that trained girls professional to be maids, and Ida considered doing the same, maybe going with Zelda if Zelda decided to go. But then there was one glitch. Ida quit talking to Zelda. Not that they had another argument. Ida pure and simple got fed up with Zelda. Not long after Joy left, Zelda moved out again, gone back with her mother. Gave no reason, just left.

But then Zelda come back the next morning—to baby-sit. And she kept coming back in the mornings just as I was running out the door to meet Elmer, and she left prompt when I come home at night.

Ida had lost all patience with Zelda, who wasn't just back living with her mother, but was also back going to the roundhouse every night, the two things—Auntie Maria and the roundhouse—hand in hand. "Probably goes and tells them all what sinners we are," Ida said. "Damn bitch," she whispered out of earshot of the baby each night after Zelda left. Though Ida kept her cool, I often wondered if the baby sensed the tension underneath. One thing was for certain: The peace that come about in the household shortly following his arrival was gone. The two sisters wasn't only at odds with one another, but one of them, Zelda, was at odds even with being in the house.

"Zelda don't know what she wants," Ida said in one of her kinder moments.

What happened? I wondered. What gone wrong?

At least me and Ida was tight. Which I never would have expected, Ida with her tough-hearted ways. Then again, who else did she have to talk to now? Who else did I have? In the evenings, after Zelda gone home to Auntie Maria and before Ida left for the camp, we'd sit at the card table and talk. Something like the old days but not the old days—no talk of happy memories.

It was high summer now. The nights was warm again and the singing of crickets so thick you could cut it with a butter knife. Above the apple trees, the stars was like the singing—everywhere—and seemed to pulse with it. Again, I found myself wandering up and down the road through the reservation, back and forth. I made a regular habit of it. After Ida left for work, I'd bundle Charlie up and out we'd go. As rambunctious as he was during the day and in the house, at night, in the open under the stars, he was calm, quiet. It was as if that odd mixture of loneliness and exhilaration that come over me on these walks come over him also. More than once we passed people on the road, probably on their way to or from the roundhouse, but they said nothing, took no notice, as if they, too, was part of this scheme, as if to them we was spirits they couldn't see.

But things begun to change. Before long, the exhilaration begun to disappear. It was the same as before when I had started to take these walks.

Only now I understood better what I only had a small sense of then. It was the memories. Not what I had talked about at the card table with the other girls, which was very little, small stories. Not the water skeeters on the creek, or the footraces on the road, not Auntie Maria's *tup-tup* or Chum's horehound candy. But memories of Auntie Maria and Big Sarah washing clothes and talking about Mama, Mama on the road to town night after night, Auntie Maria's disdain for me, and Chum's empty candy jar. And not just the pain here, or the hurt, or the anger, but the hope that gone with them things and that, in looking back, looked so foolish. Yes, the hope and the love, inseparable from one another, one and the same, a tiny golden poppy, sprouted out of season in the fall, mindless of the frost.

The memories had been on my mind since the time Zelda had come back and talked about her stay on the old Rancheria. All that talk about the strangers there had made the Rancheria seem so far away; yet, while the Rancheria seemed far away, the memories all of a sudden was close. While the Rancheria withdrawed further and further, the memories come closer and closer, and what started with Zelda progressed significant with Charlie.

I'd look at him, watch him grow, see what I never had time or state of mind to see with the others—a life that was mine—and I'd look for traces of Mama, of this or that relative, of me, and what come back smack in my face was memories. The memories was Charlie; Charlie was the memories. Which worried me. He wasn't simply a baby, but more, in a world that was more, of a mother and a people that was more. If he was just a baby, if the simple stories was all there was to things, wouldn't us four girls still be together and happy? Wouldn't there be peace in the house still? We wasn't peaceful because there was more than the simple stories, more than we talked about. There was other memories.

I'd start walking up and down the road, happy with the stars and crickets singing, with the baby the same way, all of the night in his eyes; but, before long, the heaviness would overtake me, all these thoughts and memories, the sadness, and I'd hurry back to the house and close the door tight behind me. After a while, I quit going outside at night altogether. After Ida left for work and I finished cleaning up the dinner dishes, I'd get into bed with the baby. I'd blow out the lantern and cling to him, and if I couldn't sleep, on account of how it was still early, I'd stare in the dark at the walls. But memories just painted themselves there. Charlie slept. How could I? I found the flask.

* * *

Fall come and with it the crop picking, apples and pears. Most of the reservation emptied out, as it had the year before, and Zelda gone with them. Ida insisted that she could look out for Charlie during the day, that if she was too tired to go to work after I got home, she'd take the night off. "I don't have to go every night to have enough money," she said. "Hell, half time would do. I'll eat less, drink less."

Which is what happened. She took care of Charlie days, then, three or four nights a week, she gone to the camp. Before she had complained about having to go to the camp alone, not having Joy to talk to, standing around worrying about her future. Now she had concrete complaints, reasons why she had to think here and now about another line of work. Things had changed at the camp: A gang of white girls and their Mexican pimp was running things. Since the men, no matter what color, seemed to prefer the white girls, life there was tough for Ida. Point is, Ida wasn't making much of a living, which she finally confessed to me one night.

"Which means I should probably work harder, go stand around there every night," she said. "But I can't. I hate it. It's just so humiliating being left there. At the same time, I can't stand it when a man does pick me. I hate it. I've come to hate men, even the sight of them."

"We'll work it out," I told her.

"What about when Zelda comes back?" she asked.

"Worry about it then."

Got so Ida was going no more than twice a week. And that meant most nights I had somebody to drink with. I never got to the sloppy, passing out kind of drinking, but just enough—drink, talk a little with Ida, fall asleep.

Surprisingly, we had enough money, which Ida would never have believed before, or even given us a chance to find out. Between what we got from the bureau man—both me and Ida now stood in line—and my salary and what cooked food I brung home from Elizabeth's and what Ida brought in, we had enough. Just barely, but still enough. Ida did eat less, but she drunk more, she drunk till she passed out. But she claimed none of the household money gone for whiskey; her friend, the guy that drove her at night and took her into town to get our groceries, bought her her whiskey in exchange for, as she put it, special favors.

She never drunk during the day, which of course was good because she was caring for Charlie. She didn't open the flask until after dinner, when, with the baby in bed, the two of us found ourselves sitting at the card table.

So the days and nights gone on. Same thing. At Elizabeth's I kept track of the date by looking at her newspaper on the table every morning; if it wasn't for that newspaper I might not have knowed even what day of the week it was. The headlines told me the world was in trouble: war every-where, invasion in this place and that place. But in the small world of

Elizabeth's house and the reservation, which together was all of my world, nothing happened. John wasn't any better or any worse. The baby growed. Me and Ida nipped at night. Things was more settled in my life than probably ever before. Yet I felt no peace.

* * *

When Elmer drove me to and from work, I found out something Zelda didn't tell me when she was talking about him and Ofelia: He drank. He didn't come right out and tell me. This is what happened: One day, on the way home from work, instead of crossing Main Street and heading west for the hills, Elmer turned right and we drove due north through the town of Sebastopol. "Got to pick up the stuff for Ofelia," he said, adjusting his baseball cap. He parked in front of a little bar in Graton; and, as it turned out, he done more than buy Ofelia her bottle of whiskey. He had himself a couple of snorts. And me right along with him—that's how my drinking started again—and I'd listen to him cry in his whiskey: his worries about things, his miserable life, Ofelia drinking and not taking good care of the kids. Got to be a regular event. On them days McKinley and his wife didn't ride with us—which was only a couple days a week—me and Elmer hit the Graton bar.

* * *

Crops finished and Zelda was back. I anticipated trouble: Zelda wanted her baby-sitting job back and Ida no doubt wouldn't want to give the job up. Zelda, seeing my arrangement with Ida, said nothing to her. She pleaded with me, dumped the problem in my lap, saying that, like before, her crop money would eventually run out and she needed a means to pay her way here.

"Oh, so you're going to stay this time?" I asked her.

"Got to," she said, looking down at Charlie in his blanket bed then back up at me.

Point is, she was pregnant—by another nice boy, a white boy, who, like the first, was going to come back for her. I was mad, wanting to call up her hypocrisy about white people and sin. But I didn't. Who was I to lecture? Instead, I arranged things so Zelda could have her job back. I gone to Marcellena, asked if she could do for Ida what she done for me—practice her as a maid, then find her a job. She agreed.

Ida didn't take so well to the news at first, even though I pointed out that she wouldn't have to work at the camp no more. What bothered her was facing Marcellena, who, like the others, Ida had been huffy with.

"Just be nice," I said, which Ida eventually done. And no, she didn't end up working in the egg farmer's house, even for a day, but outside with Uncle McKinley; and, turned out, she loved it—pounding nails, cleaning coops, washing eggs, which she done better than any of the men, including Uncle McKinley.

So things worked out—again.

Still, with Ida and Zelda life wasn't comfortable, for, one way or another, they was always at each other's nerves. It was no surprise that, a week or so after Zelda was back, she resumed her arrangement of living with her mother but caring for Charlie during the day. Exactly like before: come in the morning, left when I got home, followed her mother and them to the roundhouse later. She agreed to stay until me and Ida got home from work each night. Of course, I was covering for those nights I told her me and Ida had to work late, the nights in fact, me and Elmer—and now Ida—gone for our snorts after work. Oh, she must've smelled the booze when we come in; and, hell, even if she hadn't, she knowed me and Ida had our couple snorts in the evening.

She seen us before she gone back to Auntie Maria. And proof she'd gone back, she was getting in her moralizing comments about coming and going. "You're gonna be sorry you do what you do." "You know the rules, you're going to have bad luck. You'll have to sacrifice if you lead a sinful life. Charlie will get sick and die or something."

"Yeah, what about that *masan* baby in you? What are you going to do about that?" Ida screeched after her.

"Don't let her say that again," I told Ida. "I don't like it."

Cold was setting in, the leafless time, the frost-ground time, but we had wood and enough money. Zelda watched Charlie during the day. I trusted that she had done a good job, on account of how, as she put it, she was practicing for her own. I was envious. He was standing now, holding on to the wall or somebody's hand, ready to take his first step, which no doubt Zelda would witness just as she had witnessed of late all his other firsts: his pointing to the door when he heard one of us approaching; his pulling himself to his feet, using the wall or a post. Except for Sundays and a brief time in the mornings and evenings, I didn't see much of him. At night, I'd hold him to me, but before long, tired and comfortable with the whiskey, I was as sound asleep as he was. Then it was morning again. That's how it gone, the same thing day in and day out. Yes, I wanted to see more of Charlie, but what could I do? Life gone on. Things just seemed to float. Floating, floating until . . .

* * *

Three drinks. Just now and then. Another one, just a little more to take the edge off. Isn't that what we say? One for the road. So it was my fault no matter what. I should have been home. No matter what the excuse, Elmer driving off the road, which was bound to happen sooner or later, what with another, then another drink for the road, this time lucky, or so Ida claimed getting out of the car and lifting the tire out of the ditch, nobody hurt, she said, let's go. No matter what the excuse, the congregation told me with their accusing faces as I got out of the car and they drawed closer and closer, leaving me a clear view of where I would look first, the house, the rat's house that was nothing but cinders, waves of smoke, gentle and curling, rising in the black midnight from the black earth like steam . . . You left your baby to burn up. Sacrifice.

* * *

Waves of smoke, gentle and curling. He'd taken off, my Charlie. Hadn't he always wanted to run, the way he slipped out of me and growed ever busy, as if he was struggling to get ahead of me and all that I was, my memories? Wasn't he running to escape and didn't he find a way, waking and crawling toward the light, the lantern on the table that he could pull himself up to and pull down? Wasn't this in the cards? Yes, I told myself in those few moments before Elmer come back and put me under the covers again as numb as rubber.

Elmer took me, picked me up when I fainted before I could hear any of them, emptied out of the roundhouse and waiting for me, say a word, if in fact they ever did say anything. Carried me to his place, set me on the floor for fear I would fall off or roll off a bed or the couch, put blankets over me. And there I stayed for a week, closing my eyes as fast as I opened them to take water from him or Ofelia.

One day he sat me up, said, "Elba, you can't be dirtying your clothes no more. Got to take care of yourself."

Next day he sat me up again, said, "Elba, you got to eat something so you can get back to work."

Next day he sat me up again. He didn't say anything right away. Then, real quiet, he said, "Elba, you got to let it go." He paused and then said, "Wasn't much left of him. They put him under one of the apple trees . . . I'll take you there."

"No," I said, "leave him alone," and with that I took his hand and let him help me to my feet.

But I was still rubber, heavy, bound. You ever see a calf that's come out and ain't torn the birth sack, how it kicks and pushes at the smothering membrane? That's how I was, even as I took my first steps and gone on.

* * *

That was in the evening sometime. Elmer was just back from work, his overalls and work shirt smelling of cows. He got me to the table, sat me down, and served me a bowl of plain rice. Ofelia was in the bedroom with the girls. Elmer had poured himself a drink. When he seen me looking at it, he said, "You better just stick to water and rice for a while, eh?" I knowed he wanted to talk. It was time to start reconnecting me to the world. Poor guy, he had the job.

"Elizabeth done hired somebody else," he told me.

I didn't quite register what he said, which he must've seen on my face, for he gone on to explain: "Elba, you didn't show up to work. Hell, girl, it's been over a week now. She's got her father and all . . . She had to get in somebody else."

"Didn't you explain my baby died?"

"Yeah," he said, then looked down at the glass of whiskey on the table that his hands was wrapped around.

"Well, I can go back now."

"No," he said, shaking his head.

"I'm strong now. I'll be stronger," I argued.

He kept staring at his glass. I seen he was putting his words together in his head to tell me the story.

"She knows you was drinking, Elba. She smelled it on you before . . ."

"Hell," I said, feeling a small bit of life, which was anger, "you drink too. Don't she smell it on you?"

"Maybe . . . I don't know. I work outside. And I ain't missed no work."

"My baby died," I repeated.

Elmer looked up at me for the first time. He glanced quick towards the bedroom, making sure Ofelia wasn't in earshot, then whispered, "Elizabeth seen it before . . . drinking, then no-show."

Again I looked perplexed and again he seen it on my face, for he explained, whispering, "Ofelia . . . Elizabeth smelled it on her. And, you know, Ofelia, lots of times she just didn't show up. I told you, remember? She knowed Ofelia was a drunk."

"But I ain't," I protested too loud. He put his finger to his lips for me to talk softer.

The situation and the fact that I could do nothing about it begun to settle in me. I looked at him, as if asking what I was going to do now.

As if to make me feel better because he had no answer, he said, "I done got fired here."

I looked at him and he gone on to explain: "Big Sarah, she seen us come home after the accident. She seen me. You know how they was all standing around? Well, she seen me. She come up to me and seen I was drinking, said, 'You're fired,' like that." He took a drink then said, "Ah, hell with her."

"Where's Ida?" I asked, the pieces of my world starting to present themselves to me now.

"She's staying with McKinley and Marcellena."

"She still at the egg ranch?"

"Yeah," he said. He took another drink of his whiskey, then looked at me. "Elizabeth says she owes you money. She wants you to go pick it up."

"Bring it home with you," I said.

"No," he said, "she wants to see you. You better go. Tomorrow, I'll leave work early, come for you and take you back over there."

I said nothing. He took another drink.

* * *

To bawl me out, I figured. That's what she wanted to do. I was angry. Hell with that *masan*, I thought. I had no plans to talk back to her, cause trouble, but I wasn't going to let her bother me either. Her words, whatever she had to say, would roll off of me like water off a duck's back. But when I found myself sitting across from her at the table, before she even said a word, I seen in the kitchen who the new maid was and felt myself naked. In the back of my mind I'd thought that the somebody else she got to replace me was Zelda; what with Zelda's conniving ways, wouldn't she seize upon the opportunity of my shock and grief to steal my job? In my worst moments, I imagined that she burned the shack, at least let it happen somehow, left Charlie early that night on purpose instead of just going to the outhouse like she told folks, in order to mess me up and get my job. I had tried not to think about Zelda in my place at Elizabeth's too often for I was already so mad at her, blaming her—when I wasn't blaming myself—for what happened to Charlie that I could've killed her. Lucky for her, I never seen her after that dreadful night; didn't see nobody until now, really, except Elmer and Ofelia and their two kids. I was afraid to ask Elmer who the new maid was on account of how he might say Zelda and I'd go crazy. I knowed I could control myself in front of Elizabeth, but what if I seen Zelda there?

I didn't. It wasn't her. I knowed by the slender body, the long braid, the way her sweater and long old-fashioned dress fit her so comfortable that, even before she looked over and seen me, it was Nellie. Just as she was as a kid, plainer, but beautiful like Chum. And wise beyond her years, forever thoughtful. She seen me all right, but given the circumstances, she done the best and kindest thing possible. She quietly set down the dish she was holding and gone out the other door, closing it so I could hear she'd gone and wouldn't be listening.

"Do you know her?" Elizabeth asked.

She was dressed for dinner, the pearl-like buttons on the front of her black tunic gown catching the light. Clearly, her and, I supposed, Nellie was about to sit down and eat. How could I answer her? Nellie. Nellie. Nellie. Right then any trace of my angry defensiveness was gone. In its place was a sorrow greater than what I knowed at the death of Charlie; and, at the same time, shame, shame worse than I knowed walking through the reservation in whore's clothes. And them two things, sorrow and shame, married and made in me, in me and everywhere outside of me, a big hollow blackness, the cold empty hole of lonely. None of it had anything to do, of course, with Elizabeth. Maybe not even with Nellie, but just with the mere sight of her then and there, as if that vision of her was for me a key that opened the door, broke the seal, so that I could see into the house that was my life since Nellie, since childhood and Benedict's Rancheria. What happened? What bad luck had I carried with me from that place? Hadn't I carried it? Wasn't I to blame?

"Elba," Elizabeth called, seeing my mind wandering.

"Yes," I answered, startled.

" 'Yes,' you know her?"

I thought fast. I didn't want to get Nellie in trouble, have Elizabeth suspect her competence on account of her association with me. "No," I said, then folded my hands on the table and looked at her as if I was waiting for what she had to tell me.

She bit the bait. "Elba," she begun, folding her hands on the table, too, "you're the best worker I ever had." She paused, collecting her words for what come next, what she'd set me up for, the bad part: "But I need someone responsible to take care of my father. If . . . if only you didn't drink." She said this bit about my drinking sort of like a question for me to answer.

"Yes," I said.

She sighed with frustration. "Tell me," she said, "did your baby really die?"

"Yes," I said.

She sighed again. "Elba, I don't know, I feel like I don't even know you . . . You . . . if only I could tell for certain you wouldn't drink . . ."

The thought occurred to me just then that Nellie might be wanting to get back into the kitchen. I looked back down at my hands, impatient.

She bit the bait. "Well, all right," she said, and from under the white cloth place mat she pulled out an envelope with my name scrawled on it and handed it to me.

I took it, put it in my dress pocket and buttoned the pocket flap. "Thank you," I said and braced myself to leave.

"Elba, I liked you the best . . ."

"Thank you," I said, standing up.

"You know, you can do anything you want if you put your mind to it."

"Yes," I said, inching away from the table, her eyes following me.

That was about it. Maybe some stuff about how John would miss me, and then I was out the front door. She never even had a chance, if she was going to, to get out of her chair.

* * *

"Come on," Elmer said. "*Sha do.* Let's go. Ida'll be waiting."

"OK," I said, slamming the car door.

I hadn't realized how long I'd been in with Elizabeth, about twenty minutes, and just now I remembered that Elmer had been waiting in his car, that he'd finished his work early and come back on my behalf.

"Thanks," I said.

I was in a daze. Nellie. Did Elmer know that Nellie was the one to replace me? He must have. Did he pick her up from where she lived with her father's folks along the lagoon and bring her to work? Why didn't he say anything to me? No doubt not to shock or hurt me. Which is why just then I didn't bring it up with him—too touchy. Let it go.

Ida, yes he'd mentioned her, but I'd been so preoccupied with thoughts of Nellie, I hadn't realized that I would actually see her. When I did, when she got into the front seat, squeezing me between her and Elmer, I took one look at her familiar dark face, her thick arms, and grabbed on to her with all my might, as if I'd been away for years, as if we'd been separated through no choice of our own, and was now just reunited. She turned in her seat, hugging me back.

"Jesus, Elba, don't cry," she said. "Don't cry."

She patted my back and Elmer started the car.

"Don't cry," she kept saying and patting my back. "It's all right. It's all right."

My head was buried in her chest. I did not see the road, I did not feel the car turn right on Main Street, but when I looked out, after Ida took me by the tops of my shoulders and separated me from her, I seen we was stopped, parked plumb in front of the Graton bar, the WELCOME sign staring me in the face.

When I think of it now, of course, I think how stupid, thoughtless of them after what happened the last time I was here. But I don't think they was capable of thinking that deep into things at the time; no doubt, they thought, given my tears and all that had happened, that stopping for a snort was the best thing for me just then, and what they was doing was a favor. I don't know. Don't matter. I wasn't thinking either. I followed, hung on to Ida until she had me seated at a corner table staring down at the bowl of peanuts.

"Listen, honey," she said across the table, "it's going to be all right."

I heard Elmer order three whiskeys from the barmaid. She had a Spanish accent.

"Elba," Ida continued, "you're young, you can have another baby, God knows; and a job, you'll get another one. Hell, there's lots of jobs opening up these days. There's lots a girl can do."

I wasn't listening to her really, but somehow her talking on and on and my growing awareness that I was sitting in the bar again began to spook me. I felt shaky, afraid. So even before the barmaid come back with the drinks, I had my wits about me more than before. I kept telling myself that I was only feeling paranoid on account of what happened the last time I was here. Nonetheless, my nerves didn't settle. I drunk the one whiskey, but no more. I refused Elmer's offers to buy me another. Something told me to keep my eyes open.

And I seen things step by step.

First off, what I'd suspected before about Ida's long trips to the outhouse out back appeared to be true enough. Before, when we'd come here to drink, particularly the last couple times, Ida disappeared for the longest time, not once but at least twice during the evening. "Where'd she go?" I asked Elmer, who shrugged. No doubt, he knowed what was going on but let the third or fourth snort keep him blind. Hadn't I done the same thing? But now there was no question about it. I seen the thin, mustached Mexican man in a black vest by the back door give Ida the nod. He appeared to be standing casual, just another person in the crowd listening to the music, but when Ida got up and passed him on her way out, I seen him slip her a bill. Dirty work clothes and all, I thought to myself.

Elmer meanwhile was getting more and more drunk. How's he going to drive, I wondered. Was he like this before when we come here to drink and I just hadn't noticed it because I was the same way?

About the time Ida come back Elmer got up and staggered out the front door.

"Probably going to sleep in his car," Ida remarked.

"How we going to get home?" I asked.

"He'll be OK," she said, and then she was up and out the back again, leaving me at the table alone.

The fury was hot liquid in my veins. I was furious with Ida at the moment. What did she mean, "He'll be OK?" What about us? What about me? I twiddled my thumbs, refused to buy another drink from the barmaid for the umpteenth time. Finally, I broke down and had me a couple drinks, which I took each in about one gulp. I forgot the money in my pocket. I told the barmaid Ida would pay when she come back in, which seemed to be OK. I didn't feel the booze, it didn't seem to calm my rage. If anything, I was worse. When I seen the skinny bastard by the back door wink at me, I flyed out of my chair and pounded past him.

"*Señora*," he called after me.

Outside, in the black night, he was right behind me. "*Señora*," he called again.

I spun on him, yelling, "I ain't no *Señora*," then turned and called loud for Ida.

But then a hand was over my mouth—not his, for I seen him watching—and an arm locked around my neck and I was being pulled backwards, away from the building. I struggled, fought, tried to dig my heels into the wet earth, but the building with its one light over the back door growed smaller and then was no more.

Still struggling, I was in another building. It was like an empty shack of some sort, musty like an old chicken house. And there was three of them, white men, I seen that much; and then, before they started on me, when I seen what was going to happen and that there was three of them, I give up. Maybe the booze caught up with me; three drinks on an empty stomach, after all. I do remember the room spinning. But drunk or not, what use was it fighting?

They left me in there. I found my clothes, feeling in the dark on the dirt floor, and got dressed. I stumbled outside, found the light above the back door and made my way to it. Ida come bouncing through the door, no doubt to turn yet another trick.

"Oh," she said, surprised to see me. "Was that you calling me a while back?"

If I'd had my full wits about me I might've killed her. I said nothing. I couldn't.

She looked at my clothes, then back at my face, which, if nothing else, told her I wasn't happy. "What, they didn't pay you?" she asked.

I knowed what she said, but heard her say, You can have another baby.

I turned and left. I walked around the building to the front of the bar. Elmer was in his car, asleep on the steering wheel. I kept walking.

* * *

Foolish, I know. Especially given what happened and could happen again with me out alone on the road in the middle of the night. But what more could anyone do to me? Couldn't do any more. Only could do it again. Only could do it again. Only could do it again. Which kept ringing through my head. And made me fearless. All the way back to the reservation.

Ofelia was asleep on the couch, passed out no doubt. She didn't stir when I come in. I sat down at the table cluttered with dirty dishes and unfolded clothes. A lantern burned next to the clothes. I stared at it, looking from it to the clothes. And then Only-could-do-it-again become more, become what I was also hearing, more like knowing, on my walk back here. Plain and simple, a warning: Watch for it. Keep your eyes open. I looked towards the bedroom where the babies was sleeping. Light flickered there. I looked back at Ofelia, snoring on her back. I got up, seen the two babies asleep in their crib next to the bed. I blowed out the lantern above them on the dresser.

I wanted to take a bath. Two or three o'clock in the morning, no hot water. It wasn't that I felt dirty, really; I wanted to stay awake, keep the clearness of my vision. Things was all of a sudden so clear and simple. I didn't want to cloud things, let my vision get murky again. It didn't matter that there was no hot water; wasn't it cold water I wanted? I stripped off my clothes, gone into the kitchen and stood in the big metal tub and poured the two buckets of cold house water over me.

It was near daylight when I heard Elmer's car pull up in front of the house. Both car doors opened and closed, which meant, of course, that Ida had come back with him. I was at the table, the lamplight flickering. I didn't get up to look past the curtains. Elmer come through the front door. He looked at Ofelia, then he seen me.

"Gee, up so early," he said. He smelled like vomit, his eyes was at half-mast.

"Oh, yeah," I said, answering in the same tone of voice, as if the next thing I would say was that breakfast would be ready in five minutes.

I seen him looking at the clean dress I was wearing, one of Ofelia's they'd put on me during the last week, since, after the fire, I had nothing but that one other dress to my name.

"Looks good on you," he said.

He didn't know what he was saying. "Too big," I said, and with that he shuffled into the bedroom.

* * *

The clear vision I'd felt after I'd come back got squashed, first with the appearance of Elmer, then with thoughts of Ida and everyone and everything else. It retreated that morning with the light coming through the curtains, like a snail taking cover from the sun under a rock. I didn't ponder things deep then; I simply thought of Ida over at Uncle McKinley's, no doubt having coffee with his wife. It was Sunday, which I soon enough realized, and which was lucky for Elmer sleeping off his drunk. Yes, Ida at Uncle McKinley's; Zelda no doubt fixing eggs inside fat Auntie Maria's; the others stoking their fires and starting for the well with their buckets. All the world outside stirring, coming out in the light, pushing me further and further into the shadows. Except for Ida, and, of course, Elmer and Ofelia, I hadn't seen anybody since the fire. I tried not to think about them. If I had anywhere else to go, I'd go; I wouldn't stay and have to look at Elmer and Ofelia either.

So I stayed in, avoided people. Made myself busy with little Mona and Lena, which Elmer and Ofelia appreciated: Elmer because he felt assured the babies was safe; Ofelia because she didn't have to think of nothing no more and could drink her bottle empty by lunchtime and pass out. Elmer packed water, brung in the groceries. There was nothing for me to do outside, no reason for me to have to go out at all. Nobody come to see me, not Zelda or Ida. Elmer, if he knowed what happened to me at the bar, he never let on. He only talked to me about small things—the kids, the price of groceries. Trapped in that house with him, that empty talk become something I could at least partway hide behind. It made things safe inside.

But I did go out.

All was not lost. Not the memory of my clear-seeing things. That memory stayed with me. It was like a flower bud, a night-blooming jasmine that opened after I heard the last of the folks returning from the roundhouse close their doors. Thinking about it helped when thoughts of Charlie come up, and they did, what with me taking care of those two kids. Another thing it done: kept me from ever wanting another drink again. I wanted to stay clear.

I waited in the dark with Ofelia and Elmer, usually one on the couch and one in the bed, snoring behind me. I waited until the reservation, or most of it, was sleeping. Then I crept out. And it wasn't like before; I didn't feel removed from the world in that way. It was just the walking, the moving itself. I gone along. I spied. I darted from the back door to the front of Elmer's car. Crouched low, I gone then from the car to the side of Uncle McKinley's shed, and from there to a thicket of scotch broom. A secret trail that encircled the entire reservation, avoiding the two or three dogs that never got used to my rounds and barked, and any other pitfalls that might cause someone to wake up and look out their window. Of course, part of the thrill was the fear of getting caught, in which case folks would think that either I was trying to steal something or that I was some kind of spook, a werebear or weredog on my way to, or coming back from, putting on my skin. The other part of the thrill was having the guts to take on the fear, to overthrow it, and go out in the first place. I was slow at first, mapping my way from bush to post with utmost care. Within a couple weeks, I was sliding around the reservation effortless, half a dozen times before I seen the morning star.

Just as I'd come out, so did the secrets of the reservation. The secrets' time was my time. These things I spied: Sipie, Zelda and Ida's sister and Auntie Maria's one untainted daughter, had a boyfriend she was sneaking out to meet at the bottom of the road most every night, an Indian I didn't recognize, no doubt someone from another reservation someplace that she met while working in the crops; Sam Toms, my father, was back in the area fooling around with Bertha again, probably resting and eating in Auntie Maria's house during the day; and Uncle McKinley and his wife had near nightly arguments—why, in the middle of the night, I don't know—about Ida and now her brother, Dewey, living with them. Uncle McKinley, his old grumpy self again, complaining to his kind-hearted wife on the back steps that before long all of Auntie Maria's kids would be living under his roof. I could watch folks this way; unlike what I imagined I would see outside the curtains during the day—the women gathered gossiping at the well, Zelda dragging her raggedy ass here and there following Auntie Maria— what I seen at night made sense to me.

Naturally, with all this wandering at night, I got tired during the day. But I worked things out. When the babies napped, I napped; Ofelia, drunk as she was most of the time, was like having a third baby, and by the afternoon, when the two babies took their long nap, she was passed out, allowing me a long period of rest too. Then I'd get up and fix everybody dinner and wait for Elmer to come home.

The babies was actually more trouble than Ofelia. Sassy, fussing things they was; hard to keep them happy. You could've guessed they'd grow into ornery adults. To my idea they was born drunk, what with Ofelia's drinking, and lived their lives with a perpetual hangover. Ofelia, drunk or not, was nice enough, easy going. Except for her full size, she resembled

Clementine a lot, the same thin mouth, the same way of following things with her eyes, watching, as if deep down she was scared and couldn't trust what she was seeing.

Again and again, I offered Elmer money to help pay for food, and each time he refused it. I'd take out Elizabeth's envelope from my dress pocket, the one dress I'd wash and wear day in and day out, and offer Elmer the envelope. "Keep it," he'd say, or "I should be the one paying you." Like I said, my being there allowed him peace of mind. Did I have peace of mind? I didn't think about it. I had a routine. It had been a couple of months now since Charlie had died.

One night I ventured into the apple orchard behind the houses. I say ventured, but truth is, I was avoiding my cousin Moses's dog that he'd forgot to tie up. It was barking mad; I was afraid it would come after me, so I had to loop wider around the houses there, push into the orchard. Actually, this night and the night before my traveling about was tough, and not just because of a barking dog. Two days before, on a Sunday, we'd got the news that the Japanese had bombed Pearl Harbor. Folks was all astir about it, visiting back and forth in one another's houses long after they'd left the roundhouse.

In any event, I was standing in the apple orchard when it occurred to me—no doubt because I was standing doing nothing but waiting for my trail to clear—that Charlie was buried someplace nearby. I felt a weakening throughout my body, as if I would just then collapse into myself. No, I told myself. No. Don't look. Even if they put a marker, he's not here. He's not here. He's not here. I forced myself through the orchard, eyes fixed straight ahead, to its edge, where the trees ended at the opposite end of the reservation.

And that was when I seen Auntie Maria and Zelda, Auntie Maria pulling a sobbing Zelda along by the arm, more like dragging her.

Catching my breath, I watched them coming from the direction of Auntie Maria's place, moving fast until they was in front of Big Sarah's door, Auntie Maria knocking furiously. This end of the reservation, by the round-house, was quiet and Auntie Maria's loud knocking echoed through the trees, hitting me in the face like a warning, a warning that should have said, People will be waking, so go back further into the trees. But I did not. I stood and watched as a light gone on in the house and Big Sarah answered the door and took them inside. I looked at the light in the windows. What possessed me I couldn't say. Maybe I thought some kind of emergency was at hand, something wrong with Zelda, that she was sick, and I wanted to find out what it was. I knowed I could see through the windows if I gone up

close. Which was what I done. Crept to the back of the house, which I could
see clear, where the shades over the two windows was up.

Even before my nose was touching the windowsill, I seen Zelda
seated at Big Sarah's kitchen table sobbing hysterical. Sucked me right up
to that window, like a moth to the light; and when I couldn't hear the
particulars of what was going on, what folks was saying between Zelda's
sobbing, I ducked low and gone to the other window, which, even before I
lifted my head, I knowed was open a crack. Zelda wailed now so you'd think
someone had died; wailed as if she was pleading for Big Sarah to bring them
back. When I lifted my eyes, my nose was even with the open crack, making
it seem as if I was hearing with my nose, breathing in the sound of their
voices.

"Please," Zelda begged, truly like a child. She was talking in Indian,
all three of them was.

Big Sarah, seated with her back to me, no scarf over her short gray-
ing hair, said, "*Mensi*, Hush!"

"But I knowed," Zelda protested. "I knowed what I was doing!"

"See," Auntie Maria, who had her back to me also, said. "See, she's
been going on like this for weeks and I tell her the same thing."

"If some sinner's baby was going to get sacrificed like you said, I
wanted it to be hers, not mine," Zelda sobbed.

"*Mensi*, hush," said Big Sarah.

"But I put the lantern on the blankets . . ."

I pulled back from the window, caught my breath. I thought I'd
lunge forward, that I had stepped back only to launch myself off my feet and
through the glass to snap her neck with one swift blow. But nothing moved
me. I kept looking at Zelda, fearful, crying. Something akin to what I felt
in the orchard come over me, but it wasn't a weakening, a collapsing into
myself. It was an emerging, as if from an old skin, and I felt wet, alive. She
looked old, pitiful. "I forgive you," I said out loud and begun to walk.

* * *

I could say that I seen in Zelda at that moment the sum total of her
sorry life, her forever wanting her cake and eating it, too, and how I was
caught up in it: her wanting to play in Benedict's barn with me and Nellie
and then going back to her mother and Big Sarah and telling on us, giving
Big Sarah information about her supposed vision about bad girls; or, finally,
her setting the lantern on Charlie's blankets so that he would burn, get
sacrificed, because she thought somehow, for whatever reason Big Sarah and
Auntie Maria put into her head or plain scared her into crazy imagining,

that if my baby was sacrificed hers might be saved. Or I could say I seen in her, as I had before, a pitiful representative of all of us, Zelda just being more obvious about the fear and related wretchedness in each of our lives. Wasn't we all a girl at the front door offering a dress she stole from the house in exchange for a home in that house? Wasn't we all burning some baby or other so that we'd be safe in that home? Of course, if at the time I actually pondered this much on our common misery, I would've froze. Point is, all this thinking is the stuff of hindsight, what I might have said years later— or now—when I remembered it. Then, I kept walking.

Come across the lagoon, just walking. In Santa Rosa, there was no lights even though it was still dark; men was taking down the Christmas lights on Fourth Street. Roosters crowed in Benedict's barn. The creek was high.

Mama's place was gone and so was Clementine's. But Chum's stood. There was a sign on the door, a piece of wood nailed there like a warning with faded black letters that read "Hanged Woman." I stepped up, turned the rusty doorknob, gone in. Couldn't see nothing, but sat down, leaned against the wall and fell fast asleep.

When I woke, I seen light coming through knotholes and cracks in the doorjambs and boarded-up windows. I heard a car out on the road, birds. The place was cold, damp, and musty. My eyes adjusting to the darkness, I could make out the outlines of Chum's table and chairs; otherwise, the room was empty. The hole where the stovepipe had been above the stove was boarded up like the windows. Judging from the angle of the light rays coming into the room, I figured it was about four o'clock in the afternoon.

I was amazed I slept so long, sitting up, at that. I must've been tired. Then my thoughts turned to where I was. Certainly, I couldn't stay there. What was I going to do? And with that question, I reached down into my dress pocket only to find it empty and remember that I was wearing Ofelia's dress, that I'd washed my dress the evening before and that it was probably still hanging in the kitchen where I left it to dry. The envelope, which I normally kept buttoned in my dress pocket, was tucked into one of the baby's pillows, inside the pillow slip, where I would hide it while my dress dried.

I thought of Del. A dairy south of town he had said. But that's all I thought. I quit thinking anymore about what I would do. I knowed it would be different.

I got up, peered out a knothole toward Benedict's house and barn, two square specks across the winter field, a white one and the larger gray one with the corrals. I couldn't make out any people. A car was parked in front of the house. Closer to me, this side of the field, the barren ground in front of the shack and the other structures still standing was littered with rusty cans, smashed prune crates, a pile of clothes, no doubt from the Indians and others who'd come in the fall to pick Old Man Benedict's pears.

I got antsy with the desire to leave. But I worried about getting caught outside in the light. I didn't want to be stopped and have to explain myself, whatever it was I would say.

I tried to sleep again. But I couldn't. I found myself exploring shelves and cupboards, empty but still intact. I half-expected to find Chum's empty candy jar. But nothing. Then, sitting at the cold table, I felt something underneath with my foot. I pushed the chair back and blindly felt for whatever it was; rods, twined-thick willow rods, a headboard, but when I pulled it up, I seen it was one of Chum's baby cradles. No doubt about it, the bullrush and redbud star design badly faded, but even in that dark room clear enough. It had been facedown, was facedown still in my lap, the way I had picked it up. I knowed what a downturned basket meant—it was how to poison someone's baby—and you wasn't to look at it, let alone touch it. Taboo. But I didn't wonder whether or not someone poisoned Chum, or whether or not she seen it and then gone to the barn, if that was what happened and who might've done it, if it was Big Sarah or somebody else. And I didn't worry about me, what would happen to me for picking it up. I done this: turned the basket upright.

And more. With the ends of my dress, or, rather, Ofelia's dress, I polished off the mildew, wiped the willow rods clean. I pulled the broken sedge-root ties tight with my teeth and tied them. I held the basket up, shook it, testing its strength. The strings of clamshell disk beads and abalone pendants, still well attached to the back of the cradle, clinked. It was time to go.

No matter that it wasn't completely dark; still light, in fact. I gone out, packing the basket to my chest. I made for the road, a straight shot, the graveyard. I walked. Passing Benedict's barn I thought of my own cradle, how I'd left it in there. I thought of Westin too. But I didn't linger on them things; they was but passing thoughts. What come to mind just then was Old Uncle: He was in Clementine's place, saying to me, "I come to help her die," something that when he said it, and when I'd thought about it later, had only made me mad. Why now, why had this come up now? But before I could even think to ask the question, I found I'd come around the bend past Benedict's place. On them southern hills, where me and Old Uncle had parked, was a full moon. "I seen you on that road," he was saying. I kept walking. I didn't look up at the moon. I didn't check for a dark spot above the left eye. But he kept talking: "I seen you on that road." I kept walking. I gone faster. My heart begun to pound, the clam disk beads and the abalone pendants clinking and clacking against the basket with my heart, everything pounding, and I gone faster and then he was singing.

* * *

When I got to the edge of town, out of breath, things settled. I was frightened. I wondered if I had been spooked. I wondered about the basket in my arms. For the first time since I'd left the reservation my mind was sullied with thinking. My heart still raced.

I seen a newspaper stand and gone for it. I'd read the headlines—anything—to stop the thoughts in my head. The Japanese was everywhere, the headlines said, just off our coast, which is why there was no lights on at night, should they want to bomb us. War everywhere. Here. In the Pacific. Europe. Then I seen the date—December 9, 1941—and realized it had been over a month since that day Elmer took me to pick up my last pay from Elizabeth.

I was stunned. If it wasn't for a couple of white ladies pushing past me to get to the papers, I might've stood there with my mouth hung open until Christmas. Slowly, I walked up Fourth Street, past the folks bustling about to get their errands done before nightfall. I turned south on B Street. I was in a daze. Approaching the edge of town, I stopped.

I'm pregnant, I thought. What am I going to do?

There, at the end of the street, was a large old house, white with a picket fence. Over the tops of the fence I seen iris blooming, early, almost out of season, but a rich blue-purple nonetheless, the same color of the evening sky they was reaching to. And in that sky, solid and unsinkable, was the moon.

Iris.

I lifted the cradle up and called her to me.

Iris.

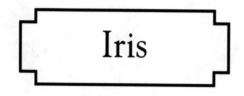

Iris

It's not enough that my mother calls and tells me that my son has been beat up, hurt. She's also got to tell me that he is leaving town. "Oh, Johnny's OK," she says, "don't worry," and then she hangs up. She leaves me out in the cold, knowing full well that in no time at all I'll be just where she wants me, knocking at her door.

My mother.

She didn't call as soon as she learned Johnny was hurt. She waited until after, until she had a second weapon to assault me with, the rope to tether me once I was stunned. How did she know to wait? Because the world opens itself to my mother; stars in the night sky roll back like stones that have been guarding secret passageways. She flies up, ascends, and just for a moment, before she travels on, she stands in the mouth of that secret cave where she has landed and looks back at the world, her world. What she sees is a chessboard. The pieces are lined up, her kings and queens and those of her opponent. She sees again where she is stuck, why she has flown to this unearthly abode. Then she turns and goes, the star door closing quietly behind her. When she returns she knows how the pieces will fall into place; she knows how to win her game. The spirits have told her.

She denies this. She says for a person so shortsighted I have a vivid imagination. She says, "Iris, you don't have to leave this earth to see what's right in front of you. Just open your eyes."

She's an Indian, old school. She keeps the white world of pious oaths and new and newer things at bay with a flick of her wrist and a girlish chuckle. At night she prays in the old language; the walls are like the ears

of a million attentive children reverently holding the high s's and abrupt
starts and stops of her language, words whose shape my throat and tongue
never learned. Of course, the fact that my mother is Indian does not automatically explain her power. Most of the Indians I know, most of the Indians
I have known, are bankrupt, and I mean in every sense of the word. If they
could as much as lift their heads to the sky, let alone see the stars, they'd
have done more in that minute than they had done thus far in the entirety
of their miserable lives.

Mother's family was known for its unusual ways. Her uncle per-
formed miracles. Maybe it was her great-uncle; I've never heard Mother refer
to him as anything but Old Uncle. His story makes that of the man who
walked on water look tame. Old Uncle didn't walk on water, he dove under
it. He turned into a frog and searched the bottom of Santa Rosa creek for
ancient medicine. He cured the sick with the medicine he found, wet sand
and slime collected under his nails. When the moon was full and bright
above the hills, he'd turn into a botfly and make his way there; people saw
him, a dark spot above the moon's left eye, the entire time he was gone.
From that place on the moon, he saw all that would take place on earth in
the month ahead, the new moon: weather, the sex of a new baby, the salmon
running. A prophet, Mother says. Month by month. He could see things.
She says he never died; he simply walked off the reservation one day. But
before he left he did two things: He told her that he wasn't really leaving,
that if she watched and listened she would see him again; and he sang her
a song.

"Do you hear it?" she'd ask. Until I was ten, she'd ask me over and
over if I heard Old Uncle singing, if I heard the song. An angel song, she
called it. "What's it sound like?" I'd ask, and she'd sigh with disappointment
and go about whatever she was doing. He was everywhere, or so she'd have
you think. Frogs croaking in the ponds and marshes just outside of town, a
hummingbird hovering above the bottlebrush plant, it was always Old Uncle. "Can you hear him singing, Iris?" "No," I yelled, fed up with the question.

I remember the last time she asked. It was a late fall day and we'd
gone to pick acorns in the hills. We always went to the same place, a spot
just off the road with an unforgettable view of the town and valley below.
Beneath the large old tan oaks that grew there, we worked furiously, knocking the nuts from the trees with long sticks, maybe a broom handle, and
then picking them off the ground and putting them into gunnysacks that
Mother dragged back to the car waiting on the side of the road with its
trunk open like the smiling jaws of an enormous dragon. She packed what
she called "a lunch," even though by the time we finished working it was

usually closer to dinnertime. Half of the lunch we ate, peanut butter and jelly sandwiches and potato chips, strips of carrots and celery; the other half we left there, an offering to the trees, she'd say.

On the day I am thinking of, we had finished late; we started late, not heading for the hills until after Mother picked me up from school. We sat together on a flat lichen-covered rock eating "the lunch" and taking in the breadth of the valley below. The sun sat low in a crimson sky behind us, casting a red hue over the land and into Mother's white cotton blouse, and already the first evening lights showed from the spreading city like tiny wildflowers strewn here and there across the valley floor. It was peaceful. I began counting the lights—one, two, three, four—out loud, the way any content child of ten might. Then Mother raised her arm and pointed to a place under the trees. I saw nothing. "What?" I asked. Her black eyes were fixed there, her arm and finger a straight unmoving line, exhorting me to follow. She dropped just her finger, indicating the ground in front of me. I saw nothing, kicked the dry, curled oak leaves and still saw nothing, and then a pattern, black and white, a design strange and unearthly, yet as regular and measured as the pattern on an old woman's basket: a snake, as thick as my leg, so long I saw neither head nor tail, and it was moving but a foot from the tips of my shoes. I froze, my throat locked. Not just because I was startled, but because seeing neither head nor tail, I had the sensation that I was surrounded, trapped, as if it had made a circle of itself around me.

"Who is it?" Mother called.

"A snake," I said, barely able to open my mouth. The sound of my voice frightened me, my words in the open air loud enough to alert the snake, cause it to rise up and strike, or tighten the circle I imagined it had already made around me.

I looked back down. It was unmoving now. The red evening had settled into the white squares and triangles across its wide back. Then I heard Mother again.

"Who is it?" she implored.

Before I had not heard her question clearly, or recognized it for what it was. Now I did, heard her and knew exactly what she was up to. How could she do this to me? Still looking at the monster a foot from my shoes, I was no longer frightened. I hated my mother so.

Slowly I lifted my eyes to her. She had dropped her arm, folded it into the other across her chest, an impatient school teacher waiting for an answer. I would give her nothing. I wanted to get safely away from the snake, nothing more. When I looked down again, I saw that it had moved, the labyrinthine pattern under the leaves several feet from me now; it was moving, and then it disappeared, suddenly, under the leaves, still never showing its beginning or end. I waited half a minute longer. Then I made my way past Mother to the car.

We drove in silence, around corners, down through the sloping apple orchards, until we were on the highway, a straight flat stretch to town. Up ahead, I saw the lights of Santa Rosa, where we lived, and said, "You knew it was there."

She said nothing. She was staring straight ahead. I wasn't going to let her brush away my anger with her silence. I wasn't finished. "You're not normal," I said. "I wish you weren't my mother."

Still nothing. In the oncoming car lights, I saw her motionless face and the smooth ridges of her knuckles as she gripped the steering wheel. "I hate you," I said.

Nothing, not a word. Only when we were home, parked in the driveway, did she talk. She stopped me just as I was getting out of the car. "Iris," she said, "you'll live life the hard way."

Of course I didn't know what she meant, the full scope of her words. At the time, I took them as a reproach I could turn my back on; I had reason to. Later, I saw what she said as a curse, her curse; and later still a vision she had, as clear as a reflection in glass, of my life up to and including this very moment.

About two weeks after the incident, I confronted her again. We were in the midst of a spat over my hair: She wanted to trim my bangs, I wanted to grow them out; bangs cut straight across the forehead were for little girls. "But they're in your eyes," she said. "Good," I snapped, "now maybe I'll be blind and step on the rattlesnake so it can bite me—like you want!"

"It wasn't a rattlesnake," she said, setting her pair of silver scissors on the kitchen counter.

I looked up from the bowl of hot onion soup she'd brought over from the white people's house and set in the center of our wooden table. "Don't start that," I warned her.

"It wasn't a rattlesnake."

"You're weird!"

Slowly, she pulled open the drawer next to where she was standing, and with one steady sweep of her hand, guided the scissors across the counter until they dropped into the drawer. "No," she said, nudging the drawer shut with the top of her hip. "I'm just your poor old mother." And with that she turned and walked into the bedroom and closed the door behind her.

Guilt. The silent treatment. It's part of the way she works. It's what you can see, a technique used by a lot of mothers. It's normal. But don't trust it. Not with her, for it's more, more than a guilt that spoils a kid's favorite lunch of hot onion soup. Yes, to look at her—if you didn't know her—you might believe what you see, a poor old Indian. Even then, when she wasn't yet thirty-five, much younger than I am now, she was old-looking. She wore her clothes like a uniform of defeat, like so many Indian women in those days: folded gingham scarves, usually a faded purple or red, that hid her thick, parted hair tied too quickly and carelessly in a bun or a roll of some sort at the back of her head, and that hooded her eyes so no one taller than her—white people—could see them; and those dresses of hers, not a one without a broken seam or an unraveling hem; even her shoes, cheap and plain old-lady blacks and browns that did nothing for her ankles and legs. Not yet thirty-five, and she looked as if she'd given up, put down the blooming rose of a young woman's body and replaced it with a bale of straw.

But don't believe it. Not then. Not now. This is the woman who works like water: Cup her into your hands and she looks pure and simple, and yet she erodes mountains, cuts wide and winding swaths through open fields. She wore me down and wore me down, sanded and filed away my resistance until I was a smooth obsidian chunk that she could carry in her hand. She worked quietly, unnoticed, plotting her moves from her place in the stars above, and when she moved, when she moved her chess pieces over mine, there was never anything to do but admit defeat, see my empty space and what she had painted there: a picture of an ungrateful daughter.

What I remember most about the day I saw the snake is that afterward, that night alone in my room, I felt separate from Mother as never before. I was angry, betrayed. What she understood and wanted for me was quite different from what I could give her—and from what I wanted for myself. I had my own life, after all, didn't I? Unbeknownst to me then, I began the silent every waking moment task of erecting a wall to protect that life. She was never at a loss for ways to tear it down.

* * *

I thought the wall was down. I thought I'd learned my lessons. But no, there's more. "Johnny's hurt," she said. "He's leaving town. You won't see him."

My son.

Everything I'm not. He's the glove that fits Mother's hand, a vase for her flowers. Wouldn't you have guessed it? It's as if he was born to her and not me. He set his eyes on her from the beginning. Five months old and he rolled from the couch to follow her out the door; I panicked, grabbing him off the floor where he fell, only to turn and find her laughing. Already they were inseparable. Oh, and from the beginning, according to her—and according to him—he saw Old Uncle in things. They've got a language of

ONE

Mother and me, sitting in the garden, and she was looking up with all of the night sky in her eyes, and I asked if she knew how to spell "pinafore." She peered down at me, to where I was sitting in a small wicker chair alongside her. It was an early spring night, unseasonably warm, and the scent of lilac and honeysuckle filled the air; years later I would know this as a night for lovers. Mother's eyes tightened, focused, and confusion showed in her brow. "What?" she asked.

"Pinafore," I repeated, hearing myself and suddenly seeing the beautiful red dress in my mind's eye.

"How do you spell it?" I said, thinking I could cover myself with the question.

Mother sighed and looked back at the stars. "Use the dictionary," she said.

* * *

Just recently, I'd won the school spelling contest; not only the contest for the sixth grade, which I was in, but for the entire Henry C. Fremont Elementary School, grades one through eight. Those rainy winter nights, before Christmas until the end of February, Mother and I had sat with the open dictionary between us on the kitchen table. She picked words from the list, pages and pages my teacher had given those of us who were interested in the contest. If I was stuck, she gestured to the thick book with her chin, and said, "Use the dictionary." But on that warm spring night I am remembering she wasn't thinking of any forthcoming spelling contest any more than I was. There wouldn't be another contest, not for me anyway, because I refused to participate; and from all that I could see just then, if Mother's sigh meant anything, it was only another show of her disappointment in me.

It wasn't that she wanted me to be a white girl. She doubted whites, was suspicious of them, and, with her offhand remarks, a finger always pointing to their misdeeds, she tried to instill in me the same attitude. Nor did she want me humiliated any more than I had been already by the school's condescending praise. "A miracle," my teacher and the school principal proclaimed with raised eyebrows that everyone could see. Not that I was just a sixth-grader, or even a heretofore undiscovered genius, but that I was "an Indian." What upset Mother was that I dropped out of the race, said no to the regional contest, because, in the language of my classmates, which Mother heard from me loud and clear, spelling contests were for ugly girls, girls who had to wear glasses. "You'll only be unhappy," she told me, "listening to other people."

Mother used her admonitions the way a smart shopper carries coupons around the supermarket, always looking for the items to spend them on. She knew just when to drop a remark, how to stop me in my tracks. Iris, open your eyes. Iris, listen to yourself. She said when she looked at the nighttime sky, she saw how simple and small the world is, even the biggest things here, people and events. You forgive and go on, she said. You see with all of Creation's eyes. You see everything. I never believed her, or payed much attention, not about that or about any of the other things she told me, stories about Indians and magic power. Before I had thought it all weird, the way my schoolmates might had they heard the same stories. Just another of Mother's quirks.

Sitting there with the stars overhead, I found myself worried all of a sudden. The thought crossed my mind that she might have seen what was in my eyes and then somehow coaxed it from my lips. How else would I have been so foolish as to blurt out the word "pinafore"? I'd have to keep talking, distract her with other questions, chatter. I had planned too carefully, worked too hard for her to grab a hold and try and stop me. It was too soon yet, not only to let her see the red dress, but to let her know where she and the rest of the world would find me in it.

* * *

We lived on MacDonald Avenue, the nicest street in town. Wide, and lined with tall eucalyptus trees that smelled so sharp and clean even a blind man would have known what street he was on. Rolling green lawns and square-trimmed privet hedges surrounded the old two- and three-story

white Victorian houses with their double front doors and long rectangular
windows. At night, with the shades drawn, the windows looked like the
hollow yellow eyes of a giant jack-o'-lantern; and during the day, particularly
in the mornings and late afternoons when the sun beamed onto the houses
at low angles, the windows reflected the green grass, the hedges, all the way
back to the street where you were standing and looking. Ten years before
the time I lived there, in the late thirties and early forties, Hollywood used
MacDonald Avenue as a location for "Every Street, America." Of course,
Mother's and my getting there was bumpy; and our presence, well, condi-
tional. We lived behind number 405 in a two-room house without a stove
or a refrigerator, the servants' quarters. Mother was a maid.

Before that it was a shack behind a house on B Street, not too far
from MacDonald, but not nearly as nice. And before that a room Mother
rented in Hotel Figueroa, a dump tucked in that stretch of neon dives,
pawnshops, and used-clothing stores on lower Fourth, where she came and
went day after day to one or more of her half dozen different housecleaning
jobs. Yes, we'd moved up, a steady climb since the hotel. But I didn't think
up or down then, merely space, more and more space. Each move from the
hotel afforded me more of what I knew before: the cabin next to the creek
and Mr. Wilson's dairy, which is the first home I remember, where I could
run to my heart's content, where I was in the world instead of looking out
at it through a single window, seeing only what Mother warned me about,
the neon-littered street with its bad men and women, people who could
harm me. So a move up meant space, a wider, safer world to run in. But
now things were beginning to change again. My schoolmates told me as
much with their interrogating glances; and, at home, the stately old couples
who strolled the wide street where I ran and played alone, the way they
looked down their somber faces with cold, charged eyes at me. I was becoming steadily aware of how little of that plant-green and sky-blue space outside
my windows was mine. Day by day the world was shrinking and, before long,
would hold itself against the four walls of my small house.

But I found someone to help me. I found a companion. Mary Beth
Polk, the daughter of the people in the big house, Mother's bosses, Mr. and
Mrs. Polk. No matter that Mary Beth was white and rich. She had everything
and nothing. She was a girl in a family where the sun rose and set on the
boy. In school she was the nerd with glasses, having graduated from her
earlier status as cootie bug.

Our friendship started one evening close to five, when her father, a
tall man, pale and austere, with a thick scar running from his temple to his
cheekbone, pushed through the swinging doors of the household kitchen
and said, "What do we do with Mary Beth?" He was talking to Mrs. Polk,

who was standing across the wide counter from Mother, dipping a finger in
the clam dip Mother had apportioned into three silver bowls for the Polks'
dinner party. Mrs. Polk sucked her finger, and when she turned and faced
her husband, it was hard to tell if what was on her mind was the clam dip
or her husband's question.

"She can come to my house," I blurted out.

We'd hardly been at the Polks' a month, and despite Mother's repeated warning to mind my place, to speak only when spoken to in that
house, I couldn't contain myself. It made perfect sense. Mary Beth's parents
were having a function for her brother, dinner for his friends and their
parents, and, after a half-minute discussion, they would decide to send Mary
Beth to her room with dinner and schoolwork—I'd seen it happen once
before.

Mrs. Polk looked up, found me—and Mary Beth—behind my
aproned mother. She held her sucked-clean finger in midair, about six inches
from her face, indicating her surprise.

"Iris," Mother snapped over her shoulder.

"No," Mrs. Polk said to Mother. "It isn't a bad idea."

She craned her head to check with her husband. The bright overhead light caught the curve of her unbelievably long neck, highlighted all
the more by the way she pulled her hair up and tight in a twist. A spray of
short bangs sprang tastefully from her forehead; I thought she looked like
Audrey Hepburn on the cover of *Life* magazine. She and Mr. Polk gave each
other the look I knew so well: what I'd seen in teachers' eyes when it was
my turn for them to inspect my fingernails, check my hair.

Mother, quietly slicing celery into uniform sticks, sensed as much
too. I saw her pause, the stained knife still a moment, before she resumed
her work and said, "Go on out, Iris."

I was suddenly embarrassed. I crammed the celery stick I was holding—and eating—into my dress pocket and turned to go.

"Wait," Mrs. Polk said.

I spun back around and froze at attention. I thought she might
reprimand me for talking out of place, even though she had said my suggestion wasn't a bad idea. Either that or she would tell me not to take food
that wasn't mine off the counter. But I was surprised. "It's OK. That *is* a
good idea," she said to me. Then she turned to Mother. "I mean, if it's OK
with you, Elba . . . They can do their homework together. They are in the
same class, after all."

You'd think she was trying to persuade Mother, but of course she
was talking for the benefit of Mr. Polk. He was inscrutable. He was always
the same, cold and austere. Except when he was turned so you could see his

scar, see only the left side of his face. Then he appeared downright sinister. Mrs. Polk looked from Mother to him and then back to Mother.

"Yes, that's fine," Mother said.

What else could she say? She found me next to the kitchen door and then turned back to her chopping. I knew I'd have hell to pay. But just then Mary Beth, who had been as still and quiet as the copper-bottomed pots hanging on the wall behind her, rushed toward me and in one clean sweep we were out the door.

* * *

A month is eternity in a child's life, and yet in that time, the time I'd lived behind 405, I hadn't known Mary Beth. We rode together to and from school every day; Mother took us in the Polks' old Ford, the extra car. We were in the same class, sat one in front of the other. But what was tacitly understood, who I was and who she was, what our parents each in their own way told us—Mother with her warning about when and when not to speak in the Polks' house, and Mary Beth's parents with who knows what—followed us to school, kept an invisible but ever present line between us. And it was the same line, like a rolling fence, that was circling tighter and tighter around my world on MacDonald Avenue.

But Mary Beth wasn't a free bird herself: big plastic blue-rimmed glasses; hair the color of pale egg yolks that frizzed even from the braids her mother—or my mother—took pains to tie tight each morning; and allergies, forever a stuffy nose, so that when she talked, and she always talked facing the ground, she sounded as if she was speaking from the inside of a tin pail. There was plenty to keep her cut off from that world too. In fact, I was playing volleyball with the other girls while Mary Beth was still relegated to the bench with her books and daffodil-painted lunch box. Despite the glances and occasional whispering I'd catch from huddled schoolmates looking in my direction, I might have done OK. That is, if Allison Witherow, the tall girl at the top of the pecking order, hadn't said out loud what everyone else had only whispered.

"What is it, anyway?" she asked. "What's an Indian?"

Even then I guessed where the word came from, who at school uttered it first. Mary Beth's brother. Who else knew what I was? Mary Beth didn't talk to anyone. Patrick, her brother, president of the Junior Demolay, knew and probably told everybody else. I watched him the way a mouse watches a snake.

"You're an Indian," Allison pushed.

It was after school. I was walking to the parking lot, Mary Beth trailing with an armful of books. Earlier, during noon recess, I'd spiked the winning point against Allison's team; I thought she was mad at me. Two other girls joined her, the three of them now surrounding me as I walked. I looked up, beyond them, and there was Mother, a red gingham scarf tied around her head, her thick brown arm hanging out the car window. Her eyes were peeled.

"My mother," I said and pointed.

I don't know if I meant to scare them, or perhaps simply to deflect their attention so I could run. Maybe both. Regardless, they ran. They didn't mention "Indian" again—not out loud—and I was careful not to cross Allison on the volleyball court. Mother scared them. With her hard, sun-blackened face and fat, hanging arm, she was ugly. She was everything they weren't.

I was lighter than Mother. At night, while taking a bath, I'd hold her white, enamel-backed hand mirror over my stomach and on my thighs, where the sun hadn't touched my skin, and imagine my entire body the fair color reflected in the round of glass. I would be almost the color of my classmates at Henry C. Fremont. And my hair wasn't too thick or black, and didn't grow low on my forehead the way Mother's did. I didn't think I was ugly, not just to look at me. And my clothes were acceptable, dresses clean and what everybody else was wearing.

But my house! I hadn't given it a second's thought until I saw Mary Beth at the door, wide-eyed. Surely she had been in the place before. Hadn't she seen servants come and go? Perhaps she'd only seen the quarters empty, between employees, never with someone living in them, never furnished. I saw what she saw: the small wooden kitchen table with its two mismatched chairs; and the folded clothes on top of the table, Mother's slips and stretched, gray-white bra, my panties, of all things; the cold box—not a refrigerator—in the corner with a dirty gunnysack of potatoes plunked on top; the couch, the bunched-up blankets there and the pillow on top of the pile, its case yellow-stained in sprawling islands that made the pillow look, from where Mary Beth was standing, like a faded and deflated globe of the world. She gazed up at the naked lightbulb over the table, then dropped her eyes to the window shades, yellow-stained like the pillowcase—Mother had talked of sewing curtains.

I thought fast. With one turn, I scooped the underwear off the table and stepped into the other room—my bedroom. When I reappeared I held, in place of the underwear, a Monopoly board.

Mary Beth still hesitated at the door. She braced herself, arms stretched out, palms pressed flat against each side of the door frame, as if someone was about to pull her inside against her will. For all her haste to get out of her house, she was in no hurry to come into mine. Then I saw her swallow, as if she'd just let down a teaspoon of castor oil. Her arms dropped and she looked at me, unimpressed.

"Sit down," I said.

I spread the board on the table and pulled a chair aside for her. She came, slowly. She plopped herself down. I sat opposite her. Her large glasses reflected the room. She held her face in the palms of her hands, elbows propped on the table, and stared at me. As if it wasn't enough to show her reluctance before, now she was challenging me.

"Loser has to take off her clothes," I said.

I counted ten long seconds, let her stew, and then rolled the dice: a pair of sixes.

"To see who goes first," I said and pushed the dice across the board to her.

She rolled cat's eyes. She was losing from the start. I rolled and moved eight spaces from GO.

And that's the way it continued. She lagged, always a good half dozen spaces behind. Around and around the board the same. I was buying more property, good property, Park Avenue, and stockpiling my earnings.

She was quiet. I didn't say anything either; I didn't have to. What would I say? It was clear I was winning.

Then Mother came in—with dinner. I pushed the Monopoly board aside, making room, and Mother set the stiff paper plates of steaming beef stroganoff on the table.

"Get a fork and knife," she said, then turned and left.

From the standing closet next to the cold box, I grabbed silverware and a couple of paper napkins, nice paper napkins, cloth-soft and embossed with fancy curlicues, that Mother had amassed from the Polks' kitchen, and that I was certain Mary Beth would take notice of. She was watching my every step. But still she said nothing, not even after I sat down and we began eating, not about the napkins, or even about the food, which, like the napkins, came from her kitchen. Her silence both annoyed and alarmed me. Was she thinking of Mother as a thief—a napkin thief—and would she tell her mother? Was she bothered seeing me eat food from her house? (Mother carried over most of my dinners from the big house.)

"Everybody's doing it," I said.

"What?" she asked, finally looking up.

"Playing strip Monopoly," I lied.

She picked a tiny thread of beef from her teeth and wiped it on the edge of her plate. She was looking directly at me the whole time. Then she picked up her fork and looked back down at her food. Not long after, no more than a couple of minutes, she got up and went to the door, and at that moment, Mother appeared, just as if Mary Beth had been expecting her. She held Mary Beth's schoolbooks in her arms. She stood a second looking over Mary Beth at me, then she left the books on the couch and disappeared just as quickly as she had come. Mary Beth lingered at the door. And after she sat down, she kept looking back over her shoulder; and once, as she turned back in my direction, I caught her wistful gaze. Then I felt sorry for her. I was about to speak. But she all at once looked up and said:

"Where's your father?"

I was stunned. Point is, I never thought of my father. I didn't know him, much less where he was. There wasn't much to know, which is essentially all Mother said: a man who didn't want a family. I thought fast. I guess I still felt sorry for Mary Beth. I told another lie. "He's with my brother," I said. "My brother was the favorite. My father left with him, and my mother and I had to come here and live like this."

I only meant to show empathy for her, that I understood her plight. But her flat blue eyes were suddenly wide; apparently I'd scared her to death. Was she seeing her mother and herself before long in a two-room hovel?

"We go and visit him sometimes," I said to mitigate the damage. But from the look on her face and imagining what she saw—her mother and her visiting her father in the big house—I realized I was only digging myself in deeper. I said what I meant to say in the first place, before she'd interrupted me:

"Let's do our homework."

Which we did. Or at least started to. Sat on the couch with our maps of Europe. We had to name each country and locate and name its capital, and, if the country was communist, put a red star next to the capital. We did Russia and Moscow and, on the other side of the map, England and London. Mary Beth helped me with a hard one: Czechoslovakia. She was friendly, and before long, before we'd filled in even half of the blank spaces on our maps, we'd let our books and papers fall aside and found ourselves talking. She told me about her piano lessons, how she hated them, and how her teacher, a flatulent fat woman with a Frankenstein-like wart on her neck, made her play the same composition over and over. "Sounds like Sister Agnes Jean," I said, thinking of the nun who was my teacher during the six months I went to St. Rose Catholic School, compliments of Mother's last boss, the lady on B Street. I hadn't thought of suggesting we do homework because I believed it would be fun, or even that it might lead to friendly talk, but only because I thought it might let Mary Beth forget that foolish game I had pulled her into. I felt bad. And now, seeing how much happier she was, I felt worse.

"I lied," I told her.

She smarted, looked at me. "About what?"

"The strip Monopoly," I confessed.

"I know that!" she shot back. "Did you think I was going to take off my clothes?"

She spoke to me as if I was an imbecile. She spoke as if she had known the truth all along and could've—and would've—stopped the game with the drop of a pin. She was hostile, challenging; I'd meant to be conciliatory. Was she embarrassed? I let it go.

"Dumb idea," I said.

There. What more could I do?

She stared at the maps between us on the couch, then slowly we began talking again, about what I don't remember. I know that when Mother came in to take Mary Beth home I was still worried she was upset with me. But as she was stepping out the door, she looked back and said, "Thank you for getting me out of my house." She was sincere, so much so that when Mother came in and called her a brat, I retorted loud and clear, "You don't know."

Mother, untying her soiled apron at the table, sighed. She bunched the apron in her hands and let it fall on the table, by the dinner plates. Gross, I thought.

Who would've guessed what that night would bring? I didn't, not at first. Mary Beth and I were in trouble. Neither one of us had completed our homework; our maps were full of blank spaces.

"How are you going to know which countries are communist?" our teacher, Mrs. Tomlinson barked in front of the entire class.

So during the noon recess we found ourselves benched, me unable to play volleyball, Mary Beth with someone to talk to.

"I don't give a damn," Mary Beth said, her eyes on the girls playing ball.

Surprising from an egghead—that she suddenly didn't care about her schoolwork and, of all things, the word "damn." She sat close to me, and though we weren't supposed to talk, confided from the side of her mouth a world of gossip: Our teacher, Mrs. Tomlinson, her husband didn't die in the Korean war, but instead found another woman before he came home (she knew because she heard her mother talking to Allison Witherow's mother); and Mrs. Kennedy, who we would have next year in seventh grade and whose baby died before it was born, how she went with Allison's father to a movie and Mrs. Witherow said Mrs. Kennedy wouldn't ever be any teacher of Allison's. When the bell rang, she stood up and shook my hand as if we'd made a silent pact—we were partners in crime. Communists.

And we played it to the hilt. Antics, anything we could think of:

simultaneously stepping out of line on the way in and out of class when Mrs. Tomlinson wasn't looking; and, at noon, switching clothes—blouses, skirts, anything, even socks, but only one sock so that we'd be wearing mismatched pairs when we came out of the girls' rest room. At night, while we were supposed to be studying—Mary Beth came to my house after dinner whether or not her family had company—we'd plot and plan the next day's activities. And I changed how she looked. Replaced the braids with a ponytail; even if her hair frizzed, at least it flew freely now. And no more buttoning up just the top button of her cardigan like an old lady.

Our classmates noticed. During those long afternoons while Mrs. Tomlinson droned on about geography or the decimal point, they amused themselves with our latest change of clothes. They laughed, seeing our syn-chronized jumps in and out of line. Mrs. Tomlinson never did find out (nor did she ever notice our clothes switch). That way, the other students joined Mary Beth and me as partners in crime. The truth, of course, is that was the way we joined them.

Success wasn't without its drawbacks. Our grades dropped, Mary Beth's most noticeably since she had been an A student. And so I shouldn't have been surprised when, shortly after our report cards arrived home, Mrs. Polk stormed into the house one night and stood wild-eyed over the table. She looked at Mary Beth and then at me. "This isn't good," she said. She ranted about Mary Beth's slipping grades and her languishing interest in piano lessons.

"You noticed," Mary Beth quipped sarcastically, at which point Mrs. Polk yanked her out of her chair, saying, "You girls must be separated."

Afterward, alone at the table, I felt like a thief who'd been enjoying the loot and just now had finally gotten caught. My free ride was over. And it didn't help that Mother came in and threw the whole incident in my face again. "See, I told you that girl's no good."

But, as it turned out, Mrs. Polk commuted the sentence and allowed Mary Beth and me one hour a day together after school, between Mary Beth's piano lesson and dinner. I don't know what changed her mind, whether Mary Beth threw an untamable tantrum or what. Point is, we made the most of that hour. We studied. Both of us got straight A's. Mrs. Polk was happy and soon allowed us all the time together we wanted. At school we kept up our silly antics, but our sudden good grades proved even more intriguing to our classmates, a new twist. We'd had good grades before our brief fall, but now they were better than ever, top of the class. The others bet potato chips and pieces of their mother's homemade chocolate cake on which one of us would score highest on the next test.

Which is how the annual spelling bee turned into such a big deal.

Mary Beth and I vowed to make them all losers. We'd tie.

The announcement of the spelling bee came sometime before Thanksgiving—I remember because Mary Beth and I were hard at work over the four-day weekend, and minutes before the Polks' Thanksgiving dinner, Mrs. Polk once again stormed into the house, this time to get Mary Beth's nose out of the pages and pages of word lists. "Iris," she said to me— she wore a string of pearls and a straight black dress—"there's more to life than books. You must learn to do other things, broaden your horizons." Again, I felt like the culprit of some crime.

Of course others signed up. But if any of them harbored any hope of winning, if they betrayed as much with their eyes, I didn't see it. Only their excitement over who would win: Mary Beth or me. So the pressure was on, not only for the two of us to stay in the race, but to hit the finish line together. Neither one of us would go down, and after the time allotted for our class contest was up, before the examiner could move on to the next class, he'd have to declare a tie—Mary Beth had it figured out. There wasn't one set of words for sixth-graders and another for seventh- and another for eighth-, but a general list passed out to all of the grades, and to assure our class victory, Mary Beth and I would have to know every word.

I was nervous. I thought Mary Beth was, too, although she had won the contest for her class the last two years. Which was the source of at least a part of my anxiety: Mary Beth had experience, and truth be known, she was a better speller than me, which became clear that Thanksgiving week- end. But the real problem for me was the contest itself, specifically the notion of standing before the entire school and being asked to spell some- thing. Someone would see that I was faking it, that I didn't know the answer, any of the answers, that I had no business up there on that auditorium stage, and the news would travel. And then nothing, not a single letter would roll off my thick tongue. I dreamed of Mrs. Polk coming toward me, just as she had the time she separated Mary Beth and me, only now it was my arm she was yanking, not Mary Beth's, and she wasn't hauling me out of the house, but off of the stage.

Mother saw my nerves. She saw me at night, long after Mary Beth had gone back to her house, hunched over the lists spread out on the kitchen table, and later, in bed, sitting up in the dark, wide-eyed. One day I came home and found a dictionary on the table. It was old, a tattered cover and all, probably something she stumbled upon during one of her jaunts to the lower Fourth Street junk shops. Still, it was enormous, a *Webster's* una- bridged with indexes marking each letter of the alphabet; and when Mary Beth and I came in, we dug through it as if it were an open box of precious jewels.

"My father has one this big," Mary Beth said, "in his office. It's full of lawyer words."

I thought Mary Beth was as delighted as I was with Mother's dinosaur, maybe even a little envious. After paging through the book for what seemed our entire study period, we finally got down to business and began going over new words from our list. And that's how the use-the-dictionary business got started. When Mary Beth or I got stumped on a word, we exclaimed, "Use the dictionary." And that way, we not only found the correct spelling of the word, but also learned its meaning. It was amazing to us how many words we could spell and yet did not understand. We had discovered something special: Knowing the meaning of words fortified our knowledge.

Use the dictionary. It's what Mother heard when she came in to take Mary Beth home for dinner. She must've figured it was protocol, a long-established study technique, because later that night, when she sat down with me, she said the same thing. She snatched the word list out from under my nose and began pitching words. Granted, she couldn't pronounce half of them correctly. Pot-poor-we for potpourri. Pay-pie-er-match for papier-mâché. We worked far into the night, past my bedtime. Then just as quickly as she had picked up the list, she set it down.

"Iris," she said.

Startled, I looked up from the dictionary, met her eyes.

"Don't let the white people impress you. Win because *you* want to win."

Her eyes were black and sharp. She sat back, resting her hands in the dirty apron she hadn't taken off, waiting as if she had asked me a question and wanted an answer.

"I want to win," I told her.

She looked at me and nodded. Then she got up, and making her way to the closet, said, "Go to bed."

But, before I could move, she was back, standing alongside the table. She opened her fisted hand, her fingers slowly unfurling, and there in the exact center of her palm sat a small square of angelica. The dried, gnarled root was about the size of a single dice and looked like a tiny house built into her palm. I saw it for only a split second, because after that, after Mother knew I'd seen it, she tilted the flat of her hand ever so slightly, letting the root roll and fall on my papers. "To protect you," she said.

* * *

I knew about angelica, the cut-up, celery-smelling pieces of root Mother kept in a brown bag on the top shelf of the closet. And in her purse;

whenever she sent me in there looking for money, I'd see it, a chunk wrapped in Kleenex and secured by a rubber band, about the size of a grown-up's thumb. For our protection, Mother always said. Against bad spirits, against bad things in this world.

I never thought much about it: just another of Mother's peculiarities, nothing obvious and embarrassing, nothing my friends could see, like her broken seams and unraveling hems, or her fat brown arms. More in line with her Indian stories, her talk about spirits and Old Uncle, that relative of hers who disappeared one day and then returned singing in all of Creation: frogs, bees, the flowers. "Do you hear him singing, Iris?" "No," I told her once and for all. But I remembered how I saw her smoke angelica once. I watched her use a paring knife to shave a piece of root into tiny shards on the nightstand between our two beds—this was when we lived in the hotel—and then fill a plain brown pipe by picking up the yellow-brown razor-thin shards with the bottom of her finger and dropping them into the pipe bowl, and then she turned off the light on the nightstand and lit the pipe with a cigarette lighter, and while the flashing red neon from the street flooded through the flimsy window curtain, she held the pipe in both hands, puffing mightily, her cheeks drawn in, and then exhaled, filling the room with blue smoke that twisted and hung in the beating light. The next day, I remembered, we moved.

* * *

Two weeks from Christmas, and two days from the spelling bee, Mary Beth asked me if I thought my mother was weird. It was after school and we were sitting at the table going over the word list, which we had gained a great command of, me noticeably so. I was shocked. I thought first of the piece of angelica root I'd stuck in my dresser drawer, then I thought better: Mother helping me late at night after Mary Beth went back to her house. Had she hung around outside the door and listened? Could she see from her window into our house?

"What do you mean?" I asked.

She'd been scanning a page of the open dictionary beneath her nose, and still didn't look up.

"Like my mother," she said finally. "She's weird."

"What?" I was genuinely perplexed now.

With her finger she marked the word she had been looking for, then slowly lifted her eyes from the book. "She has this thing in the bathroom," she said. "It's this rubber bag—Allison says her mother has one too. It's to wash out their you-know-whats down there." She gestured with the thumb of her free hand to her lap.

"How do you know?" I asked.

"Because," she answered, "I saw it. It was hanging over her shower door and Allison told me what they do with it."

As outlandish as the rubber contraption sounded to me, I neither tried to picture it nor give it a second's thought. I was relieved: Mary Beth only wanted to talk.

"That's not as weird as my mother," I said. "Look at how she dresses—rags, a hobo."

"Yeah, since your father left," Mary Beth said.

"Well," I quickly added, "she was never a great dresser."

Mary Beth shrugged and looked back down at the dictionary.

"What's the word again?"

" 'Miscellaneous,' " she said.

Easy, I thought to myself. It was her word—I'd pitched it to her—but I spelled it anyway. "M-I-S-C-E-L-L-A-N-E-O-U-S."

"Yep," she said.

After she left, and before Mother came back in with my dinner, I asked myself why I had been so alarmed by her question about Mother. What was I so afraid of? What was I hiding? Not Mother's clothes; I'd talked about them. No, it was what I didn't talk about, what I'd been hiding from Mary Beth and somehow even from myself. When Mary Beth asked if I thought Mother was weird I felt as if I might've gotten caught cheating.

*   *   *

Mother wore a dress: ink black, three white buttons the size of half-dollars in the front, low collared; I had no idea she owned it. And a white wool sweater, buttoned one button at the neck somewhat old lady-like, but, from my point of view on stage, nonetheless like a mantle of soft flowers over her shoulders. I hadn't seen her before she left the house—I had to be at the school auditorium early so I went with the Polks. But there she was, only a few rows back from the front, and if not for her wide brown face and shining black hair, which she had pulled back clean and tight, she could have been anyone's mother. She seemed still, quiet, as if she might have been uncomfortable, but as the losers in front of me drifted one by one off the stage, I could see her more clearly and knew otherwise. Her eyes were on only me.

We were in rows, me in the back row, and before long, only three of us were left; and it was then, looking at the other two contestants, Allison Witherow and Sammy Finley, a long shot, that I realized Mary Beth was no longer on stage. I hadn't seen her stumble. The school principal, Mr. Ridgeway, had been throwing the toughest words at us, going up and down the lines, hitting each student with a sinker. He was a tall man, bald; he smelled of cigars, and he sounded so bored, so uninterested, that each word he pitched seemed to drop on the floor with the spittle that flew from his thick wet lips. "Sorry," he said flatly before moving to the next student. He paused, looking first at Allison and Sammy and then at me, alone behind the two of them. I looked back at Mother. She was so close now and clear that I could see that the half-dollar buttons on the front of her dress were bone white, not pearl white or alabaster, not plastic shiny, but bone, bone white; and her eyes, they were so close that I saw how they caught each of Mr. Ridgeway's words and reflected them back to me clearly, as if they were words spelled out on giant cue cards.

First Allison was out, and then Sammy Finley. "Sluice," a short, easy word, but Sammy couldn't see it. He forgot the *i*. I saw it—a long trough of water—and remembered the *i*. For the longest time I stood there expecting I don't know what, perhaps for Mr. Ridgeway to toss another word, before I realized that I was the only one left and that all of the clapping was for me.

Mr. Ridgeway had three classes to cover, two more contests after mine. After winning, I was ushered offstage and made to wait in the dark for what seemed like forever. What had happened to Mary Beth? Where was she? It wasn't until the winners from the other two contests—seventh and eighth grades—and I were brought back onstage that I realized we were to be pitted against one another in a final spell-off. I thought we were going back out to get our prizes. Mary Beth had never mentioned the spell-off. What would we have done? What plan? I didn't have time to think what to do. Before I knew it, I was in line with the two other winners and Mr. Ridgeway was pitching words again.

The audience was still. Mother looked enormous. She nodded ever so slightly, as if she had read my thoughts and agreed. I hadn't a prayer in hell; the two other contestants were older, and yet eleven words later it was between me and the eighth-grader, a gawky boy with horn-rimmed glasses who looked like he could spell the dictionary backward and forward. "Argillaceous," of or having to do with clay, clay-like. He forgot the second *l*. I didn't.

"Iris Gonzales." My name sounded through the loudspeakers and the stunned crowd looked as if they were expected to rise up in unison and spell it back. Mr. Ridgeway handed me a certificate and then slipped a silver medal strung with blue ribbon over my head; and when I turned and found the other two contestants standing at the edge of the stage, I saw that they were looking at me just as Mr. Ridgeway was—with disbelieving eyes. You'd think a big duck had suddenly landed right in front of them and her name was Iris.

* * *

That night, Mother warned me about the likelihood of my classmates' jealousy. "The stakes is high, Iris. Keep your eyes open," she said. That and a short lecture about humility. "Humbility," she called it. "It lets you see," she said. But nothing she said prepared me for what actually happened: Mary Beth's exuberant congratulations in the car the next morning, and then her laughing at school with the throngs of others who surrounded me on the playground. Not only my classmates, but a lot of the older students had collected around me. When an older, pretty girl asked my name, finally breaking the others' silence, Allison Witherow stepped forward and proclaimed: "Iris—she's the new school dork." Giggling. Laughter. But the crowd didn't bother me just then; I wasn't embarrassed by their laughter because I wasn't seeing them. Only Mary Beth. She cut her eyes away, glanced at the ground, but not fast enough for me to miss the victory that was full on her face.

I never let on, then or in the weeks ahead, that I saw and understood what had happened. What good would it do? Mary Beth had used me. She used me to get into the world that had shut both of us out. Sure, we were using each other, but I hadn't figured it would be at one or the other's expense. She was a brat—Mother was right. I saw as much the first night she came into the house. But I never said a word, confronted Mary Beth with my knowledge. That would do no more than admit defeat. And the game wasn't over.

I let the laughter pass that horrible morning. Then, at the noon recess, I played the toughest game of volleyball ever, knocking the ball beyond Allison Witherow's reach every chance I could and scoring over and over again. Needless to say, I turned down an invitation to the regional spelling contest—no more spelling bees for me. And Mary Beth and I remained friends—on the surface. She didn't come to my house anymore—what was the need, since there wasn't a spelling bee to practice for—but I sat with her each afternoon while she practiced piano with her wart-necked, flatulent teacher so that afterward we could plan our school pranks for the next day. Mary Beth and the others never said another word about that morning. Perhaps they forgot. I didn't.

I had a plan. And I'd rehearsed it in my mind to the nth degree. And if anyone might've been able to stop me, that person was Mother. I knew she wouldn't have approved unless I figured some sly way to tell her, and that would take more calculating than I'd done already. On that warm spring night she sat gazing up at the stars, I wasn't prepared to reveal a thing. So I had reason to worry. You'd think that with some unseen power she had coaxed from my lips what was in my mind—that red pinafore. You'd think she knew my plan.

It had happened too easily, as if the news of the Junior Junior Miss Pageant had been an apple that had fallen squarely in my lap. Mary Beth and the others chatted about it over potato chips and peanut butter and jelly sandwiches. They talked as if I wasn't there, as if they were speaking a language I had no need to know. I understood: The pageant was for future Rainbow Girls, a contest to show the club members their promise. Rainbow Girls, the sorority of girls who had Christmas parties with the likes of Mary Beth's older brother and his friends, the boys of Demolay. Rainbow Girls, white and Presbyterian. I was neither. Oh, if I had any leanings toward a Christian religion, it was Catholicism, because during my six or so months at St. Rose Catholic School I'd learned the first thirty pages of their catechism, was baptized, went to confession, and made my first Holy Communion. But never mind. I'd seen enough movies. I knew the story of Cinderella. While Mary Beth played the piano and Allison twirled the baton, I would stand in the back of the room, hide in the shadows. Then, right before they announced the winner, I would take the stage; me in a red dress, bold to the point of bad, and I would sing music to their ears, a song of theirs sung prettier and more lovely than any of them could sing it.

The song was "A Closer Walk with Thee." Once, while passing the Presbyterian church on a Sunday morning, I heard the congregation singing. I stopped and listened. It was one of the songs they sang. But that's not how I learned it. I used my secret weapon—silence. I kept my eyes open. I stayed close to Mary Beth. Each afternoon, after her piano teacher left, she practiced a complicated sonata for the pageant. I encouraged her, told her she could win. Before she started to play, we'd chat awhile, mostly making fun of the wart-necked teacher who was hardly seconds out the door, and then Mary Beth would turn back to the piano, always warming up with "A Closer Walk with Thee." And that way, reading the lyrics on her sheet music, occasionally even humming along, I memorized the song. The church congregation was somber, the color gray, when they sang it. I'd be jubilant, red.

* * *

When Mother finally acquiesced with her exhausted "OK, OK." and took me shopping for a new dress, there came warnings. "Iris, they'll laugh at you." "Don't try to be one of them." "The white people have their ways, Iris." It was as if she truly had seen my scheme. And I knew what she would

314   GREG SARRIS

dislike: my motivation, my will to show Mary Beth once and for all she couldn't beat me. Still, I told her nothing. I'd made a case for a new dress by pointing out that I'd earned straight A's on my last two report cards—other kids got presents whenever they got straight A's!

That was Wednesday afternoon; the contest was Thursday, the next night. Even though I knew she'd disapprove of my reasons for wanting to participate in the pageant, I figured she'd stand behind me. Didn't she already sense something was up—why else all those admonitions—and wasn't she still driving me to get a new dress? Wasn't that the same as her leaving the big dictionary on the table, a sign of support? Which is why I wasn't bothered one iota that she headed for the used-clothes shops on lower Fourth—it was in the same part of town she no doubt found the dictionary.

We parked in front of Lido's, a corner dive. Below its red neon sign, flashing as bright as ever in the noonday sun, sat a dark-skinned woman on an upturned prune crate eating Hostess cupcakes, the corner of her mouth and her fingers smeared with chocolate. Her torn print dress was loose; it slid back from her swollen shiny knees into her lap; and, when I walked past, I saw her stained underpants. We browsed through a couple of places, Mother seemingly more interested in a rocking chair and a set of chipped dinner plates than in finding me a dress. "C'mon," I said, tugging each time she stopped. And then on a half-block jaunt between stores, walking past a corner cafe across from the train tracks, I saw Mr. Polk—probably at the same moment Mother did—and she made a point of it.

"See," she said. "See how they are. That's his girlfriend—he cheats on Mrs. Polk."

"It's his secretary," I argued. "He's a lawyer." I grabbed her wrist and pulled her past the window, lest Mr. Polk, nose to nose with a redheaded woman in a back booth, look up and see us peering in.

Probably because Mother had no friends, at least none that she saw on a regular basis, none that I knew of, she talked with me about adult matters as if I were a girlfriend and not her daughter. How much I understood I'm not sure. But I knew full well husbands weren't supposed to cheat on their wives, that infidelity was beyond wrong—it was scandalous.

"It's Mrs. Witherow," Mother snapped and shook her wrist free.

She spoke as if I'd been blind not to see as much. Truth is, I'd never laid eyes on Mrs. Witherow, Allison's mother. She'd been in the big house often, visiting Mrs. Polk—gossiping with her, according to Mary Beth—but apparently never when I was there. Certainly Mother had seen her; undoubtedly she waited on her, served her tea and shortbread in the sitting room off the kitchen.

"See how they are . . . I'm warning you, Iris. If they do like that with each other, think how they'll do with you."

We walked in silence, a safe distance from the cafe, and then I stopped abruptly. "How *they* are?" I shouted. "How *you* are. Look, you sound just like them—gossiping!"

She planted her feet, took a deep breath, about to respond, but I cut her off.

"You don't even know who my father is," I said.

Clearly, she was taken aback. She sighed heavily and started off again. "True," she said, pounding down the street with me half-running to keep up with her, "I don't know who your father is. You know why? I was a floozy—you know what that is? All the men were my boyfriends, married ones too. Any of them could be your father."

She was angry, tough, but then her voice seemed to arch, her anger crest, so that by the time she had finished talking she was flat and still, like water spilled on hot cement. If I had been older, or perhaps not so full of my own purpose, I might have understood the ramifications of what she had told me; that and her pain just then. And I'd have known, too, that she had been right about Mr. Polk—why else would a man like that be hiding in a dumpy cafe with his wife's best friend? But, focused as I was on my own concerns, what I saw in her candor was the opportunity to match it with my own. What better time to tell her of my scheme, let it out in the open once and for all.

I told her of the event to be held the following evening at the Presbyterian church, described my plan; and then she stopped again—we both stopped, facing each other. If she was surprised, I couldn't tell. But there before my eyes she'd grown large again, strong, and it occurred to me that she might argue, or worse, turn and march back to the car.

I met her in the face. "And that's why I have to sneak," I said, "because I have no father . . . and because you . . ."

But I had no time to finish. She grabbed me around the elbow with all her might, her hand like a vice, and yanked me after her down the street. Luckily I kept up with her; if I'd lagged or stumbled, she would've kept on, like a car with me shackled to its rear bumper. She stomped into a thrift shop—I don't remember which one—and pushed her way past a dozen racks of clothes and then grabbed the dress off a hanger and held it up for me to inspect. Red—I hadn't even told her red! You would think she'd seen the dress more clearly than I had. You'd think she'd been hiding it. A little too large, I could see, but exactly the dress I had pictured: a straight pinafore, small, rounded collars. She wasn't holding the dress as if waiting for an answer from me, an OK, but as if to say, Here it is, take it.

* * *

Silence. Silence on the way home, and after, while she turned me this way and that hemming the dress. Where she got the spool of red thread, I'll never know. She sewed into the wee hours of the morning—by hand. I sat opposite her studying geography. There was a wall between us, and no matter how often my books and papers brushed against the pinafore spread out on the table, no matter how close we were, her silence bid me not to cross that wall. Not anger, not even guilt with her silence, but respect, respect for the space she needed to air the hurt I'd dealt her.

If only I could sing for her, I thought. At St. Rose Catholic School I learned countless songs. "The Star-Spangled Banner." "America, the Beautiful." Christmas carols, even when it wasn't Christmas. And I had a knack for it. "You can sing, little girl," my teacher, Sister Agnes Jean, said. In the evenings, after Mother came in from her work, she would sit in a chair, my sole audience, and I'd sing songs for her, often going through the repertoire of every song I learned. She liked music. Sometimes we sang together, not the songs from school, but oldies from the forties that she'd start with a hum, maybe something from the radio. And we'd dance like chorus girls, in step, me kicking in my scuffed browns, her in her old-lady blacks. I had the urge just to jump up all at once and belt out my song, but seeing her downcast eyes and her fingers, moving like the busy legs of some small animal fully unaware of my presence, I thought otherwise.

Later that night, long after Mother finished the dress and left it folded on the table, after she finally turned off the lights, I worried that I hadn't sung for her. I never thought I'd end up keeping the entire event to myself right up until the last minute. Daily I had practiced the song, alone in my house, taking advantage of that hour between the time I sat with Mary Beth at her piano and the time Mother came in with my dinner. And at night, in the bathroom, while I was supposedly getting ready for bed, brushing my teeth, I had held my chunk of angelica and gently touched it to my lips and throat. I couldn't quit thinking about Mother all the next day. I felt plagued, a dark cloud over me, as if, for the first time, I didn't have her blessing.

And it didn't help that on the night of the pageant she didn't set a foot out of the house. I had to walk the two and a half blocks to the church alone. In fact, Mother didn't even come back from the Polks to see me off; she never saw me in the dress. She might have told me to wear a sweater or a coat, something I hadn't thought of in all the weeks I'd been seeing myself in the red pinafore. It was freezing; the weather had turned, clear but cold, the stars a thousand icicles overhead. I walked clutching my cold naked arms. And then I arrived at the church only to find it was empty. I looked through the narrow windows on either side of the door and saw nothing but darkness, empty space. Shivering, still holding to myself, I edged my way along the side of the church, crossed a cold wet lawn and came back around on the other side of the building. Cars and lights then: The back wing of the building was lit up. I groped toward the light. Luckily, there was an antechamber that was dimly lit—and warm. I stepped inside, found a spot alongside a door where I could see into the larger room—RECREATION ROOM, a plastic sign above the inside door read. It was a gymnasium, a waxed wooden floor, the kind you find in school gyms, and it was crammed with people: adults who sat in folding chairs, looming dark like a forest in front of me, the only light coming from the open aisle between them, the shiny strip of floor that led to the bright makeshift stage at the opposite end of the room. And who do you think was on that stage? Mary Beth, pounding out her number.

My eyes focused and then I could see the backs of heads more clearly. I saw hair of different colors, bald patches. And I saw that people were fidgeting, idly whispering to one another; Mary Beth's sonata wasn't complicated, as I had always imagined—it was boring. I was warm but I still couldn't stop shaking. Despite my endless planning for this moment and that, according to those plans, I was right where I was supposed to be in the dress I was supposed to be wearing, nothing made sense. And if Mary Beth hadn't finished just then and walked off the stage accompanied by unenthusiastic applause, and if a short round man the color of yellow onions, perhaps the church minister, hadn't stepped up to the microphone and called for late entries, I might've left.

There was some quiet chatter, a soft rumbling in the crowd. The round man disappeared, undoubtedly to consult with the judges regarding their decision. When he returned, he stepped up to the microphone and slowly leaned into it, as if he were about to whisper something in someone's ear. A blinding-hot strength rose up in me, and before I knew it, I was walking up that aisle, with those same rows and rows of peering faces on either side of me. I took the microphone from the astonished host, announced my name, and sang.

> Oh, sweet Jesus, just another walk with thee
> Oh, sweet Jesus, let it be . . .

I could've heard a baby's sigh. But I couldn't see a thing. White lights from the ceiling kept me blind, the audience a blur. The round host appeared when I finished and I handed him the microphone. With his lashless little pea eyes peeled on me, he lifted the microphone and said to the crowd: "And what do you say for our late entry?"

I knew condescension from others the way I knew the back of my own hand, and as much as he may have been surprised—and even charmed—by my performance, I knew he was making fun of me. Slowly, like a pile of leaves catching fire on a damp fall day, one or two leaves at a time, a dutiful applause arose. I marched offstage then and went back to the antechamber. Only now I didn't hide behind the door; I stood square in its frame. Anger—and pride—kept me there, daring them to forget me, and hadn't each pair of eyes followed me there? I'd sung beautifully. Let them try to forget it.

The host's face twisted and frowned. Finally, a band of mothers, no doubt the contest committee members, flocked onto the stage and quickly encircled him. I say committee members, and not judges, because Mrs. Polk, Mary Beth's mother, was one of the women, and so was Mrs. Witherow, Allison's mother, yes, the same redhead I'd seen in the cafe with Mr. Polk.

I stood basking in the long moments of their chaos. You can imagine how I felt when the host emerged from the circle of mothers and announced the winners and none of them was me. The winner, a name I didn't recognize, and two runners-up, one of whom was Allison.

"But before we celebrate the winners," the man said, "we would like to give a special award for effort to our late entry—the little girl, where is she?"

Of course it was an insult. You think I didn't see that? He—all of them—wanted me in and out so they could go on with their show, celebrate the *real* winners. He didn't even bother to remember—or find out—my name. Yet, I had still won something: If nothing else, I had interrupted their show. Which is why, when he bid me forward, I went back up there—to show them as much. He handed me a fake-gold statue of a ballerina. Off the microphone he said that I had to give it back, that in a week I'd receive my own in the mail, but that I could hold it for a minute now. I didn't give him a minute. I gave the statue right back to him. No curtsy. No thank-you's. I was here. I stopped your show. Good-bye. Before the audience could begin its obligatory clapping, I was off the stage.

As I marched home that night, I cherished nothing more than the thought of Mary Beth and my sweet victory over her. Imagine the look on her face when she saw me singing a song I'd lifted from right under her nose. I'd beaten her at her own game. And I was savoring that image when I walked into the house and found Mother dozing next to the radio—something on about the war in Korea. She startled when I closed the door behind me.

"How'd you do?" she asked.

I figured she still must have been half asleep, given her sudden interest in the pageant. She hadn't said a word about it—about anything—since yesterday; and remembering how she didn't even bother to see me off and how I stood shaking in that dark antechamber outside the Recreation Room, I became furious. She'd abandoned me, and now, half asleep, she all of a sudden cared?

"I won," I told her.

"What?" she asked. She was looking around the room, as if to get her bearings after a deep sleep.

"Everything," I said and stomped into the bedroom.

"Didn't you wear a sweater?" she called after me, and I slammed the door.

* * *

Mary Beth didn't ride to school with Mother and me the next morning. And she wasn't sick: From my window I could see her in her kitchen, dressed for school. So I knew something was up. I should have expected that my performance at the pageant would solidify her bond with the others, finish what my winning the spelling bee had started. I hadn't really thought it through. "Watch yourself, Iris," said Mother, who was otherwise quiet on the way to school. When Mary Beth came up to me on the playground with a pack of girls behind her, I expected, if anything, nothing more than perhaps a snide "Congratulations." But when she stopped and, a foot from my face, said my name, she was loud—and bold.

"I don't know why you did that last night," she said. "You can't ever be a Rainbow Girl anyway. That's why they had to give you that special award—because you can't ever be a Rainbow Girl," she repeated. "You know why?"

I said nothing.

"Because you're an Indian," she said, lifting her upper lip in a snarl. Still, I didn't move.

"You don't even know who your father is," she blared as if to up the ante. Then she turned to the others, saying, "Because her mother is a whore, a prostitute." She looked back at me and blurted, "My mother said so."

I glanced at the other faces, took inventory of the situation, and found tall Allison Witherow holding the volleyball with a complacent smile across her blonde face. It was only morning recess, and the thought occurred to me that this would be a very long day. I looked back at Mary Beth.

"Fine," I said, affecting great calm. "Go ask your father how he liked kissing Allison's mother across from the railroad tracks on Wednesday."

Nothing like the power of concrete details in battle. She smarted. I glared at her stunned face then.

"Tell your mother that, four eyes." And with that I turned and yanked the ball out of Allison's hands and headed for the volleyball court. After a long moment, the other kids followed, slowly, taking small, careful steps, like mules coming down a steep hillside.

* * *

I didn't hear—or rather see—the inevitable until Mother came in from the big house that night. Again, I hadn't thought of outcomes, consequences. And how in the world could I have not realized something would happen, or at least worried about it? I'd spilled a mouthful and then told Mary Beth to go tell her mother, after all. It was late, after dinner, and Mother came in and pulled the suitcases and cardboard box from the back room, my bedroom, and began packing clothes from the standing closet. Nothing, not a word; she worked quietly, her back to me. She hadn't bothered to take off her apron, and I could see where the white strings across her sides and tied in a tight bow behind her waist cut deep rivulets in the bulging flesh below her old calico. Then, as quick as you could bat an eye, she reached over and flicked on the radio. An oldie played. And, merrily, she sang along:

> He never knew the technique of kissing
> He never knew what he was missing
> But look at him now . . .

After about half a minute, she turned, still singing, and looked at me. She was smiling, radiant. Confused and then frightened, I looked down at my books and empty dinner plate, and when I looked back up, she'd turned around again and was wagging her broad rear end to the music. I was sure she was still smiling, laughing even; and, seeing her rear swing back and forth now like a huge admonishing finger, it occurred to me that she was nothing if not smug, happy with herself. Now you've really gone and done it, she was saying, went and got us kicked out of our house. Proof that what I've always said is true: There are places they don't want Indians; think how they'll do with you; watch yourself, Iris. I looked at the old dictionary next to me and thought of her encouraging nod at the spelling bee and of the angelica she dropped on my papers and of the way she stomped into that thrift shop and found my red pinafore. She'd led me to this moment just to make her point. She'd tricked me, worse than Mary Beth because even Mary Beth's game was of use to her, and now she was rubbing her victory in my face. But what victory was that? Look, we were being evicted, she'd lost her job. What power? None. Small. Nothing. I could spit it out in an instant. I'd seen it done before. I'd pick it from my teeth, as if it were a tiny thread of beef caught there, and wipe it on the edge of my plate.

Loud and clear over the music, I said, "You're nothing but a fat, ugly Indian."

She stopped, stood still a moment, and then shut off the radio; when she turned around, with the music gone, so was her smile.

She went back to her work, and, in what seemed like less than two minutes, emptied the closet, finished folding and packing the clothes. Then she untied her apron, letting it fall on the floor, and went outside and sat in the garden. I could see her through the side window, her print dress, her bare arms and face in the moonlight. She wasn't looking up at the moon. The driveway gate was open and she was looking there, as if at any moment she would get up and walk through it.

I stared at the soiled apron in a small heap on the floor. She'd left the door open and I felt a chill. The closet was empty, everything that was ours packed. I looked at Mother again. It was so cold. She couldn't sit out there for long, I thought. Then I got up and hurried out of the house, lest she get up and leave me there alone.

T W O

She was my age, about eleven, my size, her skin about the same light color as mine, and except for her oversize cardigan and dust-spotted white anklet socks—mine would never be dirty—her clothes were the same. And her mother was the same as my mother, maybe heavier, more square, but just as dark, arms and face a brown burned black by the sun, an Indian. And that's how I would always remember the girl. Not her name, but how she looked—like me—and how, sitting on the back of a pickup with her mother and a bunch of clanging, empty milk cans tied together too loosely with a rope, she grew smaller and smaller as the truck pulled farther and farther from where Mother and I stood on that empty road, until she was a speck and then no more, nothing where even the gray strip of road disappeared below an umbrella of dark pines.

She was a cousin, too, which was something else I'd forgotten. That's the first thing Mother said. She spotted them outside the feed store. She stopped suddenly, dropped everything, which caused me to look up and see what she was seeing: a woman like her hoisting feed sacks onto the back of a pickup in a dress and a pair of black rubber boots. The young girl stood nearby peering into wire cages stacked one on top of the other and full of white chickens. The woman pulled a feed sack upright from the pallet next to her, then bear-hugging the hundred-pound sack to her chest, arms strapped tight over the burlap, she lifted it and turned to the truck. And that's when she saw Mother. She froze, with the feed sack still in her arms. She wasn't looking at me, only Mother; and she seemed so big just then, and at the same time far away, as if she were standing on a hill peering at us from a distance. Eventually, she dropped her sack on the truck bed, and when she did, when she wasn't looking our way, I glanced at Mother. She was staring blankly at the suitcases and packed cardboard box on the ground, her face filled with consternation. For the first time in three days, since our eviction from the Polks', walking, camping here and there, Mother seemed apprehensive. I looked back at the woman, who was lifting another sack from the pallet, and at the girl still peering into the wire cages.

Mother didn't move, even as the woman and girl drove out of the feed-store lot and passed us on the street. She didn't look up either, but, with her head still bowed, she followed the truck with her eyes. When it pulled to the left side of the street and stopped, she sighed with enormous relief and said, "Cousins."

She grabbed up the suitcases and yanked the cardboard box with its makeshift rope handle and hurried down the street. I chased after her. The woman got out of the truck, one big black rubber boot at a time, and planted herself on the street, facing Mother. She straightened her dress, pulling it this way and that over her ample front. She was bigger than Mother, hefty, which I could see now that I was just five feet from her. She stared at Mother.

"Ain't got no place," Mother said, which the woman could clearly see if she as much as for one second looked down and saw the suitcases and box at Mother's feet.

Neither one said a word. And yet something did pass between them, some recognition or understanding, because, afterward, the woman nodded to the truck bed and said, "Get on." So we got on, suitcases and all. We secured ourselves against the stacked feed sacks, and that way, our backs pressed against the feed sacks and our hands clutching our belongings, we watched the town, first the busy streets, then the clapboard houses along its outskirts, grow smaller and smaller.

The air was thin and cool with the fields and trees on either side of the open road. It was spring: The grass was tall, patches of buttercups and lupine in the rich green like pieces of colorful silk dropped here and there; and lining the road, stretching away before us, were sweet peas a pink as bright as lipstick, as soft-looking as a baby's foot. No wonder I was not surprised when I smelled the cows, smelled them before I saw them and thought of how two days before we had visited a dairy, the dairy next to the little house between the open pastures and orchards that I remembered before all the moving with Mother, hotel room to back room, so that when the big woman turned the rattling truck up a dirt road and I actually saw the cows, a pasture filled with big Holsteins, I thought maybe I was home again. I thought maybe Mother and I could unpack the suitcases. And another thing that shaped my thinking just then: While Mother and I were at the first dairy, her friend Del, who milked the cows there, kept talking about another woman, presumably a woman Mother knew, who worked on a milk farm and might be able to help Mother get a job. He said he'd seen the woman weeks before at the feed store. Serendipity? Could we have run into the same woman at the same place? Again, I would not have been surprised. It was spring.

The woman backed the truck alongside the wood and concrete milking barn and there ushered us off the truck and into a dark windowless shack next to the barn. "I'll get your things later," she whispered. She followed us with her arms spread wide, as if she were herding a flock of turkeys. It was only when she snapped on the naked lightbulb overhead that I saw we were in her home—or somebody's home. She nodded to a small white table and then left, closing the door tightly behind her. Mother and I sat down.

The place wasn't much bigger than a horse stall, and there was no insulation, no plasterboard or padding of any kind over the dark boards. You could see the bright mid-morning light beyond the cracks and knotholes. Two pallet beds—wooden pallets identical to the ones I'd just seen at the feed store—sat on the floor with bedrolls and pillows spread over them. They took up half the room. The other things I recognized from every other place I'd been: a stand-up closet, a burlap sack half full of potatoes, and of course the small table, even if it was painted white, painted sloppily and quickly it seemed, with the same paint farmers use on their barns and fences. And it was indeed the big woman's place: Above the stand-up closet, which wasn't that tall, about eye level for an adult, was a school picture of the girl, not unlike my own from Henry C. Fremont, and on either side of the framed black-and-white picture was a votive candle, the sort you find in the alcoves of Catholic churches, the glass holders a deep crimson color. To the left of the picture sat a milk bottle filled with buttercups and lupine that sprang in every direction from the bottle's narrow neck. The flowers were so bright and fresh-looking that the woman no doubt had picked them before she'd gone to town that morning.

"Is this our new house?" I asked Mother.

She was staring at the empty wall. "Shh," she said, lifting her eyes to the door.

Three days of walking, knocking on doors, mission meals, and pitching tents with sheets tied between tree branches along Santa Rose Creek, and nothing was said about what had happened. If anything unpleasant arose, the mosquitoes by the creek, the jeering from passing cars as we stood in line outside the mission, Mother said, "Think good thoughts." And yet I felt guilt, as if it was a stick Mother owned and could hit me with at any moment, and that made me mad.

So, it was all my fault. But hadn't Mother sat back and watched? Didn't she know of my intentions? She not only sat back and watched, she led me into the trap.

"Are we going to move here?" I asked.

"Whisper," she said.

"Why?"

Her eyes focused, hardened.

"Is she going to move out of this place?"

Mother was quiet again, and then, as if oblivious to my last question, said, "Cousin . . . that's how I know she'll help us. She'll do what she can."

I knew nothing of cousins. I mean, I knew what a cousin was; I just never thought of Mother and I as having them. Mother and I floated freely. I asked her about the big woman and her daughter, and she began whispering something about her mother's mother, my great-grandmother, and how we were all related. How much I heard, or understood, I don't remember, or even if Mother finished explaining, because about that time the door opened and closed in a flash of light and the big woman was back in the room. She was wearing a clean apron, embroidered on the borders with a twirling green vine and dark blue flowers—morning glories—and she wasn't wearing her rubber boots, but flat black shoes like Mother's, and her hair was pulled back neatly off her face and neck. She reached under her apron and found two sandwiches, each in a plastic bag, which she dropped on the table. Mother said something to her in Indian, and she gave a short answer, one word, and then she was out the door.

A few minutes passed. Then, all at once a loud generator began sputtering. I dropped to my knees and peered through a knothole. I saw nothing but a sea of spotted legs and swollen udders: The cows had come in for milking. The barn and crowded holding pen were hardly an arm's length from the house. Occasionally, I heard voices, men's voices, from inside the barn, but I could not make out what they were saying over the generator.

I didn't look back to Mother until the holding pen was empty, when it was dark outside and a row of lights shone down from the barn's eaves. The generator was off then, the world quiet. Mother was looking at me. When I got up and faced her, she turned back to the door. And just then the big woman came in, and so did the girl. I stood there, not moving, and watched as they passed me on their way to the table. Just as before, the woman reached under her apron and, this time, pulled out two large hamburger patties wrapped in paper napkins and set them on the table. She reached under her apron again and pulled out a bottle of ketchup. Then, as if on cue, from under her cardigan the girl took several pieces of bread.

Mother said something to the woman—again in Indian—and the woman answered back, a few short words. Then Mother leaned so she could see past the broad woman to me and said, "Don't let anyone see you. There's another place behind this one. The bathroom is behind it. Walk between the houses."

The woman spoke again in Indian and Mother translated: "Make sure to come back the same way." She paused and then explained: "You've got to go alone. The boss can't see me with you until we tell him you're here—that I've got a daughter. Go. You'll be OK."

When I got back inside and saw the food on the table, I forgot my manners. I fixed myself a ketchup-smeared hamburger sandwich and began devouring it. The woman took a large glass jug from the cold box and poured me a glass of water. While Mother and I ate, the girl sat quietly next to her mother reading a magazine. It was *Sunset*, page after page of neatly mani-cured California gardens: beds of marigolds and petunias, geraniums in ce-ramic pots, pink and purple ice plants on hillsides and walkways overlooking the ocean. It was old, its pages stained, its corners tattered and turned down; she'd probably looked at it a million times. It was obvious that she was obeying her mother, doing just what her mother wanted her to do: Don't stare, read the magazine. She looked at each picture for the same amount of time before silently turning the page. I know because I counted three seconds for each of her stops. If it wasn't for the occasional glance she slipped past her mother, looking up at me from her pictures and letting me know the way children can with a sparkle in their eyes that she was interested in me, even excited, I might have thought her a snob.

She was perfect, a little lady. After dinner, while changing our clothes, she turned away from me, insulted that I was looking at her. I was looking because I was amazed at how much she was like me: same dark hair and, on her stomach and legs, where the sun missed her, the same light skin. When we talked finally, she was friendly. But even her talk seemed practiced, her words rehearsed. In our flannel nightgowns, we lay on her pallet bed, turning pages of the *Sunset* magazine and naming all of the flowers. It was stupid, really, but she spoke with such importance and conviction, I felt compelled to follow along. With each flower you'd think we had discovered a dying species and would be the last two people on earth to utter its name. Everything in its place with this girl. But, leave it to me, I saw that her flannel, spread over her lithe body like a cape, was stitched over in the seam, sewn and patched on the elbows. Mine was new, flawless.

While we paged through the magazine, our mothers sat at the table and talked—in Indian. I'd never heard my mother speak so much Indian in my entire life. Who did she have to talk with before? I was surprised to hear

English words surface in the flow of their talk: highway, Santa Rosa, Healds-burg, school. And reservation: reservation this and reservation that.

"Reservation?" I said quietly.

The girl looked over at me in disbelief.

"It's where Indians live," she answered finally. "We used to live there. We just came here. We—" She stopped suddenly, looking up at her mother, who, mid-sentence in conversation, nonetheless had her eyes fixed on the girl.

The girl looked back at me then. "You didn't come from the reservation."

"No," I blurted out. "We always lived in . . ." But I couldn't finish. I was stuck for words. Where had I always lived? Santa Rosa. But that really wasn't what I was trying to say. "In this," I managed, glancing around the room. "In places like this. We always had a home like this."

And then I felt the silence in the room. Both women were looking at me.

"Miniature pansy," the girl said.

She knew just what to do. I wasn't surprised; I was thankful. I quickly followed along with her, looking away from Mother and the big woman. But my mind whirled with thoughts and questions that braided and knotted themselves inside me in every way imaginable. Indians. These people were Indians. Cousins. I never thought of cousins, as I said before. And reserva-tion; sure, I'd heard of it: I knew Mother was from it and I knew she'd left it before I was born. "I wandered from there," she'd said. But I thought of it, if I thought anything, as a place like a town or street, something I knew from my own experience. Oh, I knew certain of Mother's activities were "Indian." Her picking acorns and praying with angelica root, for instance. The kind of stuff the white girls' parents never did. But just then I thought of Mother and the big woman at the feed store, what they understood with their eyes. The same with this girl and her mother just now, with all three of them. What were they saying to one another? Indians: a foreign language; a story loud and clear to everyone in the room but me. A knot in my brain.

Soon the girl said it was time for bed. I guess she had looked at the clock. It was nine o'clock. She closed the magazine, tucked it under her pillow, and then got up and reached, standing on tippy toes, for the milk bottle of flowers on top of the stand-up closet. Holding the bottle to her chest, she hesitated a moment, looking back and forth at the pillows on each of the beds. Then, having made up her mind about what to do, she began plucking the flowers from the bottle, stems of lupine, stems of but-tercups, and arranging them on her pillow, making two loose halos next to one another, where our heads would be. Only when she finished and went to the other pillow, the one on her mother's pallet, did she look back to her mother. She stood with the empty bottle in one hand and a fistful of flowers in the other. Her mother, again in mid-conversation with my mother, made a slight downward motion with her hand, as if telling a dog by her feet to stay put. The girl understood. She set the bunched flowers next to the pillow and then put the empty bottle with its inch or two of water back on top of the closet.

We got into bed, carefully, so as not to disturb her arrangements. We lay down, fitting our heads to the halos.

"Do you girls have to go to the bathroom?" her mother called across the room.

"No," the girl answered softly.

"No," I said exactly the same.

The girl said: "You are in a beautiful meadow, the stars above. And God is watching you. Now go to sleep."

And I did.

* * *

The next morning I discovered the lay of the land. "Go around the back side here whenever you leave the place," Mother repeated, letting me know I couldn't be seen by anyone outside yet. She left and went to work, doing what I don't know, with the big woman. The girl got ready for school. Sitting at the table, I made sure not to watch her dress. Then she came and sat down to slip on her tan-and-white loafers. When she finished she looked up and stared across the table at me. I thought she was going to say, Good-bye, see you later. But with that same measured talk from the night before, she picked up where she had left off then, or, rather, from where her mother had silently cut her off: "We came here because Mama got a job here. We left the reservation because of trouble there. People didn't get along. That's what Mama said. Everyone will leave soon. We left first. One day white people will take back that land."

She sat back in her chair. Then, adopting another voice, this time sounding exactly as her mother might, her words even preceded by an adult's tired sigh, she said, "White people. Can't live with them, can't live without them."

She looked at my portion of cold leftover hamburger and bread that I hadn't touched. She'd finished hers before she'd gotten dressed.

"Gee," I said, half joking, "my mother was the one who left first. She got a real head start. She—"

"Yes," the girl said, not letting me finish what I wanted to say, which was just to mention that Mother had left the reservation before I was born, which was why I didn't know everything about Indians. Perhaps I was even thinking we could talk about Indian stuff. But no chance of that. Her voice was practiced, careful again. "I have to go to school," she said and got up from the table.

It was then that a wave of sadness and self-pity swept over me. She was going to go to school; I was going to be left here alone. It seemed a few minutes passed. All I remember is that, head down, my eyes fixed on the cold hamburger, I kept thinking how I'd never felt like this before—so alone. Moving from place to place, I'd never had this feeling, at least not in the way I felt it now. Somehow Mother was there, school was there, there were windows I could look out, streets I could walk on.

When I looked up finally, I found the girl standing, as if she had been waiting for me to see her, and she was staring at the empty bottle on top of the closet.

"There will be flowers when I get home from school. Good-bye," she said, and with that she was out the door.

* * *

How long can you sit in a windowless shack? Before long, I tempted fate. I did what any kid would do. I sneaked out, peeked around corners to see what I could see. The milking barn was empty. Below that barn, and through its holding pen, I could see a man with a mustache, and another man just like him, putting hay out for a pen full of calves, the calves gathered around the wooden feeder. Then something else: the big man, the hairy man with an egg head; he was leaning on the fence, an upright pitchfork in one hand. He was looking directly at me. He must've had an eagle's eyes. I was a good distance from him, maybe a quarter of a mile, and between him and where I was standing, alongside the shack, there were two or three fences, not counting the holding pen. I kept still in hopes everything would be all right, the way you might stand in front of an animal you didn't want to scare or disturb. He studied me for a long moment and then began pitching hay with his fork alongside the other two men.

No big deal. I decided to go farther. Seeing the door to the other shack ajar, I crept forward and looked inside. On the floor was a bare pallet bed. And there was a table, painted white just the same as the one where we were staying; and, on the table, an empty roll of toilet paper. Nothing else. Next, I inched my way toward the corrals and barns that housed the rows and rows of spotted cows eating out of low troughs. I even found the bull pens, and I marveled at a bull the size of an automobile. Once, I heard the two men, the look-alike men, approach, and I skirted around a corner, hiding behind a thick post, proud of my dexterity. From there, I was able to see Mother and the big woman coming back from the main house. It was noon.

Safely back inside before they arrived, I sat at the table, a perfect lady. Mother served me a tuna fish sandwich, exactly the same as the day before, and the big woman poured herself a glass of water from the jug in the cold box and stood gulping it down. Then Mother spotted my nightgown strewn on the girl's pallet, and said to me, "Pick that up."

She looked to the big woman, who set her empty glass down and shrugged her shoulders, as if saying to Mother, What are you going to do? Your daughter is sloppy. After that, the two of them left.

Sitting alone eating my sandwich, I saw that the milk bottle on top of the stand-up closet was filled with flowers again, a fistful of buttercups and lupine. When did that happen? Had the big woman come in while I was out snooping around? Had I been caught? I could say I'd gone to the outhouse. I thought of the girl, of her routine with her mother; how her mother must gather the flowers while she was at school, and then, at night, how the girl spread them on both their pillows. Again, sadness and self-pity washed over me. When would I go to school? That was something I had meant to ask Mother just then. Would I go with the girl?

There were answers; there was a plan, which I would learn about days later, at the same time I'd learn, in a vehement argument with Mother, how I ruined that plan: to eventually tell the boss—yes, the big hairy man—that there was another kid to feed, after he saw what a good worker Mother was. Instead, he went to her, before she'd had a chance to completely work her way into his good graces, and said, "You didn't tell me you had a kid. How many more you got hiding?" And with that he told Mother to leave. But I had no idea then. Nothing was said. Even when we lugged our suitcases and cardboard box back to the truck later that afternoon, with the big man waiting in the cab, I had no idea what was happening. Both Mother and the woman—who climbed onto the back of the truck with Mother and me—were quiet, seemingly nonchalant.

It seemed routine: We drove into Sebastopol and picked up a pre-scription at the pharmacy for the man's wife. The big woman got off the truck to get the prescription and then got back on. Then, about two blocks away, we found the girl waiting outside her school. She rode on the back with us and a bunch of rattling, empty milk cans. If she knew that anything out of the ordinary was happening, or about to happen, she didn't let on. Even when the truck stopped finally on that middle-of-nowhere road, and after Mother and I got off with our suitcases and one cardboard box, she remained expressionless, staring straight ahead. If she had wanted to say good-bye or wave, you'd never know.

By then I understood that Mother and I had been dumped off. That much I knew. How could I not? But just then, standing on the side of the road and looking at the girl on the truck bed, I knew something else. She was just starting her journey, the journey Mother and I had been on all our lives, and already she knew infinitely more about it than I did. She looked at me then, as if she'd read my thoughts. Her eyes were steady and plain, silent. But I understood. I heard a tiny voice, careful and exact, say, I won't lose my home.

The truck started, gears grinding, then pulled away. The girl was still looking at me. I thought for a minute she might wave. But, of course, she wouldn't, not until she had plenty of time to check with her mother first.

* * *

Six years later, she was back—in my Spanish class.

Tenedor: fork. *Cuchara*: spoon. *Cuchillo*: knife. Eating utensils. Things of the kitchen. "What you are most familiar with. First things first," Mr. Carrica said, looking at the four or five Mexican kids whom he figured took the class to get an easy A. "I speak Castilian," he said. "You will do the same." *Servilleta*: napkin. He pronounced his s with a lisping *th*. He was Basque and, with his pointer, he showed us on a map the place his parents were from, a village in the hills, on the border between France and Spain. He was looking back and forth at the brown faces, as if to make sure they understood. He was looking at me. I was a senior and it was my first day at Santa Rosa High.

She introduced herself after class. She said she was new too. "Anna," she said, offering her hand. "Iris," I said. And then she asked if I remembered her. She gave some hints: the dairy, the old truck we rode on. And I remembered, not the night, not the next day when Mother and I found ourselves homeless again on a nowhere road because this girl's mother couldn't keep us any longer, not any of those things, but the truck, how it pulled away from the side of that nowhere road and how this girl and her mother, riding on the back, grew smaller and smaller until they disappeared. Now she was back. "Yes," I said, grabbing her hand. "Yes."

"What happened to you?" she asked.

What would I say to her? I was at a loss for words. I was so surprised, taken aback. The girl on the truck, I kept thinking. Luckily, the bell rang, and looking away from one another and finding the halls empty, all the students in their classes, we hurried off in opposite directions. But all day, as I went from each new class to the next, I thought of her.

What had happened to her? Had she stayed at the dairy? She had changed. She was polite still, the way she offered her hand, but her voice was warm; she curled her words the way a singer might in a popular song. And she was casual. She wore a straight skirt, pleated in the back, and a print baby doll blouse that, even with its banded puffy sleeves, fit her comfortably, loosely, on the shoulders. A boy at my last high school had said I looked like Natalie Wood in *West Side Story*. You could say the same about her. She was olive-complected. Latin-looking. Mexican. You wouldn't think she was Indian.

* * *

That day long ago, after the truck pulled away, Mother and I hiked to the ocean. It was about five miles from where we had been left off; five miles west over a steep and winding road. Perhaps Anna's mother had told Mother about a possible job in the town of Bodega. I don't know. Maybe Mother just wanted to see the water. She never said. Lugging our suitcases and one cardboard box, resting about every mile or so, we made it to the water just in time to watch the sun go down. Golden light traveled west over the waves forever.

"Beautiful," Mother said.

We stood on a long pier, where we'd finally set our suitcases and box down for more than ten minutes. A real rest this time. Just behind us, at the foot of the pier, was a small restaurant. It was quaint: white with yellow trim, and on this side, the back side of the building, large ocean-view windows. Certainly people sat in those windows eating dinner; but, with the low sun a uniform glare over the glass, I couldn't see them. I couldn't see anything but the reflection of Mother and myself, silhouettes, both of us dark and small, in the distance.

"Beautiful," Mother said again.

I turned from where I was looking and found her basking in the warm light off the water, head cupped in her hands, elbows propped atop the wooden railing.

Sometime after that, when the sun was just a sliver of orange above the horizon, a woman came out of the restaurant. She was a waitress: black uniform, apron. I saw her: She was carrying a kitchen tray and making her way along the side of the building. She stopped next to a tall metal trash bin, and then, right before my eyes, looking right at me, she kicked the can, making a loud hollow sound. Then she tilted the tray so that I could clearly see what was on it: plates of steaming food! But my seeing her wasn't enough. She kicked the can again; and only after Mother looked, and after the woman tilted the tray again, making certain that Mother saw, did she set it down on the bin and disappear around the corner, the way she had come.

Mother chuckled for the longest time. Then she turned to me and winked, as if I understood what it was she found so funny. "C'mon," she said, nodding for me to follow. I reached for a suitcase. "Leave it," she said.

We walked across the pier and sat on wooden milk crates and ate a delicious salmon dinner, complete with silverware and cloth napkins. It happened so easily, you would have thought mother had it all planned out. Later, the woman took us to her place. It was a neat cabin, frilly curtains, ceramic pots of African violets on homespun doilies, gleaming knotty-pine furniture. It was on a sheep ranch, down a dirt road off the coast highway. There was another cabin just like it at the end of the dirt road. It's where we would live for the next six years.

The woman's name was Peggy. A spinster. A professional waitress. She was about fifty. She always looked just so, unlike mother, but under the puff of stiff black curls, thick rouge, and little penciled crescents for eyebrows, there was the goodness that knew no bounds. Which must've been what appealed to Mother, for I'd never known Mother to be more comfortable with anyone—I'd never seen her have a friend, not to mention the fact that the friend was white. Of course, mother must've felt indebted to Peggy. Peggy saved us, after all: She got us a place to live. She paid the sheep rancher, who owned both the cabins, hers and ours, our first month's rent. She found mother a permanent job in the Sebastopol cannery and drove her to and from work every day until mother had saved enough for a car of her own. But if it was just a matter of indebtedness, Mother could have paid Peggy off, then politely closed the door on her. Instead, the two became like sisters. They cooked for each other, did each other's laundry; if one found a rip or a loose seam in the other's clothes, she'd mend it.

Peggy was like a second mother to me which, at times, felt smothering. Her cabin was between ours and the highway; if I was able to sneak past Mother, I still had Peggy to contend with. And she always found me. From nowhere—peering through an open window, rising up from her garden of enormous calla lilies, climbing out of the old Pontiac with an armful of groceries—she'd appear and call to me. Come in for a glass of milk. So I'd go, sometimes my school friends caught right along with me. Once I complained about her to Mother, and after Mother said, "Be nice," I said, "I thought you didn't like white people—you always say to watch out for them."

"Not all people are the same," she answered. "Sometimes they surprise you . . . Surprise me, Iris. Be nice."

Then we moved. The sheep rancher sold the ranch. The new owners wanted the cabins for their Mexican help. We had a last dinner. Mother insisted she cook: salmon, complete with silverware and cloth napkins.

Peggy went to San Francisco to live with a relative, a sister or aunt. I thought maybe we would move into Sebastopol, closer to Mother's work. I thought we'd rent a little cabin, something like the place we were in. I was wrong on both counts. We moved back to Santa Rosa, where Mother spent her savings on a down payment for a house. A real house, two bedrooms so Mother didn't have to sleep on a couch in the front room anymore, a front and backyard all our own.

Too bad it was in South Park.

South Park: a square mile of what-have-you's, leftovers. Small houses, batter-board dumps. An adjunct. Where Negroes lived. Poor people. At least lower Fourth, that neon strip, where, as a kid, I stayed boxed in a cheap hotel room, was connected to the rest of town; it was the main and only direct route to the train station. South Park, on the other hand, was completely cut off, out of the way, a wrong turn. Bordered on one side by the racetrack, and on the other by the highway, South Park was nothing more than a closet at the end of a dark hallway, a convenient place for the town to stash its skeletons. What it didn't want its friends and neighbors to see.

Of course Mother thought she got the deal of the century. Low down payment, easily affordable monthly mortgage. She purchased the house directly from the owner, an old, pale-looking Chinese man, after seeing his ad in the newspaper—I had no idea she was looking to buy. I wonder if even she knew, if the ad hadn't simply sparked the idea.

"The house creaks," I complained one night shortly after we moved in.

"Easy for the spirits to come and go," she answered.

"Black people everywhere," I continued.

"And Indians," Mother retorted, pointing a finger at me.

And then, the next day, something happened. It was as if the creaks in the house—the near invisible spaces between the loose floorboards, the minuscule fissures in the ceiling—connected us to the rest of the universe. Two things happened, actually. First, I went out to get the mail—it was about noon—and I found two black girls from the house across the street standing next to the mailbox.

"You got something against black folks, white girl?" the smaller of the two asked. You'd think she'd just heard my derogatory remark from the night before. She put a hand on her hip, cocked her head, challenging.

I didn't think to see the expression "white girl" as a compliment, which, in those days, I would have under any other circumstances. She had uttered it with such disrespect and utter contempt. I was frightened. I knew I was in trouble. They were colorful, these girls, bright clothing, polka dots and stripes, shiny oiled hair, and intent on punishing me. And they lived across the street; there would be no escaping them, not now, not later.

"She asked you a question," the bigger one said. She was still, her pink plastic loop earrings unmoving. Her bulged-angry eyes held me. I felt that if I as much as blinked she'd strike.

"I just moved here," I said. I wanted to mention that I'd never known black folks before, so how could I have anything against them? How could I not like them—the two of them in particular—when I'd just met them for the first time? But nothing more would come out.

"We can see you just moved here," the smaller one snapped, clearly dissatisfied with my answer.

"She asked you a question," replied the bigger girl, adamant.

My mind closed in on itself. Nothing came. All I could do was stare at the girl's pink earrings. The world emptied of sound, stopped. The way it does when, without warning, you witness something extraordinary. A shooting star. A car wreck.

"Who's that?"

I didn't hear the question, so the girl—the smaller girl—had to ask it again, "Who's that?" and still I didn't hear it, only followed her eyes back toward the house.

Then both of them were looking, and what were they seeing?

Mother, a brown sack of rags on the front porch.

"My mother," I said.

They were confused, glancing back and forth from the sack of rags to the light-skinned girl in loafers and a full felt skirt.

"Hmm," said the big one.

"You lying?" said the smaller one.

Both turned to Mother, as if they were about to ask her the truth on the matter. But there was no need for them to say a word. Mother was a mountain lion before her den. Effortless, for she gave no menacing stare, neither said a thing nor lifted a finger. She just stood there. The girls' faces softened, then tightened again in the opposite of anger: fear and amazement.

"My name is Ollie Mae," said the big one.

"I'm Roberta," said the smaller one.

Then the big one added, "You can just call me Mae-Mae," and offered her hand.

That same evening, just before dinner, Mother got a phone call from the old Chinese man's only daughter, with whom he had gone to live. The old man had died, the daughter said, and not to worry about the house payments, for he had willed the house to Mother. She would keep the down payment, however—to pay for his funeral.

She sat down at the kitchen table—which the Chinese man had left for us—and lit a chunk of angelica root. Holding the smoking ember before her, she began talking in Indian, praying maybe, but her tone was casual, easy. Which is why I must've felt no apprehension interrupting her. That and the fact I was still unsettled by the incident with the two black girls.

"What are you saying?" I asked, sitting down opposite her.

Slowly, like a clock winding down, she stopped, set the smoking angelica in an empty ashtray, her voice growing softer and softer until it was nothing at all. Then she looked across the table at me, as if just realizing I had sat down there.

"I can't understand you," I said.

"Oh, this?" she asked, gesturing with her hand to the ashtray.

"What you were saying," I clarified.

"Saying thanks," she said finally. "Grateful." She sat back in her chair, sighed.

"You knew," I accused. I figured, though at some level I didn't want to believe, that she had somehow sensed the old man's passing. Couldn't she see and hear through the cracks, come and go there with the spirits she talked about? She had unusual powers, after all. Yes, hadn't news of the old man's death come through the same crack she used to send my complaint about black people in the neighborhood out and into the two girls' ears?

I didn't hold back a word. "Oh, yes," I added. "And don't think I didn't get the lesson you set up for me to learn—being an Indian helped me out there. OK. I'm an Indian, so what?"

"Gee, Iris, for having so much imagination, you can't see two feet in front of you."

An old refrain of hers. It meant nothing. I waited. She looked down at the angelica. A wispy stream of smoke rose from the dying ember.

"Those girls," she said without looking up. "They got pride. Think how they feel when they see you, the way you are. People see things. Maybe not you, Iris. But other people do. You don't need special powers to see things . . ."

"I know," I said, imagining what she'd say next, "just open your eyes."

She leaned forward, looking at the angelica. She still hadn't looked at me.

"So why'd you come out on the porch?" I asked.

"I saw how they was looking at you. Through the window, I seen it all—trouble."

"What were you doing looking out the window?" I pressed.

She ignored me. She picked up the angelica and rolled the unlit end between her thumb and forefinger, looking at it still. Then, without moving her eyes in the least, she said, "That Chinaman, I saw how sick he was when we first come here. You did too. His spirit had already gone, left through the cracks . . . And that's how he done the kindness—he's the one who seen things. The old and dying see clear. He seen how much I appreciated his house. He seen I would take care of it. He seen my spirit here a long time." And, just then, she looked at me, making certain I heard what she was going to say next: "And, Iris, he was right."

All right, I thought, so you have no intention of moving—and you don't want me complaining about the house and neighborhood anymore.

I thought maybe that was it, she was finished.

She stood up and blew on the angelica, raising a hot red ash, a strong stream of smoke following. Then, turning to leave, she said, "I was saying thanks. If somebody or something helps you, it's a good thing to do." And with that she looked at the smoking ember and started off toward the back door.

She stopped in the doorway then, as if she had heard my thoughts, and glanced back at me. "You got it all backwards, Iris," she said, if only to have the last word. "I'm no special power, just your poor old mother." Then she was gone, down the back steps.

Just your poor old mother. How many times had I heard it? Who would believe it?

*   *   *

So what did I tell people at school? That was the question. At Tomales High, where I was before, I was popular. A Natalie Wood-in-*West Side Story* look-alike. A true contender for homecoming queen; in fact, Leslie Mathias, the reigning queen, had said the crown would be mine next year—this year. But Tomales was a small school: a collection of kids netted from the outskirts of nowhere. We'd grown up together, met in elementary school. Dairy rancher, fisherman, cannery worker, it didn't matter your background. Sure, we played the usual games—who was popular, who was in, who was out—but most of us, those who played anyway, were happy just to have others to play with. Point is, if you played well, if you played at all, you were in.

Santa Rosa High wouldn't be so easy. Who could forget the kids from MacDonald Avenue? And they wouldn't be the only ones there. Many neighborhoods poured into that one high school. And South Park, what neighborhood would be worse? I was stuck. The cards were stacked against me. To make matters worse, I was entering the school as a senior; people had their friends, all the cliques would be in place, those people who were in and kept everyone else out. This is what I planned for myself: a year of lonesome drudgery. I'd keep my head in a book and after, after I graduated, I'd start my life all over again.

Anna changed that. Funny thing, she had had the same plan. She was new to Santa Rosa High also; she'd come from Petaluma High, a small school but nothing like Tomales. I learned all this the second day of school. Not outside Spanish class, where I first talked to her, but inside the first-floor girls' bathroom, where I'd gone to check my hair; even if I wasn't ever going to talk to anyone, at least I could look my best—the mystery girl with stunning black hair and perfect perfect clothes. Anna had beat me to it. I'd walked up to the mirror, fumbling in my purse for a brush, and when I looked up, there she was, adjusting the pink hair band behind her straight shiny bangs. "Oh!" we both said to each other in the mirror. A wave of embarrassment, each of us caught in our own vanity. Then we burst out laughing.

We talked about where we'd been, the high school we went to before this one. Pushing and plucking at our hair, we chuckled, made nonsense talk the way nervous teenagers do.

"Gosh," she said in the stream of our conversation, "I told my mother about seeing you, and she wondered where you lived . . ."

She stopped suddenly. She saw I was taken aback. I'd hardly betrayed a wince, a bat of my eyes, but whatever it was, she caught it, for when I looked in the mirror I saw it reflected back in her face. She was quick, though, she handled herself well. "I'm sure Mom would like to see your mother sometime," she said. Then, without a beat, she complained about the position of the ribbon in her hair.

"I'm not sure pink's the right color anyway," she said.

"Oh, it is," I told her.

A large girl came up to the mirror. I hadn't seen her come in; perhaps she'd been in a stall. I don't know. The bathroom was busy now with girls coming and going, the bell about to ring. She was sloppy in a sleeveless white blouse. She had red hair. It was swept straight up, pompadour style, off her broad pale forehead. The ends, which drooped unevenly in loose curls down her back, were a lighter color, an orange, as if the hair had been dyed or bleached at one time. I was so amazed, so preoccupied with the girl's hair, that I hadn't noticed her looking at Anna. And then she snapped:

"Don't think your shit doesn't stink, Anna."

I looked to Anna. Again, if Anna had noticed her before, I didn't know. Continuing to fiddle with her hair, Anna was making a deliberate effort now to ignore this girl.

"*Espejo*," Anna said to me, nodding to the mirror with her fingers in her hair. "*Espejo*. Mirror . . . mirror. *Espejo*."

"*Espejo?*" I questioned.

"Yes, mirror," Anna said quickly, "look into the mirror . . . Pretend it's just you you're looking at. Tune her out."

I looked into the mirror, saw myself, saw Anna, saw the girl turning then and walking away.

"*Espejo*," Anna repeated, urging me to ignore the girl, but I saw her own eyes follow the hapless creature out the door.

"Billyrene Toms," Anna said and sighed, quickly snapping her purse shut.

I thought of Ollie Mae and Roberta, the girls across the street. Anna had found someone who didn't like her either. God, we were alike.

"Cousin," Anna whispered. "Known her a long time."

She must've seen my amazement, not in the mirror, but in my face— we were heading for the door.

"Yeah, the last of the reservation . . . they've all cleared out."

Later Anna and I met for lunch. We ate in the cafeteria, then sat on the school's front steps overlooking a sprawling lawn and tall magnolia tree. She brought up Billyrene, the girl in the bathroom. She told me how Billyrene and her sisters—apparently there was a whole slew of them, each one worse than the next—had lied and stolen her boyfriend, a guy named Joaquin, while she and her mother picked apples outside Sebastopol. It was at the tent camp there, where the Indians stayed during the apple season. This boy, Joaquin, was Indian too; as it turned out, a cousin. But Anna was crazy about him. And so was Billyrene and her sisters.

"But he liked me. He'd bring me flowers," she said.

I couldn't stop trying to imagine Anna at a tent camp, and Anna picking apples. Often, during the apple season, I'd see the families, entire families, men, women, and children, collected under trees, in the dirt on their hands and knees, picking apples. Old scarves, like Mother's, straw hats, dirty jeans. The hot sun. Driving into town from the coast with Mother, I'd see them. The kids, even the small kids working. And alongside the orchards were the tent camps, rows and rows of canvas tents, clothes propped up here and there drying in the sun, smoldering fires, a haze of blue smoke over the place. Skinny dogs. I don't know; I'd figured the workers were Mexican. Maybe some of them were. But Indians? Anna?

"Then," she said, continuing her story, "they told him all these stories about how my mother was a witch, a poisoner. He got scared. You know how Indians are."

"Yeah," I said.

"*Espejo*," she said.

"What?"

"*Espejo*. Mirror. Like we did this morning. Just don't look at her—like we did this morning. Think of something else. Put her out of your mind if she starts up again. Ignore her."

"What else?" I said.

*   *   *

Anna and I met each day at noon just outside the cafeteria. We ate lunch quietly in a corner of the crowded noisy dining hall, then, for the rest of the noon break, visited outside on the school's front steps. Watching the others, the shiny-faced brightly dressed boys and girls, lounging on the sprawling lawn before us, Anna and I discussed our futures. I wanted a career in sales, preferably in a new department store. Anna wanted to be a dental hygienist, always plenty of work in a dentist's office, she said. Both of us would go to the junior college, which was just next door to the high school. "Just like here," Anna said, "but with flexible scheduling." We talked about our classmates too; who was sitting with whom on the lawn, what boy liked what girl, who was popular, who was not. But after a few weeks, we found ourselves spending less and less time on the front steps and more and more time in the empty school library. Before long, we skipped the front steps all together, went directly to the library after eating. It wasn't that either of us was a bookworm, though we did study; rather, the library was a place where we didn't have to talk. More and more we'd found ourselves on the steps face to face with that empty quiet between us.

What we avoided, and all too often fell dangerously close to, was any conversation about our private lives, particularly where we lived, which, in fact, was the real reason both of us arrived early each day and left late—we didn't want our classmates to see us coming or going. All too often a topic of conversation, maybe just a word, stopped us cold. I'd rush in with talk of clothes, popular music, and Anna would nod with quiet relief. I remembered the look of panic on her face when the subject of where I lived slipped out of her mouth that first morning in the girls' bathroom. I had thought it was a reflection of my fear. Now I knew it to be a betrayal of her own also.

Things might not have changed. Then there was Monty. Pegged pants, dirty T-shirts; he smoked, had a cross tattooed on his forearm and, just below it, the word "Heaven." I'd overheard conversations: He smoked marijuana and sat outside the drive-in staring at girls; creepy, they said. He hadn't a friend in the world, and he fell for Anna, was obsessed with her. Dropped a note into her locker that said she was "the soul of God." Followed her, hid around corners. Creepy. Anna and I looked so much alike that I often wondered why he picked her instead of me. In any event, he discovered our sanctuary; and one day after leaving the library, we found ourselves face to face with him. Just outside the building, in the empty parking lot. Looking at us—at Anna, defying her to ignore him. Hands on hips, an unlit cigarette hanging from the corner of his mouth, he was bold.

I felt Anna take hold of my arm. "Please," she said, leaning closer to my ear, "please walk me home."

Then she must've realized what she'd said, what that meant, for she blurted out, "I live in a dump."

"I live in South Park," I answered to calm her.

"My mother's a maid, a house cleaner."

"Mine's a cannery worker!"

And that's how, following her lead, I crossed Mendecino Avenue and started up Pacific.

Until we hit MacDonald. And then I saw the Presbyterian church on the corner, and across the street, the candy store. I saw the Victorian houses, the rolling lawns and privet hedges, the windows that, at this time of day, late afternoon, reflected you on the street, and knew before knowing that a turn of fate, a trick worthy of any of Mother's, had delivered me full circle to the Polks'. I knew before Anna turned up the driveway that that was where we were going to turn. I could have told her about the poplar trees by the garage, the rosebushes along the fence, and in the garden where Mother used to sit, the gate that led to the little house in the back.

"No," I said, planting my foot on the sidewalk, as if braking a car about to go over a cliff. "No!"

We were standing at the foot of the Polks' driveway.

"I can't do it," I said. I stepped back, out of view of the house.

"What?" she asked, following me as I backed up.

I couldn't form the words.

Don't think I hadn't thought of Mary Beth. Santa Rosa High. Sitting around the house those last two or three weeks before school started, I couldn't stop thinking about Mary Beth and the likelihood I'd run into her. I'd seen a couple of the others from those days; I had a class with Allison Witherow, the tall blond, still the tall blond. Either she'd forgotten me—but then how can you forget a name like Iris?—or she'd learned to do what the rest of her kind do in the face of an eyesore, a hovel on an otherwise perfectly manicured city street—she ignored me. So be it. A truce as far as I was concerned. But Mary Beth, I hadn't seen her. The school was large; still, I figured sooner or later I would run into her, and when I did, no matter what the circumstances, I hoped she would handle me the way Allison had, as if I was thin air. But now I would be stepping into her face. Not only her face but, at the same time, plunk into the arena where our ugly little history together had taken place.

Taking Anna's hand, I turned her around and led her back up the street, almost to Pacific, and then stopped and told her the entire story, from start to finish.

"So just go on," I told her. "I'll watch you from here until you get in, then I'll walk home. Go on." I shooed her away, flicking my hands. "That Monty's nowhere around, anyway. He didn't follow us."

But she stood and argued with me. She told me that we wouldn't even see Mary Beth. She seldom came out of her room. She studied all the time. Anna had never seen her out of her uniform—she went to Ursuline, a private school for girls, which explained why I never saw her at school.

"Yes, but Mrs. Polk," I answered. "Think if she sees me, after all I said about Mr. Polk and Allison Witherow's mother—you and your mother would get evicted!"

Anna looked at me long and hard. "Mrs. Polk is dead," she said.

"What?"

"Mrs. Polk is dead."

"What happened?"

"Cancer, I think," Anna said, taking my arm, "but I'm not sure," and already she was leading me back down the street.

She was talking then, about how Mrs. Polk had died before she and her mother moved in, how her mother answered an ad in the newspaper. But I was hardly listening. I was seeing the woman with the short tasteful bangs whose long neck glistened under the kitchen lights when she turned to talk to her husband. She was beautiful. But she was ugly too. Who could forget the way she burst into the house that night and yanked Mary Beth up from the table? Her beautiful face was ugly, contorted with her determination and disregard, as she said, "You girls must be separated." Did she look that way when she fired Mother? When she died?

Dead. Gone. Mrs. Polk. That's what I was thinking as I stood with Anna outside the picket gate that led to the little house. That's what allowed me to float back down that same street so easily. The shock of it. Gone. As if somehow Mrs. Polk's death meant that Mary Beth wasn't there either. Or her father. Or her brother. Or anything else outside the scope of memory. As if I was visiting the ruins, the shell of an old building, a tombstone.

I looked at the patio behind the kitchen of the big house, then back at the brick walkway before me, beyond the gate. The garden alongside the little house, where Mother used to sit, was immaculate, the rosebushes already pruned for the winter. The honeysuckle and fig vine that grew on the wall were cropped close and cut in a straight line just below the roof. Moss grew between the bricks. Still, everything was different.

Anna tugged on my arm. "C'mon," she said, and I followed her.

The house was basically the same; I mean, what could change about a two-room servants' quarters? There were some differences, though: In place of the old cold box there stood a modern refrigerator, and next to it, where the stand-up closet used to be, was a small four-burner gas stove. The furniture was new, too, the sofa and the oak table and four matching chairs. Frilly edged curtains were tied off the two windows with matching bows.

I remembered Anna's mother two ways: first, in those black rubber boots and a dress as she hoisted feed sacks onto the back of a pickup, when we saw her that first day, outside the feed store; and, second, in fresh house clothes with a clean morning-glory-bordered apron, her hair pulled back neat and tight off her face, when she came into that little shack where we were staying and pulled two tuna fish sandwiches out from under the apron. When she came into this house, pulling the screen door back so that Anna and I turned in our seats, she looked the second way: clean, tidy. Even more so than before; she was a big woman, heavier than Mother, but she looked as tight as a drum. She wore a corset under her light-colored print dress, the binds and ties of that contraption in a line of ridges down her back, like a giant zipper. You could've bounced nickels off her. She was so neat, the short sleeves rolled up evenly, a perfect inch above her thick upper arms; and her shoes, they were old-lady blacks, yet they were polished and each tied with a tight, identical black bow.

"Ida," she said.

She leaned close so that I might see her better. She was standing next to the table now.

"Ida," she said again. "It's me, Ida."

I offered my hand. I hadn't heard her name before, when I was a kid.

"Your mother," she said, taking my hand, "how is she?"

"Fine," I said.

"There's no more reservation," she said with urgency, "no more reservation." She squeezed my hand to emphasize her words.

"I know," I said as if I knew this fact well, when, in actuality, I'd heard the news only weeks before from Anna, her daughter. I might've spilled the rest of it out—how all the Indians cleared out, but how her and Anna got a head start—if she hadn't all of a sudden let go of my hand and straightened up. Her eyes that had moved, widened with excitement when she talked, settled now. Her lips closed in a line, tight.

You would have thought it was something I said. Had she read my mind and found something wrong there? Or had she suddenly remembered the disobedient little girl on the dairy farm? Probably it was neither of these things. What I'd learn in time was that Ida, as stiff as her corset, kept herself behind the mask. That and her Bible. She was surprised to see me, taken aback, and, for that brief moment, forgot herself.

"You turned out pretty," she said. But her voice was quiet, retreating.

She made herself busy then, opening and closing the refrigerator, going into the back room and hurrying out again. Clearly, she'd forgotten what she'd come into the house for in the first place. When she left, letting the screen door slam behind her, she was empty-handed.

"My mother always wore an apron," I said.

Anna looked at me. "Oh, Mama does—in the evenings, when Mr. Polk is home."

She was quiet then. Her words hung in the air, and I heard the unspoken sadness in them. She had heard what I'd heard—the sadness that had come before, in her mother's compliment, the remorse that Ida felt because she couldn't say with all the momentary joy and surprise in her, You turned out pretty. For that would invite conversation; she'd have to stray over the line she'd drawn so deeply and firmly between herself and the rest of the world. Why it had affected me so much I don't know. But Anna felt it too. A gloom that ate away whatever shock I felt before, over Mrs. Polk's death and the odd circumstance of my return. Like paint thinner spilled on a shiny table, eating the varnish to the bare dull wood.

We both turned to the door and sat for the longest time. We didn't have words or stories to explain the sadness we felt. So we sat it out, watching, as if we would see it leave through the screen door the way Ida had.

"I should probably get going," I said after a while.

"Gee, Iris, I didn't even offer you anything to eat . . . Mom's got pie in the fridge."

"That's the last thing I need," I said, patting my hips, and letting her off the hook, for I knew the notion of getting out of that little house just then was as appealing to her as it was to me.

"I'll walk you partway," she said, getting up. "Don't you think Monty's given up by now?"

"I don't think he followed us," I said.

* * *

That night I told Mother about Anna. For over three weeks, the entire time I'd known Anna, studied each day at school with her, I hadn't said a word to Mother. I felt that it would give her a foot in my world at school, where I wanted in every way to live my life independently of her. Now, somehow, I felt it didn't matter anymore. In time, and probably with-

out any fault of my own, wouldn't she find Anna and me together anyway?
I didn't just tell her about Anna, but about my ending up at the Polks' and
seeing Ida and hearing of Mrs. Polk's death. I thought these two things in
particular—the irony of Ida now having the job she had left when Ida took
us in, and Mrs. Polk's death—would interest her. But none of it seemed to
matter to her, except for the news about the reservation.

"What happened?" she asked.

"I don't know," I answered, then repeated, "Ida just said it's no
more."

She wasn't listening to me, though; in fact, she had as much as asked
herself the question as she had asked me. She was lost in thought, her face
in her cupped hands, elbows propped on the table. We had just finished
dinner, and as I talked, she had slowly nudged her empty plate aside, as if
she'd known she would lose herself in thought and have to prop her elbows
there. She gazed past me, unblinking. There was a parade in her eyes, and
she didn't want to miss a single sight.

"Old Uncle," she said. "Old Uncle said it would happen. Said the
tribe would fall apart, every last one of us like seeds in the wind." She was
talking to herself, repeating the words that she no doubt heard the old man
saying as he sat before her on that porch or wherever it was he talked to her
so many years before.

"Was it some kind of curse?" I asked.

You'd think she'd be happy having me engage her in "Indian talk,"
talk about Old Uncle and all that old-time stuff. Mother appeared unimpressed.

"What do you mean 'curse'?" she asked.

"You know, like someone cursed the people," I answered. In so many
of her stories, when something bad happened to someone, it was on account
of someone cursing, or what she often called "poisoning," someone else.

"Hah," she said, "why would the people need somebody else to curse
them when they live day in and day out cursing themselves?" She thought
a moment and then she was gazing again. "He said, 'When the people do
bad to one other person, in no time at all they'll do themselves that way.'
That's what he was seeing—the people flying away like seeds. Poor fools,"
she said, and then she was back in the room. She was looking at me.

"There was another girl at school, light-skinned," I told her. "Anna
said she was a cousin too."

"Oh?" Mother perked up.

"Billyrene Toms. Toms, the same last name as Anna."

"Could that be Zelda's daughter?" Mother wondered out loud. "She
had a white man too."

A wave of shock ran through me. I couldn't stop myself. I asked the long-buried question: "So my father *was* white?"

Mother threw her head back and laughed and said, as if she were still following her own train of thought, "We were all wild women, each one of us, drunk and as loose as rabbits in spring—me, Zelda, Ida." Then she looked at me; her eyes were still full of glee, but she was looking to make sure she had my attention. "There was three of them. I remember that, there was three of them and they was white, and they was taking turns. So, yeah, Iris, one of them must be your father." She started chuckling again. "And three white men ain't an Indian or a Mexican, right?"

My heart sank, floated up again and bobbed like an oak gall caught in a waterfall. She did nothing to save me. She stood on the firm ground of her shore and watched.

"Yes," she continued, "Toms, see, Zelda and Ida, they're sisters. Me, I'm a cousin, Gonzales. But that's why you kids get our last name—Toms, Gonzales—no clear-cut father to speak of." She paused, then added, "Truth is, I'm a Toms too. Zelda and Ida and me had the same father. Our mothers was sisters—so we're cousins and sisters, hah!" She chuckled. "Fathers: Them's a confusing situation."

"We have Spanish in us too," I quickly countered, if for no other reason than to change the subject of fathers—mine in particular. I knew the story of Rosa, the one surviving member of our tribe who was taken in by the Mexican general, who the priest baptized and named the town after— This town, your living history, Mother always said when she used to tell this story. Rosa was the general's maid and wife.

"Sadness," Mother said, the mention of Spanish apparently cueing her to the story. Her countenance changed, the glee completely vanished from her eyes as she again began to follow the pictures in her mind.

"But her daughter, the second Rosa, got away—you always said that. She met up with another Indian man and—"

"Away, but not free," she interrupted. "Sadness, it followed. Poor fools," she said again.

Without getting up, I began to clear the table, reaching for the butter dish and plastic pitcher of iced tea. Then Mother said:

"The Mexican general had a cousin. I guess he would be what, Rosa's cousin-in-law. He used to hunt bears. He found out where they hid, them grizzlies—used to be a lot of them. He found their caves and he went there and shot them. You know what happened to him? When the Americans come and took over from the Mexicans, the Americans hunted him. They found him hiding in the bear caves and they shot him. Then I don't know what happened. He lived. He ended up living out his days in front of the courthouse, down at the square, begging for money.

"That was a sadness," she said, "that *was* a curse."

"But he was a Mexican," I said, and the thought occurred to me that the man, my great-great-great-grandfather's brother, was an uncle.

"Doesn't matter," Mother said. "Doesn't matter who you are, what you call yourself." She was looking right at me. "Old Uncle used to say that."

Then I heard it: "Keep your eyes open, Iris."

There, she had to land a lesson. But what had I done? What sin? I brought up the subject of Anna and Ida—Indians. But Mother didn't focus any more attention on me; she was staring again.

She sighed and said, "Seeds in the wind, no home. Poor fools."

Quietly, I stood up and carried away the butter dish and pitcher of tea. Mother sat at the table for the longest time, not giving me a second's thought.

I felt sorry for her in some way. And it occurred to me, as never before, that she might be terribly lonely. In those moments of memory, the talk about Ida and Zelda, her drinking and whatever, Mother must've remembered friends, people at least that she had grown up with, known well, until she left the reservation. If not lonely, then, at least, alone. A seed far from the field.

THREE

If Mother was lonely, she didn't dwell on it. She kept busy. She found joy in the smallest things. Her garden, for instance. In time, she had changed an empty yard with a few Chinese herbs into a cornucopia of flowers and plants. Roses, bulbs of all kinds, a privet hedge, winter vegetables like lettuce and cabbage, you name it and it was there. Not in rows, not in patches, but here and there and everywhere. On the weekends, and after work, you'd find her on all fours with a trowel, or standing with the hose, letting water dribble ever so gently on whatever it was she had just planted. She found cuttings left in the street, in people's garbage; she walked the streets, ambled through the entire neighborhood with an old gunnysack over her shoulder.

What people thought, I don't know. The woman across the street, Mae-Mae and Roberta's mother, gave her iris bulbs, calla lilies, and a couple of shoots of honeysuckle. In exchange, Mother made her an apple pie and a stack of fry bread, the latter of which the family went crazy over and had Mother give them the recipe. It was fall; everything Mother planted was dormant, bare bulbs, naked twigs. It rained. The winter was cold. Come mid-spring there was so much blossom and color the bees and butterflies were confused.

Mother and the woman across the street, Mrs. Clayton, visited often in the evenings, more so as the days got warmer and longer. Her name was Alice; she was a thin woman, not at all like her hardy daughters, but she had a wide, yellow-toothed laugh that you could hear clear to Sebastopol. She laughed a lot as she and Mother chatted about plants and traded recipes.

"Elba, you're the funniest damn woman," she was always saying to Mother. I never had a clue as to what in the world she found so funny.

Sometimes Mae-Mae and Roberta followed her across the street. Mae-Mae was in high school with me, a junior; Roberta was a ninth-grader, in junior high still. While our mothers dug in the yard or taught each other new dishes in the kitchen, we visited over milk and Mother's cookies or fry bread. They knew the latest dances. They knew singers I had never heard of: Dinah Washington, Etta James, Little Richard. "Elvis Presley ain't nothing," they told me. "White folks don't know no better."

White folks. How the term stung me. Wasn't I white? I mean, compared to them. Yet they never considered me so, not after our encounter by the mailbox; it was always us and them, them being white people. They talked about boys too. But they talked about boys the way they talked about music, as if I didn't know a thing. Even Roberta, the ninth-grader, lorded her knowledge and experiences over me. "You're a bookworm, poor thing," she said once as I sat amazed after she recounted yet another of her adventures with this or that boy from the neighborhood. They thought I was a nerd. They were mostly right.

Funny, how things happen. Anna and I didn't take long, out-of-the-way routes to school anymore; we didn't get to school early and stay late. We abandoned the library. For lunch, instead of standing in line in the cafeteria and then taking our usual corner seats, we left campus, walked up Mendecino Avenue past the junior college to the Foster Freeze, where, each day, we bought a deluxe burger and a Coca-Cola. Spring was in the air, the days warm and everywhere flowers and the smell of fresh-cut lawns; and, besides, in a couple of months we would be graduating. We'd survived Santa Rosa High. Nobody bothered us; I'm not sure anyone except Monty noticed us, to tell you the truth.

In the beginning, we'd eat our Foster Freeze lunch at one of the tables next to the hamburger stand, then head back to school and wait out the remainder of the hour sitting on the front steps, watching the other kids. But, before long, we found ourselves sitting on the lawn under the giant oak trees in front of the junior college instead. And that's where we'd bring up a favorite topic of conversation: boys.

It wasn't that I was completely naive. I had had boyfriends. At Tomales High I was popular; I went to dances, drove into Santa Rosa with dates to see movies, and afterward, after the boys drove me in their parents' cars down that dirt road off the highway and walked me to my front door, I might get a peck on the cheek, maybe on the lips. But that was all. Finished. It was kid stuff. Anna and I talked about the whole ball of wax, romance with a capital R, start to finish. The solitary life we had planned alone and then lived together at school was unraveling. Little did we know how much we had kept down; or, should I say, how little did we know there was so much in us to keep down. Of course, part of the problem at the high school was that boys and dating would always be associated with the larger social scene, which Anna and I tiptoed around like we would a sleeping giant.

The situation was different at the junior college. The boys were free agents. They came and went as they pleased. They didn't know this girl and that girl. If they took an interest in us and then found out where we lived and decided they didn't like us, there wasn't the whole school to tell. We'd never be forced to stand in line in the cafeteria and have people talk about us; the girl we shared a locker with wouldn't complain to her friends. It was a free world, a take me or leave me world. No dues. And the boys—how could you call them boys? They were men, a good majority of them in their twenties. Adults. An adult world. So we looked and looked, and looked some more. And it was spring.

"The blood, it must be embarrassing," Anna said one day as we sat on our sweaters under the oaks.

"Anna, it's a fact of life," I said with a dismissive sigh. "Besides, how else is the guy going to know you're a virgin?" You'd think I was Mae-Mae or Roberta.

"It must hurt."

"You're in love, you won't be thinking about it."

"You live in a dream world, Iris."

We sat in the same spot every day, not far from the small outdoors amphitheater on the lawn where lots of college guys gathered at the same time. We were in plain view. Anna had a young man picked out; he wasn't a blond, he had gorgeous dark wavy hair, and we watched him closely enough to see he drove a new red Mercury convertible, his own car, and what a car. Of course, we had no way of knowing his name; for all our talk about men, we were about as brave as mice in front of a cat—we worried that the guys would see us looking. Until one day he sat himself next to us on the lawn, not dangerously close—he wasn't obvious—but close enough. Anna panicked.

"Don't look, don't look," she said.

But it was too late. I wasn't looking; I was sitting so I could see his every move, and I saw that he had gotten to his feet and was coming our way. He'd lit a cigarette too.

"*Hola*," he said, "*Mi llamo* Mike." His Spanish was horrendous.

I nudged Anna. He was talking to her.

She jumped, found him looking at her, exhaling a cloud of smoke.

"Anna," she said, quietly introducing herself. But there was no feigning modesty or lack of interest on her part. Her red face betrayed her.

"*Come estas?*" he said.

"We don't speak Spanish," she said a little too boldly.

He looked confused, his brow furrowed. He glanced at me, as if I might explain what Anna had said. I saw his dark eyes, the small curved lips, tight when he wasn't speaking; his white letterman sweater lit his face, which was magazine handsome, strong, square-boned.

"We're not Mexican," she finally said, accusingly. She waited so he could catch the full effect of her voice, then added in the same tone, "We're Indians."

She wasn't guarding or hiding anything now, not the fluster that was so apparent just moments before, nothing. In fact, she sounded as if she wasn't interested in him in the least, as if he was a pest and she wanted to drive him away. I didn't say a word. I didn't want to provoke Anna. She was obviously bothered. Besides, what would I say?

He stood a long while. I didn't dare look at him. I don't know what Anna was doing. Now I was the one with my eyes fixed on my lap. Then I saw his half-smoked cigarette fall to the ground, and his two-tone saddle shoe rubbing it into the grass.

"Ah, well," he said, "Mexicans, Indians, it's all the same."

I looked up then. He was extending his hand to Anna, gentleman-like, and announced his full name. "Mike Bauer," he said, and Anna took his hand. Then he turned to me and did the same, and left, no doubt thankful to get away.

*   *   *

Mother loved it when Anna came over. She took off her apron, straightened the scarf on her head, or, sometimes, even took the scarf off and brushed her hair. She doted on Anna, pushing cookies and pie at her. The same way she did with Mae-Mae and Roberta, only, with Anna, I detected in Mother a desperation to please. And she'd find an empty moment in each of Anna's visits to interject, "Anna, please, hi to your mama for me." "Mama," the word Anna used. "Your mother's so sweet," Anna always said. And she liked Mother's flowers. Still, we rarely came to my house. Milk and cookies and flowers only go so far. Anna's place was much closer to school, and, besides, it offered something more: excitement.

It was like watching a movie from Anna's front window. What I remembered as an organized, very lively family—a bustle of dinner parties and social events, even if Mary Beth was often left out—was now three solitary individuals who came and went alone and without as much as a word to one another when their paths happened to cross in the driveway or on the back porch. Mary Beth, who had not yet seen me, was never in anything but her school uniform—Anna was right. It was a dorky blue-and-white shift. She left early in the morning, Anna said, and we'd see her come back in the afternoons, and, other than that, she never set foot outside the house. She had retreated to her books; she carried a stack of them, each with the same book cover, blue and white, matching her uniform. She walked with her head down, came through the back gate, then hurried up the steps and into the house, as if she knew we were watching her and didn't want to be seen. But I saw. I saw her blonde frizz top, as wild and unmanageable as ever; yes, the thick-rimmed glasses still, and her skin, once peachy smooth, perhaps her only pleasing physical attribute, now a landscape of pimples, red welts visible from as far away as Anna's window.

Patrick, her brother, had grown quite tall, and, like Mary Beth, hurried in and out of the house. His hair was darker than I remembered; then a dark blond, now a definite brown, and it seemed to be receding a bit; he had, at twenty, what you might call an aristocratic forehead. I didn't know him at all before. He was, after all, a couple of years older than Mary Beth and me, and a couple of years to a sixth-grader makes all the difference in the world. But I remembered him as snooty, the good Presbyterian gatekeeper, habitually aware of those who were in and those who were out. I know because I was out. He looked now the way you might expect a kid like that to grow up: dapper, fashionable clothes, his collar flung open and exposing a tanned neck, great tanned calves when he wore tennis shorts. Few boys in Santa Rosa could pull off such a look.

Mr. Polk had changed the least; he'd only become grayer, his countenance more sinister, and it was that air, that dark spirit, that seemed now to pervade the house. The only light came from the kitchen, where Ida worked in the evenings. The rest of the house—all of the windows—seemed always to be dark.

Anyway, that day after Anna's awkward encounter with her amour on the junior college lawn, we found ourselves as usual at her place with the kitchen table pushed up against the window so we could sit with our cookies and iced tea looking out at the Polks. Only we weren't talking about Mary Beth, Patrick, or Mr. Polk. We were still talking about Anna and her amour.

"He must think I'm a jerk," Anna moaned.

It was like that: a lot of her feeling like an idiot and what this guy must think. I mostly listened. She talked.

"You'll have another chance," I said.

I meant nothing by it, nor did I necessarily believe it. I spoke as a mother might to appease a whimpering child: The words were mere distractions, temporary balm for the pain and nothing more. I didn't know Mike Bauer was on his way. My words had no power. He simply drove into the driveway and Anna and I happened to be in the little house after school. Yes, as Anna, head down, lamented her lost opportunity, I saw the red Mercury convertible pull up and park. I saw Mike Bauer get out of the car.

"Look!" I exclaimed. Then I saw where he was headed.

"Anna," I said, tapping on the table, "he went into the house. He went into the house, Anna."

Of course, I'm sure she thought he had come to see her. And, why not?

"He's in the house," I said, ever so slowly, so my words would sink in.

"A friend of Patrick's?" she asked.

I knew she was back on planet earth then. "Yes," I said.

She had regained her senses maybe, but she wasn't the least bit relaxed. She immediately began fiddling with her hair. "He'll be back here," she said.

He never did knock on the door. She was right about only one thing: He was a friend of Patrick's. But, not to worry, she would have her chance. He was too close now, a visitor where she lived, a friend of her mother's boss, a friend of her closest neighbor. They were animals in the same small forest. Their paths were bound to cross.

* * *

That day, after Mike came out of the house and left without as much as glancing in the direction of the servants' quarters, I started home. It was late, Mother would be worried, and I was hurrying. I took the most direct route: down Fourth and then down Mendocino. At the corner there, at the square, I noticed a gaggle of girls collected around a bench. Tough-looking girls, an assortment of ill-fitting clothes and dyed hair. I passed them, paying little attention; I tried not to look, the way you might pass an army of hungry dogs. I sensed nothing good about them.

"Hey, you," the voice bellowed.

I kept walking. Then again:

"Hey, you." And more: "You, squaw."

The voice was closer, coming toward me. I couldn't run. I didn't. I turned around.

Billyrene. Her thick body, a black skirt and white blouse, mounds of red hair, coming at me. "You think you're so good, don't you, squaw?"

I didn't answer her. I stood.

"Well, you're nothing but a black-necked squaw." She snarled, her frown wound tight. "I know you," she said. "Don't act like your mother's not a fucking whore, because she is. Hear me . . ."

She started reaching for my hair, but just as her hand came forward, her entire body pulled back. There was a loud shriek, and then I could see light; the sisters were backing up, spreading out in all directions, away from me, and when I looked again Billyrene wasn't there. She was on the ground—an arm, a leg, her face—and Mae-Mae was straddled on top of her, punching the daylights out of her.

It happened so fast. Roberta was there, too, cussing at the others to stay back. Then it was like a chain reaction: Someone was on top of Mae-Mae and Roberta was backing off. It was none other than Alice Clayton, and she was pulling Mae-Mae off Billyrene.

Then it was all over. But not before a chorus of loud name-calling. Everybody was on their feet now.

"Fucking no-good tramp," Mae-Mae was hollering, despite the angry pleas from her mother to quit. Alice was holding a bunch of celery and looking for the bag of groceries while she was yelling at Mae-Mae to stop.

"God damn street whore . . . All of you," Mae-Mae said, looking at the others collecting again near Billyrene, a tattered mess now, her red hair in every direction, the front of her blouse torn, exposing the white skin punched red and splotched with knuckle marks. Her face was red too.

"Mae-Mae!" Alice threatened, lifting her fist.

Mae-Mae, finding a moment of clarity, turned to her mother, saying, "Damn it, Mama, it's true. These girls stand out here and pick up men. You see them every day, don't you?"

"Mae-Mae!"

"And did you see? They jumped Iris. That fat ugly one there." She was looking right at Billyrene, challenging her. But it was no use, even if Alice hadn't been there. Billyrene was no match; Mae-Mae had beat the daylights out of her and could do it again.

"Mama, she's a whore," Mae-Mae continued.

Alice didn't clobber Mae-Mae then. She took her by the arm and led her away, and Mae-Mae followed as gentle as a kitten. "Get the groceries," Alice yelled to Roberta.

I watched Roberta gather up the split bag of groceries in her arms, then looked back at Billyrene. I wish I hadn't. It was the strangest thing. It wasn't as if she was mad, or even sorry, but rather as if I had somehow betrayed her. She was looking right at me, and she looked so hurt, her eyes sloping sadly in her round, reddened face, that you would've thought I had taken her last dime. She didn't move. None of them moved. And when I looked, I saw that all of them were looking at me the same way. All five or six of them, light-skinned and dark, a sea of poor girls' clothes, their eyes on the thief, the unfaithful.

"C'mon," I heard Alice call, and then I walked away.

Nobody said anything in the car. Clearly, Mae-Mae was in trouble. I thought of thanking Mae-Mae, all of them, but thought it better just to keep quiet.

"You go on home, Iris," Alice said as we got out of the car.

I walked into the house and found Mother on the couch with a sobbing woman in her arms. I could see that the woman, with her head tucked against Mother's chest, was poor, a wretch, in fact. Her slip, which was so old you'd never guess it had ever been white, was the dusty brown color of moths' wings and hung below her tattered calico like a second dress. She wore nylon stockings, but they had caught and bunched around her ankles, and over the one knee that I could see, and here and there, she'd patched the runs with a brown-pink nail polish. And when Mother gently lifted her off her chest and turned her in my direction, holding her, a hand on each shoulder, holding her to me as if she were a mother proudly presenting her baby, I saw that the woman was Indian. Light-skinned but Indian. Beneath her badly permed dark hair, I saw the high cheeks, the dark eyes.

This woman's eyes narrowed and, when they opened again, they were bright and full with recognition. "You must be Iris," she said.

She swiped at her nose with a balled-up piece of Kleenex. I saw Mother's box of Kleenex on the coffee table next to them.

"Yes," I said.

Her voice was as smooth and clear as water. "My daughter knows you," she said. "She's Billyrene."

"This is Zelda," Mother interjected.

"She's right . . . You're so pretty." She turned to Mother and repeated, "Gee, Elba, how pretty she is."

I didn't trust the woman. I didn't like her. I didn't like anything in the room. But what could I say? I wouldn't give her the opportunity to go home and tell her daughter Billyrene that I came in complaining about nearly getting beat up.

"Gee," Zelda said, looking back at me, "you got the high-class looks."

I stood, letting her drink in her view of me, unflustered, unruffled. Then, all at once, with a spray of spit, she blurted out, "White girl," and began laughing uncontrollably. She attempted to suppress her laughter, covering her mouth with the balled-up Kleenex. But it didn't work. She was making fun of me.

When I looked to Mother, she was laughing too. And, then, seeing perhaps a mixture of confusion and anger on my face, she settled and attempted to explain herself. "Don't mind us." But that was it, for she then hit Zelda on the shoulder, a good punch that nearly knocked the hag off the couch, and said, "Couple of goddamned whores, eh!"

Zelda coughed. She sucked, caught in her breath then, and let out with the most raucous laughter I had ever heard from a woman.

"Lord strike you dead, Elba," she managed, reaching for the Kleenex she'd dropped on the floor.

"Ain't nobody going to strike me nothing," Mother rejoined. "Shark bite me and turn up dead, eh!"

Back and forth, the two of them. In collusion. Against me. I might have been feeling just then the way I had an hour before with Billyrene and her sisters—ganged-up on, friendless. Standing there, I might as well have been invisible. Back and forth, the two of them. Not me. But I saw something. I saw Mother as I had never seen her before, in her element, with her kind. She was common, low class; she and Zelda, in their day, just like Billyrene.

But later, sitting in my room, I got mad. Too much had happened. You could think chance and serendipity when it came to Anna and Mike Bauer. Billyrene and Zelda had to do with Mother—Indians. When it came to Mother, you thought something else. Chance and serendipity had nothing to do with her, other than as decoys she might use to avert your gaze from the truth about her, which was that she was a witch, a woman in cahoots with the stars. Face it. She'd already found that weak spot in my skin, poked her way through, as easily as you'd poke a straw through the perforated plastic cover over a soft drink, and blown herself to my core.

She'd set things up: first Billyrene, then Zelda. But why? For what reason? What had I done? In the past, when she plotted and planned with her unworldly allies against me, I had been guilty of something: selfishness, disrespect, ingratitude, laziness. But what now? I was not plotting to sneak into the Presbyterian church, a place I didn't belong, in order to crash a party I had never been invited to. I wasn't sneaking out of a house I was told not to leave. I wasn't short or impatient in any way toward someone she cared about. I'd been a model daughter, quiet, respectful. I studied. I had a nice friend, a good girl like myself, someone that Mother not only approved of, but adored. I'd even spent time—more time than I had in my entire life—listening to her tell stories about the past: stories passed down to her, stories about old Rosa and the Mexican general, stories about the old-time village on Santa Rosa Creek; and stories about her own life, memories of Old Uncle, Indian stories. She'd long given up using snakes and such to stir in me an interest in Old Uncle. But she talked, still told stories. Rosa inside the Mexican adobe, sad. Old Uncle flying to the moon. Old Uncle turning into a botfly and doing this and that. His fancy clothes, spanking-new suspenders and derby.

She'd taken to sitting in the garden again. The spring nights were warm, and it truly was her garden now, her flowers, her vines and plants. She'd carry a kitchen chair down the back steps and plant it alongside a spray of hollyhocks, the white-yellow flowers catching the night light and hanging just over her head like fat buttery stars. One night a few weeks before, I sat on the back steps, across from her, and asked her what she was thinking. It had been an unusually warm day; the house inside was as hot as fire. I had to ask twice, "Mother, what are you thinking?" She gazed down from the sky, and without looking at me, looking instead at the old wooden gate on the side of the house, said, "My people." I supposed she had time to think now. She allowed herself to think now, to remember. She owned a house. She had a permanent job. She wasn't wistful or morose when she spoke; it was more as though she was acknowledging something, her memory, say, like a party of old acquaintances suddenly gathered just outside the gate and waving to her.

Ha! She wasn't just sitting in her garden merely remembering her people—she was calling them! And when the dead—and the living—appeared just outside the gate waving to her, she did more than acknowledge them and wave back. She told them of her plans. Help me, she said.

* * *

I waited until Zelda left. I was furious. I wasn't going to forget. I sat at my desk, knees together, hands folded, and waited. When I heard the front door open and then close, I counted to sixty and got up.

She was sitting at the table. She didn't look up, even when I stood two feet from her.

"I hope you know that woman's daughter—that Billyrene!—just tried to beat me up."

She glanced at me. "Just now?"

"Don't be stupid, Mother." I could've choked her. I couldn't believe she said that. Did she think I was kidding? Was this supposed to be funny? "No," I said, "downtown, earlier." I recounted the entire event for her, Mae-Mae and Roberta showing up, everything.

She thought a moment, then said, "Good thing Alice and her girls was shopping uptown. Good thing we got friends, huh?" Then she shook her head, saying, "It's sad."

"What?" I asked.

"How Zelda come here asking forgiveness, poor thing!"

"For what?" I shifted on my feet.

"Oh, we had a problem. What you call it, a spat, years ago. I was OK with it, though. I let it go."

"But she came wanting forgiveness," I said.

"Yeah." Mother was staring across the room now. It was just as I suspected. She wasn't thinking of me, of what I had told her about my encounter with Billyrene, in the least.

"Because it's the thing to do, right?"

"Kindness is the only thing that helps us—"

"I know," I said, cutting her off. "Old Uncle said that."

"Well, maybe he did . . . That song of his works that way—kindness."

"Yes, the one I never heard. The angel song."

She looked up at me, catching the sarcasm that had slipped from my voice. I thought, Better let go now, before she has time to think and see me coming. "And you sang your witch's song to set this whole thing up. Why?"

"What're you talking about?"

"Don't say you didn't fix things—whatever hocus-pocus you do—to make it happen."

She sighed, and looking away, said, "Iris, if you had as much sense as you got imagination, you'd be dangerous."

"Mother," I said, stamping my feet, "did you hear me? That girl tried to beat me up!"

"Well, she didn't and she won't." She glanced back at me. "Would you, with that Mae-Mae anywheres around? You was scared of Mae-Mae yourself . . . Look, Iris, can't you see? Remember how Mae-Mae and Roberta was? It's probably like that. She's jealous. Probably has a hard life, like her mother. Say something to her, call her cousin."

"Can't you ever say I'm right? Can't you ask maybe if I'm hurt?"

"I can see you ain't," she answered, and with that slowly got up from the table, bored with me and wanting to get away.

I stood, followed her with my eyes as she passed, making her way to the back door.

"Mother," I called after her, "do you ever worry about me?"

"All the time," she said, opening the back door.

"Then why don't you show it sometime?"

"Quit thinking about yourself, Iris," she answered, and then she was gone. Just the open door.

* * *

You'll have another chance, I had told Anna. Just to calm her. As I said, empty words. But true.

The next day, while we were walking to my house, on Fourth almost to Mendecino, the red convertible passed. I saw it. This time so did she, right away.

"Oh, God, help me," she gasped.

"I don't think he saw us," I said. I didn't care what happened.

He passed again and didn't slow down.

"God," Anna said, "now he's playing games."

"He didn't see us," I said again, but when he passed the third time, I had to question myself. We had turned up Mendocino and were passing the square, which was empty, no Billyrene and company anywhere. He seemed to be circling the square, but what for? After we passed the square, we didn't see him again.

A mile up the street, hardly two blocks from South Park, he pulled over and stopped. He'd come up behind us, surprised us. His face beamed up at me—at Anna. "Hi. Where you going?"

The most uninspired opening line. But what did we know? Some idle chitchat and then we were in the car, Anna half-straddling the gear shift next to Mike, me by the door. Tight quarters, those old bucket seats. Three people, and no one would dare ride in the back. Anna couldn't have been comfortable, but she smiled and giggled so softly you'd think she was sitting on a down pillow. A very different Anna this time around. Awkward, yes, but pleasant, accommodating. She gave him detailed directions to my house, which amounted to about two left turns and up half a block. That was the plan: drop me off and then he would take her home. Was that OK with her? Oh, yes, that would be great, Mike. Wait until he finds out where she lives. Won't that be a surprise. She was the daughter of his friend's housemaid. Cinderella of MacDonald Avenue.

I saw nothing, not how he looked, the clothes he wore, his mouth when he spoke, how his hair tossed in the wind—all the things Anna had no doubt already typed into the first page of life's most important memories. When, following Anna's instructions, he stopped in front of "the house with all the flowers," I simply got out and managed a cordial thank you and good-bye. I didn't want to ruin things for Anna.

"Wow," he said, looking back toward the house.

I was a few steps from the car, my back to him, and when I glanced over my shoulder, he caught me looking at him; he was aware I'd heard his comment and had turned around, and he quickly shifted his eyes to Mother's flowers. "Pretty," he said.

Anna's face was empty.

"Oh," I said. "Yeah."

When I turned back and started into the yard, I saw that it wasn't only the house he had seen. It was more: Mother and Alice Clayton on the front porch shucking corn. A fat Indian with a red gingham scarf tied over her head and a bony, big-kneed, barefoot black woman. It was a scene right out of *National Geographic*. Local color.

"Looks no-good," Mother said, obviously referring to Mike, as I trudged up the front steps.

"Say that again," Alice agreed.

Which is what he thought of you two, I thought to myself.

Was I jealous of Anna? Maybe. I dropped my purse and books on my bed and hurried into the bathroom, locking the door behind me. In the small medicine cabinet mirror over the sink, which was the only mirror in the house besides my pocket-size hand mirror, I studied my face. True, boys, whether they be Monty or Mike, looked at Anna first. Between the two of us, they picked her. I didn't keep score exactly, but I would say two out of three times. Whether it was a total stranger uptown on the street or one of our neighbors just saying hello as we passed by on our way from school, their eyes fell on Anna first; then politeness and duty sent their eyes to me. Even the pudgy little Frenchman who took our order each lunchtime at Foster Freeze said, "May I take your order, please?" looking at Anna.

Studying my face, I saw why. With my index finger, I traced the contours of my lips, then my nose; I examined closely the height of my cheeks and the lift of my eyes. My lips, thin enough, turned down in the corners; my nose, while it wasn't as broad and flat as Mother's, nonetheless flared like hers, the nostrils curved high and wide. High cheekbones. Eyes that slightly slanted. I looked like an Indian. Everything about Anna was more refined: straighter mouth, delicate nose, tight little nostrils; she had high cheekbones and the same slanting eyes, but her eyes were fuller, drawing attention to their shine and not their shape. She looked more white. Even her wrists and hands, her ankles and feet, were smaller, more delicate than mine. Funny, since even Mother shrank next to big dark Ida, Anna's mother. Genes; must've had something to do with our fathers, whichever one had the strongest genes. Which was something we never talked about: our fathers. Her father, like mine, must've been white; and, like me, she hadn't a clue as to who he was, not a name, not even a maybe. The difference: Her father had the stronger genes.

So, yes, at some level, I had to be jealous. But, at that moment, I wasn't thinking particularly of boys; boys and dating, the world of Anna and Mike seemed a million miles away. And that's what I was feeling: the away, the distance between me and everything else. Who was I? I sensed a loss, a missed opportunity. I would never be a high school senior again; for the life of me, I could never tell you what it was like to be a senior, because, in a real sense, I was never there. I was left out, somewhere else. And just then, looking in the mirror, the thought occurred to me that I might be forever left out.

* * *

This is what happened. He took her home, but not right away. Yes, he was surprised to learn where she lived. In fact, she thought that's what made him turn left into Townsend's Candies for a soda instead of right down MacDonald Avenue to her house. Jesus, we can't go there then, he said, making a sharp left. He ate only half of his sundae—he had a sundae, hot fudge, and she had a lime soda. And then she thought he would drop her off, maybe a block away, because he might not want the Polks to see; not because he was ashamed of her, she was thinking, but because it might look fishy, him being a friend of Patrick's and her mother being the Polks' maid. Anyway, he didn't take her home, not right away. He drove her up into the old graveyard at the end of the street, where MacDonald ends just below the ancient columned stone cemetery entrance. Did you know it was a place for lovers, the old cemetery? Mike's wasn't the only car parked there, but certainly it was the nicest, and he kept his radio playing even when he turned off the engine. There were lots of trees where they parked, big cypress, the kind you see near the coast, and she could see water; she kept looking at the water, the square pond below the cemetery, and beyond the pond, to the Murrays' jersey cows. You could see all that, facing north away from the cemetery. Are you scared? he asked. She said cemeteries weren't her favorite thing. And she made a joke: She could live without them. Then he said, You're the dating kind, aren't you? And he said, Friday night, OK? OK. And it was his idea to double.

"No," I told her flat out.

It was nine o'clock at night, Ida was finishing dishes inside the Polks'. Still, Anna had run with a dime to the pay phone outside the Town and Country Market, where she could talk without the chance that Ida might come into the room and overhear her.

"I'm sure he'll find someone nice," she persisted.

The phone, which we had had about a month—we still didn't have a TV—was on the kitchen sink and I found myself wedged between Mother and Alice, as they diced strawberries for jam. The jars were set out on the counter before me, water boiled on the stove. Still, I was thinking clearly. "No," I said again.

That was Wednesday. Friday afternoon I was putting on my makeup. She'd gotten to my weak spot: pride. Without even trying. For the date Mike had lined up for me was none other than Patrick Polk.

"He's really a nice guy," Anna had said at lunch outside the Foster Freeze on Friday.

"Why didn't you tell me before?" I asked.

"I didn't know before. Mike only said, 'Let's double. I'll get her a date.' I didn't know who he had in mind. I didn't know it was Patrick."

"Sounds desperate: 'I'll get her a date.' What'd he have to do, scrape the bottom of the barrel?"

"Oh, Iris! No, he thought it'd be fun . . . Listen, Patrick's a really nice guy. Mike says he's a deep thinker; you know, a lot beneath the surface. I mean, of course he's going to be kind of a deep guy. Look at all that's happened to him, his mother dying and all."

"And now he's going to go out with the former maid's daughter while his friend goes out with the current maid's daughter," I said sarcastically.

But, she had me. About six paces back, I had made up my mind to go. I wasn't excited, or even nervous. I saw my advantage. Friendly, polite, attractive—I'd wear something fine—and each time our eyes met, when he opened a door for me, offered his hand and helped me out of the car, he would see that I was merely getting through the evening, quietly counting the minutes until it was over; in every glance he would see from me the word "no." And it would be my no, my victory over that world that had used the same word on me, my no to all of it—the Polks, Santa Rosa High School, the senior prom—once and for all.

So Friday afternoon I was putting on makeup. Just a trace of lipstick, red, not too dark, and the slightest touch of pencil to give the eyebrows that little lift, an arch. My hair: parted on the side, flipped just a tad on the ends. I wore my new felt skirt, charcoal gray, wide belt, and, over a pressed white blouse, a beautiful new pink cashmere sweater tucked in without a crease front or back. For shoes: white bucks with red soles. My bobby socks were turned down an even inch around my ankles. Not a single girl Mr. Patrick Polk had known would have a thing on me. I felt good. I felt confident. A girl from South Park? Maybe. But she is pretty and look at her clothes, look how well she wears them. And even Patrick Polk with his new white Thunderbird convertible wasn't good enough for her. She must be special.

Standing before the cabinet mirror, I hummed to the radio and checked and rechecked my hair and makeup.

"You look the same as you did five minutes ago," Mother quipped outside the bathroom door.

I saw her reflection in the mirror, red scarf, thick brown face. "Do you need to get in?" I asked her.

"No, I already went in the garden," she said.

I ignored her. I stared back at myself, focused on my eyes, until she was gone, out of the mirror.

The plan was to meet at Anna's at five o'clock—Mother would drop me off. The boys would meet us at six. Plenty of time for last-minute adjustments. Anna's idea, not mine; I would need no extra time. Dinner and then maybe the drive-in, Anna wasn't sure. Mike didn't say. "Whatever," I told her. "Gee, Iris, don't sound so excited." At a quarter to five I found Mother in the kitchen. She was at the sink scrubbing potatoes and singing one of her favorite show tunes:

I'm gonna wash that man right outta my hair
I'm gonna wash that man right outta my hair

She swayed her big, aproned body back and forth, singing, then humming. She was ridiculous.

"Mother," I said, causing her to turn but not stop her swaying and humming, "I'm ready."

She looked like a bear, a huge stuffed animal, electrically propelled, the top part of its body moving automatically back and forth from its two feet anchored solidly to the floor.

"Oh," she said, suddenly collapsing into herself again and reaching for her apron strings.

She pulled off her apron and tossed it on the sink. But do you think she had taken a shower or changed her dress? An hour off work and she was a living, breathing, smelling, apple cannery. What if one of the boys saw her? Forget the boys, what about Ida? Ida who she always asked about, and who might just be coming or going in front of the Polk house. What if she saw Ida? Couldn't she at least take the red rag off her head? Fat chance.

But she must've read my mind. She didn't drive down MacDonald Avenue. She stopped at the corner of Fourth. "Go on," she said.

"Don't you want to see the house?" I asked. I thought she would be curious. She said nothing.

Then I felt ashamed, thinking she knew how I felt about her. "It's OK," I told her, "just go up there."

"Can't," she said, "might cause trouble for you."

"Mother!"

"That Mrs. Polk, I might kill her."

"Mother, she's dead."

"Oh, yeah. Mr. Polk, then. Didn't care for him much either." She was grinning—I saw her chuckling under her breath.

"Good-bye, Mother," I said and got out of the car.

Just as the car pulled away I thought of the fact that Mother had never asked me who it was I had a date with. Clearly, I wasn't getting dolled up for just Anna. What would she say if she knew it was Patrick Polk I was about to have dinner with? Would she have objected? Since she'd been home from work that afternoon, I had sensed a strangeness about her. Was she up to something? I mistrusted her jokes. There was always the chance the joke would be on you. Then maybe it was nothing. Which was the trouble. When it came to Mother, it wasn't only a question as to which bush the rabbit was going to jump out from, but whether or not there was a rabbit there at all. She hung on you heavier than her odor of rotten apples. I was about to have a date with the most eligible bachelor of Sonoma County and I was thinking of Mother. That's how strong it was.

Anna was surprisingly calm. Of course she was ready. She looked like me: felt skirt and belt, white bucks, bobby socks turned down over the ankles; only she didn't wear a sweater over her blouse. "I thought I'd wear my print baby doll," she said, referring to the blouse. Which meant she didn't have a nice cashmere sweater. A great cover since you couldn't very well wear a sweater over a baby doll with its puffy sleeves. And I noticed something else: the blouse, which I'd seen her wear at least once every other week to school, had a tear in the seam under her arm. It made me think of the flannel nightgown she'd worn to bed that night many years ago when Mother and I stayed on the dairy with her and Ida. I remembered the coarse stitching in the flannel's seam, the sewn and patched elbows. Anna wasn't picture perfect. The tear was small. I didn't say anything.

We talked about small things. Where we would go to dinner. Not the Topaz Room, where the Polks and the Witherows went to rub elbows with their kind; but maybe the Saddle and Sirloin, a classy, upscale place, too, but with a western flavor, casual. Rumor had it that just inside the door you came face to face with an eight-foot grizzly bear, reared on its hind legs, its front paws arched and reaching out to grab you. Over the bar, in what was called the Palomino Room, was a set of longhorns ten feet across. "I'd like to see that," I told Anna. We wondered what the boys would wear.

"Oh, Mike will wear his letterman's sweater," Anna said with certainty. But Patrick would be another story. He had so many clothes. I'd seen him dart out of the house in Brooks Brothers suits, in blue denim jeans and saddle shoes, in tennis shorts and T-shirts.

"We'll know by what Patrick wears what kind of restaurant we're going to," Anna said.

Turns out we weren't even being picked up at Anna's. We had to walk three blocks, where the boys would meet us in front of the Town and Country Market. And dinner: a hamburger at Foster Freeze.

I was livid. From the moment we walked out of Anna's gate and past Patrick's car parked in the driveway, I was ready to call the whole thing off. Nice clothes and all, I would walk home.

"Mike set it up this way in case my mother or Patrick's father sees him going out with us," Anna tried to explain.

"What, the maid's daughter and her friend?" I retorted.

"Iris, it's because my mother is employed by Mr. Polk."

"Yeah, as a maid. Don't forget it!"

"Iris, can you be nice just for an hour or two, just for once?" she asked, trailing up MacDonald Avenue.

"Just for once?" I rebuffed her with. She sounded like my mother.

So I was nice. Nice and as cold as ice. His eyes and lips; I couldn't tell you what they looked like because I never looked. I never gave him the benefit of my full gaze.

They came in separate cars. As if it had all been rehearsed, I got into the white Thunderbird without a word; Anna climbed into the Mercury. One thing I hadn't thought of: my hair in a convertible. But not a word. He asked if I wanted the top up and I shook my head. Not a word. I held my hair down with both hands. Even while we sat in the waning light eating deluxe burgers and fries outside Foster Freeze, I said nothing, and never as much as glanced at him. But I looked at Anna. I caught her eyes and reveled in the humiliation she couldn't hide from me. I punished her. A nice dinner, the Saddle and Sirloin? Respect? Ha! Two shop girls. I was right all along, Anna.

And a movie at the drive-in? Try a ride outside Sebastopol to a godforsaken dirt road between a row of empty shacks in the middle of the nowhere. Try a ride to the reservation. Yes, the reservation, where Anna lived as a child, where Zelda and Billyrene and her sisters were the last to leave, where Mother lived until the day she wandered away, pregnant with me.

The boys parked their cars side by side before a large circular building, where the road ended. It was dark now, but there was a hint of crimson in the western sky, making the building's peaked roof look like a giant witch's hat. I could see shingles missing; the building, like the cabins on the dirt road, was disintegrating.

"It's a ghost town," I said.

And that's when Anna told me it was the reservation. We were outside, leaning against the Mercury and peering up at the sky and the large round building before us.

"What was this?" I asked.

"The ceremonial house. They called it the roundhouse."

"Did you go in there?"

"No . . . Well, I guess I did. But I was too small. It closed when I was little. The leader died or something."

Crickets sounded loud in the trees. A mockingbird squawked in the brush. The boys had left, no doubt on a walk discussing their plans for us. I was concerned: a dark deserted place invisible from the main road. Luckily, I had a steel nail file in my purse. When we turned into this place, I planned my moves, how I would grab the file and use it on Patrick should he try anything with me. Let him try, I thought, and then he wouldn't only hear no, he'd find it carved on his big forehead.

"How did they know about it?" I asked.

"The roundhouse?"

"No, this place . . . the reservation."

"Mike said people use it as a lovers' lane now."

"What people?" I snapped.

"Didn't you see the beer cans and stuff on the road back there?" She talked as if she was a tour guide for Disneyland.

"You didn't answer my question," I persisted.

"Iris, how do I know? This is the first time I've been up here with him, you know." Now she was irritated with me.

I didn't care. If going out with Patrick was a favor for her, then eating a hamburger at Foster Freeze was enough. Being stuck in the middle of nowhere was too much.

"Why were you so insistent that I come?" I asked her. "Couldn't you and Mike just go out by yourselves?"

She was gazing up at the sky. "Mike said it was fun to double. You know, do things together. You don't feel like you're the only ones that way." Her voice was hollow, the way a person sounds when they talk looking up, the head cocked back. She didn't look at me.

"Isn't that the idea, to be alone?"

She shrugged. I saw her neck was longer than mine too.

Then I finally came out with it, with what I figured she had hoped and prayed I'd left on the table back at the hamburger stand. "Nice dinner and a drive-in movie, huh?"

She ignored me, kept stargazing.

"I don't know how you can respect yourself," I said, digging deeper.

Still nothing.

"Anyway," I said, "when he gets back, I'm asking him to take me home. I don't care."

She dropped her head then and slowly craned it in my direction. She looked me full in the face. "You're a pain," she said, and then walked to the other side of the car.

"I'm leaving," I called after her.

But I didn't. The boys returned and Mike and Anna strolled back down the road, out of sight. Patrick stood by his car. I stayed where I was, against Mike's car. After a while, Patrick sat on his hood. Still, I wouldn't look at him. I was madder than ever now, mad at Anna, mad at the whole situation. Only one thing concerned me: My purse was in Patrick's car; how would I get the nail file if I needed it?

Crickets sounded in the trees. A mockingbird squawked in the brush. The sky was black.

"I never would have recognized you," he said all at once. His voice wasn't a sound, more like a bird that filled a space in the air, then disappeared.

"What do you mean?" I shot back without looking at him. But no sooner had I finished speaking than I knew what he would say next:

"Your mother worked for my parents."

"Yes," I snapped, then let out, "I'm an Indian. I'm from this place." I gestured to the surroundings with my hand.

"I'll take you home," he said. "I'm sorry."

He stunned me. Could I believe him? Was it that simple? Would he just take me home? I surprised myself. "I'm sorry," I said.

"Yeah," he said. "I know. What a mess."

I heard his voice for the first time. Clear, but it was heavy, underwater with disappointment and confusion. I thought that if I spoke more than two words mine would sound the same way.

"I don't know," I managed, "Anna . . ." I gestured back down the road to where Anna had gone, as if that might somehow explain what I wanted to say.

"Your girlfriend, Anna, right? She talked you into this. Isn't that what you're trying to say?"

I didn't say anything.

"I know," he went on, "I got talked into it the same way." He paused, then his voice lifted out of the water. It wasn't only clear now, but assured, strong. "This isn't me. I don't like this."

"Me either," I answered, attempting to match his strength and conviction.

And just then, both of us, in the same instant, turned to look at each other, as if to see for the first time who it was we were talking to, who it was we had been with all evening. It was as though a veil had been lifted from each of our faces so that now we could see what the other looked like. I saw him even though he was a good distance away, leaning on his car, and it was dark. I saw first the cleft in his chin, his strong jaw. Yet his features were soft: his small straight nose; his small mouth. I can't explain it exactly, but even while his mouth was small, his lips thin, there was something powerful about them, as if his lips were an organ he felt the world with. It was something I would notice again and again when he talked. And his eyes; I would always see them too: very blue, a twinkle, which I saw first just then, even from the distance; very blue and twinkly, but a darkness, a sadness, made all the more apparent by his thick downward-sloping black brows. Yes, very dark brows. I've described parts, but the whole added up to a handsome man; the parts mixed and blended so that he was more than handsome even: He was sensitive, thoughtful. Which, in my mind, would forever distinguish him from every man I have met since. What, in that instant, he saw in me I'll never know.

"So what do we do?" He was serious, his voice suddenly direct and flat. It was a ruler laid on the table for me to use. He wanted measurements, lengths and square feet. "Should I take you home?" He wanted an answer. No fooling around.

"I told Anna I'd wait for her."

"So we should wait?"

"Yeah, I guess." And, just as I answered him, I realized I was in the place I had never intended to be: wanting to stay.

"So, you're from this place?" he asked, his eyes scaling the large building.

"Well, no, not exactly . . ." I fumbled for an explanation.

He was looking over his shoulder now, at the empty shacks on either side of the road. "What is *this* place?" he asked.

"A reservation."

He looked at me, his eyes stopping on their way back from a cabin behind me. "That's right, you're an Indian, you said."

Then I thought of something: He didn't know what this place was. "You haven't been here before?"

"No," he answered. "I don't know. I thought . . . Well, it looked like a work camp or something. You know, for the Mexicans who pick apples in the orchards."

I thought of what Mike had said the first time he met me Anna and me: Mexicans, Indians, it's all the same. My defenses still surfacing. More questions arose, but he answered them with what he said next:

"We turned up here and I thought, Where the hell are we going? Mike isn't really a good friend . . . I've just known him a long time, since grade school. He pops over to the house now and then. He gets me in crap like this . . ."

I must've smarted, for Patrick stood up, and, gesturing with his hands, apologized profusely. "I'm sorry. I'm sorry. I didn't mean you. I mean stuff like this, like we're both in. It's uncomfortable. I don't know why I say yes."

He turned away; nervously, his eyes scaled the big building once again. "What was this place here?" he asked.

I knew he was trying to cover with conversation what he thought was a faux pas. I had understood what he meant. I understood he wouldn't hurt me. I opened like a flower, its petals spreading, breaking away one by one from the knotted bud.

"I'm not from this place, not exactly," I confessed, and then it went on from there, my whole life story, the i's dotted and the t's crossed with my fear and shame, each sentence punctuated with a brown and round woman named Elba wearing a red gingham scarf. Yes, I told him about Mary Beth and me, our mean-spirited competitions; I told him what I blurted out on the playground about his father and Mrs. Witherow. Yes, I was the maid's daughter.

"I didn't mean to pry into your life," he said, apologizing again.

"Oh, I just went on."

I could've felt stupid. But I didn't. I felt emptied and it felt good.

He turned to me. His lips moved ever so slightly. I could see them even with the distance between us. He wasn't trying to say anything. He was still hearing my words, feeling them with his mouth, testing them. Then his eyes focused.

"You're like me," he said matter-of-factly. "You're a fish out of water."

My whole face must've formed a question mark; but, more than that, the question mark was a hook that fastened to him and tore a hole where he was already weakened. He talked and talked.

He told about losing his mother, whom he loved. He told about his father, whom he hated. His father was a cold insensitive man who did little more than go to work in the morning and lock himself away in the study at night. Mary Beth was a quiet bookworm, but she had friends; away from the house, she wore loose blouses and black skirts or pants and hung out with her group of friends at the Apex. She's a poet, Patrick said. He loved her. They were close. She only had one plan after graduation: to get out of the house. Which was Patrick's plan, too; he was graduating from the junior college and entering Berkeley in the fall. He wanted to be a journalist and live in San Francisco.

He talked around and around, always landing on those points where our stories intersected, and commenting about them. He said again and again how he didn't remember me; he knew nothing about anyone, much less the maid's daughter saying anything about a fling his father might've had with Mrs. Witherow. Frankly, he said, he couldn't imagine it. He was sorry that Mother got fired, although, as far as he was concerned, it was the best thing that could have happened to us—to get away from that house.

He felt he never fit in. He never believed in all that society stuff. It stifled people, he said.

"But I remember you as so—"

"So much a part of it," he said, finishing my sentence for me. He looked to the pointed top of the round building, then back at me. "Fish out of water try harder," he said with remorse. "They're sometimes brats."

"I was," I laughed. "I still am, according to my mother anyway."

"Me too," he said, but there was no laughter in his words.

He said something else about Mary Beth, how I should talk to her, and then we heard footsteps, Anna and Mike coming up the road. He whispered in my ear, "Thanks for putting up with all this," and held me on the shoulders with his hands until the others were stopped before us, just a couple of feet away.

* * *

The phone. Neither of us could wait to hear the details of our nighttime reservation romance. What happened?

"Obviously, the two of you finally talked," Anna teased.

I was standing in the kitchen, where the one black rotary phone was on the sink, and I was already out of my clothes, in my nightgown and pink robe, brushing out my hair with my one free hand. How could I explain to Anna what I felt? How did I feel? I was in love; let's say touched, at least. But it wasn't the love of drive-in theaters or prom dates; it wasn't a silly crush. It was something else, something that made me bigger, older. Honesty. The open wounds, the Band-Aids each of us peeled off so the other could see where the flesh was punctured. Trust. And how would I say this to Anna? I wanted to; I couldn't wait to speak to her. I made the call. But now I was at a loss for words. In fact, I didn't even want to tell her, as if the mere speaking of it to anyone else was a violation of something sacred and secret. I disliked her for making the comment about me and Patrick *obviously* having talked.

"Well," I finally said, "obviously you two didn't do much talking." I was referring to her disheveled hair, the leaves and dirt on the back of her clothes, which I noticed when she turned her back to me to get into Mike's car. It came out harsher than I intended it; it came out mean and defensive. There was a long silence over the phone, and even before she spoke, I sensed a widening chasm between us, a dark space broader and deeper than anything we'd known in our time together.

"I'm sorry," she said. "I was just happy you . . . and Patrick got along. I didn't mean anything."

I'd been unkind. I didn't mean to be unkind. I didn't want to be unkind.

"No, I'm sorry," I told her. Then I gave in a little just to revive the conversation, with the hope of filling in the gap between us. "He's really nice, Anna. Thank you for getting us together."

She said nothing: The end of my sentence, her cue to talk and she didn't take it. So I continued: "I'm sorry I was such a pain." Nothing. "You know, I was just defensive on account of who he was. Turns out he really didn't remember me." Nothing. "I shouldn't have been so miserable." Nothing. "Thank you for putting up with me . . . he's really nice. We talked about all kinds of stuff." And still nothing. So I put a direct question to her.

"And Mike?" I asked.

I could sense her thinking over the telephone line. "What did you guys talk about?" she asked. She seemed interested; she wasn't simply dodging my question, not the way I had first dodged hers. But her voice was removed, as if she were speaking from another room.

"The Polks," I told her. "You wouldn't believe it." I told her everything Patrick had told me, about him, about Mr. Polk, and about Mary Beth. "Looks like before long your mother will only have Mr. Polk to cook for," I said.

"What else did you guys talk about?"

Her voice was still distant, coming from another room. But I let it go. I talked. I figured, What could it hurt? I backtracked and told her how I talked about myself, my life, and how that got him to talk about himself, his life, which is how I learned all that I did about the Polks.

"Then what?" she asked.

"You guys came back."

"But he was holding you."

I lied. "It was a second kiss."

Then I'd had enough. Again, I put another question to her, and I didn't feel a bit concerned for doing so. I'd poured out my story.

"Mike," I said. "Did you guys have a good time?"

"Boys," she said with a twinge of sarcasm. I remembered immediately how on that morning in her cabin many years before she had sat at her table and said, White people. Can't live with them, can't live without them. She sounded as if she were a forty-year-old woman with at least that much experience.

"You guys didn't have a good time?" I ventured.

"Yeah," she answered quickly. "Iris, he's so romantic, you know." She sounded suddenly as if she was lording something over me, as if what I had told her only indicated all that I had missed with Patrick.

I said nothing, for I felt the potential for a tit for tat. I wanted to be an adult.

* * *

He pushed himself on her. He was forward. He was fast. She was unsure of herself, and when he put his hands certain places, she had to stop him. That wasn't fun. That's what she wanted to tell me. But, oh, his kisses were electric, and that made it so hard for her to stop him. Oh, the closeness, the taste of his mouth, his breath. Words . . . did he speak words? That was the romance. And that's what she lorded over me. I talked, I blabbed; and there was no romance in any of what I told her had happened. Nothing.

But what was romance? Lying on the dirty floor of an abandoned shack, or being pushed up against the trunk of an old moss-covered tree? No, that wasn't romance. No, not at all; it was the stuff of drive-in theaters, prom dates, beer, and popcorn. Romance was talk, enlightenment. Romance was finding another fish out of water. Romance was the story of Romeo and Juliet, mismatched lovers, star-crossed lovers. Romance was growing.

But, somehow, as I sat in bed after I got off the phone with Anna, I kept thinking about the other kind of romance, what Anna held over me; it buzzed around me like a moth around a lightbulb. No matter how often I swatted at it, I couldn't knock it dead. I was trying to read; I had to finish *For Whom the Bell Tolls*. Would Patrick call tomorrow? Did he have my phone number?

Odd. It was late. Midnight. Mother came in and sat on my bed. She was fully dressed, still in her smelly work clothes. Friday night; weekend nights she often stayed up late. I felt crowded; I felt invaded. I thought she was going to ask me about my date. Which she never did. She might nose around, drop hints in her inimitable fashion, but no direct talk, never a mother-to-daughter encounter on the bed. Had she read my thoughts from the front room? I didn't like it. I set my book aside, ready for her. She looked me hard in the face, and said, "A TV, I been thinking about getting one. What do you think?"

Go figure.

I told her, "Finally."

She nodded in agreement and left. You'd think it was a matter of whether or not we should sell the house and move to Japan.

* * *

I didn't tell her about Patrick. As it turned out, she'd get to meet him. The next Saturday night. But the week before that night was sheer torture. Not a word, nothing from Patrick. And Anna hardly said a thing, even about Mike. She mentioned that he was busy, studying for finals at the college. "Which is what we should be doing, studying for finals," she said admonishingly. She was distant. She was cold. She didn't want to talk. The chasm that had opened between us remained. It was as if she had retreated into the quiet girl she was at the beginning of the year, the girl in the library at noon and after school, only she was alone. I wasn't with her.

He called Thursday, and asked if we could go out Saturday night. He would come by and pick me up.

"I hope you don't mind," he said, "I got your number from Anna."

"No," I said.

"Mike and Anna," he said then. "One more time. I hope you don't mind."

"No."

"But I promise: no boondocks, not that again."

Anna had been lighthearted at school that day, happy; and I suddenly understood why: Mike had called her. And, no doubt, she knew that Patrick would call me. Mike had mentioned that we would double-date again; perhaps Patrick had already asked her for my phone number. It pained me to think we couldn't talk about it. Perhaps I would have if she had brought it up first; then, again, maybe she was thinking the same thing. Pride. Fear. Shame. Boys became the wedge that opened a space for those things to get between us. We drove those things out before, closed the chasm, when the culprit had been none other than what we were: Indians, poor maids' daughters.

No, that quiet wouldn't happen again. I wouldn't let it. Not over boys, nothing. I'd put my pride on the line, bait my hook with it, so she'd have no choice but to bite and then I'd reel her back to me. Our friendship was too important. A thought occurred to me just then: what the school year would have been like without Anna. I couldn't bear it. Alone in the cafeteria. Alone on the front steps. Alone in the library. I'd be forever walking the long way home.

And that's what washed over me just then: appreciation. With a capital A. For everything. For this moment. For all moments. For Mother. The dishes: I remembered glancing at the dirty dishes from dinner stacked on the counter when I answered the phone. The dishes: Mother always did them. "Go study," she'd say. I'd surprise her: When she got back from Alice's, she'd find an empty sink, the dishes washed, dried, put away.

So I got busy. With my hands in the soapy water, a million thoughts crossed my mind. Mostly about Mother. Yes, she lived in her own small world. And, yes, she did her best. She gave me a roof over my head, enabled me to live in a world of choices, options, an older, bigger world. For all the trouble it had caused in the past, such as the situation at the Polks', she at least exposed me to that bigger world, a world that was not her world, where there was little or no possibility for her. I hadn't attempted ever to meet her halfway. I'd been too busy trying to push her back, hide her, ignore her. I pretended she wasn't there. If, indeed, appreciation had washed over me, then what it left in its wake was guilt. Guilt and grief.

I finished the dishes, wiped down the sink, then the table. Then I wiped down the sink again. But that wasn't enough. I got up on a chair and swiped the top of the refrigerator with a sponge. Then the cupboards. I went from cupboard to cupboard, taking everything out, every glass and saucer, sponging, drying with a dish towel, then putting everything back just as it was. I was amazed at how much stuff Mother had. Her rummaging through boxes and shelves at thrift stores over the past year had garnered her a full kitchen. Little matched, but there was so much of it. Flower vases, for instance. She had half a dozen of them. Why didn't Mother pick her flowers and put them in the house? Why didn't she think to use her vases? Her small world, odd. So what? So why didn't I pick flowers? I did. Took a pair of scissors and went straight for the sweet peas trailing the back fence. Reds, whites, pinks, purples, I cut a bunch of them and arranged them full and overflowing in the light yellow vase, which I then filled with water and placed in the center of the kitchen table. Mother couldn't miss it. And something more: I went back into the yard, cut a half dozen baby pink roses, the fragrant miniatures. An old vine grew below the back porch, left by the Chinese man. Those I snipped the stems off and floated in a broad teacup of water. I carried the teacup into Mother's room and set it on her empty nightstand.

I don't know what I was thinking. I expected after I had done these things that she would come home; not just come home, but be home, as if

I'd suddenly find her in the next room. When I didn't find her, I didn't know what else to do.

When Mother got home, which was at least an hour later, she bus-tled through the front room to the kitchen. It was late, a work night, and I saw she had the dishes on her mind. Only then, when she saw the empty, scoured sink, did she look back and find the bouquet of flowers on the table. She was surprised. She looked back and forth from the sink to the flowers. Then she caught me in the hallway door looking at her.

She tilted her head slightly to the side, as if studying me, then said as plain as day, "You got a boyfriend, Iris."

* * *

Anna, the next day, was a bundle of joy again, as I would have predicted, but she was still far away, hard to reach. We had a past, a gap between us, which, if it wasn't there now, at least had been there, and I wanted so much to talk about it, at least acknowledge it. We needed each other. We could help each other if only we were honest. What were friends for? But Anna never opened the door wide enough for me to send the message through. She was a floating bubble, happy and light. Who was I to deliver a pinprick?

We strolled up Mendocino Avenue, past the college, and had our last deluxe burger and Coke. As Anna chirped about what to wear, this blouse with that skirt, I thought of something: I'd let her outdo me. Yes, I'd keep talking with her, helping her decide what to wear, even suggest she borrow something of mine, if I thought that would help her look perfect. I'd make sure there wasn't a tear, a torn seam anywhere. Of course, I couldn't forget either that this was really our last full day of classes before finals, our last lunch together. What better way than to go forward with kindness?

Which I did. We decided that she would wear a blouse of mine and my new cashmere sweater. She would walk home with me, get the blouse and sweater, and anything else she needed, and then, when Mother got home from work, I'd drive her back to MacDonald Avenue.

"What are you going to wear?" she asked. She was balling up her hamburger wrapper, slowly crushing it between both hands as she gazed across the busy street to the junior college.

"I'll think of something," I said. But I was lying, for even before we had settled on a skirt and shoes for her, as soon as I saw the blouse and pink sweater on her, I knew exactly what I was going to wear: a plain white blouse and my mauve cardigan: subtle, soft, brainy. A college girl.

Then, all at once, Anna opened the door, just a tiny bit. Still gazing across the street, she said, "Hard to know what they like." She spoke so you'd think she was still talking about clothes, what boys liked to see girls wearing, what was attractive. But her voice resonated, as if from a faraway place, a deep hole. "You just worry, worry, worry."

"Talk," I told her. "It helps to talk."

"Spanish," she said. "How do you think you'll do on the final?"

* * *

All day Saturday, I studied, or tried to. Over Spanish vocabulary and California history dates, my mind kept wandering away. How could it not, with the clock ticking and ticking and Patrick's arrival at my door ever closer and closer? That was the plan: He would pick me up at my house. What did I have to be ashamed of? The house still needed paint, with its chipped walls and low windows dwarfed by Mother's plethora of flowers. But Patrick knew where I came from. What was there to hide? The inside of the house, while modest, was clean.

It was Mother I was actually more concerned with. At just the sight of Mike Bauer, she had said, "Looks no-good." What would she say, or think, when I introduced her to Patrick? Patrick Polk: I couldn't make up another name, and there was no getting around who he was. The Polks, people she told me not to trust, people she warned me about, white people. Again, I would be hand in hand with them, and in a way I'm sure she had never imagined.

She worked all day in her garden, and around five o'clock, when she came in and found me fiddling before the mirror, as she had the week before, she simply continued on her way past the bathroom to her bedroom. No quip about my vanity, no joke about her going to the bathroom in the garden. She had guessed that I had a boyfriend, and still no questions. She'd looked at the flowers on the table this morning and said, "Gee, pretty."

Turning from the mirror, I heard what I thought was Patrick's voice. Halfway to my bedroom, I knew for certain: Patrick was in the kitchen talking to Mother. I hadn't heard him come in; it was twenty minutes to six, he wasn't due for another twenty minutes, and wasn't it fashionable among the rich to be a little late? I panicked: I wasn't dressed. I bolted into my room, quickly and quietly closed the door should Mother by chance lead Patrick to this side of the house where he might glimpse me dressing, and threw on my clothes, which, luckily, I had laid out on the bed before putting on my makeup. Still, as quickly as I got dressed, I couldn't stop thinking about Mother and Patrick. I pictured a standoff, one on each side of the kitchen table, staring at each other, Mother glaring; or, Mother aloof, looking away, Patrick's attempts at conversation bouncing off her rigid body like pebbles pitched against a brick wall.

They were at the kitchen table all right, but as happy as larks. Patrick's back was to me. But I had a full view of Mother as she sat across from him listening to him talk. Her hands were folded on the table. Her face was compliant and earnest. As I came around Patrick from behind, I saw she'd given him a glass of milk, which he'd half-finished, and a plate of cookies. Cookies! She'd been in the garden all day; when had she made a fresh batch of oatmeal chocolate chip cookies?

"Good evening," Patrick said, catching me peering down at the cookies. He stood up, a perfect gentleman. Then, holding up a cookie in his hand, he said, "Your mother makes the best cookies."

"Oh," I said, flustered.

"Oh, gee," Mother said to him, "that's nothing. You should try my peanut butter ones."

"I will," Patrick answered and took a sizable bite of his cookie.

"Sit down," I said finally.

Which he did, chewing blissfully. I sat next to him. But as soon as he swallowed his cookie, which took an inordinate amount of time by my estimation, he was back talking to Mother, of all things about his family, about losing his mother, about his sister, all of the things we had discussed the previous week. She was nodding with empathy and understanding, devouring his every word with the same care and enjoyment he used to eat her cookies. At least forty minutes had passed. When I looked at my watch it was six-thirty.

I supposed I liked that Mother liked him, and that he liked her. Whatever else I thought about their rapport then I don't remember. I know I became frustrated, irritated. At Mother, of course. Go do something. Don't you have another batch of cookies in the oven? It's still light outside, Mother, go to your beloved garden.

"I don't remember these cookies," Patrick said, picking up another.

"I'm sorry about your mother," Mother said, and I thought, Oh, yeah, the same woman who bossed you around her kitchen. Didn't she? And didn't you utter "damn white" under every other breath?

At least the conversation was beginning to splay, move in different directions. I might find a way in. I was on a date, after all, and maybe somebody would remember.

"Patrick's studying journalism," I said, then thought of Mother's limitations. "He wants to be a writer," I translated.

"I know, he told me," she said. "Like Gaye LeBaron. She tells about the goings-on."

Great, now she was quoting from the town newspaper. Gaye Le-Baron: the daily columnist. Well, she was right: Gaye LeBaron was a journalist. "Yes, but, Mother, he wants to live in a big city like San Francisco and write about things there and other things all around the world."

"Oh, big-city things!" Mother exclaimed. Was she serious or was she making fun of me? It was as though we had been talking about cows and I had just informed her the subject was horses.

"Yes," I reiterated.

"But it's really all the same, Iris," Patrick said.

I glanced at him, questioning.

"If a man swindles or murders someone in San Francisco, it's the same as if he does it here. Swindling is swindling, murder is murder. The setting is different, that's all."

"Then why move?" I asked.

He shrugged. "Different settings," he answered. "See the same thing in different settings."

"Yeah, the same story," Mother chimed in. "It's always the same story, just different places—and times."

"Yes," Patrick said.

No matter if there was a break in the conversation where I could squeeze in or not. And then something worse: Where Patrick had given Mother his family story, now Mother was offering hers. And not just recent history, as Patrick had related, but the entire story, all the way back, starting with the first Rosa. "Named this town after her, they say," she told him. She was unhurried and self-confident as she spoke, her English full of its usual grammatical foibles, but nonetheless smooth and measured. You'd almost think that she was reading, and reading something she'd read aloud a dozen times or more before.

She told about when the Mexican general found Rosa, a teenager and the lone survivor of a smallpox epidemic, how she was facedown in the creek bed, in the rocks and sand, about a hundred yards below the empty village. She wasn't sleeping or passed out from starvation; she'd kept herself alive by fishing and collecting acorns and berries, and was actually quite healthy. She was scared. She'd heard the horse's hooves come over the bank and she'd collapsed with fright; she'd been upwind of the animal and hadn't heard it coming. Horses usually meant Mexicans, and Mexicans meant rape, death, and kidnapping. She was stiff as a board, even as he packed her up the bank and then tied her over his horse, behind the saddle. She expected to die. He took her far away, a day's ride, and then he left her at a small Indian camp somewhere near Petaluma. She didn't know any of the Indians there, she didn't speak their language. But they took care of her, which was the general's intention, no doubt his order.

Three months later he came back for her. No horse this time, but a wagon. And the oddest thing: Rosa wouldn't sit in the wagon. He couldn't get her to sit. She lay facedown on the wagon bed just as he had found her in the creek. They went back. About a half mile from the old village place, south of the creek, they stopped before a good-size adobe house, with adjacent high-fenced corrals for horses and cattle. That's what Rosa saw when she opened her eyes: the adobe, an enormous and dark structure, a shadow as dense as rock, made from what looked like the plucked and dried insides of the creek bottom; and horses, great numbers of them, and even more cattle, their white-spotted hides splattered and specked with the wet mud that they, like the horses, stood knee deep in. And the stench, like nothing she had smelled before, manure and hides in the hot sun; but not as bad as inside, where the general's mother and brothers and sisters lived, the smell of people who didn't bathe but instead piled on more and more clothes; and how Rosa held her breath as they drew near, the mother and brothers and sisters, after the padre stood over her and the general pronouncing them man and wife. Rosa, that was her name, they said; which meant she no doubt had been baptized years before by one of the early roving Spanish missionaries from the San Rafael mission. So there was no need to baptize her, only get her to learn of the sacraments, and that night she began to learn; and with the general, and for the rest of her life, when she wasn't working, cooking, and cleaning up after the general and his family, and ultimately her own children along with the others, she was the way she was when he first found her, not lying flat, but seated, usually in the privacy of her room, staring, her unblinking eyes hardly a foot from the wall.

Then the second Rosa, the daughter. I had never realized or known until this night that there were other children, that the second Rosa had brothers or sisters. "What happened to them?" I asked. "They're around," Mother answered. "Went Spanish or Mexican." Which Rosa number two did not do. She ran off and took up with an Indian in Sebastopol, and then another one farther west, from Bodega. From two different Indian men, she regenerated the tribe. Old Rosa, the first Rosa, had managed to pass down the language, despite the fact that she was forbidden to speak it and was always frightened of the general.

So the second Rosa knew the language and passed it on to her children. But there was something wrong with it, something wrong with the language, because there was something wrong with her, the second Rosa. A story left that place with her, and told itself in the way she spoke the language, with certain sounds, certain stresses, that old Rosa heard, that the animals and trees heard, that the spiritual people, like Old Uncle, who dreamed the old songs, heard. Old Rosa knew this but said nothing. So on and on it went. Old Rosa's story mixed with the other stories, sometimes killed them like the new animals and grasses that spread over the land at the same time killing the old animals and grasses. Sadness, anger, hatred: That was the story. It was there before, that kind of story, but this was new, a new version with details like smallpox and rifles and slavery, and would affect the people like nothing they could remember.

The second Rosa's story: She was proud, boastful. Lucky for her, she was pretty, tall, and Spanish-looking like her Mexican father. Always, she detested the way her mother was treated by her father and his family. By the time she and her brothers and sisters were teens, when they wore imported clothes and ate with the grandmother's Spanish silver, her mother, Old Rosa, older and forever Indian-looking, was encouraged to eat in her room, no longer the bedroom she had shared with the general, but a small windowless room just above the cellar stairs. But this wasn't what finally prompted the young Rosa's revolt. It was love. She fell in love with a cousin, her father's cousin's son, and he in love with her. In those days people married their second cousins. So that wasn't the problem. The problem was a conversation young Rosa overheard between the boy's mother and her father. The boy's mother, the widow Maria, told the general she did not want her son marrying his daughter. "Not an Indian," she said. "We'll send for a wife from Mexico, or look for another relative closer by." Without the slightest objection, without even a raised eyebrow, the general, straight-faced, acquiesced, which enraged Rosa as she stood listening just on the other side of the open, arched doorway. Enough that her father had all but abandoned her mother, reducing her to the likes of a servant—now he was abandoning her. If he was ashamed of her mother, he was ashamed of her, too—she was nothing but an Indian, after all. What next? Sweeping the floors? He wouldn't find her in her room, or in the courtyard, the next day when he went looking for her; she wouldn't hear what he had to tell her, which she would have no choice but to obey.

No, she didn't wait. She left that night. She stole a gold piece from her father's wooden chest and a pair of silver-studded Spanish boots, and with those things bought herself her first husband, Woodpecker, the eldest son of a headman from Sebastopol. She was home, where she was always supposed to be, among Indians, she claimed. And she vowed to rebuild her tribe. Besides her one attempt to get her mother to leave the adobe, she would, over the years, approach her brothers and sisters, appearing out of nowhere, in an orchard or on a street corner downtown, and ask them to leave with her. When they refused, and they always did, she'd holler profanities and fill the air with curses, threats about what she would do to their children and their children's children: disease, famine, deformities. Sure, she left the adobe with a broken heart, but it was spite that drove her.

The second Rosa's story, and then it went on to this one and that one, this sadness and that tragedy, mostly the women, right up to Mother's mother, Carmelita, who, on the coldest night in 1929, when Mother was just seven, froze to death on her back porch after trading a fine basket in town for a quart of crude whiskey that she polished off before she reached the porch steps.

* * *

It was a quarter to eight. By that time I had glanced at Patrick's watch at least a half dozen times. Which was easy since his exposed wrist, folded over the other on the table, was as still as the rest of him had been. He was mesmerized. It was as if her stories had cast a spell over him; as if he were a field mouse paralyzed by the sight of a large snake, he didn't move or shift his gaze from the beast lest it find and devour him.

Luckily, Mother didn't go into the kind of detail with the latter ancestors as she did the first and second Rosas. "Sadness. See, the same story," Mother said. "Sadness," she repeated. "It kills people."

Patrick swallowed hard and awoke. "But Mrs. Gonzales," he said, "you're OK. Look at you . . . and Iris."

Mother absentmindedly fingered her lips, as if she was thinking.

Patrick turned to me—Guess what? I was sitting there—and said, gesturing with his watch hand toward Mother, "This is amazing. It's history. Have you thought of writing this down?"

I detected the slightest chuckle from Mother. Then she said to Patrick, "Want another glass of milk?"

Patrick looked away from me, down to his empty glass, then up at Mother. It was as if he had finally come to his senses, just realized where he was and who he was sitting with. He looked at his watch. "Jeepers," he said, astonished, "it's eight o'clock."

"You kids better go," said Mother, getting up from the table.

She went to the cabinet and returned with a plastic bag that she filled with the remaining cookies. It was then, when she stood over the table picking up the cookies one by one, that I noticed she wasn't wearing her customary apron. Her dress, nothing special, was nonetheless clean and pressed. And something else: She wasn't wearing a scarf. Her hair, shiny and smooth-looking, was parted on one side and held off her face on the other with a barrette. When she handed Patrick the bag of cookies, I felt ashamed of myself for the anger and disregard I had felt while she talked the last hour. Luckily, I had managed my tongue and hadn't said anything. Still, I felt as if I had, as if she'd heard my thoughts.

Patrick took the cookies and then offered his hand. "Thank you, Mrs. Gonzales, thank you so much," he said.

"Gee, nice to see you," she said, holding his hand.

"You really should, Mrs. Gonzales," he said. "You really should write down all those stories."

And that way we were out the door.

* * *

Halfway down the street he pulled over.

"What should we do?" he asked.

"About what?" I wondered.

It was Mike and Anna: We'd missed them, we were almost two hours late. At Foster Freeze, we were to meet them there at six-thirty. I thought of Anna waiting, no doubt worrying. I imagined her sitting in my pink sweater, at the bench outside the hamburger stand or in Mike's car. She'd worry that Patrick had stood me up.

Patrick looked at his watch. "Who knows where they are now," he said. Then he shrugged and, slipping the car into gear, announced, "Let's have ourselves a good dinner."

And where did we go?

The Saddle and Sirloin. Top down, my hair blowing in the warm night, we pulled up and parked. Not a pair of eyes missed us—and there were many pairs. It was prom night, which I'd totally forgotten about, and half the senior class was there, decked out in tuxedos and every pale color of chiffon imaginable. When we pulled up, those couples loitering outside turned and stared. The car was enough: Remember, in those days, a Thunderbird convertible was the cat's meow. So already, even before I got out of the car, everyone was looking. But I paid them no mind. I took Patrick's arm and followed him through the swinging front doors as if I'd done this thing a hundred times before. Look how casual—and smart-looking—we were: him in a fine sweater and Levi's; me in a felt skirt and loose cardigan. Boy, was I ever glad I chose the "brainy look." It suited the situation perfectly. My generosity toward Anna—lending her my sexiest sweater—had paid off.

Patrick gave his name to the maître 'd. We had to wait. Prom night: not the best night to go out in a small town. Which Patrick complained about.

"All these loud people," he said.

But I didn't mind a bit. I had time to drink in my surroundings. I followed him into the bar and found it was everything I'd heard it was: dark, a western spectacle under black lights giving everything light—skin, teeth, the white mane and tail of the life-size palomino horse in the painting over the bar—an unnaturally vibrant deep blue hue.

"Do you want to sit down?" he asked, gesturing to a spotted cowhide sofa and chairs.

We had drinks: Patrick a scotch, me a glass of red wine. The way I carried my wine glass into the dining room—Cinderella had arrived, and on her prince's arm. Yes, turn and look, all of you, and ask: Who is that girl? Isn't that the handsome boy who drives the white Thunderbird convertible? Isn't that Patrick Polk, but who's the girl? Allison Witherow, are you watching?

We got seated in a small booth in a corner. But that's not why my prideful feelings changed—and they did. Just as quickly as my pride and spite rose when I entered the crowded dining room, so did it fall, like a balloon, its air let out, spiraling wildly, uncontrollably to the earth. It was Patrick. Nothing he said in particular, for we talked of obvious things—my finals, his finals, our graduations, that he was shortly going to start looking for a place in San Francisco—but rather just my being with him, and, as a result of that, the feelings that arose in me: an excitement, as if I was leaving the earth, or had left, and was looking back from a different place. My heart beat, and from it, generosity filled my veins, swelled the tips of my fingers, my lips.

Outside the restaurant, as we made our way through an even larger throng of prom folks collected near the parking lot, Patrick asked again about Anna and Mike.

"What should we do?" he wondered.

And again I thought of Anna and worried that she was worrying about me.

Patrick backed the car out of the lot, and halfway down the street, pulled over just as he had earlier beyond my house. "He might've gone back to that place, knowing him," Patrick said.

"What place?"

"The reservation," he answered, embarrassed.

Perhaps I looked worried or concerned; he sat up straight and said with determination, "Forget it! I told him—I told you!—no boondocks."

Obviously, he was bothered. I said to him, "We don't have to find them. We'll just tell them the truth—we got a late start because you gabbed with my mother for hours on end." I gave him a soft jab on the forearm, hoping to lift his mood.

"Right," he said, abruptly shifting the car into gear. "Let's get out of here."

I didn't know where we were headed. I knew though that I wouldn't see Anna, and into my mind a picture came: my pink cashmere sweater and Anna's face; she was seated in a car, in the dark, no doubt in a faraway place like the reservation, and Mike was certainly there but I didn't see him, only Anna's distressed and forlorn face, her soft neck and chin, her features, lit above the pink sweater. First thing tomorrow, I'd call and tell her what happened.

We drove a while, wound our way into the hills above Santa Rosa. We parked where there was a great view of the lights below. A great lovers' lane, I thought, if it weren't for the cars with their bright headlights passing all too frequently on the road. Then, as my eyes began to adjust to the darkness, I saw the grove of oak trees, and then the larger tree separate from the others and the chair-size rocks near the road's edge. I recognized the place to be none other than the spot where years before I'd picked acorns with Mother.

Patrick was distracted, still preoccupied, I imagined, with his broken commitment to Mike. With the lights looking the way they had that early evening I had been there years before, like white cottony flowers strewn across the valley's floor, I thought of Mother. I remembered. I began talking as quickly as the memory registered, for no other reason I could think of, if I thought at all, but to bring Patrick at that moment back to me, back from his troubled reverie to common ground.

"My mother once scared me with a snake," I began.

I felt the need to continue talking, my words falling like steady rain until I was emptied of them; and the as yet new and pleasurable act of talking to him ultimately drove itself, no longer my need to lift his mood or in some way bring him back to me, to common ground, if that was ever a reason other than the need to pour forth. We had been in this wonderful other universe before, and wasn't that our common ground? What was I doing by talking, if not leaping from the precipice into the magnificent and star-filled night?

"Your mother is an amazing person," Patrick said.

He didn't look at me. He kept gazing through the windshield at the valley far below us. When he spoke again, his voice was filled with a despair that alarmed me.

" 'Sadness,' that's the word your mother used. She said it kills people." Knowing I was looking at him, he nodded with his chin to the valley, to the light. "It's all the same stories."

"But they're not all sad," I offered. "I'm OK. Mother's OK. Nothing's killed us. You said so yourself at the house."

Slowly, mechanically, he rotated his head to face me. "Your mother is an amazing person," he repeated, then looked away.

"Really," I said with all the caring I could muster, "you don't have to worry about Mike . . . I know Anna will understand."

"I don't give a damn about Mike," he answered brusquely. "He's a horse's ass, excuse me." He turned to me. "It's just that I've known him all my life, him and the other guys." His eyes opened wide. "You know who I really like? Brad. He's the one my father doesn't like. Mike and those guys wouldn't like him either. Why? Because he's not all this shit, excuse me, all this cars and stuff. He's free."

"Who's Brad?" I asked.

"My best friend," said Patrick, and then he went on to describe a guy who Anna and I had seen come and go from the Polks' house, a guy with bulging tattooed muscles, in scuffed black shoes, who didn't look anything like Mike Bauer and the other friends of Patrick's we saw visiting him. My recollection of the man was of an unsavory character, to say the least. Nothing Patrick said matched my memory of him. Patrick said he was brilliant; "scintillating" was the word he used. He worked part-time on a sheep ranch, during the lambing season, somewhere near Healdsburg. He lived in the hills part of the time. The other time he spent in San Francisco in a one-room apartment in North Beach. He wrote poetry and knew writers like Allen Ginsberg and Jack Kerouac. He didn't care about money and nice cars; he detested them, in fact. He was free.

"I want to write," Patrick said then, after a moment's thought. He looked back to the light-speckled valley. "I don't want to be like my father. I'm not all this," he demonstrated, picking at his sweater, then gesturing with disdain toward his steering wheel.

I nodded agreeably.

But I wasn't just nodding to nod. I understood something profoundly. I saw in another way the meaning of what he had been saying when he called us fish out of water: He saw the world differently. He saw what Shakespeare and Hemingway saw; he saw things in Mother's stories. He felt the world in a deep way. As I saw this quality about him I also saw why he liked me, which made me at once both happy and dismayed. Happy that he liked me, first of all, and that it didn't matter that I was poor or Indian, which I'd felt already; dismayed because his liking me wasn't much different from his liking that hulk Brad, or, for that matter, Mother. He didn't care what people looked like. Yes, it didn't matter that I was poor or Indian, but did anything matter? Could I have been an Appaloosa horse sitting next to him? Was I pretty to him?

"I'm changing," he said, lost again in his private reverie. "It's like my mind is finally opening . . . I'm not what I grew up to be."

"None of us are," I said.

"None of us *is*," he corrected. "*No one* is."

I might have felt embarrassed, but I wasn't because he was looking at me and he was laughing, and the sadness and heaviness was gone for the moment. Then he jabbed me playfully on the arm just as I had touched him earlier in an attempt to lift his spirits. I lifted, easily. I felt that finally we had come together, the key comfortably fit the lock.

"What are we doing, sitting up here?" he asked.

I shrugged. "Talking," I joked.

We drove off. Not home, not right then. Dinner and a half hour parked in the hills? A date meant more. Both of us knew that much. We drove. Down the winding road, through the apple orchards, and then around and around the outskirts of town, different roads, sometimes circling close, sometimes far and wide, but always in the same direction around and around. Patrick turned on the car radio and hummed along with the popular tunes, giddy, I thought, with the same good feeling I had. Not a word between us, just the senseless driving. Was I pretty to him? The wind in my hair, the warm night, what a silly question.

I felt responsible in some way for the fun; I'd given him the first jab, after all. I gave a signal that he could use and he'd used it. I felt responsible and confident. So much so that when the time was up and we found ourselves standing below my front-porch light, I hugged him. And that's not all. I whispered in his ear, "Fish."

He pulled away. He was looking at me, his thick brows raised in confusion. But within half a second they were dropping again, his face relaxing with his understanding, his remembering.

"You understand," he said, astonished. Then, echoing what he had said earlier about Mother, he told me, "*You* are an amazing person."

I hugged him, but that was not enough. So I took the initiative. I kissed him. But it was more like I had crashed, come at him from a running start and banged into his lips. It felt as if I'd been punched in the mouth, and I'm sure it felt the same for him. I could taste my blood. He didn't thwart my enthusiasm, though; he held me still a moment, our lips pressed together, then let me go.

"Amazing," he said, slowly stepping back, his eyes still fixed on me.

And then he was gone; he turned and went down the steps.

"Good night," he called over his shoulder from the driveway.

"Finals next week," I called back. "Monday. Tuesday. Wednesday." What I was thinking I'm not sure. Perhaps my instinct was to hold on to him: remind him of our discussion about our schedules at dinner so that he would know when I would be available—so that he would call me!

"I remember," he answered, climbing into his car.

"Graduation on Saturday," I hollered.

* * *

It was still early after Patrick left, not quite eleven. I took a chance and called Anna, hoping that she would be home and that Ida would not be asleep. I struck out on both accounts. A grumpy Ida told me, "She's not here," and slammed down the phone. But the next morning Anna answered. She hesitated, as if thinking about what she wanted to say to me, or if she even wanted to talk at all.

"I can't talk," she said finally. Her voice was somber, laden with disappointment.

"Anna," I pleaded, "it wasn't my fault."

"What?" she asked suddenly.

"Being late . . . Patrick and Mother just started yapping and I couldn't get him out of here. It was eight o'clock already. I'm sorry . . ."

She didn't respond. Silence over the wires.

"Did you guys have a good time?"

"I told you I can't talk."

"Anna, I'm sorry," I pleaded again. I repeated what had happened, but, within a second or two, I was only talking to a dial tone.

She was acting as if my not showing up was the end of the world. Then again, maybe she was already in her will-he-call-me-again mode and was taking her anxiety and insecurity, out on me, as she had in the past. I didn't need it. Saturday night, after Patrick left and after my fruitless attempt to talk with Anna, I went back out onto the front porch, where we had stood, and sat down. I gazed up at the open sky. I was in ecstasy. The streetlights cast a dull whiteness above, like a worn sheet encircling all that was below—the city, the streets, me; but I knew what was beyond the sheet, for I'd been there, I'd broken through and seen the infinite stars. Thinking of Patrick, thinking of his lips on mine and his soft-spoken "amazing," I could finally identify that star-filled faraway place, that place that filled me with thankfulness and generosity. It had been a foreign territory. But now I was in it. It was familiar. And now, unlike before, I hadn't a second thought about what to call it. Love.

That was late Saturday night. Sunday evening, after a day of studying and no phone call from Patrick, I began to think that we hadn't talked enough on our date. There was no emptying of ourselves as on the first date. Patrick was preoccupied, distracted, and when we finally met in the same place, it was over a grammatical error. And then what did we do? Circle the town countless times without a word to one another.

Monday. Spanish and history finals and Anna didn't talk to me. Distant when I approached her after Spanish. "I have to go to my next final," she told me and nothing after that. Obviously Mike hadn't called her either. That night, as I sat with Mother at the dinner table, I asked Mother the question I hadn't asked her before.

"Were you ever in love, Mother?"

She looked up from her butter-oozing mashed potatoes. "Men," she said, shaking her head, "who needs them?" She glanced back at her potatoes, then quickly looked up again. "I forgot to tell him something, that Patrick Polk," she said.

I looked at her, waiting for her to tell me.

"The second Rosa, that Mexican man she liked, he's the one become the bear hunter. He hunted the bears and then the Americans hunted him. Then I don't know what happened. But he begged money in the town square. Sad, too, like Rosa."

There's one big story in Mother's head. Over time, you catch pieces of it, see how the pieces fit together here and there. But did she see me falling apart just then? Did she care that Patrick Polk hadn't called me?

Tuesday. Two more finals. Anna avoided me after school. Patrick didn't call.

Wednesday. Last final. No Anna. No phone call.

Wednesday night. A major crisis. School's over. What senior wasn't celebrating? Midnight. I'm sitting up in bed and this is what I see: a fool slamming into a boy who didn't want to kiss her. He wasn't interested in her. Except maybe as a "friend." Heck, he talked more to her mother than he did to her. He talked to fill the time. So why did he go out with her? Convenient, a double date for Mike and Anna. But not again, not a third time. Was she pretty to him? Of course not. Amazing. His voice was retreating. Like the rest of him.

Thursday. Bad news. I didn't get the scholarship that I had applied for. Who cared? It wasn't my idea anyway. When Mrs. Denham, the school counselor, called me into her office to congratulate me for making the honor roll a second time, she had suggested that I apply. She was surprised. She looked at my records, then looked at me the way the nuns at St. Rose did when they couldn't find any bugs in my hair. "The first Mexican girl to make these grades," she said. She had said the same thing to Anna. I wondered if Anna got the same rejection letter.

Mother sensed my depression. How could she not? I sat in my room all day Thursday, except to get the mail and tear up that damn letter. She tried her best. She made my favorite dinner, leg of lamb with mint jelly. She bought ice cream, made a chocolate cake, and spelled my name on top with slivers of strawberries from her garden. But instead of pleasing me, lifting my spirits, her efforts produced the opposite effect. I became suspicious of her, then angry. Had she hexed my relationship with Patrick, and was this show of food in fact her victory celebration? "Men, who needs them?" No, Mother, I thought to myself, I don't want to end up like you, an old maid, a dried prune. And if you think I'm going to live alone so that I can be company and take care of you the rest of your life, you're wrong, dead wrong! I thanked her and never let on how I felt, though she had to know.

Anger drove me. It bolstered my courage. The next day, after graduation rehearsal, I approached Anna. She was leaving, going down the back steps outside the gymnasium, and when I called after her, she kept walking, heading for the street. I marched up to her and took her by the arm. She shook loose, and spun around, facing me, daring me to talk. Her fury matched my own.

"Be honest, admit your pride," I challenged.

She smarted, cocked her head, but she wasn't the least bit daunted. Her silent eyes dared me to say more.

"This is stupid. There's nothing to be ashamed of. We're friends." I softened. "It helps to talk. I told you that before."

Still she didn't answer.

"I told you what happened, why Patrick and I were late. But that's not it, is it?" Her silent obstinance enraged me. "Be honest," I challenged again.

"Leave me alone," she said then, and walked away.

"Who cares that he hasn't called you?" I yelled after her. I meant it as a token of conciliation, but seeing how truly unnerved she was, I realized she hadn't heard what I meant at all.

"He's not worth it, Anna," I hollered with all my might, but of course she didn't hear me. She was already halfway to Pacific Avenue.

That night, Friday, I stayed in my room, pretending I didn't know that Alice and Mae-Mae and Roberta were over planning with Mother some kind of graduation party for me. When I passed on my way to the kitchen for a glass of water and found all four of them gathered at the table, Roberta looked up and said, "Recipes."

"Corn bread," Mae-Mae informed me.

"The way black folks make it," Alice added.

"Hmph!" said Mother, as if Alice had challenged her.

Nothing like being obvious, ladies, I thought to myself. Try honesty; and if you can't be honest, if you're going to hide something, try subtlety.

When I left the room, glass of water in hand, they were still talking.

From the hallway, and then through my closed bedroom door, I heard them as if I was standing next to the table.

"Jesus, what's she studying now?"

"Ain't she had enough books for a while? School's out, ain't it?"

"She's gonna go blind."

"Corn bread."

Laughter.

"The way black folks makes it."

"Hmph!"

* * *

I thought of calling Anna, but I didn't want her to have the pleasure of hanging up on me. That night no kind feelings arose in me. I was just angry. Why did I always have to make the effort? Didn't it occur to her that maybe Patrick hadn't called me either? She was so proud, so wrapped up in her own feelings, she couldn't stop to think about anyone else, and what was worse, she didn't even try. She was immature. She was selfish. She was vain. She was a frightened mouse. Me? I'll tell you: Patrick was over. And Anna, keep the cashmere sweater and blouse!

Graduation. Saturday night. It was held at Bailey Field, the outdoor stadium at the junior college. Folding chairs were set up on a large makeshift wooden platform built at the edge of the football field. Two hundred and fifty of us in caps and gowns sat there listening to teachers and administrators who stood one after the other at the podium facing our parents in the bleachers and telling them of our greatness and our promising futures. The class valedictorian was Richard Hunt, a boy from my history class whose quiet braininess and calculated manners won him A's both inside and outside the classroom. He quoted the constitution.

From where I was sitting, second row from the front, I could see Mother in the stands. Of course she was off to the side, to my left, with a group of other ladies—dark ladies, poor ladies. On one side of her sat Alice, with Mae-Mae and Roberta; on the other side was Zelda, whose slip, over her knees and hanging almost to her ankles, I could see as plain as my own hand. Thank God Mother dressed for the occasion: no scarf, and she wore her ink black dress with its three white buttons that I hadn't seen her in since the night of my spelling bee. The dress still looked good on her. Alice and Mae-Mae and Roberta dressed nicely, too, bright colors but decent enough. Poor Zelda. And where was Billyrene? She was a senior, but she wasn't at rehearsal, and she wasn't here. No doubt didn't pass her finals. Bonehead classes and still no Billyrene at graduation.

Which brought up another question. Where was Ida? If not with Mother and her friends and the Mexican parents, then where? Anna was in the back row. We were seated alphabetically, according to our last names, and Toms, Anna's last name, placed her in the back, so I couldn't see her unless I turned around, which I wouldn't do. It wasn't until I was standing, my row waiting to exit our seats and receive our diplomas, that I spotted Ida. She was up front, to my right, seated by herself at the very end of the first bleacher, next to the exit. Dressed in black, she looked so small and inconsequential—and alone. There wasn't anyone next to her or for two or three rows behind her. I watched her even as my name was called and I went up to the podium for my diploma, Mother and company cheering wildly; and later, when Anna went up, when Anna's name was called and she crossed the stage. Even then Ida didn't move, not a clap, not the slightest sign of acknowledgment or recognition. Mother and Zelda cheered and, in doing so, stirred up the rest of the contingent to follow suit. Zelda bellowed, "That's my relation! That's my niece!" But Ida didn't budge. What was wrong?

The thought crossed my mind that corset-stiff Ida with her Bible and aloof demeanor might be embarrassed by the others—Mother and Zelda—especially in a crowd of white people. According to Anna, Ida studied the Bible with a group of white women. I let out a long breath, heavily, uncontrollably, and what I took back in, what swelled in my lungs and progressed into and through every part of me, was a sorrow so overwhelming I could barely contain myself. My face flushed with its pressure, my eyes brimmed. No matter what, I had to find Anna. I had to tell her I was sorry. I had to say something. Let her reject me. It didn't matter.

There was another speech. And a prayer. When it was time to get up and march offstage, I wasn't sure that I could move. When I stood up, I found myself looking at Mother. She wasn't across the track and clear up into the bleachers, but only thirty or forty feet away, the same ink black dress with its three half-dollar buttons that were bone white, and I was standing there with the letters to a word Mr. Ridgeway had just pitched stuck to the back of my throat. I tried and tried but I couldn't unhinge them. Then I felt the girl next to me tap my arm. "Go," she said impatiently.

At the bottom of the platform students milled about, slowly moving in the direction of the bleachers, where their parents were getting out of their seats and swelling the aisles. I heard Alice and Zelda calling for me as if I hadn't seen where they were. But I paid them no mind. I looked behind me and found Anna quickly making her way though the others toward Ida. I yelled her name, loud; and I tore after her, catching my cap as it flew from my head. She had to have heard me, but she kept walking. At least this time I had the presence of mind not to take her by the arm. I got around in front of her.

"I'm sorry," I said.

Clearly, she was not of the same mind-set. She glared at me, imploring me to get out of her way.

"It's all just stupid," I continued. "Really, Anna."

Her eyes narrowed. "Don't act like nothing happened to us. You said to be honest . . . so be honest."

"About what?"

"You tell me!" she snapped and then sidestepped me, continuing on her way.

I watched her vanish into a dense crowd of laughing students, then I looked up to the bleachers. Ida was already gone.

* * *

My party. Balloons. Confetti. And food. Lots of food. Mother and Alice used the occasion for an all-out cooking competition. They didn't touch any of the food they prepared, but sat back watching as the rest of us sampled black beans, chili beans, fry bread, carrot and potato salads, pies and cakes, Jell-O, canned apples and pears, baked chicken, fried chicken, chicken-fried steak smothered in a thick gravy, mashed potatoes, fried potatoes, ham. You'd think they had cooked for half the county; the table was so piled and pushed together with food that those of us eating had to hold our plates in our laps. With peeled eyes they took note of who ate the canned apples or the canned pears, the baked chicken or the fried chicken and how each of us responded to what we ate. Unfortunately, there were just a few of us to judge, hardly enough of us to taste each dish, let alone eat a fraction of what was on the table. There was me and Mae-Mae and Roberta, and Zelda and her youngest daughter, Stella, a chubby ten-year-old who no doubt would grow up like her older sisters. She ate like a horse.

About halfway through the meal, Mae-Mae jumped up and announced it was time for me to open my presents. Of course, I had to open hers first. It was a daily planner, two of them actually, for, as she explained, this year was half up already. She didn't think I wanted to wait until January first to start planning my days. Next was Roberta's gift, two diaries, apparently for the same reason as for the two daily planners. Only Roberta didn't use standard gift wrap; on brown butcher paper she drew free-floating caps and gowns with blue and red pencils. She had taken an art class. Alice gave me a ballpoint pen, simple, nice, in its box, to which a red bow was attached. From Zelda I got a "Happy Birthday" card with a silver dollar inside. "That equals one dollar," fat little Stella informed me, "and I helped Mama pick out the card." Obviously, she knew her currency better than either of them could read.

The grand prize was Mother's gift. Mae-Mae, who'd been running the show, made sure that it was presented last. And she would be the presenter. She went into Mother's bedroom and came out with an enormous TV in her arms, a new one. Even as big and husky as she was, I had no idea how she managed to carry the damn thing. She trudged over and stood two feet from me so I could see and appreciate it, never as much as a grunt from her, then set it gently on the couch in the front room. Slapping her hands together, job done, she proclaimed, "All you got to do, Iris, is plug it in and turn it on."

"How many dollars does that cost, Mama?" Stella asked Zelda, who had turned back to her food.

"Maybe if you're good, Iris will let you watch hers," answered Zelda.

Hmph! I thought to myself.

"That's better than ours," Roberta commented.

"It's the same TV, Sears," Mae-Mae argued.

"It's bigger."

"No, it ain't. It's the same."

"Uh-uh."

Then Alice said to Zelda, "All right, Zelda, you ate both of the corn breads. Now which is the best?"

Earlier, Zelda apparently had tasted either Mother's or Alice's corn bread and now she was finishing tasting the other's.

Zelda shrugged, but what followed was an all-out food competition. With Zelda positioned in plain sight at the head of the table, Mother and Alice began lining up everything in front of her, telling her to eat and then asking, "Which one, the black beans or the chili beans, the apricot pie or the strawberry pie?" She was having the time of her life, and Mother and Alice right along with her, both of them delighting in the way unabashed Zelda relished every bite. She wasn't letting either of them win, saying, "Oh, this is good," and then about the competition, "Oh, this is good too." She just kept eating, and fat little Stella right along with her.

Clearly, by the time they got through each of the items it would be midnight. When I thought they were sufficiently distracted, laughing and preoccupied with the gorging Zelda, I excused myself. "For only twenty minutes," I said, and I asked Mother for the keys to the car. I said that I'd forgotten something at Anna's. Indeed, I'd forgotten something. It had been on my mind all through the party. I'd forgotten to tell her something, the most important thing.

* * *

Patrick's car wasn't in the driveway. But it didn't matter. That's what I had to tell her—Patrick was gone and it didn't matter. Knowing how Anna had been in the past, closed up in her pride and shame, I should have volunteered my story right off the bat. Hammering her to speak was the wrong thing to do. It was up to me to break the ice. It was up to me to bridge the chasm. I'll talk first if that's what you want, Anna. I'll do it. I'll tell you. I'll be honest.

I was in quite a state, riled and nervous, as I walked up the Polks' driveway from the street, where I'd left Mother's car. So when Anna opened her door, I just let loose.

"I don't give a damn about Patrick," I told her.

She'd opened the door wide, she was in full view, but the screen door was between us still, and because she hadn't turned on the porch light and the light in the room behind her was dull, I couldn't distinguish her features. She didn't say a thing, and in her long silence, I heard my words echo.

"What I meant to say," I said, correcting myself, "is that Patrick hasn't called me either." I waited, and when she didn't respond, I went farther. "He dumped me. Yes, he dumped me."

There, it was out. The cold truth. But still not a word from her, and now I was beginning to feel irritated. Was she punishing me? She hadn't made the slightest gesture of acknowledgment, that she'd even heard me.

"But I'm over him," I said. "I don't give a damn anymore." I turned, gestured in the direction of the empty driveway. "He's not here anyway." Then she shocked me.

"Yeah," she said with derision, "he's up there screwing Indian girls with Mike and the rest of them. Oh, and Mexican girls. Mexicans, Indians, it's all the same," she added, sarcastically repeating what Mike had said the first day we met him.

No doubt she could see me a lot better than I could see her; she had to know that I was at once confused and turned totally inside out. What was she talking about?

"Up where?" I asked finally.

"Oh, Iris, quit kidding yourself. Quit kidding me." Her voice was strident, full of reproach, yet she still hadn't moved.

"I don't know," I told her. "Up where?"

"The reservation, Iris . . . Don't stand there and act like you don't know, like he didn't take you up there again too. Or maybe he took you someplace else—for a change of scenery. But the reservation, it's their place to take Indian girls, Saturday nights, fun times. Don't stand there like you don't know. You said to be honest. So be honest, tell what he did to you . . . Or were there more than just him? Come on, Iris, you said to be honest, so tell what happened. You're an Indian, you're no different, tell what he did to you . . ."

Dumbfounded, I stared at her, a blank form. Nothing, the word that was stuck in my throat, he did nothing.

"Oh, come on, Iris," Anna continued, taunting me. "Can't you be honest? Too much shame? If you can't be honest, I will . . ."

But just then she stepped away from the door, disappeared, and in that brief instant, when I could see through the screen into the house, I glimpsed in the dull light the empty room, the bare sofa and table that belonged to the place, and the packed cardboard boxes and suitcases. Then Ida was in the door. Big and looming. She was a wall. She didn't say anything, she didn't have to. I knew she wanted me to leave. I knew, too, why she had stepped forward when she did, that she couldn't stand hearing from her daughter again what had happened, which was what Anna was about to tell me, and which, in the days ahead, I would know was the reason Ida and Anna left town later that very night. They must've agreed: Let her graduate and then, not a minute after, leave. Of course, in that instant under the lightless porch with Ida in the doorway, I didn't ponder their thoughts and plans any more than I began to piece together the details of the horrible thing that had happened to Anna, which, when I did think about it, I might've seen coming when she returned from her walk with Mike on the reservation, disheveled hair, leaves and dirt on the back of her clothes. That was the first sign. And there were others. But I didn't think about them then. I took Ida's silent cue and left. I went straight to the reservation.

I was inside out. I had to know. I had to see for myself. Blind fury. I didn't know exactly where I was going; I remembered only the road and the general area, and that, just before the turnoff, there were apple trees, on a gentle slope, which weren't that easy to see in the dark. But I drove on. Blind fury. Two wrong turns, one of them up a road that led to a sprawling ranch house with half a dozen barking dogs lined up in front. Then I saw the apple trees and, just beyond them, the road.

I should have been frightened. In a manner of speaking, I was senseless, certainly. But I was determined. I thought of everything. I parked the car just off the main road, on the shoulder where I had stopped. Easy to get away. Not only did I leave the car unlocked, but I left the door slightly ajar, imagining myself hurrying back, pulling the car door open, throwing myself behind the wheel, and tearing out of there in a flash. Then, with my eyes adjusting to the dark, I made my way up the slope, through the low-hanging apple trees, until I met the dirt road on top. It led into the reservation, past the abandoned shacks, and ended in front of the larger circular building with the conical roof, the roundhouse.

Even before my eyes registered shapes and shadows, I heard the music: Elvis Presley pounding loud and clear from a car radio. Then I saw the car: the red Mercury convertible. It was parked to one side of the building, hardly a few feet away; and behind it, I saw two other cars. I didn't see the white Thunderbird, but that didn't mean it wasn't there. Clearly, a party was going on inside. Through the missing slats, I could see firelight, the flickering of a good-size fire. Against the dark night, the place looked like a giant jack-o'-lantern, not with a carefully carved face, two eyes and a mouth, but with holes here and there, on its sides and top, as if it had been randomly hacked at with a knife or ice pick.

I slipped up to the last shack, the one closest to the roundhouse. Mike's Mercury was hardly thirty feet from me. But then I was at an impasse. I couldn't go any farther. Hiding behind one of the cars to get a look inside would be dangerous since at any time someone could wander out to their car for something. And if I just sneaked past the cars to the roundhouse, anyone returning to their car would see me standing there looking inside. I had to get to the other side of the roundhouse. I tore across the road, past the roundhouse, and caught my breath in a thicket of Scotch broom. Then, ever so carefully, watchful, I made my way to the light coming from a wide missing slat.

Shadows and flickers and a huge empty space. Crouched low, I saw the insides of the shingled roof, the round roof beams, and the large center pole to which the beams were connected. Following the center pole down from the ceiling, my eyes landed on a man, just beyond the pole; with the bright fire burning behind him, he was at first a mere silhouette, a stick figure, but when I looked, when my eyes made out color and depth, I saw that he was pushing his pants down his white legs. Then, before my eyes could reach that place they automatically went, to that center of him that was dark, he disappeared. He'd dropped to his knees, fallen behind the pole at an angle, where I could see only the soles of his shoes and the pants around his ankles. Immediately, I moved to another open slat. Then I saw everything.

I had never seen sex before, not even in pictures. The brief conversations Anna and I had had on the subject were technical, who does what and what goes where. I never pondered the graphic details that now and then flew from the mouths of Mae-Mae and Roberta. But then I'm not sure that any discussion, or even the most detailed description, could prepare you for the spectacle of sex, for at first sight there is such a mixture of

anatomy—trunk, legs, and arms—and movement, and not just that, but
what it suggests to you all at once, violence and indignity, pleasure and
unmitigated freedom. You find yourself both repulsed and immensely attracted. You are in awe.

Firelight flickered over his skin. It was him I saw, his hind end in
the air, his white shorts and dirty denim jeans twisted around his ankles. I
couldn't see her. They were at an angle, not exactly horizontal in front of
me. Still, if she were looking up at him, if she were facing him, I would have
seen her face, or at least a profile, as easily as I could see his. But you couldn't
tell where she was looking, up at him, in my direction, or toward the wall,
because her face was covered with what looked like a black sheet or towel.
I was afraid. Yes, horror and repulsion, but those things and the sight of that
person with her face covered fueled the only thing I knew just then—fear.
I wondered if the girl was dead. I watched for any sign of life, any response
from her. Her thigh, the one that I could see, and her breasts shook with
each of his thrusts, but that told nothing, for a fresh corpse would do the
same.

When he finished, he braced himself so he wouldn't touch her, and
stood up. He backed away from her, his pants still around his ankles. He
was drunk. He had oiled dark-blond hair that flopped in his eyes. I didn't
recognize him. Or any of the four others who came after him. Only Mike
Bauer. He was the last that I saw. So I don't know who after him, if anyone.
When I saw Mike come into the light, when it was his turn, I left. I didn't
trust the building to hide me, not even the night, not the stars.

* * *

I hid. Then I didn't move. Not far away, I found another thicket of
Scotch broom and pushed myself into it. I was a small rabbit and there was
a great horned owl circling overhead. I thought I would be found. I thought
I would be next. I waited for what seemed like an eternity, but, looking back,
it mustn't have been for more than an hour. The music stopped; I could
tell, even as faint as it was where I sat hiding. Then the engines started and
the cars slowly, quietly caravanned back down the road. There were three
of them—Patrick's wasn't among them. Dust swirled up in clouds and hung
in the air, in a line from the roundhouse to the end of the road, where it
turned and dropped down the hill. Silence. Then, little by little, crickets.

I waited a while longer. Then, slowly, I came out of the brush. I
didn't go back to my car. I went to the open slat where I had been watching.
The fire was still burning, light flickered inside, and somehow I knew even
before I approached the opening what I would see: the girl, left like a dis-
carded animal by the center pole, a mean and reckless offering to whatever

God once dwelled there. She was as still as before, lifeless. She was naked, with the black sheet or towel still over her head. The thought crossed my mind that maybe someone else was still there, outside and waiting to come back in. Maybe not all of the cars had left. So, looking through the slat, listening for any sounds besides the crackling of the fire, I waited.

There was an entrance to the doorway, a long tunnel-like structure attached to the building and leading into it, which had its own door, or doorway, since what remained of the actual door was nothing more than a large hinge, dark with rust and hanging from a single nail. Beer cans and broken bottles littered the place. I had to watch my step, not only because of the large shards of bottle-curved glass and the beer cans I might accidentally step on, but also because, until I was directly in front of the entrance, I could not see whether someone might be standing on the other side of the tunnel. Again I waited. Crickets outside, the fire inside. When I was sure there was nothing else, I stepped in.

The tunnel was not particularly long, about fifty feet, but the rafters overhead were low, and with the dark behind you and the firelight only in the doorway ahead, it was hard to see. You could not tell where you were stepping. You had to trust, focus on the light and keep walking toward it. Inside was different. It was big, open, and, with the fire burning, you could see everywhere. But I didn't linger then. My eyes fixed on the body and I went to it.

Suddenly, I had more courage. With each step closer to the naked girl, I felt bolder. I bent over and ripped the black cloth from her face. Then I stood holding the black cloth, which I could now see was a dress, and knew what I knew even before I reached for the dress, even before I saw the matted and tangled red hair underneath it: that the girl was Billyrene Toms.

Anna had prepared me with what she'd said. I went to the reservation with the pictures, all the information, already in my brain. There was a body at my feet and I had the horrible thought that she was dead. I panicked. What would I do? I fell to my knees and touched her hand, then the top of her chest. What I was thinking, I don't know. Perhaps I thought I would detect a pulse. She was warm and I was certain she was alive. And that prompted a new panic: I must keep her alive. I edged around behind her, lifted her shoulders to my lap and cradled her head in my arms. She was pale, very white. As I peered down at her, watching for a breath, I saw that she had vomited. Rice grains and soggy bits of carrot collected haphazardly below her chin and down her throat like beads from a broken necklace.

I shook her. I thought it best to try and wake her. When she didn't respond, I began rocking her back and forth, not gently, as a mother might, but forcefully, lifting one shoulder, then the other, pushing her this way and that way. All the while I called her name, bending close to her and whispering, lest someone be outside and hear me. She was dead weight. She was breathing, but that was about it. "Billyrene, Billyrene," I kept calling. Finally, her eyes cracked a bit, as if in the slightest recognition of my voice. And she belched. The stench of stale beer filled the air.

"That's good, that's good," I said, continuing to rock her. I thought of babies, how important it is for them to burp. "Billyrene, Billyrene," I whispered louder.

She opened her eyes full, but she wasn't looking at anything in particular, just gazing at the ceiling. Then I heard Mother calling me. She was outside and coming closer.

"Mother," I screamed, "help me!"

She called back. And then I heard Alice, and Mae-Mae and Roberta. I heard them stepping on glass, stumbling on beer cans and then coming through the tunnelway.

I looked back down at Billyrene. She was focused now, as if my loud screaming had awakened her, and she was gazing directly up at me. "Your mother's a whore," she said.

When I looked up, I saw Mother in the room, coming toward me. And Alice and Mae-Mae and Roberta, and not just them but Zelda, with Stella. They were in the same clothes, dressed up; they'd come directly from my party. I didn't see Anna until I stood up, until after the others had collected around Billyrene. She was standing against the wall, by the doorway. Clearly, she was the one who knew, or suspected, where I was. But she wasn't looking at me. She was watching the others.

They dressed Billyrene and got her to her feet. Apparently, they couldn't find the rest of her clothes. She went out with her dress on and Zelda's sweater. She went out braced up between Mae-Mae and Roberta. Nobody said a thing. The fire crackled. I saw the dark spots on the ground where she had lain, and how, splattered on the insides of her calves, the boys and the blood still spilled from her.

They were parked by the shacks. Mae-Mae and Roberta loaded Billyrene into the backseat of Alice's car and then climbed in with her. Alice and Zelda and Stella piled in the front. Anna got into Ida's car, alone. I thought of saying good-bye, but I knew at that moment not to break the silence. Mother and I walked down the hill with Alice following in her car, the car lights lighting the road ahead for us.

I drove. Mother was distracted, unnerved. She kept turning her head, looking back at Alice's car behind us, then peering into her lap. We didn't say a word. The silence was still a balloon our words would pop.

Neither one of us wanted to hear the bang, or what might follow. Finally, after the first light on Mendocino Avenue, where Alice turned to take Bil-lyrene and her mother and sister home, Mother spoke.

"Are they gone?" she asked.

"Yes," I said, checking in the rearview mirror, although I knew, as Mother must have, that they had turned.

Then she broke down. It scared me more than anything I'd just seen. I had never seen my mother cry. She sobbed out loud. "Oh, Jesus; oh, Jesus," she kept saying. And she kept asking if the car was still behind us. She didn't want Zelda to see her crying. She made no sense. "I've got to be strong. I've got to hold her up," she told me.

I thought she would compose herself at home. At least I could get her inside. When I parked finally, she did stop sobbing. But she didn't get out of the car. She wiped her eyes with a colored napkin from my party that she had found in her dress pocket.

"You're OK," she proclaimed.

"Yes," I said.

"It was foolish to go up there looking for a boy . . ."

"Patrick wasn't there," I volunteered, interrupting her.

". . . But it was a good thing you went," she continued, as if not hearing what I'd just said.

I told her everything that had happened, start to finish, from when I parked her car on the main road below the abandoned reservation to the moment I heard her from inside the roundhouse calling me. Of course, I spared her the graphic details of what I had witnessed, but told enough so that she knew what had happened and how it had happened. I suddenly felt brave.

"And you could see everything?" Mother asked, slowly turning her head in my direction.

"Yes," I told her.

"For how long?"

"What?"

"For how long were you watching it?" She was looking directly at me now.

"Half an hour, maybe more," I answered.

She shook her head in horror, in disbelief. "It went on that long?"

"Maybe longer," I told her. "I left, don't forget. I went and hid in the Scotch broom." Again I told her how frightened I was when I saw Mike Bauer in the building.

But she wasn't listening. She was retreating. In the dull, yellow-white light from the overhead streetlamp, I saw her face go from gray to boiling black. She glared at me, her eyes popped like a bull's. Then she turned and, in a single motion, was out of the car, the napkin in midair behind her. She stormed up the front steps and slammed the door behind her.

What had happened? What had I said? Done? I became enraged beyond belief. How dare she indulge in her shenanigans now? I looked down at the damp crumpled napkin that had landed on her seat, then tore into the house.

She was at the kitchen sink, drinking a glass of water. Everything was still on the table, the bowls and platters of food, paper plates where people had left them on their chairs. They had left in a hurry. Mother had to have heard me come in, but she paid no attention. I marched right up to her.

"I don't know what's bothering you," I said, "but this is no time to play games."

She kept drinking, her head tilted back, her back to me. "Silence is the coward's way out," I challenged. I was adamant, firm.

She finished her water and set the glass on the sink. Then, wiping her mouth with the back of her wrist, she turned, faced me. "Coward?" she asked.

"Yes!"

"I'll tell you," she said, visibly shaken. Her face wasn't swollen, as I'd seen it in the car, but drained, more the way it was when she was crying. But, don't get me wrong, she was fierce. "I'll tell you," she said again. "She come here, that girl, that Anna. Why? Why did she come here? To help you. She come here looking for you because she was scared you gone up there. She come here after what happened to her. Do you know what happened to her? Do you?" She paused, but only so I would listen closely to what she was about to say. "That Mike Bauer raped her," she said. "Took her up there. Only she wasn't drinking, and when them others come in, God help her, she got away. She was running, bloody and naked, down the road. That's what happened to her. Somebody seen her, found her like that, and they took her to the police. Now her and Ida's got to leave town."

Mother paused, wrung her hands. She was staring, as if seeing what she was describing. "She come in here looking for you. We're all sitting, having fun. Alice says to her, 'You look worried. What's the matter?' She looks at me, then Zelda, then it all comes pouring out of her. Jesus. Jesus." Mother began to tear up, then collected herself. "Good thing it did come out of her. Otherwise she might've gone up there alone. And good thing her and Ida's phone is already disconnected. She might not have come here at all."

She lifted her head and looked at me. Talking about Anna had made her sorrowful. Now her face was filling with anger, blackening again. "Did you know what happened to her?" she asked. But again she wouldn't let me answer. "Don't matter even if you did," she said with the utmost contempt, and then turned back to the sink.

"What?" I demanded. "What doesn't matter? Yes, I appreciate Anna. Is that it? Is that tonight's lesson? Is that what I'm supposed to see?"

"See?" she snapped, turning around to face me. "See? You don't see nothing. Nothing!" She tilted her head slightly, chin forward. Her eyes narrowed. "You know, I think I done wrong with you. Maybe I should've let you feel what it's like to be hungry. Maybe I should've let you starve like the rest of us." And with that she tramped past me to the table. She couldn't stand to look at me any longer.

I followed her. I wasn't going to let her get off the hook, have the last cruel dig. Not now, not after what I'd been through. No, she wasn't going to cut me loose now, not now. I stood directly behind her. I could see that her hands were shaking. She picked up a bowl of Jell-O, then set it down. Next she reached for the plate of fried chicken but she couldn't hold that either. Slowly, she began to move around the table, no doubt to get away from me. But I cut her no slack. I kept on her heels. Again, she'd reach for this or that, but her trembling hands could hold nothing. Meanwhile, I began to think. I saw Anna standing here telling what happened to her. Then I thought of Billyrene, and something popped into my brain. For the first time, I heard again what Billyrene had said to me when she opened her eyes.

"OK. Mother, you were a loose woman. I saw how I was made." I tried not to be angry, but instead to show sympathy.

She spun around so fast that I nearly fell back with the force of her movement. "Ha!" she snorted. "If you seen that, if you seen that much, why didn't you help her?"

"Help her?"

"You sat there and watched!"

"What could I do?"

"Gone for help," she answered. She raised her upper lip in a vicious snarl and, through clenched teeth, said, "I would've beat the hell out of them, taken a rock and tried to kill every damn one of them." Then she turned around again.

"Oh, is that what I was supposed to do?" I asked sarcastically.

She wasn't moving now.

"Risk my life?" I taunted.

I didn't see it coming. I only saw her reaching again for something on the table. She caught me off guard. She turned and tossed a handful of potato salad into my face with all her might. "I should've let you starve," she growled.

My mother never hit me. Never had I seen her riled in this way. I was stunned. She stood as if she was daring me to say another word. I stepped around her and ran into the bathroom.

I caught my breath, thought what to do: Clean my face. I grabbed a towel, turned on the hot water. I took off my blouse and started in. "Espejo," I found myself saying over and over again. Mirror. "Ignore it," Anna would say. "Think of something else." *Espejo. Espejo. Espejo. Espejo.* When my face was clean, I stood looking at myself. Even though I had locked the door, I thought I would find Mother behind me, reflected in the mirror. I turned around, as if she was there, and expected to hear another mouthful of her anger. Of course, she wasn't there. When I turned back and faced the mirror, it was only me again.

* * *

The next day, Sunday, I went to Anna's in the morning. I half-figured that I wouldn't see her, that she and Ida had already gone. But I had to try. I had to thank her for what she had done, for thinking about me, for caring enough after all that she'd been through. Ida's car wasn't parked on the street and I saw through the window as I came into the yard that the house was empty. Still, I knocked. I knocked on the locked screen as if my knocking would somehow fill the house with furniture and rouse Anna from her studying at the kitchen table.

"They moved," I heard someone say.

I jumped, spun around. Seated on the back steps of the big house was Mary Beth. All these past months I had watched her come and go and now, of all times, I found myself face to face with her. The same Mary Beth: hair all over the place, glasses, bad skin. She was smoking a cigarette.

"They left early this morning," she added. She rubbed out her cigarette on the porch step and then looked back up at me. "Hi, Iris," she said.

She made herself sound as if she'd known all along who I was, and wasn't surprised. No doubt, she had watched me come into the yard and then sat as quiet as a ghost while I knocked and knocked.

"Hi, Mary Beth," I said, attempting the same tone. I wanted her to know that she wasn't a surprise either.

But that was where it ended. She didn't open the door to our past in even the slightest way. "Yeah," she repeated, "they left this morning."

"How's Patrick?" I blurted out.

"He moved to San Francisco," she said.

She was detached, preoccupied with whatever she was thinking about. I took the hint. I said it was nice seeing her and left.

* * *

One week later, on a Sunday morning, she called and told me Patrick had blown his brains out with a thirty-eight. He had had a fight with his lover, Brad, and Brad had left him. "Brad had been a lifeline for him, you know," she said.

"Yes," I said.

She said that, when she saw me, I had asked about Patrick. She wanted me to know before I read it in the newspaper. Patrick had left my number on his desk, she said. I thanked her for calling and hung up.

The house was empty. Mother had gone fishing with Alice and Mae-Mae and Roberta. I thought of how Mother had talked to Patrick on the night of our last date. Was she feeling him out, perhaps as a way to make sure I would be safe with him? Certainly she would not have kept him there if she had even the smallest inkling that Anna was in trouble and might need us. Or did she know about Patrick? Had she seen his own sadness story and tried to help him? But it wasn't as though I wanted to ask her for answers just then. I didn't want to tell her about Patrick. I didn't want to talk. I just wanted her there, watching TV, or at the kitchen counter rolling pie dough. There was no one else.

I went outside, found her chair in the garden, and sat in it, as if that would make me closer to her. I looked at the flowers, the things she looked at. I expected to hear voices, birds, maybe Mother singing, but the flowers were still, as silent as a wall.

It was not like me to do something out of the ordinary. Or alone. I wouldn't have gone to the fair alone. I wouldn't have gone at all. Not even to the races. Especially the races. I have no interest in betting. But when Jane, my friend who manages men's suits, canceled our trip to the fair, when she called in sick with the flu and I found myself with a free afternoon, scheduled time off work, I chose not to stay home. And that perhaps is where the trouble started—with the decision not to be home. I say trouble but it never felt like that. It was as if I was joyously lost, in neither time nor space, free in that strange place between waking and dreaming, so that the crowds of exasperated mothers and frolicking children, the Ferris wheel and the barkers, the displays of flowers and fruits and vegetables and every imaginable household gadget, seemed new and unreal. Home was behind me. Home with its responsibility, with Harold's two youngest back from college, waiting for me, waiting to use the car, waiting for dinner. All of them would be waiting, and, in the years ahead, I would understand that what I was doing was running. And, once out of doors, I couldn't stop.

I meandered here and there, into the different exhibit halls, past booths of new TV's and shiny appliances, until I found myself outside the races, in line for the turnstile. Though I had a pass, I paid the extra fare, and though a friend of Harold's had offered his box seats for the afternoon, I did not go into the stands. I stayed on the ground and followed the cyclone fence that divided the track from the crowds. The fence led to the front of the towering stands and then on to the other side of the building, where there was a stable and a ring, where the trainers walked in circles their glassy-eyed, prancing horses before the next race. Other people lined the fence, I suppose to get a better look at the horses whose odds they had studied in their racing forms. What I was doing there—what I was doing at the races—I'm not sure, except perhaps following in some way my earlier plans with Jane. But, as I said, I have no interest in horses or betting; and finding myself boxed in, the fence ending at a concrete wall, I decided to leave.

Then I saw the horse. Nothing special, for I can hardly tell one horse from another. It was dark, a bay; and it had a blue strap across the top of its bridle and blue blinders over its eyes, which is what caught my attention, the color blue, after its trainer had managed the animal back to the ground from its sudden flight into the air. It had reared up, tossing its head and wildly kicking its front legs. It was nervous, defiant. Again, I would have left, but, as I stood seeing the horse with its blue strap and blinders, a row of jockeys in brightly colored uniforms appeared in the ring, each of them finding their mount. The race was imminent. Which is why I decided to stay. I wanted to see how this horse would do.

Mounted, the jockeys guided their animals out of the ring, onto the track, where they were each met by another horse and rider who would lead them to the starting gates. The trainers followed the procession on foot. People squeezed around me, wanting to get closer to the track for a better view of the race, even though, as it turned out, another ten minutes passed before the horses were in the gates. Each jockey, assisted by the other rider and horse, paraded his mount back and forth before the grandstand. Once they were in the gates, and once they were out with the bell, I was lost. I lost the bay with the blue strap and blinders in the whirl of motion that sped past me, then receded around the first turn and all but disappeared on the backstretch. I know that when they came back around with the thunderous cheer from the stands, the bay was not in front, nor would it win. Two horses were greatly ahead of the pack, one a length behind the other, and neither wore blue blinders.

Again, I would have left. The race was over. Very quickly all of the lathering, nostril-flared horses, except for the winner, came back to the ring. I saw the bay, exhausted like the others, and I watched the jockey dismount and hand the reins to the trainer. What do they do with a horse when it doesn't win a race? Does the horse have any idea of what it did or didn't do? Could it remember, or even know, a right or wrong in a race? I saw his hands; in my memory now, even the small dark hairs on the tops of his long fingers. I saw his fingers working the ties to unfasten the blinders. When the horse could see, he held his free hand a moment in front of its eyes, long enough for it to know what would touch it, and then, bending just the tops of his fingers, making a hand-size rake, he vigorously, affectionately massaged the animal's arching neck. And then, even before I heard his voice say, "That's OK, easy, easy," and looked from his hands to his face and found him looking at me, I was the horse. Yes, even before I saw his face, before I could tell you that he was handsome. I simply followed him.

I skirted back along the fence and pushed through the turnstile, out of the racetrack. I met up with him as he led his horse to the stalls at the far end of the fairgrounds. I say met up with him, but what I was doing was following him, a good thirty feet behind. It was no secret; I was no surprise. And I understood that the horse was his immediate business. He smiled when he first looked over his shoulder and saw me, and then he just kept going. He knew I was there.

I can tell you he was dark, Italian-looking, swarthy, with oiled black hair. He was about my age, thirty-five. I had plenty of time to look at him. He washed down his horse with a hose, gave it a complete bath, then walked it in a circle, cooling it down, for half an hour. I saw that he was handsome. But that is not what registered then, and wouldn't until he was a memory. All of the fair, the bothered mothers and their wild children, the Ferris

wheel and the barkers, the fruits and vegetables, the endless gadgets, all that
was new and unreal for me had gathered itself in the body of this one man,
and my only thought was to follow him.

I stood by the side of the barn, then sat on a bale of hay. After he
put the horse in its stall, he walked to the other side of the building and,
without looking back, disappeared into a room there. I followed him. I
opened the unlocked door. Inside the tiny room with nothing but a cot and
a racing form tacked to the otherwise barren wall, I found him bent over a
small sink, his back to me, shirt off, washing his hands. He must've heard
me come in, yet he neither lifted nor turned his head to acknowledge me.
When he finished and faced me, drying his hands with a paper towel from
a roll on the sink, he simply said, "Oh, please, sit down," as if his manners,
and not my presence, had been questionable. I sat on the cot and looked at
him. He peered down at me, as if now he was glad that I had sat and made
myself comfortable. Then he walked over and locked the door.

He stood there a moment, looking at me and still drying his hands.
Rolling the paper towel between his palms, he made a ball, and in one gentle
move tossed the paper ball squarely into the wastebasket below the sink, all
the while continuing to look at me. I trembled. He offered his hand.

"John," he said.

I took his hand. It was warm, big. "Iris," I said.

"You know, I'd like to take a shower," he said, still holding my hand.
"I'd ask you to come with me, you know, but it's too small." He nodded to
a small alcove in a corner of the room where the shower must've been.
Again, he was apologizing as if it was his manners, or, in this case, his living
conditions, that were questionable rather than the fact that a strange woman
was in his room who wouldn't be able to take a shower with him. I nodded
agreeably.

He took off his clothes, first his boots and socks, then his trousers
and shorts, in front of me; and when he came back out with the shower's
heat rising from his skin and the scent of Palmolive soap everywhere in the
room, he was the same way, naked, drying himself with a towel. He folded
the towel lengthwise and reached in the alcove, setting the towel on the
shower's curtain rod.

"Oh, forgot," he said with a smile, and quickly bent over the sink
again, this time brushing his teeth.

In retrospect, I was surprised I didn't think of my own hygiene, of
taking a shower also, brushing my teeth. But I wasn't thinking straight; if I
was, I wouldn't have been there.

When he set down his toothbrush and, naked, turned to me, I felt
like a small animal in a cage. I didn't know what to expect with his hands,

indeed all of him, coming for me. But when he touched me, I grew, met him equally. He touched my shoulder, and then squatted on his haunches, so that now I was looking at his eyes. He undressed me. Piece by piece, he took off my clothes, my blouse and skirt, my underclothes, my shoes, and, as if he loved each item as much as he loved me, he carefully folded them and placed them in a neat pile under the cot. Meanwhile, I played with the black hair on his chest, and, with the soft underside of my index finger, traced the contours of his hard nipples. Then he lifted me in his arms, supporting my shoulders and legs, and turned me on the cot and laid me down. Kneeling over me, he adjusted the pillow behind my head and began kissing me. And then he was moving, still kneeling over me, his lips going down the center of me; and, that way, he sucked and relished my body, as if each pore was a cell of honey. And then he showed me how to do the same with him. Back and forth we went, my turn, then his; until, at one point, when he was kneeling by my feet, he pulled me down the narrow cot, my knees bending up, and, as I met him, entered me. And then it was a carnival itself, the rides and shows of our lovemaking.

I might never have come back. But then, at some moment, while both of us were catching our breaths, time crept in and drove a wedge between us. A clock appeared on the wall, its black-tipped hands like the burned ends of matchsticks.

"The horses," he said, looking up.

My family, I might have said. But, to tell you the truth, I didn't give them a second's thought. I watched him slip into his clothes with single-minded determination. As he dressed, covering each part of his body—his legs, his penis, his chest and arms, his feet—I felt an entire world retreating from me, as if the lights of that world were going out one by one. Perhaps that is why I asked him his name: I knew I would never see him again. Not like I had. For even if I did see him again, it wouldn't be the same; it would be the second time, and at best, even if we didn't bring our own needs and insecurities to the meeting, we would still carry with us the first meeting and that alone would give us a past, place us in time. I had been out of time. So I asked his name. As if it would be a souvenir.

"John," he said, as if he hadn't told me his first name before. "John Severino, horse trainer."

"Iris," I said. I couldn't utter my last name though it was on the tip of my tongue.

He was anxious. He wanted to get to his horses. The clock said eight-thirty.

When I stepped out of his room, it was dark. The barn was lit with a row of lights. Horses hung their heads out of the stalls. The place smelled like hay and animals. He was filling a water bucket, bent over a spigot. I looked at him one more time, then came away.

* * *

I told Harold that night. I told him everything. Naturally, he and the kids were worried when I walked in. "I was about to call the police," he said.

I marched past them, went directly into the bedroom, and closed the door behind me.

Harold came in and found me seated at my vanity. I was gazing blankly into my mirror. He sat on the bed behind me. I could see him in the mirror. "What's the matter?" he asked.

I told him that I'd met a man that afternoon and had had an affair with him. That's the word I used: affair. I didn't turn around to face him; I didn't have to, for I could see him in the mirror perfectly. He didn't surprise me. He sat thinking, his head slightly lowered, his hands folded in his lap. Harold Pettyjohn, he would come up with an answer. Nothing different now, his hair more gray, the bald crown on the top of his head wider. But the same Harold. He always came up with an answer. He always found a solution. "What will the others at the store think?" I queried after he asked me to marry him. "They'll think it's wonderful; they like you; they know you're a hard worker; and this way we'll keep everything aboveboard." "And what of your three children?" I pushed further. "They love you. Marriage is the answer. Now they'll have a mother again, not just a memory of someone who left them with nothing more than good-bye. You are the answer, Iris." Always answers. Even how to deal with Mother, who regarded his efforts to placate her with reserved and quiet gratitude. "I saw a beautiful rosebush in the nursery; we'll get it for her, and what's more, plant it for her on Sunday, and while we're there, cut the deadwood out of her marguerites and pull that old ivy off her back fence." And when his children, particularly his daughter, Merideth, got angry with me and let fly in the midst of any argument the fact that I was not her real mother: "Counseling."

"Why didn't you tell me there was a problem?" he asked, looking up from his lap.

What could I say? I didn't know there was a problem. I didn't know until I bit the fruit. But it wasn't just the fruit, not just the affair, but also the garden, the not-home place I found myself in even before I saw the serpent or the tree. Unlike Eve, who left a garden, I felt as if I had walked into one, and I had no desire to return to where I had been before, or to tempt the man sitting behind me to join me. Yes, he had been perfect. He had been everything I wanted. I wanted a good husband. I wanted a family. I wanted good friends and associates. I wanted to be respected, loved, needed. I wanted a split-level home with a view, in Montecito Heights. I wanted children who went to college. I wanted to walk the streets of London, see Rome. I wanted orchestra seats at the opera and symphony. I wanted nice clothes. I wanted to learn and know more, and the more I learned, the more I wanted to know. Harold was my guide, my mentor. He opened the doors, one after the other, so that I was always walking, coming into another room, another color, another sound, another place. Until today, until now, when I saw myself as a greasy rodent, a rat, so driven by its hunger that it had fallen headfirst into a half-filled bucket of milk and now was swimming for its life to get out. So when Harold stood up and touched my shoulders, saying, "We'll work things out," I felt only that he was pushing me down, back into the bucket.

We'll work things out. Which is what he said when I told him two months later that I was pregnant. He'd have an answer. He'd have a solution. And, at almost fifty, he would raise the child as his own. He would make do. He would love the child as he loved his own. "As I love you," he told me. But that was the problem, at least as far as I was concerned, the way he loved me. Ever since the night I came back from the fair, I couldn't stand to have him near me. I couldn't stand him to touch me. I withdrew my hand every time he reached for it. When he said, "That's OK, things'll be fine," as much to reassure himself as anything else, I recoiled inside. Each gesture of affection, each reassuring word, was his hand pushing me back down into that bucket.

After I came back from the fair, I began to see things I'd never seen before, though they had been before my eyes all along. He spoke his encouraging words to reassure himself, yes; but as he said the same things over and over—That's OK, things'll be fine; Don't worry, I still love you and you love me—I began to hear them as mantras, magical chants he used, believing that if he said them enough, they would return order to his world. And order for Harold was everything. Order was what Harold loved; and he loved things in the way, and to the degree, they fit into that order. A perfect house. A perfect wife. A perfect family. A perfect life. My wants and his order. We fit perfectly. Until now. Now I saw the man, who, at family barbecues, insisted that the corn be boiled exactly ten minutes after the hamburgers were put on the grill, and proclaimed the event a failure if the salad wasn't tossed and everything else hot and ready at the same time. Because he must have the same parking spot nearest the exit in the garage, we had to leave for the opera at three in the afternoon, when it only takes an hour to get to San Francisco and the opera doesn't start until seven in the evening. This was the man who took a shower and brushed his teeth after, not before, sex.

I tried. I lied to myself, imagined a future in that house with my child. It worked, until Harold was there. I thought of the three children. The two youngest were back in college by this time, the oldest married and living in Utah. Their own mother had left them, when they needed her, when they were young. I told them everything, talked with each one over the phone. We conversed as if a family counselor was listening in. They said they understood, which is what they always said. I told them first. Then I talked to Harold. I told him I was leaving. When it became clear to him that he could not change my mind, he packed his overnight kit and went to a hotel.

* * *

Mother was the last to know.

"Do the others know?" she asked when she looked down from the sky that night.

"Yes," I told her. "They know I'm moving. Tomorrow."

But, as it turned out, I left for good that night. I stayed at Mother's, slept a good night's sleep in my own bed. The next day, I went with Mother to get my things. The house was empty, the lights still on from the night before. Harold would have a fit—wasting electricity. I turned off the lights and left with only my clothes.

Mother was good to me like never before. Maybe I should say she was good to me like always, only now I was able to see it. She cooked, made sure I had milk and meat with every meal. She'd slip chopped chicken or sausage into the omelets she whipped up every morning. There was always tuna or chicken in some form again for lunch, and, for dinner, she went all out preparing meat loafs, meat stews, and chilis, with beef or lamb. Not just one or two vegetables with dinner, but a choice of five or six spread out and arranged just so on a large serving tray: carrots, peas mixed with baby onions, steamed broccoli, butter beans from her garden, spinach—always spinach, and every way imaginable: steamed, creamed with milk and cheese, chopped and fried with bits of hamburger.

I didn't question her about anything. And she didn't question me, none of her games or tricks, none of her offhand remarks. Which must've had something to do with my being able to see and enjoy her goodness—there wasn't any tension between us. She never mentioned the inordinate amount of clothes I had, though I know she found them extravagant, waste-ful. More than once I caught her in the enclosed back porch staring at the skirts and blouses, coats and jackets hanging on the clothing rods we built there to store the clothes that wouldn't fit in my bedroom closet. She suggested I not eat blackberries or blueberries, lest the baby be too dark, and she regularly fixed me acorn mush so that it would have a long life. I obliged her in these things, small sacrifices. Once, while holding a lit piece of angelica root in the kitchen, she asked me to follow her outside. There, in the garden, she took my hand and led me in a loose circle four times through her flowers and shrubs while she sang a song. She said it was her angel song. She said it was for thanks.

She wouldn't take a penny from me. I didn't prolong a discussion about this, lest we start an argument and disrupt the peace. She was adamant. "You need to save your money. You're going to have a baby," she said. She didn't have a large salary from the cannery, and yet the extraordinary amounts of food kept coming. Still, she wouldn't consider a cent from me. I kept working. I still kept my position, with all of its responsibilities, as manager of women's accessories. Which wasn't easy. Not because of the pregnancy—I never experienced morning sickness—or because of the other employees. The employees, many of whom were my friends, particularly the divisional managers who I'd known for years, were shocked at first by the news—the separation and the pregnancy—but then accepted it without judgment or criticism, at least as far as I could see. Many took time to ask how I was getting along, if there was anything they could do. It was 1976, after all; illegitimacy, like the word "nigger," was supposed to be a thing of the past. In fact, many of the girls at the store were not married and had children.

Harold was the biggest problem. He was, of course, still my boss. He was the store's overall manager. He didn't make life difficult for me. He didn't shuffle lazy workers to my department or demand quick inventory reports at busy or otherwise inopportune times. He did none of those things. What he did do was stop by my department exactly once a week, before noon on Fridays, and ask if I had thought things over, meaning, had I changed my mind and decided to come home?

Many people came to Mother's. People I hadn't seen in years. She always warned me, if she could, if it wasn't a surprise visit, as if to give me time to leave the house or retreat to my room if I didn't want to see them. This certainly was not the old Mother, who, before, seemed to savor my discomfort with her friends. But I didn't leave or hide in my room. The house was quiet and my days off seemed long. I welcomed the visitors, even if it was just to say hello, offer them something to eat or drink. I welcomed the disruption of those long quiet spaces in that house. Alice had died of cancer a couple of years back. But the girls still came to visit Mother. Mae-

Mae was an officer in the army; she was married to another officer and had two children, and she was stationed somewhere in southern California. Roberta was a window dresser for Saks in San Francisco. She was married and had one child, a girl, who was a local chess champion. She showed me newspaper clippings she carried around in her Louis Vuitton purse. She visited more frequently than Mae-Mae, since she was closer, and she was the one who took care of selling the house after Alice died. Roberta and I had a lot to talk about, both of us being in the retail business. She never lorded over me the fact that Saks was an exclusive store and JC Penney was not. She gibed me about being pregnant, saying with a laugh, "Well, at least, Iris, I see you finally got something in you. I was starting to get worried."

Zelda came too. And her ever multiplying horde of offspring. Women with babies. Girls with babies. Babies with babies. I never could figure out who belonged to who. Zelda had six daughters, including Billyrene. That much I got. I knew their names: Rita, Pauline, Faye, Frances, Stella. I remembered having seen a couple of them, the oldest ones, with Billyrene years before; and, of course, from the night of my graduation party, I remembered fat little Stella, who grew up to be fat big Stella and, interestingly enough, the only one not to have children. So I had a handle on Zelda's daughters, but her grandchildren lost me. It didn't help matters that they were always taking care of one another's kids, so that when one of them came around with Zelda she might have with her two kids from this sister, three from that, plus her own. And what a motley crew. Like the mothers, they came in all shapes and colors, thin to fat, dark to blond. No doubt, I served milk and cookies to Billyrene's children long before I found myself serving them to her.

I was waiting for Billyrene. I figured that sooner or later she would walk through that door with Zelda just as each of her sisters had. If she remembered, if she still held a grudge against me, she could revel in the fact that I ended up no better than anyone else, pregnant, unmarried, and living back in South Park with my mother. Certainly Zelda or one of her sisters gave her the news. Then one day she came. She was a mess, poor thing. I knew who she was even before I saw her face. I saw the silhouette in the door, large, bigger than the others who had followed in behind Zelda before; and the clothes, stretch pants, a baggy blouse that hung on her the way Zelda's dresses did, raggedly, as if both of them had been dressed by a careless mother. Her face came into relief as she walked into the room and sat at the table. She was swollen, bloated, her red hair dull, tossed every which way. She smelled like wine and cheap perfume, sickly sweet. I thought she might be drunk, but she wasn't; if she had been drinking, it would have been the night before, or perhaps a small amount earlier that day, for she talked plainly and coherently. I served her apple pie and milk, and when Mother and Zelda, mindless of the two of us, began chatting in Indian, I sat down next to her.

She was easy to talk to. In fact, she led the conversation. She told me about her children. She had eight of them. Many had been in trouble with the law. One of her sons was presently in juvenile hall. Already she had three grandchildren and a fourth on the way. Then she turned the discussion to me, to my pregnancy, and began giving me advice in everything from prenatal care to early child care as if what she had just told me about her children made her an expert on parenting. She made sense, though. What she said was right, straight from the book. What went wrong? I wondered. Then, just before she and Zelda left, she pulled a rubber pacifier out of her purse and gave it to me, saying, "Here, for your baby." I thanked her. And, that way, she left with neither of us ever mentioning a thing about the past.

I knew eventually I would see Anna, and when I did, when she came into the house, I knew she wouldn't be as easy as Billyrene had been. The past was like a wall between us, and neither one of us attempted to scratch its surface, not even with a feather. Not long after she and Ida left MacDonald Avenue, a month after maybe, I received a package with no return address. Inside was a new blouse and a new pink cashmere sweater, which, to this day, I have been unable to take out of the box, or throw away.

I knew she dropped in on Mother occasionally. I knew as much from Mother. And she didn't just see Mother now and then at the house, but at work. Anna worked during the busy season at the cannery. Her husband worked outside in the yard full-time driving a forklift. They had five children. Apparently, when she and Ida left MacDonald Avenue, they went to Petaluma, where Ida took another job on a dairy, this time cooking and keeping house not only for the dairyman's family but also for all the help, most of whom were young Mexican men with little else besides a green card. Somewhere along the way, Anna met Albert Silva, who wasn't one of the young Mexicans, but a poor Portuguese boy from Santa Rosa who Ida intensely disapproved of and referred to as "the nigger." I vaguely remembered the Silvas from high school. I remembered one of the brothers, Frankie. He was dark. You would say he was a mulatto. This information Mother had slipped to me over the years. So when Anna arrived, I knew a lot about what had become of her after that dreadful night on the reservation.

But knowing these things about her didn't help me to feel less anxious about the prospect of seeing her. So much, it seemed, had been left undone between us. If she felt the same, however, she never let on. As with the others who came to the house to visit, Mother told me—warned me—in advance of her arrival. Somehow, because Billyrene had been talkative, I expected Anna to be the same, even if superficially so. But she wasn't. When she walked into the room, she was surprised to see me. She smarted, then quickly gathered herself. She said hello, of course, she was polite, but I could see behind her nod and manners that she didn't trust me, that in her eyes I was some sort of wild animal from which she would run or, if she was trapped, fight with all her might. So I took the warning. I kept my distance, respected the wall that was our past. I served her and Mother a lunch of tuna fish sandwiches and iced tea, then let them visit alone. Before she left, she came to the hallway and said good-bye and I came out of my room. "You're pregnant," she said, as if just now noticing my swollen belly. "Me too. Number six." She could have fooled me. In jeans and a sweatshirt, she looked as flat as can be; in fact, despite the five children she'd had already and, given what Mother had told me, her not-so-easy life, she looked re-markably the way she had seventeen years before. I was the one who had gained weight, and not just in the front, where I was supposed to. She said that it was good seeing me, that she had been looking forward to seeing me after Mother had told her over the phone that I was here. She kissed Mother good-bye. She looked back at me, as if questioning for a moment, wondering if she might change her opinion of me, then she left.

I had a lot of time to think and reflect, particularly the last six weeks, when I was on leave from work and found myself at home as big as a cow. Anna never did come back to visit Mother, at least not while I was there. I didn't think she would. Our past was ugly, and who was I but a blind and proud teenager who had let her down. There had to be more to say. Which I told myself as I was seeing her looking at me that last time. I worked myself into a frenzy, picked up the telephone, but then never dialed. I knew better. Turn on the television, talk to Mother, look at baby clothes, I told myself.

I thought of Harold too. Twice I called the children. They were cordial, but not particularly interested in hearing from me. I didn't sense any anger or resentment, as if they felt I had abandoned them, like their own mother before me. Rather, they were busy with their independent lives, the way Harold and I raised them to be. I had no regrets. In fact, I saw my marriage and life with Harold as just the latest and the last of what my blind and vain dreams had brought me: failure. I was forever winning the battle but losing the war.

Of course I thought all the time of John, the baby's father. Again, I had no regrets. My experience with him made no sense in the greater scheme of things. I had become everything I once abhorred and feared, the worst I might have imagined for myself: home with Mother in a poor neigh-borhood, unmarried and pregnant, or, more specifically, divorced and pregnant. And, yet, somehow it was right. I wondered if John thought of me. Probably not. He had his horses. It didn't bother me; I saw him holding his hand in front of the anxious horse and then massaging its neck, and I didn't care.

It didn't bother me that John more than likely never thought of me. But I was lonely much of the time. Not just for him but for all the others who had somehow figured in my past and now, for whatever reason, were nowhere around—Anna, Patrick, even Mary Beth. Perhaps that is why I stuck so close to Mother. Particularly as my time drew near. One night, about a week before the baby was born, I became frightened. I was face to face with the dread that all expecting mothers must experience at one time or another, over whether or not I could successfully deliver the child, and whether or not it would be healthy and normal. I told Mother. She lit a piece of angelica root and then led me down the back steps, slowly and carefully, for it was nighttime and I was so heavy. Arm in arm, we went in a loose circle through her flowers and shrubs four times, just as we had before, shortly after I had moved back home with her. And again she sang her angel song, the song I was supposed to hear all my life. This was the second time I'd heard it. The first time I didn't think much about it. Now it sounded beautiful.

* * *

It's not easy to have a first baby at thirty-five, almost thirty-six, I don't care what career women these days tell you. It was a difficult delivery. Thirteen hours in labor. But when the doctor put that baby in my arms, when I felt him on my breast, nothing in the world was better. A beautiful healthy boy. I named him John after his father, after the memory. I gave the last name too—Severino—but the hospital somehow recorded only Severe. I laughed and let it be. John Severe.

Those days home with the baby were the most wonderful in my life. With Mother cooking and cleaning, and basically spoiling me rotten, I had nothing to do, or think about, but look after the baby. I woke with him and fell asleep with him. Day and night, we were wedded to one another. Like water and shore, we made up a lake. We were the cool water and gentle sandy shore all in one. He was gorgeous; of course, every mother will tell you that about her child, but he had the fullest head of black curls, enormous brown eyes, and he smiled constantly; yes, from the time he was a week old. He was fair, with a slight olive tint in his skin, a little lighter than me where the sun hasn't hit. I felt beautiful with him. Water and sand.

Then I had to go back to work. My maternity leave was up. The world began to change. The baby and I grew apart. Slowly at first, then more rapidly, until one evening I came home and picked him up, as I always had, and found him staring back at me as if I was a stranger. His smiling mouth went slack, his eyes wide. He was actually in shock, alarmed. Of course, Mother had been caring for him during the day, but how could such a transference of love and bonding take place in the course of a mere eight or nine hours a day? I had him in my arms, or in the bed sleeping next to me, the rest of the time, not to mention full time on my days off. Still, as if it had happened while I blinked, I became a stranger, a second mother at best, to my baby. He laughed and snuggled with me, but it was Mother he was always looking for, craning his little head to find. Of course I was jealous, at times infuriated. But I tried to keep myself in check. After all, Mother did have him the bulk of his waking hours, and she was only doing her job, caring for him in a loving and dedicated manner. In fact, she'd taken a night shift at the cannery so that she would have her days free. It was only natural with all the prime time she spent with him that he would bond with her. It wasn't her fault.

Then one night, Johnny was four, maybe five months old. It was late, about eleven, and why Johnny was on the front room couch and not asleep in his crib—in my room—I can't tell you. I don't remember. Perhaps he was sick or fussing for some reason. In any event, I was sitting next to him on the couch, where Mother had laid him on a blanket, and she was standing about ten feet away, close to the door, saying good-bye on her way to work. While she was talking to me, while I was looking up at her and not down at the baby, he rolled off the couch. He banged, dropped hard. I wasn't able to catch him in time. But he didn't cry, he didn't make a peep. He turned on his back, and as I looked, still stunned and holding my breath, I saw that he had found Mother, his eyes fixed on her, and he was reaching for her. He had rolled off the couch trying to follow her out the door. I looked up, trailing his eyes, and I saw that she was laughing.

I picked up the baby, and only after Mother left, only after she was out the door, did he start to cry, as if only just then did he feel the hard bump on his head. He screamed, wailed, wriggled and writhed for hours on end. But it wasn't because his head hurt. It was to get away from me, for, when I put him down, he settled.

That night, after the baby quieted, I sat up reexamining my last year at home with Mother. I thought of her extraordinary kindness, her care not to rub me the wrong way, how hard that must have been for her, and of her prayers, the almost daily bowls of acorn mush, and the angel song. I acquiesced, fell into the trap, let her prime the child who was growing within me so that in life he would know her and her ways, so that he would respond to whatever song she sang or whatever it was that she fed him when I wasn't looking, when I was counting plastic purses and discount jewelry, and be hers forever. At three in the morning I rewrote the script for *Rosemary's Baby*. In the days and weeks ahead, I saw the situation in less dramatic terms. Nevertheless, a certain truth remained. Mother had violated my joy, my passion, once again. And this time there was no right in it. He was my baby.

Things went from bad to worse, or, rather, I should say, they followed course. He grew like her in every way. According to her, he saw things, he was different. What exactly she meant, and how she knew, I didn't want to ask her. I didn't want to engage in that sort of conversation. But it went on from there. A frog in the backyard with a missing toe was Old Uncle. And Mother confirmed this. They had a language of their own, the language I never learned, the language I failed. Indeed, he was everything to her as a child that I was not. He succeeded where I had failed. Even with Del, the Filipino dairy hand who was her friend, who arranged for her and me to live in that small place next to the dairy long ago. Unlike me, Johnny loved the cows. He asked Mother and me to take him to the dairy at least every other day.

"When he grows up he can help Del," Mother said.

"Which I wouldn't do," I testily responded.

"No, you wouldn't," Mother agreed.

"So what's the big deal about helping Del?"

"He helped us. I owe him—in so many ways."

"So you use your daughter or grandson to pay your debts."

"If they like cows."

I felt she was being smart with me, Mother with her offhand and senseless remarks. "Any boy likes animals," I said.

"He's different."

We were at the table. Mother was darning one of his socks. I looked through the kitchen door to the backyard where Johnny was playing, making sure he couldn't hear us. "Oh, that again. Different from what?" I challenged.

"Different."

"You mean different from me. But like you—all that hocus-pocus. You made him that way!"

"Oh, Iris." She sighed and stood up, "If you had as much sense as you got imagination, you'd be dangerous." Then, sock and needle and thread in hand, she walked to her room and closed the door.

*   *   *

But I didn't sit idly by. I didn't picture Johnny and me staying with Mother forever. I let her continue to pay the bills. Since, she had, in her way, invested so much in my son, let her feed him, let her help me save

enough money to buy a house and raise him in a decent neighborhood, send
him to a decent school. By the time Johnny was seven, I had enough to put
down on a house, not anything spectacular, nothing like what I lived in
with Harold in Montecito Heights, but just below there, in a clean two-
bedroom in the Town and Country Market area.

Neither Johnny nor Mother protested the move, to my surprise. It
was for the best. Johnny needed his own room; for the last year at Mother's
I'd given him mine, and I slept on the couch in the front room. I don't
know exactly what I thought, whether or not I truly believed that, even if
the bond between Johnny and Mother didn't lessen, the bond between
Johnny and me might reawaken now that just the two of us were living
under one roof. Of course, I didn't keep them apart. We saw Mother all the
time. But even if we hadn't, I saw, in time, that even if Johnny and I had
moved to Siberia, nothing would have changed between them. Nor between
Johnny and me.

He grew to be a good-looking boy, gangling and rugged, but handsome. His curls relaxed somewhat as he got older, so his dark hair was loosely
wavy; his eyes remained as big and dark as ever. He had neatly carved lips,
and except for his prominent cheekbones, which, no doubt, came from this
side of the family, he looked like his father. He'd ask about his father, but
I don't believe it was out of any genuine curiosity. Rather, it was to annoy
me, since he seemed to raise the subject only when we were fighting. I told
him the truth, adjusting the story and adding to it as he got older and could
understand more.

We fought too much. He was never a good student. He never
showed any of the aptitude that I possessed in school. Not that I wanted,
or expected him to be a straight-A student. He didn't seem to try. He spent
his time daydreaming, looking out of windows. Teachers repeatedly brought
this to my attention; and, even after I sent him to his room, after I virtually
chained him to his desk as a form of punishment for the teachers' reports
and his bad grades, I'd find him looking out the window, or staring at the
wall, rather than looking down at his books. And it wasn't just about school.
In time, we fought about everything—his friends, his clothes. He always
picked the strangest people for chums, first a retarded girl around the corner
from Mother's, and then, at the school in our new neighborhood, an obese
diabetic who was so fat Johnny had to tie his shoes. And then the clothes:
the oddest assortment of styles and colors you could imagine, nothing I
would buy for him. Day in and day out, there was something we fought
about.

Of course he went to Mother's every day after school, and, I'm sure,
she let him get away with murder. Which didn't help matters between us. I

was forever the ogre and she was forever the savior. The wedge widened each time he stomped his foot and ran out of the house, saying in protest, "I'm going to Grandma's." She kept her night shift at the cannery just so she could pick him up every day after school and keep him for the few hours until I was off from work. But then on weekends, or even at night after we got home and had dinner, something invariably would blow up between us and off he'd go, or at least want to go, to Grandma's.

And there I'd be alone. I hadn't dated seriously—I hadn't been intimate with a man since I'd been with Johnny's father. I went out with a couple of men my girlfriends from work fixed me up with, all to no avail. But then I'd done this because I felt I was supposed to somehow, or simply to oblige my friends, not because I wanted to. Working, raising a child, my life felt full. I didn't want anyone else. In fact, I began to see my friends' lives as boring. They maintained their marriages the way I had maintained mine—full of unhappy compromises. I thought more and more about Anna, even about Billyrene and her sisters. Hah!, as Mother would say, my people. Often, I felt like picking up the phone. But then what? What to say? Would they even want to talk? For the most part, though, I kept busy, didn't have time to ponder these thoughts or much else in my life. But those times when Johnny ran off to Mother's, particularly those long weekend days and nights, I was so lonely I could barely stand to be in the house. And, then, it wasn't a man I wanted or thought about, or even a visit from one of my friends. It was Johnny.

When he was twelve, I figured he didn't need a baby-sitter, and I gave him the key to the house so he could come straight home after school. I told Mother not to pick him up, that he was to come straight to this house and study after school. "Besides," I told her, "you're getting too old to be working all night and chasing around after a kid all day." To Johnny I said: "Grandma is working during the day, so you can't go there anymore after school." So what do you think happens? She discovers she's been working thirty-five years exactly and is eligible for a great pension, so she quits her job. "You said I was getting too old," she said and laughed. I tried. I still forbade Johnny to go to her after school. "Bring up your grades first," I offered as a trade off. But he wouldn't play. Tension mounted. Before long, he simply ran away. And he kept running. Not anywhere else, just to her house. It got to where he kept several sets of clothes at her place. I told her to bring him home, and she did; and as soon as he was out of her car, there he was on foot, on his way back to South Park. Eventually, I had to let him stay there permanently. He was fourteen. I lost the battle. I lost the war.

And what happens?

He barely graduates from high school. His English is bad. For em-

ployment, he works for Del, his salary zilch. His best friend is Billyrene's
sister's son, and he spends his free time helping the so-called tribe, all of
whom by now have moved into South Park, planted themselves here
and there around Mother. She's in heaven no doubt: She's got all her
people back in one place and her grandson working as each and everyone's
slave.

"What kind of work is that, working for 'our tribe'?" I once asked
him while visiting at Mother's. I could understand what a person might do
on a dairy, even if he doesn't get paid for it. But what does a person do for
"our tribe"?

With Mother just sitting there not saying a word, certain of her
firm control over him, he fed me a line of gobbledygook about how we
have been illegally terminated as a tribe by the BIA and how we must get
reacknowledged by them and obtain a land base and function as a tribe
again.

"We're Americans," I told him.

And do you know what he told me? He told me how I am one of
the lost generation, that all my problems have to do with my being lost
between two cultures, white and red. "You're on the fence, nowheres," he
told me.

"Yeah?" I said. "You're eighteen years old. Why don't you surprise
me and do something real? Get a real job. Stop living off your grandmother
here. Then come back and preach to me about what my problems are."

And what's the next thing I learn? He's started a business selling
used clothes out of Mother's house, dressing half of South Park in the castoffs
he picks up at the Salvation Army. Merchandising, it runs in the family. I
give up.

Sure, I was bitter. I was angry. And I was lonely. What had made
for empty nights and weekends before, when he was still living with me,
was now my entire life, every minute at home. When work and the television
each night weren't enough to distract me from my feelings, I'd go visit the
two of them with some reason, real or imagined, to let off steam. I'd find a
way to fight with them. Sometimes, I found myself blaming him for all that
had gone wrong of late. Other times, I thought it was all her fault. Truth is,
no matter how I saw the situation, no matter what I might or might not
have said to either of them, they were in it together, in cahoots, inseparable.

The last time I went over there, before I accepted the fact once and
for all that all I was doing was yelling at a wall, if anything, only making
myself more hateful in their eyes, I saw how solid and unshakable their bond
was. They let me see on no uncertain terms. Johnny was twenty, nearly
twenty-one by this time. His so-called clothing business had accomplished

little more than stuffing Mother's home to the seams with junk. I started off calmly, restrained.

"Johnny," I said, "it's not that I like or want to fight with you. I worry about you. I worry about your future. I've always only wanted you to have a happy, normal life," which was the truth.

Then he gave me a senseless exposition on what was and was not normal, and I lost my temper.

"All you've done is create a firetrap here," I hollered. "Do you want to kill your grandmother?"

"What do you mean?" he asked glibly.

I pointed to the clothes-stuffed back porch. "How the hell do you expect her to get out of here if there's a fire? What's she going to do?"

Clearly, this was a visit where Johnny was getting the blame, the bulk of my wrath. Then I heard Mother chuckling, and when I looked to where she was sitting across the table, I found her pointing to the front door, and she said, "I'll go out that way."

And that was it. Adios.

* * *

So it wasn't enough that my mother called and told me that my son had been beat up, hurt. She had to tell me also that he was leaving town. "Oh, Johnny's OK," she said, "don't worry," and then she hung up. She left me out in the cold, knowing full well that in no time I'd be just where she wanted me, knocking at her door.

But in her short bit of news she let drop two other pieces of information, where he was going and why: San Francisco because he liked a boy and the boy didn't like him, the same boy who beat him up. Nothing mattered then, not how things came together in my brain or didn't, not how they made sense or didn't, only that I was out the door, running to my son.

It was morning. My day off. Before she hung up, she said she was going to the bank with him, but that they'd be back. I went to the house and waited. When he walked in, I threw my arms around him and wouldn't let go. Nothing he could do would shake me free. I blurted out all kinds of things, how I loved him, over and over. He cried uncontrollably.

When we separated, after the longest time, I stood looking at him. I didn't know what to say. I glanced around the room, looking for Mother. But she wasn't there. She'd left us to ourselves. I looked back at him. Still, I didn't know what to say. I wasn't myself.

Then he told me, "It's OK, Mom."

I let out a long breath, relieved, thankful.

I hugged him again, then left.

* * *

At home, I kept thinking that I should have stayed longer, inquired about his plans, perhaps tried to dissuade him from moving to San Francisco. I thought of all kinds of things I should have or could have said, reflections on all our misunderstandings over the years, and not just that, but the good times, too, the happy times. I thought of his needs, his wants. I hoped he hadn't given up on love. I hoped that if he hadn't experienced it yet, or even if he had, that he would know time and time again the pleasure I had known with his father, and more. He deserved it—every second of his life.

I thought of Mother, too, particularly as the day's shadows grew long, and as I found myself with my TV dinner staring out the kitchen window to the evening. I hoped she prayed for him, with her magic or with her not-magic. Let her sing her angel song. Whatever. Let her take care of him. She took care of me. Mother. All our struggles, Mother and me. Her strangeness, her stubbornness. Mine. What did she want, after all? All sorts of pictures entered my mind, possible stories. Her hocus-pocus. Her conniving. But, that evening, as I thought of Johnny, wondering when I'd ever see him again, only one picture settled for long: Johnny and Mother and me sitting in her garden looking up at the stars.

* * *

Funny thing. One morning, a few days later, maybe more, I'm having my one cup of coffee before work, and he bounces in and tells me he's not moving after all, at least not for a while. He says he has a lot to do for the people first, meaning, I'm sure, the tribe. I think to myself that he wants to sit down, talk things out, take care of the business between us before anything else. I'm prepared to call work, phone in sick. Then he says, "Mom, there's a tribal meeting tomorrow night, would you like to come?"

At first, I can't believe my ears. Then I think of Anna and Billyrene. No doubt, they would be there. From Mother, I learned they attended the meetings regularly. What would I say to them? And to the countless others? I look around at my clean and empty kitchen, then back at Johnny. Isn't he an angel?

"Sure," I say, and think to myself, What have I got to lose?

* * *

Funny thing. He leaves and I pick up my coffee and go outside, think of what I can do in the backyard, my Saturday chores, even though it is a workday and I must be in the store within an hour. It is warm. Chef, my miniature collie, follows me along the patio. Weed the marigolds and petunias along the fence, rake, water the bottlebrush and primrose, I think. But I do nothing; I sit in a garden chair in the middle of the patio, coffee cup clutched with both hands in my lap, dog curled at my feet.

It is warm.

I close my eyes. I breathe, smell the day, then let out a long breath, relieved, thankful . . . Mother and Johnny in chairs on either side of me. And Anna coming through the wooden-slat back gate, swung wide open; and, behind her, Billyrene, then Zelda, yes, in her raggedy dress. Children. Mae-Mae and Roberta and Alice. Patrick. Mary Beth.

"Look," Johnny says.

But I see already.

Heaven, the far stars?

No, a wish.